Like a boil that can never be cured so long as it is covered up but must be opened with all its ugliness to the natural medicines of air and light, injustice must be exposed, with all the tension its exposure creates, to the light of human conscience and the air of national opinion before it can be cured.

Dr. Martin Luther King, Jr.
Letter from Birmingham Jail
April 16, 1963

Requiem Guatemala
A Story of the People

A novel by

Marshall Bennett Connelly

The Guatemala Historical Reclamation Memorial Project
Fall, 2019

Library of Congress Cataloging-in-Publication Data
Main entry under title:

Requiem Guatemala: A Story of the People

Based upon documented events during the Guatemalan civil war, 1960-1996

ISBN-13: 978-1-7334722-0-3

Cover image: ©
Cover and interior design: Jennifer McGuire | JEM Designs

In Memoriam

Rita Olga Navarro de Barberena
Guatemalan Teacher and Educator
1954 - 1980

Contents

Chapter 1

Three Dirges

"And then he said, `Don Lázaro'—to my face! —the Colonel himself, he said, `Don Lázaro, you've got five boys in Comitán teaching the campesinos how to read. That's subversive. That's communist. So tonight, you have to kill them.' . . . Now, what can I say? —You tell me! What can a man say to something like that, and what's a man supposed to do?"

Before sunrise the next day, the little village of San Martín Comitán lay draped, like a wrinkled quilt, over the sharp ravines that scored the floor of the valley. Nestled in a clearing in the pines that lined the slopes of the mountain range, the highland *aldea* slumbered in the final moments of a long night as the first faint glow of dawn began to trace the eastern rim of the Sierra Madre. Gently sloping patches of tile roofs seemed anchored just above a blanket of ground fog that stretched through the village and up the valley. A rooster crowed in a corner of some *milpa,* a remote cornfield behind the town.

Then, [pumpf!] —an Indian skyrocket streaked into the sky, its grey trail racing above the center of the town, followed by a pale orange and yellow burst. Its dull report echoed back and forth between the mountains.

In mid-afternoon the day before, the military commander of the garrison had been little disposed to wasting time in pleasantries.

"Sit down, Don Lázaro," he frowned, eliciting something between a greeting and an order. "You have had a very long walk from Comitán."

A weathered hat in hand, his tussled, raven hair glinting in the sunlight flooding the room through the open doorway behind him, Don Lázaro Emilio Cárdenas, a woodcarver and furniture maker by trade and the mayor of San Martín Comitán, stood stoically before Colonel Julio Alfredo Guzmán.

"There, Don Lázaro, sit down," repeated the commander, rolling a freshly sharpened yellow pencil between his fingers, never moving his eyes from the face of the leathery Mayan stooping before his desk.

Saluting the exploding rocket, its echoes reverberating through the valley, the rooster crowed again. It was answered by another more faintly on the opposite side of the village.

[BONK!] . . . [BONK!] . . . [BONK!] . . . The bell in the mission of the town began to clap in a flat, thick base. From the belfry, a flight of pigeons fluttered aloft and dispersed to roosts somewhere under the fog below.

A brilliant, ruby lining now traced the rims of both the dark, grey clouds and the flat, black mountains painted against the horizon. Another flock of birds, a sprinkle of tiny, charcoal specks, swooped out of the fields, spun once over the middle of the valley of San Martín, and drifted to perches in the pines.

Following the colonel's gesture, a wooden-faced soldier, in camouflaged fatigues with a heavy, automatic assault rifle slung over his shoulder, pulled a rickety chair from its position next to the doorway and set it abruptly beside the dusty Indian.

"Sit down!" repeated the commander as he rose from behind his desk with measured formality. The Indian dropped his eyes to the chair beside him, looked back at the colonel, and gingerly took a seat on the front edge of the chair. Twisting the pencil methodically, Colonel Guzmán walked slowly around his desk and stood directly over the diminutive Mayan peering deeply into the crown of his hat. The wooden-faced soldier stood at attention just behind the chair.

"Listen to me, Don Lázaro. Do you understand me?"

Then at once, from somewhere deep within the soul of the village, a woman's anguish pierced the still, early morning, followed by yet a duet of wails, and then a full chorus of cries. An orchestration of wrenching, penetrating lamentations began to stream from the center of San Martín Comitán and to work its way slowly, first down one rutted street and then another, passing spectre-like toward the crossroad where the graves climbed up the slope of the town's cemetery.

A solemn procession of Comitanes, in full religious regalia, followed the twelve *cofrades* in their dark, woolen *trajes*, or outfits, crimson *tzutes* tied around their heads with long silken tassels dangling behind. They marched in six files, two abreast, carrying before them in outstretched hands the sacred symbols of their rank, the silver *monstrances*, the *barras*—tall, slender staffs crowned with the embossed image of San Martín, the village's patron saint.

Colonel Guzmán continued as Don Lázaro sat before him, the Indian's head bowed to hide the increasing terror that gripped his heart.

"You have five boys—catechists working for the American priest in Comitán. They're teaching the campesinos how to read. Right?" pressed the colonel. "Maybe even you, eh?"

Don Lázaro's face froze, and his hands began to tremble. He could not face the commander before him.

"I think you understand me plainly enough," said the colonel. "Well, you continue to listen to me! They're communist subversives, these boys," said Colonel Guzmán. "So tonight, Don Lázaro, tonight you have to kill them. Every one of them . . . all five!"

Behind the *cofrades* paced the catechists, five sombre young men in sandals, musty jeans, and second-generation western jackets, in some cases too snug and in others obviously too baggy to have been their own. Following the five boys, wearing the long, white ceremonial tunics accented with a single, central woven panel of red brocading, the principal religious women—their hands over their mouths—wept uncontrollably under lacy, white veils, tinted grey in the heavy mist of the morning.

The procession of perhaps fifty or more moved with reluctance under the wrought-iron arch that was the entrance to the town cemetery. The solemn assembly flowed slowly around the faded blue and white tombs and over the crest of the hill until the five young men, each escorted now by an older man, followed the *cofrades* over the ridge of the hill and dropped down on the other side just out of sight. The small congregation then massed along the crest and peered over the hill, craning to watch the proceedings below.

"And what could I do? How could I do more?" asked Don Lázaro, as he tried to explain to the parents the imperative for waking them so late in the night.

"I took the bus that stops at the military post," he continued. "I took that same bus to Dos Padres. Then I had to run and run. Twice I fell—you can see my hands and knees! All the way I ran to reach you even now, now in the night. So, I am telling you what the colonel—what that `dog of Satan' himself—told me to my own face. He said that `all five boys' . . ." Don Lázaro choked on words trying to frame such an unspeakable crime, and, for the moment, he could not continue.

The mothers and the fathers exchanged looks of horror, unable to compass the full weight of the words they anticipated from Don Lázaro, their mayor.

"`All five, Don Lázaro, and by morning,'" repeated the Mayor to the parents of the five boys gathered before him in the candlelight of the altar.

"`And you hear me clearly,'" continued Don Lázaro, before the terrified families. "`If those subversives aren't dead by sunrise tomorrow morning, my troops will come to Comitán, and by noon they will kill every living thing in the town and burn it to the ground, and then—before nightfall—they will do the same thing to Santa María Pétzal, to Santa Luz, and to every other subversive town in Sololá!'"

The parents exchanged looks of terror and anger. The women began to moan and wail.

"That's what the colonel said to me, your alcalde!" cried Don Lázaro, choking on his own tears. "And that is the message I must bring to you!"

"But what can we do?" they cried. "Where is our priest to be away from us at such a time? But to kill our own sons! How can we do such a thing? Such a thing isn't possible!"

"But what else can you do?" asked the sons.

"Have you forgotten what the militaries did in Cuarto Pueblo?" asked Rolando Semitosa, signing the cross in benediction over his head and chest.

"Can you not remember the massacre of Puente Alto," interrupted Josúe Vállez, "how they locked all the women and girls in the school house, threw in the grenades, and burned them up? How they placed all the men in the protestant church and clubbed them to death?"

"And what they did to the small boys," added Marcos San Miguel, "throwing them into the outhouse, leaving them there to die?"

"Surely, they will come and kill us all!" cried Jaime Chopúl. "Perhaps even now, the soldiers are here, up there in the hills already, watching and waiting to see what we will do!"

"What bitches have brought these bastards into the world to do such a thing to us?" cried Don Alvaro San Miguel, lifting his fists and shaking them before Don Lázaro.

"Que putas negras! What mangy, black-souled whores!" cursed Don Pablo Santa Cruz, rising from the bench beside the altar, stomping his feet, and beating his head.

"Why will they not leave us alone?" wept Doña María Mendoza de Vallez, lifting the edge of her shawl to her swollen eyes. "And where is the Padre to speak for us?"

"He is not here," wailed Doña Lucía Sánchez de Chopúl. "Why, merciful Madre, why is our Padre not here at such an hour?"

"Yes, the Padre is not here, so what choices do we have?" asked Don Lázaro, his open hands outstretched before them.

"What choices do you have?" asked the boys, waiting breathlessly for an answer, scanning the anguished faces of their families for some sign, searching about the room for even a margin of hope.

. . . . . [BONK!] . . . . [BONK!] . . . . [BONK!] . . . . The bell of San Martín Comitán continued to clap its flat, dull refrain. From the *cofrades* rose a litany of muted, almost imperceptible prayers lifted in the air on drafts of black incense.

And then silence. Even the birds ceased their calling. The dense mist surged forward, enveloping the whole scene.

Seconds later, screeches of sharpened steel on steel sent trembles through the muted congregation, and a chorus of screams went up as women sought sanctuary against the breasts of their husbands and brothers.

Then fell the swaths of five machetes, each finding its mark: . . . . [thuck!] . . . . [thuck!] . . . [thuck!] . . . . [thuck!] . . . . [thuck!] . . . .

The dense wall of the congregation collapsed in a mass of wailing bodies. Their lamentations drifted back through the tombs, out the gate of the cemetery, up the rutted road, and back into the town. They echoed across the valley and then wafted toward the rays of morning sun just beginning their stretch across the heavens.

Somewhere away in the pine trees, the ignition of a heavy truck churned and churned and finally fired its engine. The motor revved up once and then again. After a hesitant pause, the drone of the truck slowly dissipated into the rush of a cool wind that began to swirl through the San Martín Valley of the Martyrs, flinging the drifts of clouds and the souls of five young men high into the pines.

* * *

Lydia was going to be late that day, although she couldn't have known or probably have avoided it, even if she had.

As it turned out, Lydia Penalte had enough to do for one morning, anyway. The Dean of Humanities would never understand why the non-credit public courses could not accommodate his request for more places in the fall schedule. With plans to expand the non-credit classes—particularly to enhance the women's career program which the Dean himself had approved—it was impossible to include more courses from the Humanities curriculum. It was a simple matter of room reservations and nothing more complicated than that. His continued nattering among the Humanities faculty was something more, something political among his staff, and she knew it, although, as only the student representative, she was outside that circle. Besides, she had more important things on her mind right now.

Rutilio Manuel Sanchez, Lydia's husband, was arriving later in the afternoon from Montevideo where he had attended an economic conference on Third World international debt. Rutilio was a respected member of the economics faculty at the National University. In fact, they had met there after her appointment at Tourism and she was still attending night classes. Lydia had to pick up their daughter, Vilma, from her mother's house on the way to the airport since her mother had become ill that morning and was unable to keep her granddaughter any longer during the day. She had to stop by her husband's office for his departmental mail, but if she left the National University before noon, she would still have time to pick up Vilma at her mother's home before having to leave for the airport.

"Rutilio needs to be back by Monday to meet with the Dean to settle his fall schedule and sign his contract. When you see him today, ask him to call," said Señora Elgin, the departmental secretary.

"We should be back by 4 o'clock, and I'll have him call," said Lydia. "Also, can you tell me what time the Student Association Executive Council convenes tomorrow? I'm one of the coordinators for the group, and I need to be there a little early."

"That's at 2 p.m. tomorrow in the Humanities Building conference room."

"Gracias! Muy amable, Señora!" said Lydia.

"*Para servirle,*" returned the secretary. The matronly woman watched the rushed and obviously preoccupied Lydia hurriedly exit the room and listened as her platform heels echoed down the hall. When she heard the doors slam shut at the end of the corridor, Secretary Elgin reached for the telephone.

"*Colonel Federico Altapaz, por favor,*" requested the Sra. Elgin. "Yes, a very important call. Thank you."

Lydia Penalte left the building for her car and the drive to her mother's to pick up Vilma before returning to the airport to meet her husband. Noontime traffic was manageable, and under other circumstances, Lydia would have made the trip from the campus down the *periférico*, or outer loop, without interruption. Today, however, she travelled north on her way to her mother's home, a comfortable residential neighborhood adjacent to the Kaminaljuyu National Park.

Lydia exited the *periférico* and proceeded two blocks further north to the intersection of the service road and Avenida Bolivar. As she came to a stop at the intersection, her satchel of books dropped from the seat, threatening to spill. Lydia shifted into neutral and set her emergency brake so that she might lean over and readjust her materials.

Preoccupied with her shifting cargo, Lydia Penalte never saw the two figures on a motorcycle exiting the *periférico* behind her. She never saw them checking her license plate with the handwritten note retrieved from the rider's jacket. She never heard the bullet clip slip into and catch in the chamber of the 9mm automatic pistol. Lydia Victoria Penalte de Sanchez probably never heard the first shot that tore through her back just below her left shoulder blade, exploding through her heart and left lung, or the second which crashed through her left temple, taking off the top of her right ear, as it exited, along with the whole right side of her head. She probably never even felt the remaining spray of bullets emptied into her limp body as it turned slowly and slipped around her satchel, books, and papers, now crumpled and soiled in the floorboard of her car.

Lydia Victoria Penalte de Sanchez probably never knew . . .

* * *

"*Leave* us, María!" they shouted. "Go now and take your son and free us from this terror!"

"Go *away*, María! Leave us *alone* in San Felipe!" they cried, raising their fists against the mother and her poor Felipino family.

"*Curse* you, María Xquic!" they shouted, spitting oaths and defiance. "We curse the womb that has given birth to our grief and sorrow!"

"*Bitch*, María!"

"Mother of *Satan*, María!"

"Whore of *Maximón!"*

"Leave us, María!

"Go away from us, María!"

"Go *away* from us, *tonight!* María Xquic de Xoy!"

Muffling deep sobs in a handkerchief, María Xquic de Xoy, wife of the priest of the dreaded *Maximón*—the gifted Don Andres Menchu Xoy, *auxiliatura maximo*—stood at the street corner, her hand over her mouth. Tears streamed down the face of the diminutive Tzutujíl Maya woman as she weathered the insults of neighbors and friends, threatening and cursing her and spitting across her path. They had been aroused by the frantic ringing of the parish church bell and were enraged by the report of yet another attempt by the army to "disappear" a fellow Felipino—this time their respected and beloved *alcalde*, Don Alfonso Doq, himself.

With her misshapen foot and arthritic ankle throbbing in pain, María could only stand tenuously and weep as the angry crowd swirled about her. Crying uncontrollably and on the verge of collapse, she was devastated by the savage unrelenting repression against the town and now this turning upon herself and her own stricken family.

"Could what they say be *true?*" María asked herself. "But *how?* Even her own *son?* But *why?* And how much more could a small, frail woman suffer?"

María Xquic de Xoy held onto the pole of the street sign for support and watched the crowd fall away from her as it raced toward the center of San

Felipe del Lago.

"A mad *dog* would be more a son!" cursed María, her cracked, thin lips pursed and her tiny, purple fists clenched in rage. "But my son, the *murderer* of his own brother and the agent of Felipino *death!* But *how?* Even my *own son!* And *why?*"

"Un perro del diablo y una mujer pobre!" wailed María, *"De una pobre mujer!"*

To a person, the Felipinos were nervous and frightened, but as they assembled, they became increasingly angry. Emerging from this little alley and that, first in groups of twos and threes and then by twelve's, fifteens, and twenties, they moved as in the course of an irreversible stream toward the town plaza where their usually muted voices began to swell into a chorus of hatred.

"It is a curse upon us by a vengeful God!" shouted Don J'Cab, waving his soft-covered *Kingdon Throne Bible* high into the air. "The God of Abraham knows us as idol worshippers, and He has turned His face upon the communist priest! We Felipinos must repent and cry upon the name of the Lord. Only then will He hear our prayers and lift us from this wickedness!"

At once, a small group of the freshly baptized Pentecostals collapsed on their knees, each of them followers of Kingdom Throne's new charismatic preacher of San Felipe. From a recalcitrance borne of old habits, they traced—without apparent thought—the sign of the Catholic cross over their breasts. Then raising their quaking arms high above them, the new disciples lifted on outstretched palms to heaven their prayers of thanksgiving and reaffirmed repentance.

"It is the guerrillas!" cried Alberto Reyes Benitez, seizing the initiative from the feverish Maya pastor. A retired army captain and the former civilian military attaché for the army post at Panajachél, Alberto Reyes was duty bound to speak for the constabulary.

"*Listen,* Felipinos! *Oigan me!*" shouted the military commissioner of San Felipe. "The guerrillas do these things to make the army look bad!"

"S*hut up*, you old suck up!" cried Ramundo C'jux, shoving the aging *ladino* fertilizer merchant into the crowd of angry Felipinos beside him.

"It is the *military*, and you *know* it!" cried Ramundo, a young university student whose courage was suddenly buoyed by the rousing sentiment against the military from all sides. "We know who does these things to us!"

"The *ejército*, for sure! The guerrillas, they don't have boots," added Señora Mañuela Duda, trying to shout above the growing tumult. "Only the *army* has the trucks with the tractors. Only the *soldiers* have the helicopters."

"The militaries want to *kill* us," protested Tata Paco Albanés, "and they will not stop until they have killed *each one* of us."

"Last month they took *Don Pablo!*" wept Sylvia Perez.

"Tonight they have come for our *alcalde*!" reacted Don Tupe Arredondo.

"Will our Padre be *next?*" wailed Señora Colom. "Will we see Father Jack borne to his grave at the hands of the murderous *militaries?*"

"Have we not had *enough?*" they lamented. "Are we sheep to be led to our own slaughter before the jackals of the night? Is there anyone else besides ourselves to speak to the *comandantes*?"

"Who will speak for the *Felipinos?*" they cried as a congregation with one insistent voice. "Who will speak for the sisters of the earth and the brothers of the mountains? And *who? —Who* will speak for the children of the corn?"

In the chill of the night, the stream of the Felipinos arched around the plaza and flowed back up the street toward the dusty road, the western passage that led to the detested military garrison. Señor Reyes was swept under by the swelling protests against the military, and he fell back toward the perimeter of the crowd and slipped away down a side street.

"But where are you going, Tata Paco?" cried María Xquic de Xoy, as her neighbors pushed by her.

"To *hell!*" shouted the weathered old *campesino* in anger and rage, his burnt hand gripping the handle of his machete. "I will go to the very gates of *hell* tonight, María Xquic, to tell the devil himself of a *mother's son* who has *slain his brother*, that Felipinos might be freed from his memory and liberated from the curse of his name *forever!*"

"Then, as the mother of such a one, I am *lost*, old friend!" cried María.

"And so are *we!*" protested the old farmer, as he spat into the gutter at her feet. He turned without a courtesy and sifted back among the Felipinos.

"But where are you *going*, Sylvia Perez?" cried María Xquic de Xoy, clutching ever so tightly to the post to keep from being knocked over by the tide of Felipinos, buffeting her from side to side as they streamed past.

"To raise our voices against the *evil*," sang Sylvia Perez, brandishing her two clenched fists high above her head, "and to pray to Our Lady and the only true God for protection from idol worshippers who bring *curses* upon their own daughters and *wickedness* upon her neighbors!"

"Then do you know me *no more*, after all these years, Sylvia? And is there no *pity* for a friend whose ancestors lie together and for the godmother to her own precious daughters?" cried María, as she watched her long-time friend disappear into the crowd.

The Felipinos swelled tighter and tighter. Then suddenly, the post of the street sign gave way, and María Xquic collapsed, the top of the pole and the sign, "*Via Santa María,*" stretched across her small shoulders. She began to panic, fearful of being trampled by her angry neighbors. More and more alone now, even among her own, tiny and crippled, María Xquic de Xoy sobbed and wept. Unable to rise against the seemingly endless passage and after lying prone for what seemed a night, she finally heard the familiar voice of her sister-in-law.

"Señora Manuela?" cried María Xquic, wife of the poor priest of the *Maximón*, Guatemalan mother of the damned and disappeared. María raised her hand, and Manuela Mendoza de J'Cab helped her relative to her feet.

"What can I do?" cried María Xquic.

"Your way has been very hard, María, and I fear even worse for you now and for us all. But I will speak for you, María, because I am one who remembers still the old ways!" promised her sister-in-law. "I will speak your name and raise a prayer for Don Andres! But you must tell *no one!*"

"Then, God bless you *forever*, Manuela, my precious sister!" cried María Xquic de Xoy, clutching the pole as the last of the crowd flowed past her.

"God bless your *forever, Manuela!*" María whispered after her childhood friend.

Bolstered with nothing but the simple instruments of their trade—hoes, planting staffs, and worn machetes, the Felipinos climbed up the rutted trail, through the stinging needles of scrub and brush, and over the bank onto the road.

The focus of their wrath was the "mouth of the jackal," the gates of the military garrison less than a mile from San Felipe. The moon broke through the blanket of clouds slowly drifting around the cap of Volcan Tolimán, illuminating the road's winding path, a silver ribbon weaving its way toward the post. Once upon the road, the Felipinos reorganized and turned eastward, the blades of their hoes and machetes glinting like crystal spikes against the dark shadows of the broken fields of corn.

The crest of the protestors reached the first outpost, a concrete bunker with a narrow viewing slit scored around the front and three sides of the structure. The Felipinos rushed up and around the abandoned building, clanging defiantly against the walls, flaking off chips and flinging them into the night, but the assault was only a dalliance. As the lagging trail of the Felipinos rolled back up into the pack, the angry protestors surged forward once more out onto the moonlit road, less than a kilometer from the fearsome gates of the jackal.

Inside the garrison, the young conscripts watched with increasing concern the approach of the angry crowd, perhaps two hundred or more Felipinos, turn on the road and draw up a hundred meters away from the gate. The soldiers, positioned at their posts in fighting stance for more than an hour, were looking themselves for a resolution to this outpouring of frustration. As they watched, the *alcaldes* moved silently to the head of the procession, each carrying a large hoe, their blades sparkling in the moonlight. Each of the three *alcaldes*, their heads covered with *cofrade tzutes*, moved into a forward position ahead of the pack and stepped several paces in front of the rest. At once, the grumbling crowd dropped to silence as the *alcaldes* continued their march toward the gates.

"You are ordered to stop, disburse, and return to your homes—*immediately*," barked a loudspeaker in Spanish. The *alcaldes* stopped and lowered the blades of their hoes, although none sought to retreat from the impending confrontation.

"You must leave immediately or accept the consequences," insisted the military voice. The stone-faced *alcaldes* stood motionless. To the others, already angry at the soldiers, the order was a challenge. Again, the ultimatum was repeated:

"You must leave *immediately* or accept the consequences. You have five minutes to disperse."

The Felipinos brandished their machetes in front of them as the *alcaldes* readjusted the hoes across their shoulders. Slowly, a rumble of Felipino voices crescendoed into a swell of angry repudiations, and the crowd surged forward, engulfing the hapless *alcaldes* who would have been their spokesmen.

"*Down* with the repression!" railed the inspired Ramundo C'Jux. "*Close* the garrison! *Out* with the soldiers!"

"*Curses* on the killers of Don Andres!" cried Doña Mañuela Mendoza, crossing her breast as a blessing for herself as well as for her sister-in-law and friend, María Xquic de Xoy, a woman whose own anguish and sorrow told the story of the people themselves.

"Stop *murdering* our sons and *raping* our daughters!" wailed Tata Paco and Sylvia Perez. Don Tupe Arredondo spit vehemently at his feet and lifted the twelve-pound hoe high above his shoulders as he shouted oaths of defiance. Señora Colom ripped the *tzute* from around her head and shoulders and jerked it up and down in front of her face, shaking her fist, and wailing at the soldiers behind the low stone walls.

The angry crowd had become a mob, bent on crashing through the gates to occupy and close down the garrison. They wanted to be free of the military and liberated from the constant state of siege. They wanted to be free from subjection to whimsical abuse and the brutality rained down upon them, lifted from the fear and the intimidation, free to rise each morning to attend their chores and to climb the mountain to tend their fields. They prayed to be freed to conduct their worship services, to manage their schools, and to celebrate their *fiestas* without fear that the militaries would suddenly appear afterwards to take away their healthy young sons for service as wild dogs in the evil *ejército*.

"*Go! . . .Go! . . . Go!*" chanted the mob as they swelled toward the gates.

[Crack!] [Crack!] [Pumpf!] [Crack!] The soldiers began to fire, this time not from orders, but rather from a white terror that gripped them as they realized that no walls or gate would deter the enraged Felipinos. They fired wildly into the crowd, scrambling for new clips of ammunition, shouting in panic to one another, and shoving each other for more secure positions.

Startled and panicked by the unexpected fusillade of soldiers' fire, the Felipinos tried to fall back, scattering as they could into the dark shadows of the fields and trees, but not all could escape. Tata Paco was the first to fall, collapsing on both knees and then toppling face forward across the blade of the machete that had served him so well for the past seven years. Her fists still raised above her head, Señora Colom was jerked off her feet and flung into the Felipinos behind her by a bullet that tumbled through her chest. Then fell Ramundo C'Jux and next to him a black-headed little boy in his brown and white-checkered *capixay* and fresh straw hat. Then, old Mercio Steinholder, the pharmacist, dropped, his whole face suddenly awash in blood, and then Señorita María Menudo de Somosoto, the third-year teacher from the American school, who was spun completely around by a missile that ripped through her breast.

One by one, in defiance of the bullets that tore away their lives, fifteen Felipinos fell in the flush of the very moment that they had reasserted their own dignity and the community's sense of its fundamental humanity.

And then it stopped. Just as quickly as it had begun, the shooting ended. Just as the earth had opened to receive the fresh sacrifices of furious, hot blood, it was over. Each Felipino and each soldier stood frozen in the repugnance of the moment. One by one, the young soldiers laid down their guns and faced their neighbors, and the Felipinos, stoned in horror at the realization of the murders at their feet, relinquished their hatred for unbridled grief and anguish. Laying down their crude weapons—the hoes and machetes and their planting sticks—they gathered up their dead and wounded and cradled them in their arms. Then turning their backs on the damned, the Felipinos slowly coursed their way back up the silver ribbon of road to San Felipe del Lago.

María Se Va

We are coming, María, with a sacrifice
to lay at your crippled feet.
We are coming, María, with our sacrifice
nursed at the devil's teat.

Receive us, María, with our sacrifice,
how rigid and cold in death.
Receive us, María, as a sacrifice,
now void of life and breath.

Leave us, María, as a sacrifice,
that we may live in peace.
Leave us, María, for a sacrifice,
that our curse may find release.

* * *

Chapter 2

The Uniforms of Satan

Manuel Xoy held the mouth of the plastic urn under the spigot of the water hydrant. He gripped the two handles on either side of the bottle and leaned his bulging stomach against it, his fragile little thigh and knee positioning the heavy vessel against the hydrant pipe.

Hugging the bottle brimming with the water, Manuel managed to slip his tiny hand up over the mouth of the bottle and turn off the tap. Awkwardly but quickly, he grappled with the bottle, suddenly threatening to fall, and water spilled over his white muslin, handwoven trousers. His thighs slid under the bottle, and with the newly established point of leverage, he was able to reposition the heavy urn and lift it onto his right shoulder.

Manuel turned slowly and deliberately away from the spigot, testing his uncertain balance. His calloused feet gingerly sought the otherwise familiar path down the trail which lurched left, then right, then left again toward the main street of his tiny *aldea*, San Felipe del Lago. Pedro, the family's dog, blithely scampered ahead, smelling at clumps of grass in the path and corners of the crumbling concrete walk flanking the dusty, rutted street. Manuel stepped up onto the sidewalk and assumed a soft glide as he continued the struggle to maintain his balance.

Colata Toj, an aged weaver, was closing her sidewalk stall. She had just managed the knot on the thick cords that secured her bundle of textiles as Manuel Xoy approached her along the sidewalk. She rolled her heavy bundle out of the little boy's path and inside her store front as he approached and grunted an expletive as he splashed a little water on her twisted, tortured feet. He followed his dog up the street past the *panderia*, then the *farmacia*, and turned right at the door of the evangelical church.

The path divided into a series of deep, dust-filled ruts, the erosion of the heavy highland rains that drench the western slopes of the Sierra Madres between July and November. In these early days of February, the corn is parched, and the soil nothing more than a powder that billowed around each step up the path as he lurched back and forth toward his home.

Up ahead, beyond his sight, Manuel heard his dog growl and snap, apparently at another animal on the trail. A litany of barks and grievous, low-toned drones marked the animals' respective territorial claims as Pedro moved further along the path. In his concentration on balancing the water, Manuel seemed to move independently from his feet which knew their own way from the spigot to the front door of the hovel that was his home.

Bamboo poles, lashed together, fashioned the four walls. Laced thatch in great flats formed the layered roof. Chickens scratched and pecked at the dirt yard surrounding the house. A light-grey wall of sandy clay towered behind the fields that stretched down the slope in back of the house. Great concave shallows had been dug out of the face of the hill. Manuel's older brothers sold the clay to a concrete merchant who brought his truck into the village once each week to collect the earth. His brothers had to carry the soil in sacks over their shoulders down the same trail which Manuel now struggled to compass with his vessel of water.

As he approached the turn off from the path that led to his house, Manuel Xoy, the great grandson of the village's most legendary *auxiliatura*, spied the flat rock where the older youths would sit at the end of the day to wait for the girls coming back from market. Manuel set the plastic urn on the rock, shook his thin little arms, and looked up and down the path and toward his house up on the hill, fearful that someone might have observed his fatigue.

He was safe. Damp fog had rolled in from the upper reaches of the mountains, enveloping the breaks of trees and obscuring the trail on either end. Through the tingling fog, Manuel Xoy, whose great grandfather Don Andres Menchu had healed Don Diego Xic, the *alcalde* of San Mateo Cuchumatán, brother of General Francisco Palma Sierra, Manuel Menchu Xoy, the curator of his father's name in the village, gripped the handles of the plastic jug with its diagonal green and white stripes and raised the water back on his shoulder. The smell of his mother's wood-burning fire and fresh tortillas drifted through the damp fog, into his lungs, into his veins, up through his skin, and filtered into his clothes.

Corn, earth, water, mothers, the green leaves of the chichicaster, the twenty maguey seeds of the sacred bundle, *Santo Guzmán*, *Santiago*, and the blessed saints of the mountains, the *alcaldes* of the lake and high sky above, *El Mundo* and the saints of all good work, and the blessed *Virgen*—the likeness of which he wore on his sleeves and in the lining of his woollen jacket—Manuel Xoy, son of the *Tzutujiles*, was bringing water to the fire of his mother, María Xquic de Xoy.

The footpath ended at the entrance of his *casa*. The dusty, grey feet of his mother passed across the threshold in front of him as he approached the door. The skirt of his mother's *corte* was coated in the same dust of her feet, and pasty patches of dry *masa* checkered the front and side of the wrap-around fabric. The brocaded lozenges of her *huipil* were frayed and faded from the years of wear under the open skies. She wiped her leathery palms against the sides of her skirt as she turned to receive the great grandson of Don Andres Menchu.

The little boy struggled across the threshold, trying with resolve to avoid spilling his cargo, but the sinews of his tiny arms twitched in spasms as he lowered the jug. His mother reached for the exposed handle and helped him lower the vessel to the ground before the hearth. Tears welled up into the eyes of the great grandson of the renowned Don Andres, friend of the fearsome Generalisimo Francisco Palma Sierra (the "rat") whose troops had ripped through the valley of Salamá. The "rat" would be embarrassed to see him now, struggling with only a jug of water, and he would laugh at him, and following in kind, the *ladino* troops would wink at one another on the backs of their horses, and they would laugh, also. They would laugh long and hard at the foolish little water bearer's anemic plight with a plastic jug of water.

His mother recognized Manuel Xoy's chagrin and turned away to her chores, so that she might avoid seeing the tear slip from the corner of his eye. Wiping it dry against his T-shirt sleeve, he had managed to save face. Thanks to the Mother of God, Lucita Maria and Ana Fabiola were away. They would cover their mouths and laugh at each other to see him struggle so. Thanks to the Mother of God, they were away in the market with Tanolito and Miguel Mapa.

Miguelito and Tanolito, Manuel Xoy's two older brothers were preparing to leave for the coast. Every year, for the past five seasons, they would leave the highlands with the other Felipinos and the *Atitecos* from Santiago Atitlán to cut sugar cane in La Paca and work the shrimp hatcheries up the coast of Retalhuleu. It was hot, hard work that would take its toll on the laborers who weren't used to the heat. Don "Pimi" Xcix died on his first trip to La Paca, and the workers had told how, while trying to meet his quota, he had collapsed in the cane from a heat stroke. Don "Pimi" was delirious for more than three days, and then he died. The government took him away and buried him at Los Arboles before Doña Tacha even learned of his death.

But Miguelito and Tanolito were strong in their youth at twenty and twenty-one, and they could do anything. Manuel Xoy knew that, too, because he had watched them dig out the old ceiba roots when the bores had finished their work on the ancient tree.

Manuel Xoy slipped quickly out the door and chased the cat off the rack of corn piled twenty-one rows high under the eave of the straw roof.

The cat was a grey, striped stray that had wondered into the field below the back of the house more than two years before. It thrived on chicken bones and tortilla scraps, just like the other animals—domestic and otherwise—that always meandered into the *Tzutujil* Indian yard. It bounded along the edge of the weathered adobe wall of the house, across the open yard at the rear, and into the parched stalks of maize. Manuel skirted the first three rows of the harvested maize to surprise the cat as it settled between the rows in the soft hillocks of hoed earth. He slipped silently to the ground, flat as a tortilla in his mother's palm. The cat amused itself just beyond his reach, rolling over and over on its back, slapping at the air with its front paws.

Manuel Menchu Xoy was patient. He waited as he watched. The cat, in its distraction, would work its way playfully just next to him in the adjacent row. Manuel Xoy relaxed completely. He felt the fullness of the very tips of his fingers and the relaxation of the tense muscles along his spine. If he were discovered, it would not be of his own doing.

The cat rolled in the earth against a mound of finely hoed volcanic soil. Then it spied a small beetle tumbling over and around the fine granules of dirt. [Slap!] The paw of the cat crashed over the insect which, stunned, revived momentarily and proceeded on its own path.

[Slap!] [Slap!] The cat lurched upright, and standing, arched over the insect, watched it intently as the beetle fumbled ahead. The cat methodically and slowly matched the pace of the insect, unaware that it was moving within arm's reach of the wily young Felipino prone flat in the row beyond the next head of corn.

"*Aheee!*" squealed Manuel Xoy as he sprang upon the preoccupied feline.

Startled, the cat hissed and raised its pelt, falling back and rolling over and over. Suddenly, the cat regained its composure and tore away down the row of corn toward the house. Manuel fled after it, hoping to cut it off before it reached the ravine behind the house.

The cat bounded across the compound, racing across the threshold of the house, and disappeared into the brush and brittle corn stalks. Manuel Xoy followed accordingly, unable to keep pace. He rounded the corner of the path out of the abandoned cornfield. He turned the corner of his house and hurtled over a net of cabbages. Startled by strange voices, he lurched to a halt at the rack of corn and flung himself backwards on his heels. He crouched low behind the bin of corn.

"Sí! El capitán! Por su puesto!" said the familiar voice. It was the high-pitched voice of Miguel Mapa Xoy, Manuel's oldest brother.

"We can make arrangements," offered Miguel Mapa, "no, problem, for sure. No problem, for sure. My brother, Tanolito, we're a team, you can count us. You just say, and we'll be there."

"You Felipino *tacos*," said the other, "you're all the same. Every one of you sound just alike. Someone can piss all over your feet, and you Felipinos apologize for it missing your faces. Monday, *four o'clock, Monday. Got it?"*

"*Four o'clock, Monday!*" confirmed Miguel Mapa. "Four o'clock, Monday. *Sure!*"

The stranger turned and walked away. He was a *ladino* that Manuel had never seen before. The stranger was wearing a green plastic rain jacket over jeans stuffed into his high-top boots, and he stepped briskly down the trail, jumping nimbly from side to side to avoid the ruts.

Manuel Xoy watched the stranger work his way down the path over which only an hour or so earlier he, himself, had labored to bring the water jug to his mother. He was puzzled by the bit of conversation he had overheard. His brothers were strong and could move heavy rocks and turn great mounds of earth with their hoes. They had respect in the *aldea* and could drive a bargain in the city market. He didn't understand the stranger's words. They seemed rude and hostile, and Tanolito and Miguelito had not responded as he expected. He crouched behind the corn rack until he saw the stranger pass from sight. His brothers had walked away around the corner, muttering to themselves. The cat coursed its way through their feet as they proceeded haltingly, pausing from moment to moment to whisper a confidence between them.

Manuel Xoy was confused again. One or two days before—he wasn't sure—he had seen his brothers on the plaza in front of the evangelical church talking with two soldiers. One had slapped Miguel Mapa on the back of the shoulder. They seemed to joke with Tanolito and Miguel Mapa, and the *ladino* soldiers' heads snapped back in a crackling laugh.

María Xquic de Xoy had advised—*no! pleaded*—with her sons to avoid the soldiers. They were *evil* people. Sons of the earth put on the uniforms of Satan, and then they do terrible things to their mothers and fathers and to the little ones and to the neighbors. They forget their friends. They forget the land. They spurn the soil. They forget the *alcaldes* and make fun of *la costumbre*. With their guns slung about their necks, the soldiers mock the funerals of the poor Indians and gamble with the *ladinos* during the Holy Mass.

"Avoid the *soldiers!*" protested María Xquic. "Don't go near the *soldiers!*"

And Manuel Xoy was confused again. The stranger's boots were high top boots that the soldiers wear. And Tanolito and Miguel Mapa were talking with the man in the high-top boots, and the soldiers were joking and slapping Miguel Mapa on the shoulder and making fun.

"Don't go near the *soldiers!*" María Xquic de Xoy whispered over his shoulder, and Manuel Xoy was confused.

Chapter 3

Hail the Saints

"We've got two of them. They should be coming from outside the Palace in the next five minutes or so," said Rooster. "This traffic is going to make a pick up difficult."

Rooster stroked his rib cage, reaching inside his polished cotton long-sleeve, pale-blue shirt which he wore unbuttoned to the third button so as to reveal his muscular torso. His hand glided from his rib cage up to the gold chain that he always wore around this neck. He glanced from side to side through his aviator sunglasses and reached cautiously at the driver's jacket slung over the back of the front seat between them. Inside was the notebook with the names of those "clients" already "serviced" and those yet to be "processed." He found the black spiral with his thumb and index finger and worked it out of the jacket pocket. He leafed quickly through the pages to the latest entries.

Ramiro Alvarez
Pedro Bustamante
Rutilio Martinez
Beatriz Villagros
Tano Xoy
Miguel Xoy

"What's the agenda with these two peckers?" Rooster asked.

"Delivery to the shop," returned Taco.

"*Delivery?*" he asked again.

"Yeah, *`delivery,'*" said the bored driver.

"How are we going to recognize them?" asked Taco.

"One of them is tall—*powerful* guy for an Indian. He's *really* strong—about six feet or so. The other is shorter, but he's a tight nut, also. They haul sand," he reported. "He's the one with a scar across the top of his forehead above his left eye. The older one—the *big* guy—always wears a cap. Look for a `Saints' cap with the French thing on it."

"`*French* thing'?" asked Taco.

"Yeah, you know, the `*fleur-de-lis,*'" explained Rooster. "The *devil,* man. Don't you have any *class?*"

Rooster laughed. Taco was silent.

"Hey, Chaco—*Chico, Chaco!*" Rooster urged over his left shoulder. "We're looking for two muscular Felipinos, Tano and Miguel Xoy. We're just picking them up. We're supposed to take them to `the shop' for the Colonel, so no *rough* stuff. You *got* it? Don't make a scene. Just show them your `piece' and bring them in."

"What do they *look* like?" asked Chico.

"The big one—that's Miguel—he always wears this New Orleans `Saints' cap with the gold insignia—the *fleur-de-lis*," explained Rooster.

"The `*what'?*" asked Chaco. Chico stared straight ahead, but he, too, was alert for the answer.

"A golden *shit hook*, you dumb *sticks!"* roared Rooster in his moment of triumph.

The Cherokee inched along in the late afternoon traffic down the one-way, three-lane avenue toward to the great plaza and the National Palace. The sidewalks were packed with files of people walking briskly with purpose from corner to corner. Others browsed in shop windows or smoked cigarettes in casual conversation just inside the shop entrances outside the melee of pedestrians. The Cherokee came to a stop several vehicles behind a red light. A drab, green city bus arched its rump just in front of them, its limp tail pipe pulsing to the rocking rhythm of the idling motor.

Next to them in the left lane, a young professional couple sat compromisingly close together on the back of a motorcycle. The driver, a suave, thin young man with thick, black hair sweeping back and over in a duck tail, set up straight, tipping casually from right toe to left as he revved his engine impatiently. Squeezed tightly to his back, a rider, a woman in her twenties, wearing tight grey pants, a white blouse, and grey jacket, held him securely around his chest as she rested her right cheek against his left shoulder. On the right, a dilapidated taxi, a rather weary, dark-brown Ford sedan, pulled to a stop. Its unmatched, musty grey tires were unevenly inflated, and the whole vehicle tilted precariously over a collapsed shock on the driver's front side.

Wearing a filthy straw hat, a grizzled old man, his vision impaired by a thick leathery cataract over his left eye, shuffled forward between the Cherokee and the taxi. As Rooster watched through the heavily tinted window, the drunk took a position over the left front tire of the taxi and unzipped his pants. He bent over slowly and leaned against the hood of the taxi, and then braced himself on his left elbow for support. Oblivious to the city rush swirling about him, the old man began urinating over the tire. The driver bellowed a curse that was lost in the roar and belching fumes of the bus and a cacophony of horns anticipating the changing light. In revenge for the public insult, the taxi driver lurched his vehicle forward twice and then a third time, braking suddenly after each, sending the old man wheeling to the pavement. Slowly, the traffic moved around the still, wasted progeny of Tecún Umán.

The Cherokee glided forward, pulling away from the pedestrians who had clamored past the van only a block before. Taco watched carefully the traffic to either side through the side mirrors. Space—he always wanted more space at a time like this. He was always anticipating the need to turn quickly either left or right to get away from a pick-up point. That was out of the question in traffic this heavy. Rooster pointed toward a parking space a block ahead just in front of the National Cathedral on the right. Both knew it was nothing more than a mirage, that some vehicle would slip in before them, and it happened just as they approached the corner.

"*Shit!*" said Rooster. "We lost the best possible *spot!* And so *close!*" Taco guided the Cherokee past the lost parking space and pulled to a stop once again behind the belching bus. Diesel fumes seeped into the cab. In the rear, Rooster and Chico broke into coughs.

"Mother of *G-God!*" protested Chaco. "You fart *again*, Chico?"

Chico never smiled. Nearing a "service," he was all business. He squeezed the shoulder holster under his left arm just enough to confirm its presence. Even though he never removed it (except in the shower), he sometimes found himself taking the pistol for granted, and he needed to remind himself occasionally; from time to time, he needed to pull himself back on guard. Chaco had sobered again from his coughing spasm and his spurned quip, and he began flipping a rubber-coated truncheon. The outline of his own hand gun holstered in his belt, bulged through the back of his leather jacket. He remembered how Sergio Rivera had almost shot his ass off coming back down the deeply rutted road from Comalapa two years before. The truck had bottomed out, almost ripping away the drive shaft, and Sergio's pistol had discharged, burning his buttocks and ripping a hole through the back of the seat and out the underside of the cabin. The Colonel had called him "flash ass" after that.

"*There!*" Rooster gestured. "Pull up there on the *corner!* That's even *better*." He had spied a space just on the next corner next to the National Palace just across the street from the National Cathedral.

Chaco drove the Cherokee into place and shifted the gear into neutral.

Everyone sighed. Now they began the waiting. No one said a word.

Rooster scanned behind Taco's head and gazed intently at the people milling around the Great Plaza just across the street in front of the National Palace. There would be two of them, two brothers, two Felipinos—one tall and muscular, the other shorter and wiry, but reportedly just as strong. The cap was the key, and Rooster peered over the clusters of people, looking sharply for caps. An *elote* vender was wearing a cap; two young teenage boys were wearing caps; an old mechanic emerged from beneath a pickup truck parked way across the plaza—*he* was wearing a cap. The clusters of people drifted from place to place, intersected by the play of youngsters chasing each other around the concrete benches. A soccer ball went flying into the air, launched from somewhere beyond the benches near the center of the plaza.

Every time the light changed, the passing traffic blocked his view, and Rooster arched his neck, backwards and forward, to see around the passing trucks and busses. It was impossible. They would have to exit the truck. Rooster looked back and snapped his fingers, the signal to go. Chaco and Chico exited the rear and left side, and Rooster from the passenger side of the front seats. He tucked his shirt into his pants and pulled his jacket together at the bottom and zipped it up about five or six inches. He adjusted the sunglasses on his nose and walked toward his two "administrators" in the rear.

With a nod of his head, Rooster, "the navigator," signalled his team to work their way across the two lanes of traffic and to enter the plaza. The three of them wound single-file in front of a car and behind another bus and stepped into the plaza. They had lost sight of the Cherokee, and that wasn't good, but that's the way it was.

"*Here,*" said Rooster. "We're looking for a tall Felipino and his brother, Tano and Miguel Xoy. Miguel is wearing this black and gold cap. The design looks like *this.*" Rooster took out a ballpoint pen and outlined the fleur-de-lis in his palm.

"I'll take the left side, you guys, the right, and we'll meet back at the fountain in the middle over there," Rooster directed. Then the two groups fanned out. They made three large loops around the plaza, checking off each time at the fountain, but with no success. After another twenty minutes passed, Rooster began to think that they had failed. The sun had already set behind the buildings and was drifting beyond the volcanoes to the west. The incandescent arc lights were already humming around the plaza, warming up to check the darkness around the National Cathedral, the plaza, and the National Palace itself. They had obviously missed their pick-up, and the team retreated back through the lingering traffic toward the still purring Cherokee and the ever-reliable Taco.

"*Shit!*" exclaimed Rooster as he stepped back into the passenger seat. "I guess it's going to be a long night. We'll have to refuel before we leave for the lake. They'll probably be taking the last bus back to San Felipe."

Chapter 4

Two Sisters of Patozí

"How many do you think we'll find today?" asked Marcus, as he fumbled deeply through the bag for the small package.

"Probably thirty or forty," Father Mike responded.

"Is that fairly *typical?*" continued Marcus.

"It's down from more than 300 a night five or six years ago when the Casa was over at San Benito."

Marcus Finley's fingers found the small package with the microphone battery. He pulled it through the tangle of audio wires and loose video batteries and into the light. He bent the package across the sealed battery and forced the tiny power pack through the back of the wrapper. He was doing the right thing, starting with the fresh battery. He didn't want to miss a moment in the compound.

"Have you ever lost an interview?" asked the priest.

"Once," confessed Marcus. "I taped an entire health fair last spring. I got pretty decent video, but not a sound. The damn battery was dead—the whole *time!*"

Marcus wished he could retrieve the previous observation. Mike continued, his eyes fixed on the ribbon of weathered asphalt stretching straight out before them. They had met earlier in the morning at a restaurant parking lot just north of the international bridge between McAllen and Reynosa to travel southeast to Brownsville. There they would review the precarious situation at Casa Libertad.

Citrus orchards pealed by them, punctuated by stately royal palms, towering on either side of the road at irregular intervals. The Valley was greening in this early flush of spring with its seasonal rains. They passed orchard after orchard of lime, orange, and grapefruit. On the other side of the road, stretching northward as far as the eye could trace in the dim fog, lay aloe vera fields; the spiny, medicinal succulents marched in rows toward the grey horizon.

"There's a good chance the new bishop will close the Casa," offered Father Mike. He had missed the idiocy about the dead battery, noted Marcus.

"*Close* the Casa?" asked Marcus, free from exposure.

"Appears possible," said Father Mike.

The young priest was on temporary assignment for the Brownsville parish in Mexico just across the border. Tuesdays were free days, usually, and he often met Border Watch volunteers like Marcus Finley on Tuesday mornings. He was still drowsy this morning. He had worked in the rice bins for more than six hours the night before, when he was already just about to collapse. He lacked the energy to spell out the details, but felt compelled to do so.

"With the war technically over, INS has pressured the new bishop into some premature concessions, including *closing Casa*," said Father Mike. "We've tried to get an appointment, but that hasn't worked. He's always `too busy.'" The priest smiled sardonically.

"The best bet," he said, "is just to go there. You can usually find him walking across back and forth to his office during the week," explained Mike.

"INS has been trying to close in on Casa Libertad ever since it opened in 1980. They have a tower just behind the back fence. It's really rather humorous. They worked for days to construct the thing. They manned it twenty-four hours a day on the Friday, Saturday, and Sunday after they finished it, and it's been shut down ever since."

"What was the purpose?" asked Marcus.

"Intimidation, pure and simple," explained Father Mike.

The car entered the city limits of Brownsville. Two pickup trucks with Hispanic workers passed them going the other way. The men waved limply to Father Mike's greeting on the horn.

"They're Valley laborers. They pretty much float from job to job. They're probably on a construction crew today," said the priest.

Marcus adjusted the Velcro strap on his camcorder. He wanted to be ready the moment the car approached the drive at Casa Libertad. They continued down the stretch of highway, passing truck after truckload of workers. Two blocks past the intersection of Highway 12 and FM Road 1266, they saw the fenced compound of Casa Libertad. They slowed and turned into the side road leading to the entrance.

As they came to a stop outside the padlocked fenced gate, they could see only two or three young men milling around within the grounds. Then two women, wearing aprons, emerged from one building and began clearing dishes from outside tables under an awning that connected the kitchen complex to the barracks. One of the young men saw Father Mike and Marcus as they stepped from the car and walked slowly toward the gate.

"*Buenos días, señor,*" greeted Father Mike. "*La Directora está en casa?*"

"*Sí, señor. Como no! Pasen adelante, señores,*" welcomed the young man.

The three of them entered the open green stretching from the gravelled entrance to the main house and the rest of the compound. Two more men came out of a work shed carrying trash cans and brooms. Both smiled and waved at the two strangers in their midst. Father Mike and Marcus Finley followed their guide to the Director's office. They stepped up on the front porch just as Sister María opened the screen door to greet them.

The plump, good-natured Dominican nun smiled as she greeted her friend, the priest. María had served as the Director of Casa Libertad since its inception nine years earlier when the flood of her people from El Salvador arrived in the valley in the tens of thousands. Born to a devout, second-generation Salvadoran family in Chicago in 1934, María Pascual had made her commitment to the Church as a young girl. For the first twenty-five years of her life in the Church, she had worked in the Dominican Republic and later in Puerto Rico. For another fifteen years, she had worked a food bank and street kitchen in a Chicago parish dominated by poor blacks and Hispanics and had come to the Rio Grande Valley in 1978 as hostilities began to sharpen in El Salvador.

Since her tenure at Casa, María had witnessed unspeakable suffering among the Central Americans and had personified, in her own commitment to service, the spirit of the Church's outreach to the poor and disenfranchised. Moreover, María was a good administrator. She knew how to manage large groups—how to shelter and feed them. She knew how to coordinate staff and, most importantly, how to arbitrate the inevitable conflicts that erupt between desperate people. Additionally, she was sensitive to public relations and the necessity of "good press"—something Casa had not always enjoyed. After so many years in "the refugee business," María had an intuitive eye for reporters, and this morning she had a cheery smile for the priest and his young companion with the camcorder and clipboard.

"Welcome, Mike. It is so very good to see you again so *soon!*" enthused Sister María. "What brings you back twice in the month?"

"María, I want you to meet Marcus Finley," a reporter for the *McAllen Star*. He's new to our area and is interested in getting more familiar with the Valley. Refugees are of particular interest to him, and I thought today might be a good time to bring him over to Casa."

Marcus Finley shook the nun's outstretched hand.

"*Mr. Finley!* Both of you are most welcome," María encouraged them once more. "What do you want to know, Mr. Finley?"

"Well, I guess to start with, just a little bit of the history would be helpful. I know that must be an old story for you, but it would be helpful to me," explained Marcus.

"*No, no.* Not at *all,*" apologized María. "Casa Libertad was of the Church from 1980 in San Benito. We had a house there already, and we decide to open a kitchen for the refugees who were here by the thousands in the first few months of the civil war in El Salvador. It was very difficult, because you know that word got out very quickly, and every day, more and more people, *thousands* of people begin to come. And it made some trouble for us, too, with the people in the neighborhood."

"*Trouble?*" asked Marcus Finley.

"People really weren't very sure about what was going on in the house," explained María. "They could see all the Central Americans, and some of them began calling INS and the police. They were afraid of the crowds and that some of them might make trouble for the neighborhood. One day when one refugee got in a fight that went out into the streets, some nervous neighbors begin to call the police, and that is when we had to abandon our small house in San Benito and find another place, *this* place."

"But you know, *really,*" said Sister María, "that was a good thing for us, because you know that that house was so very *small*, and we have to try to feed *so many* people."

"But the Church owned this land in Brownsville," said María, "and it had two houses already on it. We only have to add the two dormitories and the kitchen to make what you see here. And we can keep maybe 1,000 people—with a little crowded, *okay?* But sometimes we have just to do that."

"How many are here now?" asked Marcus.

"Maybe sixty, seventy maybe," returned the nun. "Some people of Honduras and Salvador. We have two from Guatemala."

"Can I ask you some questions without compromising the refugees here?" asked Marcus.

"I don't understand," said María.

"I mean . . . well, can you *talk* about the refugees?" stumbled Marcus.

"*Claro!*" said María. "Well, I can say *some* things. You know that many of the people are very quiet. They have a lot of trouble coming here, and many of them are still afraid, so they don't talk too much. But I know *some* things. *Sure!*"

"What do you want to ask?" interrupted Mike.

"Well, why are they here? I guess that's the basic question," said Marcus.

"Well, for many reasons. They are hungry. There are no jobs or work," reflected the Sister.

"They can't say *that* to Immigration," observed Marcus.

"But *of course* not, but you asked why they are here, and that is a reason. Some of the people are starving at home. There is nothing for them at all. The people from Honduras, especially," said María.

"And *Salvador?* The Salvadorans?" persisted Marcus.

"The war, it has left everything so *bad.* There is no work or jobs, no food in many parts of the country. The crops, they were destroyed this year in the fighting . . . many thousands of acres," explained María.

"And the *Guatemalans?*" continued the priest.

"Well, that is different. We have two Guatemalans . . ." said Sister María, somewhat hesitantly. "Their stories are very hard."

"What can you share with us, Sister?" asked Father Mike.

"Come inside," offered María. The three of them entered the Director's office and took a seat in the small reception area. María selected a straight-backed chair, her hands spreading her dark skirt smoothly over her knees.

"It is very bad, their story. They came here; they came together two days ago, and they are very frightened, very frightened by what has happened to their families. They say they are all dead in Patozí." Sister María was obviously deeply disturbed and having difficulty relating what she knew. Her face became deeply lined and wrinkled as she struggled for words.

"In Patozí, they say the *ejército* killed them *all*, more than *two hundred!* They say," said María, "that the people came to the center of Patozí to protest the taking that land, the taking of their land by the government."

"These were people of *Patozí?*" asked Father Mike.

"From Patozí, yes," said Sister María. "They were all from Patozí, and they had just gone down to the military . . . the military post outside the village. They said that they were going to have a protest the following weekend, the two hundred of them."

"What happened?" asked Marcus Finley.

"Well, the *ejército*—the army—learned about the protest, and the day before they sent two tractors, *not* tractors, not *tractors*—those with the big front, the big *blade* . . ." María struggled.

"*Bulldozers?*" asked Marcus.

"Bulldozers, *yes!*" said María. "They sent in these two bulldozers, and they dug two deep lines, two, uh . . . two `ditches.' They dug these two ditches just outside the city on the day before the protest. The next morning the Patozites got together at the evangelical church at the end of the street, and they were just waiting there, sitting there in front of the church. They waited maybe an hour—maybe two—I don't know. But then the army came. They had two trucks with soldiers, very heavily armed—they had *machine guns*. The soldiers got out of the trucks and pointed their guns at them, and they told them to go behind the church. One of the boys, he began arguing with one of the soldiers. Some of the women were very frightened, and they started to cry and pulling their *tzutes* over their faces. They put their little babies under their *tzutes*. Then the soldiers ordered them to sit down behind the church. At the other end of town, people said they heard the army start to shoot. They fired shoots—*shots*—for maybe ten minutes. They killed *every* person, the old men, the women, the little girls and the boys, even the *babies*, they killed them all. *Nobody* was left alive." For a few moments, Sister María was too choked to continue.

"The soldiers," she began again, "these soldiers piled all the bodies in the back of the trucks, and they drove them to the two ditches, and they just threw all the bodies . . . those little ones, the little *babies* and some of them *still crying*, they said."

Tears began to trickle down the Sister's cheeks.

"They threw them all into the ditches," she said. "Then the bulldozers covered them all up, and the soldiers left, and that was all. It was all over."

The three sat silently, completely stunned by the nun's story. Sister María could control her feelings no longer, and as she covered her mouth with the palm of her hands, she broke into uncontrollable sobs, a flood of tears streaming down her face.

Father Mike rose and walked to the window of the Director's office and stared out across the green toward the barracks of Casa Libertad. The muscles tensed in the back of his neck, and he felt a shiver drift from the nape of his neck out across his shoulders.

"*Why?*" asked Marcus Finley. "Why did they kill them?" he asked as he looked deeply into the swollen eyes of Sister María.

Sister María wiped her eyes with a handkerchief. It was seconds before she could respond.

"Why?" she repeated, as she searched within herself as much for meaning as an answer.

"*Why?*" Sister María returned the question to Marcus Finley. "I cannot tell you *'why?'* But I can say this: I can say there is an *evil* in that land. I can say to you that there is *burning pitch* where the heart of that people should be. I can tell you that the heavy chain of the militaries has dragged down the spirit of the people. Maybe I can say—to find the words—for forty, now for forty years and more, there is a demon fever raging in the *soul* of a dying nation."

"You know," said María, "everything in that country, it is turned around. You just can see it. Guatemala is supposed to be `the land of eternal spring,' they say. The national flower, you may know, is the orchid. But the *monja blanca*, the white orchid, it is just a *parasite*, sapping the life from the beautiful tree. And this tree, tall and proud, is the *gente*, the precious *people.* The white orchid has become the *white hand of death and destruction* of the Guatemalan people!"

"Sister María," said Father Mike. "Are the Guatemalans who told you of these things, are they *here*, here in Casa *now?*"

"Yes," said María vacantly.

"Well, is it, I mean, do you think that they would be willing to talk with us?" asked the priest.

"Oh, *Father!*" cried the distraught María. "They are so *terribly* frightened. I don't know."

"You must be the judge, María," confessed Mike, reluctantly. "You obviously are the one to know better."

"Well, let me talk with them. Wait for me here. I will go and see them. Perhaps they will talk with you since you are a priest," said María. She rose slowly and left the room.

Mike turned to Marcus Finley, still deep in shock from the report. He had never heard anything like such a massacre. He couldn't begin to visualize such a senseless, brutal act.

"If they decide to talk, Marcus, I probably will need to see them privately," explained Mike.

"Oh, I understand!" returned Marcus. "I'll leave now and go back to the car and wait for some sign from you. It will probably be better if they don't see me at all." Marcus Finley rose and gathered his camera and equipment and quickly exited the room.

Mike slipped back toward the window and peered out across the green. His thoughts drifted southward to Guatemala and to the Guatemalan department, or state, of El Quiché. He never travelled to Patozí, the little village in the far northwestern sector near the Mexico border, but he knew quite well the parish priest, Father Alejandro Méndez, a Guatemalan. He had met him at a meeting of Central American clergy four or five years before, and they had spent several hours together discussing the difficulties of pastoring in a violent land. Two earlier priests had been threatened and one, Father Julio Dombey, assassinated. He had been seized by four armed men, according to one eye witness, on the streets at the outskirts of Chichicastenango and driven away in a black Jeep Cherokee. His body was discovered two weeks later almost forty miles away on the road to San Pedro Itzamná. His hands had been tied behind his back, and his body showed signs of brutal torture from cigarette burns and beatings from a heavy, blunt instrument of some kind. Apparently, he had died from a stab wound through his ribs. The other priest, Father Montenegro Bulask, fled to Costa Rica, after the death of Father Julio. Additionally, more than a dozen catechists had been murdered or "disappeared" in the last ten years.

"If you want to give a believer the kiss of *death*, just install him as a *catechist*," Father Méndez had told Father Mike. "We bring the Gospel of Christ to the people, they begin to examine their lives from the point of view of the Word, begin to *act* as servants of God, and collect their reward—a *bullet in the temple* if they're lucky, or otherwise, they're brutally butchered with a machete."

"Sometimes, I have to ask myself and the Church, quite frankly," confided Father Méndez, "for what life are we saving these poor people *now*—never mind salvation and the hereafter. Eschatology they *understand.* It's making sense of the *here and now* in the light of the Gospels that they struggle with so desperately every time they suffer another attack. These are the bravest people I have ever met. For without a doubt, confession of *faith* is the surest path to martyrdom in *this* world, in *this* country. The military has declared us all `subversive.' I simply don't know how much more a people can stand."

Father Mike remembered the conversation so well, for his liberal zeal had been sobered substantially by Father Méndez's confidence with him. He himself suffered considerable anguish from Father Méndez's reflections, for while he was living stateside in comfort and security, the Guatemalan priests were living, day by day, with their hands already tied behind their backs and lined up against the wall. They lived not only with the continuous threats to their own safety and security, but they had to live constantly aware of the consequences of active faith for the *campesinos* they served. Mike had made a pledge—of a *kind*—that he would "work daily to support his martyred brothers in Christ and those who followed them, *as long as* . . ." As long as he *himself* didn't have to go . . . His unspeakable conclusion to that idea was interrupted by approaching footsteps and a knock on the office door.

"Come in," said Mike. Sister María entered and stepped aside as two diminutive Guatemalan Quiché-Maya Indian women, shawls over their heads, entered timidly and stood in the door.

"*Pasen adelante*," encouraged Father Mike. "*Siéntense, Uds., por favor.*"

The two Indian women looked at him blankly, walked over to the couch, and sat down, occupying almost the same cushion. Slowly, both withdrew the brightly colored, handwoven shawls from their head and placed them in their laps where their hands might find warmth and refuge.

"*Señoritas*, this is Father Mike," said María to the two Guatemalans.

"Father Mike knows and loves very much the people of Guatemala," she continued. The two Guatemalan girls stared vacantly at her.

"He . . . he wants *very* much, *señoritas*, to hear your stories," pleaded Sister María.

A look of horror washed over the two Guatemalans, and their faces turned down to their laps. Swallowed up in their grief riding so close to the surface of their emotions, they seemed even tinier and more pitiful.

"I *told* you, Father Mike . . ." reminded María to the priest, this time in English.

"I *know*, Sister," said Father Mike. "I am trying to understand." He turned patiently and with marked reserve to the two frightened Guatemalans.

"The Lord receive you in his peace and bless you in your suffering," the priest offered in Spanish, and he laid his hands on both their heads. "May the Lord lift this heavy burden from you and send his guardian angels to wash your feet and to soothe the thirst for peace in your hearts."

Mike withdrew his hands from the top of their heads and passed his fingers down the outside of their faces, and turning them under their chins, he gently lifted their faces to meet his own.

"The Lord loves you and feels your pain and suffers your anguish and accepts you as His own," whispered the priest, as he made the sign of the cross across each of their foreheads.

"Peace be with you, Sisters," said Mike.

"And with *you*," returned the Guatemalan on the right. They were Catholic, and he had found a way into their confidence.

"Sisters, you are safe now in this land. No one wishes to harm you any more. Sister María, I, the others here at Casa Libertad—we are your friends, and we are here only to help you," he explained. The two timid girls turned their heads slightly to each other and exchanged the swiftest glances.

"It may help now," continued Father Mike, "to share your stories among those who love and care for you."

"It is very *hard*, Father, to know *how* to say it," struggled the girl on the right, as her friend looked at her silently. The wall of their anxiety was beginning to come down. They did, in fact, need desperately to share their stories, to cry out against the inexplicable evil that had crushed their families and friends.

"Why don't you tell me your names," said Father Mike.

"Noelia Tenox," said the girl on the right.

"María Colín Pérez," offered the other in barely audible tones.

"Donde viven, Ustedes?" he asked. "Where are you from?"

"Patozí, Patozí Vera Paz, El Quiché," they revealed.

"`El Quiché' I know," explained Father Mike, "but Patozí—I have never been to your *aldea*. It must be a *beautiful aldea*."

"Oh, Father, it *is* beautiful, along the road to Sumpatenango," said Noelia.

"Cuantos años tienen, Ustedes?" he asked. "How old are you?"

"Nineteen—*she* is," said Noelia, answering for Maria. "I am twenty-one."

"Tell me why you left Guatemala," coaxed the priest.

"Father, we have no one, and the soldiers said they would come back for the rest of us if we stayed. And so we fled. We left *everything*: our *homes*, our *belongings*, the *old* people who are crippled, and those who were working in the fields who we couldn't stop to *tell.* We left them *all* to come here."

"What happened in Patozí Vera Paz, Sisters?" Mike asked directly. "What did the militaries do to you and to your *aldea*?"

"My father, Don Carlos . . . Carlos Tenox Villagro, he was a farmer for the owner of the *finca*. He worked in the fields with the cattle to feed them, to drive them, to look after them. Maria's father, *too*—Don Fernando—they both worked for the *finca* with the cattle and livestock. They heard the cooperative director say that it wasn't right that the government took our lands the year before, and now a large road was coming through our fields to take the trucks to the north, to the rain forests. The cooperative director told them they should fight the government, to make a protest to make them give back the land."

"My father," said Noelia, "he believed the government was wrong for taking the land, the Indian land we had been living on all our lives and so *too* our fathers and their fathers before."

"Who is the director?" asked Mike. "Is he *Guatemalan?*"

"No," said Noelia. "He was an American, a `Mr. Bradlaw,'" she offered.

"Mr. *`Bradlaw'*? Mike repeated.

"Yes, Father," Noelia reconfirmed. She looked puzzled.

"No, go *ahead*," urged the priest. "So, what happened?"

"Our fathers talked to the other men in the village, and they had a meeting with Mr. Bradlaw. Mr. Bradlaw told all of them that it was wrong, what the government did when they took our land, when they began tearing up the land with their tractors and machines. Mr. Bradlaw, he told us to tell the government to stop the tractors from ruining our fields and destroying our crops. He told us we should stop work on the *finca*, to let the cattle run loose.

He told us we should meet with the government to tell them to give the land *back*. So our fathers met among themselves and with the *cofrades* and went to the church to ask the priest, a young Guatemalan catechist . . . we didn't have a priest in our town. Only twice a month the priest would come. Sometimes only once. So they met with Don Benedicto at the church, the *cofrades* did, and they asked him what to do. Don Benedicto said `*No!'* that there would be lots of trouble. But our fathers and the *cofrades* were very strong and didn't like what the government had done, and they told them what Mr. Bradlaw told them, to make the protest. Don Benedicto said, `Well, to do that would be to give our lives away!' That's what Don Benedicto told our fathers."

"And what did they do?" asked Mike.

"*Bueno,*" said Noelia. "Our fathers prepared to make a protest. They went to the *alcalde* and told him to give back the land. The *alcalde* is *ladino*, and he just *laughed* at our fathers and at the *cofrades*. He told them that he could not give them back the land, that he had not taken it from them."

"Our fathers and the *cofrades*, they were *very* angry, but they only held their hats in their hands and told the *alcalde* that they would be back tomorrow, that they wanted to have back their lands, and they would bring more people to tell them to give back their land. That's what they told them," explained Noelia.

María sat transfixed, lost in the story of her friend.

"And what happened?" continued Mike.

"The rains came," Noelia explained. "Heavy rains came for three days, so our fathers and the *cofrades* decided to wait for another time. So, when the rains stopped, they went back to the *alcalde* to tell him to give back the land, but the *alcalde* would not see them. Then our fathers said that they would return with the *cofrades* and the other people of the town on the day after the Sabbath, and they would come, many of them would come to the office of the *alcalde* to ask him to give back the land."

"On Sunday morning—it was during the Mass—we heard sounds from tractors, the machines that make the roads. They sounded very close. We were so very angry," explained María, "that the road people were working during our Holy Day, and we prayed to God and to the saints that they would stop the work on the road. . . . But, Father, they weren't working on the *road.*"

María dropped her head and raised her shawl to her eyes. Tears filled her eyelids and streamed down her cheeks. Mike moved closer to her and stroked the tiny head buried in her lap.

"So, the next day," continued Noelia, "our fathers and the *cofrades* and the workers from the fields came to the church with their families."

"And *you*, and *María?* Where were *you?*" asked the priest.

"We were washing our clothes at the *pila* with some of the other women when the soldiers came. We weren't at our houses when our fathers came for us, so we didn't know to go to the church."

Noelia paused for a moment and looked over at Maria, and then spoke so softly that Mike strained to hear her.

"And then the soldiers came. They came in two trucks with the covers over them. They passed the *pila* where we were washing the clothes. And the men in the back had *guns*. When they reached the church, the trucks stopped, and the soldiers came out of the backs of the trucks with their guns. We couldn't hear what they said, but we could see our fathers and the *cofrades* in their red *fajas* and white pants and our sisters and mothers and the *little* ones, we could see them running quickly around the church and to the back. That's when the soldiers started shooting their guns. We all began to *scream*, and we ran and ran down the road away from the *pila* and away from the church. We ran to the fields, past the tractors, and then we saw where the tractors had been working on Holy Day. We saw the long trenches in the earth where the young corn had been growing. So, we saw that the tractors with the big yellow blades were not making the road. They were just *sitting* there with the big yellow blades high in the air. They were just *sitting* there behind the huge mounds of earth that had been the mother corn for the *masa* in the fall."

"So, we ran and ran," Noelia continued. "So, we ran until our hearts jumped within our breasts, as if the bullets were exploding in *our* breasts, as if the soldiers were ripping out our *hearts*. So, we ran through the fields until we fell over our feet and into the earth and collapsed in the fresh, young corn. We were so *frightened,* Father!"

"When the shooting stopped," said María, "we clung to the earth where we were, there where we were, deep in the young corn. We were away from the road that the soldiers had to take to leave, so they would not see us. So, we stayed where we were. After a few minutes, we heard the tractors and the voices of the soldiers over the rise in the hill above us. We were so afraid that they would come for us, too, come for us down there in the fresh, sweet corn. We heard the roar of the tractor engines and the voices of the soldiers. We heard the roar of the tractors starting up and stopping and starting up and stopping and the voices of the soldiers."

"After a while," continued Noelia, "we heard the tractors and then the trucks with the voices of the soldiers pass over the road above us. We listened to the sound of the tractors and of the trucks until we could hear the voices no more, and then the trucks, and finally the sound of the tractors no more. And we cried and cried, still afraid to move, afraid to be the first to reach out to another that we might weep together in the rows of fresh, sweet young corn."

Chapter 5

Pepe's Grave

"If you will wait here, *Señor*, the Colonel will see you shortly," said the pert, petite secretary. She smiled winsomely and passed toward the door of her tiny outer office.

Miguel Mapa sat down slowly, his "Saints" cap in hand, and placed it by the bill over his left thigh. He had followed the New Orleans "Saints" since his teacher's visit there many years before. Tanolito waited below at the entry to the guard station of the National Palace.

Miguel Mapa turned his head slowly, gazing at the immense inner plaza of the palace. Sprays of sparkling water of a central fountain pattered incessantly in the large circular pool, splattering in a wet ring a foot or more beyond the wall of the basin. Sixteen huge concrete planters were stationed around the edge of the plaza. Each hosted a single, spindly, though carefully manicured royal palm stretching three stories tall and higher. At both ends of the plaza and facing inward toward the central fountain, two immense Maya stelae, with their ornately carved glyphs and feathered chieftains, stood erect on marble bases, their corroded brass plates interpreting the splendid subject and age of each. Rows of Spanish arches lined the outer walls of the eight floors of offices. Floor by floor, walnut partitions and carved panelled doors led to small outer offices where young female clerks greeted the steady streams of petitioners and made them wait for colonels who would, of course, "see them shortly." Occasional benches and a few rickety, straight-back wooden chairs, each painted—at one time or another—a mouldy military green, set against the walls outside a few of the offices. Some barefooted, others in bruised, sockless shoes—a few old, wrinkled Indian men, their elbows on their knees and straw hats in hand, waited and waited. Brown, conscripted soldiers in tightly laced boots and mottled military field uniforms guarded the corners of the long corridors and were posted at each stairway. With their feet slightly apart and automatic rifles slung over their shoulders, they peered from side to side at the few Western tourists herded by dress-shirted guides from hall to hall to see the heroic Salazar murals.

Inside, Miguel Mapa was a confusion of anticipation and impatience. Outwardly, he was stoic and solemn, conveying the appropriate mien of his class. He had been born a Felipino, but he was *ladino* by choice, and caught between his desire to make some money and the necessity to respect the *costumbre* of his *aldea* and the *cargo* mandated by his birth, he was confused and angry. Now, in the National Palace for the first time, Miguel Mapa was a new man with a new charge.

The Minister of Education was a colonel, Col. Dominico Alejandro Misabál. The Minister of Economic Affairs was a colonel, also—Col. Rodolfo Calles Soto Longe. And so, too, the Minister of Internal Security, Col. Federico Altapaz, and the Vice Minister for Interagency Directives and Protocol. The leaders of the entire country were here, all about him, and Miguel Mapa Xoy was present. He had not met a colonel before, and the Felipinos would be proud of him on his return. He had weathered the insults of a messenger and had proven his worthiness. Was he not here—here in the very National Palace itself? Had he not been summoned for something special. Was he not to be trusted with a mission of state?

No! No! The call had not gone to Victor Luis, or Dicho "Caca," or Ramundo Xic. Three—maybe four others in the town might have been tapped, but who did they come to? Hey! Miguel Mapa Xoy is here. He's the *one!* But why? Was it a good report from the garrison? He had never missed a patrol. He could count on that for something, *no?*

Three years before the first general amnesty, guerrillas were operating in and around the lake. Miguel Mapa remembered the night the militaries had arrived. For more than an hour, you could hear the heavy trucks moving slowly around the lake. It was the rainy season, and after the heavy squalls had subsided, the air was so still, as they say, that you could almost hear the mites on the chichicaster.

Just before midnight, in the dead silence of the slumbering San Felipe del Lago, a scream pierced the night air followed by the muffled [pumpf] . . . [pumpf-pumpf-pumpf] of automatic rifle fire, and an eruption of barking as the animals echoed their alarms. Moments later, the barking subsided and Miguel Mapa could hear then only muted, short whimpers. And then, an eerie silence.

Nothing, no one stirred in the village, not even the animals. After about ten minutes, Miguel heard the scraping of the boots against the rutted streets and the occasional soft, low-pitched commands of the squad leader passing behind the house near the square below.

For more than two hours, no one stirred in the village, even after the soldiers had departed. About three o'clock in the morning, Miguel was startled once more by the cranking of the truck motors which seemed frightfully close by. The military squad was apparently retiring. It was not until late into the morning that the community heard the wailing of Pirata Muñez, the mother of labor organizer Remigo Peolido and wife of Pancho Tierez, the village baker. Almost at once, the doors of the houses creaked open, and several of the village elders dared to move into the street.

Doña Pirata lay in a heap at the entrance to her son's house. She had fainted completely away. Miguel Mapa had cautiously watched the *auxiliaturas* move through the plaza across the market stalls, pass the evangelical church, and rush to the hump of an Indian woman in the street. Doña Petra rushed to her side, lifted her head into her own *tzute*, and pulled the matted hair away from her nose and eyes. When Doña Pirata tried to speak, a look of horror came over her face, and she could only gurgle deeply in the pit of her throat. The face of Doña Pirata seemed frozen in a mask of terror.

Inside the shadow of the door frame, human debris was scattered about the room. Flies ringed deep pools of blackened blood under the bodies of Lupe Sanchez Diaz, school teacher, the headless stump of her infant daughter, and her husband, Remigo Peolido. The half-clothed body of Lupe Sanchez Diaz sat against the wall, her shattered head and left arm across the small wooden chest that held the family papers. Her face had been peeled with a machete from the crown of her head, down behind her right ear, then under her chin, and upward to a point just beneath her left ear in an attempt to rip the face from the skull. Her blackened, severed hands lay crossed over her *morga* skirt pulled high up above her thighs.

Remigo Peolido, chief operator for the Pate Bottling Company and associate director of the Workers Labor Coalition for the past three months, husband of Lupe Sanchez Diaz for the past five years, lay stripped on his back across a work bench in the corner of the room, his arms dangling over the sides of the bench. Thick, clotted blood was still dripping from beneath his buttocks through cracks in the table planks onto the floor below. He had been castrated. His throat had been slit from ear to ear; his testicles stuffed into his mouth.

Don Alfonso Doq, former mayor of San Felipe and *auxiliatura maximo*, the most esteemed of the "traditionals," backed trembling from the doorway into the bright light of the blue day, staggered away from the growing crowd, and retched along the curb.

Miguel Mapa had returned there that same day. He had been so exhausted from packing the cement bags down to the trucks. He wondered how even the gunfire had awakened him, but he could say that he had witnessed it all. He had heard the [pumpf] [pumpf] of the soldiers' guns that had run off the guerrillas. Everyone said that it was the guerrillas. The guerrillas were butchers. "They don't have the guns. They have the knives. They have the machetes." That's what they say. The people could be thankful that night for the army that had saved the village from even more attacks by guerrillas. That's why he cooperated with the militaries in accepting a leadership role in organizing the civil patrols of San Felipe del Lago. That's why, he was now certain, he was to be appointed for a special mission of state.

Certainly, the Colonel understood his commitment and gratitude, thought Miguel Mapa. He could wait a little longer, perhaps. The Colonel must be a very busy person.

A guide passed by with his flock of Club Med Germans, sparkling with their new cameras on straps over their shoulders and dangling below the women's breasts. Guides were lucky. They made lots of money during the tourist season. Most lived in the capital and directed groups up the Pan American highway to Salamá or west to Xela. They were usually home by early evening. Or shacked up. He knew of a guide like that. He could usually get a woman at least by the second night. His guide friend preferred the rich Europeans. They're all looking to "get a good fix," his guide friend had said.

Miguel Mapa flipped his cap in his hands. The Colonel wouldn't keep him waiting much longer. Tanolito would be wondering what was happening. The telephone rang in the outer office. Miguel Mapa watched through the door as the receptionist leaned over, reaching for the telephone. Her full breast filled her sweater and caught against the edge of the desk as she reached for the receiver.

"Claro! . . . No tenga pena. Por su puesto. A sus órdenes, Colonel," responded the receptionist with the full, cupped breasts.

"Señor Miguel?" called the receptionist, turning her head toward her voyeur.

"I beg your pardon, *Señor*, but the Colonel's secretary has no record of your appointment. I am sorry, but I think I had you confused with another gentleman. I'm afraid I can't help you," confessed the receptionist, somewhat perplexed by the situation.

"There must be some *mistake,*" said Miguel Mapa. "You see, I was *summoned,* told to be here at 4 o'clock. There's no mistake about it. Today's the *day*. The soldier told me *himself,*" Miguel pleaded. Miguel Mapa Xoy was stunned.

"How could this have happened?" he wondered. Surely, he had not misunderstood the soldier. He felt dazed. This wasn't happening to him.

Hastily, Miguel Mapa reviewed his conversation with the soldier: the insult, the smirk on his face, and then the instructions. He remembered them all. There could be no mistake. Suddenly, however, he felt very out of place in the National Palace. He was an intruder into a world for which he had no admission, no credentials, and no authority. It was only a fleeting sensation, but for a flash he had panicked, was completely out of control and at the mercy of the cir-cumstances. In short, he felt lost and very alone. When he gathered his composure, he realized that he had drifted to the edge of the railing overlooking the immense central plaza. He looked down and saw his cap on the slabs of the ground floor, the golden *fleur-de-lis* of the New Orleans Saints' insignia brilliant in the wash of sunlight across the gleaming Spanish tiles.

Outside, Tanolito was entertained by a variety of late afternoon attractions. Tanolito liked the ladies, and university women were breaking from classes just as he and Miguel Mapa had arrived at the National Palace. Several had passed in front of the great doors of the palace with its wrought-iron gates. Tanolito felt his fingers running through their long, brown hair, over their shoulders, and around their waists. He liked the idea of his fingers slipping under the elastic bands of their slacks.

"Oh, *my!*" he said to himself. "Oh, my *goodness!*" he thought, as he followed their steps past the gates, listening to their laughter, oblivious to his fantasies. He watched them move away, slowing and stopping periodically to turn and laugh with each other.

Tanolito looked at his watch. He had been waiting for Miguel Mapa for more than an hour. He wondered what he and the Colonel could be discussing. He imagined the Colonel in his crisp, fresh uniform sitting formally across the desk from his older brother, pencil in hand and his fingers drifting back and forth along the edges from the eraser to the precisely sharpened point. He could see Miguel Mapa, behind his coy mask of compliance, nodding in agreement to the heavy affairs of state inferred by the soft-spoken "military."

Tanolito really looked up to his brother, Miguel Mapa—"Miguelito," the "tiny one." The "*tiny* one," *indeed!* Miguelito with his 6' frame; Miguelito with his huge, round shoulders and quivering biceps; Miguelito with the puckish twinkle, his playful smirk that disarmed adversaries only a flash before he decked them with his hammer-like fist; Miguelito, "the *tiny* one," who bit the living heads off fighting roosters to impress the locals.

"Miguelito, *indeed!*" he caught himself saying aloud.

Tanolito began to pace back and forth in front of the National Palace. The street was crowded with people coming from work. The fumes of the dieselfuelled busses and trucks choked the dying afternoon. Small children wheeled around an ice cream vendor across the plaza. Their mothers, in tight black jeans and complementary sweaters, fished throughout their purses for wallets.

"I'm going to make *me* a `mama' someday!" Tanolito pledged to himself.

Tanolito surveyed the great plaza, the National Library to the right, the great National Cathedral with its tall spires and to the left, and the busy shops across the street. At each corner of the plaza, pairs of conscripted Indian soldiers, brown as charred flesh, stoically watched the pesky traffic inch along from intersection to intersection. The late afternoon was cool in the shadows, and he shivered as he turned back toward the jarring gates of the Palace. Miguel Mapa was stepping through the narrowly spread bars held in place by the Palace guard. Capless and with his shoulders slumped, somehow Miguelito looked smaller and flattened in his defeat.

Miguel Mapa approached his brother and passed him without saying a word, looking straight ahead across the plaza with only a vacant stare in his eyes.

Tano followed closely on his heels.

"*Qué pasa?* What *happened?*" he called to his brother.

"*Qué pasa? Qué pasa!* What happened? *`Shit'* happened! *Stupid!* We've been *shit* on, brother!" exclaimed Miguel Mapa, wheeling around to confront his incredulous brother.

"Come on, Miguelito! *Talk* to me!" Tano cried. "What are you *talking* about?"

"I mean just *that!* We've been *had*. We're nothing but Indian *shit!* And they're going to get us, *man!* We've been set *up!* We've got to get out of this fucking city right *now!*" said Miguel Mapa.

Miguel Mapa grabbed his brother by the shirt sleeve and pulled him around toward the facade of the National Cathedral. They began running toward a fleet of five or six cabs parked parallel along the great fence skirting the front of the edifice, this center of Guatemalan Catholicism. They raced between the slowly moving cars jamming the intersection at the south end of the plaza and approached the first cab at the end of the line.

"The bus depot, *man!*" directed Miguelito.

"Sí, señor. Pasen," invited the cabby.

Miguelito shoved his smaller brother into the back seat ahead of himself and slammed the door behind.

The lethargic cabby stirred the engine, slipped slowly into reverse, and glanced through the rearview mirror at the traffic jam behind them.

"*Move* it, *man! Come on!* We've gotta get to the *bus!*" shouted Miguelito as he grabbed the shoulder of the driver.

"Easy, *hombre*! We're not going to get there any faster. There's the street, *amigos*!" offered the cabby.

"*Disculpe, señor!* I'm sorry!" retracted Miguel Mapa, realizing he had stepped beyond the bounds of normal courtesy in an exchange between a *ladino* and an *indigena*. Miguel Mapa, for all his *ladino* ways, was very Indian in appearance.

"I'm going to take you to the bus depot, yes?" asked the cabby.

"Sí! Sí, señor!" confirmed Miguel Mapa.

"*Okay!* We *go!*" said the cabby as he pulled into the slow-moving stream of traffic.

"Why do you think we've been set up?" asked Tano.

"*Shut up,* brother!" insisted Miguelito. Almost imperceptibly, he slipped lower and lower into the back seat.

"Where's your cap?" asked Tano.

"My cap? My *cap!*" exclaimed Miguel Mapa. *"Chinga la puta!* I lost my cap in the Palace!"

"Hey, *brother!* You lost a good cap!" said Tano, sympathizing with his brother's fondness for the North American keepsake.

"Chinga la puta chingada!" said Miguel Mapa as he hit the seat with his fist.

The cab continued its creeping pace behind the buses, motorcycles, and autos as the evening traffic ebbed on through the congested streets of the city. At almost four million people, it seemed as if most had congregated between the Palace and the bus depot. After about thirty minutes of exasperation, Miguel Mapa reached into his pocket and pulled out five *quetzales.*

"Aquí!" he said to the cabby. "Here, take *this!* Let's *go!*" he said to Tano as he flung open the door, pulling his brother's shirt sleeve. The cabby flipped through the folded bills and stuffed them in his shirt pocket as the two brothers exited.

"I'll tell you how I know we've been *set up*," said Miguel Mapa to his brother as the cab inched away from them, gagging in a cloud of exhaust from the dilapidated Vega.

"That little *puta* in the Colonel's office. She looked very disturbed all of a sudden after she received a call from the Colonel. She had my name on her schedule, for sure. She never showed me any other reason to think different. Something's fucked *up*; that's for certain, and I think it's *us,* brother!" explained Miguel Mapa. "So, the thing for us is to get to that bus, if anyone's looking for *us.* We can be home in three or four hours, and it'll be dark if we have to jump."

"What do you think it's all about, Miguel?" asked Tano, now clearly disturbed and frightened.

"I don't *know!* But what have we *done?*" asked Miguel Mapa. "We're a *team*. We're the best damn team in the patrol, *you and me!* So, I don't know."

"Maybe it was just a slip up . . . maybe, maybe . . ." queried Tano.

"`Maybe,' `maybe,' . . . `maybe,' *shit! Madre de Diós*!" exclaimed Miguel Mapa.

"You don't think it was some kind of dodge just to get us out of San Felipe, do you?" asked Tano. That was a possible new twist to the dilemma.

"Oh, *shit no!*" retorted Miguelito. But it was a frightening possibility. Anything was possible with the militaries, and they both knew it well.

At the end of the day, the street merchants that surrounded the bus depot had just about completed packing away their trinkets and paraphernalia for another day. Little urchins were chasing each other through the boxes and bundles being stacked together for movement to invisible shelters probably many blocks or even miles away. Miguel Mapa and his brother picked their way through the bundles down a side street, a short cut to the rows of busses on the other side of the warehouses.

"We'll just get home and work this out," reassured Miguelito. Within an hour they were on the way up the Pan American highway. Periodically, the driver would pull to the side of the road to pick up another Indian woman and her kids or a small gang of teenage boys on the way back to Sololá or El Quiché.

As the bus approached Chimaltenango, Miguel Mapa could see the National Police post up ahead to his left. The bus began to brake and slow as it moved over a *tumulo*, a traffic bump, in the road toward the check point. Rather than regaining momentum, however, the bus moved to the side of the highway and stopped. "What the hell now?" thought Miguel Mapa to himself, and he stole a nervous glance at this brother, Tano.

Two soldiers entered the front of the bus, their submachine guns slung waggishly over their shoulders. The first military moved to the rear of the bus while the second began at the front. They were checking *cedulas*—the Indian's registration cards—and passports of the two or three European-looking passengers. The two brothers, sitting two rows apart from each other, sifted through their pockets for their identifications. The soldiers looked slightly at each and passed on to the next person.

"Where are *you* from?" asked the soldier of Miguel Mapa.

"San Felipe," answered Miguel Mapa. With his *cedula* in the hands of the soldier, there was no reason to lie.

The soldier returned the registration card to Miguel Mapa and continued his review up the aisle of the bus. When they were finished, the two soldiers moved slowly and cautiously to the front, turned toward the passengers, and ordered everyone off.

An immediate clamor went up from the passengers. Miguel Mapa looked furtively toward his brother, Tano, who returned his glance. They were deeply anxious, but they didn't dare panic. They had been checked before—many times, and they had done nothing; both their registrations were in order.

In a moment like this, each passenger wished to blend into the other so as not to attract attention. Each Indian woman, her baby in her *tzute*, the men in their straw hats—some smacking gum, and the young people, smiling and jabbering to each under their breath, stepped from the bus and congregated in a bunch just outside the door.

The two soldiers ordered the group to step away from the door and to line up against the side of the bus opposite the highway.

"You Indian women are all *putas*!'" shouted one of the young *ladino* soldiers as he walked down the line of the passengers. "You Indian *men*—nothing but cattle licks! You *understand?*"

The Indians drew into themselves behind glassy, pale exteriors.

"And we're looking for two cattle licks, two *`women' sons of bitches!*" he continued. He smiled sardonically, as he paced back and forth down the line of passengers.

"*You* two! *You and you!*" said the other soldier, pointing to Tano and Miguel Mapa. "You come with us. Maybe you can help us find these two *`women.'*" The first soldier lowered the barrel of his machine gun, as his right hand assumed its grip on the trigger guard.

Frozen in terror, the two brothers stood horrified momentarily before they took two halting steps in front of the lineup.

"The rest of you *putas* can get back on that piece of shit *bus!*" barked the other soldier. The little Indians rushed to the door of the bus and fled as far back into the rear of the vehicle as possible.

"Come with us," said the first soldier, as he motioned for the two brothers to walk in front of them. They stood back as the bus belched and backfired once and then moved back onto the highway. The two brothers felt very alone and abandoned and embarrassed by the close scrutiny they were under from the curious on-lookers gathered around the ambulatory police post on the opposite side of the highway.

On the other side of the road was a military jeep. "Get in," ordered one of the soldiers. With the fingers of their hands interlocked above their heads, the two brothers stepped up into the rear of the jeep and waited directions to sit.

"Sit down, *fools,*" ordered one of the other guards. The two soldiers who had boarded the bus were still busy in discussion.

Miguel Mapa tried to counsel his increasing fear by thinking of Mildred, his girl friend, but Mildred's face was lost in a shower of detail and intellectual debris which he couldn't control. He was terrified, plain and simple, standing erect beside his military escorts at six-feet, three inches tall.

After some hesitancy, as they continued their brief conversation, they both boarded the front of the jeep. The first soldier from the bus fired up the engine, and the jeep lurched forward. They travelled down the Pan American Highway almost due west behind the bus for perhaps a quarter of a mile, but when the jeep reached the intersection with the Antigua highway, it turned onto a rough, rutted road down which they travelled for nearly a half hour before it reached the military post.

"Welcome to my office," said a military officer at the station where they stopped to check in. "My name is Lieutenant Varos. Please be seated, *señores*."

The two brothers took two of the four plain wooden chairs sitting in the middle of the room before the officer. At a signal from the Lieutenant, the first two soldiers retired to positions outside the office.

"Why didn't you keep your appointment with the Colonel today?" asked the officer. The two brothers looked at each stunned and dumbfounded. Neither could say a word.

"Orders are *orders*, *Señores* Xoy," said the officer as he rose and moved around the desk to stand before them. The brothers remained speechless, too horrified to even anticipate what might come next in such a bizarre circumstance.

The lieutenant kept slapping a short riding whip across the palm of his left hand as he paced back and forth in front of them, mocking them both with his taunting smile.

"The Colonel is a very busy man," said the lieutenant, "and you let him *down!* The Colonel—with a very special mission for the *both* of you. What do you have to say to *that, señores*?"

Miguel Mapa was clearly perplexed and couldn't find the words to engage the officer.

Tano finally found his voice. "But we were *there!*" he protested, "*there,* at the gates of the National Palace—*at 4 p.m.* just like they told us—*the soldiers!*"

"*Shut up!*" said the lieutenant. "If I want a word from you, I'll ask a *question!*"

Tano's response was visceral. Anger tightened into a wad of nerves in his stomach, and the muscles of his shoulders drew up across his back. He would jump the "son of a bitch" if he messed with him. He hadn't done anything. Just let the bastard touch *him! He'd* show him what Indian stuff was made of, the *ladino chingado!*

Miguel Mapa was more reflective. His mind was racing with solutions. There was a reasonable explanation for this mix up. Clearly, this was a part of a larger scenario which had its origin in simple conversations with the soldiers back in San Felipe the week before, thought Miguel Mapa. But what could it mean—this nonsense, this idiocy of the moment?

Miguel Mapa suddenly realized that there was to be no verbal resolution of their dilemma, that something else was going on in which they might not even be the focus. Miguel Mapa began to drift. His mind was swirling, looking for meaning to this surrealistic setting and encounter. It was a very bad and terrifying dream over which he had no control.

"I think you two can't explain yourselves," continued the Lieutenant. "I think you two may be enemies of the army, not to keep your *appointment!*"

Tano jumped from his chair only to accept a slashing blow from the Lieutenant's riding whip. Shocked, Tano's eyes almost jumped from their sockets, and he staggered, falling clumsily into his chair.

This *blow!* This *attack!* This was a new dimension to their situation. Miguel Mapa found himself gripping his chair, his knuckles white with fury. He was rising in defence of both himself and his brother and was ready to split the Lieutenant's head with the chair beneath him. And then he heard a footstep behind and felt a sharp jab in his left kidney. It was the barrel of the soldier's rifle. Miguel Mapa froze in terror and slowly inched his way back onto the edge of his chair. Any moment he expected to have his side ripped away by the explosion of a bullet through his gut, but the Lieutenant raised his hand, and the soldier withdrew his muzzle.

"Take them away," said the Lieutenant.

"`Take them *away'!* `Take them *away'!* What could be the *meaning* of this?" thought Miguel Mapa. `Take them away' *where?* What the fuck was going *on,* anyway!"

"*Lieutenant!*" cried out Miguel Mapa. "*Surely* there is some *mistake*, here!"

The Lieutenant stared through the eyes of Miguel Mapa all the way to the back of his head, never flinching, at once in complete control.

"Take them *away,* Corporal!" repeated the Lieutenant.

Tano rose slowly, holding the collar of his shirt against the wound across his cheek that was bleeding freely. The corporal urged him along with a push on his left shoulder, and Tano fell to the floor.

"Get *up!* Indian *shit!"* barked the young soldier, and he gave Tano a severe kick in the buttocks. Tano lurched forward, his wounded cheek still in his palm against the floor.

Miguel Mapa resisted the urge to assist his younger brother.

"Blindfold them and take them to the closets," instructed the Lieutenant.

Moments later the second guard entered with two leather hoods with draw strings which they pulled down over the brothers' heads and secured them with the strings beneath their chins.

"Tie their *hands*, Corporal!" ordered the Lieutenant. The corporal reached behind him for several cotton cords looped on nails in the wall above him, stripped two from their moorings, and grabbed the left wrist of Tano. The soldier jerked it away from his cheek and wrenched it behind the stunned Felipino. Almost as if he had given up, Tano dropped his other hand behind his back and yielded to the seizure.

As the second soldier trussed up the hands of Miguel Mapa, the older brother's mind was swirling, seeking alternatives to their desperate station. Mechanically, he followed Tano and the first soldier behind him and shuffled down the corridor of the hall.

One dim light bulb illuminated the shabby, filthy hallway of the concrete block building. They passed a series of doors secured with large, industrial padlocks on their hatches. They followed the hallway around a right turn, past more locked doors from which they could hear low groans from deep within. At the third door, the first soldier stopped, rested his gun on the floor beside the doorjamb, and reached in his belt for a set of keys. He fumbled through the keys until he found the right one, slipped it into the lock, and turned the key to the right. The lock sprang loose, and the soldier removed it from the clasp.

As the dingy door fell away into the room, the soldier shoved Tano into windowless darkness. The young *indígena* fell to the floor and rolled instinctively until he reached the wall, stretched out the length of his body along the wall as the only available security, and then lay still and rigid against the dark.

The second soldier pushed Miguel Mapa along down the hallway, around a second turn, and slammed him against the wall next to another entrance. The first soldier arrived with another key with which he unlocked the holding closet. The second soldier grabbed Miguel Mapa by the shoulder and spun him into the tiny room. There was barely enough room for the bound and hooded Felipino, from a sitting position, to extend his feet. As Miguelito eased down against the back wall, the soldier wheeled around and slammed the butt of his rifle stock into the Indian's groin, and as Miguel pitched forward, he sent a second blow crashing into the back of his shoulders. Miguel Mapa collapsed in a heap onto the floor, and inside his hood, a small stream of blood began trickling from his mouth. The first soldier shut the door and locked the closet, and the two returned down the hallway to report to their superior.

He could never quite catch his breath. Every time he tried to breathe deeply, Miguel Mapa gagged on his own blood. He vomited twice and had to throw his chin up so that it would seep slowly out of the hood tied loosely around his neck. For the first few hours, even a shallow breath was accompanied by jabbing pain across his shoulders that twisted deeply into his throat. His legs were cramped in the tight space, and at first, Miguelito had a great urge to try to kick out the wall, but fear stole every incentive to make a sound or other disturbance. The only comfort he was able to secure was the ability to maneuver his buttocks inside the circle of his arms, so that he found that he was able to sit up with his tied wrists caught up under his knees, making it possible for him to relax his arms and shoulders. He didn't dare any longer to question his circumstances or to try to rationalize his future. His total focus now was on management of the moment. After what seemed like hours of torture, Miguel Mapa rolled over on his right side and drifted into sleep.

Up above him—in the darkness of the closet—the jacket on its hanger began to rustle, even though there was nothing to disturb it. Something was messing with it, fixing the collar and the pocket lining bulging out of its mouth.

"Leave the jacket alone!" said Miguel Mapa. It was Mildred—he knew it was. She was always trying to tidy things up. It was the only thing about his nóvia that always made him nervous. He was messy, and she was organized. Miguel Mapa could just make out the fine, thin outline of her fingers pressing down the wrinkles of the jacket and straightening the garment on the hanger. . . . Mildred . . . Mildred with the long, black hair that he liked to brush against his face. Mildred . . . Mildred with the tiny midriff, so small that he could touch his own thumb and fingertips around her waist. Mildred, who was so tight he thought he would die as she slipped down on him, and he pulled his knees instinctively under his chin to hide his growing erection.

"They cut Tano's jacket into little ribbons. When I tried to hang up his jacket, it just fell apart in my hands," explained an exasperated Mildred. "What am I supposed to do?" she cried.

She held the front panel of Tano's leather jacket—the one he had purchased at the market from the Quiché merchant a year before. Mildred reached into the pocket and pulled out Tano's tongue and wrapped it in a warm tortilla.

"See!" she tried to explain. "What can I do, Miguel, with just the pieces of a jacket?" And she tried to place the strips of Tano's shredded jacket over Miguelito's swinging above his head.

"Leave the jacket alone, and come down to me!" Miguel ordered his girl friend. "Come down to me so that I can tell you something."

Mildred dropped from the hanger above his head and perched on his shoulder, pecking a mite from his ear that had been irritating him so. Her claws clamped into his shoulder and neck muscles as she tried to adjust to his collapsed position.

"Listen to me!" ordered Miguel Mapa in a loud whisper, so as not to disturb the sentries who might be listening outside the closet. "Listen to me carefully!"

Mildred readjusted her position, anchoring her sharp claws into the exposed flesh of his neck.

"Don't go near the soldiers!" he said.

"Don't go near the soldiers!" said his mother, María Xquic.

"Don't go near the evil soldiers!" said little Manuel Xoy, cradling the grey cat over his shoulders.

María Xquic lifted the bird from his neck and placed it inside her huipil under her breast. She reached back down to her son's neck exposed beneath the hood and massaged the wounds from Mildred's claws, then reached under his head and turned his hooded face to her own.

"Don't go near the soldiers!" she whispered. "They are evil people. Sons of the earth put on the uniforms of Satan, and then they do terrible things to their mothers and fathers and to the little ones and to the neighbors. Don't go near the soldiers!"

"I won't, mia madre! I promise not to go near the soldiers!" pleaded a terrified Miguel Mapa.

Manuel Xoy, Miguel's little brother, nuzzled under his mother's arm and slipped his tiny hand into her huipil, groping for the bird. "Don't go near the soldiers, Miguelito!" he teased playfully. "Don't go near the soldiers!" he began to sing.

Miguel Mapa was startled and awakened by a kick against the door of the closet. A small stream of light was shining faintly under the door. He shook his head and felt a sharp pain in his right shoulder as he turned to acknowledge the interruption. His limbs were numb; except for an electrifying tingling, he had no feeling in his legs or arms. He knew that he would fall if he tried to stand.

Miguel Mapa heard the soldier fumbling through his key ring. If only the soldier would wait long enough for him to regain some circulation in his legs, he could make himself presentable, stand at attention just as he did before the captain of his civil patrol. Perhaps the soldier was bringing him something to drink. His mouth was parched and throat raspy from his gagging earlier in the evening. He heard the key slip into the lock and the lock arm spring open. The door creaked open on its rusty hinges, and dim light from the hall flooded the floor of the closet.

"Get up, *turkey shit!"* ordered the soldier.

Miguel Mapa rolled over to a sitting position, facing the light which he could see around his collar.

"Get up, you putrefied, Felipino *shit!*" repeated the soldier, and he kicked Miguel's feet with his boot. "Get *up!*"

Miguel Mapa maneuvered himself into a crouched position and felt the blood rushing back toward his feet. He shifted on both knees in an attempt to force the blood through his limbs. He wanted desperately to scratch his wrists where they itched severely above the cords that tied his hands. As feeling returned to his legs, he became aware that he was urinating in his pants, the warm stream collecting in his trousers around his left knee. He panicked, but he couldn't stop the flow. All at once, he saw a burst of light explode before his eyes followed by a wash of red and a screeching whining in his head. And then he blacked out.

When he came to, he felt a sharp, pulsating pain in his left jaw, and he realized he was on his right shoulder.

"You Felipino *shit!* You piss on *that.* See how you like *that!*" shouted the soldier, and the lights went out.

Miguel Mapa was stunned. He had no idea where he was or what was around him. It wasn't the hard, concrete floor of the closet. He reached out and then upward to feel his swollen, tender jaw, racing with fever and throbbing pain. He tried to open his mouth and then resisted as fiery pain sent him reeling backwards against the wall. His jaw was broken, he was sure. The soldier must have kicked him or struck him with the rifle stock. Then he realized, for the first time, that his hands were free and he no longer wore the hood. But he could not see.

It was pitch coal dark. He could make out nothing around him. He reached out in front and felt nothing. He fumbled about cautiously to the left and then to the right. Once more, his right hand touched a moist, earthen wall. He could feel crumbly, wet dirt and small, spindly roots protruding from the earth.

"My *grave!*" thought Miguel Mapa. "They will bury me *alive!*" My *grave!*" he mumbled aloud. And he fled backwards against the earthen wall, slipping down onto his knees in the corner.

Slowly, Miguel Mapa began to feel with his hands to both sides of him. How wide was the area? He could feel nothing but the damp earth around him. If only he could see something . . . *anything!*

But was he *alone!* What if he was not *alone!* The thought terrified him, and the pain in his jaw was forgotten in the horror that he was being watched. He reached slowly in front of himself and felt nothing but dirt. He moved into a crawling position and, inch by inch, worked his way forward, feeling cautiously around as he began to explore his surroundings.

Each slight touch of his fingers revealed cold, wet dirt. He could smell now the sweet clay as he became more sensitive and secure. He was not in a grave: the area was too wide. He was in a pit of some kind. Perhaps he could stand. Perhaps he could pull himself *out!* The idea became a project. He would try to stand and lift himself out. It was a plan. Now he knew what he had to do.

Miguel Mapa rose carefully to his feet. He placed the palms of his hands flat against the wall of earth in front of him. Cautiously, he felt his way upward. The walls extended straight up. It would be impossible to climb up the wall without some kind of foothold. He finally extended his right arm as high as he could reach, but could feel only the earthen wall. He was in a deep pit, so it seemed. Then he began to slide along the wall of the pit, reaching as high as he could with both arms, patting the sides of the pit with his hands up and around him, hoping to find something for a support—a heavy root penetrating the wall, anything that might be used to move him a little higher.

Side-step by side-step, Miguel Mapa maneuvered himself around the hole—surely something . . . and then he fell, collapsing into a heap. He had tripped. His foot had hung up on something, and he had fallen again. His head was exploding with pain, and he reached up to his mouth to cradle the jaw in his hands. He stroked the jaw lightly, trying to test for a fracture. His fingers gingerly nudged the swollen flesh, and he reached back with his left arm to brace himself and to lift himself to a sitting position. As his left hand reached backward, he touched a body.

Miguel Mapa screamed at the realization. He rolled over and shinnied backward against the wall. It was a dead body, and he was *not* alone! He tried to breathe, but he was hyperventilating and unable to control the pounding in his breast.

"*Madre de Díos!*" he cried. "*Oh, madre 'Díos! Soy muerto! Soy muerto*!

I am *dead!* Oh, *save* me, Mother of God! Oh, *save* me blessed Mother of God!"

Miguel Mapa sobbed and sobbed, each convulsion shooting rivets of pain through his jaw. He was completely lost and helpless for the first time in his life. His chest heaved as he struggled for breath, and finally he was able to catch a spasm of oxygen. He grabbed his shirt in his clenched fist and rolled over onto his left side, sobbing and moaning.

He reached once more for his jaw and slipped his finger into his mouth under his tongue to see if he could sense more precisely the point of his injury from within. He coursed his finger gently against his gum line, but could feel nothing, when all at once he felt a tug at his pants leg!

And then a hand gripped his ankle!

"*Ahheeee!*" cried Miguel Mapa. He kicked violently in an attempt to throw off the attack, but the hand locked its fingers inside his shoe and pulled for life to hold on.

"Let *go!* Let go, you *son of a bitch!* Let *go!"* cursed the distraught Miguel Mapa, but an arm stretched out and seized his belt. Instantly, he felt the weight of a full body upon his own, and Miguel Mapa rolled over and over, fighting to free himself from the desperate clawing.

At once, he felt a sudden surge of strength tear through his shoulders that raced into the palms of his hands. He doubled his hands into two mighty fists and began flailing out against the groping body, crashing over and over at the mound of a face, pulverizing the head with three hammer blows that stunned the body and sent it quivering into the damp earth beside him. Instantly, Miguel was on top of the body. His deadly hands found the throat which they squeezed into a vice of death. Instinctively, he began pounding and pounding the head against the wet ground until he felt jets of warm blood splattering on his hands and heard the death gurgle rolling deep from within his limp adversary. Miguel Mapa released his grip and fell backwards against the wall of the pit and passed out.

When he came around, Miguel Mapa looked up to discover himself on a gurney in a small medical clinic. His jaw was numb, and his face was wrapped in bandages, his mouth barely able to open. A soldier was standing beside him, and a civilian in street clothes was reviewing notes on a small tablet.

"Well," said the civilian, "you are very strong for a Felipino, *eh!*" He smiled at the aching heap of a man prone in front of him.

Miguel Mapa tried to move his mouth to respond.

"*No! No!* Don't try to say anything just yet," warned the civilian in his khaki pants and plaid, short-sleeved shirt.

"Just relax as you can," he said. "You've got some mending to do. My name is Dr. Monsanto. Corporal Díaz will assist you if you want something to drink or eat. You're going to be on liquids for a day or two, but you're going to make it just fine. I'll be back tomorrow to check on you."

Miguel Mapa was a different man. For the first time in his life, he was out of control and completely dependent on others. A sense of great uneasiness—worry, fear, and anger—stuffed his chest like an *apaste* of wet *masa.* The walls of his tongue felt dry and fibrous, a patch of cotton against the walls of his mouth. His mind was dull and listless. He had no energy to promote himself. His consciousness seemed to drift down his arms, through the palms of his hands, and to dissipate at the ends of his fingers. He wanted to sleep, but he was afraid to close his eyes completely, fearful that at any point he would slip into death.

And then, as though it had been a week or more, he remembered Tano, his brother. His memory churned, racing back and forth through the bus trip and the anger he had felt toward the two soldiers. Then he remembered stumbling down the passage through the muted corridors of the garrison, but Tano himself was only the faintest recollection. He thought he saw—no, *heard* his voice in front of him, but he couldn't see him. Miguel was struggling to remember something—the hood he hadn't recalled. Only the darkness and the fear behind the darkness washed in waves through his forehead, and he struggled to remember something—even *anything*—of Tano. But Tano was lost to him, only a sound tripping on the end of his tongue.

"Ta—, Ta—, Ta—," he kept trying to say, but Miguel Mapa was drifting, struggling to maintain attention to the quest for Tano, but he was losing his grip. His head was getting blurry, and he seemed to retreat into his chest and shoulders. An awkward, pounding throb began pulsating over his left eye, and Miguel "Pepe" Mapa faded into a deep sleep.

"Can he move? Does he have any sense of response?" he heard them saying. He felt a sharp pain in his foot, and he jerked back the violated heel.

"*Look!*" said another voice. A wash of red drifted across the dark curtains of his eyes. Miguel Mapa was fighting consciousness. His face was cold, and he realized that the bandages around his head were gone. He reached up slowly and felt his jaw with his right hand. He allowed one eye to squint open—just for a moment—and then closed it tightly, disturbed as he was by the blinding light flooding into the room.

"*Pepe!*" barked a stern voice.

"*Pepe!*" the voice repeated.

Miguel Mapa turned his head slowly to the left toward the voice.

"*Pepe!*" said the voice. "*Look* at me!"

Miguel Mapa opened his eyes and stared blankly at the fleshy, pock-marked face of a uniformed *ladino*. He was the doctor.

"Get *up!*" ordered the *ladino* doctor, as he stepped back from the side of the gurney.

"You can get up. *Do* it!" he ordered more explicitly.

Miguel Mapa tried first to move both hands. He felt the warm sheets covering his legs and extended his hands from his sides outward to the edge of the gurney.

"Get *up!*" repeated the *ladino* doctor.

Miguel Mapa lifted his head and pulled his elbows under his sides and propped himself up. He turned his head from side to side to better assay his situation.

"You're ready now," explained the *ladino* doctor.

Slowly, Miguel Mapa picked himself up, turned, and sat up on the side of the gurney. He shook his head as if to settle his vision and looked around.

"Well!" said the *ladino* doctor. "I think you're going to be a very strong man once again."

"Stand up," ordered the *ladino* doctor, "and let me examine your jaw."

Miguel "Pepe" Mapa's left jaw was swollen and blue, but much of the initial pain had subsided.

"A little punchy still?" asked the *ladino* doctor.

"*Sí,*" said Miguel Mapa.

"Well, it's going to take a while for all the swelling and the color to go away, but you'll be all right, *okay?*" said the *ladino* doctor. He pointed to a stack of new clothes, a khaki outfit of some sort, lying across the back of a chair at the end of the gurney. "Here. Put on your clothes," ordered the *ladino* doctor.

Miguel Mapa slipped off the gurney and took the hand of the doctor to steady himself. He took a hesitant first step and then a second toward the chair. His steps felt strange and uncomfortable, something familiar rather than anything natural. He reached the chair with the clothes and stood before it for a moment. He reached for the shirt—a military fatigue—and slipped his right arm into the sleeve, then eased into the left and pulled the shirt tightly around his waist. He buttoned the shirt from the top, skipping the first three buttons out of habit. The *ladino* doctor reached over and corrected the mistake, buttoning first the top, the second, and then the third buttons respectively.

"You are *military*, now!" the *ladino* doctor offered. "You do things very differently now, *understand?*" His remark was more an order than a question of the new recruit.

Miguel Mapa was beginning to gather his senses and to assay his situation, but he perceived an uncertain future. The tablet was blank, and he had no crayon, much in the same way he had stared at a blank piece of paper at the *ladino* school so many years before. It was two days before the teacher discovered that he had no pencil, and without a pencil he could not write his lesson, and without a lesson he had no future in the school. Once again, he had no pencil with which to write, and for the first time in his life, Miguel Mapa sensed that he had no future. Pointlessly, he pulled up his trousers and fastened the buttons up the fly.

"Sit *down!*" ordered the *ladino* doctor. "The lieutenant will see you shortly."

Miguel Mapa sat down mechanically into the chair beside the gurney. Staring at nothing, he dared not think of anything but the present. The lieutenant would see him shortly; that was enough. The past was a blur that had no meaning or significance to him. The chair beneath him—that was enough. The crack across the concrete floor that slipped between the wheels of the gurney—that, *too;* that was enough. And the lieutenant would see him shortly. That was enough.

"Bastante!" said Miguel Mapa to himself. That was enough. He reached to his shoulder under the sleeve of the khaki shirt. Something was crawling in a small circle with a thousand tiny feet just behind his bicep. He rubbed the spot where the tiny feet were crawling, an *insect*—it must be—dancing in a circle with its tiny feet. And it stopped. He withdrew his hand, but at once, the feet began to scratch even more feverishly into his skin, stabbing their tiny claws into the muscle. Miguel Mapa slapped at his arm.

His arm tingled as he rubbed it so vigorously. Miguel Mapa pulled back his sleeve to observe the spot where he had slapped the tiny feet, but there were no feet—only a flaming, red patch of skin which he had agitated in his petulance. In the center of the patch were small red scabs where he had received the injections.

Chapter 6

Two *Quetzales*

For more than five years, the Cherokee Jeep had been the G-2 vehicle of choice. With the back seat removed, two guards could maintain control in the rear while the driver and forward guard could maneuver the traffic and city intersections. Two "commissioners" in the rear, a "captain" and a "navigator" in the front, then, constituted the personnel supporting standard operating procedure.

"Taco," the driver and veteran, had been a "captain" for almost three years. He knew his business; there were rules:

"Don't get caught in traffic."

"Leave room in front of the vehicle to maneuver."

"Keep access to the sidewalk or the outside lane."

"Don't speed, so as not to attract attention."

"Keep a record of the mileage."

"Always return the vehicle to the military garage; never
park the vehicle on the street or leave it without at
least one `commissioner' when on a mission."

And then one of his own rules: "Always collect the twenty *quetzales* in small bills." He didn't want his wife to get suspicious of his little extra income. If she found a large bill, she would want to know what he was doing, what was going on. He really didn't want to have to explain. She would get ideas, and she would start making demands and plans. He had his own plans, however, and some of them didn't include hers or *her*, for that matter.

"Rooster" rode "shotgun" as "navigator." It was his role to protect the "captain," to watch the traffic patterns, and to keep an eye on the rear. If things ever got out of hand or "difficult" in the back, then he was the "arbitrator": it was his job "to fix things." It had happened before when they had picked up a large, well-built priest who had decided to press the issue on the spot. "Rooster" had had to "arbitrate" with a hammer to the back of the priest's head. The priest crumbled against the back of his seat. The thing was to disable the subject and to avoid a "mess." And then the navigator always had one more job.

Rooster was the "public affairs" agent in the vehicle. It was his responsibility to relate in any way with the public, the military, or local officials—and with any of the above only in an absolute emergency. He carried G-2 papers, the red card with the Colonel's personal signature. He carried the authority from "the shop," as they called it. When he carried the card, there wasn't a chicken-shit in the country safe from his reach. He was one of the most powerful men in the country, and he knew it.

Chaco was one of the commissioners, otherwise known among the guys as a "dick." "Jobs" were what he lived for. He had worked for the Colonel for five or six years. He was a specialist in "communication"; he knew how to "get a statement." He knew how to make a chicken-shit sweat. And he was a master of "technique"—he knew how to make a chicken-shit die "real slow."

Chaco was retired military. No one "on the team" knew much about him, and that's the way it was designed to be. "Team members" floated from unit to unit every month or so, so that camaraderie would never become an issue on "a job." Most of the city guys could tell he was a *zopelote,* or buzzard. "Birds" had only one place to "roost" and one "menu" to feed off. They were doomed to the crumbs discarded by the military. Castaways from their *aldeas* after tenure in the military, "zopelotes" were the dregs of society, at home nowhere except among other paramilitaries. They constituted a notorious brotherhood whose numbers had swelled during the 80's. Most of them lived on the fringes of the capital. They were the notorious "death hands" who thrived as informants and "hit" men, the *comisionados*. They lived among the bars and the brothels in the *colonias* and were used to infiltrate local villages before the *militaries* would move in for their predetermined "initiatives."

Chaco's partner was "Chico," a conscripted Mam Indian from San Marcos, who had worked for G-2 for more than twelve years. Chaco was "Big Dick"; Chico—"Tata Dick." Chico's story was dark. Few ever questioned him very far; they knew better. When guerrilla activity centered on Puerto Barrios and Zacapa back in the `60's, Chico had earned a reputation for ruthlessness. In boot camp in 1968, Chico was training in the same camp as his step brother. Both had been sitting around a smoldering fire when his step brother, Roberto, had asked Chico for a match to light a cigarette. Upon cue from his captain, Chico got up to hand Roberto a match with one hand and drew his bayonet with the other. As Roberto fired the match and lifted it to his cigarette, Chico stepped behind. As Roberto inhaled a drag and was starting to remove the cigarette from his mouth, Chico reached under his step-brother's chin and slit his throat from ear to ear. Never moving until the end, Roberto just sat there, staring in front of himself into blankness, his arms collapsed to his side, the cigarette still clutched between his thumb and first finger. Washed in a fountain of cascading blood, Roberto's uniform turned black. Chico wiped both sides of his blade on first the left and then the right shoulder straps of Roberto's uniform as the life leaked away beneath his chin. Then, with a single blow, Chico lifted Roberto's head off the torso with one swift swath of a machete. The torso jerked nervously once, maybe twice. Chico gave it a single nudge with his boot, and it fell forward, following the head into the burning coals.

Stunned speechless by the horror of the unexpected demonstration, the young recruits sat frozen in fear as the captain drew his pistol and rose.

"When I rise, you snap to *attention*, you little *shits!* Do you *understand* me, you puke *bastards?*" shouted the captain. "Maybe I ought to just come over here and put a bullet through your fucking *ears*, you worthless piece of *shit!*"

He grabbed the slower of the recruits by the collar and threw him to the ground, straddled the frightened seventeen-year old, pulled back the hammer on his 45 cal. automatic pistol, and fired. The ground exploded inches away from the head of the ashen face of the recruit. The captain roared with laughter mixed with disgust and kicked the cowering recruit in the testicles.

"Get up, you sorry son of a *bitch*, you little *chicken thief!*" yelled the captain, and he booted him twice in the buttocks as the horrified recruit staggered once more to his place in line.

The captain turned to Chico and barked, "What's your name, *dog shit?*"

"*Dog shit, SIR!*" snapped Chico.

"D-O-G-S-H-I-T, *SSSIIIRRR!*" snarled the Captain.

"D-O-G-S-H-I-T, *SSSIIIRRR!*" echoed Chico.

"Kick that putrefied *crap* into the fire, Dog Shit, and put some more wood on it. And all you other *shit heads*, you stand at attention till noon tomorrow until you piss all over yourself as a salute to Dog Shit here, the only *real* man among you. Do you hear me, *chicken shits*?" yelled the Captain.

"*YESSIR!*" returned the chorus. The Tenth Brigade/Squad "Homero Guzman" had its first lesson in military preparedness and discipline, a lesson in authority they would never forget. And they had witnessed for the first time a soldier's initiation into rank; "Dog Shit" was promoted to Corporal Chico.

At noon the next day, the squad buried the charred remains of the step brother among the coals of the smoldering fire. In turn, each soldier was required to file past and urinate over the mound. Corporal Chico and the squad broke camp and disappeared into the jungle.

How he found his place into G-2 is only surmise, for Chico never talked about his "work," one reason probably why in, his line of work, he was still alive. What was known, however, was that he had survived Zacapa while in the army and, early on, had satisfied the lieutenant of his squad. He had a medal and commendation to show for it.

Chico had distinguished himself in the 60's for his work in counter-insurgency. The guerrillas had first emerged in the east in 1962 as the Rebel Armed Forces when Col. Juan Barco and Col. Bartolome Portillo had failed to engineer a coup against Gen. Hector "Pepe" Stig two years earlier. The colonels commanded two divisions in Zacapa and Puerto Barrios. They had demanded reform within the military, protesting endemic corruption, and the use of Guatemalan territory for the training of Cubans for the "Bay of Pigs" fiasco. The night that the rebel forces began attacking the military posts in Zacapa, Chico was a guard at the gate of his garrison. He had been grazed by a round on the back of his thigh, but he had insisted on returning to duty only two days later.

When a few of the rebel troops were captured days later during preparations for another attack on his post, Chico assisted with interrogation. Even with a raging fever, contracted as a reaction to his wound, Chico had been most successful in his "demonstrations" before the terrified prisoners. He had forced them to watch while he brained senseless one of the largest and strongest of them, slit his throat, collected the dying man's blood in a glass, and drank it dry in front of them. He learned much later that day "in conversations" with the detainees. Two weeks later, he was employed by his captain as one of three "escorts" who accompanied the wretched rebel troops in C-47's out over the Caribbean. Making more than a dozen flights, the plane would climb to 5,000 feet at forty miles out and then level off. When any rebel even hesitated, Chico would shoot him in the leg as "a little incentive" to jump and then deliver a quick kick in the ass to boot the bastard into oblivion against the moon-blanched waters below.

For the past year and a half, the "team" had been working the Lake District under orders from the *comandante* of the *"Bruceros,"* the name adopted by the troops of the Military Post #14 north of the town of Sololá. The *Bruceros* had taken casualties continuously from guerrilla activity in the area for more than five years, and the military had responded in kind, sending patrols out every morning and late afternoon that worked the back trails well into the evenings. At Panajachél, the post commandeered boat sheds and several tackle shops which they employed as launches for night patrols along the coast and for quick excursions across the lake to San Felipe del Lago, and several other communities suspected of serving the guerrillas. The colonels had redlined the whole Lake District as insurgents and their sympathizers, most notably—according to the *Bruceros'comandante*—the North American priest.

Father Jackson "Jack" Heller was one of the most beloved of the clergy to serve the San Felipe Indians. He had taken the parish as a diocesan pastor after his first assignment in Oklahoma thirteen years before. Actually, he had sought a Central American post after he had met a Salvadoran family living in sanctuary outside of Oklahoma City. The diocese had placed more than a dozen priests in mission fields over thirty or more years, and Jack Heller had been intrigued and challenged by both the beauty of Central American traditional cultures as well as the challenges faced in serving in a subsistence economic setting. He had arrived in Guatemala in July of 1973, and on his first afternoon had taken a second-class bus out of the capital to the lake. He hitched a lift on one of the tourist boats the next morning for San Felipe and had been there ever since, returning only four times in his thirteen years with his adopted family of the Felipino community.

"*Buenos días, Padre*," said Diego Poppe, as Father Jack meandered past him beside his father in the Felipino market.

"And good morning to you, *chico*," responded the good natured, kindly priest.

Don Pablo, the boy's father, was sorting peppers from the basket beside him, tossing out those that had turned bad on him since he had brought them to market a week before. An *Atiteco* before his marriage to the daughter of a fellow merchant in the market some twenty years before, Don Pablo had become a respected member of the *cofradia* of San Felipe over the years and was in the fifteenth stage of his cargo. In four years he would become only the fifth *cofrade maximo* in the present memories of the Felipinos, not too shabby for a "foreigner."

Don Pablo had resented the North American priest upon his arrival, but he had been won over by Father Jack's help when his daughter, Blanca, had miscarried during the priest's second spring. Father Jack had rushed her to the hospital in Sololá, probably saving her life. From that point on, Don Pablo had worked part-time in the Catholic Church, doing odd jobs around the grounds, going for the mail and packages that came intermittently from the Father's family back in Oklahoma. But since 1985, Don Pablo had assumed an even more important role, that of a confidante to the priest, a kind of security scout for potential trouble.

The guerrillas had seized the village of San Felipe in 1984, highjacking two busses on the road late one evening as it was making their last runs around the lake. The guerrillas had ordered everyone off the busses and into the bushes where they lectured them on the importance of resisting the militaries and the necessity to provide the guerrillas with shelter and food while they were operating in the area. Then, they took their busses back to San Felipe where they seized the *alcalde* and four catechists and ordered the whole town to gather in the town plaza.

The leader of the guerrillas was a tawny young man in his late twenties who went by the name of "Lupe." Lupe was introduced by a strikingly beautiful young woman dressed in a black T-shirt, khaki pants, and a badly worn pair of Reeboks.

"Lupe has come to you from the people and has a message from the soul of Guatemala," cried the young woman, pressing her clasped hands between her breasts.

"Lupe" worked the gathering crowd for an hour or more, calling for the people to choose, to take the side of freedom from oppression and tyranny, to continue the resistance against the wealthy thieves who were seizing their land, to struggle against the rape of their wives and their daughters, to be vigilant in their watch for traitors and informers among them, to collect their produce into secret hideouts so that they might be sustained if attacked, to donate a portion of their harvest to those who had left their families and their homes to take up the cause of liberation, to fight against the soldiers who were burning their fields and slaughtering their livestock, to wait for the day of revolution when their lands would be returned and their *costumbres* reinstated and peace would come again to the people of the lake.

"Lupe," the khaki-pants girl, and the dozen or so guerrillas left San Felipe that day as quickly as they had come, taking the vehicles back up the road. An hour or more later, the same busses returned with the villagers, shaken by their ordeal and angry at the interruption of their commerce. Within the hour, three army helicopters swooped down into the plaza and at both ends of the road out of town, sealing off any exit. Minutes later, five military troop transports rumbled up to the first *tumulos* across the road, their heavy cargos lurching over the road bumps, as they crawled into town and to the plaza. Quickly, squads of soldiers, armed with heavy machine guns and automatic rifles, leaped from the back of the trucks and took up positions around the square. Two of the squads moved hastily down the side streets throwing open the doors of the surprised Felipinos sitting at their work or eating at their tables.

Father Jack had been occupied with a young Felipino couple, discussing with them plans for their marriage still several months away, when a young boy had bounded into his study with news of the arrival of the guerrillas. Father Jack jerked the little messenger into his study, quickly bolted the door and windows, and pulled the couple and the little boy into the corner of the room that was adjacent to the door. There they waited out the visitation of the insurgents.

Father Jack had made it a point to avoid discussing the guerrillas publicly. While privately he championed various points in their human rights agenda, he decried all killing and maiming, and openly, he took the middle way, teaching the "love of Christ." Some of his more visible activities, however, suggested a more complex commitment.

Through Catholic Action, Father Jack had initiated a language school to teach the young Felipinos Spanish, a little English, and some basic arithmetic. He had developed plans for a health clinic in the *colonia* that had sprung up at the western edge of the town, and he had openly called for civic registration for voting in the upcoming national elections. He had procured the help of an American Peace Corps volunteer in introducing the concept of grafting and other techniques of fruit tree propagation and care of cash crops useful in even the small private plots that some of the Felipino families maintained through the local cooperative. If he didn't carry membership in the *Guerrilla Army of the Poor* or the *Organization of the People in Arms*, Father Jack must have seemed to some to exhibit all the signs of a "subversive," and it wasn't more than a year or so before he had become the focus of some uninvited attention.

"Stop helping the enemies of the Republic!" the first note had said, quite simply. He had found it slipped under his study door more than two years before. He kept the note secreted away in a Bible commentary in the library, for he was sure it would not be the last, and comparisons might be helpful when future "correspondence" developed. No one of his staff seemed aware of the note, and he didn't press the issue, fearful that it might otherwise make him appear weak and less authoritative among his parishioners. Nevertheless, he had hastened to inform his Bishop in Sololá across the lake, and Bishop Marroquín had summoned him for a conference days later. The Bishop, too, had been targeted for similar warnings, but the scrawl of Father Jack's note was meaningless next to the typed one that Bishop Marroquín had shown him.

"Watch *out*, Jack," urged the Bishop. "If you are attacked, it will probably come indirectly—maybe one of your workers, one of the catechists. They won't attack you personally, at least not at first." Father Jack stayed over that evening to celebrate the Mass with the Bishop and then returned the next morning across the lake.

"How is my favorite merchant of peppers today?" asked Father Jack, as he paused to greet Don Pablo. Father Jack reached deeply into the basket of peppers, stirred through them with his fingers, and brought a handful to the surface.

"Too much *water*," observed Don Pablo. "It rains too soon or not enough. It rained hard, but it has been so dry for the past four or five weeks, and the peppers are burning on the branches!"

Father Jack was still learning, and there was so much for him to observe and understand among his adopted community. He had learned a basic handbook of Tzutujil within a year or a little longer upon his arrival in 1973, and he had been refining his plebeian use of the language ever since. Catholics among the Felipinos came to adore him, partly because, even from the beginning, he had not insisted on saying the Mass in Spanish.

Father Jack knew that he was "frontline fodder" as a Catholic priest in such a hotly contested territory in Latin America. He had no illusions about security. While he grieved deeply for the more than a dozen other priests of various orders who had lost their lives in the highlands over the past decade, he knew that his continued work with Catholic Action and other social service programs had been deemed "subversive." He knew also that his support of the people of San Felipe del Lago only aggravated the difficulty and security for them as well.

"What can we do, Bishop?" asked Father Jack. "What can we do to serve our mission to these people and, at the same time, provide them some relief from the constant state of repression they live under when they try to apply the Gospel to their lives. Every leader that rises up among them is cut down and in the most savage ways! I see nothing in all of our programs—or in the Gospel of Grace that we live by—that is any answer for a bullet in the head! What can we do, Bishop? What can I do?"

"There's only one thing, Jack," observed Bishop Marroquín. "There's only one. You, we—we've just got to keep planting seeds."

Father Jack returned to San Felipe and to his adopted family, serving them day by day in both the small and momentous events of their lives together. As he could take the time, he would write to his mother, father, and sister back in Oklahoma. He knew of their constant worry for him, and he made it a point to downplay the increasing violence around the lake. He couldn't be sure his letters weren't being intercepted from time to time. His sister Mildred had read of the attack on an Indian bus weeks before when four people had been killed, more than a dozen severely wounded, and all robbed of their valuables. The inveterate clipper of Guatemalan bad tidings, Mildred Francis, he knew, kept the rest of the family on edge, and that frustrated him. So he always made the effort in his own correspondence to mask the anguish and increasing urgency that he felt for his people every day.

But for all the worry and the occasional horrific interruptions of the daily routines, Father Jack's programs continued to grow. His literacy project was successful beyond his expectations. Within only four semesters, he had acquired a reputation as a sympathetic language instructor, and he even had to begin refusing students. There simply weren't enough teachers and materials to go around.

The health clinic continued to grow. Several parishes stateside were now supplying supplemental medical equipment and cases of various, basic antibiotics. He had arranged with a Guatemalan doctor and nurse to visit the clinic once a week from Panajachél, which was no small feat in itself.

Father Jack's Sunday Masses were always packed and were becoming something of the social occasion. More and more young people were attending as well, and he felt as though the Church was maintaining its own leverage in the face of persistent pressure from several evangelical groups building chapels in the area. For his programs, then, Father Jack was pleased, but he had cause to be ever wary.

Several of his parishioners had whispered their fears about the expanding military presence around the lake, and the post—only five kilometers away—had augmented its troops tenfold, numbering almost two hundred. While on patrol the soldiers were stopping more and more of the *campesinos* and demanding on-site verification of their *cedulas*, or registration cards. Many without their cards were being detained, and several had been badly beaten, accused of being guerrillas or their supporters. To add to his own personal concern, Father Jack received a second clandestine note: "Stop your subversive support of the Indians, or we will send you back to Oklahoma in a *jar!*" As before, Father Jack immediately reported the death threat to Bishop Marroquín who advised him to increase his security precautions around the church. He might also consider moving his sleeping quarters every other night or so within the compound itself. The military was beginning to widen its influence in the region, and reports of intimidation, threats, and disappearances were coming in from just about all the *cantones* throughout the department of Sololá.

"We have a problem in that priest," said the *comandante* to his lieutenants at the pre-dawn meeting. "He has completed the clinic and has expanded the language classes. I think we need to do something else to get his attention, Lieutenant Gomez. Work out the arrangements with Taco and the Rooster. I want a report by the end of the week."

"*Sí! Comandante!*" saluted Lieutenant Gomez as he snapped from his chair and sprang to attention. After he was dismissed, Lieutenant Gomez called the Rooster for a briefing and strategy meeting. Such meetings with captains typically were brief and secret, called together usually in the mess hall after lunch as the garrisoned troops were retiring for their early afternoon posts.

"Get this little greeting to the priest," ordered the lieutenant. The officer handed a dirty piece of tablet paper to the Rooster, "And eliminate the pepper belly on your way back, but whatever you do, don't bring him to the post. You might want to use the shed or whatever; I don't really care. You can handle the drop in the city or somewhere off the highway. You know what to do," explained the Lieutenant, and he handed the Rooster an envelope containing Q200 quetzales, Q50 quetzales apiece, payable in advance to a trusted, reliable team.

The Rooster usually initiated responses to orders. Procedures were pretty straight forward. They began with instructions to Taco, the driver. He'd sign out for the vehicle and its supplies and have it prepped at the garage. His primary responsibility as a driver was to check out the gear that was assigned to the van. Each of the *comisionados* would be responsible for his own "piece." Taco would make sure the vehicle contained the necessary physical restraints—belts, ropes, a couple of nets. Of course, he would bring extra ammunition for the pistols and clips for the Uzi that was assigned to the unit. And then there was the rest—extra batteries for the flashlights, a car battery and electrical cords, a tarpaulin and blanket, two machetes, razors, two *capuches*, a can of insecticide, and a bag of lime dust. When Taco was satisfied he had secured all the materials, he sent the truck on to the garage for servicing.

Rooster made up the assignments. He had a new man to work into the schedule, and this little job was a good opportunity to check him out. He sent the corporal to the compound for "Pepe," the name that had been assigned to the young Felipino. This one should work out. He had made it through the training and was "independent." Participation in a job or two would usually complete the training. Although this fellow had proven his metal in the civil patrol, a kid with strength and commitment didn't fulfill all the criteria for a member of "operations." The single, most important factor was ownership, the critical element in the mix of a successful member of an operations team. "Ownership" meant just that: a man belonged to the unit and to no one or anything else. How that ownership was achieved varied from person to person. The key was compromise. "Fear" alone worked for most; conscripts from the villages could be compromised by a "demonstration" or two. The captain would dispatch the weaker member of a squad in front of the rest as an example of what losers faced. A second demonstration usually wasn't necessary.

For others—like this kid who had come from a strong family—"compromise" meant breaking the bond within the family irrevocably. That had been accomplished in the pit. At Chimaltenango, "Pepe" had received the usual treatment—with one exception. He had become his own brother's executioner. Once the Felipino had been paraded before his own brother's pulverized corpse, "ownership" was complete: he could never return as a member to his village or even to his family. The task remaining was "introducing" the young initiate publicly. That would happen through reassigning him to the post nearest his village.

Very rarely were conscripts reassigned to their own department. Common soldiers were never sent back and usually finished their eighteen-month hitch far from their own *aldea*s. "Commission" units were much different. There could be no question of the loyalty, for they constituted a secret component that made rule by repression so successful. A member of an "operations unit" was a member for life. While a member could enjoy numerous military-sponsored "benefits," there was no retirement plan other than an unmarked grave twenty miles out to sea.

What had distinguished the Felipino was his eager leadership and dispatch in the civil patrol. The kid assumed responsibility from the first night. Within the first two outings, he had fingered two of the most prominent catechists in the area and had lifted the head from the second and tossed it to the jackals at the community garbage dump. A tall, burly figure for an Indian, he was respected both for his physical prowess and for the family name he bore. His father—like his father and grandfathers before—were *brujos*, that is to say, traditional priests whose dark secrets were passed along the family lineage by the gods they worshipped and with whom they conspired from generation to generation.

It was Madagascar Pecho—"El Pesado," the "heavy one"—who witnessed the second return of the patrol and who had first noticed the Felipino's potential. "El Pesado," the civilian military commander of the San Felipe civil patrol, had brought his name before the *comandante* at the regional garrison. It seemed clear that this particular Xoy brother would break the string in the *costumbre* cycle, although it probably wasn't yet obvious to the young man himself. Nevertheless, he was reputed to be most respectful of the stature of his family. If there was a weakness in the boy, it was his affection for his younger brother, Tano. Colonel Herrera, *comandante* of the Felipino and the other Sololá post, was the director of the ruse at the National Palace which had taken the two brothers away from their village duties. If the present assignment worked, this operations unit would acquire a valuable new member. "Pepe" would begin his first assignment as the only "administrator" for this job. "El Pesado" had confided his interest in the Felipino to Rooster and suggested he be integrated into the unit as quickly as possible. Rooster sent for the new conscript awaiting instructions in the post's holding room.

"You are essential to the success of this little job, Pepe," said Rooster. "You know the village. Your task is to get this message to that fucking *priest*. Pick out a kid—one you can depend on—you *got* that? And get this to him. We're moving out at dusk."

Rooster handed Pepe the folded slip of paper with the crude threat scribbled across it.

"Here's two quetzales for the kid," he said. "Make him come back to you after he's delivered the message, but tell him to meet you at a different site. You don't want anybody trailing you back to the truck, but make the last stop within a block or two of the truck anyway, so you can get the shit *out* of there, you *understand?*"

Pepe took the two bills and stuffed them into his shirt pocket along with the note.

"Don't put the goddamn *note* with the *bills!*" Rooster barked. "What if you drop that note and the *wind* catches it?"

Pepe shuffled through the bills and retrieved the note and placed it inside his pants.

"Be ready in twenty minutes. We're going to pull out of here just after dark," Rooster explained.

Miguel "Pepe" Mapa was only beginning to recover from his ordeal. Physically, he had survived the broken jaw and two cracked ribs, but memory of Tano's body dumped unceremoniously on the compound grounds in front of the Colonel's quarters had seared his soul. Had the target not been either he or his brother? What choice had he *had?* He had been *crazy* in the pit. How could he have known? But of course, it had not been meant for him to know. He had been set up—*both* of them, from the beginning. He had had days to think about it as he lay in the compound recovering. He knew he had been tested, and he knew he had passed. But the idea of killing his *own brother* kept working on him. But would not his brother have done the same? But *of course!* That was clear. He knew that he could never reveal the truth to his family or even to his lifelong friends in San Felipe. He would never be able to associate with them again. Even so, he knew that his very survival now required him to get beyond any concern—personal or otherwise—he might still feel over the death of his brother. He was now entering a world that he had only fantasized, a world in which he would join the Republic's elite, the most feared and respected echelon that made and unmade the very presidents themselves, and he had joined it. He was now a member of the most fearsome corps in the whole country, and if he played it right, he was fixed for life.

It wasn't difficult to accept his role among the team. He was beginning to get a little heady with his newfound respect and position. In time, if he proved well, he might move up the ranks: he might even be offered a captain's post in his own commission unit. Still, the idea of returning to his own village chilled him, and he began to reflect on a possible candidate among the neighborhood runts for ferrying the message to the priest. Whom could he trust? And then it dawned on him. Little Manuel, his own brother, was ideal! Manuel Xoy idolized his older brother. He wouldn't say a word to anyone, but the idea of him participating with his brother as an agent for the military would command his allegiance and quick response. And of course, the two *quetzale*s would cinch the deal perfectly.

The truck pulled out of the Sololá garrison just as the last faint glow dimmed out completely on the opposite side of the lake. The drive around the lake to the post of the jackals would take more than three hours. The first stretch would take them into Panajachel where they would radio the post at San Felipe. Then they would proceed around the lake, past San Rafael del Carmen, past Tupotenango, and finally through La Colema on the far southern flank of the lake. From there they could drive straight to the garrison with only a few of the *campesinos* to notice them as they maneuvered up the rutted road.

The passage around the lake was uneventful. The road, under any other circumstances or for any other work, would have been unpassable in the night. Deep ruts crisscrossed the surface of the road, and several times, the team had to exit to push the vehicle out of the washed out slips.

"*Damn!*" said Rooster. "What a *ride!*"

Pepe felt bruised at every angle of his body, but on his first assignment, he wasn't about to express any aches and pains. The team entered the military post outside San Felipe at almost one a.m. in the morning, their entrance noted only by the single pair of guards at the front gate. Rooster pulled the Jeep into the middle of the post and stopped at the captain's compound.

"Why don't you get out and take a leak," said Rooster. "I'll check in with the captain, and then we'll do the job."

Pepe didn't mind the opportunity to stretch or to relieve himself. He had been miserable trying to hold it back for the past hour. He stepped out of the jeep and made it only as far as behind the captain's building.

"No *noise!* No *commotion!*" said the captain. "Make it clean. Take the old man outside the town, but leave his body where it'll be found in the morning. Most important, get the note to the priest. The whole idea is to reinforce the pressure on the goddamn Yankee priest."

"*Sí! capitán!*" said Rooster as he saluted the officer.

"I want this kid to work out, understand?" said the captain. "He's from a big shit family in San Felipe, so he knows everybody. But I don't want anybody to see him, not on this first job. You can remember your first commission, *no?* Nervous as a *whore* on a first *date!*"

Both laughed at the little joke, but in a glance, the captain was all business again.

"*Sí! capítan!*" reiterated Rooster.

Rooster stepped outside into the night almost to run into Pepe returning from the back of the building.

"You got two jobs," explained Rooster. "First, you're going to get a kid to deliver the note. There'll be a few street kids. You can rouse anyone you want."

"No," interrupted Pepe. "I've got just the one—my kid brother. I can trust him to keep his mouth shut. He looks up to me, and we'll be going in close to our house."

"That's okay—*whatever,*" agreed Rooster. "If he can keep his mouth shut, then that's just one more *shit stick* we won't have to pitch in the stew later on."

The idea of silencing little Manuel hadn't entered his mind, or the killing of any other Felipino kid, for that matter. He shuddered at the thought of it, but then he knew his brother. He knew he could depend upon Manuel. He wasn't so sure of the street urchins who wandered in and off the streets and into San Felipe from other towns since the beginning of the big violence several months earlier. He wasn't sure he had the stomach for killing a kid. Priests, catechists, pepper merchants who passed around notes to the guerrillas—they were something else. They were all subversives, guns or no guns. In fact, you could respect a guerrilla combatant who would stand face to face and fight you. There was something of honor in that. But these others—they were even more vile, even more wretched and to be feared because they worked to destroy the country from behind lies and smiles. Cut out their fucking tongues! They seemed to understand that. Slit their goddamned throats!

"That's the trail that leads up to my house," said Pepe as they entered into the eastern end of the town. "Just pull on up to the first corner—two blocks more, and I'll come back. On nights like this, my brother sleeps with the cat in the corn bin. There won't be any sound. I won't disturb anyone. He can meet us here, so we don't have to go anywhere else."

Rooster pulled the Jeep Cherokee up to the first intersection and stopped. Instantly, Pepe slipped from the car and was bounding away into the shadows away from the glow of the light streaming from the one street lamp in the plaza. Within moments he was up the trail and in sight of the corn bin at the edge of the clearing to his house. All was still, but he could make out the profile of the body of his little brother fast asleep at the foot of the bin.

"*Ssst!*" whispered Pepe between his teeth. "*Ssst! Ssst!*"

Little Manuel stirred once and rolled over. Pepe would have to risk awakening him, and in a moment, he was at his side, his big hand clamped over the little boy's mouth.

"*Shhhhsh!*" ordered Pepe. Manuel was terrified at the rupture in his sleep, but instantly, he recognized the figure of his brother, and his little eyes brightened with surprise.

"*Shhhhsh!*" repeated Pepe.

The little boy raised himself to his feet and followed Pepe's signal to leave with him back down the path. At the foot of the trail, Pepe pulled his brother aside and explained his mission.

"You can't tell *anyone! Understand?*" said Pepe.

Manuel nodded in compliance. Pepe explained in the simplest of terms the commission for delivering the note and showed his brother the two *quetzales* he promised to give him upon his return. He then pointed down the road toward the town where the little boy was to report after delivering the message. Manuel shoved the note in his shirt pocket and away he raced into the night.

"That's *good!*" said Miguel Mapa to himself as he drifted back toward the Jeep. No one had seen them, he was confident. "That's a good *job!*"

"How did it go?" asked Rooster as Miguel "Pepe" Mapa eased back into the cab of the Jeep. The older brother smiled and snapped his fingers. "Just like *that!* Just like I thought it would."

"That's good," said Rooster glancing out the side window and behind them in the rearview mirror.

"My little brother, he's going to meet me in back around the corner there," said Pepe, "so I better get on over there."

Once again, as quietly as Manuel's pet cat, Pepe slipped from the truck and disappeared around the building. It wasn't more than five minutes when he returned, a broad smile across his face.

"Let's go pick some *peppers!*" said Pepe.

Rooster started the ignition and eased the car back out into the street.

"Go around the plaza to avoid the light on the corner," said Pepe. "Just stay in the alley and go about two blocks. The pepper guy sleeps beside his bundle in the alley every night. I'll just pop his neck and he'll never know a thing. Then we can take him outside town, and I'll dress him like a fucking *stag*. I'll have him carved up in five minutes. Then we can just dump his ass on the road and be on our way."

Chapter 7

La Familia

María Xquic de Xoy finished rinsing the kernels of white corn and sprinkled pinches of lye into the kettle in order to clean the husks from the meat of the corn during boiling. She set the kettle over the hearth and slipped another stick of wood between the stones. With a smaller branch, María stoked the coals to liven the fire. Instantly, the flames flared under the kettle as the bark peeled and crackled. The exposed wood beneath the vanquished bark splintered and burned in the withering heat and sent sparks exploding out the ends of the hearth. Slowly, the water began to churn, and the kernels of corn relinquished their husks which floated to the surface of the pot, swirling around the smooth strokes of María's wooden spoon. María scooped up the husks and flung them out the window over the hearth to the expectant chickens congregated on the ground below.

After drying the cleaned corn, María began the arduous task of grinding the kernels into *masa*. She placed a handful of white corn on the grinding stone and mashed it into a thick, even dough. Then she kneaded the growing mound with her leathery hands, blending into the *masa* globs of tasty pork lard, in preparation for the tamales. Satisfied that she had prepared enough for the evening meal, she wiped the sticky paste from her palms and shook the gummy little balls of residue from her fingers. She walked to the door of her one-room hovel and peered out across the fields. She watched her two young daughters gathering the banana leaves for wrapping the tamales.

Steadily in the late afternoon, the air continued to thicken. Veils of clouds poured slowly through the tall, stripped shafts of the pines that ringed the *milpa* and drifted across the ground, enveloping the corn shed and the pile of faggots for the evening's fire. The combed, red head of the rooster bobbed up and down, disappearing under and then reappearing from beneath the layers of ground fog as the petulant fowl foraged around the hut for bits of refuse and grains of corn.

The pungent smoke from the cooking hearth and the hot, fresh aroma of white corn tortillas mingled with the heavy, cold air of the morning with the gossamer shreds of cloud. Ana Fabiola and Lucita María passed ghost-like through the fog, crossing their arms with the broad banana leaves used for wrapping the little loaves of tamales. María Xquic returned to the heavy bowl of *masa* and began shaping the thick Tzutujil tamales, bland mounds of white corn paste and pork lard wrapped over a thin layer of shredded meat and tapered to an edge on each end.

Ana Fabiola and Lucita María entered the doorway with their arms loaded with the broad, smooth banana leaves and laid them on the flimsy little table next to the cooking hearth. Then, Ana Fabiola returned her brother's *machete* to its place just inside the door. As she walked back toward her mother, she pulled her fingers through the thick strands of her long, flowing dark hair.

"You are too *silly* at the plaza, Ana Fabiola María Xoy!" scolded her mother. "You aren't acting like you're a daughter of mine. You're too *silly* with the boys, and you've got to be more careful, or you'll give wrong impressions."

"Yes, mother," confessed the embarrassed young girl. How would she know such a thing, she wondered? Ana Fabiola looked behind her mother's skirt, her heavy, dark denim *morga*, toward her older sister Lucita María to confirm her sister's attention. It would be the most her mother would say about the subject for the present. It was always like this. She didn't talk to Lucita this way. It wasn't fair!

Ana Fabiola was fourteen, two years younger than her sister, Lucita María. Ana Fabiola was proud of the two little mounds of breasts beginning to show under her *huipil*. She was proud of the looks the boys were beginning to give her.

"Come, Ana, you better come *on* now!" Lucita would tell her as they finished with their washing at the *pila*, the community washing tank. She knew that her younger sister was the more attractive and beginning to flirt with the young men in the community. She knew that she was breaking with the traditional courtship patterns of her village and with the instructions of their mother. Mostly, though, Lucita María was simply embarrassed by her sister's attention and uncertain of her own relationship to the increasingly separate and restricted world of the males. She felt violated by the leers of the "wild boys," and she was revolted by the heavy drinking among the older boys in their twenties. On the other hand, Lucita María was drawn to her mother and her aunt and cousins. She enjoyed market days with them and preparations for holy days when for more than a week she and her cousins—all the girls—would work with the nuns in the church to wash the floors and dress the saints for the periodic devotions. The boys were not interested in a girl so tall and thin and so flat in the chest, and that was all right with her. She was comfortable in her work with her mother and in her evolving new religious duties.

Between the two daughters, Lucita María was the weaver. She worked for hours at the *tejida*, the backstrap loom, as her mother had taught her so many years before. Lucita could remember, at four, the thrill she had for the little *huipil* that her mother had finished for her. She was fascinated by the rows of intricate, many-colored animal figures that paraded across the dark-blue blouse, outward from the center *randa*, or seam, to her left shoulder, and the same to the right. She had given them names after her favorite fowls in the yard and would talk to them as her small fingers stroked the designs fabricated from floating threads that, at regular intervals, emerged from between the vertical warp threads of the ground fabric. The bright, mercerized threads from which the designs were made wrapped across the face of the ground fabric over three and four of the warp threads, and then plunged again into the dark, indigo fabric only to rise again and then disappear once more an inch further as the next arrogant, piquant chicken, turkey hen or pea hen.

Lucita's favorite toy as a small child had been the drop spindle, a shaft of wood—perhaps seven to eight inches long—that extended from a point on one end, then expanded into a whorl or ball at the other. Twirled by the finger tips from the pointed top, the drop spindle was used to spin a thread from a clutch of cotton or wool held two or three feet higher by the weaver in her other hand. The filaments of the fibers wound into a thread, the density controlled by the amount of tension maintained between the clutch of raw fibers and the point of the spindle.

Lucita could spin thread by the time she was only seven and a half or eight, and even when most women had begun purchasing more and more commercial yarn from the new *tienda* that opened at the end of the market, María and her grandmother, Doña Audelia, always accepted her skeins and worked them into the bundles that they would send to Don Fernando, the dyer who had served the Xoy family for more than three generations. As she grew even more experienced, Lucita's technique produced finer and finer, more uniform threads. Lucita was always proud when her yarns came back from Don Fernando almost indistinguishable among the other yarns spun by weavers many times her own age.

"Lucita María is the daughter of a *weaver!*" Doña Audelia would say to her neighbor when her granddaughter walked past them down the trail on the way to the church. The implication was clear, of course, to all who saw her work that the traditions were being passed successfully in the young protégé.

María had labored herself for more than three months at the loom in weaving the first panel of the *muestra*, the model *huipil* for Lucita María. María had prepared carefully for the creation of the *huipil*. On the evening before she was to select the shafts for the warping reels and shed rods for Lucita's loom, Maria had knelt with her husband before *Santa Mesa*. They lit candles and placed them in pairs on the ground before the sacred table and prayed that the two of them—mother and daughter—might find harmony in the ancient lesson of the village's art, that the *costumbre* of San Felipe might be passed with grace and skill from one generation to the next. Don Andres rose and swung the censor above the candle flames and then sealed the ritual with a pass to the four cardinal points, pacing softly from the north to the east, then south and to the west, returning in solemn reverence before *Santa Mesa*. They left the candles to burn as a gesture of their abiding faith in exchange for the enduring guidance of *Santa Mesa* as the mother and daughter began one of the most precious chapters in the relationship of a San Felipe family.

On the following morning, María had risen earlier than usual, more than an hour before the crow of the rooster, and had begun preparations for cooking the beans and tortillas. The day that a San Felipe mother sits down at the loom with a daughter for the first time is a moment both remember for a lifetime. Even little Lucita had been skittish the evening before, obviously awaiting the next morning herself with great anticipation. Doña Audelia would come by during the morning after she judged that the young student would be well beyond the first throws of the hettle. By custom, the girl would be weaving at her new loom off to the side of the house—still within sight of her mother, albeit—and working with the *muestra* that her mother had presented to her just at dawn so that the first light of day would illuminate the model and engrain upon the young girl's imagination from that day forward the particular patterns of her village.

It wasn't as if, of course, that Lucita hadn't already studied the weaver's art. Each step in the process had always been an abiding fascination for the eager child. She had been at her mother's side every day of her small life, watching her lift the warp threads with her pick, following her mother's deft fingers, chasing the pattern weft threads throughout the warp and coaxing them up and under again across the face of the loom.

In the afternoon before her lesson, Lucita had sat beside her mother, gently nudging the winding reel, releasing the long yarns as María had carefully wrapped them over and under, over and under, around and around the rods of the loom mounted in their slots on the warping board. It took more than an hour to complete the warping for Lucita's loom.

When she had finished, María carefully turned the warping board on its side and gently removed the rods, now intertwined in the warp of the loom. María carefully raised the hettle rod to expose the first shed and gently slipped the waxed batten into the wide space between the alternating threads of the warp. Her daughter would learn first to set the selvedge at the top and bottom of the warp before initiating the first few inches of the ground fabric.

In the market, María had purchased Lucita's small backstrap, the belt that wrapped around her hips to secure the base of the loom at her waist. Now the laced, maguey band was folded and lying in the basket of multicolored balls of pattern yarns and the ropes that would tie the top warping rod of the loom to the rafter under the eave of the house. All was ready for the next day when Lucita would take up the loom for the rest of her life.

La tejida was more than basic technology for the hundreds of little Indian hamlets that dotted the highlands. The backstrap loom was to the woman what the machete was for the man. Early mastery of each demonstrated the metal of the user and marked the passage from childhood to youth. Each *tejadora*, or weaver, would learn the respected art from her mother or her godmother, the second most sacred obligation—after childbirth—in the *cargo* of an Indian woman. To be able to make the tortillas in the style of her village and to be able to weave the material of her *huipil* and of her husband's *cotón*, or traditional jacket, completed a young woman's apprenticeship for marriage.

More than a craft, however, the practice of weaving had even deeper roots in the psyche of *indigenas*, the "real people." The threads of weaving wound throughout the Maya world of myth and legend. It was said that the ancient ones had initiated the tradition of weaving, and they had learned it directly from the fierce goddess of *Xibalba* herself, the gruesome *Ixchel*, dark princess of the underworld, the bitch goddess who attended the initiation of each young pupil and communed with the warp and the weft, guiding the fingers of the girl, quickening to life the menagerie of knotted, little animal forms that traipsed back and forth across the ground weave. With her attention to every movement of the yarns, every earnest, little apprentice worked to win the goddess's approval. Each learned to dread the ancient deity and with cause. Sloppy craftsmanship might mean everlasting back pain and the curse of arthritis in her hands before marriage. The goddess would not be trifled.

Later in that first morning—in fact, just after María had returned from the market, Lucita's grandmother, Doña Audelia had stopped in to visit the young weaver at her work.

"*Ahhh, reina!*," droned the wise, old lady. "The little one will embarrass the silly boys when they return from the mountain!"

It was a compliment, of course. It was all her grandmother would say, but in so doing, she had completed her obligation to the family. Lucita was very proud. She loved and respected the majesty of her grandmother, the wise one who had taught her mother so much. How could one come to know so much, to command such respect among the other members of the village? And to think—even to *think* that her grandmother would attend her at Lucita's work *this* day! The little girl had not dared look up for fear of offending her grandmother, fearful that she might seem negligent to the present duty at her fingertips.

"Ahhh! The little one will embarrass the silly boys when they return from the mountain!" repeated Lucita from her memory of those rarefied words already folded and tucked safely away in her small breast. She would come, in time, to remember her grandmother by those words, but for now, however, Lucita was preoccupied with secret desire, an unspeakable yearning that she would never dare to express before even her mother or—her husband of some nebulous future day. It was this: she would weave every day to honor *Jesucristo* and the saints and the benevolent *San Felipe*, Saint Philip, the patron saint of her village. She would weave for the ancient *Maximón*, the terrible one who could steal the fever from suffering heads or shake the waters of the lake when he was angry. She would weave for the four cardinal points, dedicating her very best efforts each time to *El Mundo*, the lord of all the world, and before *Santa Mesa* and beg her father to light candles, one each for both her eyes that she might better see the loom, one candle for her mother's health, another for *Jesucristo*, and one candle for Doña Audelia, the wise one.

That was many years before. Lucita had grown both in her faith and in the weaver's art, but she could see in her younger sister, Ana Fabiola, a spirit very different from her own, a temper of rebellion against the old ways and against the wise ones. Doña Audelia, she sensed, didn't care for the ways of Ana Fabiola.

"*Sassy* one!" Doña Audelia had said when she watched Ana Fabiola neglect her catechism. And there was something else.

Lucita María worried about Ana Fabiola's drift from her early mentors among the nuns in favor of more trifling things—lounging at the *pila* and coaxing favors from the boys. Ana Fabiola was already a young woman. The earth had been spotted for more than a year. The younger sister enjoyed her new-found attention, and she hoped somehow she might attract the eye of Isaiah Xolop, the son of Don Sergio Enric Xolop, at one time, before the arrival of so many *ladinos*, one of the town's most prominent merchants. Isaiah was popular among the girls who admired his carriage on the horse and the confidence of his position among the other young men. His presence was giving her a new value to the Mass, and Ana Fabiola maneuvered in the pews so as to catch a glimpse of Isaiah. She always hoped that she might exit after the Xolop family, for Isaiah liked to hang out with his friends after the service on the concrete benches around the plaza. She always tried to walk on the outside of her family as they passed by the benches so he would see her as she went by.

Isaiah would make quite a husband. He looked so handsome in his straw hat and store-bought shirt. On Sundays he wore the traditional wool jacket with the insignia of the village stitched across the back, the stylized image of the bat. Isaiah would sit in the long row of boys and talk about village affairs. Ana Fabiola had an idea of what those might be, overhearing Miguel Mapa and Tanolito sometimes laughing, sometimes arguing over their *frioles* and tortillas: the traffic of commerce around the lake, *girls,* Catholic Action and its new training programs, the priests and their conflict with the evangelicals, *girls,* and—more quietly, the military presence in their community and rumors of horrible things at the military post, and of course, *girls.* Ana Fabiola was hopeful that, even at fourteen, she might somehow become a topic of the boys' Sunday conversation.

Ana Fabiola assisted her mother in wrapping the tamales. They sat each one on top of a spread banana leaf and folded it over the top. All the tamales were then placed snugly in a cooking pot and steamed just before the men were scheduled to return from the fields. The men usually returned an hour after sundown, the time it took them to work their way from the fields draped over the steep slopes of the mountain, down the road, through the northwestern path to the village, and to the plaza where they parted to make their respective ways to their families.

Despite her frivolity, however, Ana Fabiola had always revered her father. She was in awe of his position as an *auxiliatura* and healer in San Felipe. When she was just a little girl, she remembered many villagers would speak of him with great respect as the family returned on its way from Mass.

"Good day, Don Andres, and may you be blessed and your family enjoy health and happiness, Don Andres." That's what they would say.

"Remember me at *Santa Mesa*, Don Andres, and here's a *quetzal* for your petition," old Doña Concha would plead as they passed from the church.

These were the things that she had heard from childhood. As a tiny little thing behind the folds of her mother's skirt, Ana Fabiola would stand back away from *Santa Mesa*, the sacred table, and tremble at the sight of the sacred beans when her father would cast them over his *tzute*. It was general knowledge throughout the village that her father controlled the universe. Was he not the privileged servant of *San Simón, the Maximón*? Could he not call upon the gods, the saints, and *El Mundo*? Could he not visit the *dueños de las montañas* and negotiate the harvests? Her father, Don Andres, had the ears of the earth and the eyes of the skies above. Long into the evenings after laborious, sometimes torturous work in the fields, her father would sit at *Santa Mesa*, pouring over the divining beans and coursing his way through the universal plan that only the gods and those few, specially anointed priests to the gods could ever hope to understand. Don Andres Menchu Xoy—conversant with *San Simón, with El Mundo*, the Lord of the Earth, with the Christian saints, Jesus, and with Santa María, the mother of God—her father was a great and revered man, and his word was authority in the house. Don Andres, the *auxiliatura máximo*, entered the doorway and, nodding slightly to his wife, removed his hat and slung his bag over the back of his chair.

Don Andres was a diminutive Tzutujil Maya, not unlike most of the other men of San Felipe del Lago, and like them, his body exhibited the sinewy and wiry muscular frame under his worn shirt and frayed trousers. He wore the traditional *tráje* of his village. His shirt was handwoven blue cotton, festooned with the tiny brocaded abstractions of birds, people, and animals in yellow, greens, reds, and purple yarns. His pants were the simple handwoven cotton with the alternating half-inch bands of purple two inches apart running up and down the length of the garment. The faded, red sash around his waist held in place the brown and white checkered *capixay*, a heavy woolen cloth that folds in front through the sash, worn only by members of high rank in San Felipe. For years, perhaps a decade and more, Don Andres had worn the same sandals, fashioned from an old tire, with wide leather straps crisscrossed over his dusty arches.

Within his own home, away from his fellow *campesinos*, Don Andres could exhibit the day's fatigue. He allowed the strap of his bag to slip softly from his shoulder into the crook of his arm. Then he reached over and lifted it by the mouth of the bag to keep it from dragging on the ground. He moved into the shadows of the cooking fire, crossed his feet, and squatted against the wall. He closed his eyes momentarily and wiped the perspiration from his eyebrows. Stretching his arms out over his knees in front of him with his bag of ancient relics before him, he bowed his head between his elbows and rested.

Doña María folded a handful of fresh, hot tortillas in a *servieta* and brought it, along with a cup of sweet corn broth, the traditional *atole*, before her husband. But Don Andres lifted his head and through squinted eyes accepted the bit of food. Typically, the head of the house was the first to eat, followed by the other male members, if present, then the children, and last of all, the women. Don Andres was disturbed, and he would eat alone tonight. Ana Fabiola and Lucita María huddled across the room in the warmth of the hearth watching their father and waiting for him to speak. When the male householder had eaten, he would indicate both the subject and tone of the conversation for the meal, but there would be no conversation tonight.

Don Andres rolled his tortillas and dipped them into the pasty loaf of refried black beans that his wife had placed before him. The mound of black beans was garnished with his favorite goat cheese, graded and sprinkled generously over the surface. On cue from her mother, Ana Fabiola reached into the bowl of steamed tamales and took one to her father, who acknowledged her courtesy with an abrupt, but not unkindly nod. Hungry and tired, Don Andres ate slowly and deliberately. After a third or fourth bite of tamale, he brushed his lips and looked up at his wife, the gratuity of the householder to his spouse and the sign for them to begin.

Each girl threw her hands deeply into the ceramic pot containing the thick tamales. María Xquic took her traditional place by the hearth where she could continue to warm the tortillas. She dipped a cooking spoon into the bowl of black beans and spread the paste over a tortilla, rolled it, and began to eat slowly off one end. María waited for her husband to speak.

Don Andres continued to chew vacantly at the end of the tamale. He was deep in thought and obviously troubled. At last he finished and looked around for his shoulder bag. Without a word, he lifted the bag by the shoulder strap, then rose, and left the hut.

"Don J'cab has always been a good and faithful man," Don Andres mused to himself. "He's always been faithful to his *cargo*, and he always understood his duty to our family and to the saints, and to the lords of the mountains, and to Jesucristo. It isn't right that he should turn against us all."

Don Andres walked away from his house and down the path toward the plaza. He was exhausted from his work in the *milpa*, but he was also worried. He had prayed before *Santa Mesa*, and he had divined the Sacred Beans. Don Chamchot, also a priest for San Simón, was worried. He had brought three turkey eggs for the *diós regalo*, and together they had lit candles as *costumbre* prescribed. Had he not *prayed*, and had he not presented his petitions? Was he not pure *himself?* He would consult Don Diego and Don Soto. He would propose next a sacrifice of divination, if it came to that. Don J'cab had always been a fine, decent man. Maybe he had been singled out by the *evil eye*, a *death* threat by an enemy. This was no small matter between two lifelong friends—indeed, between two *brothers*.

The clouds had swallowed up the trail completely, and Don Andres worked his way meticulously down the rutted path. Dimly, but then with more assurance, he began to make out the faint, white glow of the single light bulb on the plaza over the water hydrant as he inched along the trail. Dogs growled and occasionally barked as he passed the stone walls outlining the entrances to his neighbors' houses. He approached the trail leading to the house of Don J'cab on the hill above and stood for a moment peering up the path through the blighted corn stalks toward the entrance. Through the mist, Don Andres could make out faintly the orange glow of the electric light, flickers from the hearth, and the occasional pass of a ghostly silhouette before the doorway.

Kneeling down, the priest placed his shoulder bag in front of him. In the swirling mist, he slowly retrieved his censor, a perforated metal can to which was attached a clothes hanger wire and a leather strap. Returning into the bag, Don Andres fumbled in its folds for a paper wrapper containing chips of *copal pom*, incense mixed into small cakes of charcoal, used for centuries by the Mayas before their gods. Carefully, he unwrapped the *pom* and took a generous handful of the crumbly cakes and placed them in the bottom of the censor. He withdrew a package of matches, tore away two from the packet, and lit them. He tipped the censor and slowly placed the burning matches against the dried incense. Instantly, the coals flashed, and Don Andres held the can steadily until the flame engulfed all the chunks of the *pom*. Then, while still on one knee at the entrance to his friend's home, he began a litany of prayer, swinging the censor back and forth beside him.

"All gods of the sky and earth, and all the saints in the heavens, all the *Alcaldes* of the high mountains and the *Alcades* of the mountain streams and of the lake; hear me now, your servant Don Andres, poor minister to your will. Jesucristo and mother of god and the Christian saints, hear me now. Bless the entrance of the house of this good man, Don J'cab, and all his family. Bless his wife, Doña Manuela, that she may serve her husband and her children, that they may know health and happiness, and that through this door no evil may come their way. Hear me now, all you *Alcaldes* of *Santa Mesa*, and of the Holy Earth. Hear me now, oh mighty *San Simón*! *Ah, malaya*, *Maximón*! Pardon this servant his sins and make his heart pure that you may hear this petition for a faithful man, Don J'cab. Come now to this place at this time and in this day and at this hour, that your power may be with this man that he might this night be of service to his family. *Ah, malaya*! *San Simón*! Ah, mighty *Maximón*! Do this for me, and I will burn five candles and sprinkle rose petals as a gift appropriate to you and to *El Mundo* and to all the saints and the

Alcaldes and to the *dueños de las montañas*. This I pray, your poor servant, Don Andres Menchu Xoy of San Felipe del Lago."

In the course of his prayer, Saco, the bony hound of Don J'cab, awakened at the sense of disturbance down at the roadside and let out a mournful howl. Finding at last the energy and curiosity to move, it gathered its back paws beneath its haunches and rose to check out the problem. The dog loped down the path toward the priest still on his knees. When it reached Don Andres, lost deeply within his prayer, the old, familiar friend playfully bounced around the shaman, sniffing at his clothes and licking at his face.

Without disrupting the rhythm of his litany, Don Andres reached out with his left arm and gathered the old comrade to his side, continuing to swing the incense with the other. At the conclusion of his prayer, the priest set aside the censor and hugged the animal with both arms and scratched the pet behind its ragged ears.

"*Saco! Saco!* Old friend!" said Don Andres. "And your master! Where is he that he cannot come to stand by his brother in prayer—a prayer for the well-being of his own family? Go back to the house and tell a poor priest's brother that he shames him so not to honor a prayer to mighty *San Simon* and the gracious *El Mundo* who protects him and gives his family health and life! Ask a poor priest's own brother why he has allowed the jumping *evangelicos* to sway him from the gods and the earth and the faith of his family and ancestors! *Heh? Go! Go* now, and ask your master, old friend, why a brother will not greet his older brother on the street or speak with him in the market. And then, come back to me, Saco, and tell me why his own children tell stories and make the jokes about their little *primo*, their own cousin and my precious little boy. *Heh,* Saco? Can you do that one thing for a poor, sad priest?"

Don Andres hugged the old dog and pulled his sagging jowls to his cheek. Just then, he heard a cry at the door of his brother's house. The old hound bolted away from the priest's embrace and bounded up the path to the house. Don Andres could make out the hound's pawing at something near the door. For a few moments, the dog barked and pranced around. Then it picked up something in its mouth and came loping again down the path toward the priest.

As it reached him, Don Andres could make out a small, plastic *bolsa*, a soda bag sold in the *tiendas* at the market. Saco padded confidently up to his visitor and deposited the bag on the ground just in front of the priest. Don Andres reached forward and picked up the bag. It was filthy and greasy, and wet from the slobber of the hound. The priest lifted up the bag by a corner and turned to one side to face down the trail toward the dim light shining through the mist enveloping the plaza far below. Against the faint light, he stared intently through the bag for a moment and then, in surprise and shock, flung the bag away.

"*Ratón!*" cried Don Andres. The hound leaped over to the discarded bag, picked it up in its teeth, and gave it a shake. Out fell the rancid remains of a giant field rat.

For a few seconds, Don Andres stared at the dead rodent. As he gasped deeply to catch his breath, he caught the full draft of putrefied animal. Then, as if suddenly realizing its meaning for the first time, Don Andres collapsed to his knees, sobbing and crashing his leathery fists into the earth.

"*Ah, malaya!*" cried the priest. "*Ah, malaya, malaya*!" Almost catatonic in his grief, Don Andres lay prostrate, his mind racing to make sense of the affront from the house of his own brother.

The lethargic hound ambled over to the distraught priest, sniffed at his crotch, and then nosed up his jacket, licking his friend in the ear. Don Andres collected his senses and rolled over to stroke his old companion. He rubbed the animal again behind its ears and scratched up and down its tick-infested rib cage.

"*Sssst!*" a strident whisper intruded from somewhere above and behind him.

"*Sssst! Ssssst!*" it came again.

Don Andres sprang up onto his elbows, now surprised and embarrassed to have been discovered in such a moment. The hound turned its head and growled, and then, moving back from the priest and taking a set, the old dog let out a long, piercing howl.

From behind a bush, laughter of children erupted, and Don Andres's canister of smoldering incense came flying out from behind the scrub and grass along the path. As the can rolled toward him, the handle caught in a rut, discharging the glowing fragments of crackling incense across the path. Don Andres lurched aside to avoid being burned by the cascading coals.

As he was pulling himself up, Don Andres heard the now familiar voices of his two nephews and niece.

"*Brujo! Brujo! Brujo!*" cried the children, and then giggling to themselves, obviously pleased with their mischievous, little assault, the youngsters fled away, racing back up the path toward the house of Don J'cab.

Don Andres picked up his censor and walked back to secure his bag with the mixes and his figurines, only to discover them scattered widely over the ground. The priest collected the small ceramic and jadeite images and placed them carefully back into the woolen bag, but the ground fog was too dense to enable him to recover all the mixes.

"*Ah, malaya*!" cried Don Andres. "What has happened to my family, to my own *brother? Ah, malaya*! What is happening to *San Felipe!*"

Chapter 8

An Army of Righteousness

"Three minutes to `standby,' Mr. Farrell," said Dottie Smith, the televangelist's floor director.

"Thank you, honey," said the media-smooth preacher as he passed his comb for the last time through his mound of sweeping, gold and platinum locks.

"*Jack!*" he called to his administrative assistant. "Jack, tell me again how to pronounce this guy's name."

"`Julio Francisco Mátiz Soto,' with the accent on `MA'—the first syllable," explained Jack Murphy.

"`Soto' would be easier, don't you think?" asked the preacher as he adjusted his tie in the mirror.

"But not correct," said Jack.

"`Not *correct'!* How *come*, Jack?" asked Farrell.

"Well, `Mátiz' is his family name; `Soto' is his mother's name. You always address a man by his family's name."

"Just a bunch of trouble, don't cha think, Jack? Just a bunch of *trouble!*" laughed the preacher. "How do I look?"

"Just fine, Brother Rafer, just *fine!*" exuded the young assistant.

"One minute, Mr. Farrell!" cried Dottie Smith.

"Let's go, Jack," urged Farrell. "Tell me again this guy's title."

"He's the Special Assistant to General Bustamante, the President of Guatemala."

"And `Guatemala'—that's somewhere around the Canal?" asked Farrell.

"No, sir, Brother Rafer. It's the first country south of Mexico," he explained as they raced down the hall from the dressing room to the studio set.

"How long . . . what kind of Kingdom staff do we have down there now?" asked Rafer.

"Yes sir! We have thirteen pastors, five clinicians, and five or six teachers—maybe 24-25 people on staff—and anywhere from 80 to 120 volunteers coordinated out of Quetzaltenango," said the assistant.

"Well, it's hard to keep up when you've got a growth curve of 250% *annually* down there! Right?" said Farrell.

"Yes, sir!" said Jack.

"*Praise the Lord!*" exclaimed the preacher, rather perfunctorily.

"*Amen!*" Jack responded.

"Is Mátick already on set?" asked Farrell.

"`MA-tiz,' it's `MA-tiz!'" repeated Farrell's assistant.

"`MA-tiz,' `MA-tiz,'" said Farrell. "Okay, I think I've got it."

Rev. Rafer Farrell and his assistant rushed through the wide doors of the television studio, across the wires and cables, and between the cameras. All the crew was at stand-by as their boss entered the set. Every element in the darkened set complemented the large, blue translucent cross mounted over fuzzy-focused clouds projected on the backdrop. Between the cross hanging in front of the cyclorama and the plush, carpeted platform with its ornate, glass and gold coffee table and cushy swivel chairs, a mask of stage flats, linked together in front of the massive cross, suggested the silhouetted arabesque rooftops of old Jerusalem.

Farrell approached the chairs on the set and made an obvious, though somewhat over-embellished gesture to shake the outstretched hand of his guest from Guatemala, then kissed the cheek of his co-host, petite, little Missy Magnum, and took his place to the right of the platform.

"We're at stand-by, Mr. Farrell," said Dottie. "Count to ten in your mike for a sound check."

"Right on *time!* Why that gal doesn't miss a *lick!*" thought Farrell to himself. He was a man who never liked to lose a minute. He clipped the microphone to his tie and passed the cord under his coat and slowly counted to ten.

"Okay, Mr. Farrell," said Dottie. Her headset adjusted and her clipboard on the ready, Dottie was relaying the count to the set.

"Five . . . Four . . . Three . . . Two . . . One . . . We're *rolling*," processed the floor director.

The set lights faded up and the center camera dolly rolled up with its center of focus on the axis of the translucent cross. The clouds began to roll from right to left against the rear-projection backdrop. An upbeat Christian chorus intoned praises in major chords as soft-edged spotlights began to drift across the platform and its guests.

Farrell stared into Camera #2 and at Dottie's uplifted hand, waiting for the cue to his opening. Dottie watched the monitor overhead and at just the precise moment dropped her hand, pointing her finger at her boss. "*Go!*" she said.

"God has a *blessing* for you *today!*" effused the Rev. Rafer Farrell, his sparkling eyes twinkling into the camera, his toothy smile fixed in its episcopal promise as the camera dolly flowed up and back to take in the whole set. "DVE moves"—animated graphics combined with swirling panels of live video—wheeled across the screen with scenes of a "live" congregation previously taped at a remote location. Row after row of true believers—their arms outstretched, their faces rolled upward, and their eyes pinched shut, strained for the surge of the rapture to move across the arena—all slick graphics suggesting to the viewing audience a house of thousands in the otherwise empty studio. The chorus of praise built on roll after roll of crescendos of an organ, a synthesizer, and horns as the camera dolly locked onto the center of the cross which began to glow from a rear-projected halo.

"God . . . Loves . . . *You!!!"* wailed the announcer in rhythm to the chorus, "and here, from Kingdom Throne in Macon, Georgia, with his special message of praise and promise is Brother RaferrRR*RAH FFFFAARRELLLLLlllll!*"

"Aaa*MMEenn!* And *GAWD*-uh! certainly *loves* you *today!*" cried Farrell, his eyes glistening with excitement and expectation.

"And *GAWD*-uh! has a special *miracle* today for *YOU!*" smiled the preacher.

Another DVE move of the frozen face of the preacher went wheeling and drifting around the set as the camera dolly coursed its way once more up over the evangelical team and across the outstretched beam of the translucent cross.

"*Yeh*-yus! And welcome to our service of praise today. And what a message of hope we bring to you today from the Mission Board of Kingdom Throne with the people of Guatemala. And joining me with our special guest from Central America is my lovely co-host, Missy Magnum. Say `Hello,' Missy!" Farrell appealed to his partner.

"Praise *God!* Brother Rafer! What a *thrill* it is to share the miracle of praise again with you and our viewers *today!*" squealed little Missy, just a twitch and a twitter, bouncing with a charming little early-morning ecstacy for Brother Rafer and their more than 13 million estimated viewers in twenty-four nations.

"A miracle it is, Missy, and tell me, sweetheart. You have just returned from Central America, and you bring a special blessing to us today," anticipated Farrell.

"Brother *Rafer!"* stammered little Missy Magnum. "God is moving in wonderful and powerful ways in the land of eternal spring." [Video insert of the old Spanish ruins of Antigua with the towering volcanoes in the background.]

The voice track rolled behind the visual inserts, and a more subdued, somewhat academic-sounding "Missy" voice in a slightly lower pitch continued the explanation, obviously read from script. "In the collapse of Catholicism in the 1700's with the great earthquakes," explained the "little Missy" voice, "the Gospel of our Lord is being restored to the poor people [insert of a beggar on the steps of San Francisco Church] who have hungered for so long to hear the Word of Hope."

"Across the mountains of Mexico, Guatemala, and throughout the highlands, the Lord's blessing is finding its way into the lives of millions who have followed, until now, the false gods of paganism and Christian heresy. That's right, Brother Rafer," continued the canned "little Missy" voice track, "through `The Kingdom Throne' cassette ministry, the love of *Jesus* is saving thousands of souls each week through the generosity of `Kingdom Throne Prayer Partners' around the world who make the `Kingdom Throne Cassette Ministry' possible."

"Yes, *viewers!*" returned the preacher to the "live" broadcast. "The Word of *Faith* is reaching into the depths of misery and suffering in the mountains of Central America and particularly for the people of Guatemala because of your continued prayers and support of this wonderful ministry."

"Missy, tell our viewers what you have seen with your *own* eyes!" invited the enthusiastic evangelist.

"Brother Rafer, the people of Guatemala" [Video insert of an Indian *campesino* in a white shirt, straw hat, and ragged jeans, entering the sanctuary of a village evangelical church followed by a woman—his wife—with a covered basket on her head, a baby on the tit beneath her *huipil*, and a filthy, five year-old boy hanging onto his mother's skirt] . . . "are finding a new hope in a country that has been abused for so long by *false gods and idols!*" claimed little Missy [Video insert of the same family kneeling before a coatless "Kingdom Throne" American evangelist—with a loose tie and rolled up sleeves—waving an open Bible over his head].

"And *today,*" beamed little Missy, twisting a lock of her hair over her ear, "the Lord has *blessed* this people, and thousands now call upon the name of the Lord and have been *saved.*"

"PRAISE*GAW*-ud!" exclaimed a squint-eyed Brother Rafer as he raised his left hand (the one behind his head so as not to block the tight camera cutaway of his face). "PRAISE*GAW*-ud!" he exuded again, as his hand slowly descended, palm forward, and he regained his sightline back on Camera #2.

"Yes, Missy. *GAW*-ud is certainly working out his miracle of salvation among this poor people," exclaimed the preacher to his television audience.

The "1-800-" number of "Kingdom Throne" began its repetitive, slow scroll across the bottom of the viewers' screen. "And we are not alone—all of us and our vast television community of saints—we are not alone, because for the first time, Missy! I say, for the *first* time, sweetheart! The Lord has found His Way into the heart of the very President of Guatemala, himself. And with us today is Brother Julio *MAAH*-tiz', special assistant to the President of Guatemala to tell us how *GAW*-ud! has so richly blessed this poor people. And we'll be back with *GAW*-ud's special emissary from Central America right after this special `Kingdom Throne' message."

The camera dolly pulled back and up to refocus on the beam of the translucent cross, the golden halo beginning to pulse slowly as the image dissolved into the "Kingdom Throne" promotion.

"`Kingdom Throne' is bringing the Gospel of the *true* faith to the people of Central America!" encouraged the radio voice track as the visual followed a "Kingdom Throne" missionary up a rutted road, handing out Bible tracks to a handful of little, ragged children chasing around his heels, then drifting slowly toward the hovels of their mountain village.

"For centuries these poor people have survived ruthless torture and misery, but they are now *rejoicing* [Video insert of Indian families in the village church standing, lifting their outstretched palms above their heads during a `Kingdom Throne' worship service] in their new-found faith in the *true* Jesus."

"That's *right*," continued the slick commercial. "The *true* Jesus is bringing the light of his love and grace, and we are seeing His miracles of healing and *love* changing the wretched lives of these forgotten and abused ones—thanks to `Kingdom Throne Prayer Partners' like *you*."

"Won't you help spread the love of *Jesus?*" began the appeal, as the visual raced around the beaming missionary bending over to embrace his little converts. "Won't you send a `love offering' *today* to see to it that the Word of God continues to shine in the lives of these precious little ones?" [The 1-800-number begins its steady scroll across the bottom of the screen over the kneeling missionary surrounded by his small entourage. The "Kingdom Throne" chorus begins to swell to its resolution of major chords as the 1-800-number freezes and starts to pulse. Then, the image dissolves once more to the "Kingdom Throne" set in the Macon, Georgia, studios.]

"And what a *blessing!*" puffed the preacher. "And joining us on our show this morning is one of *GAW*-ud's special ministers to our brothers and sisters of Central America. Welcome to `Kingdom Throne,' Brother Julio!"

"Grácias a Diós! Claro! Dales todas la alabanza al Señor! En nombre

de la Presidente de la Republica de Guatemala y la Iglesia de la Palabra Vivienda," said Sr. Mátiz.

"You speak-a-duh-*English, Señor?*" whispered Brother Rafer, still audible in his worldwide microphone.

"*Cut!*" cried the producer in the sound booth above. The producer winced and banged his fist against his forehead three quick blows.

"Don't *do* that, *guy!* Why did he *do* that?" whispered the producer into his headset mike from the sound booth over the set.

"I can't help it!" whispered Dottie, the floor director. "I couldn't get to him in time. Brother Rafer is going to be really *angry* with us!" she confided.

"Well, he looks pretty foolish in front of 16 million viewers right now!" returned the producer. "'You speaka da Eeengliss?' I mean, *JEEZZ!"*

"I *know!* I *know!*" said Dottie, and then turning to the evangelist: "Mr. Farrell, we're standing by!"

The young floor director moved to the set. Farrell and Mátiz were already into it.

"Yes *sir! Señor!* I speak English, *sure!*" said Mátiz.

"Well, this is an `*English*' show here, `*Señor'!*"

"Stand by, Mr. Farrell," said Dottie. All directions were channeled to the boss; everyone else had long since learned to take their own cues from him, usually intuitively.

"Well, let's get it right this time, sweetheart," urged the boss.

"Yes, *sir!* Mr. Farrell," acknowledged Dottie.

"We're standing by Camera #2 for retake of welcome to Mr. Mátiz—`Welcome to Kingdom Throne, Mr. Mátiz,'" directed Dottie, as she adjusted her headset and raised her hand. "Five . . . four . . . three . . . two . . . one—*Go!*"

"Welcome to `Kingdom Throne,' Mr. Mátiz," gushed Farrell.

"Thank you. Glad to be here with you, sir!" returned Mátiz.

"Mr. Mátiz is our guest today from the country of Guatemala. Tell us about Guatemala," instructed Farrell.

"*Bueno* . . . well, Brother Farrell, Guatemala is a very small, but very beautiful country just below Mexico. And it is the country of Central America most friendly, you know, to the people of the United States. Everybody love the United States in Guatemala. Guatemala have very beautiful mountains—volcanoes—lakes, monkeys, many wild animals," continued Mátiz.

"But many *problems*, too," interrupted Farrell. He needed to get to the point—the quicker the point, the quicker the pitch, and he wanted to get through this segment. He was noticeably uncomfortable relating to this diminutive, mushy-faced, slick-haired little emissary who had come calling with his handout. "You got *communists*, too!"

"*Bueno* . . . well, that is correct, Brother Farrell," responded the emissary. What else could he say? "We have for many years now been fighting the communists who want to take over the free people of Guatemala. The communists, they don't know the Lord."

"Aaa*MEN!*" sparked Farrell.

"The communists, they don't know *Jesus!*" offered Mátiz. He sensed he had finally struck a vein of common interest.

"Aa*MEN!*" chimed little Missy Magnum, as she shifted forward to the edge of her chair, thrusting her little bird-like breasts into the conversation.

"We can all say `AMEN' to that, can't we, Missy! We can ALL say `Amen' to that," retorted the boss, reasserting his role as "point man" in the conversation.

"Mr. Mátiz, I know that Guatemala has new leadership, and that you bring to our American and worldwide viewing audience a special message from your country," said Farrell.

"Yes, that is correct, Mr. Farrell," responded Mátiz. "The people of Guatemala have a new leader, a Christian man. His name is General Jorge Bustamante. This man is a `reborn' person."

"`Born again,'" corrected Farrell.

"`Born again,' *sure!*" emphasized Mátiz. "This man is promised to make a new country, a Christian country. This man is promised to raise up the name of `Jesus' in everything he does to help the people of Guatemala. This man is promised to be strong against evil communism and lies of the priests. This man is promised to . . ."

"To attack the heresy of the false cult of Catholicism and the `dupe' *priests* who support the communists under the guise of helping the poor," clamored Reverend Farrell, uncomfortable with his guest's broken English and unsteady message. "To root out the heinous *lies* of false doctrine that nurture the godless *guerrillas* who worship a Marxist-Leninist atheism that is committed to destroying the *free world.* This brave General, this President Jorge Bustamante raises up *Christ,* Mr. Mátiz, raises . . ."

"Raises up the *Christ, yes!*" interrupted the Guatemalan.

"I said `Raises up the name of the Son of *God!*'" returned Farrell, unwilling to relinquish the text of an evolving appeal that his guest, in his simplicity, couldn't begin to appreciate.

"And lifts the *crucified people* of Guatemala above their *sin* to the *glory* of the resurrected *Lord.* And Kingdom Throne Prayer Partners, you should know that *you* can help in this ministry. *You* can help this courageous disciple of God's Word. Let us raise an `Army of *Righteousness'* to stand side by side the simple Guatemalan soldiers who must prosecute holy *war* against the legions of *satanic communism* and their Catholic *dupes!*" Brother Rafer Farrell was beginning to get stirred up, and he felt "the Word" welling up in his soul. It was time—just *now!*—to make his appeal.

"And we shall raise *up* this `Army of Righteousness,' and we shall raise it *up* from the souls of our brethren in the faith *today!* Is there any better time than right now to lift up the name of *Christ?* Is there any better time than right *now* to commit our resources in the fight against evil? My `Kingdom Throne' partners, can there be a better time than now—right now!—to halt *atheism* and *heresy* in our hemisphere once and for *all.* Dare we wait for another messenger of God to rise up to draw the sword of *righteousness*? Can we wait another *moment* to save a nation dying in *sin?"*

Rafer Farrell was in his element, as he turned with supreme confidence to the camera to deliver his charge.

"In the name of *JEE*-sus! I am pledging $1 million dollars today to the save the soul of Guatemala, and I know that *GAWD*-uh! can depend on *you!* Now, as the Kingdom Throne Chorus sings its call, I want you to examine your soul and your commitment to this divine ministry—in the name of *JEE*-sus! I said, `in the name of *JEE*-sus! What did I say, brothers and sisters—`in the name of *JEE*-sus! *JEE*-sus! *JEE*-sus! I said, `*JEE*-sus'! Now, let me hear that *chorus!—Dottie!*" instructed Brother Farrell . . . . "That's *it!* Let the Kingdom Throne Chorus lift up the name of *JEE*-sus!"

"And friends—our brothers *in Christ*—" and Camera #2 zoomed slowly into the earnest, languid, expectant eyes of the good Brother Farrell. "I want you to pick up the phone right *now!* That's *right,* you don't need to waste another moment of the miracle of your life to return this little favor to our Lord—I say, pick up the phone right *now* and call our number—you see it now on your television screen—and root out godless *communism* in our own neighborhood once and for *all!* That's *right!* Our phones are ringing *now!"*

"Praise *GAWD*-uh! Missy, sweetheart! Can you hear our phones, sweetheart!" Brother Farrell was crying now, more intensely as the phones continued to light up.

"Oh! Brother *Rafer!* I feel God's hand moving across the Kingdom to slay the *evil* of vicious *godlessness* in Guatemala! Oh, Brother *Rafer! I . . .*" and little Missy Magnum could no longer contain the spirit, and she rose from her chair, her eyes squinted shut, and lifted her hands high above her head, arching her palms in soft salutations to the movement of the spirit, tears of joy streaming down her cherubic cheeks. And then she collapsed in a flood of tears at the feet of Señor Mátiz. Farrell himself rose from his chair, his face awash in tears.

"Praise *JEE*-sus!" Brother Farrell stammered to his television audience. "Praise *JEE*-sus! For the first time in the history of this small nation, the President is putting down wrong-doers and punishing those who are evildoers. Let it be an example of what *God* can do when *His* people are in charge. Now we'll see what can happen when the disciples of *JEE*-zus take over a suffering country!"

As the Holy Spirit moved through the studios in Georgia, in Guatemala, young military conscripts were already loading their ammunition clips as American-made helicopter gunships, flown by United States military advisors, began lifting off their bases for sorties into the highlands.

Chapter 9

Scented Waters

"The Latin American Bishops, Your Eminence, understand all too well the position of the Congregation. Where I think, Your Eminence—if I may be free . . ." said Cardinal Mueller.

"Of course, Cardinal Mueller, of *course!* We mustn't mince words among ourselves," said Cardinal Von Zurmuellen. "We have worked together *far* too long for that kind of thing."

Old warlords in European theological circles since their elevations as Cardinals more than twenty-five years before, the two understood each other well. Since his appointment as Head of the Congregation for the Doctrine of the Faith, Herman Von Zurmuellen had pursued the orthodox course tenaciously. At eighty-one, Peter Mueller, for six years *Cardinal Emeritus*, was an old ally, though he was approaching his colleague on a most delicate issue, the rescinding of a declaration of silence of a Latin American Bishop and a fiery, controversial American priest. But these two thorns were only agitants in a larger, more sweeping concern over "liberation theology" and the emergence of hundreds of thousands of so called "Christian base communities," the *comunidades de base*, throughout Latin America. Not that he was abandoning orthodoxy a whiff, Peter Mueller was seeking to test the strength of the Congregation's commitment on this specific, though very complicated and highly controversial decision. In fact, the real purpose of his meeting was to hear specific assurances from the Congregation that might bolster proposed options for the Mexican Archbishop Pablo Ramirez.

"We are entertaining perhaps the most critical issue confronting the Church in this century," continued Cardinal Von Zurmuellen.

"Your Eminence, some have suggested that this `liberation theology' is the first serious challenge within the Church since 1517!" offered Cardinal Mueller.

"Well, perhaps, perhaps. But I . . ., I'm sorry. Please continue," continued Cardinal Von Zurmuellen.

"Your Eminence, in my opinion—but of course, you have sought my council—in my opinion, having communicated at length with Archbishop Ramirez—who understands clearly and respects the Congregation on all points regarding this `liberation theology'—it is my opinion that nothing short of silencing will curb the critical voices within the schism," said Cardinal Mueller.

"And of course, it is in fact a `schism' from any understanding of the word. Peter, let us speak plainly with one another: The Holy Father understands the implication of Vatican II and daily intercedes on behalf of the world's great impoverished masses. In this the Congregation joins the Holy Father and offers its unbridled offices in embracing the Church of the Latin world and awaits its instruction to us all that we all might be more Holy ministers to those in need. Likewise, the Congregation appreciates the role of tradition, liturgy, and doctrine through which the Holy Spirit has been manifested in its ministry of Christ's reconciliation of the world to Himself. Within this understanding, Cardinal Mueller, the Congregation for the Doctrine of the Church has taken under advisement the interests of the Latin American Bishops, and enjoins them to reaffirm their commitment to the understanding of the Holy Father and their clarifications through this office. The Bishops will understand our meaning, I think, Cardinal Mueller?"

"Without exception, I am sure, Your Eminence. And if I may offer one other query, the issue, Your Eminence, the question of Father Michael Justice," offered Cardinal Mueller.

"The Bishops will understand our meaning, Cardinal Mueller?"

"With respect, Your Eminence . . ." questioned Cardinal Mueller.

Cardinal Von Zurmuellen spun slowly in his plush leather desk chair, abandoning the incredulous petition of his colleague, and from behind the invisible mantel of absolute authority, the Head of the Congregation for the Doctrine of the Faith repeated his question with finality intended to be understood officially and without recourse.

"The Bishops *will* understand our meaning, Cardinal Mueller."

"Without *exception*, I am confident, Your Eminence," apologized Cardinal Mueller.

"Cardinal Mueller, my brother," said Cardinal Von Zurmuellen, as he retraced the circuit of his chair, wheeling back around to face his fellow prelate.

"Let us retire, not in an `understanding' but in the embrace of our mutual affection for the Holy Mother and the Grace of Our Lord," returned Von Zurmuellen. "Peace be with you."

"And with *you*," responded Cardinal Mueller, rising to receive his old colleague's hand. He was feeling the full weight of ecclesiastical power and had witnessed at this moment one of its most severe penalties: the silencing of one of its most vigorous voices in the Americas.

The message was clear. The Head of the Congregation for the Doctrine of the Faith was in no mood to compromise with the Latin American Bishops on a single point. After twenty years of "dialogue," the censorship would not be rescinded, and Father Michael Justice—more specifically—would report to the Vatican for "consultation and counseling." Cardinal Mueller bowed his head respectfully, turned, and walked slowly from the study of the chief Inquisitor. Upon exiting the Office of the Congregation, Cardinal Mueller walked to his office where his secretary led him into his parlor.

"Peace be with you," said Cardinal Mueller to his visitors.

"And with *you*, Your Eminence," returned his guests.

"Please . . . please be *seated*, won't you," offered the Cardinal.

"My good Bishop Ramirez," began the Cardinal to his collaborator among the Latin American congregations. "It is a beautiful day, is it not? I think I see a smile in the clouds," reflected the Cardinal. "My good Bishop, . . . my good Bishop," he paused for effect, "we have played our cards with finesse, and my good friend and brother, you should know that we have won!"

Archbishop Ramirez smiled widely as he savored the meaning of the announcement. "We have won, indeed, Your Eminence! We have won, indeed!"

"When Bishop Montenegro issued the imprimatur, knowing as he did, the contents of the Congregation's letter to you," said the Cardinal, "well, he sealed his fate. I thought so, and this afternoon Cardinal Von Zurmuellen confirmed it. You need to return now and see to it that the American Bishops get the fuller picture. Father Justice will recant or be *damned!* He will appear now, without question," explained the Cardinal.

"I will make plans to leave at once, Your Eminence. Know full well that we shall keep the faith in Mexico, and that that faith will be rekindled in our most rebellious brothers. They will now come to `understand,' or they must accept the consequences."

Archbishop Ramirez rose to receive Cardinal Mueller's dismissal. They clasped hands and smiled triumphantly, and the Archbishop turned and glided to the door.

A flock of pigeons swept into the air as the Archbishop walked confidently to his official car. He would return to his suite at the North American College for two, maybe three days of rest and some light correspondence before returning to Mexico City.

The driver opened the rear door, and the churchman slipped smoothly across the back seat to the middle of the vehicle. Sitting in the center of the car gave the Archbishop a sense of balance, as though he were the fulcrum from which he could maintain a certain equilibrium. And, for that matter, that's the way he felt about himself: *he* would be the fulcrum, a point of balance and harmony. *He* would be the vehicle for curbing the factionalism and disaffection so dividing the Church. It was no small responsibility, but he felt the flush of commitment to the critical challenge. Furthermore, he recognized the point of attack: the wretched, little priest's "liberation theology."

But there would be time sufficient for that. He had other, more immediate concerns for the next two or three days: a little R&R. The Vatican limousine cruised comfortably through the mid-morning traffic. The driver would take him to the North American College where he would rest the remainder of the day in one of the guest suites.

The Archbishop watched the pedestrians casually strolling around the parks along the Roman sidewalks—mothers with their pre-schoolers and pets on leashes, hurried businessmen in their grey silk suits and leather brief cases. The good prelate was a world away from the squalor of the Third World, and he was comfortable. That's what it was: *"comfortable"!* Comfort was satisfying. You could never quite *relax*—"feel *comfortable*"—when you knew that the drive home would take you through the suffocating fumes of the *barrios* and *colonias*. He wouldn't see any poverty on the way "home" today.

The limousine wound its way through the business sector, through the diplomatic zone, and to the up-scale neighborhoods of the estates surrounding the grounds of the College. He was coming home after too many years, and he was looking forward to renewing old ties with the Dean of Canon Law, Father Guiggio Palo.

"Welcome, your Excellency," said Beatrice Lerna, the receptionist at the official residence. Sister Beatrice had spent much of her Christian life in service to the prelates at the College, and the Archbishop was an acquaintance from many years back.

After signing the registration log, the Archbishop followed Beatrice down the corridor of the first floor where the official quarters hosted, at one time or another, the most important Church emissaries from around the world.

"I hope your Excellency will find these quarters to your satisfaction during your stay with us," said the nun.

"But *of course!"* insisted Archbishop Ramirez. "*Por su puesto!*" he repeated in Spanish, as he delivered a good-natured slap to the Sister's shoulder from behind.

"Good day," responded Beatrice as she left the Archbishop in the middle of the entry way and closed the door behind him.

"*Por su puesto!*" repeated the good Archbishop to himself under his breath. Why *wouldn't* he find "these quarters" to his satisfaction! Satisfaction, indeed! These were the little "bonuses" that he always found so . . . so *deserving!*—that was the basic truth of the situation when you got right down to it. He had earned this little three-day "bonus," and he certainly meant to take full advantage of it.

"*Por su puesto!*" he repeated aloud.

For an extended moment he stood in place and scanned the apartment. Behind him and then to the left and right, Medicci tapestries hung from beneath twenty-foot wide cornices and drifted down eighteen feet to within six inches of the elaborated molding that dressed the foot of the walls. Angels sang above the suffering body of the martyr Stephen, while children removed the stones from his mortally wounded body. To his left Peter swooned in his third denial of the Lord as Satan sneered from behind a Venetian garden wall. To the right, the Lord stood poised at Ascension, the disciples at his feet staring in awe and wonder at the rarefied expression of the Savior about to be lifted into Paradise.

The heavy tapestries of the parlor muffled his footsteps as he stepped toward the deep plush, blood-red carpet that stretched beneath elegant legs of baroque lounges, side tables, and desk sets. The Archbishop untied his cape and draped it over his left arm as he passed toward the sleeping quarters. He pushed open the heavy oak doors to reveal the high canopied bed with its seal of the Church woven in the center of the gold-fringed bedspread. That was all well and good, but what he *really* needed to do was to relieve himself, and he unbuckled his skirt and stepped out of it as he walked into the restroom.

The lid on the basin of the commode was cushioned as was the ringed seat—much more "comfortable," even, than the staff facilities of the Cardinal's administrative offices at the Vatican itself. The roll of bathroom tissue was mounted on a gold-plated fixture that complemented the inhabitant's rank in even the most personal of arenas. As he completed his toilet and flushed the commode, scented water circulated through the fixture, refreshing the air of the closet. The good Archbishop rose and adjusted his garments, checking his organization in the gilded, floor-length mirror just opposite the towel cabinet and sink with its Venetian marble counter. Such "poverty" he could understand and appreciate.

Archbishop Ramirez dried his hands on the monogrammed towel and returned to the dressing area in the sleeping quarters. His plan was to sleep, but as he laid his jacket over the back of a chair, he noticed the blinking red button on the base of the telephone on the desk across the room. The bishop stared at the button quizzically for a moment and then walked over and reached for the receiver. The ringer sounded three times before the College's operator responded.

"May I help you, your Excellency," asked the operator.

"Thank you, *Señorita*," said the Archbishop. "I believe I have a message."

"Yes, your Excellency," said Beatrice. "Just one moment please." Beatrice fumbled with three or four notes before she found the right one. It was an urgent call from Cardinal Mueller.

At first, Archbishop Pablo Ramirez was irritated by the interruption of his extended Roman weekend, and then he was angry—angry, first, that the interruption would come from his own hemisphere and secondly because, in a surreptitious way, the clever Jesuits—in all their learned intrigue—had *invited* it!

But to be shot and brained in their own garden! And the housekeeper—along with her own daughter!

Of course, the Archbishop had been moved. The tragedy of Salvador was the agony of both the Church and her people. But this savage, stupid act of aggression amounted to nothing less than the continued attack on the Church of the Savior which itself had somehow insidiously gone awry. Was he not in Rome at this precise moment to address the very issue that continued to foment so much division and suffering among the Western congregations?

Those simple, romantic *Jesuits!* Why must they waste their remarkable talents in a lunatic radicalism that at best would survive in future histories as only a wrinkle in the raiment of the Church! As he walked toward the western fountain on the grounds of the College, he watched the doves fly into the late afternoon glow of the Roman day. Like the doves, peace had fled Salvador, but they would come to roost in Mexico in days to come, he could now be assured, with this reaffirmation from the Congregation. At a deep, personal level, of course, he grieved appropriately for these fresh martyrs. Their blood was his blood, and together they shared in the mystical, tortured blood of their Savior and Lord. But that blood would live, even thrive in Mexico, not be spilled just to rot in the quagmire of some Marxist-Leninist twist on Grace! He would return to Mexico City on the first available flight.

As he made his arrangements for departure, Archbishop Ramirez became more and more frustrated with the interruption in his visit. He wasn't a `fool Jesuit', but this Father Michael Justice was as much an irritant—nothing more, however, given everything else on his agenda.

"*Scented waters*!" smiled the good Archbishop as he flushed the commode in his suite for the last time. "To be able to cruise home someday on *`scented waters'*!" How much more comfortable his job would be—just after he finished with this Michael Justice affair.

Chapter 10

The Room Key

"Brother Farrell, this is one of the most *moving* moments in the Kingdom ministry! I feel the Lord moving so deeply in this crusade," said little Missy Magnum, first among the "Kingdom Throne" true believers. "Oh, Brother *Farrell*, I know we'll see the fruits of this ministry in *thousands* of saved children who have lived in this godless *wasteland!*"

The plane was in its final approach to La Aurora International Airport. Through the window, little Missy peered out into the towering ridges of the Sierra Madre. She followed the silver ribbon of the Motagua River twisting and turning through the deep green valleys. Powdery fluffs of grey-white clouds hovered above and around the peaks of the volcanoes Acatenango, Fuego, and Agua. The river turned abruptly to the west, and the ground began rising sharply under the plane as it passed almost directly over the crater of the steamy, tremulous volcano Picaya, belching plumes of noxious gasses a thousand feet into the air.

"Praise God, Missy. Praise God," said Rafer Farrell rather perfunctorily, his mind preoccupied with some taunting administrative details at the moment.

"Oh, Brother Rafer, what is *that?* Is that a *volcano?*" asked Missy. Rafer Farrell was churning through his satchel for his accountant's record of the month's receipts and for the more than $8,000 in traveller's checks that he had purchased two days before.

"What is *what?*" mumbled Brother Farrell.

"Oh, Brother *Rafer,* look at the *smoke* coming out of that *mountain!*" gushed little Missy Magnum. "How absolutely *exciting!"* she said. "But I'll bet it's pretty hot down there in the bottom of that *hole!"*

"Yes, `magine so," said Farrell, trying to acknowledge his assistant's enthusiasm, as his fingers found the packet of travellers checks in the bottom of his satchel. Much relieved, he turned to Missy, placing his hand on her smooth, round knee.

"Oh, *yes!*" said a newly inspired Brother Rafer. He sensed the blush of a little fever racing through Missy Magnum's pert little knee as he squeezed it with the tips of his pulpy fingers.

"Very pretty, *idn't* honey!" said Brother Farrell, giving Missy's knee a firm pat before withdrawing his fleshy palm.

Little Missy Magnum turned her head toward Brother Rafer's face and looked appreciatively into his eyes as she ran her thumb and first finger up and down the edge of the plunging neckline of her baggy blouse.

"I just feel so . . . so *blessed* to be here with the Kingdom Ministry—and with you, Brother Farrell," confessed little Missy Magnum, never moving her deep blue eyes from her partner's. "I just feel the spirit moving so *deeply*," she said as a hot shiver drifted through her chest.

"Missy, I'm going to need your help while we're down here, honey. I want you working by my side throughout this crusade, sweetheart," whispered Farrell with an air of hope if not expectancy.

Caught up in the moment of her first international travel, the close proximity of her spiritual mentor, and the enthusiasm for her work, little Missy Magnum placed her hand into Brother Farrell's and gave it a heartfelt squeeze. Farrell seized the opportunity and slipped his hand up Missy's wrist and forearm and into the wide, open sleeve of her blouse. He passed his fingers around and over her shoulders and introduced one finger beneath her arm pit and into the elastic band of her exposed bra. He leaned over and whispered, "I'm going to need you working very, *very* closely with me, Missy. You *understand* that, don't you?" Farrell pressed.

Missy was surprised and shocked and on the verge of hyperventilating. She locked her hand onto his arm as his finger slipped forward inside the elastic band and under her left breast. Her eyes penetrated his own gaze as her mouth dropped open, and as Farrell's index finger reached her nipple, Missy suddenly sighed audibly and closed her eyes, her breath rushing into a quick, little pant. She reached into Farrell's lap, touched the inside of his thigh with her finger tips and then quickly withdrew her hand, fearful that she might lose complete control of herself. Embarrassed, she felt the onset of an orgasm and a sweet, slippery evacuation between her legs. Farrell withdrew his finger from her blouse, reached up behind her head, and drew her to his shoulder. She shuddered as she yielded to the irreversible orgasm, and she sank against his chest as two tears streamed down her face.

Farrell reached into his coat pocket and retrieved a handkerchief with which he wiped Missy's eyes and cheeks. Then he reached below her chin and lifted her face to his and kissed her deeply, rolling his phlegmatic hands over and around the back of her head, pressing her mouth into his.

"Do you *understand?*" whispered Farrell as their embrace dissolved.

"Oh, *yes!*" said Missy, her tearful, grateful eyes locked like radar into his own surprised gaze. Farrell never expected to express his interest so publicly, but there was no one within five rows on the plane, he knew, who would have recognized them as anything but husband and wife. Missy readjusted herself into her seat face forward and then turned to stare out the window. Encouraged once, Farrell's hand drifted again, this time to Missy's thigh and stroked her leg downward toward her knee. Without shifting her head for even a moment from her gaze out the window, her right hand found his, and they slipped together into a tight-fisted embrace.

The plane banked sharply to the left, and from her vantage point, Missy could now see the wide, expansive Guatemala City some five thousand feet below. The plane was making its final pass over the city before returning up wind to make its landing.

"Ladies and gentlemen," said the recorded attendant's voice over the intercom. "The captain has announced our final approach into Guatemala City. Please return all seats to their upright position and lock your trays in front of you. We will be landing at *La Aurora International Airport* in five minutes. Please return to your seats at this time and remain seated until the Captain has turned off the seat belt lights. Thank you for flying Aviateca. We hope that you will enjoy your stay in Guatemala, the `land of eternal spring.'"

The plane leveled off and began its smooth descent toward the runway. Below, wrapped over and down the slopes of the deep ravines, the *barrios* of Guatemala City raced by; then the expansive houses in the diplomatic quarter with their guard stations and swimming pools; next, the military hangers, and then the foot of the runway itself. A spattering of applause greeted the pilot's near perfect touchdown. As the nose cone of the jet dipped down to the runway, Missy felt Brother Rafer's hand once more on her knee. A little shocked, Missy jumped slightly and then placed her own petite hand over his and began to twist the tiny hairs on the back of his hand.

"Missy, as soon as we get to the hotel, I want you to come to my *room*," said Rafer. "I have some things . . . I want to go over, I want to go over some *things* with you before our first meeting with the counselors tonight."

At once, Missy began smoothing out the twists of hairs, stroking Farrell's hand warmly. That was exactly what she was somehow expecting to hear and something that she had been fantasizing for the past few minutes.

"Yes, Brother Rafer, I want to . . ." Missy caught herself. "Sure, I'll just drop off my things and come over. Where do I get the key?"

"I'll leave the extra key in an envelope for you at the front desk," explained

Farrell.

"Okay," said Missy. "I'll be there as soon as I get settled." She squeezed Brother Farrell's fingers and stroked the outstretched open palm back and forth with the edge of her thumb. And then she caught herself. She had to stop before she embarrassed herself again.

The plane cruised to the end of the runway, turned, and rolled toward the gate dock. As the jet engines wound down, people rose quickly to retrieve their overhead luggage and immediately jammed the aisle of the plane. In the rush to secure their belongings, only one noticed the Rev. Rafer Farrell stroke the left breast of his assistant.

The other members of the Kingdom Throne Crusade rose from their respective seats and began collecting their jackets, carry-on bags, briefcases, and luggage.

"What do you think about the trip, *now!*" asked Benny Johnson of Mendy Parker, two of the Kingdom Throne staffers. He obviously had missed the withering flash of white-hot anger that only seconds before had blistered the soul of his fashionable, attractive, middle-aged colleague.

"Oh, I'm so . . . so *excited!"* managed a stammering Mendy Parker, Brother Rafer's accountant. "I've . . . I've never been *south* before!"

"This should be a successful crusade," confided Benny Johnson, Kingdom Throne's popular organist and one of the ministry's most fervent believers in the good Brother Rafer. Benny had traveled to Canada and twice to Mexico with the Kingdom Throne Crusaders already this year. Thousands had "received the Lord" in Guadalajara and Guanajuato, and the Mexican *pesos* were still rolling into the coffers of their Crusade office in Mexico City. With any luck at all and certainly in the dry season, the Guatemala Crusade would net at least $250,000 and that wasn't bad for four days of work. Mendy's public records, of course, would show no more than $45,000 after "expenses," while the real accounts that she and she alone logged personally with Brother Rafer would be organized stateside weeks later. Only Mendy and her boss understood the fuller meaning of Christian charity as it applied to the Kingdom Throne ministry.

Mendy Parker had worked personally for Brother Rafer Farrell for the past eight years. She had come highly recommended from the West Coast office after Farrell had put out the word for an accountant following the death of his former bookkeeper in an automobile accident. Brakes had failed on a sharp turn overlooking the coastline north of Pebble Beach under very suspicious circumstances that had never been resolved; the car's brakes had been checked just hours before the alleged accident. But no official concern was ever registered over the incident.

Ms. Parker was a most attractive forty-two-year-old Viet Nam widow. Her husband, a Navy flier, had been lost over Haiphong Harbor in 1972. She had been left with a small child, a girl, who had been born mongoloid. She had first attended a Kingdom Throne Crusade with an apartment neighbor just after the memorial service for her husband and had been deeply moved by the fiery confidence and charisma of Brother Farrell. She attended every meeting for the following three evenings and met him coming out of the stadium men's room still zipping his fly. She became very acquainted with his fly over the next few months, for Mendy Parker not only kept the secrets of the Kingdom Throne accounts but a number of other very personal secrets as well.

Before Brother Farrell had completed the divorce of his second wife, Mendy had already enjoyed various Kingdom Throne perks. Kingdom Throne generosity had placed her daughter in a private home for the mentally retarded in the Midwest which freed her mother to become more "personally committed" to the Crusade's ministry. She had secured her place as Brother Farrell's mistress on a cruise to St. Thomas three months after they had met. She had "stowed away" in an adjoining cabin which shared a common doorway that remained unlocked for her own brand of ministry. Mendy had had the opportunity to play nurse to a queasy Rafer Farrell hours into the cruise, inadvertently discovering the Reverend's most personal fetish. Mendy had resolved his "situation" with a soapy enema, administered from her douche kit, only to have him return to her cabin no more than an hour later in the afternoon to request an additional "application." The good Brother Farrell remained in cabin, pre-occupied with his newly acquired nurse and unrequited "distress" for much of the remainder of the cruise.

For weeks on end, following the cruise, Brother Rafer would find reason to consult his accountant. It was during one of their late-night trysts that Brother Rafer had discussed the possibility of "augmenting their records." At first, it was to be a backup fund for emergency operations abroad, something he or she could tap without having to work through the normal appropriations channel. It was to be Brother Farrell's own "money reserve" for Kingdom Throne "donations" which he liked to drop into the hands of deserving though certainly unsuspecting recipients, a ministry whose reputation had spread widely in little time. Publicly, of course, Brother Rafer was depleting his own salary, much to the embarrassment and frustration of his estranged family. The fund, which had begun with a discretely misdirected $500, had swelled to more than $230,000 since "Nurse" Mendy had begun her services to the good Pastor.

While some probably suspected Brother Rafer's affair with his accountant, no one who valued his or her job dared enter the rumor mill. It had happened before when Brother Rafer had been caught in a compromising position with his secretary almost ten years earlier. The complainant had not only lost his job, but had been taken to court, sued for slander, and had lost all his personal belongings in a fire that blasted through his trailer home back in Florida on the morning the Kingdom Throne Crusade had opened in the Astrodome in Houston. But if Brother Farrell had suffered any decline in support over that tawdry little incident, a member of the congregation would never have known it from the next month's receipts. There were plenty of "true believers" who had seen Brother Rafer at work—on the television, on the Crusade platform, passing out the Kingdom Throne tracts at foreign orphanages, true believers who had seen their small contributions at work around the world, reaching out to rescue sinners from the manacles of demons abundant, others who had felt the warmth of Brother Rafer's healing power right through the top of the radio and who had been healed, and healed *forthwith!* And the money kept pouring in.

But Mendy Parker was in a circle of two that had no counsel for a third, and the interesting little nuzzle that she had witnessed four rows in front of her as she had stood up from her seat was enough to send tremors through the very foundation of the Kingdom Throne Crusade in Guatemala—or anywhere *else!*

"I believe there's a message for me," said a nervous little Missy Magnum to the receptionist at the Front Desk of the Eldorado Hotel, almost an hour after their arrival.

"Of course, right away, Miss . . . Miss, uh?" asked the smart, collegiate-looking young man in his dark grey suit and black-rimmed glasses.

"Magnum," stammered Missy, new to the intrigue of an affair. "Miss Magnum," she said.

"May I see some identification, please?" asked the receptionist.

"Some *what?*" asked a startled little Missy.

"Some *identification*, please," repeated the courteous but resolute young man.

"Oh, I'm sorry, sir," confessed a now flustered little lover. "No, I'm sorry. But *wait!* I have my room key. I just registered thirty minutes ago, you see. *Here!*"

Missy Magnum slid the room key from her small hand purse to the young man. He took the key and flipped through the new registrations and confirmed her name and number.

"Very good," he said. "Please wait right here."

The receptionist walked slowly—too slowly, thought Missy—to the message bin at the other end of the Front Desk, reached into a top slot and retrieved a sealed key envelope. Missy blushed as he turned and approached her behind the counter. She felt a tremble rumble through her spine, and she sensed her knees start to slip and the first faint urges of another orgasm.

"Thanks . . . *Thank* you, sir!" Missy managed, and she took the envelope, assured by the weight of the key inside. She would wait until she stepped into the elevator to open the small package and confirm the room number. She would punch the button for the top floor, open the package, examine the key, and then press the button for the correct intervening floor. It was a plan that would preserve some modesty and a little privacy.

With all the reserve she could muster, Missy Magnum walked toward the elevator in the center of the ornate lobby of the Eldorado. She reached the polished brass elevator doors and pressed the "up" button. The elevator light was flashing on the basement floor; it would arrive momentarily. She was looking nervously at her watch and fingering the small envelope, caressing the chiseled edge of the key through the paper when the voice repeated itself.

"Going up, Señorita?" said the attendant.

"Uh! . . . *Yes!* Why, *yes!*" she stammered.

"*Pase adelante*, beautiful lady," he offered.

Missy Magnum had not expected company on the ride to meet her first lover. She stepped into the elevator, her head already swooning with a combination of embarrassment and fright.

"What floor, miss?" asked the attendant. Missy continued her grip on the key.

"I beg your pardon?" she asked.

"I said `what floor?' miss," he repeated.

"Uh! . . . Uh, the *sixth,* the *sixth* floor!" she blustered as the elevator raced passed the seventh floor on its way to the tenth.

"Oh, I'm very sorry," he said as he reached for the panel of buttons. "I'll have to get off and send you back down," he explained, obviously proud of his English and fascinated by the pert little American.

"Yes, uh, yes . . . That'll be fine, just fine!" said Missy. "Thank you. Thank you very *much!*"

The attendant stepped toward the door of the elevator in front of the distraught little Missy Magnum. When the elevator slipped to a halt, he turned and winked at the frustrated American girl, bowed his head slightly, and stepped through the door.

"He *knew!*" thought Missy, and she felt an urgent sense of shame and discovery. "But how? Oh, that's foolishness. He couldn't possibly have known *anything!*"

The door of the elevator began to close, and Missy stood alone in the compartment. It jerked at the beginning of its descent, and after regaining her balance, Missy looked down at the envelope, now a wad of paper and metal in her sweating little fist. Nervously, she straightened it out, tore away the slightly sealed flap, and slipped her finger into the mouth of the envelope.

Inside the paper envelope, Missy felt the sharply defined edge of the shaft of the key and along side it a piece of folded paper. She pulled out the key and quickly noted the room number engraved in its shank.

"Fourteen-thirty-five," whispered Missy audibly. "Room 1435 . . . I still have to go up," she said, feeling, for some inexplicable reason, a little relieved. She reached forward and scanned down the panel until she located the button for the fourteenth floor. She pressed it quickly in order to secure control of the elevator's course.

The door opened on the sixth floor to a vacant lobby, paused in its cycle—forever, it seemed to little Missy—and then slowly closed in front of her. As it jerked again and started to rise, Missy let out a little sigh.

Relaxed for the first time since she had started up the elevator to her rendezvous, Missy leaned back against the rear of the compartment and slipped her finger into the envelope for the note. The elevator was very slow, and she would have time at least to savour her new-found lover's encouragement.

"What would he say that he must have written so hastily?" she thought. "What would so *spiritual* a man convey in a note to both a loyal staffer and now such a very personal confidante?" "What would he be thinking right now! Perhaps wondering when she would actually tap on his door and slip the key into its slot, thinking what she would look like as she entered his suite?"

Little Missy Magnum pulled out the note, opened it with her thumb and index finger, and moved toward the reflected light from the side mirror of the elevator. The note was upside down, so she turned it around and strained to catch the message as she readjusted it.

"Honey," said the note in the delicate pen of a woman, "Brother Rafer likes a warm, soapy . . ."

Little Missy Magnum reeled backwards, her heart racing and her breath expiring. She clutched the note tightly as she felt the compartment of the elevator begin to spin to the left, faster and faster, and little Missy Magnum, with her two little bird-like breasts heaving just above her dilated diaphragm, passed out cold in the middle of the Eldorado's golden logo woven into the carpeted floor.

Chapter 11

Don J'cab

A shower pelted the drivers working their way along Avenida La Reforma in Guatemala City. Behind their stalls and carts, flower merchants on the corners of the busy intersections cowered under plastic sheeting to avoid the steady downpour. The windshields of the cabs parked along the avenue had fogged over as their drivers nodded off to sleep. Trucks and cars inched along, creeping from one light to the next. The traffic was unusually heavy for so early in the afternoon. It was only as the cars moved closer to Zone 1 that the reason became clearer. Both city and out-of-town busses were converging on the old stadium and sports arena just opposite the modern national theater complex and convention center.

A caravan of the belching, fuming vehicles maneuvered through the narrow gates and deposited their legions of disciples before the banners of the Kingdom Throne crusade. From the busses, streams of the indigenous drifted through the sheets of rain to shelter beneath the towering arches of the stadium. For many, this first trip to the capital of the Republic was a disturbing, disorienting excursion and, albeit, a costly interruption in a rigid cycle of labor that most could ill afford; if they were here, it meant that no one was tending their *milpa* or stock.

At whatever the sacrifice, however, they had come, partly out of the enthusiasm for a change, some because they might find additional opportunities or contacts in the city, and still others who came, of course, in celebration of their new faith. These new believers had come with expectations on the promises of the Kingdom Throne ministry. Out of the rain under the shelter of the stairwells, the *naturales* from more than fifteen of the departments of Guatemala huddled together, orchestrating a cacophony of disparate idioms as the rain continued to fall. Twelve, perhaps thirteen different Maya dialects competed in the swell of enthusiasm that began to build when, after a little more than an hour and—as most expected—the rain subsided and the clouds began to dissipate, revealing, in time, a broad, spotty pattern of pale blue sky above.

As the incredulous Mayas continued to huddle together in their various church groups or among friends, a squad of Kingdom Throne "Kounselors" came walking hastily through an entrance from some place deep in the recesses of the stadium and began handing out flyers printed in Spanish. Each of the Indians took a copy and smiled graciously at the assistant and slowly scanned the tract. Few, if any, could read the message, but the four-color photographs and especially the glossy reproduction of Brother Rafer Farrell, with his arms outstretched, one hand lifting the massive Bible aloft, was impressive. Even more so was the photograph of Brother Farrell with his arm around some indigenous person in what was obviously an indigenous community not too much unlike their own. If they couldn't read the words, they got the message clearly nevertheless that they were in the right place.

With only two hours before the scheduled opening of the Kingdom Throne crusade, maintenance personnel began unlocking the gates to the great arena. At once, thousands of Mayas jammed the entrances as they began filing into the wet stadium to take seats on the weathered, splintery benches. Many of them were young men, rounded up from among the indigenous communities by their Pentecostal pastors. Because of the remote locations of many of the villages, the military had provided covered trucks for transporting them to bus terminals, sometimes as far away as a two or three-hour drive. At least a few brought their wives and toddlers who hung on their fathers' jackets or pulled at their mothers' skirts. Tottering, old men and their wrinkled wives, grandchildren chasing through the rain and splashing in the puddles of water, young girls—tremulous in their first excursion into the city—all were caught up in the sense of something special about to happen. Nothing from their background, however, could have prepared them for the spectacle that would confront them from the floor of the stadium.

In the rear of the arena grounds, taking up the whole eastern half of the complex, the Kingdom Throne speaker's platform had been assembled with its massive pulpit and choir loft at the center. The floor of the platform rested on a four-foot-high bed of interlocking scaffolding more than one hundred feet long and almost as wide. The pulpit, set in the middle of the platform, was a special break-apart unit designed for quick dismantling, shipping and storage, and reassembling for use in such traveling crusades. A flight of more than forty steps looped around from the rear of the pulpit, rose up the left side, and then curved to the top directly again behind the pulpit. This unusual external staircase had been designed intentionally as the point of focus so that everyone would see Brother Farrell as he entered the arena. As the swirling spotlights came to fix on the pulpit, Rafer Farrell, missioner of God, was elevated through a trap door constructed in the recesses of the scaffolding just behind the pulpit. From there, with his large, heavy black Bible under his arm, the evangelist would walk slowly and distinctly up the stairs to take his position before the expectant and fawning crowds.

On the front of the pulpit was draped an oversized Guatemalan national flag ornamented on either side by buckets of gladioli sprays stacked on racks so as to loop from below and up the sides of the flag. On upright stalks, their fiery orange and bluish-red tongues flared in every direction, hundreds of bird-of-paradise blossoms were being amassed in a water basin some twenty feet long, extending from one end of the base of the pulpit to the other.

The tank of flowers provided a festive headboard for a three-foot-deep baptismal pool. Forty feet square, the pool could accommodate more than two hundred new Kingdom Throne disciples and their "Kingdom Kounselors" at a time. The "Kounselors" would route them from left to right, in on one side and out the other. Hundreds of *campesinos* usually responded to the calls for baptism or reconfirmation and would make their way down the aisles to receive baptism in the tank. Vents in the floor of the platform drained the water from the feet and clothes of the soaked converts as they exited the pool. Sometimes a call lasted for more than an hour at the end of the service for the Guatemalan *campesinos*.

Directly behind the pulpit, the bleachers for the massive Kingdom Throne crusade choir spread in a full semicircle, stacked to the rear of the platform and extending back and up for more than twenty tiers. The choir of three hundred would stand throughout the service, singing their newly instructed lyrics of charismatic praise. Large loudspeakers—projecting in every direction—hung from the crisscrossed spans of two towers of scaffolding looming more than forty feet tall over the ends of the risers. Framing the platform over the pulpit and mounted across the stage from tower to tower, a forty-foot-long light bar bristled with hanging spots.

Two whole sections of stadium seats behind the platform and choir loft were closed. No one would be permitted to enter that area which had been carefully rigged for the most impressive fixture of all. Up the center aisle lay a sixty-foot aluminum cross—edged in blue neon tubing—that would be raised by a hydraulic lift just as Brother Farrell began walking up the steps of the pulpit. Flood lights mounted above the base and to the sides of the cross would fade up on the two intersecting beams just as the stadium lights dimmed. An image of Christ's barren tree—in aluminum and neon lights—would then float up over the pastor as he began to preach his gospel message.

But all that was yet to come.

In the steamy, wet afternoon, the freshly transported *campesinos* continued to file off the busses and into the stadium. Each arriving busload was greeted by bright, bouncy American gospel music, its unintelligible English lyrics enlivening the crowd, nonetheless, as they made their way up the ramps of the stadium complex and entered the arena.

Every few minutes, crusade managers barked directions over the speakers in Spanish to the disciples newly arrived inside the area. Their instructions were interspersed with North American gospel recordings of the Statler Brothers, the Judds, Johnny Cash, and evangelical hymns sung in English by various North American church ensembles.

Don J'cab was nervous but excited as he inched his way along up the steps of the entrance way near the south end of the stadium. It wasn't just the newness of the experience; it was that, of course, but more, something which he couldn't even articulate clearly for himself. For the first time in years, he lacked confidence, had lost his moorings. Though proud and independent, he was uncertain of the future. His recent rejection of just about all his family had taught him about things religious—and, still to come, the inevitable confrontation with his more celebrated brother—forced questions for the first time in his life about everything else. Rather than renewed and secure in his recent conversion, he felt only confused and somehow unrewarded. So today, at this place and at this time, Don J'cab was searching, looking for reconfirmation and reassurance. He wanted to experience again what he had felt three months earlier when, kneeling before the railing of the Pentecostal altar, with those massive hands of the Kingdom Throne "Kounselor" clutching the crown of his head, he had "given his life to Jesus." In fact, he was expectant; Don J'cab awaited a miracle promised but yet to come.

"Why not *today,* Jesus? Why not *today?*" Don J'cab whispered his prayer just under his breath, and with the extended thumb of his right fist, he made the sign of the cross across his chest.

Throbbing gospel music rolled across the floor of the sports arena as he stepped through the south entrance of the stadium. Like the other indigenous around him, Don J'cab could only stare at the expansive layout of the platform before him. Two men in a bucket worked atop the arm of a crane adjusting lights hanging from a bar more than twenty feet above the platform. Technicians were stretching microphone cables across the floor. Two groups of women, one at each end of the flower tank, were bent over on their knees tending the flowers, straightening the hundreds of bird-of-paradise stalks. The speakers seemed to be buffeted by the heavy base chords throbbing behind the high-pitched tenor strains of the gospel hymn.

"Maybe *today*, Jesus!" whispered Don J'cab. "Maybe *today*, ah, *ma—!*" He had caught himself. "Oh, *Jesus!*" he corrected himself. He would have to break an old heathen habit, and that would not come easily.

Don J'cab felt a nudge behind him, and he took another step down the aisle. Looking up and ahead, he watched the long row of his colorful countrymen turning left and right off the aisle to take seats in the stands, and he was proud that so many, like himself, had found the true path. At once, he felt a sharp pang of regret as he thought about all the wasted years lost to ignorance and false belief. He thought, too, of his brother, damned in his heathen worship, and how such remarkable gifts could be so *wrong*—and so *dangerous!* Don J'cab was so frustrated, so really *angry.* To think that Andres—Pastor José had called him a "witch doctor"—that a *"witch doctor"* could enchant so many people with his false gods! Secretly, he looked forward to using that new term—"witch doctor." There were other new words to learn and practice as well. And then he was afraid. Don J'cab knew that the God of Jesus would certainly bring destruction on the family of such a one as Don Andres. Would it be a plague of locusts? Would it come as a flood? Would the mountains tremble and collapse upon him? Or would fire sweep down and consume him? Don J'cab played with the fanciful images he had learned from the sermons of the evangelicals, and he imagined Don Andres writhing in the throes of Biblical tortures. His brother was just a fucking *brujo*!

Don J'cab followed a *campesino* family up a flight of narrow steps about ten rows above the main aisle below him and took a place on the end of a bench. He was sitting more or less directly in front of the platform with its massive pulpit before him. He could not even begin to imagine what lay ahead, but as he settled on the wet bench and looked around at the long lines of the Maya around him, he knew that he was where he was supposed to be.

For the moment, however, Brother Rafer Farrell was not so comfortable. On the north side of the stadium in what was usually the office outside the men's locker room, the evangelist was entertaining a rather animated business partner.

"You goddamned *sonofabitch!*" continued Mendy Parker. "I *mean* it, Rafer! This is the *third time* you've tried to pull this crap on me, and I won't *have* it!" she reiterated as she flung the hymn book at the cornered evangelist. "If that little *bitch* isn't on the plane in the morning, I'll break this goddamn scam all to *hell*, and your princely little wavy locks'll be published in every fucking *paper* from New York to *Los Angeles!* And *Ted Kopple'll* be knocking at your goddamn *door!* Do you *get* it, Rafer! Do you think you've got the goddamned *picture?*"

Mendy Parker was angry—hot and furious, but most definitely in control. Brother Farrell sat stoically through it all; he'd heard it before, and he'd most assuredly weather it all this time—and probably the next.

"She's already *gone,*" explained Farrell, trying to collect himself. "Benny took her to the airport this morning."

Brother Rafer rose from behind his desk, walked to the front edge, and sat down against the top.

"Look, *sweetheart.* I made a *mistake.* I let her go too far. She's been after me for more than a year now. Look at the tapes. Look how she's always worshipped me. I'm no goddamned *saint!"*

"*Amen!*" barked Mendy. "Amen to *that* Brother *Rafer Farrell!* I *mean* it, Rafer! Don't you *ever . . .!*"

Rafer hoped to check what was warming up to be another eruption.

"I'm *sorry*, sweetheart! I *really* am!" The Reverend Farrell lowered his head, squinted his eyes up tightly, a trail of tears, streaming down his cheeks. "God *knows* I've wronged you, honey. God knows I've *wronged* you, sweetheart."

The gold and platinum preacher waited for his mistress to make the inevitable move toward him when he knew he could resolve the scene with a little massaging.

"I *mean* it, Rafer!" said Mendy Parker, now sobbing herself. "I really *mean* it!"

"I *know* you do, sweetheart. I *know* it, and so do *I.* So do *I*, honey," reiterated the pastor, beginning once again to charm his partner into submission.

With tears still tracing her cheeks, Mendy Parker stared at her lover from across the room, her fists nailed tightly against her hips. How could he *do* this to her? Right there in the aisle seat in front of the whole plane full of passengers. What did he *take* her for, anyway? Did he really think she couldn't see right in front of her what was going *on?* She *would!* She *knew* she could do it. She would expose him for what he *was*—she knew she could do it, *would* do it, if she ever got mad enough and fed *up* with it all. She had the goods on him, and he knew it, too. She had him by the *balls.* But she had a lot to lose as well. Brother Farrell was about the only golden prick in town with a slush fund of $200,000 grand a year in "fun money."

Mendy Parker took a step toward the pouting pastor. It was in her best interest, having nailed the sonofabitch, to get him ready for the evening's crusade.

"I *mean* it, Rafer," she said softly, and then she crossed over the floor of the dressing room and reached into his crotch. "Right *there*, honey!" she whispered against his ears. "I've got you right *there*—any time I want you!" And Mendy Parker gave the evangelist's scrotum a little squeeze. "I kinda want you *now*, Rafer," she whispered, and she felt his large, puffy palm begin stroking slowly around the right cheek of her ample little ass. Brother Farrell would enter the crusade arena tonight—cleansed, renewed, and refreshed.

The familiar chorus of "Amazing Grace," sung by the Statler Brothers, began to swell through the stadium. More than half the stadium was already full, and still the busses kept coming. Plans for the week-long Central American Crusade had been in the works for more than a year. With only a handful of minor exceptions, all details had been worked out with remarkably little conflict due ultimately to the goodwill of the Guatemalan military.

The military had provided initial liaison support, coordinating all international correspondence and setting up initial meetings between United States and local staff. From their first trip into Guatemala City, military attachés had made them feel welcome, meeting them at the airport, arranging all local transportation and hotel accommodations. The very first night, Kingdom Throne associates had been entertained lavishly by military personnel at a reception in the penthouse of the Camino Real, treated to the strains of an eight-man marimba band, a style show of indigenous costumes modelled by young *ladino* students from Landivar University, and rounds of delicious "native" hors'd'ouevres and spicy Guatemalan soft drinks.

And in a sense, the party never stopped. Military transportation eased their movement throughout the country. They were provided "safe passage" through previously contested territory and had been informed along the way about the devastation caused by the guerrilla movement throughout the highlands. The Indians were looking for peace, they were told, but they had been confused by the guerrillas. Only a well-organized operation like the Kingdom Throne Ministry could reach masses of people. This first crusade was a much-welcomed alternative to the "Catholic/communist scenario" that had been undermining the country's security for more than thirty years. Certainly, the "real people" of Guatemala would welcome Kingdom Throne.

Little Missy Magnum had diarrhea for a week after her return from Guatemala, and the problem wasn't the one meal she had had on board the plane on the way from Miami. Her queasiness began after she found herself in her hotel room with the Guatemalan doctor the Ministry had summoned for her after she had fainted dead away in the elevator. The next morning, she had a message from Brother Rafer confirming her return flight. The good pastor also apologized for being unable to see her before her return. Little Missy Magnum had read that note and promptly threw up in the commode. She was too upset the rest of the night to eat anything.

Little Missy Magnum recovered quickly, however, after she submitted her resignation to Kingdom Throne Ministries, Inc. The first day back, she had called in sick as an excuse originally for such an abrupt return, and no one seemed the more concerned. When she resigned three weeks later, Missy cited nerves and the need for a rest. Several of the associates called or stopped by her apartment to see her. She told everyone that she was thinking about returning to her mission work in San Diego where she had worked before joining Kingdom Throne, and while expressing regret, none of her colleagues seemed to suspect anything more. On a morning that she knew that Brother Rafer would be in a staff meeting, Missy stopped by the offices of the Ministry to process her termination papers.

"Oh, *honey*," said Linda Butler, the good-natured secretary who managed the administrative office corps, "I am so sorry that you won't be with us any longer. Brother Rafer was telling me just yesterday how sorry and shocked he was to learn that you were leaving the Ministry, but that he knew well how the Spirit moves us in His service. I just *know* that the Lord has a *special* blessing in store for you, honey!"

"Yes, I'm sure," said Missy rather perfunctorily, as she returned her ballpoint to her purse. She smiled at the innocent woman, slung the strap of her purse over her left shoulder, and walked out the door. She had entered a side entrance on her way to the office so as to avoid having to answer a lot of questions of associates who might try to engage her in an explanation, but as she walked past the front entrance for the last time, Missy spied a pallet of boxes that apparently had just been delivered from a printer. A sample that had been taped to the top of each carton revealed a brochure advertising the Kingdom Throne Ministries videotape of the Central America crusade.

"That's pretty fast," thought Missy as she pulled away the sample brochure taped to the top of the carton. She recognized the cover picture as a file photo and the art work that the graphics department had developed more than three months prior to their departure. There was the evangelist with his arms outstretched, the expansive, floppy Bible opened and pouring over his puffy palm. Behind him the neon-enhanced cross rose high over his shoulders. A map of Guatemala with the quetzal bird resting on the north-eastern corner of the Petén was superimposed in the lower right-hand corner of the brochure which announced, "God's Speaks to a Heathen World."

"Are these available?" asked Missy to receptionist at the front desk. The girl was new and didn't know Missy as a former associate.

"Well, I guess you can take that one," returned the girl.

"No, I mean the *tape* . . . is the *videotape* ready?" said Missy.

"*What* videotape?" asked the girl.

"This one, the tape on the Guatemala crusade," explained Missy Magnum.

"Ohhh," squealed the girl. "I don't know anything about that. I'm new here. I just started last week. I can call down to `video' and see. I'll just do that for you right now."

The receptionist looked to be in her mid-twenties. She dressed with reserve in a grey suit and high collar and wore her short hair with a stylish flip of her bangs. Even so, there was nothing about her probably that Brother Rafer might find engaging, thought Missy. She was probably safe.

"Do you want one?" asked the girl.

"I'm sorry," said Missy Magnum. "I guess I was day dreaming."

"Do you want a copy of the *tape?*" the girl clarified.

"Yes, yes, I *do,*" said little Missy Magnum.

"Just *one?*" she asked.

"Yes, that's fine. Just one," explained Missy.

"Just one," said the receptionist into the telephone. "Okay, that's just fine. She's waiting at the desk now. Okay."

Missy Magnum wondered, for the moment, who the girl was talking to at the other end. She wondered if Mike and Annie were still in the stock room. They were truly good people who had such a strong faith in the Kingdom Throne Ministries. She would never be able to tell anyone like them what she had been through in Guatemala, but for some compelling reason—something more than her own aborted involvement in the crusade, little Missy Magnum really wanted to see this tape.

Grand chords of the crusade organ brought the strains of "A Mighty Fortress Is Our God" to a climax as the swirling spotlights swept to a single focus on the outstretched arms of Brother Rafer Farrell wearing a glistening, light-blue silk suit, his platinum locks of hair flowing in the breeze that coursed its way across the stadium. Behind him—just at the close of the opening anthem—the cross completed its ascent and locked in a towering plane up and over the choir and the massive pulpit. Brother Farrell raised up his arms again and again as he turned in the pulpit, saluting the massive crowd that was standing on its feet, clapping and clapping. Suddenly, a gasp rolled across the floor of the stadium as the brilliant, neon tubing flickered and then flashed in a brilliant blue outline. The Kingdom Crusade Choir followed the introit of the organ into "Jesus, Jesus, Praise His Name." As the song developed, a dark-haired man in a flashy brown and gold-trimmed ensemble took his place beside Brother Farrell in the pulpit. He, too—his head arched back—raised his arms, his palms stiff and uplifted as he drifted from side to side. His eyes tightly shut, he seemed to be crying and lifting his joyful praise to the high beams of the neon-enhanced cross above them. José Alfonso Bailón would be the official interpreter for the crusade sermon.

To get a better feel for the production of the crusade video, Missy began fast forwarding through the tape, pausing at intervals to catch various elements of the service. She stopped at one point where incredibly long lines of Indians were inching their way along and up onto the platform for baptism. She turned up the volume to catch a little of the actual sound of the ceremony.

"And I baptize you, *Don J'cab*, in the name of the Father, the Son, and the Holy Ghost—oh, *thank* you, *Jesus!"* and down he went! Down went the Mayan *campesino* onto his knees and into the pool of water, the Kingdom Throne Kounselor himself kneeling beside the Guatemalan, forcing his head momentarily under the crystal water. "Rise, Brother J'cab, to serve your *Lord Jesus Christ!*"

As Missy continued to watch the crusade tape, she became aware of a growing nausea. She felt chilled and began to perspire. Suddenly, she realized that she was about to faint.

"Oh, *my!*" she exclaimed. She dropped the VCR remote control and fled to the commode in her bathroom. After a fourth convulsion, she propped herself up against the wall beside the basin of the commode. For a minute or two, Missy tried to wipe out all thought, concentrating on catching her breath and easing the spasms in her stomach. Her throat was burning from the acid she had discharged.

"What . . . what is the *matter* with me?" she suddenly cried. "What's going *on?*"

And then she knew. It was the tape. It was the Guatemalan crusade. It was Rafer Farrell and the whole Kingdom Throne ministry. It had all come together as she was watching the baptisms. It was all so mean and arrogant. For the first time in all her years of work in her church and later in the crusades, she felt like a crook, like the "queen of rip-off"! What had she been *doing?* What was Rafer Farrell and Kingdom Throne ministries *doing* to these people? It all seemed so fake, so orchestrated, so manipulated. And Rafer Farrell—his little thing with Mendy Parker, whatever *that* was! For a fleeting moment, she felt the evangelist's pudgy fingers slipping once again inside her bra and maneuvering around to stroke her breast, and she just shuddered. She felt so cheap and worthless, and tears began streaming down her face. How *dare* that man—that *creep!* How *dare* he take advantage of her trust and her *faith!* Suddenly, she felt angry. She *hated* Rafer Farrell! She just *hated him* and *herself* and *Kingdom Throne Ministries* and *all those people in the studio!* All those stupid, gullible people who let themselves be so persuaded by such a *fake* as Rafer Farrell!

"*Ohhhh!*" she just wanted to . . . just wanted to, wanted to—

"*Ohhh!*" she didn't know what she wanted to do, maybe except to call Benny—*Benny Johnson! That's* what she had to do! Call Benny Johnson! She had to talk to him. She had to tell him about what had happened! He was the only one who was worth even a word about any of this. He was so nice and kind and loving. She *had* to save Benny!

Slowly, Missy raised herself from off the floor, wiped her mouth and chin with a stream of toilet tissue, and then flushed the commode. She was shaking still and very unsteady, but the convulsions had subsided, and she felt she could make it back to her lounge chair and the telephone beside it.

"Well, I'll tell you something else," said Benny Johnson, some hour and a half inside their telephone conversation. "I'll tell you something *else.* Broth—Rafer, you know—he raised a *million dollars* on the show when the Guatemalan guy was on. But that wasn't *enough!* What that guy—*Matiz*, I think his name was—what he told Rafer was that the Guatemalan government wanted the money to buy military supplies and equipment, but that they really needed *$25 million!* So Rafer picked up the phone and called Senator Freeman—*right there on the spot!* I was there in the *room* when he picked up the phone and called the Senator and made an appointment with hi—for Matiz—to go to Washington, D. C. to ask Congress for $25 million for military aid."

"What *happened?*" asked Missy Magnum, now very much engaged in the international backdrop.

"I don't know," said Benny Johnson. "I think it's coming up next month. And I'll tell you something *else* I heard. There have been whole *massacres* of villages down there!"

"What do you *mean?*" asked the puzzled little Missy.

"*Massacres!*" exclaimed Benny Johnson. "I mean where the army has gone into these villages and wiped out everything that moves! Kids, animals, the old people! A lot of the priests—the *Catholic* priests!"

"The *priests?*" asked Missy. "Why the *priests?*"

"Because they say they're 'comunists,' that they're part of the guerrillas, or at least supporting them."

"I can't *believe* that!" cried Missy. "That just doesn't make sense, that the *priests—*"

"Well, that's what I heard, anyway," said Benny Johnson.

"I'll tell you *what!*" said Missy, suddenly taken with an idea. "I've got a cousin—a second or third cousin or something like that living down in the Valley in Texas—the Rio Grande Valley? I haven't seen him for years, but when we were kids, we always played around at family reunions and stuff. He's about seven or eight years older than me, and he always baby sat me. But *he's* a priest! I'd be interested in hearing if *he* knows anything about this. Anyway, I've always thought about calling him. He just might *know* something!"

"What'd you say his name was?" asked Benny Johnson.

"Michael—" said little Missy Magnum. "*Michael Justice.*"

Chapter 12

Bugs and Plants

"*Buenos días, Señora Belamonte y Señor,*" sang the petite Lydia Penalte, the young receptionist for the *Dirección de Turismo*. "May I take your coat, *Señora*? Please, follow me."

The Belamontes trailed politely behind the svelte, sloe-eyed college student completing the third semester toward her Licenciada degree in public affairs and administration. In her dress and makeup, Lydia represented the chic styling and care for sleek femininity the Director of Tourism sought in his young subordinates.

A bright, unusually attractive Guatemalan student, Lydia had parleyed an early career in modeling with an almost insatiable fascination in her studies, following the successful collegiate work of her two older brothers at the National University. She now supplemented her student work/studies program with duties as a receptionist for the Department of Tourism. Usually, she worked the front desk, receiving dignitaries (and their ladies) arriving for consultations, meetings, and receptions.

To all who might have noticed—which would include almost all of the men whom she received, Lydia seemed to enjoy her work with Tourism. She liked to say that it gave her "a sense of a larger world community," removed from the narrower interests of academic pursuits and the demands of faculty and other students. Lydia Penalte also seemed to enjoy the added attention she received from older men who knew how to appreciate the effort she invested each afternoon at her dressing table. With her liner pencils, she played the arch in her eyebrows for as much as it was worth, and the ruby lipstick she had used to accent her full, pouting lips.

On evenings like this, Lydia wore one of four sets of tight, low-cut blouses that plunged between her voluptuous, firm breasts, tanned to a deep olive brown. Braless, she knew her swelling breasts were her strongest economic and social assets. She was confident in the fact that "the two blessings" had kept her in well-paying jobs since she was fourteen, but at the age of twenty-three, she had learned to exercise her attractiveness for political favors as well.

Lydia Penalte had little trouble in earning a position of responsibility, if not respect, among the male-dominated University Forum at the National University as well as a seat on the University's Student Council. As a member of the University Forum, she sat with both deans and department heads among a small complement of students like herself whose task it was to determine university-wide academic themes and program directions, approve recommendations for guest lecturers, and suggest student program activities. Since January, she had served as the Third Vice President of the Student Council, which placed her in line for the Presidency in three more years. If things continued on course, Lydia would be President in her second year of law school—if she survived!

The question of survival was far from a moot concern for anyone associated with the National University. Five student leaders, two from the Council and three from the University Forum, had been "disappeared" in only the last year and a half, and thirteen had been murdered outright over the last five years. Silently, Lydia was deeply bitter and angry at the ruthless and flagrant attacks by paramilitary death squads aimed at intimidating, for almost fifty years, the students and faculty of the National University. Long a nurturing ground for anti-government sentiment and restless agitation on behalf of a long agenda of social causes, the National University had maintained a defiant, though bloody posture in Guatemalan life for more than fifty years. A coalition of National University students and faculty, supported by several companies of disgruntled soldiers and a phalanx of some of the most respected entrepreneurs, had overthrown the thirteen-year-old Ubico dictatorship in 1944 and, in 1946, had installed a democratically elected president, Dr. Juan José Arevelo, selected from the ranks of the National University itself.

Lydia Penalte drew strength from the close-knit relationships she had fostered on the University Forum and Student Council for which both her beauty and brains had secured her respect. She had enjoyed at least two opportunities to mould university life since she had begun her service. First, she had been instrumental in achieving an equitable grading scale for undergraduate students enrolled in optional, dual-credit undergraduate/graduate courses. Undergraduates would now be graded separately on the basis of an undergraduate course outline, a new academic policy, adopted, in part, in response to her petition before the University Deans' Council more than a year before.

The second contribution for which she could take more direct credit was her petition drive to extend scholarship and financial aid to indigenous students living outside their own University districts. For decades, the National University had divided the country into six districts, each served by an extension campus of the National University system. Many indigenous students, however, migrated in and out of their own districts, following the harvesting cycles of the seasons, and many had resettled outside the jurisdiction of their home district, making them ineligible, according to previous regulations, for financial support from the local branch of the university. Lydia had petitioned students and faculty to relax regulations limiting support for out-of-district Indian applicants to the University. The proposal was finally approved after long debate, and the University chancellor had honored her efforts with a National University Award of Distinguished Service, one of only three conferred that year.

For all her visibility as both a student and receptionist at Tourism, Lydia Penalte was something even more complicated, for the ever-so-popular Lydia Penalte had a private, dark side: secretly, she was an urban guerrilla, fundamentally committed to the overthrow of the Guatemalan military complex. As such, she was a member of a small cell of four soldiers—two men and two women—who were "plants" both in the National University and in two branches of the government for the *EGP*, the "Guerrilla Army of the Poor." Simply described, they were "intelligence officers." Lydia's position in the Department of Tourism, therefore, was no accident. In fact, she had groomed herself carefully for the appointment.

"I want to be with you, Señor Marcos Juarez. I want to be with you tonight," she had whispered intently over the rim of a crystal goblet, two years earlier, as she stared into the eyes of the now deceased, middle-aged Associate Director of Tourism. Within a month after his death, Lydia Penalte had slipped comfortably into the sheets of Pablo Manuel Rigoleto himself, the Director, often bringing along with her Alma María Vargas, her own lover and the second woman, a corporal, in their guerrilla cell.

Lydia Penalte had never thought of herself as bi-sexual. She had always enjoyed the lusty challenge of male partners and felt equally avaricious in the pursuit of a climax, but with Alma María, something was different. She had met Alma María Vargas in an evening humanities course at the National University in the same semester that Carlos Alvarez, the secretary of the Student Council and Alma María's boy friend had been "disappeared." When news of his abduction had reached Alma María, she panicked and, near collapse, had rushed to Lydia Penalte with whom she had been studying the previous week for their exams.

Long into the night and well into the next morning, Lydia had tried to console the distraught girl. While massaging the back of the reclining girl's neck and shoulders and combing out the wet tangles from her long, black hair, Lydia Penalte discovered a deep stirring and desire to lie beside Alma María and to press her own body into every pore of the sobbing soul that stretched so closely and so vulnerably before her on the couch. That newly quickened love, born on the breast of empathy, swelled into a full tide of passion between them both. For long hours after classes, the two retired together where, amidst embraces, they confessed, little by little, the fear they shared for their colleagues as well as their own security and their growing conviction that a silent, passive vigil was deadlier perhaps than an alliance with an "established alternative." Within in two months of Carlos's disappearance, the two lovers, with the help of a confederate, had enlisted in an urban unit of the Guatemalan Guerrilla Army of the Poor.

Their first assignment was the observation of traffic patterns at the main entrance to the National University in the early mornings and afternoons. Attacks on students and National University faculty had occurred twice at peak periods in early morning hours and three times during afternoon arrivals and departures of large numbers of students. Not many years before, medical students stepping from a city bus at the entrance to the university had been gunned down by assailants from the rear of a pickup truck. When one student, wounded in the back, attempted to flee toward the nearest building, the driver of the truck wheeled sharply back over the curb and drove the student into shrubbery where the killers finished their work with a burst of automatic rifle fire.

In reaction to such a bold assault, the University had cemented steel pylons deeply into the sidewalks at all entrances to avoid direct attacks at those strategic points, but such blockades were helpless against determined abductions of individuals which had continued periodically over the past months. Alma María and Lydia Penalte took up posts at two entrances where they observed traffic patterns at the heaviest periods for more than three weeks. Their notes were later incorporated into a security paper distributed to students during the following terms.

Not long after their enlistment in the guerrilla unit, Lydia Penalte had been invited to a reception honoring the graduation of one of the grandsons of the oligarchy who had completed an advanced degree in engineering from the University of Madrid. The young man had returned to Guatemala with about twenty fellow students who were coming to the "land of eternal spring" to join him in a jaguar hunt in the Petén on one of his father's many *fincas*. His parents had arranged a grand reception through the Department of Tourism to celebrate their arrival. The Associate Director of Tourism was the first to greet her as Lydia Penalte completed the ascent of the steps from the street and entered the reception gallery.

"You must be the first bloom of the *monja blanca*, Señorita," intoned the entranced and fascinated Marcos Juarez. "I must join you later for a glass of champagne," he pleaded.

After her first sexual encounter with Marcos Juarez, Lydia Penalte had rushed to her apartment and to Alma María where she attempted to amuse her not so enthusiastic lover with little anecdotes about her something less than "entertaining" fling in the bed earlier in the evening.

"He has a pencil with a lollipop for a *rod!*" she laughed. "He coughed every time he started to come. I wanted to duck, but I was afraid I might break him off! But I was easy with him, and Alma, you'll never *guess*: he offered me a *job*, Alma! He offered me a job as a receptionist. Do you have any idea what that can mean?" she asked. "We're *in!*"

Alma María Vargas was neither amused nor quieted. She was churning inside, and her mind was blank while her heart reeled in terror.

"I can *help* you, Lydia. I want . . . I want to *be* with you if you must do these things," whispered Alma, as she clutched her lover's hand and slipped Lydia's fingers against her cheek and into her long braids of hair. "I can *help* you do what you have to do," said Alma María Vargas. When Marcos Juarez died from cardiac arrest nine months later, Lieutenant Lydia Penalte took an apartment with Alma María only blocks from the residence of Pablo Manuel Rigoleto, and soon, the two of them were paying visits to the Director.

Alma María was, in many respects, quite the opposite of her vivacious, outgoing partner. Outwardly, she was a very quiet woman and reserved, but intellectually quick and observant. From German great-grandparents, Alma had derived her strong, angular profile, and from her Maya-Quiché grandmother, her thick-bodied, raven hair. In a three-way tryst with the Director Rigoleto, Alma was a merchant of supple words that flowed in an offertory from her dark, rich voice like thick honey over a bite of gin. Alma María would lie beside their male partner, twisting the ends of her hair, gazing into his eyes and describing what she knew he would enjoy, while Lydia was the puppet, led by her lover's cadences, enveloping their client in her warm, moist cavities and wrapping herself around every inflamed appendage. Periodically, Alma María would touch both of her partners with her long, manicured nails and then drag them deeply through their flesh, tracing her fiery fingers from zone to zone until Lydia pounded the Director into a writhing climax.

As a receptionist in the Department of Tourism, Lieutenant Lydia Penalte had direct access to the most important figures of CACIF and the whole Guatemalan oligarchy. As an information agent, Lydia was charged with collecting data on the movement of the elites and members of their families. Without questions or unnecessary attention, Lydia roamed daily through the Director's mailing lists, agendas of meetings, notification of travel plans—including both arrivals and departures, and even more discreet information, such as the oligarchs' preferences for less formal and more personal "entertainment," which Director Rigoleto kept in a small notebook in his desk drawer, along with the keys to the office vault.

Luncheons were especially useful occasions for Lydia Penalte because Guatemala's most influential entrepreneurs seemed to favor them. Meetings of *CACIF*—the Guatemalan Confederation of Agriculture, Commerce, Industry, and Finance—and the Guatemalan-American Chambers of Commerce were frequented by both the established and the rising stars. At any such activity, members of the conservative press, representatives from the diplomatic corps, the large landowners of the *latifundios*—the chief architects of the nation's economic infrastructure—and delegates of certain "other elements," to be sure, mingled and renewed acquaintances and reinforced their sense of a common direction.

"We have a real opportunity," said Jaime Alvarado, as he stirred his martini slowly. "`*Opportunity'*—that's all we need. Isn't that what this is all about?"

Marco Peneda nodded his head in a particularly knowing way, setting his own dripping, plastic swisher aside, staining the white cotton tablecloth of the service table. His business as a banker was about "opportunity" and nothing more.

Col. Mintor Albanes Rojas looked deeply into his Chivas Regal on the rocks, shaking the glass lightly to settle the cubes of ice. "Opportunity" was Guatemala's national treasure, as yet, an unfulfilled, precious commodity of inestimable value—if marketed appropriately. The military understood this. It was the army's responsibility to keep the gate from would-be poachers without and from subversive elements within who refused to appreciate the significance of Guatemala's "opportunity."

Lydia Penalte also appreciated "opportunity," and luncheons with the Guatemalan-American Chamber of Commerce constituted such advantages. Off the shoulder of her escort, Director Pablo Manuel Rigoleto, the vivacious guerrilla lieutenant was a stimulating addition to any conversation among her male admirers.

"*Buenos tarde, Señorita,*" said Fernando Morales, Associate Executive Director of the American Chamber of Commerce and chief assistant to Martín "Bucky" Watermann, the current president of the Chamber. For the moment, the eyes of Fernando Morales were lost within the cleavage of Lydia's exposed bosom.

"I must say—from one staff to another—that the *señorita* knows how to impress the company, *eh?*" said Morales.

"She knows how to support her boss, *eh?*" Lydia retorted.

"And *please* him, I understand," Morales pressed winking, as he reached for her hand. Raising her fingers to his lips, Morales turned his own wrist so that in passing he might stroke the loose sweater as it slipped past her left breast. Lydia smiled coolly at her assailant, never blinking her eyes at his as he finished his caress.

"I have a jealous *chief, Señor* Morales. A very *jealous* chief, indeed," said Lydia. She touched her cheek to his in the familiar greeting, but on retreating, brushed his nose with her own and puckered her lips in a feigned pout.

"Perhaps just this very *moment*, he is watching everything and is *very* hot, don't you think so?" she teased.

"He may be *hot*, but does he have my *passion*," pursued Morales.

"I am afraid as to where all this may be leading us," cooed Lieutenant Penalte. "Perhaps we should *chill the flames* with another drink. Why don't you be my hero and fetch me another!"

"If you will take it in my *room, señorita*," pressured Morales.

"Only if my Director says `okay,'" teased Lydia. "Shall I *ask* him?"

They both laughed at the finale of the retorts.

Lydia Penalte was most adroit at managing her unusual beauty and attractiveness in a culture dominated by a *machismo* that was used to orchestrating the tempo and the tenor of its pursuits. Women expected abuse periodically, and Lydia had learned at an early age the irony of both the special strengths and vulnerabilities of her uncanny sexuality. Her distinctive beauty had afforded her a certain distance from most men, had actually placed her out of their reach. She might be the subject of every man's quest, but she was a prize out of bounds except to those upon whom she might bestow her interests.

Fernando Morales refreshed Lydia's drink at the bar and returned to her side. He was not on her list for "favors." Coy bantering with a probing male colleague was a clear sign of her rejection. Lydia never negotiated serious "foreplay" in a public arena, and Morales knew as much, knowledge which, of course, afforded him a little verbal slack. Still, he could enjoy her substantial presence, while his own shielded her from the obnoxious sorties of others.

"Why don't we take a seat a little further up in the room so we can hear better," coaxed Morales. "There's a lot of traffic out in the restaurant around this time. Even with the door closed, sometimes it's hard to hear."

"Yes, that's a good idea," said Lydia. "Why not over there." She was angling toward a table next to one already occupied by a familiar party, Sidney Gallagher of the I.G.A.

"I'm going to sit a little closer to the front," Lydia explained to her boss as she passed him near the cash bar in the rear of the salon.

"That's fine," said Pablo Manuel Rigoleto. "You take good notes, *eh*?"

"*Sí, mi amor*!" teased Lydia, as she took the available hand of the Associate Director of the Guatemalan-American Chamber of Commerce and began drifting slowly and deliberately through the chairs toward the front of the room.

"I want to welcome each of you to our luncheon today," said Lic. "Peri" Alfonso Montoña, the Director of the American Chamber of Commerce, speaking against the microphone on the small speaker's podium that had been placed on the decorated head table.

The company of middle-aged Guatemalan men, some of the most important investors in the country had assembled for their monthly respite. Slowly, they made their way to the tables to hear remarks from Col. Federico Altapaz, the Minister of the Interior, from the National Palace. Lydia and her escort of the moment had taken seats at a table for eight just off center near the head table. Within a few moments the Guatemalan beauty had been joined by five other men and a woman.

"General Tierez, may I present to you Señorita Lydia Penalte of the *Departamento de Turismo*," offered Fernando Morales.

"It is my *pleasure*, for *sure!*" returned the officer as he shook her hand respectfully and took his seat.

"Licenciado Snider, this is Señorita Lydia Penalte of *Turismo*," repeated Morales, obviously pleased with his little assumed social obligation of introductions.

Gustavo Bethancourt, the General Manager of *La Prenza Libertad*, one of Guatemala's oldest newspapers, sat down beside Morales. He was joined by Doña Patrocinia Rendón, the widow of the founder of the newspaper, René Juanmanuel Rendón Gramajo, who still retained majority ownership of the paper and was one of the few women to attend the invitational luncheons regularly. Doña Patrocinia, smiled graciously across the table, and then turning her attention to the folds of her napkin, she assumed the familiar inscrutable countenance by which she maintained her presence among her male counterparts.

Doña Patrocinia Rendón was the heir-apparent to her late husband's political machinery as well as his substantial media holdings. René Juanmanuel Rendón Gramajo was the co-founder of the MLN, the party of the National Liberation Movement, the first right-wing, anti-communist political party to grow out of the revolution of Castillo Armas in 1955. Generally known as the *padrino de las esquadrones de la muerte*, the sponsor of the death squads, Rendón was thought to have collaborated with the military in the brutal repression of 1962-64 which rounded up more than 7,000 guerrillas of the Rebel Armed Forces and their alleged sympathizers in the eastern departments and dispatched them over the Caribbean. In fact, the guerrilla insurgency had included no more than 150 men or so, and probably as many supporters. If no one cared to address Doña Patrocinia on the subject of the family's heritage in Guatemalan politics, it wasn't because the good lady was negligent in the shadow of her late husband. It was common though unspoken knowledge that the inheritance of the Guatemalan matron was the primary underwriting for a wide spectrum of paramilitary activity throughout the country and sponsorship for continued surveillance of the Guatemalan refugee community from Miami to Los Angeles, from Mexico City to Toronto. Doña Patrocinia Rendón spoke little and answered to no one. Behind her back, the good widow was affectionately referred to as the "admiral of the fleet"—a fleet of unmarked four-wheel drives, that is.

"And Señorita," offered Morales a last time. "It is my pleasure to introduce a special guest of the Chamber today. This is Captain Daniel Manheim Rosenberg, military attaché of the Israeli embassy. He has been with us in the `land of eternal spring' only for the past two weeks. Captain Rosenberg is an expert on main-frame computer systems."

"It is my distinct *pleasure*, my dear," cooed the young captain, rising partially from his chair. "My *distinct* pleasure to meet such a . . . such a *lovely* representative of your beautiful country." He resettled in his chair, never removing his eyes from the sensational vision of Lydia Penalte.

The "Salon de Libertad" was small and cramped for most Chamber luncheons which usually were packed by the addition of numerous guests of the members. The room lay just to the left and behind the entrance to the restaurant of the old Pan American Hotel and served as the meeting place for a number of business groups with offices in the capital. Its tall, floor length windows once looked out onto the busy downtown street, but since the latest remodeling more than twenty years earlier, the windows were draped and corniced. The head table, covered with the hotel's yellow tablecloths trimmed in green fringe, was mounted on a foot-tall platform that extended across the drapery along most of the side of the room. Twenty circular tables jammed across the floor below the platform could accommodate six patrons comfortably and up to eight out of necessity.

Most notable, the seals of commerce and fraternity were featured against a backdrop of Guatemala nationalism. Embossed facsimiles of unfurled United States and Guatemalan flags crossed staffs at the base of the circular seal of the Guatemalan-American Chamber of Commerce that was fastened to the front of the speaker's rostrum. The actual flags hung on their staffs at either end of the head table. Attached at regular intervals across the top of the dark green cornice flew a thirty-foot banner—absconded from the 1978 Guatemala-Belize campaign—which read, "*Guatemala es Primero!*"

The cacophony of tingling utensils and cocktail glasses flowed incessantly as a backdrop for the staccato chatter of entrepreneurial Spanish as the members and their guests began to file in to the dining room from the cash bar just outside the door. Once seated, members usually found it virtually impossible to move from their places while waiters were serving the plates or removing them. Dressed in white shirts, black slacks, and cummerbunds, both the young men and women moved quickly with an air of common purpose in and around the tables, serving first the head table and then the dons throughout the room.

Lic. "Peri" Alfonso Montoña returned to the microphone.

"Please find your places," he urged. "Please take your seats, and we will begin our program. I know some of us have only a short time today, and we want to give Col. Altapaz every moment possible. Please take your seats, ladies and gentlemen."

Lydia Penalte turned her head slightly in order to watch the final members and their guests enter the room. Some slight enthusiasm at the doors turned heads as a lithe, elegant young lady entered the room. She wore a stunning, navy-blue sequined "midi," with a high-collar choker and a plunging neckline swelling at the apex of her deep cleavage. Rosalia Mendoza, the reigning "Miss Guatemala," stepped slowly around the chairs as the men rose ahead of her to assist her to her place at the head table.

Rosalia Mendoza was the twenty-one year old daughter of Arturo Riobles Mendoza, the head of internal medicine at the Roosevelt Hospital and reputedly one of the military's consultants to the *Kaibiles*, Guatemalan's elite military corps. Rosalia had completed pre-med studies at Landivar University and would leave in the summer to begin medical school at Johns Hopkins University in the United States. More than her two predecessors, Rosalia, behind all the rose flush on her cheeks and the deep, cherry-red lipstick, was becoming a national centerpiece on the official dining circuit.

Lydia was pleased with the instant competition. She was now officially off the hook and could concentrate on matters other than deflecting the aggressive masculine competition for her attention.

The final members of the Guatemalan-American Chamber of Commerce entered the room, and, following a signal from Licenciado Alfonso Montoña, a waiter closed the door. Light conversation continued as the last few stragglers found their seats. Satisfied that all were in place, the host rang the Chamber bell next to the rostrum, and all rose for the Guatemalan national anthem.

Rosalia Mendoza led the singing, her heavy, sculptured lips lining each verse against the recording reverberating from a small audio cassette player on the table beside the rostrum. Patiently, the gathering completed the six stanzas and applauded enthusiastically at the finale. Then, once again, the waiters, who had stood silently at attention during the anthem, slipped back into the tables with their remaining dishes and pitchers of tea and water.

Rosalia Mendoza picked politely at her plate of *frijoles* and *pollo al carbón*, wiping the corner of her mouth slightly every other bite or so, smiling demurely at observations thrown her way from up and down the head table. At the same time, Lydia Penalte was making careful mental notes about the conversation and particularly focusing on the table behind her.

"Oh, *yes!* Of *course!*" said an American voice just behind her. Lydia strained to catch every word.

"I think that's the continued value of such a cooperative enterprise like the IGA," continued the familiar party. The IGA provides a much-needed service in a setting where we hope our Guatemalan constituents will always feel comfortable. It's always an educational institution first, you know. But its salons have hosted many voices that have done much to seal the friendship between Guatemala and the United States. I think we would be open to a proposal."

This conversation was, perhaps, the very one that lieutenant Penalte had been anticipating in the last two weeks.

Sidney Gallagher covered his assignment as the acting C.I.A. station chief with the veneer of another federal appointment as the Associate Director of the Instituto Guatemalteco-Americano, or the Guatemala-American Institute, better known to the locals as the "IGA." In its twenty-second year of operation, the Institute was a bi-national center for the study of English, a cooperative venture between the Guatemalan and American governments. Like such centers found throughout the hemisphere, the bi-national centers were built and initially directed by United States foreign service personnel and staffed by Guatemalans, always with the understanding that on a predetermined schedule, the directorship would be turned over to a mutually acceptable national. Still the director of operations, at least in practice, Sidney Gallagher was completing the two-year training schedule with Armando Peneda, a Harvard-educated Guatemalan who was one of the bright comers in the Christian Democratic Party and already a respected jurist in the Guatemalan appellate courts. Peneda had been chosen as the second Guatemalan to accept the directorship of the IGA after the assassination of Ricardo Sandoval two years earlier in 1987.

It was Lydia Penalte's sense that Sidney Gallagher was a very busy man, having tried unsuccessfully to telephone him for her boss several times in the past year. He was a familiar figure at these luncheons, however. This was the third time that she had seen him at these afternoon occasions in just the last month. Armando Peneda sat to his left and listened while his mentor continued a discussion with Col. Leopoldo Lopez, the newly appointed Vice Minister of Education and Culture for the Ministry of Education.

"By the way," said Gallagher. "I think I have some news that you may find interesting. We're going to be able to work things out, and we should be able to make shipment possibly as early as August or September."

"`Work things *out?*' did you say?" asked the colonel.

"I said *`work things out,'*" repeated Gallagher.

"*Bueno!*" returned the colonel. "*Esta bien!*"

This portion of their conversation was not lost to Lieutenant Lydia Penalte who had been apprised of Gallagher's possible double role. She was alert to coded signals in conversation with the American Embassy staffers. Her report of the plans to recall Abraham Brasewood, the former C.I.A. station chief, in fact, had alerted the guerrillas to the impending step up of the repression against the communities of population in resistance in Huehuetenango the previous spring. Only days after Brasewood's return to Washington, D.C., Lt. General Charles "Charlie" Hendricks had been sent down from the *School of the Americas* at Fort Benning. He was carried on the books as an ESL—that is, an "English-as-a-second-language"—instructor and even had an office at the IGA. Within two weeks of his arrival, however, "Charlie" had been spotted entering the compound of "B" company at the command post of the *Kaibilies* outside San Marcos. He was accompanied by Colonels Hernando Francisco Monterosa and Hector Meija Ruis, two former graduates of the *School of the Americas* and former Directors of the Palace Guards at the National Palace. Under the command of Col. Monterosa, security troops had stormed the offices of the University Student Union at San Carlos University, destroying equipment and seizing records. Before a week had lapsed, more than two dozen students and three professors had been disappeared. They didn't wait that long, however, to restrain Guatemala's "merchants of death." Within a day, the *Kaibiles* unleashed coordinated attacks against the indigenous of seven villages. With devastating ferocity, the troops had used recently purchased *Galil* field rifles and the new M-16 1A's purchased through intermediaries in Israel.

Lydia had been apprised of the impending purchase of more than 16,000 M-16 1A's from the United States, a $13.8 million dollar package that had been carefully developed to fall just under the $14 million dollar ceiling imposed by the United States Congress on direct military hardware sales to Guatemala. It was hoped that the shipment might be intercepted or its distribution harassed at least for propaganda purposes. The former was not highly likely, but their mole in Washington, D.C. was monitoring the development of the "package" very closely, and Lydia knew that it was only a matter of days when the decision would be passed along to the Guatemala military. Col. Leopoldo López was generally acknowledged by the guerrillas as the liaison between the Guatemalan military and the United States Pentagon and Administration.

"We're going to be able to work things out" was obviously code, indicating that the full sales package was intact. But Gallagher had not said "have been worked out," as much to suggest that the final schedule might be the hang up.

Lost in a whirl of reflections, Lydia was startled to find those around her completing a round of applause. Col. Federico Altapaz had already found his way to the podium.

"*Señoras y señores*," began the Colonel. "You must forgive me for I am no speech maker."

"Speech maker" or not, the suave, lithe, carefully tailored and manicured officer stood erect behind the podium, his supple hands gripping the sides of the rostrum. Clearly, he was there on purpose and seemed quite comfortable and self-assured.

"Throughout my career in service to the Guatemalan people," continued the colonel, "I have always preferred action to words."

The tightly fitted audience broke into its first spontaneous applause. They were obviously ready to reward apostrophes complementary to their own commitments on the most serious issues. No one in the room failed to understand the Colonel's reference to his own "action."

"However, this afternoon, I have heard much about *`opportunity'*—a `*Guatemalan* opportunity,' and on this subject I have a few words that I wish to say: I have always thought of `opportunity' as something to `seize,'" insisted

Col. Altapaz, backing away slightly from the microphone as warm applause again filled the chamber.

"So, I am here today to help you inaugurate a joint campaign to `seize a Guatemalan opportunity'!" bellowed the Colonel with an evangelical fervor which elicited his first standing ovation.

"I am speaking of the Northern Transverse Territory," explained the Colonel. "For the past decade or so, we have become increasingly aware of the rich deposits of minerals in the area, and we have begun to develop the infrastructure including settlements and highways deep into the mountains for accessing them. But today, I have been asked by President Bustamonte to share with you one of the most important developments in our continuing exploration of the territory."

The luncheon audience sat hushed and poised. This, perhaps, was to be the announcement a number of the investors in the group had been awaiting.

"At the Ministry of the Interior," said Colonel Altapaz, "we have been able to confirm the discovery of `sweet petroleum'—perhaps a pool of more than *500 million barrels!*"

The audience broke into spontaneous applause and cheers which the Colonel accepted and allowed to run its full course.

"`Sweet *petroleum*' and *millions* of cubic feet of natural gas," added the Colonel, "enough natural gas to supply the needs of the country for the next *twenty decades!*"

The audience began to buzz back and forth across and between their tables.

"Now, if my assistants will come forward," cued the colonel to two young military attaches standing just inside the doors of the Salon, "I'll give you some idea where we have located this band of pools, and other areas which exhibit the same geological faults found in the Northern Transverse, particularly on the south side of the Lake Atitlán."

The two attaches moved forward with a folded easel and rolled chart which they propped up at the end of the head table. The room was astir with excitement.

"Lieutenant," instructed the colonel. "Point out the two areas there . . . no! further to the right . . . *there! That's it!* There you can see the sites—just along the eastern edge of the Ixcán. The other area courses along a thin fault line stretching through San Marcos to the base of Lake Atitlán and then straight south for about sixty miles."

The guests were buzzing eagerly.

"I am no petroleum engineer," continued Colonel Altapaz. "My profession is one of service to the engineers and to the Guatemalan workers and to you, the Guatemalan investors whose faith seems now rewarded. So, I am here only to complement this wonderful discovery which may be the `opportunity' to move Guatemala into a position of new, unprecedented authority among the Central American nations."

More buzzing.

"Let me say this," begged the Colonel. "Let me beg your sympathetic understanding: there is a lot to do before one drop of petroleum can be extracted from the Northern Transversal. Before we can bring the engineers and geologists into these zones, we have to build roads. We have to raise shelters. We have to construct camps. Before we can do anything, the entire area must be made *secure*, and I think that there must be no one in this room who misunderstands what I am saying."

The implication was clear to everyone in the room and brought yet another cycle of boisterous applause as the members and guests rose to their feet, nodding from side to side, gathering mutual support for the unfortunate inevitabilities of maintaining the state.

"The insurgency is still strong in several sectors of the Northern Transversal, and we know of at least three guerrilla groups operating in Sololá," emphasized the Colonel. "We have evidence—*indisputable* evidence of Cuban support for these continued hostilities. But you should know that we have our finest troops on station, and we are doing what we are trained to do and what we have to do to maintain a free Guatemala!"

Once more the audience broke into energetic applause.

"Now, no doubt," confided Colonel Altapaz, in measured phrases. "No doubt, during the next few weeks—as we step up our security activities—you're going to be hearing some *blather* and *nonsense* from the international press and from some of our own self-proclaimed `*human rights* advocates' whose souls bleed *incessantly* for our home-grown communist *traitors!*"

Grumbling and catcalls erupted about the tables as the entrepreneurs registered their disdain for the revolutionaries.

"We can expect the leftists in the church to *wail* and *moan*," mocked the colonel, and the room itself swooned and moaned as if on cue, a response not lost on the good Colonel Altapaz.

"And we can probably expect the *MR*, the *Guatemala Women's League*, and the other communist agencies and their *dupes* to file various petitions in our esteemed courts . . .!" offered Altapaz, and the members and their guests hissed, laughed, and clinked their glasses.

"And we may suffer one or two *disruptions* here in the capital—and we will let them have their *say!*" The colonel had stumbled into a rhythm that was taking its effect as the diners strained toward the podium.

"We will *let* them have their marches!" exclaimed the Colonel as he pounded the podium for effect. "We will *honor* their demonstrations! [Slam!—down went the open palm of his right hand!] And as they *do!* [Slam!] . . . As they *do!* . . . As they march, and as they wail, and as they slop at the trough of the international socialist media, we will be very *patient!* We will *give* them their *say!* And all the while, my friends, all the *while! We will be there!* [Slam!] We will be *watching!* [Slam!] And we will *make lists!* [Slam!] And we will *take names* [Slam! Slam!], and in the night—after they have had their say—we will come into their homes, and we will cut off their communist *heads!*" [Crash!!!]

No one appeared to regale more lavishly in the ensuing explosion of cheers and applause than did the beautiful lieutenant of the insurgency. The enthusiastic chorus washed in waves around the room. Lydia lifted her shoulders high, perched on her toes, and vigorously clapped in keeping with the occasion. Within, however, she was making her *own* list and taking her *own* names. So-called "subversives" would surely die, but each bloody blow would be answered—that she could *guarantee!*

"I think that if I should leave with you any parting observation," said Colonel Altapaz, "I think . . . I *think* . . ."

The colonel paused to allow the final flurry of applause to subside. Confident in their renewed attention, Colonel Altapaz suddenly scowled and slowly panned the room with a gaze that penetrated the mien of even Doña Rendón.

"I think that I would invite you . . ." offered the colonel, "I think that I would *encourage* each of you to watch your *own* ranks and the staff you choose to serve you."

A murmur began to stir about the room. Heads turned and eyes dropped as the heavy import of the colonel's admonition began to register.

"But I think we know each other well, *no!*" returned Colonel Altapaz to end his remarks on a positive, cooperative note. The gesture was not unappreciated as the guests rose to a final standing ovation.

Colonel Federico Altapaz made his way from the podium down the aisle behind the guests at the head table, placing his burnished hands on each shoulder of Rosalia Mendoza. The Guatemalan beauty reached across her ample bosom to touch his hand as he gave her a little squeeze, whispering gratuitously in her ear. Then he moved on, shaking each extended hand of guests at the head table as they stood and turned toward him at his passing. His two attaches folded the chart, disassembled the easel, and awaited their commanding officer at the end of the platform. The applause and cheers almost lifted them from the floor as they made their exit through the doors at the rear of the *Salon de Libertad.*

The luncheon lasted a half hour more, filled with chatter and shop talk. Everyone finished dining, comfortable in the knowledge that the present security concerns reflected only temporary discomfitures that would be resolved in the customary way by a most dedicated, highly trained, and well-paid military. Professional soldiers wore carefully manicured uniforms with starched shirts and shiny shoes. Their officers could write polished, literate reports. On occasions like these, some of them could rise to oratory comparable with the best. The CACIF trusted their military implicitly. And the colonels reciprocated; they stayed out of each other's business. If the nation's chief investors ever found reason to complain, they seldom questioned means, only results.

Chapter 13

Revolutionary *Cargo*

URNG, the Guatemala National Revolutionary Unity, was more than a coalition of disaffected Guatemalan *campesinos*. It was more than a movement against repression and terror. URNG had taken on a soul, become a spirit capable of firing a new will to respond and react that seemed to draw its strength in proportion to the horror to which it was subjected. Every new "disappearance" of a father, brother, sister, or daughter, every pound of freshly mutilated flesh bound and dumped like garbage off the side of a road, every budding leaf that rotted in place from the sprays of defoliant rained down on the crops and fruit trees by the military aircraft, every conscription of a young *campesino* son into the detested Guatemalan army, every young catechist chopped down by the long machetes of a civil patrol, every charred, exploded skull lifted from another clandestine grave became, in time, the elixir which nourished and charged the very roots of their souls. The *campesino* insurgents had crossed the line. They drew more determination from every new horror and fresh energy from each reported assault against their *aldeas*.

"URNG" became synonymous with a patriotism that united the highland *campesinos* with the aggrieved of every community, from the Mames porting their cargos of *tinajes* over sharp ridges snaking their way through the Sierra Madres, to the tanned and fevered Cakchiquels stripping the tall cane from the steaming coastal planes of Jutiapa; from the stoic, grizzled workers packing the *piñas* and bananas across the prickly foothills of El Progreso, to the remote Kanjobals tending the stands of sparse maize against the towering slopes of Huehuetenango.

In the beginning, the guerrilla "movement" was more of a continuous flight of small cadres of ragged *campesinos* dodging both the civilian and army patrols from one valley to another across the Cuchumatanes and the Sierra Madres. In truth, if one were to assay the dominant spirit of the few guerrilla combatants, it would plumb the dregs of constant fear, not so much out of a concern for themselves as for their communities in resistance, and an anger—

exhibited as an austere vigilance in the face of the loss of friends or family members to the savagery of the army, but a seething anger also for the displacement and interruption of the course of their lives by a long litany of social, political, and economic abuses.

"I joined the Guerrilla Army of the Poor because the *ejército* drove my family from our land, the only home we have known in more than 100 years," explained Monroy.

"They didn't give my little brother a chance. He was seventeen years old when they came into our village," explained Humberto. "The soldiers took him straight from the *church*, right in front of the *priest*, and we never saw him again. Fileberto said that they chopped him with a machete. They said they split his head in half with just *one* blow, one *blow* while he was asking for forgiveness. So I joined the Guerrilla Army of the Poor."

"The head of the civil patrol of Santa Lucía Paoquil came for me in the night—just after I had placed my baby in her little hammock," said María Sanchez Monroy, a *ladino* school teacher who had been with the guerrilla movement for the past three years. "He told me that I was a widow. I wouldn't—*couldn't*—believe him, for my husband had left me only an hour before to take the cured pork to Pablo, the tailor. I told him there must be some mistake, and then he drew open the cord on the bag over his shoulders. He grabbed it by the corners, and turned it upside down. Out fell the head of *Pablo*, the tailor, and the *head* of Francisco Monroy, the father of Sonja, my little baby girl, and my *husband* of thirteen years. The chief of the civil patrol told me that I needed a `new husband' for the night, and he threatened my baby with his sharp machete. He told me I had to do what he said, or that he would kill Sonja. All through the night, he did terrible, *unspeakable* things to me. He hurt me badly. So the next morning, just after he left, I found the old lime merchant, and I became a guerrilla for the Army of the Poor."

"Lupe," the *comandante* of the Cabracán squadron of the EGP, looked up from the circle toward the Indian boy on the other side of the basket of corn. Pedro Gutierrez Suchite never spoke unless commanded to do so by his lieutenant. Lupe called to him.

"Pedro, you have a story worthy of your sacrifice. Tell us *your* story and why *you* have chosen to serve the Guerrilla Army of the Poor," ordered Lupe.

Pedro continued to stare down at the ground through his crossed forearms resting atop his knees. It would be so hard to say what he knew and had seen with his own eyes.

"What is the word from such a young *campañero*?" asked Lupe, urging the boy to unburden himself of the terrible story of his flight into the mountains.

"My grandmother, Vilma Petrona Hernandez, they killed her. She was 79 years old—maybe older—and she was very feeble." Pedro spoke softly and deliberately. "She couldn't say to them, `I am no subversive' because she has the cancer in the roof of her mouth. So, they took my grandmother Vilma Petrona, and they *nailed* her to a board and tied it up to a tree, like the Lord Jesucristo, and when they beat her with their rifles, she *died!* So they cut down the tree with my grandmother still tied to the cross beam, and they trimmed off the bottom of the tree and propped it up into a hole in the ground—just *there*, just in front of her house so that Anabella, my mother, would have to see her when she returned from the market, and she would be the first to see my grandmother stuck up next to her *own* front door."

"When my mother came back with the nets of cabbage and a chicken," said Pedro, "she dropped everything when she saw my grandmother. My mother, she just fell down into the dirt by the fence. We could just see her body jumping and jerking, her arms stretched out in front of her and her face down in the dirt, just jumping and jerking. She just lay there, her voice gurgling. Alejandro Putzeys, our neighbor, came to remove my grandmother. He had to chop the ropes that tied her up with his machete. She was—I mean her body was swollen and stiff when they took her down. *Black*—that is, most of her body was black and purple. My mother couldn't speak to anyone for many days."

Every evening the soldiers retold their stories, their horrifying testimonials to the events that had brought them together. These stories acted as reminders, but more than that, they lanced the old wounds of hate and vengeance that had driven most of them to the hills in the first place, and slowly, one by one, each combatant had come to see himself or herself in a unique relationship with this debilitating war. They were soldiers, true, and each expendable in the cause, but some would survive, and could witness the day when peace came to the Ixcán, to the Petén, Huehuetenango, to Chimaltenango and Zacapa. Perhaps they might even be a factor in the national healing. So, it was important for them to step out from their own misery and, from time to time, to watch themselves from right angles to gain the more perspective. They were not operating in a vacuum. They had a revolutionary past, a militant present, and a deeply longed-for future of peace and tranquility. But for now, they would continue to tell their stories and sing their songs of the repression and their glorious revolution.

Each guerrilla carried a special pain, but what each suffered individually, they shared, and that suffering gave them, as a revolutionary unit, a strength and resolve. The recitation of their stories also gave them patience and filled the long hours on the trail and in the mountains as they waited for their opportunity to strike a significant blow for their cause. To help them channel their grief and to outline their plans, the ragged, little band deferred to the educated among them. In short, they had adopted "Lupe" and María Paloma as their leaders.

Comandante "Lupe" was a reconstituted elementary school teacher from San Pedro Ixteucán, a small *aldea* several kilometers north of Los Encuentros on the Pan American Highway. He had studied at the more conservative and private Francisco Marroquín University for his first year but had transferred to the National University, following his girlfriend, María Paloma Escobar, another education major who, like her admirer, had vowed, somewhat idealistically, to return to Santa Lucía, her parents' childhood village, to work in the local school there.

"Lupe" and María Paloma became engaged, following the customary negotiations between the two families. The young girl had attracted the attention of the dance supervisor in the Department of Aesthetic Education in the City. María had studied dance at Escuela "Justo Benito Fernandez" and had impressed her young teacher. Featured in the lead position of the school's Christmas ballet, María Paloma had thrilled her audience and the visiting supervisor, Doña Sonia Baillez, the grand dame of student dance for more than thirty years. Doña Sonia arranged a small scholarship for María Paloma to study at the National University of San Carlos, but her budding social consciousness had widened her interests. When the army burned the church and school on the plaza of her parents' *aldea*, María Paloma determined to be a part of the school's reconstruction program. But that rejuvenated program would be postponed by the *barrera*, the great fear that came into Santa Lucía and the surrounding highlands, and the charred school house and the church remained as they were, moot reminders of the heavy repression for which there apparently was no recourse and which could be revisited upon them at any time.

Of course, María Paloma had not noticed him at first, but "Lupe" had watched María Paloma practicing dance at the conservatory and had been attracted immediately. He stayed around to talk with her after her lesson, and within a week, was seeing her at the National University almost every evening. He decided to transfer to San Carlos when travel back and forth across the City began eating into his own study time.

"Don Jorge," said Emilio de Leon, "you know that your daughter María Paloma is an angel sent from God to bless us all."

"*Sí, amigo,*" acknowledged the young girl's father. "This is true, and it is a good thing that others have enjoyed her blessings." Don Jorge was somewhat amused but flattered at this third visit of his old friend from Sololá. It was good when the young people respected the old ways enough to speak with the parents. Of course, Don Jorge was aware of his daughter's interest in the boy from Patrocinia del Quiché. He had met the boy several times when his family had come to Santa Lucía on market days to sell their pottery. He was an educated boy; he would be something. His parents were poor, and the expected dowry would probably be nothing more than an honorarium. But they had offered two sows and a first-born calf, a treasure under any terms. Of course, he would amuse his old friend, the go-between in these delicate negotiations.

"And you know very well the good faith of Don Tubercio—and two sows, the first-born of his only heifer! Well, I have to ask you, with all respect, my friend: Don Jorge, what do you say for your daughter?"

"In the name of Santa Lucía and the mother of our little angel María Paloma, I accept the generous offer of Don Tubercio. You must tell him of our desire to meet and to ask the Padre to say a Mass to bless the new union of our two families."

The marriage ceremony was orchestrated in the traditional way. At an appointed hour, one of María Paloma's uncles launched a rocket high in the sky to announce the beginning of the day's activities. María Paloma's friends went to the church to inform the priest of the impending arrival of the wedding party, a task prearranged, of course, for all details had been worked out with the priest and payments to the church collected well in advance. But the little act was part of the tradition that had been played out many times before.

On schedule the two wedding parties met at opposite ends of the plaza in front of the church. The priest walked slowly out onto the porch of the church and raised his hands, the signal for the two families to come together and to enter the sanctuary. To the squawking cacophony of the *chirimia* and the *tambor*, or drum, the two parties paraded into the church, each genuflecting just inside the door and making the sign of the cross.

Before the altar and the priest, the young couple stood, dressed in their wedding attire. María Paloma wore the long wedding *huipil* that stretched from her neckline to the floor. The ground fabric was undyed, white muslin against which paraded rows of festive animal figures—male and female—turkeys and their hens, peacocks and theirs; each was carefully brocaded with imported purple silk threads. In decades earlier, the silk threads would have been home grown on the local silkworm farms of the weavers and dyed from the *pupura patula*, a deep, royal purple dye extracted from the glands of a mollusc harvested off the coast of Nicaragua.

Over her head, María Paloma had worn the wedding *tzute*, a brilliant red square of fabric composed of two panels of backstrap cloth attached by a heavily embroidered *randa* featuring a train of white silk doves zigzagging between the two panels of cloth to make the seam. Against the red ground fabric, the same animal patterns featured in her *huipil* raced back and forth in a ritual mating parade. In an earlier time, the pattern was widely accepted as a bit of sympathetic magic intended to insure the couple's fertility and the young bride's conception of a male child in the first year of marriage.

Kneeling beside his bride, "Lupe" wore a dazzling jacket made of the same bright red ground fabric with the same silken animals trotting from row to row across his back, under his arms, and stretching to the hem lines in front. One exception in the male designs was the stalwart, noble, dark-blue deer with their parallel racks of antlers parading across the middle of the field of animals. On his head "Lupe" wore the customary clean straw hat, the traditional gift from his godfather in San Pedro Ixteucán.

In their hands the young couple carried the large wedding candles, three-inch thick tapers that towered more than three feet tall and wrapped in red and white ribbons that streamed in parallel paths down and around the candles. At the appointed time in the Mass, "Lupe" and María Paloma rose and stepped to the altar, placing their two candles before the image of Santa Lucía and the *Virgin* before taking their first Communion together as husband and wife.

An explosion of marimba and rockets greeted the wedding party as the revellers stepped out into the bright, noonday sun. The guests and family members broke into joyous dances in celebration of the new union, a fiesta in full swing as the troops approached the ridge overlooking the small village, hidden in the tree line along the summit.

The first mortar fell into the open market just to the south side of the plaza stretching in front of the church. The flash and explosion sent splintered rocks and building debris high into the air, showering the wedding party with dirt and pellets of flying stone. In the settling dust where the mortar had exploded, five bodies could be seen in clumps on the ground, flung like rags in a circle perhaps twenty feet apart. Wild wailing punctuated the canopy of clear blue sky above as the second and third mortars screamed into the plaza, one exploding near the marimba, splintering the instrument and splattering its two or three straggling players in bloody heaps against the wall of the church.

"Lupe" grabbed his bride and raced back into the church. They fled to the rear of the altar and down the steps that led deep into the old catacomb beneath the sanctuary. They forced the lock from the rusty gate that sealed off the four or five sarcophagi and raced to take cover behind the heavy tombs.

As soon as his eyes had adjusted, "Lupe" spied three deep slots carved into the mother rock that constituted the northern foundation of the sanctuary. Obviously, they had been carved out just large enough to receive the caskets of future priests that would be honored by interment within the hallowed walls of the church they had served.

"Venga aquí!" cried "Lupe," as he grabbed his bride's hand and slipped into the left slot just behind the larger of the five tombs. María Paloma stifled an urge to cry and buried her face deeply under her new husband's arm. Outside, the mortars continued to screech into the plaza. They could hear the loud, muffled explosions and the incessant wailing of their friends and families struggling to flee the area. About four or five minutes into the attack, María Paloma and "Lupe" could hear the drone of an approaching plane—a low flying plane racing toward the small village, followed by the explosion that ripped apart the church above them. The floor of the altar came crashing down around them, knocking the great tombs from their pedestals and covering the young couple with a blanket of rocks and dirt.

It was deep into the night before "Lupe" and María Paloma felt like moving. "Lupe" had been knocked out by a large block of ceiling masonry that had bounced off the tomb and landed on his back and shoulder. It was more than an hour before he regained consciousness and realized that he had not suffered serious lacerations or a broken back. Feeling was once again restored to his right leg and foot. Even with his feeling renewed, however, they had decided to avoid any movement that might attract attention. A military patrol had entered the village in the late afternoon just before sundown. The soldiers had moved from house to house, shooting at anything that moved and then set house after house on fire. After about an hour, they left in the heavy trucks that had brought them up the road to Santa Lucía. They had heard the soldiers poking around the rubble of the church, but apparently no one else had had time to seek sanctuary in the church before the bomb had destroyed it. As it turned out, the stairwell leading down into the now exposed catacomb was filled with rubble, so the soldiers had apparently decided not to risk further cave-in by venturing down into the crater of masonry and debris.

The smell of burning cane and wood still blanketed the village as the fog moved in after midnight. "Lupe" and María Paloma turned cautiously in the walled tomb and slowly began lifting out the debris that caked them. "Lupe" pushed up on his elbows and forced the large block of masonry, the one that had knocked him unconscious, up and over the edge of their receptacle. Then carefully, he maneuvered himself from the grave and lifted out his bride who fell trembling and sobbing into his arms.

Through the stench of the burning village, the couple slowly picked their way around the perimeter of the town and up into the hills overlooking the silver, smooth lake. María Paloma knew the site of a small cave where once she and her classmates had taken refuge from a driving rainstorm. There, for a few hours, they found a peace between each other and consummated their vows in the twilight of the stars.

It had not taken the couple long to find support among the cadre of guerrillas that had been working the towns in the area. Their ranks had been decimated in the last month, and only a dozen or so of the more than forty had survived, and four of them were so weak that they couldn't walk for more than an hour each day. They had been reduced to eating berries and roots, and three of them had almost died from amoebic dysentery but were slowly rebuilding their strength. María Paloma had been able to enter the village of Santo Domingo just on the other side of the mountain and had obtained some dried meat and two chickens, a small pot, matches, and a little money from her sister's god-parents. On that the ragged little band had been able to begin its restoration.

In Santo Domingo, María Paloma had been able to learn what had probably triggered the scorched earth attack on Santa Lucía. The notorious Madagascar Pecho, "El Pesado," had fingered the town as a probable community in solidarity with the guerrillas. "El Pesado" was easily the most feared *ladino* in the Department of Sololá. He was reputed to have dispatched his own parents, sister, and brother-in-law with a grenade tossed into his own boyhood home as proof solid of his allegiance to the *ejercito*. "The Heavy One" was the leader of the civil patrol in San Felipe where he ruled as a warlord over the affairs of the people. Each mysterious disappearance, each brutal attack upon the villages in the area were traceable, it was said, to Madagascar Pecho.

One particular story had sealed the *campesinos*' dread for "The Heavy One." He had put out the word that he needed a woman for the evening. He liked young teenage girls particularly. He would send word through a little runner to the family of the girl he had selected. It had become every mother's dread that her daughter might be tapped for the terrifying evening.

Madagascar Pecho weighed upwards of 350 pounds. On hot days, he would sit on the side of a 55-gallon steel drum that he had rolled up against the wall of his concrete block house and listen to his cassette tape player, the first of its kind in the village. He liked especially the disco beat of the "BeeGees," and the strains of the same three or four tunes filtered for hours across the cornfields that surrounded his house. Young girls whom he expected to attend him throughout the day and overnight were made to prepare his meals of beans, tortillas, and tamales and to bring a six-pack of bottled sodas with them in preparation for his ministrations. The bottles became instruments of his various pleasures and the terror of the young girls whom he forced—with threats to their families—to perform unnatural acts upon both him and themselves. One of the young Filipino girls had died from internal hemorrhaging after he had broken the neck of the bottle off when pounding it into her vagina.

Rumors had it that at least four families had disappeared in other villages in the last two years and that the daughters, the single survivors, had been forced out of fear to move into the awful house in the middle of the cornfield. Others said that the corn itself was supported on the blood of their lost families. "El Pesado" was a natural, initial target in the area for the Guerrilla Army of the Poor.

María Paloma had volunteered to risk her own life to assist in the attack on Madagascar Pecho. "Lupe" and María Paloma moved into a small adobe barn that had been abandoned on the property of the church in San Felipe. María volunteered as a housekeeper for Father Jack following the retirement of his elderly assistant a month before the planned assault. She had told him, somewhat truthfully, that she and her "brother" had survived the assault on Santa Lucía only because they had been out of the village on the evening of the attack. Word soon filtered throughout the village of the new housekeeper, and just as promptly, word came in a scrawled, rumpled note that the girl was to report to "El Pecho" "for questioning" on the morning of the following Wednesday.

Father Jack had managed to keep the note from María Paloma for a couple of days, but when the girl came before him trembling one afternoon, he shared with her the portentous note that he had been afraid to discard, fearful that it might resurface in the wrong hands. Father Jack called María and her "brother Lupe" into his quarters late in the afternoon to talk to them both about the dilemma. In his innocence, Father Jack explained to them the rumors about "the Heavy One," and confided in them his great anxiety about their remaining in the town. He reached into his pocket and took out a handful of *quetzales* and gave them enough for bus fare out of the village on the evening route. María Paloma and "brother Lupe" expressed their deep gratitude and took their leave with the clear understanding that they would depart the same night.

Instead, "Lupe" sent word with a young runner that María Paloma would comply with the interests of Madagascar Pecho on the next day. As the evening bus began its circuitous path out of the city, the young couple were huddled together with their confederates watching its lights trail in and around the curves of the rutted road far below them. They would have already moved down the hill behind the house of "El Pesado" before it turned completely out of sight on the far side of the lake. Of chief concern was the dog, the pet of "The Heavy One." To counter any interruption from the animal, they had made plans to lure the dog into a trap of poisoned meat, a dead rabbit whose carcass they had laced with rat poisoning that María Paloma had secreted away from the storeroom of the church.

The plan worked. Late in the evening, they removed the rabbit from a plastic trash sack and laid it on the path the animal usually took when drifting away from the house to relieve itself each evening. Almost on cue, about one o'clock in the morning, the dog stretched and ambled up the path from its place beside its master's house and soon picked up the scent. In less than an hour the dog was lying on its side among the corn rows, its legs extended and twitching, and in the final throws of its poisoning. María would approach the house just after day light almost before "The Heavy One" would have time to miss the animal, and the guerrillas would have moved in to surround the house just out of sight. Only four or five rows back from the dying dog, the guerrillas fanned out to take up positions behind the house where they could watch to see if any pre-dawn contacts with soldiers might otherwise interrupt their plan. They knew that on days that Madagascar Pecho took his girls, no soldiers or anyone else ever dared to disturb his rendezvous.

An hour before sunrise, María Paloma moved away from her husband and began to back track up the hill directly behind the house of "El Pesado" so as to avoid detection by the commander, should he, for any reason, be up and around and looking out either of the other side windows. Just as dawn was breaking, María Paloma was approaching the front of the house on the footpath that led from the road through the corn rows to Madagascar's door. Snuggled warmly in her *tzute* drawn up under her arm, she carried the customary six-pack of orange sodas. María reached the end of the path and stood at the edge of the small dirt compound that stretched from the corn rows to "The Heavy One's" door. There she would wait for his discovery.

María did not have to wait long. After the third crow of the cock behind the house, "The Heavy One" appeared in the door and looked about. He wore only a sleeveless undershirt that was rolled up over his enormous belly to suggest a bra. He spied the beautiful school teacher standing almost in front of him at the end of the compound, her face wearing an expression of meekness and submission. He liked that. Madagascar Pecho liked his girls dependent upon him and submissive to his every whimsy.

"El Pesado's" affairs with these girls would be orchestrated throughout the day. He was never in a hurry, but liked to watch their anxiety increase every time he had them approach him. He would sit against the front of the house on the steel drum and turn over his "Bee Gees" tape. He would have the girls come to him several times, and before dismissing them with some innocuous instructions, he would feel them up and have them reach below his rolls of fat to tweak his penis and caress his testicles. When he, himself, was in sufficient heat, Madagascar Pecho would order the girls to bring him two bottles of soda, cooled in the stream that ran through the cornfield, one drink for him and one for her. They would drink the sodas throughout an hour of teasing foreplay in which he would introduce the bottles. "The Heavy One" would then manage the bottles—and the girl—for the rest of the day.

"*Ah, señorita!* I see that you have come to Madagascar! And so *early* in the morning! I like that in a beautiful young girl!" exuded the commander.

Madagascar Pecho wobbled a little toward the girl who, still feigning reluctance, waited with her head slightly bowed for a second encouragement.

"Heh! heh! heh!" laughed "The Heavy One" with an expectancy justified by previous engagements. "You want old Madagascar to come to you, young one! Old Madagascar is going to `come' to you, sweet *reina*!"

The lethargic blimp turned aside and wobbled to the end of the house, looked around, and crossed to the nearest corn row. Then he turned his back on the girl and began pissing at the roots of the first stalk. Just then, a single shot rang out, and "The Heavy One" threw up his hands, wheeled backwards, and fell with a single bounce upon the ground. In a moment "Lupe" and five other guerrillas came crashing through the corn rows, joined by María Paloma who had dropped her *tzute* and rushed toward the mound of flesh, twisting and retching on the ground.

The bullet had ripped open the center of the belly, and a furious stream of black blood and bile was issuing from his bowels. Just as the guerrillas arrived, "The Heavy One" was gagging on his own blood, and his eyes were rolling wildly in their sockets. With his hands pawing the air in uncontrollable spasms, he squirmed on his back from side to side, suddenly sprouting a tremulous erection. With one well-aimed swath of his machete, a fascinated Pedro dispatched the abhorrent member with the point of his blade and pitched the violated, little prick back over his head into a corn row. Then, two black streams spewed into the dirt below him as the spasms contracted into one final seizure that sent a gasp of blood exploding from his mouth and a string of feces coiling from his anus. And just like that, it was over. Turning his face into the dirt and vomit, "El Pesado" rolled slowly on his side. His legs curled up beneath the mound of flesh and moved no more. The Guerrilla Army of the Poor had cut down the most feared demon on the mountain.

So that their act might not be confused with a common robbery and assault, the guerrilla band removed nothing from the house or compound. That single act, unviolated by semblance to any "common crime," would become the band's trademark in future assaults. The guerrillas would pick their targets with care and make sure that their act of aggression would be clearly differentiated from the banalities of the criminal.

With a corn stalk, María Paloma drew the insignia "EGP" in the dirt at the feet of "El Pesado." For a few moments still, the guerrillas savored their triumph, staring at the mute mound of death in their midst.

"`El *Pesado'* . . . `El Pesado,' *shit!*" said Monroy, and he spit an angry fountain of saliva at the purple lips of the limp giant.

"He don't look like so much now, *huh?*" said Humberto. "He won't be diddling any more chickies now, you *bet!*"

María Paloma winced at the suggestion and drew up tightly against her husband as they stood aside, wondering what to do next.

"We have to leave now," said "Lupe." "We'll go into town and talk to the *alcalde* and tell the people of San Felipe that they are free from the hands of `El Pesado.'"

The younger soldiers jumped up at the suggestion, laughing and yelling their approval.

"Let's *go!*" ordered *Comandante* "Lupe." And with that, they slipped back deeply into the corn rows.

Chapter 14

Valley Protocol

"I'm *sorry*, sir, but the Bishop is in conference this morning," said the portly Hispanic lady sitting at the antique-styled Spanish-colonial computer desk. A middle-aged woman in her early fifties, Mrs. Perez had served two previous Bishops of the diocese in the valley. She knew all about appointments and schedules, and most assuredly understood the necessities of deflecting the periodic and usually suspicious-looking drop-ins.

"What time do you expect him to be free?" asked Father Mike.

"Perhaps in about two hours," smiled Mrs. Perez. Two hours was a realistic proposal, too long to encourage them to linger, too long to put her response to the test. She returned to her keyboard. She would think of something to type that would communicate her reluctance to field further interrup-tions. The new Bishop would come to appreciate her deft defenses.

"We'll wait, then," returned Mike, winking at Marcus as he pulled the straight-back chair slightly away from the wall and under him as he backed into it. "Have a seat," he invited Marcus. "We have the time."

Fingers began to fly across the keyboard.

Father Michael Justice was a Maryknoller, a free-lancer and something of the "pariah of the parish." The young people delighted in his wit and dry assessment of Valley politics in the church. He had attracted a small coterie of young adults in their twenties who were stimulated by his direct statement and encouraged by his open challenges to the evangelical fervor that was spreading through the diocese.

A friend of Central America and Central American refugees, Mike Justice was an angry young priest who identified with "the struggle." His God was an impatient God whose children had been tested sufficiently and "were due a little grace," he liked to say in front of the Monsignor. His "brothers in Christ" understood him, and the Church hierarchy be damned.

"If he closes Casa Libertad," offered Mike, in easy hearing of Mrs. Perez, "we're prepared to open a new one with ecumenical support in San Juan."

"Do you think the Bishop actually wants to close Casa?" asked his young companion. Marcus Finley was a new reporter for the *McAllen Star*. He had moved to the Rio Grande Valley from Pasadena where he had attended community college and the University of Houston's Clear Lake campus. He had majored in public affairs and minored in journalism. Just after graduating from U of H, he had attracted some attention with an exposé he had co-authored in Pasadena on refinery pollution along the channel. He wasn't very popular with the blue-collar community that made its living off the chemical fertilizers, petroleum refining, plastics, and paper processing. He had met Father Mike at a press conference called earlier regarding the possible closure of Casa Libertad, a sanctuary house and complex in Brownsville sponsored by Catholic Charities. He was new to refugee issues and felt a little out of place and somewhat uncomfortable with the prospect of authoring a story on such a controversial issue in just his first few months on the job in McAllen. Mike had reassured him, however, with his ironic, cheery pessimism and obvious bank of knowledge that he seemed more than willing to share with the novice reporter.

"Well, probably," said Mike. "We think the INS and some `influentials' have already got a hold of him. He's not going to do anything that's in any way confrontive, and the idea of legal support for refugees has always been a little confrontive for a lot of the Anglo `pioneers' in the Valley. It's interesting how many people can live here for decades and not see anything."

"Who's the power in this area?" asked Marcus.

"Rafael Nuñez," said Mike, "and this guy's something else. His family moved into the Valley from Reynosa around the turn of the century and started buying up property for cattle grazing along the Rio Grande. It was always a matter of folklore about those cows. They'd jump river and disappear and then suddenly reappear back in Texas around `round up' and market time—just after old man Nuñez had submitted his income tax. That guy learned the system pretty well. He never paid taxes on more than a nickel's worth of his property."

"How much—what do they control today?" asked Marcus.

"*Hey!* Just step outside and look up the street. There isn't a town in the Valley that the Nuñez family doesn't have a stake in. Rafael Nuñez has been mayor of three cities at some time or other in the last thirty years. And *power!*" Father Mike smirked. "Did you hear about his speech a couple of years back at the university?

"No, I guess not," said Marcus.

"Well, Nuñez was giving a talk at the annual convocation," said Mike. "Now, you really need to get the picture: the convocation lecturer was Peter

Rustow, the Nobel Prize winner in physics back in the early sixties, and he's sitting right there on the platform with Nuñez. Well, Nuñez has been asked to present the key to the City of Edinburgh to Rustow after the talk. When Nuñez gives him the key, he just waddles on over to the podium and takes over the mike and begins extolling the virtues of the Valley, especially opportunities for investments by multinationals—the `maquilas,' you know—well, one of the young assistant professors in economics is sitting about two rows back—you're not going to believe *this!*—and asks Nuñez to explain the wage scale proposal that Cardenas's supporters were promoting."

Marcus Finley smiled with anticipation.

"This guy, Nuñez, never flinches, *right?*" gestures Mike. "He walks right over to this assistant professor and asks him his name. Then he asks him what he teaches. When the prof answered `economics,' Nuñez looks him right between the eyes and retorts, `Not any *more!'* Right *there* in front of Rustow and the whole *public!* I mean, this guy has *balls!* He doesn't answer to anybody. He brings fruit trucks and all his Mexican farmhands back and forth across the border, and as long as the trucks say `TEXAGRO' on the doors, nobody—U.S. or Mexican—says a word. This guy is in *complete* control. It wouldn't surprise me if Nuñez *himself* hasn't hand-picked this Bishop."

The fingers continued to fly across the keyboard, the clatter getting heavier and heavier. Father Mike was thirty-eight years old and was serving his third parish in ten years. Ordained at twenty-eight, Michael Emanuel Justice nurtured the tag of "trouble maker" in Church circles. "He liked to make waves," they said. "He has no respect for protocol," they said. Father Mike liked to break icons. He had grown up in the Church, but he had always seemed to resist counsel, and he had little use for administrators blind to what he perceived to be the Church's new mission. That mission had emerged from Vatican II and from 1968 at Medellín, Colombia. He had read Peru's Gutierrez in first edition and broken the spine so frequently that only rubber bands held the book from complete dispatch. He was an occasional correspondent with Boff in Brazil. He had been in El Salvador for three years and frequented the Central Highlands of Guatemala through his friendship with the late Father Bill Arnold. Bill's murder in El Quiché three years before had galvanized his solidarity with the *campesinos* no matter where he found them, and there were plenty in the Texas Rio Grande Valley who needed his support. He used every opportunity to seize attention for his passionate commitment to the refugees, even the innocence of a Marcus Finley.

The young reporter represented a new avenue for the advocate priest. Rarely, did he ever run into a reporter so "ripe and ready." Mike was eager to introduce Marcus Finley in the subtleties and the intransigence of evil in the Guatemalan culture, but he himself had no popular voice. The nuances of Central American prejudice regarding Catholic clergy extended to the United States popular perceptions as well: clergy were supposed to be concerned about man's inhumanity to man. Writing pronouncements, directives, epistles, apologies, edicts—those kinds of things belonged to the domain of the clergy as much as liturgies, the sacraments, and popular devotions. But "white papers" came from the media. It was the popular media that could turn up the heat, and if he played it right, he had a new voice in Marcus Finley.

Mike was not very sophisticated in working with the secular media. He had enjoyed only marginal cooperation in seeking previous assistance in his human rights work. More specifically—and to the point—the *McAllen Star* (and the three other newspapers in the new Taylor-Smyth consortium) had not been particularly receptive to his "Valley sniping," as one editor had confided to another regarding Mike's numerous editorial submissions. That the editor would hire a young activist reporter like Marcus Finley gave the priest at least a window of opportunity.

"If you think you want to do something—maybe a story on Guatemala after this," said the priest, "I can get you an interview with one of the most respected workers in the country down there—Father Jack Heller."

"`Heller'?" asked the reporter.

"Yeah," said Father Mike. "He's an Oklahoman diocesan priest working in San Felipe. He's been down there for a few years. I've got an American Peace Corps worker down there with him right now—Susan Simpson. She's working on an agricultural project with a couple of the experimental cooperatives. She's supposed to be there for another two years, but she may stay on longer. She's got the option for renewing her two-year hitch."

"He has connections?" asked Marcus Finley.

"`*Connections'?*" said the priest.

"Yeah—I mean, he knows enough people to get me some interviews—for the story?"

"Oh, *yes!*" said Father Mike. "I should say *so!* I've been working with him for the past five years. He knows people all over the country. And he's not new to drop-ins. He's taken two or three other Americans down there to stay on for awhile. But he's used to people coming down all the time. He's working with a small community of Mexican nuns who are helping him in San Felipe right now."

"Would I have a place to stay?" asked Marcus.

"Oh, yeah. I'm sure," said the priest. "But I can write him and let him know you're coming and how long."

"How much should I take down there with me—`money,' you know?"

"Well, maybe a thousand or so," said Father Mike. "You don't need much to stay a long time."

The priest looked at his watch and then over toward Mrs. Perez.

The clock on the secretary's desk showed 9:48 a.m. They had been waiting for almost forty-five minutes. The Bishop's schedule included Friday visits to at least one church in the diocese, a perfunctory chore at best, being the new bishop and all that. It made sense "to be present" in impression, if not in person. Those who had business knew better than to contact his office for appointments. Mike figured that the Bishop would probably be returning shortly to gather his satchel for his weekly outing.

Every line in the face of Mrs. Josefina Perez protested the presumption of the two men in her office. [Rip!] went the first page. [Rip!!!] went the second, and the third. Mrs. Josefina Perez was so angry she couldn't concentrate, but she knew better than to cross wills with this notorious little priest. She'd seen more than one like him in her three decades of service to the church. She used to let them intimidate her, but not anymore. She knew for whom she worked. Still, these . . . these `bad' priests who went around stirring up *trouble!* Well, if they kept hanging around the office long enough, they'd meet the bishop, all right, and *this* priest, for one, would get more than he *came* for!

"Good morning, Mrs. Perez," said Bishop Blanchard. "How are you this morning?" The Bishop breezed into the office, laying a copy of the *Brownsville Register* on her desk.

"Very well, Monsignor," said Mrs. Perez in a rather surly response.

"Ohhh! Some—" said the bishop. Mrs. Perez caught his eye and pointed with her pencil to the two visitors sitting on the couch behind the door.

"I'm sorry!" exclaimed the bishop. "I wasn't expecting any visitors this morning, I thought."

"I'm *sorry*, Monsignor, but . . . " apologized Mrs. Perez.

"Oh, *Father Justice,* I see!" said the bishop. "Look, Father Justice, I'm very busy this morning. I just stopped by . . . "

"*Monsignor!*" interrupted the priest. "Just a moment of your time—I'd like you to meet Marcus Finley, reporter for the *McAllen Star*."

The genial reporter reached out, pressing the bishop for a handshake which the prelate reluctantly accepted.

"Mr. Finley . . . " said the bishop.

"I'm pleased to meet you at last," said Marcus Finley. "I've heard very good things about you."

"Hmm," said the bishop.

"Yes, well . . . " continued the reporter. "Look, Bishop Blanchard, I have just one question I'd like to ask you, if you don't mind."

"*Look,*" said the bishop. "I don't mean to be rude, but check with Mrs. Perez here. She'll be happy to schedule an appointment with you. I really have to be going."

"We'll do that," interrupted Father Mike, "but we have scheduled *three* appointments in the past month only to have them cancelled at the last minute. Mr. Finley, here, has just one—"

"Well, one question, Mr. Finley," said the bishop, brushing his coat sleeve back to check his watch.

"What can you tell me, Bishop, about your plans to close Casa Libertad?"

Bishop Blanchard was clearly taken aback by the question. "I don't know what you're *talking* about, Mr. Finley. I have no plans to . . . "

"Bishop," continued the reporter, "isn't it true that the director for the INS in Brownsville has discussed the refugee center with you in just the last few—"

"Well, yes," said the bishop. "As a matter a fact, I have had several conversations with Mr. Promise—about Casa Libertad and many other topics."

"And isn't it true that Director Promise has encouraged you to close Casa?"

"We have had some serious and very frank discussions about Casa, Mr. Finley," said the Bishop, preferring obviously to dodge the details if possible.

"But to close the Casa . . . " pressed Marcus Finley.

"Mr. Finley, let me just say that . . . "

"*Bishop!*" interrupted Father Mike, "why can't you just give us a *direct* answer? Why can't you just come right out and say that you're planning to *close Casa?* It's rumored all over the Valley. It's no real secret that you favor closing the center. The only question is *why?* How can you just *come* into the Valley and, with no more experience or information about the issues here, be bought *off* by the *feds?*"

"Mr. Finley," said the bishop, "will you please excuse Father Justice and me. There are some things we need to discuss in private . . . *No*! better yet, why don't you join us. Mrs. Perez, please be so kind as to hold any calls for me. I don't want to be *interrupted*."

"Thank you, Monsignor," said Mrs. Perez. "Of *course!*"

"Gentlemen," said the bishop, indicating for them to follow him into his private suite.

"Sit down, please," said the bishop. "Mr. Finley, you're free to report anything I have to say. Excuse me just a moment while I pull some things together."

Bishop Blanchard reached into the side drawer and lifted out a folder and bulging, legal-sized envelope.

"I'm going to be very frank with you both," said the bishop. "It is my intention, gentlemen, to return this diocese to a path that reflects the *Holy See's* vision of the Church. Let me be very clear—there should be no misustanding in what I am about to tell you. The Holy Father's displeasure with the radicalization of a wide segment of the priesthood throughout Latin America has been articulated precisely and unmistakably—as has his will regarding its return to Catholic piety. The politicization of the priesthood is an abhorrent aberration that, like a cyst, has spread its roots throughout the entire body of the Holy Church. Only the most *stringent* poultice can dissolve and eradicate this putrefying cancer."

"`Liberation theology,'" said the bishop as he rose from his deeply padded leather chair, "has led only to widen the schisms that divide people and to separate them irrevocably from the ground of their faith. `Liberation theology' has led only to *more* murder, *more* bloodshed, *more* suffering on the part of the very people it has always purported to save. And *you*, Father Justice . . . *you* have continued to function under the guise of `liberation theology' from behind your sacred charge as a voice of constant disaffection and disharmony. Let me present this case. *Look!*"

The bishop opened the clasp on the large brown envelope and dumped its contents across the top of his desk. Dozens of newspaper clippings, photocopies of articles and stories, brochures, tear copies from books—obviously the product of someone's close scrutiny and consideration over an extended period of time—was reflected in the mound of materials.

"*This . . .!*" offered the bishop. "*This,* Father! All *this* speaks for itself. *Publication after publication*, each a *prostitution* of your sacred charge and office, each in the service of social ferment and political intrigue! And *this!*"

Bishop Blanchard made a flourish of the other envelope and opened it slowly for full effect. "And *this*, Father Justice, is the response of the Office of the Congregation of the Doctrine for the Faith . . . "

Father Michael Justice was stunned. He couldn't believe what he was hearing. The Congregation! The Congregation to Michael Justice! Just the idea was incredible! Nothing in his experience, nothing in his background ever anticipated a response from the Vatican! He knew what it was, of course. And this wasn't anything particularly new. His work had attracted abuse from various circles, both from within and outside the church. Every rebuke had been for him a badge of honor. He had fought and fought all his life for a more humane world and a church that was committed to social justice. He was proud that he had been a thorn, the tweak in the side of the institution that was supposed to be the model of grace and which, for him, had always fallen so short. But a letter from the Vatican? This should be good! He didn't care about the details of the next few words of this . . . this administrative toad, this ecclesiastical fool! As far as he was concerned, an admonishment from the Vatican was a sign that all his work for peace and justice had at last paid off at the highest possible levels!

" . . . your *censorship and silencing, Father!*" proclaimed the Bishop, the shadow of a scowl drifting across his face.

For a moment, Father Michael sat staring at the bishop. Then, he broke up in an outrageous laugh, slapping his knee, and rising up over the edge of the bishop's desk.

"`Censorship and silencing'?" cried the priest. "`Censorship and silencing'! Let me see!"

The bishop slowly turned the single-paragraph letter around before the gesturing priest who ripped it from the desk. Father Michael peered over the letter for a few seconds, wadded it up, and crushed it into the top of the table.

"*Censorship and silencing!*" growled the Father Mike. "Let me tell you something, Monsignor! You can take your `Opus Dei' and all that refined and reconstituted piety directly to *hell, Bishop! Who* do you think you *ar*e behind all that . . . all *that, that* diplomatic *cant*? What do you know about the lives of the people? What do you know about the suffering of the Church—I mean the *real* Church! The church whose hands bleed from daily sacrifice because the 'church fathers' are afraid that if they speak the truth in the presence of evil, they might bloody their own noses a bit! '*Censorship and silencin*g'! Really now, how do you propose to 'censor and silence' me, *Bishop?* Cut out my *tongue*—cut out my *tongue* like they do to peasant women and children, students, priests, and labor leaders down in Salvador and Guatemala? Cut out my *tongue* like they do to those who speak out against injustice and repression? Cut out my *tongue* like they do to people who speak up for the poor and the disadvantaged? Cut out my *tongue* like they do to the community leaders and human rights workers? Cut out my *tongue*—is *that* what you plan to do? Because if you don't, *Bishop!* Because if you aren't *willing*—if you don't have the personal *fortitude* to do *just that*, you pious, sanctimonious *fool!*—you'll never *'censor and silence' Michael Justice!"*

With that last rebuke of his superior, Father Michael reached back across the desk and seized the crumpled letter from the Vatican.

"Come on," said Father Mike to Marcus Finley. "I have *plans* for this!"

Then turning back to the bishop, "Haven't you ever heard of `Brer Rabbit and the *briar patch*'? This letter of censorship, Monsignor, is the one thing that is going to bring international attention to the Valley. You might just want to stay far away from your office, Bishop Blanchard, because your phone is going to start ringing off the wall! You might have a lot of explaining to do for some people a long way from here! But I'm sure the good Señora Perez, here, can handle all of that! Come *on,* Mr. Finley!"

Father Mike turned in triumph from the bishop and slapped Marcus Finley on the shoulder. "Thank you, Mrs. Perez!" said the priest as he passed the secretary at her desk. "I hope you'll have a good day and a *nice life!*"

The two walked out of the bishop's office and across the grounds to their car. "It's supposed to be snowing and icy in Washington this weekend. If this letter doesn't get me into the Senate Foreign Affairs Committee, it'll get me an audience with the *Washington Post* for sure!"

Chapter 15

Lessons of Monkey Skull

Above the *mayordomos* were the *regidores*, and beyond these trusted aldermen—among these leaders themselves—the honored *principales*, the three most respected ruling elders of the community of San Felipe del Lago. Sitting in court together on the long, unvarnished bench of the *cofradia* house, they displayed the unmistakable emblems of their rank. Around their heads and streaming over their shoulders they wore the intricately handwoven *tzutes* of hand-dyed *papura patula*—the royal purple—silk-enhanced scarves. In their weathered, right hands they held the tall, silver staffs mounted with the gilded *monstrances*—hand-beaten silver reliefs of the saints centered at the focus of radiating, gold and silver rays, glinting in the copper sunlight drifting through the doorway of the compound. On their feet, the four *principales* wore the stylized sandals, the high braces of which arched up over the back of their ankles, a pattern dating to their ancient Mayan ancestors. Seated in their positions of responsibility, the *principales* and their court governed through consensus, receiving in order each petition of the Felipinos waiting patiently for their hearings before their village elders, and handing down their judgments in every arena of religious and social obligation laid upon them.

For more than 1,000 years, according to the ancient stories of the community, the ruling body of San Felipe had gathered at the sacred places, generation by generation, passing the *barras,* their staffs of office, to those assuming new ranks and positions of honor and responsibility.

Through the orderly service to their various *cargos*, the *alcaldes* held the community together, both politically and religiously, orchestrating the services and ceremonies of the several *cofradias*, the religious duties of which dominated much of their social activity. Some devotional, in fact, was prescribed daily as obligatory homage to designated Christian saints as well as to the ancient deities of the Maya highlands which still jealously commanded their uncompromised allegiance.

The ancient gods were as old as the mountains that surrounded Lake

Atitlán. They were, in fact, the very spirits of the mountains themselves, and of the streams, and the trees. Gods inhabited the promontories and little peninsulas. Every path had a soul; likewise, every lookout, and every cavern. Deities drifted just under the surface of the water or slept under the hillocks of maize in the *milpas*. They floated through the air, sweeping away or gathering up the clouds. They bellowed petulantly in claps of thunder and flashed in the streaks of lightening around the summits of the volcanoes late in the evening, threatening those who might somehow have disturbed them rudely during the day.

And there were yet other gods—those spirits ripped from their natural moorings and captured in the carvings and statues, or locked in the little clay figurines shaped by the priests who had conjured the spirits unaware. The Lacandón priests to the north fashioned great clay god pots, formed little faces on the sides, and placed them in rows on racks in their thatch-covered god houses. Day by day, the Lacandón priests retrieved the appropriate pots and served them a stew of incense and candle wax. Old Mateo Chanking, the withered Lacandón—in his white *topee* and stringy, black hair—communed with his pots, negotiating privileges or scolding them for favors unrewarded. For those god pots most recalcitrant, the priest would rip them from their honored places in the god house, dispatching them to the roadside stands above the village for sale to the first travelers who might come along. No penalty more repugnant could be imagined for a failed deity than to be banished among the tourists.

The shamans of the *naturales* passed on their precious collections of little jadeite or clay gods from generation to generation and maintained their altars and shrines high in the hills above the village. In the caves of San Jorge across the lake, they would gather every eighteen days of the twenty-month Mayan year for services before day break, sacrificing turkeys and hens, and divining the entrails of the same. Every ceremony was an appeal to *El Díos Mundial*, the World God, that commanded great respect and attention among the Felipinos who had kept their traditional faiths. They trusted their shamans to maintain the spiritual equilibrium of their universe. Through the proper rituals, madness might be diverted, and the warm, life-giving forces coerced in dissipating deathly cold. The evil eye could be turned inward on its perpetrators, and good fortune coax the flow of the divining seeds across the seer's table. To the *naturales*, the gods lived and worked among them, and they took every pain to acknowledge them, burning their candles daily according to ancient *costumbre* of San Felipe. No obligations were more seriously ministered than those honoring their gods.

Before the colonization and the Christian evangelization of "San Felipe," city leaders and their charges always met at the top of the hill overlooking their Mayan city of Uxpatán where the ancient idols had been transported on *paseos*, small, richly carved wooden platforms, resting on the shoulders of the *rezadores, the prayer makers*. There, at the appointed site, the wooden statues were placed behind the *quemador*, or burning place, and presented gifts of life—the sacrifice of selected fowls and the burning of *copal pom*, a thick piñon resin extracted from the pom tree, and green twigs collected from the huge ceiba tree in the center of their plaza.

Many of them venerable even before the arrival of the Spaniards, ceiba trees were sacred throughout the Maya world, and the giant ceiba of San Felipe was one of the largest, measuring more than fifty meters around with branches extending completely over the plaza and beyond the small stalls that sprouted and disappeared each market day under its protective shade. Lovers might dally in its late evening shadows, but children told stories about horrible, frightening sightings under the old tree late at night, images and happenings reputedly dating to the mythical age of Cuchmaquic, old "gather blood," and the other Lords of *Xibalba*, the underworld, and his daughter Xquic, or "little blood," when Hun-Hunahpú—his severed skull hanging from the branches of the ceiba—seeded the earth with his potent spittle. One of the oft repeated rumors reported the laughter of the ghost of Generalisimo Francisco Palma as he dispatched the Indians of Salomá. Another recorded the rumbles of the ancient ball game deep in the earth beneath its roots.

The old men of the town recounted other traditions, sometimes repeating the horrible death of the Maya priests who were stripped and then slain by the marauding Spanish who hung their flayed skins to dry over the lower limbs of the tree, and how under its shade much later—sometime around the turn of the century—the Felipinos had drafted their plans for attacking the *ladinos* who used to steal from them along their paths.

These ancient gods and their myths were familiar to the Tzutujiles who kept them alive in their consciousness through the endless cycle of their storytelling, governed by the movement of their calendar, the Sacred Round. On the peaks of the mountains or at turns in the rivers, in a clearing here or there in a *milpa*, the shamans would clear a place on the ground, unfold their bundles, and set up the little figurines before them. Beginning the chants, they would call the gods before them to those very spots of now consecrated earth, set momentarily apart for their sacred devotionals. They would call upon the gods in reference to their various duties, recounting from the old, familiar legends. Gesturing from side to side to those Felipinos in their service, the shamans would remind their supplicants of their duties—respective to the particular god and their requests—and advise them frequently in aphorisms that helped fix for their clients the specific functions of the various deities addressed. The familiar stories and sayings were then easily transmitted from the mountain shrines, down the steep paths, and into the domestic settings where mothers could admonish their young sons and daughters:

"As Puc'ah Maquix, the goddess of the field reminds us, my sweet princess: remember the elders who have come before and to learn from their wisdom, my little bird," María Xquic de Xoy would tell Lucita María, her eldest who seemed to shrink from duties whose instructions she hadn't clearly understood or might be reticent to accept.

"Study the ways of *Xibalba*, Miguelito," admonished María, "so that old `blood chief' won't *trick* you and steal your heart in a *gourd!*" And the paunchy little five-year old, already twice the size of his village comrades, would stare at his mother in wide-eyed distress that sometime in the night he might lose his heart or awaken with his head swinging from the branch of a tree.

Some years later, María would educate her daughters as she had her sons before.

"Why do rats' eyes stick out, Ana Fabiola?" demanded an irate María Xquic, cornering her pouting little daughter whom she had caught whipping the cat with a swath of sugar cane. "Because—are you *listening* to me, Ana Fabiola? Are you *listening* to me, or would you like to explain yourself before old `monkey skull,' who would like to swing you high up into the trees! Old `monkey skull' knows how to treat little girls who *whip the cat!* And then to *lie* to your mother, when you're standing there with the cane in your hand! Why *Ana Fabiola!* Look at the eyes of the *rat* that lied to the magic twins!" Her mother rolled her eyes back in her head and projected them forward up under her eyelids to affect the appearance of the protruding sockets of the rat.

And a terrified little Ana Fabiola would flee into the corn stalks, wailing for her father or Tanolito or Miguel Mapa to save her from old `monkey skull' and the curse of the bulging eyes.

The lore of the ancients registered in the simple terror and astonishment of the children who learned early the necessity of keeping strict attention to the machinations of the unseen world, a universe that bristled in their imaginations. They learned to be alert always to the pesky spiritualities that might jump them at any moment on a trail or trip them and send them tumbling into the *cenote*. Without any warning, even the family pet, afflicted with the spell of some deadly spirit, might turn on them and hex them with the evil eye. The gods dwelled among them, sitting in court at the corners of their experiences, their exploits chronicled and catalogued, and recited in a vibrant, living tradition and cloaked in layers of folk belief and ritual that defined each Mayan in his or her identity, place, role, and time.

The family of the gods was extensive and their service exhausting, but among the Felipinos, no fixture in the pantheon of the underworld gave them more cause for alarm—especially among the youngsters—than the presence of the idol, *Maximón*. An ancient, carved idol, the *Maximón* of San Felipe del Lago was the fact of the evil underworld in their very midst from which there was no escape and from whose attention there was no recourse.

Not, of course, to be confused with the *Maximón* of Chimaltenango, the *Maximón* of San Andrés Itzapa, the *Maximón* of Patzún, the *Maximón* of Xejajabi de Tecpán, the *Maximón o*f San Jorge la Laguna, the *Maximón* of Concepción, of Nahualá, of Santa Catarina Palapó, San Andres Xecúl, Zunil, and Patulul, the *Maximón* of San Felipe del Lago was the fearsome manifestation of their belief, the nexus of all their ancient folkways and history.

For as long as any Filipino could remember, the celebration of *Maximón* coincided with the traditions of the Christian Holy Week. In the procession of the Christ during *Semana Santa*, the *Maximón* was mounted atop a crystal casket and bedecked with streams of flowers. On Good Friday the *Maximón* and the *Cristo* were paraded side by side, led by the *alcaldes* of their respective *cofradia*s. Some obscure tradition attached the *Maximón* to the disciple Judas Iscariot, but rather than abusing the traitor—as a more orthodox Christian posture adopted in other cultures, the *Maximón* was hailed and feted throughout the course of *Semana Santa*.

The *Maximón* was still, by far, then, the most feared of the ancient gods which retained a center of spiritual prominence in the San Felipe community. For more than two hundred years at least, the ward of the *Cofradia of Santa Cruz*, the *Maximón of San Felipe* had been carved from a single block of a hard wood and stood about four feet tall. It wore a handwoven *traje*, or ensemble. Its trousers were constructed from two backstrap-woven panels—narrow purple stripes running the length of the legs to wide bands of embroidered animal figures parading in three files or rows just above the bottom edge. Supporting the pants was a typical leather belt accented by a *capixay*, a square piece of checkered, brown woollen cloth that draped over the belt and hung down to the knees of the pants. Its long-sleeved shirt was backstrap weaving of *jaspe*—tie-dyed yarns with alternating bands of white and color, configured into designs of lyres or alternating animal and human block forms. Their corners tied to a silver ring around the idol's neck, more than thirty multi-colored rayon head scarves completely masked the shirt and most of the trousers, leaving exposed only the head and the black, polished shoes. Over its wooden pate, the *Maximón* wore two *sombreros*, one nested into the other, with several scarves dangling in back from between the two wide, black brims. From its carved-out mouth protruded a fat cigar.

Of the native wooden figure itself, only its austere, sinister face was visible. In contrast to the fine, polished carvings of the Catholic saints and other pious icons that line the alcoves of the church's sanctuary, the *Maximón* was fashioned for some inscrutable purpose of its long-forgotten sculptor. The idol was, to be sure, a primitive form, and to the outsider, only crudely finished. The face was splintery. The eyes, only roughly shaped ovals, were set adjacent and to either side of the straight profile of the nose that extended away from the face not more than a quarter of an inch at the base. Notches sliced around the perimeter of both eyes suggested crudely fashioned eyelashes; the same gouges ringed the hollow mouth, something hardly more than a half-inch wide hole carved several inches down into the head through which *aguardiente* was poured during ceremonies of worship and healing.

Of all its reputed acumen, the *Maximón of San Felipe del Lago* was most respected as a deity of immense healing power. Day after day, the "traditionals" among the Felipinos sought solace and relief from a plethora of ailments. Hour by hour, they lined up outside the door of its chapel in its adopted compound for that year, waiting their turn to be presented before the idol and ministered to through its priest and his assistants. Don Andres Menchu was the *jefe maximo*, the chief or head priest for the *Maximón of San Felipe*. From the New Year's Day procession of the *alcaldes* to the last, terrible five days of the Mayan Sacred Round, Don Andres Menchu kept his solemn *cargo* to Maximón by which he held at bay the whimsical wrath of this evil deity, maintaining the very fate of his village. No man bore a more solemn responsibility than Don Andres Menchu Xoy, the priest of *Maximón*, an undisputed honor that apparently had been established by the gods themselves.

What had singled out Don Andres from the other priests were the voices, generally acknowledged by all Felipinos as a spiritual gift. In his early childhood, Don Andres had first heard his voices. Initially, he attached nothing particularly special to them, and during his first years, the voices were as much a companion as the little friends whom he chased up and down the streets and through the cornfields. It was when he was about seven years old that his father happened upon a "conversation" between Andres and what he assumed at first were his village school mates. The little boy seemed to be entertaining an invisible host in a lively exchange just as his father, Don Pablo, returned from the fields. What his *campesino* father overheard was startling and terrifying.

"I want the *green* rock! I want the *red seeds!*" said young Andres. "I want the *bag* and the *red seeds* and the *green rock!* I want the *bag* there in the *dark!* You give me the *bag* with the green *rock* and the red *seeds!* You can keep the big egg, the big egg there under your arm. Let go of the *bag!* Give me the bag from your cold, black *hand!*"

Don Pablo fell back from the door. What he had heard was impossible. The "bag" and the "red seeds," the "green rock," the "bag there in the dark"—the images were impossible for young Andres to know, let alone to comprehend, for these were sacred relics of the grave that Don Pablo himself had placed in the cold, steel grip of his father's corpse before interment in the San Felipe graveyard more than twenty years before his son was even born.

It was to the cemetery that Don Pablo fled.

"What if *somehow* . . . what if *someone* had disturbed his father's *grave!* What if the sacred relics of the grave had been *removed* . . . or worse *yet!* What if they had been *stolen?*" queried an anguished father as he raced through the streets of San Felipe, beyond the city gates, and up the hill toward the graveyard.

Out of breath, his heart beating furiously, and on the edge of physical collapse, Don Pablo was shocked to find the cemetery quite peaceful and intact. The tranquility only raised his suspicions, however, that the apparent orderliness masked a heinous injustice and sacrilege to the memory of his father. As he approached the cemetery entrance, his exhausted run tapered into a staggered, broken walk, and just inside the archway, Don Pablo collapsed in the damp grass beside a crumbling tomb. He pitched backwards into its shadow, grabbing at his chest which was heaving in deep spasms. He tore at his shirt and rolled over on his side, struggling to regain his breath. Soon the heavy pitching subsided, and Don Pablo began a long, though labored recovery.

After a few moments of frenetic gasps, Don Pablo sat up on his elbows and then clutched the corner of the tomb beside himself and pulled himself up into a sitting position once more. From his upright position, Don Pablo could look far up the hill through the graves that stretched before him. He would find his father's now and check it out. He was worried; he halfway expected to find the sarcophagus opened and the elements of the grave long since removed. As he came closer and closer to his father's tomb at the rear of the cemetery, he discovered, however, that such wasn't the case after all; that, in fact, everything seemed in perfect order.

Don Pablo stood looking down at the crest of the low tomb before him, a concrete case half buried in the ground, its vaulted top six to ten inches higher than the few vagrant weeds that had grown up around its perimeter since his last visit. Nothing seemed amiss. Nothing suggested any of his suspicioned foul play, but how was that possible? He thought of what he had heard from his small son with his own ears. He hadn't made up any of it any more than, as clearly now, his father assuredly was in the grave before him.

"But what *if . . .!*" thought Don Pablo. "What if he was *wrong!* What if somehow the remains of his father had been spirited away? What if, in fact, his father's body was nowhere near or gone forever, the tomb's surreptitious secret the emptiness which it now guarded before him. There was no alternative: he must have the grave exhumed.

For the moment, Don Pablo stared at the exposed surface of the tomb as if trying to penetrate the bricks and mortar to peer into its very depths.

"*No!*" he thought to himself. His fears were only tricks. Had he not visited the tomb almost every month since his father's death? Of *course!* Then there had to be some other explanation. For a few moments, he rested beside the grave of his father, picking at the few weeds within his reach. Then, Don Pablo rose, turned slowly, and began to retrace his steps through the graves.

"And the *egg*, the big *egg!*" thought Don Pablo. How could his little son know about the *egg?* How could a little boy—just a *small* boy and so *young!* How could he know of such a thing! The contract of a turkey egg in the mysterious ritual of a dying *brujo* was probably the most personal expression of a man's faith at the end of a long life in the service of the gods and his people. Surely, his young son was gifted. It was less than a year that Don Pablo also confirmed his son's *regalo de los luminos sagrados*, the "gift of the sacred lights."

Only in the most holy messengers were both the voices and *los luminos sagrados* confirmed in a single person. By traditional belief, such lights were the faint shadows of the dead. Any claims to such illuminations were to be entertained with critical skepticism and investigated thoroughly, for they were much too serious to be regarded lightly. When questioned sternly by "Tata" Joaquim (Don Gebrew Joaquim X'úm), and the other *alcaldes principales* of his father's generation, little Andres spoke of the *luminos azules*, the blue lights, in the room just over his shoulder and behind him. After the "blue lights" had appeared, the voices became strong enough to be understood. The innocent boy—too young, the *alcaldes* believed, to have pretended such wonders—was undeniably gifted. Little Andres was obviously blessed with some strange and awesome power in his short experience. No man among them could remember—had even heard such a thing in his or another village.

Andres began to sense the uniqueness of his gifts, he revealed before the council of *alcaldes* some years later, only after he confessed "seeing the lights" during a ceremony before *Maximón*. At that time, before the *alcaldes principales* and the young initiates of the *Cofradia of Santa Cruz*, Don Andres would recall softly, almost imperceptibly, the early visitation of the lights as "faint, bluish halos"—the indistinct outline of faces—which had drifted across the back of his shoulders and flickered down his arms. He described, also, urgent but likewise unintelligible voices whispering to him from somewhere behind his head as his late uncle, also a priest of the solemn idol, petitioned the austere *Maximón* on behalf of a client. It was about six months before she died: Doña Lupita, a withered, old crone, had come to seek relief from debilitating arthritis in just about every joint of her body. As his uncle had approached the climax of the ceremony, Andres remembered a tingling sensation that raised the hair on his neck, and he felt a cold chill tremble along his arms. He had actually seen the faint, blue veils of light drifting off his shoulders and down his arms. As "Tata" Joaquim passed the *chachales*—the hand beaten, silver-beaded Indian necklaces, over and over her beleaguered limbs, Andres felt a tingling beneath his scalp and down his shoulders and then heard faint, undecipherable, but nevertheless insistent whispers behind him.

For the first few years of his service in the *cofradia*, Don Andres experienced only sporadic visitations. As he grew in his patronage of *Maximón*, however, the apprentice priest was able to commune spontaneously and upon command with his spiritual hosts. Sometimes in the litany of a prayer, the voices would spew from his own tongue, often in ejaculations of strange-sounding communications that sent all those around him to their knees in awe and wonder. The voices set the young priest apart from the rest of the hierarchy of leadership in the *cofradia* and spread his reputation as a shaman, or traditional priest, soaring among the pines and over the steep mountain passes throughout all the surrounding villages.

"They say Don Andres has the gift of *spirit voices!*" whispered Colata Toj, the old weaving merchant on the plaza of San Felipe.

"They say Don Andres communes with Generalisimo Francisco Palma and the spirit of his father, *Don Pablo!*" said Tata Paco and Sylvia Perez.

"It is not good for one man to stand apart, but who can say to the spirits—the spirits come and go and select this man or that," complained old Ramundo C'Jux, an *alcalde* in the competing *Cofradia of San Augustine*.

"*Madre de Díos!* Don Andres is surely a man of *god!*" said Señora Mañuela Duda, as, bowing her head in deep reverence, she crossed herself over the forehead, the shoulders, and then her heart.

From his tenth year, young Andres took his education in the salons of *Maximón* and with the legions of the *Cofradia of Santa Cruz*. He began his apprenticeship as an *alguacil*, a runner and custodian of the compound with its four concrete-block buildings, otherwise a private homesite of Don Mateo X'új, one of the most revered among the *mayordomos* and an *alcalde primero* for more than a decade.

The highest honor for an *alcalde* is to have his homesite selected as *la casa sagrada*, the "holy house," set aside for a year of service to the *Maximón*. Don Mateo had worked through the stages of his *cargo* and, upon selection among the *alcaldes*, had registered his compound for official consideration as a *casa sagrada*. Then he went to work. He was one of the first among the *naturales* who had dared enter into contractual arrangements with the few *ladinos* who had settled in San Felipe during the past two decades. He negotiated a partnership with Jesse Mendoza, a *ladino* who had opened a freight line between the lake area, Xéla, and Huehuetenango. Don Mateo arranged the labor for loading and unloading produce and built storage facilities for fresh vegetables. All proceeds from the storage were dedicated to the *Maximón* and the *Cofradia of Santa Cruz*. The bulk of profits from his labor pool Don Mateo set aside for the year when the *cofrades* would accept his offer for use of his compound.

Apprentice Andres Menchu Xoy watched at the gate of the complex as the *paseo* bearing the image of *Maximón* crossed into the home site of Don Mateo, supported in procession by the files of the *rezadores*, the *alcaldes*, the *mayordomos*, and their acolytes—the *regidores*. Following in the court came the members of the women's auxiliary and the population of the *cofradia* membership and other Felipinos, hangers-on who always arrived for the inevitable *fiesta*.

No other day among the Maya quite matches *la día fiesta*. At 6:00 a.m. rockets streak into the air and explode high above the *aldeas* to mark the beginning of activities. Every quarter hour, the church bells clap their frenetic call to the faithful. Around the village, marimba music erupts in festive rhythms that break the lethargic tone set by the formality of the processions. Couples of men and others of women respond to the familiar and favorite *sons*, dancing the slow, simple two-steps learned as children at the heels of their parents and passed along from one generation to another. Metal caps twist and pop from bottles of *aguardiente*, as the men begin a serious contemplation on an evening of rededication, hallowed, of course, by deep swigs of the potent brew offered as a greeting between each of the *cofrades*. By early afternoon, their intoxicated, limp bodies are slumped against walls of the *tiendas*, under the eaves of the houses, or even stretched out in the middle of the street. Engaged in a continuous stream of community chitchat, the women gather around the steaming pots of tamales, while the souls of their inebriated husbands fly into the mountain tops to commune with the *dueños de las montañas*, the mysterious owners of the mountains and the mighty Mayan powers of destiny. In the *casas sagradas*, clouds of incense billow around the base of *Maximón* as devotees await their turn to present their petitions through the priests and their assistants who interpret the enigmatic god's every whimsy. Season by season, the *Maximón* is marshalled by its constabulary, and year after year, the devotees flock to its shrine to submit their humble requests for its solace and support.

Fiesta day means more, however, than "party." *La Fiesta* is also a solemn occasion for taking stock of one's *cargo* and for reinforcing relationships within the community that are so essential in subsistence economies that follow the demands of seasonal cycles. On fiesta day, women gather in their respective auxiliaries, and while their hands are busy patting out the mounds of tortillas that will be devoured during the day, they are careful to exchange respectful greetings to the elders who among them take their places as acknowledged matrons of honor within the designated kitchens. No one has to remind the women of their responsibilities relative to their ranks or stations, activities which they have observed generation by generation at the skirts of their mothers and grandmothers before them.

Up before the others, the newly appointed assistants in the auxiliaries have been gathering the stands of sugar cane, grinding the corn, cleaning the hearths, and sweeping the streets. Those of higher station arrive, knowing full well that the earlier preparations have been completed and that they may proceed with the making of the tortillas, the ceremonial tamales, and gallons of *batido*—a fermented chocolate drink used to honor the patron saint, San Felipe, following the procession of his image from the sanctuary.

The older women of station have likewise kept their *cargo* in honor of the saints. They have worked for weeks to complete the ceremonial *tzutes*—small, handwoven panels of fabric with carefully fashioned images of the *naguales*—the animal soul mates—of the village, each figure brocaded in the finest silk available from the *ladino* merchants upon their return from the Mexican frontier.

By 9:00 a.m., all preparations have been completed, and both the men and the women return to their respective chapels to witness and participate in the passage of the saints to their respective *casas sagradas*, or holy houses, where they shall be awarded the annual tributes of thanksgiving and prayers for blessings in the coming year.

The Felipinos have always adored their religious relics. Young girls look forward to the third and fourth stations of their *cargo*—somewhere between their fifteenth and twentieth year when, like their mothers before them, they are appointed as keepers of the images. Every day for three to five years, the women of the third and fourth stations will gather at the churches to sweep the altars, to dust the images, and to clean the ceremonial garments of their beloved icons. Devotedly—and in the privacy of the sanctuaries—they whisper softly to their images, greeting them as sacred friends and confidantes. The ears of the idols indulge all the little incidentals of the women's lives in their families, the small communities of their associates in the village, and within the *cofradia*. Periodically, these statues are charged with the keeping of grave secrets, the little passions and jealousies, and sometimes the particulars of even private vendettas that both intimidate the women and keep the various factions of their village segregated and at times belligerent.

On fiesta day, then, each woman accompanying the *paseo* of her *santos* reconfirms both her social as well as her very private relationship with the spirit of the saint. With every *quetzal* donated to the *cofradia*, the supplicants are careful to keep their secrets secure, while under their breath they entreat their spiritual partner's continuing allegiance for the coming year.

Like the women, Maya men live in accordance to the cycle of religious duties that are some of the most solemn responsibilities of a lifetime. Rank among the women corresponds with the placement of their husbands in the *cofradias*. Upon recommendation of a sponsor, the men enter the hierarchy of *cargos* at the age of fifteen. Their first responsibilities are educational; they must complete a series of courses in which they are instructed in the calendar of obligations, the ritual litanies and prayers, the levels of authority and their respective responsibilities, and their exercises in the service of the *mayordomos* and the *regidores* to whom they are assigned a period of assistance and apprenticeship. It was at such an instructional meeting, that Andres Menchu Xoy experienced from among his own peers the anointment as *compañero sympatico*, a title that he held deeply to his heart.

The voices and lights made Andres Menchu Xoy a wonder among the other apprentices. He was always reluctant to talk of them for fear that someone might say, "Andres is proud! Andres Menchu Xoy thinks he is better than his peers!" He could never have suffered such shame for himself or his family. Still, people learned early to respect his reputation if not his exhibitions, for he harkened to the voices only in the service of others.

"He is a fine young man," said Doña Ester.

"Yes," agreed Doña Francesca. "He will make some Felipino *reina* a lucky husband. How many young girls could ever hope to marry a seer like Andres? No. He'll make a fine husband, *indeed!* And who will stand against such a family as *that!*"

Even before the homely girl had ever seen the famous apprentice priest, María Xquic had heard the tales of the awesome visitations of Andres Menchu Xoy. She had never met him, however, until one day in the town she spied him on the plaza, eating an *elote* beside the bins of freshly cooked corn-on-the-cob. Then, the strange young man, some seven years her senior, only smiled as the frail, little girl took water from the town hydrant. María had never forgotten the energy and excitement she drew from that one moment in his presence.

As a young girl, María Xquic was shy around boys, deeply embarrassed by prominent physical abnormalities. Because she had been born almost a month prematurely, she had grown up a slight, tiny child with something of a limp, and therefore she was unable to participate in the heavier work and play of many of her friends. Compounding her difficulty in size and carriage, during infancy, María had suffered lesions on her arms, chest, legs, and face from malnutrition. Upon healing, the lesions had left the little girl permanently scarred with light patches of skin over much of her frail body. But María was a bright girl, and she learned to compensate in ways that won for herself the modicum of respect she so deeply craved.

As she grew older, María drew strength from her ability to weave master works of precise patterns and embroidery that set her loom apart from that of every other girl in San Felipe. Word spread to regular buyers from the shops far across the lake in Panajachel and Sololá. She had been surprised one morning to find a German couple asking about her work. She had nothing completed to show them, but they gave her an order for five *huipiles*, almost a year of work for the young girl. That contract and a subsequent one the following year confirmed her growing reputation in the region and shut down more than ten years of mean whispers and humor about the little "marked" girl.

By the time she was sixteen, María Xquic had managed to corner enough respect and admiration that she was no longer too shy to be seen in the market. Nevertheless, she was resigned to the belief that she would never know the face of a man. She knew that as long as her weaving could sustain her, she would be accepted unquestionably by the community, but she knew also that if she should lose the ability to maintain herself economically—if she should suffer, for instance, from some crippling or debilitating disease—then, as an unmarried woman without the support of a primary extended family, she would be an outcast, a person seen as a burden and a curse to her community.

María remembered "Doña Estúpido"—as the young girls had so cruelly tagged the unfortunate spinster of San Felipe. In the face of her community's ostracism, she had committed suicide, drowning herself in the throes of the *Xocomíl*, the fierce wind storms that wrack the lake each afternoon in the summer months, making navigation in the small, unstable *cayucos* impossible. Adrift on her own sea of shame, the old lady shoved out far into the middle of the lake, against the blackened, churning waves, never to return. If such cruel rejection were to be her own fate, María would probably have to leave the village to seek employment as a maid or cook in some *ladino* home, perhaps even as far away as the capital. The thought of such a prospect frightened her, for she knew how fickle the health of a *naturale* could be, even when one faithfully observed her *cargo* and *costumbre*.

The fear of never marrying and raising a family drove María more deeply into her weaving. Hour by hour, she would sit silently in the shadow of the eave of her family's house, her mottled face in the shade, her loom and frantic, little hands in the bright sunlight working the pick in and out the sheds of the warp, creating the intricate, tiny stick figures of birds and human forms with her mother's own bone needle. Lost in the intricacies of her work, María could pass the hours without a trace of thought for her future. Among her friends, however, she was not so easily distracted.

From the time she was thirteen or fourteen, the primary concern among her friends were the boys and those most eligible, to their own ways of thinking, for marriage. It was not unusual for a girl to be married by the time she was fourteen or fifteen, and for a girl to enter her twenties without serious considerations for matrimony meant, for some, an embarrassing social stigma. For some young women, unable to bear the shame, the single life meant ultimately a self-imposed banishment from the village, often to a life of housekeeper among *ladino* tenants in larger, mixed communities. In other—less fortunate—cases, girls were known to have been forced into prostitution and a life on the streets. Once such a rumor had been established—much less confirmed—those girls would never be welcomed into their villages again.

At first, María feigned delight in "boy talk" among her peers. To keep face, she would giggle with the others when the names of certain boys were mentioned and echo the other girls who went so far as to single out particular young men for their prowess. The best catches were always those who had a good work ethic and who demonstrated their physical strength in the natural course of the day's activities. Girls considered silly boys as "show offs" (or worse!)—perfect material for the military draft! As she anticipated her future, no girl really ever pictured herself married to a soldier except those girls who had been seduced by enticing images of the *ladino* lifestyle. Soldiers who had been forced to enter the *ladino* world—perhaps at the expense of their own village's *costumbre*—represented a passage out of the austere and difficult world of the *naturales*.

Otherwise, marrying a soldier usually meant being ostracized by the older members of the community. Any girl, it was thought, could catch a *soldier*. The pariahs of their own villages, young men so unfortunate as to be drafted were considered dirty and used. Certainly, no young man compromised in any way by his stint in the military would ever be considered for appointment among the higher ranks of the *cofradias*. Worse, they might never be welcomed home if it were learned that they had performed acts of violence that went against the codes of the village. The histories of the young soldiers were inscrutable and risky. No girl would want to settle for a former soldier. There were *stories*.

Under Ubico's tyranny, village girls were often forced by the soldiers to attend special "parties" given by the dictator for his elite corps of personal guards. Dressed in their best village attire, the girls would be paraded in "style shows" and chosen for the evening's entertainment. Many of the young girls so selected never returned home. There were many stories.

As she grew older, however, María became more cautious about her remarks. Inwardly, the plain, little girl was frantic and frightened, and she often fought to hold back tears as her friends filled more and more of their conversations with eager stories of love and marriage. Friend after friend fell away from the childhood group as they entered the various stages of courtship. One by one, María watched her closest companions drift from the circle of playful confidantes to accept their places beside their young men. From a distance, María began to witness the wedding processions of her former playmates, and sadly she resigned herself to a life of the spinster, a widow only to her fading dreams. It was not surprising that she all but fainted away when one evening her father informed her of a petition he had received on her behalf.

"*What,* papa!" María exclaimed.

"Yes, *reina*, my precious little princess, it is *true*," explained her secretly delighted father, Don Vincente Marcos Xquic, outwardly, however, feigning distress and deep concern. "I have received this very day an inquiry regarding your hand. Of course, you understand my shock and surprise. Why, I had no idea that some *tigre* was lurking under the very eaves of my house to pluck the brightest chick from the nest. Ah! *Madre de Díos*! What can a poor father do to save his family always under assault from those lions that would rip from his heart the seat of virtue of his very *soul!*"

Don Vincente was about to make too much an issue over the whole affair, and he began to back off from his protestations, worried that he might have overplayed his part. María, however, was never so much aware. Her heart was full and overflowing for the first time in her life. She sat stunned before her father, her head bowed, masking a grin that spread across her face. The fragile little girl had to clasp her hand over her mouth to keep from bursting with joy.

"But *who?*" she wondered. "Who is the person who would seek out a poor little weaver?"

And then she panicked! Certainly, it would not be the crazy son of Don Fernando, not the one given to the strokes of madness that sent him tumbling into the streets without warning. Certainly not the one who would drool from the corner of his mouth during class. Certainly *not*, this same Jaime T'uj who once dropped his pants in the middle of the morning lesson by the new *ladino* teacher on his first day at the village school!

"Oh, Lords of *Xibalba!*" cried María, deep within her pounding, little heart! "Let it be anyone but the *crazy* one!"

Certainly, this was not some kind of joke!

"Oh, let it not be some awful joke played upon such an unfortunate one as I!" she pleaded. "Spare me, *Madre de Díos*, oh Holy *Vírgin!*" prayed María. "Let it be anyone but the *crazy one* who dropped his pants before the new *ladino maestro*.

". . . if you have been with someone such as *this!*" demanded her father, obviously speaking to a young daughter otherwise preoccupied.

"I . . . I . . .," stammered María, suddenly aware of her father's concern.

"Is it?" asked her father.

"Is it . . .?" repeated María.

"*`Is it?' `Is it?'*" repeated her Father, knowing full well of his young daughter's embarrassment. "*`Is it?'* she asks her own *father!* Would a daughter *mock* her old *father?"* he pretended to scold her.

"Oh, *no!* Father!" responded a sobered little girl. "*No!* Of *course* not, Father!"

"Listen to me, my little bird . . . my little weaver bird who brings such acclaim by her loom to her poor Maya family," soothed the flattered, old man. He could no longer maintain his composure at what was for himself also a very happy moment.

"Does a little weaver bird know of any young lad in San Felipe who might have an interest in a poor father's little daughter?" queried Don Vicente.

So, it was a *Felipino*, to be sure, thought María.

"*No,* Father! I have no knowledge! How *could* I, Father? I work, as you know, here with Mother. My friends, they have all gone to other things, and I am busy every day at my loom. Every *day*, Father! *Every* day! How could I know such a thing!" she pleaded as her heart most burst within her small chest from excitement.

"Who, *Father*, who might be interested in such a little thing as I?" she asked.

Her father felt his own emotion catch in his throat, and for a moment he was unable to speak, fearing he might not be able to utter the young man's name. He placed his hands on each of her shoulders and drew her close, face to face.

"Would my little weaver bird know a young man by the name, by the name . . . by the name of, of '*Andres*' . . . 'Andres Menchú Xoy'?" he asked as his eyes swelled with tears to name the most respected young man of San Felipe del Lago.

María's eyes flashed in fright. She fell back from her father's grip and scooted backwards against the post of the house, her loom and threads falling away in disarray. At first, she could not fathom the significance of words which, as a name, was the utterance of one who belonged to the gods and heaven; that his name might be mentioned in the same breath as her own was unthinkable, inexplicable. She was struck dumb, and she could only stare at her father, frozen in a moment of complete neurosis. Her small lips began to tremble.

"Did you *hear* me, my precious one?" asked her father, unable to appreciate the depth of his daughter's breakdown.

"*María!*" said Don Vincente. The girl could only stare wildly at her father's face. *María weaves at her loom. In and out. In and out. The needle in her hand. The threads. Red threads. The shiny red threads of silk that the chickens in the loom against the white ground fabric. In and out the needle picking up the threads where the chickens hide in the red, silk threads. In and out. The brilliant yellow threads that eye the chickens parading in a row across the ground that the Alemanes wanted in the huipiles that the Alemanes wanted. The chickens. In and out the chickens for the Alemanes. The shiny, silk red threads. In and out. In and out.*

María rolled over on her left side and drew her knees up under her chin. *In and out the chickens in the silken, red threads the Alemanes the threads the chickens in and out the needle carrying the threads of the chicken in and out the proud, poor chickens all in a row in and out and in and out.*

María's eyes stared wildly across the yard where the chickens pecked in the dirt for little kernels of corn discarded by her mother long before the sun had risen so many hours before; stared out into the corn rows of the milpa and followed the line of the path through the dense, green stands of maize; stared past the corn rows and up the side of the slope of the volcano over the tiny patches of corn, the high mountain fields scratched into the towering slopes of the mighty volcano; stared up into the sky at the line of clouds beginning to amass in the late afternoon around the summit of the mountain with its yawning mouth, its plumes of ash rising slowly into cool, crisp air; stared into the deep blue sky where she could just make out *the faint outlines of the chickens in the silken, red threads and the loom that the Alemanes of the chickens in the sky.*

María Xquic could not hear her father—would not hear the words her father said; could not bear such words—such precious words that she dared not utter, would never have to say if only she could fix on *the chickens in the red silk threads against the background that the Alemanes!*

"*María!*" snapped her father, his hands stroking the shoulders that had fallen so sharply from his caresses. "*María!*" returned Don Vincente, trying to secure his daughter's confidence.

Chapter 16

Frijoles de Brujo

The *frijoles de brujo* rolled across the striped *tzute*, clustering in more or less five areas on the Sacred Table. In small, deliberate circles, old "Tata" Joaquim passed the shaking palm of his right hand slowly over the red maguey beans, turning them gingerly to even them out, and he spread them into a clearly discernible pattern.

"*Ah, malaya*! On this day, *k'mane*. Come, *alcaldes* of the mountains, great chiefs of the sky!" said the wizened, old priest. "Come, oh, sacred saints of the church. All the *alcaldes* of the heavens! *See!* I light my *candles!* I light the candles for each of the cardinal points that you may hear my voice, that you might come on the winds and hear this prayer of a poor *indigena! Ah, malaya!* Now, I pray for your forgiveness of all this poor servant's sins. Make him straight and right. Make his heart and soul pure that he may be an inspiration to his family and to his small town of San Felipe. Oh, *alcalde* of the west! *Ah, malaya!* Come to us now. And you, sacred *alcaldes* of the north, the east, and of the south! Come *here!* Come *now,* and hear your faithful servant. Listen to his prayers, and speak of this loving servant here beside me, this Andres Menchu Xoy."

"Tata" Joaquim squinted through the cataracts of his eyes, catching the light glinting on the edge of the red beans before him. Slowly and deliberately, he rolled his head to this side and that, examining the position of the dried seeds strewn over the *tzute*.

"Come over here," said the old *alcalde*. "Come over here, son," he said, "and you can see for yourself. You can see the shape of the beans. *Look!*" he said, as he pointed to the configuration of seven beans—three of them angled away from the sun, four of them toward the sun.

"You will have a family, Sr. Andres. *See!* Look at the way the beans read from the sun and from the north. Now," said the priest, "we will cast them again—this time from the north."

The old man's hand slowly gathered the seeds into his trembling grip, and from the head of the *tzute*, he cast them carefully and deliberately back toward his lap from the top of the table. The seeds fled across the *tzute* and rolled to a stop in two, somewhat distinct groupings.

"Well?" the priest queried his young apprentice.

"Here?" asked Andres, as he pointed to the group of beans which had rolled closest to the edge of the tzute.

"Well?" repeated the priest, without yielding. An apprentice must read the beans with confidence and commitment.

"Yes," said Andres, "this is the cluster, and these are my children."

"So they are," acknowledged "Tata" Joaquim, "so they are—and? . . . and?"

"And?" asked Andres, respectfully.

"The children? What are the children? You can *tell!* You can tell from the crotch of the beans to the north—*see!* See what I mean? You can *tell!*" exclaimed the old man. "*Now!* You tell *me!* Tell me about your own children!"

Andres peered over the *tzute* toward the configuration of the seeds. Clearly, he need not strain; the cluster always revealed itself. He need only be present and alert. He must read them carefully. The earnest young man winced, however, in a momentary flight of recognition, and a shudder raced down his neck and across his back. There they were—his very future—his own family configured on the stripes of the *tzute* before him. This was *real!* This was his future, and he sensed the gravity of the revelation. There would be no recourse from this reading.

Andres extended the point of an imaginary finger across the face of the *tzute* toward the cluster of the beans gathered toward the head of the cloth. The phantom finger hovered over each of the beans, and then he dared to begin the count. First, "one"; then, "two"! He would have *two* children! Andres trembled again, his breath catching tightly in his chest, for, quite obviously, there were others still to come.

Then, "three"—a *third* child! And then, a *fourth!* The ghostly finger continued to move across the grouping of the seeds. He dared not miscount or duplicate any one of them—or *skip* one! For there would be only one more roll of the seeds in the reading.

"*Four!*" he counted to himself. And then, "*Five*!" He was sure.

"*Cinco*!" he said silently to himself.

"That's *right!*" intuited "Tata" Joaquim. "Five, it *is!*"

Andres was moved to tears of pride.

"*Five!*" he said to himself. "I will have *five* children!"

Andres stared at the *tzute*, transfixed in the presence of the profile of his own life, marvelling that fate could be revealed so pristinely and irrevocably through the natural order of rolling of the mixes of seeds.

"Tata" Joaquim sensed the poignancy of the moment for his young student who was learning so quickly. He gave him a space of time to appreciate the circumstances of his own future. After a couple of moments, he turned to him.

"Again," said the priest. "Now, only those . . . those five, and from the north, just as before."

Andres reached to the table and slowly swept away the other beans and set them to the side of the *tzute*. And then the fingers of his phantom hand rushed into position across the back of his own right hand, and the young man sensed a fullness or weightiness as he reached toward the five beans at the upper left of the cloth.

One by one, Andres picked up each of the seeds, turned them, and let them slip into the clutch of his palm. When he had retrieved them all, he closed his fist tightly and scanned the *tzute* for the appropriate spot to release them.

"Tata" Joaquim watched the apprentice as he prepared to roll them for the last time.

"Easy," said the learned mentor. "Let them flow from your hand. Don't sling them or just let them drop. `Flow' . . . *`flow,'* son; just let them *`flow'* from your hand. *Okay?*"

Andres loosened his fist and passed it in slow circles above the opened area in the center of the *tzute*. At the end of the third pass of his fist, he slowly released the seeds, one at a time, to the surface of the sacred cloth. As they struck against each other, the beans popped and bounced and rolled to a quick stop against the wrinkles of the *tzute*. With both hands, Andres spread the corners of the *tzute* tightly to remove any remaining wrinkles that might otherwise intimidate a clean reading, and there they were—the five seeds aligned unmistakably in reference to the north and the sunlight from the left.

"Three beans to the top; two to the bottom," he said, looking quickly from the corner of his eye at his teacher.

"Tata" Joaquim retained the inscrutable expression of the master teacher awaiting the interpretation of his student.

"Cinco niños," said Andres. "Tres hijos . . . y dos hijas!"

"Tata" Joaquim never flinched as he awaited a reconfirmation.

"*Tres hijos y dos hijas*!" repeated the future father.

"*So!*" said the priest. "So, it *is!* Five children—three boys and two girls for Andres Menchu Xoy. May the gods attend them as they certainly have heard the prayers of one young man so dedicated and so blessed as you."

Andres trembled to hear such accolades from his mentor. His heart was full, and he bowed his head in an expression of deep, unbridled respect for his teacher.

"Well," said "Tata" Joaquim. "I think it is a time to express our thanksgiving, *heh?*"

Moved by the solemnity of the moment, Andres reached for his bag and retrieved a clutch of candles. Meticulously, he untied the wicks and separated out from them five pairs which he set aside and then returned the remainder into his woolen shoulder bag. He picked up two of the candles and held them together in his left hand as he took a mechanical lighter from his shirt pocket and fired the exposed wicks. Then beginning his prayer, Andres stepped back away from the table and the *tzute* with its revelation of divining beans, knelt before the table, and tipped the two candles to allow a spot of wax to spill to the floor of the *quemador*. After three or four drips had congealed in a spot, Andres secured the base of the candles in the molten wax and reached for the second pair, repeating the process of mounting them in place before *Santa Mesa*, the holy table. In barely audible whispers, the proud young man muttered his deep prayer of thanksgiving to *El Díos Mundial* and all the other divine powers that held court over his destiny.

"*Alcaldes sagradas, oigame a su servidor pobre*," prayed the young priest. "*Ah, malaya!* Hear this poor servant and receive his small gifts of gratitude."

Andres reached to the candles to adjust them in the wax to keep them from toppling.

"Hear me, your servant, *Santo Mundo*, *Santa Mesa*, *Santo del Cielo*, and *Santa Justicia! Ah, malaya!* Hear me, old sacred *alcaldes* and receive my offerings of thanksgiving for my family yet to come. *Ah, malaya*! My children—my three sons and two daughters yet to come: bless their souls that they, too, may serve you in thanksgiving and humility."

Andres Menchu Xoy placed his last set of candles in their place on the *quemador* before the sacred table with its mix of revealing beans. As he secured the candles, he withdrew his hands and placed them over his knees, lowered his head, and framed the most important request of his service.

"*Ah, malaya! Santa Mesa, Santo Mundo, Santa Justicia, y los Alcaldes del Cielo!* Hear, now, this poor servant," pleaded the young priest, "and answer his prayer. Reveal to him now his companion and precious wife, the woman who will bear his children, that she—like they—may know your gifts and love, that they—that we together—may never forget to walk in love and respect and worship in humility!"

Yes, he had dared to extend his request, to push for full disclosure of his fate. But he felt confident in his words and expression. No candle had fallen; the flames burned steadily. And this day—the first day of the calendar—this day of *k'mane*: would it not prove fortunate? Why would he expect anything other than a full answer to his prayers and request?

"Tata" Joaquim laid his hand on his young protege's shoulder and motioned him to move aside. Then, the older one approached the side of the table, careful to avoid disturbing the burning candles, and took up the mix of seeds from the side of the *tzute* and the five that still rested on the cloth. With the same patience and slow, deliberate movements of his right fist, "Tata" Joaquim passed his hand in shaky but determined circles over the center of the *tzute*, releasing the maguey seeds in two's and three's. He would throw the mixes this time through the full cycle of the calendar, pairing each set of seeds by the day beginning from the name of each day in sequence, watching carefully as each mix resolved itself in even or uneven combinations throughout the cycle. It was critical to move smoothly through the bad days when the mixes could be unkind to a client—the third, sixth, eighth, the twelfth and thirteenth, and the formidable fifteenth day of the month—*kimex*, the day of the pig, a day ruled by desolation and death.

One by one, the old *chimán* flung the mixes. For more than an hour, he paired the red seeds in their little clusters, praying as he passed his quaking right palm over the inevitable configurations before him on his sacred table.

The path of the mixes coursed their pairings through the complete calendric cycle, avoiding each threshold of evil from day to day. At last, "Tata" Joaquim led his young disciple around the *quemador* to join him before the end of the table.

"There," said the priest, pointing to the small pot of granulated *copal pom* incense. "Place two pinches in the *pichacha*."

The young man did as he was instructed and placed two small pinches of the resin into the clay pot over the bed of burning coals in its base. Instantly, a vapor of incense rose in a towering column, its rich aroma wafting throughout the room. As his attention turned again to his mentor, Andres noticed that the pile of seeds to the right had been divided evenly—the best possible sign for the divination! Nevertheless, "Tata" Joaquim never smiled, but continued his ceremony.

The old man began a slow, methodical, though undecipherable litany. With his head bowed, the silken tassels streaming down the back of his head and over his shoulders, "Tata" Joaquim began to rock back and forth, the mumbling of his chant dripping from his lips. Only the drone of his humming could be heard against the crackling of the *copal pom* in the *pichacha*.

Periodically, he motioned to Andres to place more incense over the coals, his prayer becoming more insistent as it proceeded. Beads of sweat began to appear on his forehead as his eyes closed tightly and his head began pitching slowly from side to side.

Then, without hesitation, "Tata" Joaquim reached to the table and began counting out four separate piles of the seeds—sixteen seeds in each of the four quadrants of the table, the remainder deposited in a fifth cluster in the middle. Upon completing the mix, "Tata" Joaquim turned to young Andres and motioned him to take his place at the side of the table.

"The name of your wife, Andres . . . *look! There!* There in the mix. There you will discover your wife, my son," explained the old man. "I must leave you now, for you must listen to the seeds alone."

And with that, the old *chimán* rose stiffly and retired from the room.

For more than a minute, Andres stared at the configuration of the seeds before him on the sacred table, moved by the awesome solemnity of the moment, and then he began to pray.

"*Ah, malaya!*" he cried deeply from within the very pit of his soul. "*Santa Mesa, Santo Mundo, Santa Justicia, y Santo del Cielo!* Hear me now, your poor servant, who asks forgiveness of his sins. *Santa María y Jesucristo*, come and hear my prayer, that your names may be blessed forever among we poor *naturales! San Simon!* Oh, *mighty Maximón*, lord of healing and patron of the sacred cross! Hear my prayer and reveal to this poor one the name of the mother of his children!"

Andres passed his right palm over the mixes, circling each time over the cardinal points and then spreading the central pile into an even blanket of red seeds. With his right index finger, the young apprentice moved his imaginary course through the seeds, the phantom digit coaxing the seeds to give up their name. Over and over he watched the imaginary extension of his own hand filter through the seeds, and then his hand stopped. His actual hand began to shake in an inexplicable and completely unexpected trembling. He watched the few hairs on the back of his hand dance as if electrified, and then, all of a sudden, a faint, blue glow began to effuse from the tips of his fingers, flow over his hand, and irradiated the whole table. Then he heard the voice.

Behind his right ear, Andres heard the first, faint, soft whisper of his voices. All but indecipherable at first, slowly, the voices—as in times past—began to coalesce in a clearer, much more pronounced explication. Then in a rush, as if as shifting winds, he heard the name distinctly and unmistakably.

"*María*, Andres! Take *María Xquic* from her father! María is to be the mother of your children. They, too, shall know the gods, and they, too, with their mother María Xquic, shall speak for your faith and bring honor to the gods and to the Holy Mother, *Jesucristo*, and *Santa Mundo*."

Suddenly, Andres began to gasp. He clutched his throat, unable to draw a satisfactory breath, and fell backwards, almost in the smoldering patches of the melted candles. The blue light drifted in little bursts over his collapsed shoulders, over his head, and down his arms. Then, as quickly as they had come, they dissolved into the column of smoking incense, and Andres Menchu Xoy lay still before the Sacred Table.

"*Andres*, my son . . .? queried old "Tata" Joaquim as he returned to the room upon hearing the confusion.

"Andres? *Ah malaya!"* he said. "Andres!"

Chapter 17

Washington Follies

The airplane had arrived in the nation's capital just before midnight during a blinding snowstorm. It was the last flight to Washington, and Father Michael Justice watched the two Guatemalan girls grimace in fright as the plane touched down at National Airport. So, they were here, here at last where they could make some waves. So, they were here where the very leadership that had prosecuted the war against their Guatemalan families could see first hand and hear from those who had suffered for so many years from their arrogant handiwork.

Father Michael, María, and Noelia took a cab from the airport to the Margolis Hotel, an older, rather seedy establishment in the northeast section of the capital. The girls nodded off to sleep as the cabbie engineered the car through the swirling snow. Father Michael thought it best to let the girls sleep-in the next morning when he went to the office of Senator Freeman to double check the arrangements.

"Here's your pass, Father. You'll need to clip it on your coat pocket. You will have thirty minutes for your presentation," said the aide. "If any member of the committee wants to question you in detail, of course you'll have longer to respond, but don't count on it. You need to be in the chamber by no later than 10:30. You'll probably need to eat something before you go. They may break for lunch or not. The Senator is in the mood to get on with the hearing. He's very busy right now. Do you have any questions?"

"Well, *yes!*" said Father Mike. "What about the two Guatemalans? the two girls from Patozí?"

"I don't know what you're talking about," said Ms. Price, looking puzzled and a little irritated. She had hoped to dodge this one.

"Well," began Father Mike, "I thought that was all *cleared.* I've talked with Miss Peters at least three times—in fact, every time I've called. She said there wasn't any problem, that they could tell their story."

"Well, I'm sorry," said Janice. "This is the first *I've* heard about any

Guatemalans. I'm afraid it's impossible at this point. We already have a full schedule for the morning at this point with other speakers who have requested appearances. They've come at their own expense and at great distances like yourself to be here. There's just no way. I would have had to have known at least three weeks ago."

"But you *did!*" insisted Father Mike, becoming quite irritated himself. "It was all worked *out.* Miss Peters said that she had cleared the schedule with you, that they would speak and I would translate for them, and then I would be able to give some wrap up or final remarks. I'm sure there's some mistake here. We've had groups of kids doing car washes, candy sales just to pay the airfare for these two very desperate people. They're the whole *point*—they represent the Guatemalan people. I'm sure that if you talk with Miss Peters . . . "

"*Father!*" interrupted Janice Price. "Miss Peters is unavailable, and perhaps I need to clarify something else to you before we go any further. As far as the Senator is concerned, this hearing is not about `the people of Guatemala.' This hearing is about America's interests in the region and the stability of American investments there."

"With all due *respect*!" protested Father Mike, his neck splotched with angry, red whelps, "However, you may want to couch it, the `people of Guatemala' is the only agenda item! Maybe you . . . "

"Father . . . *Father Mike!*" interrupted Miss Price. "There's no way at this point I can get them on the agenda. I don't know what happened, but the best I can do is give them a pass into the chamber, that is, if we have any left."

"`Any *left'?*" asked the priest, growing more and more upset. "`Any *left'?* What kind of a person *are* you? These people have fled for their *lives!* The *kids* in Texas!—They've worked so hard! We had this all worked out, and I'm sorry! These two ladies will speak in the Senate hearing tomorrow, or the good Senator's image is going to be blackened all over the evening *news!*"

Ms. Price was seething, but her sense of professionalism masked the indignation and affront she felt at this mealy, little priest's insolence. Who did he think he was, anyway, to challenge a Senator's aide? She comforted herself in that Senator Freeman himself would bring the cleric to heel if he carried the same attitude into the hearing. He'd take a lesson back he wasn't likely to forget.

The buzzer sounded under the desk.

"Excuse me," said Ms. Price rather perfunctorily, and she turned to enter the Senator's outer office.

"What's that all about?" asked Senator Freeman, stepping briskly out of his private, interior suite.

"Well, it's about your hearing on Guatemala tomorrow," said the aide.

"Jan," said the Senator, dropping a sheaf of loose folders into his satchel. "Let me make something clear about tomorrow. I want this hearing to move along. How many we got on the schedule?"

"We have four, Senator," said Ms. Price.

"*Jesus!*" said Senator Freeman. "Look, I've got a lunch date with Bustamante's representative today. I'm inclined—going into this right now—to work with this bunch of cutthroats, but I don't want any surprises at the hearing. You get my drift?"

"Yes, Senator," said Ms. Price. "I don't think we'll have any *surprises.* I've already seen to that."

"Good girl, Jan!" said Senator Freeman. "I like a lady—how'd that bumper sticker go?—`Fifty-one percent "sweet thing," 49% "bitch," so don't *push* it!'"

"Well," said Janice, "I've got one out there right now that's `pushing it.'"

"How's that?" asked Freeman.

"Oh, it's the priest—that `Father Michael Justice' from Texas," said the aide.

"Oh, *shit! That* one? The one the Pope's censored?" said the senator. "He made it after all, *huh?*"

"Yeah," he made it all right," she said, "and apparently with the two Guatemalan women."

"*No! No! No!* We're not gonna have any `*Guatemalan* women'! Didn't you talk with Janie? We've got that covered, don't we?" he asked.

"Oh, yes, Senator," said Ms. Price. "I put on my position as `lady cop' and told him I didn't know anything about that and that it would simply be impossible. I lined up a couple of Pentagon people who'll fill the gap just nicely."

"Who are the Guatemalans?" asked the Senator.

"They're two women from a mountain village," explained Ms. Price. "They witnessed a massacre or something like that."

"Oh, *really?*" said Senator Freeman rather disturbed. "Well, even more so, I don't want them in the chamber. I don't want them anywhere near Bustamante's aide. I really don't want that priest . . . "

"*Senator!*" protested Ms. Price. "I can keep the two Guatemalans out, but the agenda has already been announced and distributed. You may run into more trouble. He's already threatening some kind of press conference or something if the Guatemalans don't testify."

Senator Freeman slammed his satchel against the back of the receptionist's chair. "That little *weasel!* That goddamned little *sonofabitch!"*

Father Mike wasn't any happier. He was getting the bureaucratic run around and wasn't going to be very surprised if he and the whole opportunity to testify were about to be cashiered right off the agenda. If that happened, he was going to raise a little holy hell for sure. The *Washington Post* might be happy to take his story, and he could be thankful, in part, to Marcus Finley for the contact.

"I don't want you to worry," said Father Mike to his two Guatemalan guests back at the hotel. "When you go in, you'll be sitting right next to me until I have to speak. You have to wear these badges—just clip them anywhere on the front of your *huipiles*."

The two sisters of Patozi sat very still. They were obviously very uncertain about the whole affair and particularly frightened about the idea of speaking before a group of strangers. They couldn't possibly comprehend the setting in a Senate hearing room—all the lights, the phalanx of reporters and television cameras, and Father Mike had decided not to take the chance of intimidating them any more than necessary. They'd find it all out soon enough, and he would be dealing with those insecurities as he had to.

The next morning was one of the coldest days of the season, and they bundled up tightly to brace themselves from the blustery, icy wind. They took a cab ride from their hotel several miles away from the Capitol Building. All along the route, the two girls stared out the back windows at the Washingtonians crowded about the street corners waiting for busses or the next cab. They looked strange to the two girls, sort of tight and stuffed up in their suits and snappy ensembles. María Colín snickered at a woman in a long fur coat but frowned as she spotted occasional pairs of street people huddled together under plastic sheeting and straddling gratings over sewer drains, the fumes of vapor puffing about them. At one intersection, paramedics were kneeling beside the body of a black man stretched out on a bus stop bench. Father Mike crossed himself, and the two girls followed in kind.

The cab turned right onto Pennsylvania Avenue and pulled into the loop circling the Capitol Building. The two girls looked at each other with featureless expressions and closed their lips tightly. The car stopped smoothly behind three other cabs in front of them, and the driver opened the door and stepped outside to assist them. Father Mike paid the fare as the two tiny girls huddled together against the curb, their hair whipping about their faces in the strong wind.

"*Hurry!*" cried Father Mike. "Let's get inside as quickly as possible."

María Colín Perez took a step back to allow her older counterpart to take the lead beside Father Mike. María deferred in all things to her friend, Noelia, who, at the time of their flight from Patozí, had been two stations higher in her *cargo* in the auxiliary of the *cofradia de San Juan* and, in fact, almost ready for her next charge. They stepped briskly around the long sidewalk that led them to the side door, the closest entrance, to the Capitol. Once inside, they kicked the frozen ice and snow from off their feet and climbed the long flight of stairs to the main hallway.

"We have a way to go," said Father Mike. "We'll take the elevator up to the next floor to get to the room where we're going."

The girls looked puzzled but fell in line behind the priest. As the elevator doors opened, a swarm of media crew members rushed out, laughing and barking at each other. One large, heavy-set African-American man with rounds of cable and a television camera perched on his shoulder had been joking with a colleague behind him when he stumbled into María Colín.

"*Jeezus!*" the man swore as he spun around to catch himself from falling backwards into the others. "What th' *shit!*"

"Easy, buddy," cautioned Father Mike. "Watch where you're *going!* You just about ran over the *lady!*"

"`*Lady'?*" he grumbled as he spied María. The man sneered at María Colín standing in front of him in her native ensemble.

"Wha's she up here fo', t' get my *job?*"

The crew moved on out into the hallway, snickering at the two girls and the priest. "They gonna have t' 'abla th' Eeeng-*lace'* fo' they gonna get *my* job, *huh!* Gonna have t' 'abla th' Eeeng- *lace'* fo' they gonna get *my* job, ya herrah? *Hah! Hah! Hah! Hah! Hah!* `Abla the Eeeng-*lace'*! No *shit,* man!"

"Come on," said Father Mike as he escorted the two girls ahead of him into the elevator. Then, something dawned on him. That was it! The *huipiles*, their deep, black blowing hair, the wide expanse of their foreheads, the high cheek bones, the glimmer of suspicion twitching their eyelids. He had been trying to pull it all together. He knew that the girls were the key in Washington and that this forum was the lynch pin in the argument against funding that had been raging within in him for months. It was the personal contact, but not just the contact as much as the power of the nuances. They couldn't help but catch the blackness of their bankrupt policies in Guatemala. The girls' stories were one thing, their obvious dishevelled fear the other—*that* was the clincher. The elevator was too slow! Surely, there was someone about to leave the foyer of the hearing room who needed to see these two girls if only in passing. No one was exempt; these girls would convict them all. They would see the girls; the girls wouldn't have to say *anything*—just the *fear*, just the *stares*, the flitting of their *eyes* back and forth across the chamber.

Father Mike was glad that he hadn't attempted to explain what they were getting into, what the chamber looked like. Of a sudden, he was even grateful for the ass who had just accosted them on the floor below. When the girls walked into this Senate hearing room, when they saw all the lights, the crews tripping over the cords, the photographers crouched below the pounding rostrum, their backs to the heavy grained, oak panels. They would be swept away, lost completely in a brown swirl of indecipherable abstractions, the lethargic pulse of tired tradition, the banalities of all the ritual pleasantries, and throughout the morning the crescendo of political bantering, and the chorus of limpid chatter snipping about them in the balconies. And *these*, *these* who had never felt the pulse of hot young corn, *these* who would never smell the ether of a pre-dawn fog sifting through the blackened smoke of parched husks igniting the new hearth of an all-saints eve—they would come to *know* this day!—before this morning was out, before the last *fool* among them had sauntered out for his lunchtime double martini, ogling every skirt left and right that preceded him—every *one* of them—in the presence of these two simple girls—was about to catch at least some sense of the gross injustice of their easy games so glibly played out in sessions like these inside the Beltway!

The elevator door opened on the second floor of the Senate corridor, and Father Mike held the door open so that the two girls might pass in front of him.

"Let's see," he said, as he looked left and right. "I think we go this way."

Father Mike turned to the left and began walking briskly, almost forgetting the two girls. "Down here," he said. "`The Franklin Salon.'"

The trio turned heads as they proceeded down the corridor. Haughty, bright young aides with aggrieved, sophisticated little frowns glanced at the colorful girls in their fancifully woven, bright red *huipiles*, and pleated, multicolored tie-dyed skirts streaming from their waists. The girls slipped cautiously in step behind the priest, two diminutive shadows dependent on his every step. As they approached the Franklin Room, they began to pick up the din of voices and commotion. Several men and women stood at the entrance, speaking animatedly in solemn, knowing ways about "Senator so and so" and the "Director of this and that." As they turned to enter the room, Father Mike noticed that, oddly enough, the room was bristling with people and the gallery already filled.

"Wait here," he said. "Don't leave. I'll be right back, *okay?*"

His shoulder bag bumping against each person he squeezed past, Father Mike worked his way through the room toward the railing that separated the gallery seating from the witness and respondents' section. He grabbed his own clip-on pass to keep from losing it in the press of the people. As he inched his way up to the railing, he turned to peer past the shoulders of those crowded around him to check the seating. He was relieved to notice the first three rows were empty, but then he spied the ribbon that sealed them and the placard reading, "Reserved for Press."

"That's not going to *work!*" swore the priest to himself. "We had an *agreement* and that's simply not going to *work!*"

"*Excuse* me!" said Father Mike, nudging into the most immediate conversation next to him.

"I beg your pardon," said Artemus Jaffe, a lobbyist for the Association of Arms Manufacturers, who turned rather perturbed at the intrusion, flipping her smart, sculptured bangs back off her left eye.

"I'm sorry to interrupt," explained the priest. "I was looking for Ms. Price, the aide to Senator Freeman . . . maybe you've seen her?"

"I'm afraid *not*," she snapped as she turned back to her disinterested companion, raising her hand over her ear to rearrange her hair line, obviously put off by the outsider's interruption. "*Excu* . . .," Father Mike began again with the next couple, but then stopped, thinking that he had caught sight of the aide at the entrance. Once again, he began his press through the crowded chamber.

"This just won't *do!*" he protested once again, working up his own response to the affront. "These girls will testify, or I'm going to the *Washington Post* within the hour! The secretary herself told me the first row was for the *respondents*, not the *press*. You don't have *press* on all *three* rows of the gallery!"

Finally, at the entrance once again, the priest strained to spot the senator's aide, but to no avail. The "Ms. Price" turned out to be someone else whose short, curled up nose belied any resemblance to his antagonist in this whole affair. Now exasperated, he stepped outside the doorway to find the two girls, María and Noelia. He found them huddled together against the wall, all but ignored as anything more than trifling or bothersome curiosities to those who even tolerated them with a glance.

"*María! Noelia!*" cried the priest over the dense hallway chatter.

The two Guatemalans stepped forward toward the priest, querulous expressions across their faces.

"Yes, *Padre?*" said Noelia.

"Look," said Father Mike. "I'm afraid that there is a problem."

The two girls tried to follow the tell-tale lines of his face and eyes.

"The chamber is closed," he tried to explain. "I don't think that you will be able to tell your story today. I don't know if I will be able to tell your story."

María and Noelia exchanged looks of shock and apprehension.

"We cannot tell our *story*, Father?" asked Noemia. "We cannot tell the story of what happened at *Patozí*?"

"No, I don't think so," said the priest. "Well, but I will try to tell the story as best I can if they let me speak today."

"I don't *understand, Padre*," said Noelia. "You told the people of the church that we could come to tell our story. So many people were happy about that. So many people have given us help to come. What can we do? They will not understand."

"*Noelia! María!*" said Father Mike. "You will tell your story in Washington. I promise you that. If I am unable to speak today, then we will go to the newspapers, and they will print your story."

Noelia looked thoughtfully at Maria who was embarrassed by tears beginning to show in the corner of her eyes and to slip down the side of her face.

"But for now," said Father Mike, "I think you must stay here in the hall. Perhaps someone will offer you a place to sit, or you may sit on the floor."

The two girls looked at each other and turned back toward the oak paneled wall. Father Mike smiled supportively and began to work his way back into the hearing room which was already filled to capacity—with the exception of the first row reserved for "the press." The second and third rows, as usual, were filled with members of the media; the first—normally reserved for respondents and witnesses—was occupied by State Department types, military brass, and lobbyists.

Father Mike bristled as he looked down the front row to spot Ms. Jaffe and her partner, a smug "Marlboro man"-type about fifty who seemed to be her supervisor. She reached over, laid her hand on his forearm, and whispered something in his ear. To her right was an Army colonel and Assistant Secretary for Latin America, Bill Boyer himself, whom the priest had recognized from various media reports on Latin America over the past two years. Then it struck him: "The deck's *stacked!* No *wonder* they didn't want the girls! The whole deck's stacked *against* them! They're going to fund the military and *that's* clear!"

Slowly, the members of the committee and their legion of aides filed nonchalantly into the hearing chamber. The aides slipped piles of reports and ledgers onto the desks as the fifteen senators settled in. The hearing clerk, a frumpy, matronly artifact from the Kennedy era, motioned to Father Michael to take his seat at the witness table. The priest stepped forward and sat down behind the microphone ensconced in the middle of the table.

Senator Freeman picked up the gavel and hammered the room to order.

Slowly, the mumbling and restlessness subsided.

"This hearing of the Senate Foreign Relations Committee of the 105th Congress will come to order," barked the Senator. "This committee will entertain information relative to the extension of aid to American allies in Central America. This morning will hear testimony regarding American interests in Guatemala."

The Senator fumbled through his papers momentarily looking for the schedule of witnesses. Ms. Price pulled the agenda of testimonies from out of a manila folder and placed it before the appreciative legislator.

"Thank you, Ms. Price," acknowledged the Senator. "We will first hear testimony from Texas. Will you state your name for the record?"

For a moment, the priest felt strangely disoriented, sitting in the witness chair before Senator Jesse Freeman, his old ideological nemesis.

"Father . . . Father Michael Justice," said the priest.

"And your address?"

"Holy Cross . . . Holy Cross Emanuel Catholic Church in Harlingen, Texas," said Father Mike.

"Well, Reverend," said the Senator, "I understand that you are here to address the situation in Guatemala, is that correct?"

"Yes, Senator."

"Well, Reverend, why don't you go ahead, but remember that we have a tight schedule this morning, so keep your remarks to the point."

"I will, Senator," said the priest.

"Now, Reverend . . . *Father? (Aside)* How do . . . I mean, what do people usually call a *priest?*" Senator Freeman asked Ms. Price poised on the ready at the edge of her chair behind him.

"`Father,'" returned the aide.

"Well, *`Father,'*" said the senator. "Have you ever been to Guatemala?"

"Yes."

"When were you last there, Father? *(Aside again)* I sure feel strange calling a *boy* almost three times younger than me *`Father,'* you know what I mean?" quipped the Senator to his colleague, Senator Mark Littlejohn, two positions to his right. The two exchanged a round of chuckles. "Excuse me, Father. Let's see. Where were we?"

"In *1985*, Senator . . . that's when I was last in Guatemala."

"`1985'—that's been a little while ago, wouldn't you say?" pressed the senator.

"Six years, Senator."

"Six years, six years, ummmmm," mused Senator Freeman. "Well, six years ago . . . were you a `father' six years ago?" Ms. Price snickered audibly behind the Senator's embossed leather chair.

"Yes, Senator."

"That's a little surprising, wouldn't you say?"

"How's that, Senator?"

"`A little *surprising,'* I was saying."

"I don't understand, Senator."

"Well, you don't look that old, that's all I meant. I mean it takes you boys a long time to *`make priest,'* I think, no?"

"That's right, Senator," returned the priest rather testily. "Look, Senator, with all due respect to you and this body, I am here to testify regarding the present situation in Guatemala, and . . . "

"That's right, Father Justice," interrupted the Senator, "but I'm just trying to get some background here for this committee. I think they have a right to know something about your level of *expertise*, Father. And I have to tell you that I haven't heard anything so far that answers some pretty fundamental questions I have right now about your qualifications to address this committee here today . . . "

"*Senator*!" said Father Mike.

"Don't interrupt me again, *son!*" roared the Senator, his fist slamming down on the rostrum. The gallery erupted in a rumble of surprise and shock. Father Mike sat stunned by the attack and, for the moment, lost his guard. He was not about to be sabotaged, however, by the intimidations of the Senator and his rank.

"*Senator!*" returned the priest. "I am here to testify today about a continuing practice of *genocide* being *perpetrated* against the Maya people in Guatemala. I have been scheduled for this appearance and have come at great expense to myself and to two young Guatemalan asylum applicants who are scheduled to speak in detail about what is happening to the Maya people perpetrated by the United States *government* and *military* . . . "

"Mr. *Justice!*" barked the senator as he rained the gavel on the desk.

". . . two young girls who have been *locked out* of this hearing this morning . . . "

"*Mr. Justice!*" cried the senator.

". . . by your own *staff*, this `Ms. Price' here, and by you, Senator, because you and this committee don't want to hear the *truth* . . . "

"*Mr. Justice!"* roared Senator Freeman. "You will come to *order* in this hearing, or I will hold you in contempt of *Congress!* Do you *understand* me, *Mr. Justice!*"

"*Senator Freeman!*" cried the priest, rising from his chair. "You and the American voters are *killing* the Guatemalan *people*, even as we *speak!*"

"*Mr. Justice!*" cried the senator. "One more outburst like that and I will have you cited and arrested for contempt of Congress . . . "

"Why cannot you all *see* what . . . "

"Mr. Justice . . . "

". . . what you are *doing* to the Maya people . . . "

"Mr. Justice! You are in contempt of . . . "

"Just give these girls a *chance* . . . "

". . . of Congress, Mr. Justice, and I order you to . . . "

". . . just *a chance* to hear their stories . . . "

"*Mr. Prothrow*, will you remove *Mr. Justice* from this *hearing* and hold him over for the *federal marshals!"*

"You can't *do* this!" cried the priest. "You can't *do* this to an entire race of people! Can't you *see* what you are *doing*! *All* of you! Can't you *see?*"

Clarence Prothrow, the Senate sergeant-at-arms, stepped forward from his chair at the side of the hearing room and approached Father Michael Justice who was now standing and waving gestures toward the Senate committee and the reporters behind them.

"*Please*, Father Justice," urged Mr. Prothrow. "Why don't you come along peacefully now." Two federal marshals came running down the aisle to assist in the priest's removal.

"Let's go, *bud!*" said one of the burly officers, all but lifting the priest off the ground with his grip under the arm.

"This hearing will be in recess for thirty *minutes!*" bellowed Senator Freeman, and turning to his aide, he ordered abruptly, "Come with me."

Ms. Price and the Senator rose as a unit, passed quickly behind the chairs of the other aides, and slipped through the side door of the hearing room.

"Tell the marshals that I intend to revoke the contempt citation after about five hours," explained the Senator. "I just want the little *sonofabitch* to stew in his own *juice* for awhile, but I want the three of them back on a plane and out'a this town *today*. You're going to need to go back out there in a minute and apologize to the others. Tell'em we'll get on with this thing as quickly as possible, but I want to clarify the situation with `Mr. Guatemala' in there—Bustamonte's boy—what's his name again?"

"`Julio,'" said Ms. Price. "`Julio Francisco Mátiz Soto.'"

"`Julio'—*what?*" repeated the Senator. "*Jeez—whatever!* I just want `Soto-Soto' in there to understand clearly that he's *got* the goddamned arms. After I go back into the hearing, I want you to work it out. Tell him we'll go for the $25 million, but to get around the $14 million Congressional ceiling on arms sales, tell him we'll draw up a contract through State for, say, $13.8 million right now and accept an application from the Guatemalan government for "Peace scholarship" monies for the remainder. Then, in five or six months, he can come back through this office and request a reallocation for a general ESF grant that he can use to purchase guns, strawberries, or *condoms* for all I care!"

Senator Freeman turned away from the aide and reached for the door.

"*Oh!* And one *more* thing, Ms. Price," said Freeman.

"Yes, sir!" said the aide.

"If any of those *jaimies* from the *Washington Post* call me for comments on any of this?" said the Senator.

"Yes, sir . . .?"

"Yeah," said Freeman. "Tell'em to *kiss my ass!*"

Chapter 18

Notes & Queries

Noticias
para Chico
1.11.90 Simon Chical (Comalapa)
Diego Cenas Lix (San Andrés Semetabaj)
Arnulfo Morales (Poaquil)
Oscar Rivas Martinez (ciudad)
Chan Rabinal (Zaculeu)
Meda Zamora (ciudad)
3.11.90 Yagil Hernandez (Jilotepeque)
Velasquez Soto (ciudad)

"*Oh, my God!*" Lydia exclaimed under her breath. "*Oh, my God!* This is *it!* This is the *ledger!* The *sonofabitch* is *G-2!* I *knew* it!"

She slapped the folder shut as she stared blankly across the room.

Lydia had rifled through no more than two shelves of the safe before she had found the ledger, the first of four or five worn manila folders containing lists of *Guatemaltecos* and their respective locations on lined, yellow tablet paper, each page cumbersomely annotated with cryptic lines, scribbled dates, and abbreviations. Transfixed, she found herself mumbling each name, people whose fate she only dared to imagine. Now things began to fall into place—the untidy schedule each week, the occasional flurries of *militaries* in and out of the office, the inexplicable deliveries she was never allowed to open. The office of the Director of Tourism was a clandestine station of G-2. Pablo Manuel Rigoleto was an intelligence agent, and the ledger confirmed it.

The list continued:

Felipe Vicente (Costa Rica)
Miguel Xom Calel (Chichicastenango)
Pedro Shon Catiz (Chupol)
Carlos Guillermo Ramirez Galvez (ciudad)
Telesforo Ramos (Playa Grande)
Carlos Rodrigos Mendez (Olintepeque)
Jacabo Lopez (Tactic)
Salvador Juarez Telon (ciudad)

Lydia flipped through more than twenty pages of smudged and abused names, looking for those of any friends, colleagues, or other familiar references. When she had absorbed the names of the last page, she collected the loose-leaf stack together and carefully placed them in their original place in the first folder. Then slowly, she retrieved the second folder from under the first and set it before her on the side table next to the Director's desk. She pulled his chair from behind the desk and sat down, hesitantly opening the cover.

Nervously, for a few seconds, Lydia turned through what appeared to be multiple copies of a brief, three-line statement. At first, she caught only a phrase or two:"*. . . of the freedom of . . . notified that . . . are hereby . . . the agents of . . . leave the country . . .*"

Then she began to reconstruct each message in its fuller construction. "agents of subversion of the freedom of the people . . . notified that they must leave the country . . . or die! . . . will perish if you continue . . ."

What she read sent her hands over her face in disbelief.

Eliado Tucubal Salazar

Tecpán

The agents of subversion of the freedom of

Oscar Rivas Martinez

Guatemala

The agents of subversion of the freedom of the people of Guatemala are hereby notified that

In almost disbelief, Lydia was reading the photo copies of the actual death threats delivered to those students, labor leaders, *campesinos*, and other "subversives" targeted for repression and execution. As the significance of the messages, the place—in her own office—and the immediacy of it all coalesced. Lydia began to tremble and her stomach churn. Suddenly, she felt nauseated and realized that she was about to faint. That couldn't *happen*, she tried to convince herself. She stared for a moment at the embroidered flowers around the framed Patzún huipil hanging behind the director's desk, all in an attempt to divert her attention from the horror before her, and she pulled the box of tissues from the Director's desktop into her lap—and not any too soon. She felt a chill wave wash over her face, neck, and shoulders as the rush of vomit exploded from her throat and mouth.

Lydia was successful in catching most of the discharge in the box of tissues. Only a spot or two had reached her skirt and the inside panel of the file folder on the desk before her. Then she felt a second wave rising within her throat, and rather than resist it, she relieved herself in the same box and collapsed over the desk in a flood of tears and exhaustion.

After a few moments, Lydia began to feel a little more comfortable. The nausea had subsided. She closed the folder and sat back in the chair. She heard voices—clerks from the legal department—coming down the corridor outside the Director's office. She was satisfied that they would never have reason to intrude on her discovery. She reached for a rag inside the safe and wiped up the residue from her seizure.

Lydia Penalte had stumbled upon the tangible evidence of an evil, the magnitude of which now, stretching well beyond her own incidental encounters, extended into an incomprehensible and overwhelming relentless pursuit of targets. Before now, Lydia's own conception and experience of Guatemalan violence had been limited to highly personal reactions and constantly shifting positions to cope with the after-effects of the horrific hits themselves—the lonely vacancy and sense of loss of a friend or colleague, the startling silence in a room where she had expected some response, the abandoned stack of unmarked papers across the desk of a dean who had been "disappeared."

Lydia sensed her intrusion into the inner workings, the planning and the processing of the very administration of evil. She sat stunned in her realization. As if the flesh had dissolved from her own hands as they drifted over the pages, this Guatemalan evil seemed to radiate in icy fingers from the papers in her lap outward in all directions, twisting and probing in a seething, frenetic, tenacity that accepted nothing short of its own brittle ends. Lydia Penalte shuddered as she sensed the poignancy of the moment, that in her lap and across the desk were the visible traces of the very demon itself. Only now, it had a name.

ChanRabinalZaculeuTheagentsofsubversionofthefreedomofthepeopleofGuatemalaareherebynotifiedthattehymustleavethecountryordieYouwillperishif . . . ChanRabi . . . Chan Rabinal . . . Zacu—!

Once again, Lydia was drawn to the photocopied death threats. At first, her eyes raced across the entries, attempting by quick scanning to capture the essentials of the texts, searching for any distinctions between the entries.

youcontinueyourcommunistactivitiesTheWhiteHandSimonChicolComalapatheagentsofsubversionofthefreedomofthepeopleofGuatemalaareherebynotifiedthattheymustleavethecountryordieYouwillperishifyoucontinueyourcommunistactivitiesTheWhiteHand DiegoConos Lix SanAndresSemetabaj . . . Theagentsofsubversion ofthefreedomofthepeopleof Guatemala are herebynotifiedthat they must leave thecountryor dieYouwill perish ifyoucontinue yourcommunistactivities. TheWhite Hand

But her effort was futile. Lydia's attention was too unstable to scan the texts with any recognition. She took a deep breath, spread the loose pages of the folder across her lap, and began to read each text word by word.

Oscar Rivas Martinez (ciudad)
The agents of subversion of the freedom of the people of Guatemala are hereby notified that they must leave the country or die. You will perish if you continue your communist activities.
The White Hand

And the next:

Arnulfo Morales (Poaquil)
The agents of subversion of the freedom of the people of Guatemala are hereby notified that they must leave the country or die. You will perish if you continue your communist activities.
The White Hand

And another:

Chan Rabinal (Zaculeu)
The agents of subversion of the freedom of the people of Guatemala are hereby notified that they must leave the country or die. You will perish if you continue your communist activities.
The White Hand

The next:

Meda Zamora (ciudad)
The agents of subversion of the freedom of the people of Guatemala are hereby notified that they must leave the country or die. You will die if you continue your communist activities.
The White Hand

Lydia Penalte turned each notice slowly, scanning annotations for any suggestions of outcomes. The second folder contained more than fifty separate notices. After scanning the last of the messages, she straightened the pages and set the folder aside for the third.

The third folder contained only one sheet of tablet paper. Lydia slipped the page from the folder and held it closer to the desk light. The page was written in the unmistakable hand of her boss.

~~Simon Chirol~~ 15.11.90
~~Diego Costa Lix~~ 13.11.90
~~Ernesto Morales~~ 13.11.90
~~Oscar Rios Martinez~~ — released 5.11.90
12.11.90
~~Chon Rabinal~~ 21.11.90
~~Pedro Zamora~~ 19.11.90

The list included the names of more than forty people dated and deleted. Slowly, Lydia traced her fingers down the page, pausing and stroking each name as if somehow to reconstruct the contours of each face. A confusion of feelings gripped her—the constant, blanching fear of discovery and exposure was now complicated by a searing, white anger that almost unstrung any shred of reason. She struggled against destroying all the folders, when her eye caught sight of the last file, this one labeled on the outside.

"`Deliveries' . . . " Lydia said softly to herself. "`Deliveries,'" she repeated. "*`Deliveries'* . . . maybe *this* . . .!"

Lydia's anger warped into an eager curiosity as she lifted the last folder from the pile. Quickly, she flipped open the cover to find a disarray of notes and a fragment of a small tablet that fell out over her lap and scattered about the floor on both sides of the chair. She pushed the chair back and began to crawl about the notes, first trying to reassemble them face upward but found the scanning of the irresistible.

The first:

Col. Altagoz 3.11.90 bring directory

Another:

Wait for confirmation / base 14 - Sololá
~~Bruceros~~ condo
Bruceros alert 3.14.90

Another:

Gallagher to notify 3.2.90

Another:

Call Gallagher (330766)

Another:

Altapaz (OK) Gallagher confirms relay
16,000 units
Congress OK early fall (September?)

Another:

Gallagher — ~~yes~~ not sure
~~[illegible]~~

And then:

16,000 units ammo Aurora 15: 7.90
9, 11, 14, 21 — Poly technique

~~250 for Base 14?~~
500 — Sololá
250 — #14

Lydia stared at the small note, stunned by the implication. This was *it*—the note that confirmed the conversation she had overheard months earlier at the luncheon! This was the tell-tale note that revealed it *all!*

Lydia jumped up from the floor, the note in hand, and looked across Rigoleto's desk for anything to write with and a piece of scratch paper. Then she spied the small note pad in the folder itself, removed a slip, and began copying the brief notice.

"This is *it!*" cried Lydia to herself. She had finally confirmed the shipment and probable points of delivery for hundreds of M16-A2 assault rifles approved earlier in the spring by the United States Department of State.

"*No!* Better copy *all* of it," she thought to herself. She could use the copy machine on the next floor and have all the materials back within ten minutes. That wasn't too much to risk.

Lydia was beginning to feel queasy again and knew that she needed to complete the copy work quickly and return everything to order inside the safe.

"Oh, *damn!*" she exclaimed. "The machines are down!" It would take more than five minutes—or longer—for the copiers to warm up, and the idea of standing there, perhaps even being surprised by fellow workers with such files wasn't an option. Lydia had no choice but to return the files and to try the next day.

Now Lydia concentrated on her orderly exit from the office. She looked over the desk for any item that she might have overlooked from any of the folders. She picked up the rag and wiped the dark spots still visible on her dress. Then she withdrew the second folder from the stack, opened the cover, and rubbed the rag vigorously over the stains in a last, vain attempt to eradicate any traces that might expose her. The acid, however, had already seeped into the fiber of the paper, and there was nothing more to do.

Exasperated with her failure to remove the stains, Lydia looked into the safe for any other folders that she might use to replace the soiled one. She shuffled tablets and other familiar files of Tourism data and found a used one. Residue from old labels and erased notes, however, rendered it useless. She jumped from the chair and rushed to the front drawers of the desk. The lower left-hand drawer was a filing cabinet. Sure enough, she found perhaps twenty unused files together in the back of the drawer. Eagerly, she withdrew one from the collection, secured the notes and items from the original folder, and returned the new one to its place in stack on the shelf in the safe. Now she was satisfied, comfortable that her untimely seizure had been masked.

Hurriedly, Lydia locked the safe and returned the slip of paper with the combination into the top desk drawer and placed it under the deck of cards. She picked up the old manila folder and the box of tissues with its cargo of her vomit and left Rigoleto's office, pulling the door behind her. Once again in her own office surroundings, she felt more comfortable and secure. Her only dilemma now was to remove the folder and the tissue box without arousing suspicion of the guard in the lower parking garage or anyone else in the office who might chance to see her exiting on a Saturday. Her own trash can contained a plastic liner. Surely, she could deposit both the folder and the tissue box in the liner, tie the top of the liner in a knot, and place the liner in the dumpster in the garage.

"*No!* Not in the *dumpster!*" she thought. "That might be too risky."

Lydia decided to place the trash liner in her car and to carry it home with her for a more private disposal. Just as she was about to collect her purse and lift the liner from the trash can, she glanced, quite by accident, at the back side of the folder. She was startled at the sight of a telephone number casually scrawled across the back.

"*Shit!*" stammered Lydia. "*Goddamn* it! *Goddamn* it! . . . *Goddamn!*" She flung the folder down on the desk. "There's no way! I've got to return the folder, smudges or *not! Goddamn* it!"

Hastily, she fled again into Rigoleto's office, quite frightened now that her time might be running out. She fumbled at the combination, failing to unlock the safe on a second and then a third attempt. Her hands began to tremble as she cleared the tumbler in a free spin to the right and cautiously tried the lock again. This time she heard the pins release, and she grasped the brass handle and pulled the door ajar.

"*Oh, my God!*" she thought. "I forgot to wipe off the *handle!*" She reached into the floor of the safe, grabbed the rag, and began to wipe the handle and the top of the safe where she had placed her fingers. Then she withdrew the stack of folders and lifted out the second file and slipped it from the others. Careful not to disturb the order of the notes within, she emptied the contents of the new folder once again into the original and returned the ledgers into the safe.

"Now," thought Lydia. "Now, I'll just have to wait and see. If the *niño de puta* wants to pursue this, I'll be ready. I'll cut the bastard's *fruit* right off the *tree!*"

Lydia was resigned to the inevitable, whatever the folder might bring her. She resolved, however, to begin carrying her pistol in her purse. She wouldn't be surprised, whatever the outcome. Unable to control the fate of discovery, Lydia turned her attention to her memory of the ledgers, and her mind began racing with the details. She had to communicate the discovery to Alma María.

Quickly, Lydia sought her brush in her purse and combed back her disheveled locks while glancing at her reflection in a framed tourist poster on the wall next to the entrance to the Director's office. She rolled a streak of lipstick across her upper lip and mashed her lips together as she gathered the knotted trash sack with the tell-tale box of tissues and her purse and headed for the door.

The hallway was empty as Lydia closed and locked the receptionist's office. She turned down the corridor toward the elevators. She planned to drop the opaque plastic trash bag in the incinerator shoot halfway down the hall. Her heart was pounding as she approached the shoot, fearing that she might yet be discovered before she could make the drop, but she sent the bag to the basement dumpster without discovery. Lydia sighed as she turned and continued her passage to the elevators.

"Lydia?" came a voice behind her. Lydia almost froze with horror.

"Lydia? Are you *okay?*" asked the voice. Lydia couldn't think. She couldn't remember a name for the familiar intonations and was too fearful to turn around. She was completely shut down and vulnerable.

"*Lydia?*" said the voice. "*Lydia!* What's the *matter?*"

"Máte?" Lydia responded. Then she remembered—"Mate Rivas de Ramirez."

"*Máte!*" cried Lydia. "Oh, you *scared* me so!"

"You're okay?" asked Lydia's office suite mate, a secretary for the legal staff in the adjoining office.

"*Oh!* Let me catch my breath," said Lydia, buying a few moments of time for recomposing herself. "Yes, of *course!* Why . . .?"

She knew her question gave her inquisitor an opening, but it was too late to retract or to speak without appearing to cover up.

"Well, you look . . . " stammered Máte, trying to retain some diplomacy. She wouldn't mention Lydia's languishing odor or the large spot of residue on her dress that her colleague had apparently missed in cleaning up. "Lydia, you look so, so `pale.' You're all flushed. Are you sure you're okay?"

"Oh yes," claimed Lydia. "I was just doing some cleaning up in the office, getting up and bending over and all, and I started having these heat flashes. I guess it's the *bitch goddess*!"

Both shared a feigned laugh.

"I had to sit down," confessed Lydia. "I really thought I was going to faint."

She had gone too far with her explanation. Lydia hadn't intended to reveal anything about her mission that morning, and she was perilously close to a confidence.

"Well," said Máte. "Be sure and stop by the restroom before you leave and check your dress there on the side."

Startled by the shock of exposure, Lydia pulled the side of her skirt around to reveal a large coagulated spot about the size of her fist. Máte smiled forgivingly and continued on toward the elevator.

Alma María Vargas disappeared exactly two months, four days, fourteen hours, and thirty-six minutes after the marriage of Lydia Penalte to Rutilio Manuel Sanchez, an economist for the National University of San Carlos. Lydia had given little thought to the extended ring on her comrade-colleague-sometime lover's telephone, or, for that matter, even the second. The third telephone call later in the day produced a disconnect which wasn't possible. Something seemed very wrong.

"I don't know what might have *happened!*" cried Lydia to her husband,

Rutilio. "She was supposed to contact us by today if everything was on course."

"And you didn't get any other word?" asked Rutilio.

"No!"

"And Lupe didn't come back into the city?" he asked.

"I don't think so," explained Lydia. "He was supposed to wait in at the lake in San Filipe, and the rest were supposed to get word from him before they started the operation. If *Alma* . . .!"

Lydia Penalte de Sanchez gasped before she could finish the sentence.

"My *God!*" said Lydia. "What if she's been *discovered!* Oh, *God!* What if she's been taken *in!* What if they've `disappeared' *Alma!*"

Lydia was horrified at the prospect of Alma's capture, and from the kitchen where she had been looking through the telephone directory she ran to their bedroom. She raced to a side table next to the bed and began tearing through the small pile of papers and pamphlets in the bottom drawer.

"It's *gone!*" Lydia cried, as she turned in fright to Rutilio.

"It isn't *here!*" she repeated.

"*`What'* isn't here?" he asked.

"The . . . the *ledger,*" Lydia blurted out. "It's *gone*—the one from the *safe!*"

"You're *joking!*" returned Rutilio. "You've got to be *joking!* I thought you were going to copy it before you brought it here! Surely, you haven't lost the original."

"*Yes!*" cried Lydia. "The *original!*"

"*Shit!*" exclaimed Rutilio. "Why didn't you copy it at the office? I thought you weren't ever supposed to take that ledger from the *office!*"

"I had no *choice!*" cried Lydia, her face now colorless as she sat trembling on the side of the bed. "There was no way for me to slip it back into the office because they were having a meeting—some kind of hearing with a Texas group or something. It was going on and on, so . . . "

"Why didn't you take it down to the copy room, make a copy there, and leave the original in the storage closet—like we did before?" asked her angry and nervous husband.

"There was no *way!*" cried Lydia, her face a mask of terror. "I went to the copy room, but the copier was down, and the locker room was locked. The only key was back in the office, and I was afraid to walk back in on the meeting. So, I brought it home."

"That's why the door wasn't set yesterday when we got back," remembered Rutilio. "I thought it was María coming back from the bakery, but she told me that she never went, that she had changed her mind and stayed here.

Then Rutilio panicked. "We've got to get *out* of here! They *know!* God*damn* it, if they've picked up Alma! *Shit!* They've got to *know!*"

"Well, she would know, then, if anyone came into the house," offered a relieved Lydia. "That's got to be *it!* That's got to be the *answer!*"

Surely, she had only misplaced the ledger, explained Lydia, because María would have heard anyone coming in and out of the house.

"*No!*" said Rutilio. "María left later. She must have forgotten, because she went to pick up her daughter for about an hour late in the afternoon. That would have given anyone an opportunity if he knew what to look for, if he knew what he was doing. Come *on,* Lydia! We've got to get out of here *now!* Go to the back, and I'll check the front."

Quickly, Lydia fled down the short hall of the house toward the tiny kitchen. Light poured into the room from the wide, open window. She stopped just at the door so as not to be seen through the doorway or window by anyone who might be lurking in the back on the adjoining roof. For the first time, Lydia felt as though she were an intruder in her own home, as if all the familiar, little accoutrements of her life were strangely distant, items for sale or discarded now and forever. The rags drying over the basin, the plastic dishes—long scratched and stained—that her mother had left her, the bent and dented grey pots and pans hanging on pegs driven into the wall over the sink, the wobbly preparation table, etched and scored by twenty years of chopped chickens and diced vegetables. Now, in this moment of panicked flight, all seemed strangely obsolete and pointless.

If she and Rutilio were being observed directly, it would be from the front, in the street—probably a car or van parked down the street, a couple of guys wearing sun glasses with jackets stuffed with guns or rope. If from behind, anyone could be positioned on the roof line of the adjacent house, poised for a leap into their small back court. Lydia was relieved to note, as she stood at the entrance to kitchen, that anyone attempting a jump from the neighbor's roof would have to fall through the tarpaulin that María had erected as a lean-to over the bags of seed corn that Rutilio had purchased for his uncle's *finca.* Still, she had to confirm their security.

Lydia scouted her options for moving around the kitchen. If she stepped left, she would be unable to catch a glimpse of the roof line above them. If she moved right, she could crouch beside the oven and peep between the coffee pot and large pan of beans already boiling on the stovetop burners. She would be exposed, however, for at least two steps, but that seemed her only option.

Lydia clutched tightly the open neckline of her blouse just under her chin.

She took some sense of security that her blouse was a dark blue and long-sleeved garment and that she was wearing her tight, black stirrup pants. At least from the waist down, she felt thinner, but suddenly got the urge to mash her breasts deeply behind her ribs. Still clutching her blouse tightly at her neckline, Lydia Penalte pulled her arms over her breasts as she stepped backwards against the door jam, bent over slightly, and took two bounding steps, landing in a crouched position against the side of the stove.

Her heart was suddenly pounding, and Lydia thought she might faint. Her head was spinning, and her feet slipped out from under her, landing her unceremoniously on her behind. A sharp pain stabbed through the fleshy cheek of her right buttock, and she grabbed the top of the stove to keep from reeling over. Recovering as she could, she drew her knees up quickly against her chest and tried to catch her breath. She shut her eyes, fighting back the image of her possible assailant that she might discover peering down upon her.

But what would she do if he *were* there! Suddenly, Lydia Penalte de Sanchez felt a soul-blackening tremble of terror rip from the glands in her throat and twist through her spine, settling in knots behind her knees, and leaving her without feeling in her sweating hands and cold feet. She didn't dare move, but she had to. If only for a moment, she had to crane up just high enough to peep through the utensils.

Lydia backed squarely against the wall beside the stove and drew her feet and knees up under her. Then she placed her hand on the floor beside her to establish a new point of balance. Suddenly, she was aware of the dust, dirt, and grainy grime that had collected on the floor and which had accumulated in the corners of the room. Her stretch pants were stained and her fingers now smudged with kitchen grease and grit.

Momentarily, she had suddenly lost completely her sense of purpose and train of thought as she felt repulsed by the seamy squalor of her own kitchen. She felt the need to wipe her hands but the sudden inclination to reach for a towel drying over the sink brought to focus once more the terror of the moment, and Lydia began to cry.

Squatting in the shadows of her own kitchen, Lydia Penalte de Sanchez shuttered as she felt for the first time the ineffable sentence of death that so many of her friends had tried to explain. Her heart pounding, she was now experiencing what, in wrenching anguish, they had never been able to convey save for the sense of terror and abandonment racing in their eyes. Lydia did not want to die. Not *here!* Not *now!* Not on a *Wednesday!* She wasn't *prepared!* There was so much *more* to *do*, so much left to *dream*. And *Vilma*, her little daughter—what would become of *her!*

With the rush of horror that had just swept through her, Lydia had completely forgotten her child, but she was relieved to remember that she was safely away with her mother who kept the little girl during the weeks when Rutilio and Lydia were busy at the university. The thought of her tiny daughter was the one factor that now comforted her as she sighed in the realization of the infant's security far away in another part of the city, far away from the agents of death she now engaged. Thoughts of her daughter gave Lydia a new resolve, and taking two deep breaths, she gradually eased up from behind the stove and dared to look upward toward the roof line above the patio.

It was clear. Only puffs of a cloud drifted slowly against a canopy of blue. Could it be true? She scanned the roof line back and forth and gradually rose to her feet. She could wipe her hands now and brush off the back of her slacks, but before she could make a move toward the sink, Lydia felt herself turned around, and at once she was wrapped in the security of her husband's arms. Lydia Penalte de Sanchez gave it all up, sobbing uncontrollably against her husband's strong chest.

"It's *okay!*" Rutilio reassured his distraught wife. "It's *okay!* It's all *clear!* Nobody's *out* there!"

Rutilio stroked the length of her long, flowing hair and wiped the tears streaming down her cheeks.

"It's all right, all *right!*" he repeated. Lydia turned her cheek away from his face and rested her head on his shoulder, her chest still heaving from the trauma.

"I *lost* it!" she sniffled. "I really lost all *control!* I really thought I was stronger than that."

"Well, we're okay," reassured Rutilio. "Let's look again for the ledger."

"Yes, you're right," Lydia agreed. "Let's try again."

Finding the ledger wasn't difficult. The small folder had slipped to the back of the top drawer and fallen behind the desk. Lydia had forgotten placing it in the desk to keep it out of the inquisitive little hands of Vilma, their toddler, who loved to rifle the lower drawers.

"I *found* it!" cried Lydia to her husband across the room looking once more under the bed. He jumped and turned around to see a recomposed and obviously relieved wife smiling excitedly, the bound sheaf of pages from her hands.

"Here it *is!*" she offered excitedly.

"Thank *God!*" returned Rutilio as he accepted the loose papers and the folder from Lydia.

"Check it over and make sure that it is in order," he suggested, "and then let's figure out how to get it back."

Lydia slipped back deeply into the short sofa, took a deep breath, and relaxed for the first time in the past half hour. Tears of relief streamed down her cheeks.

"I can go in early tomorrow," she said, brushing away the tears. "I can return the ledger to the safe before Rigoleto arrives. He's supposed to meet with an American group until ten o'clock, so he won't even suspect."

"What about Alma María?" asked her husband. Lydia looked shocked. She had forgotten Alma completely in the frenzy of the last few minutes.

"Oh, my *God!*" said Lydia. "Alma is the only one who knows the transportation schedule. That was her signal last night—the two rings. She was with Rigoleto, and she was supposed to let me know if she was able to get a sense when the shipment was leaving the Polytechnic. She's the only one who *knows!* We've got to reach Lupe *tonight!* If they arrive too *early,* they'll alert the *Bruceros* for sure. They'll be trapped on the *highway!* We've got to get to Alma right now to find out if she got *word* to him!"

Then she blanched. "*Oh, my God!*" cried Lydia. "What if she's *taken!*"

"Then we'll have to get to the radios," said Rutilio.

Lydia Penalte was on her feet and moving toward the closet to grab her jacket.

"We've got to get to *Alma's!*" said Lydia.

"*Goddamn* it!" cried Rutilio. "If Alma María has screwed this up, we're *all* dead!"

"Oh, *no!*" protested Lydia. "She knew exactly what to do. It was all perfectly arranged. Rigoleto was after her all day yesterday. He was really worked *up!* He was chasing her all over the *building!* He really *wanted* it! All she had to do was to get him to tell her what time he was leaving the apartment. We already knew from the schedule he was going to the Polytechnic. He had the whole day blocked out. We just didn't know when he was leaving. Every time they've moved a shipment, he's been there about two hours before. The decoy always goes out about two hours after he leaves for the institute. Then the real thing about an hour later. Alma María is good. She got that information, for *sure!* She wouldn't have signaled last night if there had been any doubt. She *knew* all that!"

Both Lydia and Rutilio knew that they were working the edge, that at any time they might be discovered. The plan was to finish this job and reassess their security. They could leave the country within eighteen hours on any day, from any time. But this job was critical. The EGP hoped to seize the shipment—perhaps as many as a thousand American-made M16's—but if that proved impossible, then to destroy it. In either case, the ancillary effect had propaganda value in embarrassing both the American Embassy and the military.

But clearly, timing was everything. The "mechanics" would secure two LAWS rocket launchers to the frame of one of three outgoing busses from the capital scheduled for the lake. They needed only the word from Lupe in San Filipe to know which vehicle.

At best, the plan was a little convoluted. The bus station in the city was under constant guard. G-2 had plants in the scheduling office, so there was no way to discover the bus assignment directly from the city. The night manager in San Filipe, however, was one of Lupe's men. The idea was to get the signal identifying the correct vehicle from him through Lupe. He would contact Alma María who would telephone Lydia. Lydia would then contact "Hector" at the service garage who would delay the bus to check the drive shaft and grease the U-joint. During the fifteen-minute delay, "Hector" would attach the launchers. The guerrillas would be waiting for the launchers at the first turnoff from the Sololá highway just south of Los Encuentros. Lupe's team would be reinforced by more than two hundred units who were already standing by in Sololá and awaiting the signal for movement up the highway in the night. Lydia had to assume that they were moving toward their rendezvous right now. Lydia and her husband had no time to lose.

Alma's apartment was only two blocks from Rigoleto's. She had taken a small efficiency in the same building as Lydia's after Lydia's appointment to Tourism. The problem today was accessing it. The two-room apartment was on the second floor of what was once the Cacique Hotel. After the `76 earthquake had split the foundation, making renovation for renewed tourist use too costly, the Cacique became a kind of hostel, catering to married USAC students and an increasing number of the internally displaced seeking refuge from the highlands.

Rutilio and Lydia would have to enter the building from the underground parking stalls in order to avoid observation from the street in front of the building. They decided to take a bus rather than to risk the more visible use of their small Datsun. Rutilio made a last check out the front window and then through the open door. Belching clouds of blackened diesel fumes, two commercial trucks ground past with a load of paving stones headed for street repairs around the corner and up a block or two. A couple of taxis drifted by, returning to the airport across the city. The muted roar overhead of a Miami-bound Aviateca jetliner broke the ordinary cacophony of busy street activity. Satisfied that all was normal, Rutilio and Lydia, disguised only behind pairs of sun glasses, stepped onto the sidewalk and sauntered casually for the bus stop two blocks away.

At the corner, five young, uniformed teenage school girls, giddy in their early morning reunion, shared gossip and boy talk mixed with the inscrutable admonitions of a Cakchiquel Maya mother and her two filthy urchins in soaking underwear cavorting about her feet. A *ladino* street merchant stood with folded hands beside a hefty bundle secured in opaque plastic sheeting and an expandable, hemp net. Rutilio and Lydia approached the converging congregation of passengers with an air of nonchalant preoccupation.

Behind them a white Cherokee Jeep with darkened windows and license tags bearing the official "O" prefix turned the corner and parked beside the curb just before the intersection. Rutilio spied the vehicle from two blocks away just as he stepped into the city bus behind Lydia and the others. Although startled, he kept his jaunty gait as he moved on up into the bus, and he continued to fix on it as he strained to peer between bobbing heads of the seated passengers. He was relieved when the Cherokee turned left with the change of the light. Having observed its departure, Rutilio decided the non-issue wasn't worth the insecurity his relation of it might elicit in Lydia, so he merely turned to her, bestowing a somewhat simpy smile of self-confidence, meant only as a gesture of reassurance as the bus inched its way through the traffic, intersection by intersection. Rutilio himself never noticed the dark blue van which slipped in behind the bus two blocks further up from their point of departure.

Alma María's apartment had been ransacked. The door itself had been kicked in and was hanging from a top hinge. Furniture was knocked over, the single, ceramic, Maya-style desk lamp shattered in the corner. The drapes were billowing out the broken window behind the small couch which had been slashed and pulled apart.

"*Move!*" whispered Rutilio, as he grabbed Lydia by the elbow, turned her around, and fled with her down the corridor.

"What should we *do*?" asked Lydia. "They've *got* to *know!* Should we *leave?* Do you think we should just *leave?* Go to Mexico? Go to Philadelphia? Houston? We could live with my uncle in *Houston!* What do you *think*? . . . *Rutilio?*"

Rutilio paced back and forth across the room. They had fled Alma María's apartment and escaped though the kitchen of the adjoining restaurant and out the back alley. They took the bus loading at the corner, transferred on another, and returned to the university. They felt confident, unseen.

"Look," said Rutilio as he took control. "We've got time to think about that. We've got to get this transmission to Lupe, if we're not already too late."

Lydia opened the third drawer from Rutilio's filing cabinet and lifted the mask of fake files from the back of the drawer, revealing the olive-drab transmitter beneath. Carefully, her husband lifted it from the secreted niche and sat it down on the desk. He unwound the power cord, plugged it into the wall socket, and turned it on. He raced through the frequencies several times to avoid giving away his signal and then slowly locked back into the correct frequency for their clandestine communication. He knew he had no more than twenty seconds at the most to complete the transmittal.

"Two tamales, three," Rutilio pronounced distinctly into the built-in microphone.

"Two tamales, three," he repeated, and then he shut off the power, unplugged the unit, and sat it inside the drawer. Lydia carefully slipped the fake files back into place, shut the drawer, and repeated her questioning.

"Well?" she begged.

"Look," said Rutilio. "We haven't been followed. If they were after us, they would have reached us by now. We'd already be picked up. I think we just go on as if nothing's happened."

"What does that mean?" asked Lydia, obviously shaken by the ordeal of the morning.

"Well, I think you go on back to the office and your night class," explained Rutilio, "and I'll go on to the economic conference in Montevideo tomorrow."

Chapter 19

School Days

"You've got a leak," suggested Col. Federico Altapaz, tapping his pencil against the edge of the Guatemalan mahogany desk stretching out before him. Suddenly, he leaned forward and remarked, more insistently, "You've got a leak, and it shouldn't be a big surprise. It's got to be someone in the office."

Pablo Manuel Rigoleto stared over the officer's shoulder at the outline of the emerald and ruby-breasted quetzal bird with its long, cascading tail sculpted in the national seal. The symbol of Guatemalan liberation was illuminated in the stained-glass window behind the colonel's chair. As he swiveled around, the officer's dark silhouette eclipsed the seal. The words of Col. Altapaz only confirmed Rigoleto's suspicions. He had a mole in the office, between the sheets, or both.

"It can't be more than a dozen people or so," said the Director, feigning a count on his fingers in an attempted dodge. "We've placed two people in transportation, a couple in records. We just added three in the last few months in the legal department."

As the sunlight outside shifted, Altapaz became an immobile shadow against the interlocking puzzle of stained glass behind him. From an otherwise stoic mein, the colonel stared at Rigoleto with an incredulous smile. Methodically, he put down the pencil, reached into his shirt pocket, and retrieved a package of cigarettes.

"Pablo . . ." interrupted Col. Altapaz. "Just . . . just *stop* it. *Look* at me . . . who are you talking to, anyway? That's just a *line*, friend, and you know it."

Altapaz fired a cigarette and took a long drag. Rigoleto tried to follow the tail feathers of the quetzal and up the back of the bird, but his view was blocked by the colonel's head.

"Well, Pablo, let me ask you this," continued the colonel. "Or better yet, let me just get to the heart of the matter and drop all these little niceties: who are you involved with in that office, *huh?* If you're poking anybody in that office of yours, *that's* where you need to start!"

Rigoleto wished he could finesse the question and avoid what was obvious to them both. With the officer's slight shift, the national bird had now disappeared completely behind Altapaz's head.

"That's your first suspect, *friend!*" said Altapaz, tapping his pencil rapidly now on the desk. "Huh, Pablo?"

Inwardly, Rigoleto was seething. Who the hell he was screwing and on what terms was nobody's business, least of all this patronizing *son of a bitch!* He had the two finest cunts in the capital, and he wasn't particularly interested in compromising the good times just yet. They both could be subversives, maybe even plants, for all he knew. As a matter of fact, it wasn't the first time he had thought of it himself. Indeed, every time he shoved it home, even the fleeting suggestion of such a possibility intrigued him and made him even hotter.

"Feel my stomach," whispered Lydia Penalte in his ear. He remembered tracing his finger playfully around her navel and noticing the extended girth and the stretching skin. She threaded his fingers through hers and then turned and flattened his open palm against her flared midriff.

"Embarasada!" she whispered and blew in his ear teasingly.

Startled, Rigoleto had jerked his hand away only to have her pull it back where she led his palm in a slow, languid circle over her stomach.

"Whose?" he asked.

Never blinking, Lydia Penalte only stared at her lover with dark, steely eyes and coaxed his hand between her legs.

"Does it matter?" she asked, as she began to writhe from under the excursions of his probing fingers.

"Not at the moment," the Director said. He rolled her over on her side and nuzzled up behind her, forcing his knee into her groin. Slowly, she began to grind against his thigh until she shuddered in a wrenching orgasm.

"I . . . I didn't think so," she stammered into her pillow, as Rigoleto began a rhythmic penetration. Her little teases during sex excited him. He often fantasized his self-confident lover mounted over him, clad only in the open, camouflaged shirt of a field uniform, her pendulous breasts cupped seductively in the shadows behind each pocket. He projected now the hefty, distended belly protruding over his own as he speared her from beneath. Pregnant women were sexy; he imagined them bloated with his own semen. They always reminded him of the little erotic carvings of pregnant women for sale by the street vendors in Barbados, Jamaica, and Bermuda, and the come-ons of pregnant prostitutes turning tricks on the corners of the side streets.

A fly landed on the Director's ear.

"Why? How do you know it's coming out of Tourism, anyway?" Rigoleto quizzed the colonel, tweaked abruptly from his reverie. "It might be the post office, Immigration, the National Bank . . . I mean, *shit!* It could be any *one* of the offices. Why *mine?*"

Increasingly impatient with the tiresome, ineffectual little charade, the colonel flashed and turned on the petulant Director.

"Because Alma María Vargas *said so!* " barked Altapaz, "just before they *`polled'* her!"

Pablo Manuel Rigoleto blanched. The words ripped through him like a shot. He felt the blood drain from his forehead and slip back from around his eyes. His heart raced, and he lost his breath. He started to swoon and had to grip the back of the chair beside him to keep from collapsing. For the moment, he could only stand there, trembling, stone cold, and speechless.

"*Alma?*" he finally managed under his breath. "*Alma María?* How could that *be?* I mean, *Jesus! Alma María?*"

Cool as ice behind the discomfiture of the Director, Colonel Federico Altapaz blew a pair of smoke rings slowly into the air as he watched Rigoleto fainting before him.

"Perhaps you've been a little careless, my friend," said the colonel, a little disingenuously. Altapaz sensed the start the revelation had affected in the Director, but within his orchestrated pose, he wasn't ready yet to risk the loss of his confidence.

"Look, Pablo, sit down, catch your breath. We've known about the girls for quite some time," offered the colonel gratuitously. "We knew before she and Miss Penalte began visiting Juarez. We certainly knew before the two of them began `servicing' you, my friend."

"*Goddamn!*" Rigoleto thought to himself. "Isn't there anything this fucker *doesn't* know!"

And then he exploded.

"Why didn't you let *me* know?" fired the Director, throwing his hand wildly over his head, then drilling his forefinger repeatedly into his own chest. "Why didn't you say something to *me*?" he protested, rejecting the offer to sit down.

The colonel moved from around his desk and approached the Director, now furious and combative.

"Pablo, my friend," soothed Altapaz, reassuringly. "We've been *sympatico* for many years. We don't keep things from each other . . . we never have, *right?* That's why I'm telling you *now* . . . now, before the *Minister of Defense* arrives. Don't worry, Pablo, *amigo*! Your office has been most successful.

Your two little doves have worked exactly as we thought they would after the October affair at San Carlos when we picked up Alma María's boyfriend."

Rigoleto sat stunned by the office disclosures, the compromise of his privacy, but more so, by the obvious affront to the independence and integrity of his own activities for military intelligence. Of course, he had known, but until now had failed to realize the extent to which G-2 functioned at various levels of operations and administration. From the perspective of these new revelations, his own intelligence station now appeared nothing more than a rather unsophisticated little chop shop, a small, two-bit mechanics stall on only the back lot of a much larger playing field. Simply put, Rigoleto felt humiliated and violated. "Justification" never crossed his mind. He was angry to the point of exploding.

"You know, Pablo . . ." said the colonel, sizing up just how far he might penetrate Rigoleto's self-esteem. "You know, we knew that as long as Alma María and Lydia were putting out, you wouldn't screw things up!"

Altapaz chuckled at the pun and his small attempt at levity.

"No, I'm very *serious,*" he said. "Eventually, we knew that they'd make a move on your operations or that they would lead us to the *real* connection at the university," continued Altapaz, "and that's exactly what happened. We needed to get one of them into your office, and, as it turned out, that was Lydia Penalte. She was the best—being outgoing and all. We knew she'd be watching operations, who all was coming and going. But we'd be watching her watching you, you see. Your operations, Pablo . . . your operations have worked well. You're doing okay. In just the last two days, we've flushed out the whole network . . . here, up in San Felipe—well, you'll see momentarily. Colonel Molina-Saloj will join us with the whole report from Sololá."

Hesitantly, with the restoration of only a guarded confidence, Rigoleto sat down in the chair, crossed his legs, and lit a cigarette, trying to maintain some semblance of composure, as he attempted a personal assessment of the moment. At first, he was angered at the idea that all this might be pretext for a judgment of his own operation? He would have no part of that. But now—*No!* That couldn't be the purpose, he was satisfied. He had been performing exemplarily. Operations at the post office had been exposed because of stupidity. His own cover was still intact, he was sure. *No!* If Alma María and Lydia were plants, then he and the girls had been set up, just like Altapaz was suggesting. If he hadn't known, that wasn't his fault; he'd been "kept out of the loop" intentionally. He wouldn't be held responsible for what he didn't know—*goddamn!*

Rigoleto exhaled a deep draught of smoke, comfortable that all was still in order in his own office. He had always maintained careful records that were securely locked away in his own private safe. No one had that combination but himself. He was certain that no one had ever even witnessed his working in the office while the safe was open. He was always careful to lock both the receptionist's office door and his own before ever moving to open it.

Colonel Altapaz turned away from the Director and took his seat once more behind his desk. He had said all that he would for the time being, and he pretended to address a little work, shuffling through some incidental correspondence from the "in" tray on the desk. Both of them had exhausted any interest in further conversation for the moment and obviously were only marking time before the arrival of Colonel Molina-Saloj. Rigoleto lit another cigarette and, after a minute or two of ineffectual puffing, rose from the chair. He began a casual tour of the spacious office, moving to the shelf of the colonel's military displays, campaign trophies, and combat memorabilia. Most impressive were Altapaz's "Presidential Citation for Distinguished Service" and the *Orden del Alvarado*, knighthood for valor in the 1978 Belize campaign. The letter of commendation was signed by former President Lucas Romeo Garcia and outlined the essential features of the colonel's contribution. Altapaz had organized the base camps along the disputed borders and had directed the intelligence network that established the coordinates for the *kaibiles* in the event of a British attack by the Harriers.

The solid gold medallion was suspended from a wide, blue and white ribbon that flared upward from the clasp to the top of the framed mounting board. The blue and white matted letter was offset to the right of the medallion and both finished in a thin, Japanese black-lacquered frame. In a set of matching framed displays were other letters, also in the pen of General Garcia to his "friend and colleague in the quest for Guatemalan freedom": one signed photo with the colonel and the President's brother—Benedicto Romeo—the Minister of Defense, standing beside the bodies of two guerrillas killed in San Felipe, and a second featuring a much younger Lt. Federico Altapaz at a field radio directing an armored assault against guerrilla targets above Esquintla. Rigoleto was projecting his own national decoration—something that he had always coveted—when the door of the Colonel's office swung open followed by the entrance of Lt. Juan Baldor Herrera, the attaché to Col. Molina-Saloj, the Minister of Defense.

"Gentlemen," said the smart, young soldier. "I apologize for keeping you waiting. Colonel Molina-Saloj requests that the two of you join him at the Polytechnic. If you'll come with me, please."

Rigoleto looked at Altapaz for some interpretive signal for this unexpected turn, but the Colonel was already reaching for his uniform cap from the hall tree near his desk.

"After you, Licenciado," offered Colonel Altapaz, and Rigoleto turned, resigned to follow the unfolding script, obviously (at this point) written in another's hand.

At the exit to the military parking garage, the guards raised the gate pole, and Lt. Baldor saluted the heavily armed soldiers as the vehicle passed out of the National Palace.

"What's the agenda at the Polytechnic?" asked Rigoleto as their jeep pulled out into the busy afternoon street.

"You'll—*we'll* find it instructive, I'm sure," said Colonel Altapaz, as he picked up a clipboard stuck between the center console and the seat and began flipping through charts and texts. That assurance was the last word he shared with Pablo Manuel Rigoleto as they coursed through the afternoon traffic toward the Military Training School.

As the vehicle inched along, from intersection to intersection, Rigoleto reflected on his long, though interrupted relationship with Altapaz—growing up in the same village of Suchitepequez, their fathers' jobs in the same trucking firm, attending classes together in the public school. He also remembered, still with some small clot of chagrin, the military scholarship that went to the cocky, little Altapaz, the one for which the two of them had applied. Rigoleto had never pursued the frustrating question that had lingered for more than thirty years: why not *he* as well as Altapaz? Why not *both?*

It was Altapaz's scholarship and later, selection for training among the *kaibiles* that separated them, both personally and professionally. Before his appointment at Tourism and subsequent tapping for G-2 operations, Rigoleto hadn't seen his boyhood friend more than four or five times over the years. On those few occasions, the taut and wiry, up-and-coming military man had had little more than stiff small talk for his former classmate.

Following an uneventful passage through downtown traffic to the Polytechnic Military Academy, the car entered the gates, cleared the perfunctory check in, and proceeded into the interior of the military yard. The attaché parked the vehicle in front of the base infirmary and forensics laboratory. He stepped out, smoothed his coat, and opened the rear door for the Colonel and Rigoleto. Col. Altapaz slipped easily from the car and stepped briskly ahead of the attaché. The Director of Tourism flashed in anger at the apparent rebuff. As Altapaz entered the front entrance to the laboratory, the attaché assumed doorman duties for Rigoleto who, thirty or more paces behind, lumbered down the sidewalk and into the building.

"Where . . . where are we going? What's all this *about?*" he asked.

"Follow me, please," returned Lt. Baldor courteously, though non-committal. It was not his to say, even if he knew.

The two passed down a patchy, painted concrete floor through only a dimly lit corridor striped in the traditional, two-toned military green drab. First left, then right, and then left again, the hallway divided into a maze of narrow passages, each intersection posted with a heavily armed conscript dressed in battle fatigues and banded with grenade belts. Overweight and unused to rapid walking, Rigoleto was already soaked in sweat and irritated by the unseemly circles of perspiration expanding under his arms and around his collar.

"What's the goddamn *hurry?*" he thought to himself. The two made one more turn and approached a doorway midway down the hall lit by only a single, naked bulb burning over the entrance. Two guards posted on each side of the door were the only signals of the importance of circumstances on the other side. As the two men approached, one guard stepped in front of the door, took the doorknob, and pulled the door open for the two men.

Lt. Baldor entered and stepped to the right, giving Rigoleto a full view as he followed into the room. At once, the Director was surprised by the thick air in the chamber. The place was damp, and a heavy, sweet odor of blood seemed to cling to the walls. About to gag on the unexpected stench, Rigoleto almost slipped as the concrete floor began a gradual slope toward a central drain in the middle of the room, apparently some kind of laboratory.

Lic. Rigoleto fought to refocus his sight against the exposed glare of a medical spotlight mounted from the ceiling and hanging low over a stainless steel gurney positioned over the drain. On the gurney lay a body draped in a blood-spattered sheet. Rigoleto winced when he discovered matted strands of long, brown hair hanging out from under the sheet. In contrast to the glare over the gurney, the remaining figures were recessed deeply as only vague silhouettes against the walls surrounding the tables.

"Over here," directed Lt. Baldor. "Licenciado, why don't you step over here. The Minister will be joining us shortly."

"Where is the colonel?" asked Rigoleto.

"He's accompanying the Minister of Defense. He'll be with us in just a few minutes," reiterated Baldor.

Rigoleto's eyes flashed back to the body before him. The feet flared apart from the heels under the sheet. He followed the contours of the legs from the knees upward over the thin outline of the thighs, over the small pubic mound and flat stomach, up to the flattened breasts, and then to the sharp point of the chin turned slightly to the right. Rigoleto shuddered and felt his hands begin to tremble. He suddenly realized that he might not be able to stomach the revelation of what lay directly under the sheet.

"Look," Rigoleto explained, "I've got to sit *down!* I don't know what this is all about, but I need to sit *down, see?*"

Lt. Baldor snapped his fingers, and a soldier standing in the shadows five feet in back of the table, stepped forward toward the head of the gurney.

"Bring the Licenciado a chair, please."

"*Sí! Como no!*" said the soldier who exited at once into the hallway.

As he peered slowly around the room, Rigoleto suddenly sensed the smallness of the place. The heavy air of the room was beginning to overcome him. The sweet, pungent aroma of coagulated blood was an odor he had experienced only once before when he was asked at the military post in Xela to view the bodies of subversives just delivered from the highlands the night before. He had been just as repulsed and unsettled then, even in the open air.

From the beginning of his governmental double-dipping in both Tourism and G-2 some three years before, Rigoleto had always had difficulty squaring the various physical "necessities" of the counter-insurgency with his sense of national responsibility. But whatever his own visceral squeamishness at the operations level, monthly payoffs from the military over the period had been helpful in massaging his "sensitivities." He had never found service to his country difficult from his sixth-floor carpeted office. Names in a ledger were just that and nothing more.

As quickly as he had retreated, the young soldier returned with a short-backed wooden chair and placed it at the foot of the gurney just beyond the perimeter of the floodlight illuminating the body.

"Go ahead," urged the Lieutenant. "Take a seat. The Minister and Colonel Altapaz will join us shortly."

Rigoleto slipped into the chair, wiping his perspiring hands on his trousers. And then it hit him—

"*Madre de Díos!*" he exclaimed to himself. "What if—what if this is *Alma María! Jesus!* Mother of *God!* Oh, my Mother of *God! Not Alma María!*"

The Director suddenly had to fight back the urge to jump up and rip back the sheet. He now stared intently at the strands of hair that appeared glued together in rusty, bloody patches.

"Jesus *Christ!* Oh, my *God!*" he cried within himself. "What have they done to *Alma María?*"

Rigoleto reached into his hip pocket and retrieved his wadded handkerchief. He wiped his forehead and heavy eyebrows, panting now as he seemed to be sweating from every pore in the unventilated room. Moments later—and with no help to his growing confusion, the Director heard footsteps approaching from down the hall.

"Jesus *Christ!* It's about time," said Rigoleto just under his breath, and he spread his feet apart preparing to rise.

"That's all right," said the lieutenant. "Just keep your seat."

Rigoleto was grateful for the forgiven social amenity and reached backward for his handkerchief again. The footsteps drew closer, and Rigoleto recognized the sound of military boots. They paused as the guard stepped forward to open the door. A party of seven or eight entered the already cramped quarters. Rigoleto looked up to see four soldiers—each carrying M16's—enter the room and assume positions in a formal phalanx behind the gurney. They were followed by a Guatemalan captain wearing the maroon tam of the *kaibiles*, armed with a holstered automatic pistol, and behind him, a most unexpected figure.

"Come in, captain," said Col. Altapaz. Through the doorway entered a uniformed American officer, in his mid-thirties perhaps, sharp and alert, and wearing captain's bars. Behind him, silently and unobtrusively, stepped Col. Molina-Saloj, the Minister of Defense.

"Thank you, captain," said the American to the Guatemalan officer. "Colonel Molina!"

The Minister of Defense nodded formally and then retreated to one side of the soldiers and took a position next to Col. Altapaz. When all seemed in place, Federico Altapaz signalled the Guatemalan captain.

"Gentlemen!" he said. "You have been assembled here today to witness the prosecution of subversion against the liberty of the free people of Guatemala."

Inexplicably, the captain's words chilled him, and Rigoleto's hands began to tremble. Embarrassed that they might be discovered, he crossed his arms over his protruding waistline, only to become aware of the uncontrollable twitches in his shoulders that rumbled down his back.

"You have been called together to witness the punishment of *corruption* and the heinous threat that *evil* people have perpetrated," continued the captain, "against those citizens who sacrifice *everything* they have *every day*, those people who risk *all they own* and the well-being of their *families* for the development and growth of Guatemala."

The young soldiers stood at rigid attention in a line behind the gurney, their eyes riveted to the wall over the captain's shoulders.

"These people will stop at *nothing* to ruin Guatemala. They are agents of the *satanic Soviet Union* whose goal is to *dominate the world!*" elucidated the captain. "They start with the little countries, like Guatemala, which they believe are ready for their revolution. They start with the common people, working on their hearts and minds, trying to convince them that communism will give them a better life. They tell the little people—the *hard-working* people of our country—that—just like *that!*" [the captain snapped his fingers]—"that just like *that*, just by killing their landowners, that just like *that* . . . [snap again], "they can take over and successfully *run the country!*"

The captain now began a slow pace back and forth down the gurney, cracking a short riding whip against the edge of the metal table.

"These people care *nothing* for Guatemala and will send *anyone* to the slaughter house if it will serve their *own* selfish and evil purpose!" continued the captain.

"Who are these people?" he asked the young recruits. "Who are these people who would sacrifice you, your fathers, your mothers, and brothers and sisters of Guatemala?"

Rigoleto found himself beginning to get caught up in the rhythms of the articulate, young officer. His message was a familiar one, and one which, for that matter, he thought to himself, ought to be lesson #1 in any national primer.

"Who *are* they?—[snap]—I will *tell* you!" said the captain. "And you shouldn't be so *surprised!* Some of them are your *brothers and sisters*, your *own mothers and fathers* who don't understand the difference between what is right and what is wrong, who can't see the big picture, those who sing the great national anthem of Guatemala but don't understand its meaning; for that matter, those who put *themselves* before their country, those who love *themselves* more than their mother, *Guatemala!*"

"*Who* are these people?" repeated the captain. "*Listen* to me! I'll *tell* you who they are! They are those people—in our *own country!*—who want to get *rich* off the *misery* of others. They are people who want to get *rich* from the *labor* of others, those who won't lift a finger to do the work *themselves!*"

"*Who* are these people?" asked the captain. "I'll *tell* you who they are! They are the *communist teachers and professors* who misguide our young people and lead them into the *evil beliefs of Marxism!* They are the *communist priests* who hide behind their cloaks of religion while they encourage their *paisanos* to work *against the people* and *against the Republic!* They are the leaders of the *trade unions* who want to wreck the economy to fill their own dirty pockets at the expense of the very *life of the nation!*"

"And they are the stupid *guerrillas in the mountains*, those who hide out in the fields, those who lurk at the roadsides, or brazenly walk the streets of your *aldea* and even *here*, in this, the *capital!*" snapped the captain. "They must think they are *invisible!* They must think that they can hide in the *air!* They who think they can fight the Guatemalan army and *win!*"

The young officer was really worked up now. His American counterpart stood somewhat removed from and perpendicular to the line of conscripts receiving the lesson from the captain. Face erect and his eyes fixed before him, the American advisor listened intently to the Guatemalan *kaibile* as he walked vigorously about the small laboratory, snapping his whip and delivering definitions of every kind of "subversive" to each of the four young conscripts standing at attention before him.

Trembling and his guts tied in knots, Rigoleto had waited as long as he could, and he passed a fart that punctuated the captain's last remonstrance. He was weathering the onset of diarrhea, and he felt as though he were about to explode. He knew he couldn't sit there in the room much longer, and the nausea only added to his growing anxiety.

The captain had ignored the Director's untimely eruption, never pausing in his lecture.

"And what are *you?*" asked the officer of each of the conscripts. "And what are *you?*"

The captain peered deeply into the mossy eyes of the soldiers as if searching for any tremble of weakness.

"*You* are the *protectors of the nation!*" pronounced the captain. "*You* are the *shields of the people! You* are the only *hope* between the life of Guatemala and those who wish to destroy it! And *gentlemen! There is no middle ground!* Some of you *dogs growled* when you were asked to leave your homes and to come to serve your nation. But you did not *understand!* How *could* you?"

The captain was maneuvering closer to his point, alternately slapping his whip against his right thigh and sticking it under the chin of the Indian soldiers.

"There is no middle ground in the battle to save the nation from communism!" continued the officer. "There is no middle ground in the battle to save the people of Guatemala from destruction! There is no duty, then, but to serve and—by serving—but to save!"

Slowly and deliberately, the captain scanned the eyes of each soldier.

"But no mangy *dog* can save a *free nation!*" barked the captain, his eyes now glinting and his lips pursed. "Only *dogs of war* will save the nation! Only *dogs of war* will route the *jackals of communism!* Only *dogs of war* can rip the lies from the throats of those who would turn the minds of a *free people!*"

And with his last protestation, the captain ripped back the clotted sheet on the gurney. He had made his point, and the soldiers stood face forward, their lips sealed, and their eyes now tense and black with rage.

Rigoleto's mouth flew apart as the sheet slipped from the foot of the gurney, landing in a heap at his own feet. Bathed in the white glare of the flood lamp, there lay before him the pallid body of Alma María Vargas.

But something was very *wrong!* Even in death, something about Alma María was unexpected and bizarre; small details refused to coalesce, to make any sense. The body on the gurney before him retained only the most general resemblance to that of his former lover. The expanse of the forehead and the tiny chin were the only two features that, at first, suggested any familiarity at all. The remainder of the body appeared contorted in death and savagely violated. Still fighting to make some sense of it all, the Director would have to take notes, add them to his ledgers—*that's* what he could do! He began drafting mental notes.

1) patches of dried blood around the mouth, eyes, ears,

2) the face—pale and waxy;

3) the lips grey, almost translucent.

4) The mouth slightly agape and one eye seemed to stare straight up, and the other? . . .

5) Five? Five!—no other, only the bloody socket and the collapsed eyelid.

6) The right breast slipped to the side beneath the arm, and the left? . . .

16) no "left,"

17) . . . only pink flesh and two exposed ribs.

7) . . . 17) The splintered end of a broom handle protruding from between the legs, shit? no shit—just thick blood,

17) the other end—more than eight inches of the shaft—sticking out just below the right clavicle, blood . . .

18) deep, brown hack marks sliced across the chest and muscles of the arms and shoulders.

19) left ear gone,

20) the right, too.

21) severed hands lying crossed over the sternum,

2) skin of the wrists slipped up more than an inch above the raw stumps of the forearms.

3) the tip of the bloody tongue sticking out of the left hand.

4) face on the right side stretched, bruised red blue, pulled loose from the skull—tried to peel it off? machete? had to be—

14) Alma María Vargas . . . butchered! 14) blood, not shit. . . meat, not lover, not lover, 14) Alma María . . . Alma María, chopped meat.

Rigoleto could not move, but only stared, transfixed by the massive horror before him. His lips were locked slightly open, and everything within him was screaming. But he could not move. His eyes were drying, and he tried to blink, but the Director could not move. A fly had found his ear, dancing in and around his earlobe, but he could not move.

It was the eyes! The poor eyes of Alma María! Pablo Manuel Rigoleto felt himself screaming deep within his throat, but he could not actually hear it. Then he realized he could hear nothing at all.

The captain continued to move back and forth behind the body, jabbing at it with his riding whip and slapping the whip over and over again against the side of the gurney. But Rigoleto could hear not a word or sound. Pablo Manuel Rigoleto was suffering a stroke.

The Director's scream subsided into a groan that extended deeper and deeper into his viscera. It filled his lungs like a heavy fog. The eyes! He sensed it oozing, like a thick cud, from his throat, down his spine, and from out his anus. But the eyes! Down his shoulders it slipped and wrapped around his elbows. Down his forearms and dropped like globs off the tips of his fingers. "Alma's eyes! Alma's eyes! Her poor eyes!" he screamed, but no one heard. His whole body was racked by a screech that whirled about the top of his head. And the captain still pacing back and forth, poking at what was once his Alma María, the splintered staff exiting just below her collar bone, the tongue in her severed hand. Clotted patches of blood on the sheet, in her hair, the beautiful, brown hair of what had been Alma, Alma María, Alma María Vargas—skewered on a fucking spit!—and the captain whom he couldn't hear with the mouth working up and down and the riding whip, flailing and slapping at what was left of Alma María. And the part of her face that wouldn't hold and the ear that wasn't an ear any more the soldiers with their pursed lips the American captain at attention slap! slap! slapping the table—the riding whip the mouth of the captain with the gun shiny under the light, the glinting barrel of the captain's gun, the frothy mouth of the captain gripping the tight handle of the gun over what was left of Alma María, the bloody, crisscrossed stumps of the forearms of the former Alma María the gun glinting in the light, the soldiers' pursed lips, the American captain, Lt. Juan Baldor Herrera smiling, the Minister of Defense behind Col. Federico Altapaz as the gun glinting, the barrel, the Captain's mouth pursed, his terrible eyes squinting, the barrel of the gun that Alma María the gun the gun of the fierce captain's eyes his shouting and the gun the whip and then the gun! the gun barrel! Oh, my God Almighty! the gu

Chapter 20

Sweet Breads and Coffee

"I wouldn't put it exactly that way, Mr. Finley," said Mrs. Townsend. "Our family was always very active `socially,' I guess I would say, but we always had to take precautions."

"Why don't you try one of these sweet breads," she interrupted. "It'll taste very good with Antigua coffee, don't you think?"

Mrs. Phillip Townsend poured Marcus Finley a cup of stiff, black Guatemalan coffee, placed the steaming cup on a small, pale-blue, handwoven napkin with the delicate, white, brocaded quetzal on the center fold, and passed the young journalist a platter of pastries. She picked up a small bell from the side table beside her chair and rang it sharply.

"Thank you, Mrs. Townsend," said Marcus Finley as he watched the "fiftyish" Guatemalan matron take her place on the plush love seat across the coffee table from the reporter. She was a most attractive lady with refined features, elegant posture, and a lithe, trim figure.

Drying her hands on a damp dish towel, Mrs. Townsend's housekeeper, a diminutive Mexican woman dressed in a modest blue and white plaid housedress and full white apron entered from the kitchen and stood at a discreet distance from her patroness and guest, waiting for directions.

"*Sí, Señora,*" said the housekeeper.

"María . . . excuse me, Mr. Finley . . . María, would you bring that small cup of cream from the counter? I forgot it when I brought in the tray."

Sí, Señora," said María, and she turned and walked slowly back into the kitchen.

"You were about to say something about `precautions,'" said Marcus Finley.

"Well, I was trying to remember, now," returned Mrs. Townsend. "Let's see . . . the communists killed my uncle, I remember—God rest his *soul!*—when I was only five or six. We were in Europe with my cousin, and we were very frightened for Daddy who was in the North at the time. We couldn't reach him because the communists had cut the lines. We learned later that they were really after Daddy and not Uncle Luís. But, of course, that was too late for Uncle Luís."

María returned from the kitchen with the cup of cream on a saucer and placed it on the coffee table.

"*Grácias,* María," said Mrs. Townsend.

"Sí, Señora. Algo más?" asked María.

"No, that's fine. Thank you, María," said Mrs. Townsend.

"*Muy bién,*" said the servant, and she took two steps backwards, nodding diffidently, turned, and walked softly back to the kitchen.

Marcus Finley hadn't anticipated the warm reception or the detail Mrs. Townsend was willing to share about her childhood in Guatemala. Mrs. Townsend, the former Señorita Miriam María Belamonte of Guatemala City, for the past twenty years or so had been the wife of a successful physician and internist, Dr. Phillip Townsend, in residence at Wilson Jones Hospital in Martin, Texas. Little about the simple, understated elegance of their expansive, ranch-style home suggested her deep ties to Central America, except for a matching pair of *huipiles* framed on the wall, a handwoven runner down the center of the formal dining room table, and some family photographs mounted in hand-carved, wooden frames nestled in the book shelves.

Don Roberto Fernando Belamonte, her late father, explained Miriam, had been a successful farmer and rancher in Guatemala. At one time, he operated more than a dozen large *fincas*—or *latifundios*—in the highlands and in the Southern coastal plains, in Zacapa and Puerto Barrios in the East, and most of two Indian townships and the surrounding lands—more than 80,000 acres overall. In the highlands, just west of Guatemala City near Antigua, Don Fernando, Miriam's father, owned and worked seven large coffee plantations. In the South, forty kilometers west of *Volcán* Picaya in the steamy department of Esquintla, he drove five large herds of cattle. In Retalhuleu, the expansive and entrepreneurial Don and his brother Luís grew cotton and sugar cane. Of late, after the murder of his brother, Luís, Don Fernando operated a shrimp hatchery on the coast. There was more, of course, Mrs. Townsend continued: the mineral rights, etc. The explanation became tedious in its cataloging. The family estate, she suggested, was one of the most extensive in the country. Her biggest difficulty, now with the death of her father, was to find a way somehow to work around the tight estate laws of Guatemala which prohibited the removal of substantial inheritances. To liquidate her assets for exportation to Texas, Mrs. Townsend had become the second largest cattle producer in Guatemala. Her plan was to sell her stock abroad and return the profits stateside.

Marcus Finley turned the page in the Belamonte-Townsend family picture album. "So, the guard dogs, the soldiers on the roof—these were just part of your growing up in Guatemala?" he asked.

"Mr. Finley, you have to know that, for . . . well, for the `more established,' shall we say, the `better-off,' Guatemala can be a very *dangerous* place to live," offered Miriam. "Security is always a major concern. There are so many thieves. The people like Daddy and Mommy who have taken all the risks in developing the country, those who have tried to raise the standard of living, the ones who have built the highways, and the many schools—*well!* my grandmother brought radio to Guatemala in the 1920's—you see, Mr. Finley, in a small country like Guatemala, a person who is willing to make an investment can watch it grow on behalf of many, many people. In a small country like Guatemala, one person can have a very large impact. Well, I lost my train of thought; I'm sorry. What I was going to say is that there are always people looking for opportunities to take from you everything that you have developed for a lifetime, and the communists are the worst."

"How is that?" asked Marcus.

"The communists have been trying for more than *forty years* to take over the country!" said Miriam, as she collected a crumb of coffee cake on her blouse with a napkin.

"What kind of *power* do they—the *`communists,'* I mean, what kind of *real* power do they have?" asked the reporter.

"Oh, no *real* national power. The army is too strong, *grácias a Diós!*" and she snapped her fingers. "But the communists are always a threat to individuals, especially high-profile business leaders and politicians," said Miriam.

"When did the communists get their start?" asked Marcus Finley.

"Well, in the 1940's, just after World War II. The communists began organizing in Guatemala during the Presidency of Juan José Arévalo in the late `40's."

"He was a communist?" asked Marcus.

"Oh, *no!* Certainly *not!* I don't think any of us thought that," suggested Miriam. "But he tried to make some changes. You see, the people had become sick and tired of President Ubico. He was a tyrant—but *really* a tyrant!—in every sense of the word. He controlled everything and everybody. No one was safe. The people wanted a change. Everything was bad—the economy, the schools—he was a thief. He really ripped off the people; *everyone* suffered because of him."

"So, they elected—`Avalo'?" asked Marcus.

"'Arévalo'," Miriam corrected him. "Dr. Juan José Arévalo. And he was good for the country. He established a minimum wage law, and he did a lot of good for the people. But that's when the communists began operating in the country. They took advantage of the young Guatemalan democracy and the climate of freedom that developed. They wanted to take over the whole country. They were for seizing all the private property."

Miriam offered the reporter a cigarette.

"No, thank you," he said. Miriam picked out a long, thin cigarette from her pack and lit it.

"Do you mind?" she asked.

"Oh, *no! No!*" he said. Miriam took a long draw on her cigarette and exhaled.

"They got started in the labor unions first," she continued. "And we had a new constitution that gave everyone the opportunity to organize, so what could we do? The communists were ruthless, too. They would kill anyone who got in their way. You know, we had a young communist who became very disillusioned and turned the tables on them back in 1948 or so. He had to go to Mexico, but he wrote some—how would you say?—'exposes'—on them. He told what they did and how they lied to the people and how they would kill some of the people who went against them. They were *ruthless!*—but *really ruthless!*—the *communists!*"

Miriam Belamonte Townsend reached into her sleeve and pulled out a small tissue.

"They still attack the power stations; they kidnap people. My father was kidnapped and held for more than a year." Mrs. Townsend wiped a tear from the corner of her eye. "It was awful not knowing about him . . . not knowing whether he was dead or alive, not knowing if he was in pain or suffering. The communists are very evil. We had peace in the country before the communists wanted to change everything. Our family had to pay more than a million *dollars* in ransom before Daddy was released! For thirteen *months*, they held him!"

Obviously under a deep emotional strain, Mrs. Townsend fought back more tears. She picked up the pastry dish from the coffee table, rose, and carried it into the kitchen. Moments later she returned with the platter reinforced with freshly sliced coffee cake.

"Well, Mr. Finley, how are you doing with the photos?" she asked, her composure newly restored.

"What is *this*—what is *this* picture?" asked Marcus. Turning the subject, he thought, might help her regain her confidence in the interview.

"Let me see . . . oh, *that* one! It's out of place. It must have fallen out of the other section. Let me see," said Señora Belamonte. "Oh yes, here it is," she said, reinserting the photograph into its proper slot.

"Yes, these are a series of pictures of Mommy and Daddy's United States reception in 1973. That was a beautiful evening . . ."

Miriam began to drift. She became lost in the memory of a glorious moment in the life of her family. In 1973 she had escorted a delegation from Texas and other parts of the United States on an official junket to Guatemala. Her father and mother hosted the trip of business and professional people from the States as part of a cooperative educational and economic program between the two countries. Miriam, thirty-three at the time, served as the translator and tour guide for the group of seventy or so North Americans. Because of her father's close friendship with the President, her father had been successful in arranging a Presidential reception for a small number of the delegates at the National Palace. Of course, the United States Embassy officials would also be present.

Securing a Presidential reception was no small feat, and its materialization was a sign of the especially close ties between the First Family and the Belamontes. "Daddy" had been a close, lifetime associate of President Marcos Antonio Osuna and his family. They had grown up together, although they had pursued two distinct courses in their lives following their graduation from different universities on the Continent. Don Fernando, Miriam's father, held degrees from the National University of Mexico and the University of Seville in business and economics. General Osuna held a degree in political science from the University of Madrid and had continued graduate studies in military administration and planning from West Point and from military academies in Buenos Aires and Santiago.

The friendship between Don Fernando and the General had been cemented years before when the Don had "acquired" wide tracks of land in El Quiché, acreage rich in mineral deposits and a vast swath of uncultivated properties following the break up the United Fruit Company in the early `60's. Don Fernando and the General—then "Colonel" Osuna—exchanged certain "interests." Don Fernando gave up sections of land to the Colonel's family while Osuna agreed to provide "security measures" that he could arrange for various "sensitive" sectors of the Don's vast holdings. When labor incidents began to break out on Don Fernando's holdings in Zacapa, Colonel Osuna brought in the C47's and moved swiftly to "tidy up the situation."

"Don Fernando," said the Colonel. "We're going to lift the birds from your trees tomorrow night and take them east on a little moonlit flight!" Miriam's Daddy liked to recall the incident in selected circles.

"Well, my good friend," said the Don, "we do what we have to do, *eh?*"

Miriam returned to her guest who was still turning through photos of that distant reception.

"It was a lovely, but truly *lovely* evening," explained Mrs. Townsend, as she focused on another photo from the reception, and Miriam was adrift again.

"The Honorable Judge Arnold and Mrs. Ferris, Baytown, Texas," announced the Presidential Secretary.

"The Right Rev. Parker Stewart, Houston, Texas."

"The Honorable Mayor Walker and Mrs. Bumpass, Jacksonville."

The Presidential Secretary continued to introduce the forty guests of President Antonio Osuna and the First Lady of Guatemala.

The National Army Marimba Band continued its lively, melodic strains as the President and First Lady received the delegation.

"Daddy and Mommy have worked for many months with the Presidential staff in coordinating plans for this evening. I think it is very lovely, don't you," asked Miriam Belamonte as she took Claudia Ramos of Brownsville by the elbow and escorted her guest around the corner to the living room.

"Miss Ramos, it is my pleasure to introduce to you Señora Matilde Barcos de Palmieri, the wife of the late President of Guatemala and former First Lady of the Republic."

"I assure you, it is my pleasure to meet you," said the First Lady to the Brownsville realtor. "I hope you are enjoying your stay in Guatemala. Is this your first visit?"

"Why, yes, it is. Thank you, and it is certainly an honor to meet the wife of such a distinguished family of Guatemala. I know that your husband was a close friend of the people of the United States," said Mrs. Ramos, as she adjusted the cup of her bra while taking a sip of her martini.

"My husband was a martyr to freedom and a very dear, special friend, yes, indeed," said Señora Barcos de Palmieri, in flawless English. "He was dedicated to stopping communism in our country and restoring liberty to all the people of Guatemala. Thank you, Mrs. Ramos, for coming to our small country. I hope you enjoy your visit. How long will you be with us?"

"Only five or six more days," returned Mrs. Ramos.

"Well, I am very, very sure that you will find a warm reception throughout the country," said Señora Barcos de Palmieri. You must see Lake Atitlán and our Indians."

"Yes, thank you. I believe the lake is on our schedule," acknowledged Mrs.

Ramos, "and I just adore the weavings! Don't you think they're just wonderful! Everywhere you go, you see the Indian women under the trees or beside their houses weaving. I think that is just so lovely and picturesque. I saw the most gorgeous table cloth this morning. I may just have to buy it before I leave. I bet if you were with me you'd know how to get the very best price. I just couldn't believe they were asking twenty dollars for the set. Twenty dollars `American'!"

The former First Lady smiled politely and extended her hand. Mrs. Ramos was holding up the reception line that had continued to form behind her.

"Well," she continued, "it has certainly been a pleasure, Mrs. Palmieri!"

Across the reception hall and around the corner from the patio and the lively marimba music, a young university professor was engaging the American Chief of Staff, William Chafin, who listened somewhat restlessly to the enthusiastic educator. On his first trip to Guatemala, Dr. Chalmers Brinkley was outlining a list of exchange proposals he hoped to discuss with Guatemalan college and university representatives in a day or so.

"Yes," said Chafin. "That's all very nice, I'm sure. Look, Mr. Brinkley," he said, clearly and intentionally ignoring the young professor's doctorate. "Let me give you some advice, okay?"

"I beg your pardon?" said Brinkley.

"I've been down here awhile—in three other posts in Latin America, but you can take it for what it's worth: tuck those little notes back in your brief case and leave'em at the hotel. Enjoy yourself while you're here. Have a good time—that's what these little get-togethers are all about—and then go on back to the States and get back to work. Nothing'll ever come from any of that. Now, if you'll excuse me . . . ." Chafin was a busy man with two more receptions still to attend that same evening.

"Mr. Chafin . . . !" the academic responded, but Chafin had already engaged a newspaper publisher and a couple of lawyers, gentlemen more to his own age and taste than the university types, especially like Brinkley, who had a persistent way of annoying him. If nothing else, Chafin derived a little humor in making them squirm. He could always count on usually one or two of these "Latin America `wannabe's'" to needle him about this or that—always something that was none of their business or completely out of their frames of reference. Basically, the narrow interests of academics bored him. They rarely, if ever, had an appreciation for the broader, "American" view of things. New to Guatemala, Brinkley was an easy target. Chafin knew how to walk off and leave the new ones, like him, twitching like a lizard stapled to the side of the barn door. Let Badger have him.

". . . you know how many people you can get in a Guatemalan bus?" offered Badger.

A couple of the two-stepping Texas matrons—who were hanging on his every word—strained for his answer.

"Dos mas!" he said, raising two fingers. "Two more!" he offered as a courtesy. When she got it, Mrs. Blackshear almost lost her self-control in a guffaw that disturbed the strained, formal ambience of the others attending the Presidential reception who turned as a group toward the corner of the reception hall.

At 6'2" tall and 240 pounds, Jim Badger was a large, gregarious ten-year veteran of cultural affairs in Latin America and fluent in Spanish, German, French, and Russian. Though it had only been hinted as a possibility, in fact, he would be in Moscow before the end of the year. The foil to his suave, sophisticated boss, Badger was the "good old boy," the "glad hand" at any reception who could easily put the "folks" at ease. He liked to appear approachable and social; he liked to come off as the "neighborly" type. He had perfected the little pose over the years.

At this point, Jim Badger was trying to juggle a cup of coffee, two sugar cookies, and a conversation with Sissy Blackshear of Fort Stewart, Texas, and he was about to drop one of three. Sissy Blackshear, a buyer for Helman's Foods, was laughing so hard she was about to slobber her martini down the front of her exposed bosom. As she raised a napkin to her lips—to salvage her reputation as the genteel sort—Chalmers Brinkley made his move.

"Let me help you," said Brinkley. "Let me take that glass," he said to Mrs. Blackshear.

"Oh, thank you, honey," she said. "Oh, me! I am so embarrassed! Oh, my! That is just a precious joke, Jim! I must remember it!" exclaimed Sissy Blackshear, as she squeezed the Cultural Attaché's arm in a charming, winning way.

"Oh, thank you so much, Dr. Brinkley," said Sissy Blackshear as she retrieved her martini.

"Jim," she said, "let me introduce you to Dr. Chalmers Brinkley of Central State College over in Thompson County."

"`Dr. Brinkley' is it?" asked the friendly official.

"Well, `Chal' . . . `Chal Brinkley,'" offered the sociology professor.

"I'm pleased to meet you," said Jim Badger, in an expression of genuine interest and courtesy. "Is this your first trip to Guatemala?" he asked, the requisite opening question at these functions.

"Oh, yes," said the professor. "I'm pleased to meet you. You sound like

you might be from the South yourself."

"Houston, actually," said Jim Badger. "I grew up in West Houston—over in Bellaire—you know that part of the city?"

"Generally. I've only done some work at the University of Houston once or twice and get lost outside the downtown area and the airport," explained Brinkley.

"Yeah, I grew up in Houston before moving out to the West Coast—UCLA for my undergraduate and masters work," said Badger.

"You're at the Embassy? Is that right?" asked Brinkley.

"Yeah. I'm in Cultural Affairs," related Badger. "I'm really doing some double duty as the Information Officer at Embassy."

"You'll have to forgive me," said the professor. "I'm completely new to all this foreign service thing. What do you do as an `Information Officer'?" asked Brinkley.

"Well, to be perfectly honest," said Badger from behind a wide, puckish grin, "it's my job to disseminate United States propaganda."

"Okay . . .," said Brinkley, trying not to appear as unsettled as he felt at such a revelation. He wasn't very successful.

"Well," said Jim confidingly, trying to be a little charitable as well as informative, "you know, Chal, it's never in the best interest of the United States to reveal everything about every subject to just everyone."

Brinkley smiled gratefully.

"Things can get pretty complicated down here, and we try to do our part in the Information Service to help keep the lid on, if you know what I mean," explained Badger. "Embassy is sort of a lightning rod for a lot of different groups and interests down here. We get our share of clowns down here as well as people who are really out to do some good, get some things done. So, we try to be as much a help as we can without `stirring the pot,' you know."

"Yeah, I imagine," said Brinkley.

"Listen, if I can be of any help to you while you're down here, Chal, here's my card. It's always good to see some home folks in Guatemala," said Badger as he pressed his large, puffy hand into the grip of the professor.

It would be more than a decade before `Chal' Brinkley would become sophisticated enough in foreign affairs to realize the professionalism of a `Jim Badger,' that while charming his way through a crowd for an hour or two, he could say nothing and reveal even less.

The marimba fell silent and the old septuagenarian, maroon-suited musicians retired into a private alcove across the patio. The professor drifted over to the tuxedoed attendant bearing a tray loaded with more than a dozen styles of bite-sized hors d'oeuvres. Joining him were other members of the Texas delegation—State Senator Toddie Lee Wyndham, Hudspeth County Commissioner Elsworth Privit. Other Texas notables were just gravitating to the pastry trays when a loud blast from a chorus of conch shells startled the guests. Everyone turned toward the entrance of the reception hall as a quartet of conch players from the hallway behind the doors of the hall blew four long "chords." With the last blast of the shells, the Army marimba band began playing the deeply melodic and melancholy strains of the "Paabanc," the folkloric dance rhythms of the Spanish Imperial City of Cobán.

After a short marimba introit, a figure emerged from the dark hallway and into a soft spotlight that illuminated the top ramp that stepped down into the reception area. Gasps and sighs greeted a tall, elegant, twenty-year old Guatemalan girl, her arms extended straight out from her side. She wore a simply-tailored, long, white homespun tunic, not unlike the male topees of the Lacandon Maya of the Petén, that extended from her neck to the floor. Around her neck was an authentic, ancient Mayan jadite bead necklace selected from the private collection of the Belamonte's treasures. Towering from her head was a fan of exotic pheasant feathers, a spray of iridescent browns, reds, oranges, and beige.

Looking straight forward and smiling demurely, the model moved in rhythm to the center focus of the spotlight, turned slowly to reveal the full effect of the headdress, and then passed down the flight of steps into the middle of the reception hall. Just as she reached the lowest step, a second model appeared from the shadows of the hallway and into the spotlight. In a white Maya tunic like her partner before her and wearing a black Mayan axhead pendant on a hand-beaten silver necklace, the beautiful, young college student turned full circle to accent her headdress of emerald peacock plumes that extended in a corona more than four feet in circumference.

A dozen Guatemalan ladino beauties paraded through the reception hall, each in step with the soft, melancholy strains of Mayan sons played wistfully by the marimba band on the patio outside the hall. As each girl moved among the delighted guests, she was greeted with spontaneous applause and cries of pleasure.

"Yes, sir! That's some gal!" said R. C. "Bubba" Burke, rancher from Pala Duro Canyon. "Whoo-eee! Go it, honey!"

"My word!" exclaimed Ms. Diane Meadors, Austin socialite, who habitually kept wrestling her bracelets up her wrists and over her elbows each time they slipped. "I never realized plain muslin could be so glamorous!"

"Hot damn! Don'cha wisht we could git somethin' lak'at for the drill team

nexyur!" exclaimed Ponder "Pokey" Macmillan, superintendent of the Piney Grove I.S.D.

Flowing with the sad strains of the marimba, the girls mingled easily with the crowd, charming everyone with their smooth, olive complexions, narrow sloe eyes, sculptured lips, and rehearsed English greetings. The Texans formed somewhat distant rings around each model who turned slowly, dipping her eyes if not her head, stealing the show completely from the President and First Lady still fixed in place at the head of the reception hall, accompanied by their formal guards and attendants.

Four or five minutes after the entrance of the final model, as if on silent cue, each model bowed deeply, dropping on one knee, bending her head forward until the tips of the headdress swept the floor in front of her. Then, just as gracefully, each lifted her head, rose again, turned and drifted toward the center of the reception area, and passed in single file in her original order out of the hall. The Texans exploded in a round of gasps and applause at the closure of the unexpected display and then returned to their respective pleasures around the bar, as, from the alcoves, the servers slipped into the hall once again with their lacy trays of hors d'oeuvres.

The musicians continued selections of traditional Mayan music. Like the clinking of a gaudy trinket, the tight little sticks beating out the tenor melody of the marimba measured out the tune, echoed in the strong, deep, resonate base keys at the opposite end of the keyboards. The drummer rolled the sticks around the rims of the drumheads in steady rhythms, complementing the strong, reserved, pulsating beats of the string base just behind him. The lead musician reached the coda of the last son and nodded his head, the signal to take the ending. The melody turned right, and the tenor sticks tripped to a crescendoing climax punctuated by a quick roll of the drum heads and a crash of the cymbals. As a group, the six musicians crossed their sticks at their waists and took one step back from their instrument.

Comfortable chit-chat rattled in little clusters about the reception hall. The black-vested servers slipped from group to group hawking their fancy pastries. After a few moments, the Presidential Assistant strolled to the center of the floor, stood erect as he faced the President and First Lady and announced:

"Señoras y señores, ladies and gentlemen!"

The Texans turned from their chatter, jowls bulging, with martinis at their lips or in easy range. The room silenced once again.

Satisfied by their attention, the Assistant proclaimed, "His Excellency General Marcos Antonio Vale Osuna and the First Lady of the Republic of

Guatemala!"

Once again, the Texans broke into warm and enthusiastic applause. Now flanking both the President and First Lady were their Guatemalan hosts Sr. and Sra. Fernando Belamonte and their daughter Miriam, the official translator for the reception, who moved into a position just next to and slightly in front of President Osuna.

"Nuestros estimados amigos de Texas . . ." began the President.

"Our esteemed friends from Texas . . ." returned Miriam.

"De parte de la gente de la Republica de Guatemala . . ." said the President.

"On behalf of the people of the Republic of Guatemala . . ." Miriam repeated.

"En esta ocasión tan amable . . ." said President Osuna.

"On such a pleasant occasion as this . . ." said Miriam.

"The First Lady and I wish to welcome you to our small country, the `land of eternal spring,' with wide arms and an open heart for our United States friends," continued President Osuna.

"As you know, Guatemala is a land of three civilizations and many wonderful and mysterious traditions. But Guatemala, like so many other Third World nations, is striving to assume its place in the world community. In that development, we have relied many times on support from the United States. We are deeply in debt for the foresight and the help that Guatemala has always received from the people of the United States," Osuna said.

"Most of all, when we, the people of Guatemala, think of the United States, we are thankful for your model of freedom, and we are grateful for our own liberty—our freedom from the manacles of oppression and slavery," said Osuna. "You are aware, I am sure, of something about the blackest part of our history when Marxist-Leninist communists attempted to take over our country. They wanted to rob us of the most precious gift we can give to one another outside of life itself: that is our freedom."

The Texans were loving it.

"Together—with the help of your government and the support of you, the American people—godless communism was set back," so the little lecture continued. "The people of America and la gente—the people of Guatemala—learned a very important lesson: we must always remain vigilant; we must always remain on guard against communist aggression!" cried Osuna. As Miriam translated the last statement, the Texans broke into a spasm of vigorous applause. President Osuna took it as his cue. Almost evangelically, he continued:

"To fight communism, you know from your own experiences in Viet Nam that sometimes we must do things that are difficult to justify outside the context of the fight," explained the President. "Because the communists fight dirty, sometimes we must fight dirty, also."

The American Chief of Staff William Chafin, standing to the side of the delegation, smiled benignly and applauded politely. Jim Badger, on the other hand, like a senior on the high school cheering squad, clapped heavily, winking and smiling from side to side, quick to catch the eyes of his own paisanos.

"Wars are never pleasant, but unfortunately, war is the only thing that the communists understand!" explained the President.

The Texans bestowed more enthusiastic applause. The "beehive" salad ladies of the Sweetwater Women's Auxiliary knew all about "commynists." Austin stock brokers, Dallas bankers, and East Texas state senators knew all about "commynists," too, as did West Texas ranchers and South Texas realtors: they all knew about "commynists"—always wary and on guard for them, of course, just as they were for gays, lesbians, atheists, "libbers," and other suspicious minority types trying to break up their neighborhoods, running for positions on their school boards, teaching freshman English over at the community college, slipping into Democratic party caucuses, influencing the Ruling Body of Elders in the local churches, even organizing programs for their P.T.A.'s. No Guatemalan president need instruct them on "commynists." They could tell you some "war stories" of their own! They knew how to "red line" a city map or how to turn out the dogs on a "wet back." But "scorched earth" probably wasn't a term in the vocabulary of most Texans attending the reception that evening; "Jim Badger," however, enjoyed a broader education.

"And this guy?" asked the reporter.

"His name was 'Jim' . . . `Jim Badger.'" said Mrs. Townsend. He was a wonderful man, a really friendly person. He was killed by the guerrillas in 1979 in Chimaltenango while he was escorting a musical ensemble to Antigua for a concert. The guerrillas stopped the Embassy car on the turnoff to Guatemala City when they were coming back from a trip to 'Chichi.' They pulled Jim out of the car and shot him—*shot* him! Right there in front of the *ensemble!* It was really *awful*. The musicians just panicked. It made all the newspapers, you know."

"Why did the guerrillas attack him?" asked Marcus Finley.

"I really don't know. Probably because he worked at the American Embassy. You know, Mr. Finley, the communists are doing everything they can to ruin our country from inside and outside. They attack people who work in the American Embassy just to show how vulnerable the people—*really*, how vulnerable all of us are in the country," said Mrs. Townsend. "So, they killed Jim Badger in cold blood, *really!* Really, in *cold blood* just so they could show they could *do* it! They are completely *ruthless,* and that is really what we're up against in Guatemala!"

"Mrs. Townsend, who are the `communists' you are talking about?" asked Marcus Finley.

"Who *are* they?" asked Mrs. Townsend. "Who *are* they?"

"Well, I mean . . . I mean are they 'Guatemalans' or outsiders, foreigners, I mean?" explored Marcus Finley.

"Well, 'Guatemalans,' *sure!*" said Mrs. Townsend. "They're *all* Guatemalans. They get help, though, from the outside . . . from Nicaragua—the Sandinistas, you know, from Cuba, from Czechoslovakia—that's what we're up against in Guatemala. It's an international communist conspiracy to take over a free country with *so* much history and tradition."

"Mrs. Townsend?" asked Marcus Finley, rather unsympathetic with what sounded so much like an official party line. He wanted to talk about some specifics.

"Yes," she said.

"May I ask you some other questions . . . questions about some, well, some news stories . . . I mean you might have a more informed opinion than what American readers might have," explained Marcus.

"What *questions?*" asked Mrs. Townsend.

"Well, I guess you would have to say they are about some of the stories that have appeared in newspapers and in other publications," he explained. "Stories about the military attacks on the Indian villages like Patozí in the highlands and the killing of students—"

"Mister *Finley!*" interrupted Mrs. Townsend. "Those *stories*—you just can't *believe* those *stories!* The North American media always portray the army as the villains, and I am really tired of all this liberal attempt to discredit my country and its government. The truth, these stories—even *questions* like *these!*—just make the situation worse, because they encourage the guerrillas to do more killing."

At this point, Miriam's right fist clawed with white knuckles the cloth napkin from her pastry dish.

"Guatemala is a *civilized country!*" she protested. "Don't you think if those things were happening, the world would know about them?"

Miriam Belamonte-Townsend was deeply disturbed and about to lose her composure. For years she had had to deflect such reports, and she was understandably a little battle weary. It was difficult to maintain composure any longer, but "there was too much at stake." She had to remind herself constantly, "to let down her guard," particularly before a young, enthusiastic reporter like Marcus Finley. Any kind of bad press could have severe and long-term consequences that could lead to increased hostilities and difficulties for her family, not to mention her inheritance. She simply had to be careful.

Miriam Belamonte-Townsend would try a different tactic.

"It's what I was telling you before, Marcus—may I call you `Marcus'?" she asked. She knew that she was inviting liberties, but a more personal rapport might check some of the urgency she sensed in the young man.

"Yes, of course," offered Marcus Finley.

"Well, *`Marcus,'* then . . . ," Miriam responded.

"Marcus," she continued, "may I share a confidence with you?"

"Well, of course," said Marcus.

"Marcus," said Mrs. Townsend, as she leaned modestly forward, crossing her elbow over her knee. "You must know that my family is one of the first families of Guatemala. We have always loved our country very deeply, and you know that we have had some problems—like I was explaining to you. But these reports of the military killing the *people!* Marcus, you *must not* believe them! They are simply *lies*—every *one* of them! They are lies planted by the guerrillas to stir up trouble for the government. The guerrillas put on Army uniforms and go into the villages and do these terrible things so that the people will be afraid of the soldiers and take the position of the guerrillas. Now that is documented *fact!* All the officers in the Army come from some of the finest families of Guatemala—from good *Catholic* homes! Many of our military leaders have trained in the United States—at Fort Benning, *Georgia!* I mean, right here in the *United States!* For goodness *sake,* Marcus! Now, what sort of `atrocities' do you think they are learning at Fort Benning, *Georgia?* If the Guatemala militaries are committing atrocities, where do you think they have learned how?"

Of course, Miriam's peculiar slant and subsequent ironies were founded, at least, on documented "family fact." Miriam's brother-in-law was a captain who had trained at Fort Benning and who, in subsequent years, was decorated for leadership in "counter-insurgency campaigns" in the Ixcán, El Petén, and San Marcos. And for the Catholic allusion: was not the Archbishop himself a frequent dinner guest during their childhood?

"You know that we have a democratic constitution," said Miriam, turning the thrust of her rebuttal to the Republic.

"The people vote for whom they want for the Congress and for the

President," explained Miriam, "and there are many, many people *still* who don't want to see democracy grow and flourish in our country. They are very greedy people who are dedicated to the overthrow of everything that is fine and decent in Guatemala."

"So, the report of the killings of the *Indians* in Patozí in *El Quiché*—that didn't *happen?* The story that we heard came from two refugees, not from the newspapers, but from two Indians who fled from Guatemala who were *there*, who *saw* what happened!" said Marcus Finley.

"*Marcus!* . . ." responded Miriam Townsend. She had to catch herself. Eye witness reports were something else. It was always much easier to fight the more amorphous "liberal press."

" . . . who *were* these two people?" asked Miriam Townsend, as she settled back into her chair with her fingertips to her chin, slipping now behind the mask of the gracious doubter.

"Well, they were Indians from Patozí," said Marcus. "We interviewed them at Casa Libertad just last month."

"*`We'?*" asked Miriam.

"Father Michael Justice, a priest who works in the Valley with the refugees," explained the reporter.

"And these . . . these two *Indians:* they said they were *from* Patozí?" asked Miriam. Mrs. Townsend knew of the report of the massacre at Patozí. She knew it very well, indeed. The government had plans to develop a large section of the territory for extracting rich veins of nickel that geologists had recently discovered. Small families of Indians had lived on the land for generations—and probably for centuries (family grave sites dated at least to the mid-nineteenth century)—but they had no legal titles. Very few Indians ever had such titles. They were squatters, the land—open frontier. The government always tried to persuade these people to leave peacefully, to find other properties. What was the government to do? You can't have a handful of squatters holding back the development of a whole *country!*

"Besides," said Miriam, "the incident had been fomented by a drunk Indian in the first place. The Indians had been complaining for weeks about the government's plan to seize properties. They had gone to Guatemala City and had tried to stir up a lot of trouble. But the government had the full right to develop untitled land and to enlist corporate support and the assistance of the Guatemalan investors and growers in the industrial and agricultural sectors."

There was no question, in Mrs. Townsend's mind, certainly, that the government had been most patient; the protests had gone on quite long enough.

"When the government officials decided to hold a hearing at the church in

Patozí, these *Indians came armed with machetes,"* explained Mrs. Townsend. *"One of them actually* attacked one of the soldiers who were there to maintain peace during the talks. And then these Indians went *crazy*, running all over the town."

"That's not what they *said,*" interrupted Marcus.

"Well, who *are* these two Indians?" asked Miriam, curious as to how two such keen eyewitnesses could have escaped! "Those *Indians* come up here to take American *jobs!* They pick up these stories along the way and start spreading them around so when you and I hear them again we can say, `Yes, that's what I heard, too. So, it must be *right!*' Marcus, I've heard these stories for years. These Indians will say anything, *but anything* to get here to the United States, and they'll put on a pretty good act, too. Fortunately, we have very experienced judges in our immigration courts who can detect these filthy, little *frauds!* They're nothing but *vermin, Mr. Finley! Filthy, little communist vermin!*"

Miriam was on her feet now, shaking her fist and napkin before her. "And you better know, all of you . . . you, you *reporters* who are always so ready to write up every little wretched, lice-infested Indian *slut*—we are not just going to roll over *dead* and give up everything we've worked for all of our *lives!* It's not going to *happen, Mr. Finley!* Not for *them!* Not for *you!* Not for those . . . those *`priests'!* Not for all those human rights . . . those, those *`internationals'* coming in from God knows *where,* thinking they can run our country—not for *them!* Not for *anyone! Never!* And that's the way it *is!*"

Miriam María Belamonte-Townsend had finally lost it, lost it completely. She had become louder and louder. Now tears were streaming down her face, much to the embarrassment of Marcus Finley. This whole situation was starting to get very personal between two strangers who obviously had nothing in common—background, income, education, politics, religion, or even sentiment. And it was sentiment that was making the difference.

Marcus Finley, liberal reporter, had heard enough, and he began to fold his notes and place them in the briefcase which he closed and clasped shut. He rose and said politely but determinedly, "Mrs. Townsend, thank you for allowing me to see you this morning. These are very difficult topics to talk about, but I must tell you, with all due respect: what I have heard you say this morning tells me that the killings of the Indians will not stop for a very long time."

"*Mr. Finley!*" exploded Mrs. Townsend. "Will you please *leave!*" And she rose and stormed across the den to the adjoining hallway and released the alarm to allow him to exit.

"*María! María!*" cried Mrs. Townsend, as she stood next to the study door at the alarm panel, her arms folded across her breasts. Marcus Finley wiped his mouth and placed his napkin next to his coffee cup on the table. He picked up his briefcase and turned hesitantly toward Miriam, anticipating the opportunity at least to shake her hand, obviously an unwelcome gesture, from the expression and posture of his host. María entered quietly once more from the kitchen.

"Sí, Señora?" asked the housekeeper.

"Mr. Finley is just *leaving!* Will you please show the *gentleman* to the *door!*" ordered Mrs. Townsend, a trace of a tear still streaking her cheek, and she recrossed her arms to reinforce her determined closure of the interview.

Marcus Finley followed the housekeeper out of the den, past the formal living room, down the corridor, and to the door. As María reached for the door, Marcus Finley could hear the muffled sobs of Miriam Belamonte-Townsend.

Chapter 21

A Time For Us

Ana Fabiola could be irritable. A year later—a year after the arrival of Susan Simpson in San Felipe—little things were beginning to frustrate her. Little things like Remigo Toreo talking about her with Patricia Lopez and Meri Batos, that "bitch"—*there!* She had said the *word!* It wouldn't be so hard a second time, because that's what she *was*—just a *"bitch"!*

Ana Fabiola was relishing the sound of the word as it rolled off her lips—"Meri Batos, the `bitch.'" She would have to be careful where she used a word like that. If she heard it, her mother would be so hurt and *angry!* Lucita María would be horrified to hear such a word as that!

"She's *so!*—Lucita María, the *Saint!*" Ana Fabiola whispered caustically just under her breath. Sometimes she just *hated* her older sister—well, she really didn't `hate' her. Not like *that!* Nevertheless, Lucita María thought she was just "so *good!*" She was always "so" . . . *"so"* . . .! Anyway, the convent might be a good place for her. She would make a good "sister" in the church someday. But a life in a convent wasn't for her. Ana Fabiola would have her man and she would be a woman and she and her man would have a family and they would be the pride of San Felipe and then she would show that nosy Patricia Lopez who couldn't mind her own business and that Meri Batos who always liked to go around talking out of both sides of her mouth and telling vicious stories about other girls she didn't like and all, trying to make trouble for everybody.

Ana Fabiola's suspicions about both schoolmates were well founded, but they weren't the only two young friends feeding the rumor mill, nor was there anything particularly out of the ordinary in the vicious frenzy for repeating them that often overtook a community of friends. Stories about so outgoing a girl as Ana Fabiola Xoy were nothing new to the social circuit of San Felipe. The target of such tales, however, had reason to resent them because they often tagged a person for a long time, in some cases even for years. Fabricated or not, little stories were passed along with relish, sometimes generation after generation, taking on a dynamic of their own. The incessant, undulating pool of such *fablios* constituted, in fact, a kind of living reservoir of an *aldea's* identity and its meaning. Without the endless rounds of little stories, life for the villages had no memory, presence, or a frame on which to envision a future.

At the highest level, tales idealized the past and honored the ancestors. With measured grace, though only in the security of carefully orchestrated circles of confidantes, the old folks would relate the familiar, worn-out stories, always to the renewed joy and enthusiasm of all around them. In turn, and out of unbridled respect, their listeners among the junior ranks were always more inclined to tolerate the little inconveniences necessitated by a mentor's weakening eye or arthritic limb as together they celebrated through the stories the revered prowess and lusty adventures of the ancestors.

Tales also served less honorable but no less essential roles as well. Even a plausible lie could function as a cathartic, a corrective, or both. With little more than a saucy smirk and haughty wink, San Felipe matriarchs wove the threads of well-timed little rumors that secured their influence among their peers, usually at the expense, of course, of village fools and outsiders. At the other end of the social scale, young girls were judged in the society of their friends to the extent that they could finesse the most vicious innuendos that one might make of another and somehow best an adversary. In school or on the playground, dull-witted waifs were ostracized by their betters and relegated without mercy to the social trash heap. Always on the periphery of school life and community activities, these poor creatures stood apart and suffered immeasurably.

What might have been described in a more urban setting as a "streetwise kid," Ana Fabiola always rode the crest of popularity among her friends, most of them a year or two younger than herself. Though none would admit it, they drew reassurance from little Ana Fabiola's neighborhood savvy. She always spoke her mind, said what she thought, and friends always knew where they stood around her. She knew about the other girls in San Felipe and never took anything off of them. Ana Fabiola was a natural leader who wasn't anybody's pet dog; nobody led Ana Fabiola Xoy around. And it was always interesting how she could control the conversation. Most of the time, the topic came quickly around to Felipino boys, and it was never very far in a discussion before Isaiah Xolop came to dominate everyone's attention. "Isaiah did this," and "She saw Isaiah when he was," or "You wouldn't believe who Isaiah was laughing with today." All she could talk about was "Isaiah *this*" and "Isaiah *that*."

It was all quite a change. When she had found herself initially attracted to Isaiah, four years older than she, Ana Fabiola had refused to speak about him, fearful that she might be thought pretentious. That all changed when Pilar Suarez began seeing Tonsol Agusto Chol, the nephew of the former *alcalde* of San Felipe, who was almost three years older. Ana Fabiola suddenly realized that she had better stake her claim among her friends. It would have just about killed her to have overheard some other girl talking about Isaiah Xolop.

"Once she had her man," Ana Fabiola kept telling herself, "she could have it all." There wasn't a question of a better choice. As soon as he began to notice who she was, surely this fellow would realize what she had to offer. Who looked as `promising' as she, anyway? She could make a hearth and prepare *frioles*, grind the *masa*, and make the tortillas. She could keep a place and clean the clothes. True enough, she wasn't much of a weaver, but with a little practice, she probably could execute passable work. Most importantly, Ana Fabiola knew that she could keep a man as good looking as Isaiah Xolop from straying. No other girl was as attractive as she, not even Meri Batos, the *"bitch"!*

She knew it was *Meri*—it just *had* to be, the girl who was spreading the rumors. Manuela wouldn't just come right out and say it, but that didn't matter. Ana Fabiola knew it had to be that *Meri* girl. She was probably the one who said that Ana Fabiola was an "available." She could just about *hit* her for saying an awful thing like that. She was always prissing around; she wore too much jewelry—the *tourist* kind. She looked like some kind of "cheap, North American *tramp!*" That's what her aunt had said.

"You better watch that `*Meri'* girl," her aunt had cautioned. "She's not very careful about the way she looks. She won't even wear the *chachales* any more. She's already *ladino!*"

Ana Fabiola would never think of wearing anything else. Besides, she liked the set of heavy silver and red coral beads and old coins that her grandmother had bequeathed her, especially given her two primary assets. The heavy necklace lay between her breasts and made them more pronounced. Nobody among her friends looked quite as developed as she, and her two prominent little charms certainly figured in her plan.

Although that plan wasn't very complicated, Ana Fabiola's little scheme just *had* to work. While the peripheral details were constantly shifting, the principle focus always remained the same: to get as close to Isaiah Xolop mentally and physically as she could and to make him her own. She had often thought about rolling up strips of chichicaster and slipping them in one of his tortillas or soft drinks. She had thought about pulling threads from his jacket at the Mass. She would put them under her *petate*, right under her head. That would make him think of her, for sure. There were all kinds of ways to make a boy turn his head. The only thing that Ana Fabiola had refused to try was asking her father to cast the mixes. She had doubts about many of the little engines of domestic magic, but she feared she would never survive a negative reading of the maguey seeds.

"What you need is for old Colata Toj to work things *out!"* teased Lupita Samayoa, Ana Fabiola's little *ladino* friend.

"*Yeah!* Get old Colata Toj!" echoed Sandra Serrano. For four generations and longer, Señora Toj was the reputed match maker in the town. The village girls were unrelenting in their fun at the expense of the decrepit old woman whose reputation for gossip and rumor-mongering had atrophied her role and service to the community. No one much cared for the grouchy weaving merchant, and only lesser lights of San Felipe even bothered to greet her as they passed by her on the streets.

For several weeks Ana Fabiola had been looking forward to this particular weekend. A popular *conjunto*, or rock band, from the capital had been scheduled to perform for the *fiesta* of Santiago, the patron saint of Guatemala. Ana Fabiola would press her issue on the square. She had worked out all the details. She had enlisted the help of Isaiah's younger cousin, Celina Marquez, a girl two years younger than Ana Fabiola herself. Celina had agreed to approach Isaiah during the concert and to tell him of his admirer, a girl who would like to dance with him. Because she was family, Isaiah wouldn't dare ignore her. Of course, while the information certainly wouldn't obligate him, at least he would then know of Ana Fabiola's interest. Ana Fabiola could take it from there herself.

The festival would last for nine days in San Felipe. By far, the celebration of Santiago was the largest festival of the year and easily the most eagerly awaited, particularly for the youngsters. Workers were given the actual saint's day off, and families used the occasion for renewing ties, catching up on the news, and some much-needed relaxation. It wasn't unusual for families, as a matter of fact, to save for months, secreting away a few precious *quetzales* for celebrations among their relatives and closest friends. They could lavish the few worn bills on food in the market, rounds of beer and liquor, a fresh, new blouse or *huipil* for the woman, or a carefully selected utensil for the hearth. Most would gather at the homes of the oldest members where they would be regaled for hours by the endless recycling of favorite tales, feasting on sumptuous mounds of banana leaf-wrapped tamales, swigging six packs of beer, or imbibing countless pints of the ceremonial *aguardiente*.

All through the day before *fiesta* and well into the nights, the paths and roads were packed with people. Little children tripped along, absorbed in the simple pleasures of the moment, somewhat comical to any outsider in their miniature costumes and replicas of their fathers' straw hats still too large for their heads. The little girls on errands looked dwarfed underneath their mother's large, plastic water pitchers balanced precariously above their lollipop faces, round distended bellies, and wiry little frames.

Fiesta days were market days as well, and the children were eager to case the stalls or to make a few *quetzales* selling trinkets and handwoven items—belts, head ribbons, friendship bracelets, and the like. Just the sight of a tourist would send them into a selling frenzy, and they would mob a customer, swirling about her, ejaculating a frenetic barrage of merchant patter:

"Two for *one!* Two for *one!*" they would screech, jostling each other and maneuvering for attention.

"You *buy!* You buy from *me!*"

And the always "heartfelt" confidence of a more seasoned merchant:

"Para Ud., Un buen précio! For you, my friend—a very special price!"

The tourist traffic in and about San Felipe always swelled on market and fiesta days. Greeted by the women and older girls scrubbing their washing on the rocks around the landing, the large tourist ferries and smaller boats usually arrived around 9:00 o'clock each morning from Panajachél. Sightseers from around the world clamored up the beaches and poured into the streets of the town. San Felipe women would sit at their backstrap looms working only so energetically as to inspire a photo or two, keeping, at the same time, a close eye on their merchandise, a spread of handwoven belts, blouses, shawls, and decorative looms draped over the short fence or low stone wall separating their tiny houses or shops from the busy streets.

It had been a year before. Taking passage on the "San Pedro," one of the more modest of tourist launches out of Panajachel, Susan Simpson arrived in San Felipe on the first day of *fiesta* in June, 1989. A shrill chorus from ceramic whistles and bird calls greeted the thirty or more French, Belgian, American, and an assortment of foreign *latinos* as they stepped from the side of the boat onto the peer. Eager to sell a bauble or two, more than twenty Felipino girls swarmed the tourists, quickly isolating members of the tour group, making them more vulnerable to a highly practiced patter of intimidation.

"No thank you," said Susan Simpson as she clutched her large, baggy Guatemalan purse tightly under her left arm.

"Two for *one!*" mocked the Felipino urchin. "You buy *one*; I give you *two*. Two for *one!* Two for *one!* You buy from *me! Here! Here!* You buy from *me!* Two for *one!*"

"*Okay!*" Susan Simpson had caved in. "Just *one!*"

"*No!*" returned her little tormentor. "You buy *more. Here!* You take *all!* Just *veinte quetzales—veinte quetzales* for *all!"*

"Miss! Look here, Miss!" interrupted a small competitor. "Very pretty to *you! Look! Miss! Miss!* Look how pretty to *you!*"

"*No!*" Susan protested as she turned to the first. "Just one and from you. *Here!*"

The young American college graduate lifted a *quetzal* from her coin purse and pointed at a dark blue and green, hand-woven friendship bracelet.

"*No! No!*" countered the practiced little Felipino merchant. "You take *all! Veinte quetzales para todos*!

The little girl was growing increasingly irritated when two more of her village entrepreneurs moved quickly into her established territory.

Suddenly realizing her predicament, Susan decided to reject all opportunities rather than become the point in these swarthy little domestic hostilities.

"No!" returned Susan. *"No quiero nada!"*

Susan returned the knotted bracelet to the San Felipe girl who spurned her would-be client with a snarl and lashed out against her interference with a tear and a curse.

"Go home! *Yankee!*" protested the Felipino. "You're just a Yankee *whore!*"

Susan Simpson, on whom the slight in Tzutujíl vituperation never quite registered, turned her back on the quartet, and retreated toward the boat. Four girls followed her, however, intent on closing a sale.

"No!" she cried. *"No compro nada! Nada! Me entiende?"*

The four scowled at the affront and muttered to themselves as they began to move away.

Susan Simpson watched the girls climb back up the steep concrete steps to the street above the landing. Satisfied that she was free for the moment, at least from the onslaught of the little street vendors, she turned back toward the lake to get a fuller sense of the beauty of the spot.

To her left towered the 9,000-foot peak of San Pedro and the range of mountains beyond that plummeted into the lake. She scanned the ridges and from the base of the volcano, followed the little patches of the *milpas* up to where they dissipated in the spotty tree line near the summit. She tried to imagine a climb up the ragged slopes to the peak. The boat captain had explained that many people climb the three volcanoes throughout the week, but he recommended against it now because of the increased guerrilla activity around the lake.

Just the idea of small guerrilla bands operating around her gave Susan Simpson a little rush of excitement. She felt—how to put it otherwise—she was on site where something, something really *glorious* was going on—That was *it!*—Something *noble* was happening among these people. She panned the breadth of the lake, knowing full well—just for herself at just that point—that somewhere out there, somewhere out there where her eyes were just then passing, small, hidden cadres stood on guard, watching and waiting, dedicated to their comrades and to the little people who had been suffering so much and for so long. Susan Simpson winced as a sweet little rush of empathy swelled within her. She complimented herself on the idea that these poor people were beginning to exert themselves, to wake up and reclaim something of their integrity.

"These people are so *brave!*" whispered Susan Simpson to herself. Self-satisfied with her private little reassurance, she could now move more comfortably among the Felipinos in the town above her. She understood why it was important for the tourists to come there, why it was important to buy a little something-or-other to help out, if just a little.

"Buy a `weave' and help save an Indian," thought the American. It sounded a little crass, even as she framed the idea, but that was the essence, wasn't it?

Susan tucked in the quetzal-emblazoned T-shirt that she had purchased in the gift shop at the hotel back in Panajachél. Then, just to double check, she felt inside her right thigh through her baggy trousers for the money sock where she kept her credit cards and United States driver's license. From the foot of one of her father's blue dress socks and the sash to her own bathrobe, she had fashioned an impromptu little money bag the night before she had left home in Brownsville. The secreted credit cards would assure her another ticket out of the country if she ever lost her bag and the original tickets.

The little assault by the Felipino girls had separated Susan from the other tourists on the launch, but that wasn't particularly troublesome since she really didn't know any of them anyway. Nevertheless, the sight of a familiar face in a strange community could be reassuring, and she would feel more secure if she could see one or two of them out in the streets. What she really wanted to do, however, was to find the church. She had overheard others on the boat saying that she would find the *cofrades* preparing for the processions later in the afternoon, or the following day—they weren't certain about the schedule. Even if she had to miss the processions, though, she hoped to snap some pictures of the Indians dressing the icons, something she had noted in her guidebook.

Once she completed the trek up from the landing and moved two or three blocks into the community, Susan Simpson found herself free of the irritating little sales girls. She walked up a broad street paved with bright, white, interlocking concrete paving stones, a relief underfoot from the deeply rutted paths that had threatened to wrench her ankle as she stepped off the pier.

Along the street Felipino women walked to and from the market still several blocks ahead of her. Susan marvelled at the women carrying the large, woven baskets filled with produce on their heads. Small children played at the curbs and chased each other around the short, stumpy trees in the tiny yards. In one such yard she spied two women working slowly but meticulously at large backstrap looms. One was weaving a tie-dyed *peraje*, or shawl. Susan Simpson had read about the tie-dye process—or *ikat*, as the woman at the museum had called it—and had seen the large rolls of yardage for sell in the Central Market in Guatemala City on her first afternoon in the capital, but this was her first observation of the colorful work in process on the loom.

Three children scurried around the woman working at the *ikat* as Susan stepped inside the courtyard. They giggled at the long-haired, blonde American student as she fumbled around inside her purse. When she managed to find the strap, Susan pulled out her camera. At once, the children began to yell, almost in unison.

"Pagado! Pagado!" they cried as they ran from behind their mother. *"Pagado! Dos quetzales para fotos! Dos quetzales!"*

Susan Simpson picked up on the "*dos quetzales*" and understood clearly. After securing the camera strap around her neck, she reached into the recesses of her bag once more for her coin purse, pulled out four or five Guatemalan bills, and handed two ragged *quetzales* to the weaver herself. The woman folded them in half between her fingers and slipped them down the front of her *huipil*. Susan set the zoom on her camera, stepped back, and snapped two photos, one of the weavers, including the full ensemble of the loom, and the second over the shoulder of the Tzutujíl weaver to capture a close up of the intricacies of the alternating white and crisscrossing color patterns.

As she was returning the camera to her bag, Susan Simpson thought to ask the woman for directions to the church. Before the weaver could return a word, her children once again sprang to life, each offering services as her guide.

"Mira! Mira!" they chattered. *"Sigueme! Sigueme!"*

And off raced the triumvirate into the street, dancing about the gate impatiently, waiting for their ward to join them for the walk up the street and through the community market to the church at the crest of the hill.

Susan Simpson had read with interest about the Indian markets, but even the glossy, four-color illustrations seemed sterile and artificial against the experience itself. Stepping out of the glaring sunlight into the subdued shadows of the covered marketplace, she was suddenly struck by a confusion of heavy aromas in an arena of spirited entrepreneurial chatter. Small chickens and other pullets pecked at kernels of grain around the base of boxes and crates. As she stepped too close, a dilapidated dog limped away from Susan's foot and, at the expense of two outraged hens, negotiated a new spot for itself under a rickety table. Odors from baskets of small, dried fish competed with racks of tropical fruits—mangos, papayas, and spongy, black, over-ripened avocados, some as broad as a cantaloupe.

Susan was drawn to the small basket of an emaciated, wrinkled woman whose mottled skin suggested the malnutrition of her childhood. Behind cataracts that all but blinded her, the woman's languid stare belied the careful work of her fingers as she crocheted the neckline of a red *huipil* spread across her lap. She was a resident of Patzún, a Cakchiquel village on the far northeast side of the lake just over the north side of the continental divide. The small woman was selling *pitaya*, one of the delicacies of the highlands available only during the summer months.

"*Qué es eso?*" asked Susan.

"*Pitaya,*" said the woman, darting a quick glance first left, then right, never raising her eyes to address her customer directly.

"*Pitaya?*" asked Susan Simpson for clarification.

The old woman's head bobbed only once as she glanced over at her Tzutujíl neighbors in the adjacent stall. Susan had heard about the luscious, sweet fruit. Cut open, the *pitaya* displayed a moist, deep-purple meat laced throughout with tiny black seeds that gave it its light, distinctive texture against the roof of the mouth.

"*Cuánto cuesta?*" asked Susan Simpson.

"*Cincuenta,*" muttered the toothless merchant, almost inaudibly.

"*Cincuenta?*" the girl asked again, checking the muted response against her rather marginal lexicon of Spanish.

The woman only nodded again as she reached hesitantly into her basket, gingerly nudging two of the fiery red and yellow-tinged fruits. Susan Simpson fingered the change in her purse, fetching two coins, 25 *centavos* each which she handed to the woman. The old lady took the coins in her left hand and rubbed them together momentarily with her thumb against her palm and then dropped them into the basket of fruit. Susan Simpson bent over and selected a modest piece of the delicate fruit. She thanked the grey-haired old woman who only dodged the gratuity, staring across the market floor and wiping her fingertips on her faded apron.

"It's hard to grow old," thought the American. "I guess she's had a pretty rough life."

Susan Simpson was startled from her reflection by several fingers jerking on her pants. Her hands flew instinctively to her money belt, only to be embarrassed at the discovery of her three guides urging her on through the stalls toward the church. Immediately, the American girl gave in to her small mentors and slipped cautiously through the dense crowds clogging the aisles and out the other side of the market again into the almost blinding daylight. Only upon reaching the open air did she realize that she had been breathing through her mouth during the whole excursion through the market. As she inhaled again, this time deeply through her nose, she gagged on the sudden rush of the fetid, sweet stench that still lingered from the stalls she had just passed and from the urine—human, animal, or both—coagulated along the curb at her feet.

As she struggled to regain her breath, Susan Simpson wondered at first why the heavy odors seemed so disturbing. Then, she remembered the smell of the ink as she had pressed pages of her travel book to her nose when she opened the volume for the first time many months before. From childhood, her first experience of any new book was always olfactory. Until the shock of the moment, as she stood there outside the market, Susan Simpson's Guatemala had been transported on the clean, crisp aromas of newsprint and enamel papers. Disorienting so, this Guatemala wasn't typeset, and its smells had taken her completely off guard.

By 11 o'clock, the streets were swelling with *campesinos.* The band of four worked their way along, moving closer and closer to the central plaza of San Felipe. Women visited behind their *tzutes* spread over the small patch of street as others bent over their produce, fingering the fruits and vegetables or turning the slaughtered fowls hanging from cords on makeshift racks. An ice cream vendor attracted a steady entourage of anxious, impatient urchins poised expectantly around his two-wheel street cart. Tape cassettes blared across the way from portable players, and a loud speaker crackled with the staccato announcements about various activities scheduled for the festival that afternoon and evening.

As Susan Simpson and her small guides turned the corner facing the central plaza, a wedding party was exiting the steep, circular tier of steps leading down from the tall, narrow doors of the sanctuary. As they reached the foot of the steps, fireworks erupted somewhere within the crowd below, and the dull clap of the church bell began an energetic peel announcing the new Felipino couple. Two rockets shot into the sky and exploded almost simultaneously over the revelers. It was all very exciting for the American girl, and Susan Simpson was beginning to get caught up in the ambience of the Felipino celebrations.

The American enthusiast caught up with her young guides at the steps of the church, and she paid each of them a *quetzal* for their services. The two older girls snickered and winked, laughing at each other as they stuffed the bills in their *huipiles*.

After waving off her little guides into the marketplace crowd, Susan was suddenly engulfed by a swarm of short Maya men and women, and for a fleeting moment, she felt very exposed and vulnerable. She struggled to move away from the center of the steps to allow the remainder of the Indian families to evacuate the church. She was fascinated by the older men, some wearing what to her seemed the almost effeminate black brimmed hats and carrying the black canes. After reaching the foot of the steps, they had turned and formed a line to witness the passing of the bride and groom, their respective families, and the other guests. They were obviously of some importance to the town, and Susan Simpson couldn't help but stare at them as they posed so formally before the departing guests.

After a few moments, satisfied finally that the rush had passed on, Susan Simpson began the ascent of the steps, almost slipping on the dark-green pine needles strewn over them and the peels of fruit and discarded plastic drink bags that the crowd had dropped behind. The wind had shifted, and as she reached the top of the steps she could smell the strong scent of the market again. Once more, the smell made her uneasy, even a little nauseated, and she decided to enter the sanctuary. It was only then that she caught her first glimpse of the soldiers on the periphery of the crowd in the central plaza.

Three young *militaries* were entering the square, each armed with large assault rifles which hung from slings over their shoulders. Their belts were girdled with grenades, holstered automatic pistols, and sheathed bayonets. The Felipinos gave them space as the troops began a slow amble through the crowd across the front of the church and on into the market stalls beyond. Just as they completed their course across the plaza, a second squad of three more soldiers, similarly outfitted, emerged from the right, and the Felipinos began to disburse. Susan Simpson noted their movements and the crowd's reaction but saw no particular cause for alarm. She turned away and entered the sanctuary.

Just beyond the wide alcove at the entrance to the sanctuary, two rows of ten-foot long, straight-backed wooden benches extended up the length of the vaulted building almost to the shadowy altar that rose at the other end. All along the walls, effigies of the saints wore the familiar, flowing robes of the Spanish iconography, accented this festival week with the *tzutes* and *perajes* of the San Felipe *cofradia* of Santiago draped around their shoulders. A thin carpet of pine needles was scattered at their feet, running on both sides, up and down the length of the sanctuary. Although the smoke had dissipated, the aroma of incense and pine remained heavy on the air, a pleasant alternative to the odors of the street.

At the front, Susan could see three or four Felipinos walking up the steps and then descend behind the altar, and she decided to follow them. As she advanced toward the front of the sanctuary, a dozen or more women entered from the side of the room bearing on their heads the now familiar diagonal blue and green-striped plastic pots. Almost on cue, each reached up, secured the handles of the pitchers, and began pouring water onto the floor toward the altar. As the first round emptied their vessels, a second phalanx of laughing, playful Tzutujil women entered the same door and released their small floods. Then, a third group appeared with straw brooms and began to push the water toward the opposite side of the sanctuary. From behind the altar, twenty some odd men drifted down the steps and began stacking the wooden pews against the walls beneath the icons. All were members of the *cofradia* of Santiago and their women's auxiliary who were beginning to wash out the church as part of the preparation for the procession of the *paseos* later that afternoon and evening and throughout the community during the next day.

Susan Simpson stood aside as the men filed past her, and then she commenced her exploration behind the altar. Far to the left and behind the pulpit, she could see a small group of men mumbling a litany of personal prayers and kneeling before a glass-encased effigy of the Christ in repose. Behind them, three of their party swung censors of billowing copal pom. Against the wall, their wives and daughters, apparently the leaders of the auxiliary sat formally on benches, holding heavy burning tapers wrapped in swaths of wide, red ribbons.

As Susan stood back to get her bearings, the men began reciting a fervent liturgy in Tzutujíl, periodically crossing themselves and bowing their heads before the icon. After a few minutes of the pious ritual, they rose slowly, and the two men on the end reached forward and unlatched the pins that served to secure the front glass panel in place. Carefully, they removed the pins and lifted the six-foot framed glass front, holding it up while the men between them reached under the wooden platform on which rested the carving. The four men slipped the whole assembly forward until it had cleared the glass frontispiece which the two outside assistants carefully lowered back into place. What followed was the solemn dressing of the effigy in preparation for its mounting on the *paseo*.

Susan Simpson wanted badly to take a few snapshots of the preparations, and she approached one of the men who was refilling his censor from a crumpled page of newspaper containing crushed copal and charcoal.

"Se permite hacer los fotos?" asked the American.

"*No,*" came the answer. "*No se puede.*"

"Bueno," persisted Susan. *"Mire, Ud. es la jefe de esta cofradia? No?"*

"*No,*" said the assistant as he pointed to one of the men on the far end in the red *tzute* tied with the long, silk tassels behind his head.

Susan Simpson decided on a new tact. She would make an offering to the *cofradia* in honor of St. James and any additional contribution as she might be directed. Then she would request the photos.

"*Perdón,*" said Susan as she stepped to the turbaned *cofrade*.

"*Sí, mujer,*" said the man still preoccupied with the activities of the adoration of the Christ, and she offered him her proposal.

"*Sí, se puede*—that's *okay!*" agreed the *auxiliatura* of the *cofradi*a as he accepted a wad of *quetzales* from the American girl, more than twice what they had agreed upon which pleasantly surprised the Tzutujil leader.

Susan stood back, positioned her camera, and snapped a half dozen photographs as the assistants began lifting from a collection of musty, old cardboard boxes the various elements for the adoration—a barbed-wire crown, ornamental sprays of metal leaves, and canisters of varnish. Assistants lined the branches upright in a row against the side of the reclining Christ figure and sprayed them with the varnish to enhance their brilliance in the open light and from the glaring lights in the evening during the processions.

Susan finished one roll of film, replaced it with another, and turned once again to the *cofrade*.

"*Grácias, Señor,* and can you direct me to the priest of this church?" asked the American.

"*Sí! Cláro!*" said the leader in, at best, a broken English. "His room are there. Just behind, *okay?* You going in that door there. *Okay?*"

"Thank you," said the girl.

With a smile, Susan Simpson offered her hand to the diminutive Maya and turned toward the exit at the front of the church. As she approached midway down the center aisle, she was startled by the silhouettes of two soldiers entering the front of the sanctuary. Alarmed by the unexpected sight of the heavily armed men in the church itself, Susan almost dropped her shoulder bag with her camera. The strap slipped off her shoulder, and she struggled to keep her balance as she intercepted her bag before it struck the floor.

The soldiers seemed not to have noticed the girl as they glanced from left to right and peered over her head at the Indians shuffling the furniture about her. After looking casually about the sanctuary, they passed slowly down the aisle toward Susan Simpson. Suddenly, she got the idea to photograph them.

"Mira!" she said as they met. *"Me permiten Uds. un foto?"*

From their high cheek bones and wide foreheads, the two soldiers were obviously Maya conscripts, and they looked at each other as if to seek each other's permission. They smiled sheepishly at the attractive blonde and grunted their approval.

"*Allá,*" said Susan, directing them to a position against the wall. An eight-foot, larger-than-life figure of the bruised and dying Saint Sebastian, the first-century martyr, loomed over them, wearing a mask of anguish and frozen in a posture suggesting his impending death. The two soldiers moved into a position side by side in front of the statue, swinging their long, automatic field rifles with their curved magazine clips dangling below the firing chambers.

Susan Simpson adjusted the zoom lens to take in the two young men and the satin-robed, bleeding icon above them. She snapped two photos, thinking of the double prints that she would make from both. She was planning scrapbooks for Christmas presents that she would assemble on her return for two friends and her mother and father, people who had loaned her money to make the trip.

"*Cómo se llama?* What are your names?" she asked.

"Juan," said the first.

"José," the second.

Susan jotted down their names in her small note pad that she kept in her shirt pocket for such opportunities.

"How *old* are you?" asked Susan.

"*Cómo?*" asked Juan.

"How old—*disculpe!*" said Susan.

"I'm sorry—*cuántos tiene anos*?" she asked, confusing her syntax. "How—how many years? How old are you?"

"*Dieciseis,*" said the soldier, overlooking the grammatical indiscretion.

"*E yo?*" asked Susan, committing her second error. The two soldiers smiled at each other.

"*Veinte-uno,*" said José.

"Twenty-one," she said as she wrote the annotation on her pad.

"How long have you been in the army?" asked Susan.

"Two years," said José.

"Six months," offered Juan.

"Where are you from?" she asked.

"San Marcos," said Juan.

"San Pedro—San Pedro, San Marcos," said José.

"San Pedro—*S-a-n-M-a-r-c-o-s*," said Susan aloud as she scribbled the hasty addendum to the names. She'd have to look up the places on the map at another time.

"How do you like it in the army?" asked Susan. "How do you like army life?"

The two shrugged their shoulders.

"It's okay," said José.

"*Grácias!*" she said, and the two soldiers smiled, looked at each other with puckish grins, and waved to the photographer.

"These aren't *killers!*" Susan Simpson remarked to herself. "They're just *boys!*"

The reports of Father Mike and her interview with the Guatemalans in Brownsville about the brutality of the military just didn't square comfortably with the impression of these two, rather unsophisticated young men. The guns themselves seemed merely playthings-writ-large, slung over the shoulders of the two albeit muscular and fit young teenagers who should be returning to afternoon classes in the senior year of some public school. As she watched the two troops walk casually out the side entrance, Susan Simpson realized what was missing. It was the swagger, the "military" arrogance that she had expected. In fact, what she perceived was something closer to a childish innocence in the two, a good-natured humor rooted in the banter between two young high school students on a holiday at the Brownsville fair. She decided to follow after them, if only to the doorway of the sanctuary.

The soldiers had moved into the garden by the time Susan Simpson reached the door. The women were huddled around the one water hydrant next to the wall of the church's commissary as the soldiers entered the grounds. Immediately, they fell to a hush and turned immediately to the task of filling their pitchers, looking from one to another and whispering in undertones. The two soldiers seemed not to notice and continued walking across the grounds to the steel gates which separated the compound from the streets beyond. Once the soldiers were out of sight, the women continued with their brisk chatter and playful asides. Susan Simpson watched the exchanges for a few moments, then removed her gold-rimmed "John Lennon" frames and wiped the lens with a tissue from her pocket.

"Well," said Susan to herself, "maybe Father Jack can answer some of my questions."

Susan watched the soldiers exit and the women break once again into their routine as if nothing had ever interrupted them. Susan Simpson proceeded out the courtyard and on to the door that led to the private quarters of the priest.

"It's nice to meet you," said Father Jack to his American visitor. "I wasn't sure what day you might arrive, so I instructed Sister María to keep the room ready for you. Did you just get here?"

"Yes . . . well, about an hour ago from Panajachél," said Susan Simpson. "I came over with the tourist boat."

"Well, you might be a little thirsty," suggested the priest. "Why don't you help yourself to a drink over there in the refrigerator, or María will have some fresh coffee brewed in about five minutes."

Sister María had escorted Susan Simpson from the more formal parlor of the priest's quarters to the kitchen in the rear where Father Jack was preparing a pot of coffee.

"How is Father Mike and everybody back in Texas?" asked the priest.

"Oh, very well, I think," returned the girl. "He's always so busy, you know. But his real love is his work with the refugees. He's really committed."

"Yeah," said the priest. "*Committed.* Committed for *sure.*"

Father Jack reached into his pocket and retrieved a cigarette. "Do you smoke?"

"No," said Susan. "No thanks."

"Well," said Father Jack, as he lit a strong Guatemalan Rubio, "Mike keeps sending us volunteers, and we can always use them. What brought you here?"

"Well, I guess I just wanted to be of some help," explained Susan Simpson. "I worked for a year in the Peace Corps in West Africa, but I had to come back after my father had a heart attack. I came home to help my mother with my dad's wholesale business. I met Father Mike at a demonstration for Salvadoran TPS—you know, `temporary protective status'—outside Casa Libertad. That's in Brownsville. That was the beginning. Then, I had a chance to meet a Guatemalan for whom one of the churches in the Valley was providing sanctuary. I just couldn't believe what he was saying about the killings. I was planning to go on back to graduate school to start my doctorate, but I just couldn't get past his story. His whole family had been killed during a raid by the army. He had lost everything. He was so nervous when I talked with him. So that was it; I just decided to come down. But I had to wait and save some money and still had to borrow a little to make the trip."

Susan Simpson brushed back her hair and took a long draft on the bottled drink. She was happy to find the old reliable soda available in the highlands. It had kept her alive in West Africa for her one-year tour of duty.

"Yeah, it's been pretty rough down here for sure," said Father Jack. "We've lost five people in the past year just in my parish alone around San Felipe. The army has increased its activities in the area ever since the guerrillas moved in here about two years ago. These guys may be few in number, but they make up for it in *cajones*!"

"`*Cajones*'?" asked Susan, unfamiliar with testicular humor.

"Well, never mind," said the priest, somewhat embarrassed by the liberty he had taken.

"Anyway, they shut down all the hotels at Panajachel for over a year about two years ago because of the guerrillas. They walked right into the lobby of the Del Lago, sat their guns on the table in the dining room, and ordered breakfast. They brought in a radio transmitter and started broadcasting from out by the swimming pool. It was the craziest thing."

Susan Simpson sat transfixed. She had just spent the night in the same place. It made the revolution seem so *real*.

"It was a Sunday morning," continued Father Jack, "and there were about 100 people staying at the hotel the night before—most of them having breakfast—and the guerrillas held a prayer service. Then, they preached a sermon to everybody on the importance of the revolution and how they should all go back to their countries and tell them how bad things were for the people of Guatemala. That was a little hard for some of those tourists to understand, I guess—from a balcony in the Del Lago!"

Father Jack laughed at the idea as he poured himself a cup of the freshly brewed coffee.

"Things got really rough after that," he continued. "The army came swarming into Sololá, and a lot of people started disappearing. They started night patrols, and the people tell me that you could hear the screams and cries from all the way across the lake—from San Martín, from Santa Catarina, all the way from San Jorge. They said the wind picked up the cries and carried them all the way up into the volcanoes. It was *bad*. It was *really* bad."

Father Jack started to back off. He had had second thoughts about the rather romantic anecdote, but the emotion it seemed to transport in his young visitor reminded him why it remained one of his favorite stories. It was a story he liked to tell among the "natives" back in Oklahoma, too. Whether it had happened or not, the reality was so much worse. But who could talk about *that*?

"Look," Father Jack pleaded. "I guess I got a little carried away there. It's just a story, you know. You hear a lot of stories. The people tell these tales, you see, and maybe it makes them a little stronger as a community. See what I *mean?* Who knows, you *know?*"

Father Jack sipped again at his steaming coffee, set the cup down, and added another teaspoon of sugar.

"It can get a little *stout!*" he exclaimed, wiping his mouth on a napkin.

"Father Jack," said Susan. "These *soldiers*—the ones I saw this morning in the market. They're so *young!* They don't even look *real*, if you know what I mean. I took their pictures!"

"Check your prints before you *pay* for them!" laughed the priest. "They say around here that you can't take a picture of a *devil!* It'll just ruin the film!"

"But these are just boys!" exclaimed Susan Simpson. "They can't be more than seventeen, eighteen. They don't *look* like killers!"

"Neither do *you*, sister!" returned the priest pointedly. "Neither do *you!*"

Susan Simpson sat stunned, not fully registering the import of the comparison.

"Well, I *hope* not!" Susan laughed at the idea in an attempt to deflect the heavier suggestion.

"But then neither do *I—I* hope not, at least!" laughed Father Jack. "But do you get my meaning?"

Susan Simpson waited for the clarification.

"None of us is *born* a killer, and very few of us, I dare say," said the priest, "would take much pride in killing a fellow human being. But we can *learn.* We can be *taught.* We can *all* be compromised. That's our condition, and that's their situation. Most of them believe probably they're fighting for Guatemala—that's what the guerrillas believe, *for sure!* And for those who aren't particularly complicated by *principles* . . . well, they're more willing to kill than to be killed, and many of these young conscripts are more afraid of their own *captains* than they are of the insurgency, and that's a *fact!* With their captain holding a gun to their heads—quite *literally*, *most* of the time! Why would they think twice about blowing away a *kid?* or a whole *family,* for that matter?"

Susan Simpson sat horrified at the implications as her mind raced back through the images of the morning—the young children who had led her through the market, their mother at her loom, and the old merchant of *pitayas* in the market.

"These boys . . ." said Father Jack. "How did the people react to them, *huh?*"

Father Jack paused.

"Don't forget it for a moment, Susan," said the priest as he looked sternly at her across the kitchen table. "If their captain snapped his fingers—just like *that* [snap!]—these *`boys,'* as you call them . . . these same `boys'—in just two minutes! —would cut off your head and stick it on a pole in front of this very *church!*"

Outside the church and Father Jack's orientation of Susan Simpson, Ana Fabiola sat on the fringe of the young people. They watched eagerly as they waited for the rock band to complete the assembly of their equipment for the concert later that evening. Members of the band carried box after box from the back of two vans and out of a pick-up truck parked just off the steps of the church. The band had erected a portable platform about thirty by twenty feet. Two towers bristled with speakers aimed in every direction at either end of the platform. Ana Fabiola and her friends found it all very exciting. Few bands made the long, rough trip around the lake except when a town could guarantee a large turnout, so that the festival of Santiago was always looked on with great anticipation.

The drummer was the first of the musicians to complete his preparations, and a long, frenetic roll across the heads and cymbals sparked a wave of shouts and a spattering of applause. The clamor gave Ana Fabiola a chance to look intently about her as she waited for the arrival of Isaiah Xolop, but the initial crowd was mostly female. The boys often came around later in the evening, sometimes more than an hour after a concert began, preferring instead to sit around in small groups in the surrounding bars to drink and loosen up. It wasn't unusual for them to arrive quite drunk and a little rowdy. Ana Fabiola was hoping that a few drinks would make Isaiah a little more favorably inclined to dance with her.

The merchants began to strike their stands just as the sun began setting quickly behind Atitlán, the taller of the three volcanoes that loomed over and around the village on the south side of the lake. Free from the work of the busiest market day of the year, they and their families could relax with their neighbors for the remainder of the evening. Those from out of town could sit where they were and watch the revelers pass by and then fall asleep amidst their bundles of hardware and produce. As the crowds continued to grow, the streets became clogged and all but impassable as those who planned to leave bunched around the last outbound busses at the intersections of the main street that cut through the middle of the town. Members of the blue-uniformed national police whistled to the crowds to move along, and soldiers kept posts at a distance just outside the fray.

Seven or eight busses would take the final passengers from the town. Every inch of both sitting and standing room would be doubly parked. In the past, children were known to have suffocated, crammed under the seats with only hot, tight little pockets of putrefied air to breathe. The passengers would have to wait sometimes more than a half hour before departing, jammed as they were, while the driver and his assistant finished securing baskets and boxes of freight on the luggage rack on the roof of the vehicles. When ready, the busses would inch forward through the remaining crowds, belching clouds of diesel fumes behind them.

As sunlight diminished, strings of bright lights, tied to telephone and light poles at the corners and suspended through the limbs of the giant ceiba in the middle of the court, stretched across the plaza, illuminating the fountain and the surrounding concrete park benches. A crackling voice announced the entertainment for the evening and the outcome of the *ladino* beauty pageant that had been held next to the Esso service station earlier in the afternoon. The *paseo*, or large platform which had carried the reclining Christ that morning and the evening before still rested temporarily against the side of the church just off from the stage of the band. Members of the *cofradia* of Santiago were wiping down the platform and polishing its rich carvings before storing it in the rear of the sanctuary.

The concert began after eight o'clock, almost forty minutes late, but no one seemed to notice. The young people around the plaza had been enjoying themselves for several hours. Ana Fabiola had never moved from her post just off the main artery into the plaza. From there she had been able to observe almost every group as it passed in and out the area. Her only distress was echoed by many others as a canvas-covered troop transport arrived and deposited more than a dozen soldiers in the square. Minutes later, an armored jeep sporting a testy-looking fifty caliber machine gun, wheeled in at the rear of the transport, and two soldiers took their positions behind the gun. Not more than a half hour later, another squad of soldiers arrived in a second truck. Immediately, the militaries began to disburse among the young people, and the long-awaited fervor that had been reserved for the opening of the concert began to dissipate in a smothering mantle of resentment.

But Ana Fabiola's anxiety was lifted the moment she spotted Isaiah Xolop enter the plaza. There he was—in his finest Felipino shirt of alternating bands of dark blue and green *ikat* opened almost down to his navel, his gold chain and crucifix dangling from his neck, and the crown of a new straw hat perched high over his deep brown face. There he was—the finest catch in the town, strutting like a randy cock between two of his cousins, one the brother of little

Celina Marquez, her trusted confederate in this fateful evening. Ana Fabiola watched as the three meandered over to the concrete wall of the fountain and took places between two other groups of young males. She liked the confidence he exhibited as he accepted a cigarette from one of his comrades, lit it, and took a long, first drag. Ana Fabiola watched intently every expression on the face of her intended. She was infatuated with his every move and gesture. She laughed at Isaiah's clumsy cavorting. Ana Fabiola crossed her hands tightly over her mouth, as Isaiah slapped the other on the shoulder, almost plummeting him into the fountain behind. Obviously, from their fun and jaunty movements, they had been drinking and seemed unconcerned about the troops that had so disquieted the women in the crowd on their arrival an hour earlier.

"*Chee! Chee!*" signaled young Celina between her teeth. "*Chee! Chee!*"

"What?" cracked Ana Fabiola to the girl who had worked her way beside her client in the evening's romantic escapade.

"*Mira! Mira!*" ordered Celina as she pointed to her cousin.

"I see him!" returned Ana Fabiola. "I already *see* him!"

"Is it time? Is it time yet?" asked Celina, eager to begin the adventure.

"*No! No!*" snapped Ana Fabiola. "The concert hasn't even *started!* We have to wait until the *music* starts!"

Celina Marquez was anxious and increasingly irritated by the delay. She settled back down against the curb to finish the last bites of an *elote* she had purchased from the vendor a block away.

A riot of yells and screams erupted across the square as the first warped strains of the electric guitar signalled the beginning of the concert. Shrill whistles and cat calls complemented the crooning, rhythmic strains of the singer as he all but swallowed the head of the microphone. Two *ladino* dancers, sporting tight miniskirts and high white leather boots, swayed back and forth to the rolls of the guitar and drums. The Felipino girls had never seen anything like this before, and Ana Fabiola was embarrassed by the howling of the men who had assembled immediately around the stage. Other *ladino* boys with their dates broke out in rolling gyrations toward the rear of the crowd, and the concert was on.

Ana Fabiola suddenly panicked.

How could she compete for attention with something like this? She had never expected this pounding sensuality. How could she even pretend to dance like that? For the first half hour, the band hammered away in the unrelenting rhythms of hard rock, something totally unexpected by the young philanderer. Ana just wanted to die and would have retreated in hysteria if Isaiah Xolop had exhibited even the slightest interest in the concert. Rather, he and his two cousins seemed content to joke and drink from their cups of hot *atole* beside the fountain, and Ana Fabiola took some comfort in being at least in the same arena as her lover.

After the first half hour, the rock band was ready for a break. The *ladino* mayor of the town, Don Fernando Fajardo, took the stand and the microphone to welcome all the people to the festival of Santiago and invited the priest, Father Jack, to say a few words to the celebrants that might seem appropriate to the occasion.

"I want to join with our *alcalde*, Don Fernando, in welcoming you to this festival of Saint James, the patron saint of Guatemala and her people," said Father Jack in his always disarmingly articulate Tzutujil. A spattering of applause broke out among a few of the participants in the crowd who were caught unexpectedly by the American priest's practiced Guatemala voice.

"I want to invite all of you to the Mass tomorrow," he continued, "to celebrate with us in our town the sacrament of Our Lord and to pray for peace across our beautiful country."

Polite applause fluttered over the crowd as the host took the microphone once more from Father Jack. The priest stepped down from the platform and joined the American girl who had waited for him just a little beyond the stage. As they turned away, two soldiers moved aside to let them pass, and the MC announced the return of the band and the remaining groups scheduled for the program.

A large smile spread over Ana Fabiola's face as she caught the name of *Ko'jom*, one of the most popular groups around the lake. The marimba band always played the favorite old *sons* which brought the people from their chairs and into the dance floor. The band was scheduled to play after the next break. It was time for Celina to make her move.

"*Go!*" instructed Ana Fabiola. "Go on, *quick!* Before they *leave!*"

Ana Fabiola's willing little messenger jumped from beside her friend and moved deftly into the crowd of young people returning once again to the front of the platform. Ana Fabiola reached back to the knot of hair where her ribbon began its course around the crown of her head. She positioned her fingers between the wraps of the ribbon so that the spacing would be perfect. Then she reached down and tugged at the *chachales* and thrust her little chest outward. "Everything" had to be just right.

Ana Fabiola's heart pounded behind the little mounds of her breasts, and she felt weak in her hands and elbows. She didn't dare turn her face in the direction of the boys. She would have to wait until Celina returned. All of a sudden, she felt a sudden urge to defecate. Her stomach was knotted and churning inside. What was she to do! Ana Fabiola was about to lose all composure. Surely, she would be sick if she had to wait another moment. She had to turn her head. She *had* to *know!*

Celina Marquez was standing among the young men, her back to Ana Fabiola. The young lover couldn't make out what was being said, but she could see the strong, angular features of Isaiah Xolop under the wide brim of his straw hat every time the spotlight that was directed from the stage passed over the crowd. As she caught his features, Ana Fabiola could see him clearly, standing with his arms folded across his chest looking at Celina, his little cousin almost two feet shorter than he. Then Ana Fabiola saw Celina point toward her and caught the glimpse of Isaiah Xolop which he passed in her direction.

Ana Fabiola was mortified. What if he had seen her looking at him so *intently?* What would he *think?* Tears began to seep from the corners of her eyes until her cheeks were awash. Ana Fabiola turned her head away toward the band, but then fearing exposure under the swirling arch of the flood light, she put her hands to her face and collapsed beside the little wall.

"*Ana!*" the distraught girl heard overhead just moments later.

"*Ana Fabiola!* Where *are* you?"

It was Celina Marquez.

"Celina? Celina?" called Ana Fabiola. "*Here!* I'm down *here!*"

Celina Marquez squatted down to speak with her friend and burst out laughing.

"Why?" she asked. "Why are you down here? You can't dance on the *ground?*"

"You *talked* to him!" exclaimed Ana Fabiola, quickly wiping her cheeks. "You told him *about me? Tell me!* Tell me *exactly* what you said! Tell me what *he* said! What did he *say?*"

"He said he liked to *dance!*" returned Celina Marquez.

"`He said he liked to dance,'" repeated Ana Fabiola, as if to compass the meaning of the remark.

"But did he *say?* . . . What *else* did he say?" pressed Ana Fabiola. "Did you mention my *name?* What did he *say* when you mentioned my *name?*"

"He didn't say *anything*," said Celina Marquez. "He just said `he liked to dance.'"

Unsatisfied, Ana Fabiola pulled her little persona next to her and grilled Celina repeatedly for the details of the conversation. Each time, she repeated Isaiah's response, only, however, to the increasing frustration of her mentor.

"But what do I *do?*" asked the distraught Ana Fabiola. "Do I just *wait* here? Is he going to *come* for me? Should I go to *him?* What did he *say?*"

And Celina Marquez, sensing that she had perhaps failed in her high mission, began to cry.

"You *forgot* what he said!" accused an angry Ana Fabiola. "You won't *tell* me what he said! I *know* what he said! He said that he *didn't want to dance with me! Didn't* he? *Didn't* he say that, Celina Marquez? You're just *lying* to me!"

The desperate little Celina Marquez was horrified to hear the accusations after she had done what she thought had been expected of her. For a moment, she just stared at Ana Fabiola, then turned and ran, and Ana Fabiola dropped her head between her knees and wept. Her whole world—all her plans were crushed.

When she finally regained something of her composure, Ana Fabiola rose to hear the strains of the *Son del Lago*, one of the most popular, soulful pieces in the marimba repertoire. As she turned to take her bearing, she saw a number of the *campesinos* dancing slowly to the familiar refrains. Two old ladies were turning together beside a young brother and sister. Several teenagers were floating in little circles beside her, and over in front of the platform, Don Alfonso Doq, the *alcalde* himself was circling gracefully around his wife.

"*Chica!*" said a voice beside her.

At first, Ana Fabiola was petrified, unable to turn to acknowledge the unmistakable voice behind her.

"*Chica!*" said the voice again, this time with more insistence. "I want this dance with you, *okay?*"

Instantly, Ana Fabiola's little soul swelled with sunshine, and she felt a little white-hot passion flash through her breasts, as she turned to accept the dance with Isaiah Xolop, the first and only love of her life. Her long-awaited moment had come in an unexpected rush.

"I want this dance with you, *okay?*" repeated the soldier.

Ana Fabiola was so stunned by the unforeseen twist that her mouth fell open, and she began pawing the air behind her as if plummeting into a chair. Thinking that she was falling, the young soldier lurched toward her, taking her by the shoulders.

"I want this dance with you, *okay?*" repeated the soldier again.

"Okay," said Ana Fabiola mechanically, though terrified and very angry.

"My name is Juan," said the soldier, as he adjusted the automatic rifle over his left shoulder. He reached toward Ana Fabiola, placing his left hand lightly on her waist and taking her spongy, left palm in his right. Slowly, he began to move his feet clumsily to the rhythms of the marimba and the *Son del Lago*, a piece so popular with audiences around the lake that the bands usually extended it, sometimes as long as ten minutes. It would be the longest dance of her life.

Ana Fabiola was trembling. What if Isaiah Xolop should see her dancing with the soldier! What would he think after Celina Marquez had confessed her secret desire that she had so carefully cultivated for just this evening? Ana Fabiola began looking past the soldier, straining to sweep the crowd for any sign of Isaiah Xolop. He wouldn't be hard to spot, being so tall as he was even without his new hat.

Slowly, the incongruous couple continued to turn throughout the *Son*. A round of applause went up as Don Alfonso Doq completed what he could at his age and escorted his wife to a small chair that had been reserved for her. She turned to acknowledge the sound, but as she passed her gaze before the band's platform, Ana Fabiola caught a glimpse that froze her in her little circle.

Isaiah Xolop was dancing with *Meri Batos! Meri Batos, the bitch!* There he *was!* —his hands crossed behind his back, drifting back and forth before the swaying, prissy little Meri *Batos!* Ana Fabiola was seething. How *could* she! How could she *dare* such a thing! But *he!* Her lover, *Isaiah Xolop!* How could he even *think . . . do* such a thing within minutes of her *own* confessed *devotion!* Ana Fabiola's little heart was exploding within her. She suddenly blanched with embarrassment, however, when the soldier strained to pull his hand away from her tight, trembling grip.

Ana Fabiola had never felt so much anger for another human being as long as she lived.

"Meri *Batos*, the *bitch!*" She just spit out the words.

"What?" said the soldier. "What did you say? Is something the matter?"

All of a sudden, Ana Fabiola had an idea. What a clever *idea! She* knew how to fix all this! And *she'd* show that Meri Batos something, too. But how to say it?

For the first time in her life, the young girl sensed the elixir of power over another, and that power made her bold. Ana Fabiola drew herself closer to the soldier, so close that the silver cross and coins at the end of her *chachales* began to clink against a grenade that hung from his ammunition belt. Then she reached up and put her right hand up behind his shoulder and drew the young military up against her left breast.

"*Mira!*" said Ana Fabiola, at the ear of the soldier. "*Look!* . . . Look over *there!*"

The soldier turned in the direction of the crowd.

"Where?" he asked.

"Over *there!*" she whispered with growing confidence and self-control. She shifted her hand in his and turned so as to lead his line of sight squarely in the direction of Meri Batos and Isaiah Xolop.

"I'm so *afraid!*" whispered Ana Fabiola. She swelled with pride and self-satisfaction at how easily her little subterfuge was unfolding.

"Afraid of *what?*" asked the soldier, pulling his face closer to her ear.

"That *guy!*" said the girl. "That guy over *there! See!*—that couple dancing over there by the platform."

"*What? . . .* What's the *problem?*" questioned the soldier.

Ana Fabiola reached behind the soldier's neck and drew his cheek beside her face and whispered in his ear:

"He's a subversive!"

"*Who?*" asked the soldier.

"That *guy* over there," said Ana Fabiola. "That *tall* one in the straw hat dancing with that *ladino* girl. He works for the guerrillas."

Juan, the soldier, never said a word, but kept his fitful, slow pace while the *Son del Lago* wound to a close. At the end of the dance, he stepped back politely from Ana Fabiola and thanked her.

"You are a very good dancer," he said. "Thank you for your information."

The soldier smiled at Ana Fabiola in a knowing way, readjusted his rifle, and turned back into the crowd.

It wasn't as she would ever have dreamed, but for the first time all evening, Ana Fabiola felt satisfied. *That* would fix that Meri *Batos* and that *two-timing Isaiah Xolop!* The *soldiers* knew what to do. They'd fix *their* little "party"!

Ana Fabiola could just imagine Meri Bato's face when she got word that Isaiah had been picked up. She knew about the soldiers. They didn't take anything off of *subversives*. They'd pick him up, probably rough him up a bit. And then she just *might* stop by his home and offer her services to the humiliated Isaiah Xolop. *That's* what she would do! She could become a little *nurse* to him. In that way, he could see just what he might be missing, and furthermore, she would be there if that Meri *Batos* decided to come around, that Meri *Batos*, the *"bitch"!*

María Xquic had been up for more than an hour. Don Andres, her husband, was already on station before the Maximón and the auxiliary of the *Santa Cruz Cofradia*. Lucita María would come home from the convent for dinner. Manuel was still fast asleep, curled up around the cat. All her little world seemed in place that morning. The only thing perplexing was Ana Fabiola's unexpected return the night before and her fresh enthusiasm for helping her mother with evening chores while the rest of her friends remained at the fiesta on the plaza. Hot coals kept warm the fresh pile of tortillas that she had finished already. The sun had not yet broken the line of clouds on the far side of the lake when she was startled by sounds behind her. She turned back in time to see Ana Fabiola and Celina Marquez racing from the doorway and down the path. The flight of the girls set the neighborhood dogs to howling. Moments later, María Salinas, the wife of the tailor at the foot of the hill, came struggling up the path, clutching the front of her *huipil.*

"Doña María!" cried Señora Salinas. "Doña María! Come! Come quickly!"

María Xquic de Xoy turned to the voice as she wiped her hands down the sides of her *morga.* In the dim light of the corner of her kitchen, she couldn't see the party calling to her from the yard outside.

"Why Señora Salinas!" cried María Xquic. "What could be the matter so early in the *morning?*"

"*Quickly!*" her neighbor pleaded. "You must come *quickly*, Doña María!"

"All right!" she agreed, "but what is the matter? What is the problem to rouse the neighborhood so early in the morning? What is all the commotion—and the two girls just now?"

"Oh, *Doña!*" cried Señora Salinas, sobbing deeply. "It is the *children!*"

"The *children?*" cried María Xquic, her heart beating tremulously. "*What* children? *Your* children? *My* children? *What* children?"

Ana Fabiola and the little Marquez girl were just with her only a moment before. Surely, her neighbor had seen them as they raced past her on her way up the hill.

"We must *hurry!*" cried Señora Salinas.

The two women lurched down the rutted path, making their way along the trail as quickly as possible through the dense, early morning fog. By the time they reached the smooth paving stones of the alley, María was panicky.

"What has *happened,* Señora?" she pleaded.

Señora María bent over and then leaned back against the pick-up truck parked at the curb.

"*Isaiah . . .* " she gasped. "Isaiah Xolop and little *Meri Batos! . . . Dead!* Both *dead! . . .* Dead by the *militaries!* You have to *come!* You have to *see!*"

"Mother of God!" gasped María Xquic. "Isaiah! Isaiah Xolop! But he was the friend of Ana Fabiola! And Meri Batos! Oh, Mother of the Gracious Savior!"

Once again—their breath restored—the two women began their brisk walk, half a run. They passed the boarded-up marketplace and crossed swiftly through the plaza in front of the church.

"Where *is* it?" cried María Xquic. "Where are we *going?*"

"On the road to the military post," answered Señora Salinas. "They dumped them just on the road to the *post!*"

Twice again the women had to stop to regain their breath. Others apparently were now alert to something gone wrong. The women could now hear dogs barking ahead of them, the sound of doors being unbolted, and frantic, though indecipherable voices increasing around them. Two men turned the corner just ahead of them, shouting something as they ran. Two more joined them in the street at the service station where the street forked, breaking away to the right toward the military garrison.

"Oh, we must *hurry!*" said María Xquic.

"Yes, we *must!*" insisted her terrified companion.

Following the men now well ahead of them, the women turned past the Esso service station, its streamers from the beauty pageant the day before drifting lightly in the early morning breeze. They could see a small but growing congregation of Felipinos at the end of the street where the paving stones gave way once more to the dusty road. The people seemed grouped to the right, standing in a bunch and looking down.

"*María Xquic*!" said Toribio Alfaro, the gentle cobbler who rushed up from the group to meet them when he saw the women approaching.

"*Doña* María and Señora Salinas! *Please*!" he said. "It is *very* bad! Perhaps you don't want to see this!"

"*But!* . . . " cried María Xquic. "But . . . we *must!* We *have* to see this, *whatever* this horrible thing might be!"

"*Please!*" cried Señora Salinas. "We *have* to see! These children are *our* children. They are *Felipino children!*"

And she pushed her way past the poor cobbler. "*Come* María Xquic!"

The two women looped around the group of men to the right who, in their own morbid fixation on what lay before them, discovered the women's intrusion too late.

At once, Señora Salinas gasped, and flung her open palms over her startled face, turning in horror toward María Xquic de Xoy.

"*No! No!*" cried Señora Salinas. "*No!* Such a thing *can't be!* Not to the *children!* Not to the *children of San Felipe!*"

María Xquic grabbed the arms of the distraught neighbor, bracing Señora Salinas against her own crippled body to keep her friend from collapsing, and then peered around her toward the ground.

"Oh, my God!" she cried. *"Oh, my God!"*

And María Xquic de Xoy swooned herself against her comrade, throwing *Señora* Salinas off balance, and together they fell at the feet of the two headless children. It was almost two hours later that Susan Simpson discovered the body of Ana Fabiola hanging from a rafter behind the altar in the sanctuary.

Chapter 22

La Sopa de la Muerte

Marcus Finley's preparations were hurried. He had had to cover many details before he could take off a week in the middle of the month to go out of the country. His passport had arrived in only two and half weeks, which was one hassle out of the way, and the credit union had approved his loan application for a $1,000 to cover his anticipated expenses and flight down. It wasn't the anticipation of problems there. Father Mike's contact with his long-time friend, Father Jack Heller—at least his initial focus for a story, then Susan Simpson, the peace corps worker from Brownsville being down there and all—arrangements in Guatemala weren't the problem. The biggest problem was Tammy, his present "item," who couldn't believe that he would drop *everything*—including their weekend in *Cancún*—to go to *Guatemala,* of all places!

Tammy worked as a waitress in the non-smoking section at "Cheeter's," an up-scale little restaurant near the airport in Harlingen. She did very well, serving a good number of arriving businessmen each afternoon and evening, gentlemen who knew how to treat a girl with her looks and attention to their service—most particularly, her looks. Marcus Finley had certainly been smitten. He monopolized the back booth every day for an hour and a half starting around 11:00 or 11:15 a.m., just before the lunch rush arrived. Marcus Finley knew how to string out two or three glasses of iced tea and a hamburger—with the proper tip—for an hour or more without arousing consternation from management. He would always bring along his note pad and work at a story or use the time to proofread some galley, any visible excuse to catch once or twice the eye of the popular little waitress.

And he had. Even with his slightly bent nose, Marcus Finley was a very good-looking young man for his twenty-five years. He kept in shape. He wore the right clothes. The new 240ZX didn't hurt anything either. He was a "package," as some of the bar ladies had called him before, intentionally within earshot. With his looks and apparent means, the liberalism of Marcus Finley was never an issue—at least not initially. It was only when trips to Cancún were interrupted that his more private convictions got in the way of good partying. Tammy liked to party and dated only those who could keep her entertained.

After more than a month and a few pitches in the sack, however, Tammy was becoming something hardly more than a dalliance. She didn't care much for *priests*, anyway, and increasingly, she had sensed her interests being compromised in favor of "this *Catholic* thing," as she liked to disparage it. Marcus Finley could tell Tammy to bug off easily enough, but he was getting a little addicted and didn't want to close off all chances for a little more T&A when he returned. That all changed with a phone call.

"You might want to go with me," said Father Mike. "I can pick you up in about an hour."

The trip to El Chamayo would be a turning point for the young reporter and a sustaining encounter for the troublemaking priest. Gib Harris, a *pro bono* attorney had called Father Mike requesting his assistance as an interpreter for a Guatemalan singled out by INS for immediate deportation. Harris had been able to secure a restraining order from the Court, but he needed immediate assistance in translating the detainee's story.

"He's some Guatemalan they've ordered for immediate deportation. That's unusual, to say the least," explained the priest. "The judge had issued the deportation order after the first interview, but this guy got word from his bunk mate that he had the option of requesting a `hearing on the merits.' That's the only thing that saved him, I guess. I can't imagine what this guy's all about. It must be something pretty stiff, though."

It was a drizzly day, and the highway was very slick. Produce trucks all along the route to El Chamayo were taking their time to avoid skidding. Several pickup trucks passed them carrying pickers up the highway and inland to the orchards of San Medina. About an hour after they had departed Brownsville, Father Mike and Marcus Finley arrived at the entrance of El Chamayo.

The guard was on the telephone as they pulled to a stop at the entrance check point. Father Mike looked to his left past the guard station to the block of buildings about a quarter of a mile down the boulevard that led to the Central Office.

"It'll be that two-story building between the two dorms over there," the priest explained.

"How can I help you gentlemen?" asked the guard as he hung up the receiver.

"We're here to interpret for a *pro bono* client. I'm Father Michael Justice. You should have our name on your roster there," said Father Mike.

The guard returned to his roster on the clipboard, scanned down the morning's clearances, and checked off the priest.

"Go right on to Building G. That's the Central Office. Your attorney is already there and waiting for you. You can park anywhere in a visitor's slot."

Father Mike waved a salutary gesture of thanks as they pulled past the guard station.

"This should be interesting," offered Marcus Finley.

They pulled into a parking space just adjacent to the handicap ramp leading into the Central Office, entered the building, and approached the hispanic receptionist preoccupied at a computer terminal.

"*Disculpe!* I'm sorry," she protested. "I didn't see you come in. How can I help you?" she asked.

"We just need to sign in. We have an appointment in the interview room," explained Father Mike.

"Oh, Father," she said. "I'm *doubly* sorry! I know you from your work over in Colonia Villa. I'm Gracie Hernandez—the one who took you to the teachers in the Colonia about two months ago!"

"Oh, *of course!*" exclaimed the priest. "I'm sorry I didn't recognize you. I guess I was a little pre-occupied myself."

Gracie handed Father Mike the clipboard on which he signed in his time for both of them and returned it to the receptionist. Their anxiety began to mount as they walked down the corridor to the interview room.

"I can't even venture to guess what we're about to hear," said Marcus Finley.

Gib Harris greeted the two as they entered the small reception room. Two years out of law school at the University of Wisconsin, Mr. Harris was new to the Texas Rio Grande Valley, although he had elected to settle here after a couple of earlier college excursions to South Padre Island. He had taken a position with *Johnson, Merrick, Stanford & Coats*, a San Antonio firm, and had been transferred to the Brownsville office only six months before. This curious situation represented only his second *pro bono* case and his first asylum application.

"Hello, Father," said the attorney. "Thanks for coming on such short notice." He turned to Marcus Finley and introduced himself.

"Oh, this is Marcus Finley," offered the priest. "He's a reporter with the *McAllen Star*, and we've been covering the situation at Casa Libertad—you know, with the threatened closing of Casa. We had a pretty heavy interview with Sister María a couple of weeks ago, and Marcus has become pretty interested in this whole Guatemala human rights subject."

"Well, I think this case will thicken the whole pot," explained the attorney. "I've never heard anything so bizarre in my life. I asked the attorney for INS to clarify the judge's decision about this fellow. I tried to follow with the client himself, but I just don't speak the Spanish. The best I can make out from the report and from what INS has said is that this guy is a member of some sort of government-sponsored `hit team,' or something like that."

"Un esquadron de muerte," said the priest.

"Say *what?*" responded the attorney.

"*Esquadron de muerte*—a `death squad,'" interpreted the priest.

"That's *it!* That's what they *said,*" said Gib Harris.

"Oh boy!" exclaimed the priest. "Where is he now?"

"Oh, just here—right through there," said the attorney as he pointed toward the adjoining parlor.

"Well, let's get on with it, I guess," said Father Mike.

The three of them walked down the corridor to the interrogation room, opened the cold-grey, industrial steel door, and walked in. Wearing the standardized orange overhauls of the detainees, a small, wiry hispanic man of about 130 lbs. sat with his head in hands, obviously quite shaken by his situation and very much isolated in this intrusion of officialdom.

"What is his name?" asked Father Mike.

"His report says `Hector Mario Linares,'" said the attorney.

"`Hector Mario Linares,'" repeated the priest to himself, just barely audible. He turned to the detainee.

"Señor Linares," said Father Mike to the quiet, reserved detainee. *"Me llamo Padre Miguel. Estoy aqui para ayudar a Ud. con su papeles de migración. Por favor, explicame la situación."*

The detainee looked up quite disturbed, and said, *"No se puede regresar a Guatemala! No se puede!"*

"*Por qué*? Why?" asked Father Mike, as he sat down across the table from the young man who looked to be no more than twenty-four or twenty-five years old.

"Por que? Por qué!" he exclaimed, as he grimaced in a mock death mask. "Why!" And Hector Mario Linares drew an imaginary knife blade across his neck.

"Why? Who wants to *kill* you?" Father Mike continued to probe. Marcus Finley and Gib Harris stood to one side against the wall, their eyes fixed on every nuance of the distraught figure before them.

"Who wants to *kill* you?" the priest asked again.

"Los esquadrones de muerte!" revealed the detainee.

*"`Esquadrones de muerte'?* The `death squads'?" asked Father Mike.

"Sí, esquadrones de muerte," confirmed the young man in almost a whisper.

"Why?" asked the priest. The detainee sat with his head buried in his hands, sobbing silently as his shoulders trembled.

"Me esperon . . . esperon," said the man.

The detainee looked up at the priest, then turned to scan the reporter and attorney. Both looked down to avoid his glance. As if by collusion, the interrogators adopted a community of silence, waiting for the man to explain himself. He would get no help from the team, outside an opening, perhaps, from the priest.

"Ellos estan esperandome. Ellos estan esperando para matarme al momento regresar al aereopuerto Guatemala!" The man read the expressions of resolve on each face of his interrogators. He would have to tell more . . . much more.

"He says the death squads are waiting for him at the airport in Guatemala as soon as he returns. He's saying, I think, he won't even get out of the airport alive," explained Father Mike. He turned again and looked into the eyes of the detainee.

"Why do you think they are waiting for you at the airport?" asked the priest.

"Por que conosco tan mucho . . . tan mucho! mucho! . . ." paused the man.

"About *what?*" probed the priest.

Silence.

"You know much about *what?*" repeated the priest.

More silence. And then, *"De ellos,"* mumbled the man.

"*About . . .?*" asked Father Mike.

"De ellos—los miembros de los esquadrones de muerte," said the man.

"What do you know about them?" asked Father Mike.

"Everything," said the man.

"*`Everything?'"* pressured the priest. The man nodded silently.

"How would you be in a position to know `everything' about `them' if you weren't one of `them'?" asked Father Mike.

Silence.

"You were one of them?" asked the priest.

The man didn't respond.

"You were one of them?" repeated Father Mike. The attorney and reporter were frozen in expectation.

The man nodded, confirming their suspicions.

"I think we need to talk about this," said the Priest. "*Okay?*"

The young man nodded again.

"So, you were a member of a death squad in Guatemala?" pursued the priest.

"*Sí,*" acknowledged the man, obviously embarrassed by the whole confrontation.

"What is your name?" asked Father Mike.

"Hector . . . Hector Mario Linares."

The attorney checked the name again on the initial report against what he just heard.

"And you go by . . .?" asked the priest.

"Mario . . . Mario Linares."

"Mario. Mario," said the priest. "Well, Mario. Tell us about this death squad and what you know about it. How long were you with this death squad?"

"Tres años."

"Three years. I see. Who . . . what was . . . whose squad was this? Was this a military unit, or . . . or was it, was it? Well, was this an *official* military unit?

"Oficiál," mumbled the man.

"*Military?* An army unit, or what?" asked Father Mike.

"*Ejército, Sí!"*

"Then, were you `Army,' too?"

"Yes . . . well, yes . . ." came the tentative answer. *"Bueno, Policia Ambulatory Nacional."*

"Okay, I see," said the priest as he turned to the attorney. "He is member of the `National Mobile Police.' I think that makes him `retired military.'"

"Were you drafted into the Army?" asked the priest.

"Sí."

"Cuando?"

"Four years ago."

"Como?" asked Father Mike. "Did you volunteer?"

"No. They came to my *aldea*," explained the man.

"And what? . . . what happened?"

"They came on fiesta day four years ago. Some soldiers in a truck came into the plaza in the afternoon. They told me and José . . . José and Rutilio and Paco to get in the truck," explained the detainee. "They just pointed their guns at us and told us to get in the back of the truck, and that was it. We were in the Army."

"And you just left. You never had time to tell your family goodbye?" asked the priest.

"No," said the man.

"He says that the Army came into his village on fiesta day—I guess when there were a lot of young men like himself around the village square," explained Mike. "So, the soldiers pointed guns at him and some of his friends and told them to get in the back of the Army truck. They were drafted, just like that! They never even had time to tell their families goodbye or anything."

"Have you been back to your village since you were picked up?" asked the priest. The man shook his head.

"So, you went into the military—into the regular Army?"

"Sí," said the man.

"And you were assigned to a death squad?" asked Mike.

"No . . . no," said the detainee.

"Did you *fight?* What *happened?*" asked the priest.

"Well, after training, we were assigned to a unit in the Petén," explained the man. "We had to fight the guerrillas in the jungle and along the border with Mexico. We had to kill the subversives who were helping the guerrillas."

"Along the border? You had to kill the subversives *along the border?*" asked Father Mike for clarification.

"Sí, a la frontera," said the man.

"You had to kill the subversives along the border . . . do you mean those in the villages?" asked Mike.

"Yes, in the villages . . . sometimes in the villages, sometimes when they were running," said the man.

"Did your unit ever chase them across the river?" Mike asked.

For a moment the man was hesitant, but then he responded: "Yes, sometimes across the river."

"In Mexico?" asked the priest.

"Yes."

"How many times would you say? Frequently? You chased them many times across the river?"

"Yes," said the man.

"Father?" said the attorney. Father Mike turned around.

"Where is all this going?" asked the attorney, obviously picking up something of the conversation.

"Well, this is good," said the priest. "I mean, I really want to find out just what he knew and how his army experience is tied to his death squad work."

"I see," said Harris. "Okay."

"So, you chased subversives across the river, right?" asked Mike, returning to the detainee.

"Sí."

"Did you engage them in combat . . .?

The man didn't answer.

"I mean, was there fighting on the other side of the river?" asked the priest.

"Yes, sometimes," he said.

"The Army fought with the subversives . . . the guerrillas, on the other side of the river?" asked the priest.

"Yes," said the man.

"You, too? You fought with the guerrillas in Mexico?"

"Sometimes," said the man.

Father Mike paused for a few moments to catch the interest of or possible cues from the attorney. With no visible response from Gib Harris, the priest continued:

"How did you become a member of a death squad?" asked Father Mike.

"Through the military," replied the man.

"Through the military? How `through the military'?" asked the priest. The questions were starting to get very close, and the man was beginning to withdraw. He made no response.

"`Through the military,' you said?" queried the priest, unwilling to back away from the line of questioning.

"Yes," said the man.

"How?" pursued the priest.

"The commander of my unit, he recommended me for special duty," said the man.

"`Special duty'?" asked Father Mike.

"Yes," said the man.

"And this `special duty' . . . that was the *death squad?*" asked the priest.

"Yes," said the man.

"To move into `special duty' . . . was that some kind of *promotion?*" asked the priest.

"Yes," responded the man.

"You made more money? a higher rank, maybe?" asked the priest.

"Yes . . . more money. I was made a corporal," returned the man.

"Why were you selected?" asked Father Mike.

"I don't know," said the man.

"You were just . . . singled out, singled out for no reason?" he asked.

"No . . . well, the commander recommended me because of my service record," the man finally volunteered.

"Your `service record'?" asked the priest.

"Sí," said the man.

"What did you have to do to become so `distinguished'?" asked Father Mike.

"I . . . I killed a lot of subversives," confessed the man.

"How many did you kill?" continued the priest.

"I don't know," responded the man.

"Many?" Mike pushed.

"I don't know," persisted the man.

"Maybe *thirty . . .?*" offered the priest.

"Maybe . . ." said the man.

"Maybe *more . . .?*" asked Mike.

"I guess so," said the man.

"Maybe a *hundred . . .?*" Father Mike was trying to establish some kind of window.

"I guess so," agreed the man.

"Maybe a hundred . . . and that was more than the other soldiers killed?" asked the priest.

"Yeah," said the man.

"Did you *like* to kill . . . kill these `subversives'?" responded the priest.

"I don't know," said the man.

"A hundred or more," said Father Mike. "Men . . . were most of them men, these *subversives?*"

"Yes, some of them."

"Some of them . . . some of them were *women?*" encouraged the priest.

"Yes, I guess so," said the man.

"Children? Did you kill children, too?" pumped the priest.

The man was hesitant.

"Children, *too?*" asked Father Mike, more forcefully this time.

"Sometimes," mumbled the man, barely audible through his hands which now cupped his face.

A shiver ran across the shoulders of Father Mike just like it always did whenever he was stunned by another example of unexpected cruelty or inhumanity. He sensed that he had finally struck a nerve with the detainee, one that he intended to pursue to its grim resolution.

"And as a member of the death squad," said Father Mike, "as a member of this death squad . . . you killed . . .? Who did *you* kill?"

"Subversives . . . communists, subversives and guerrillas," said the man, still mumbling into his fists.

"Men . . .?" asked the priest. Father Mike was angling toward the horrific clue about the children.

"Yes," said the man.

"Women? Women, too?" continued the priest.

"Yes," came the response.

"And *children?*" asked Mike.

There was no response.

"And *children?* You had to kill the *children, too?*" asked the priest. He could hardly believe he was hearing himself speak such a blasphemy against life.

"Yes, sometimes," admitted the man.

"As a member of the death squad, you had to *kill children!*" said Father Mike more emphatically to make sure the man understood him clearly and precisely.

"Yes," came the response.

"Why was it necessary to kill the *children?*" asked the priest.

"Sometimes we didn't have any choice?" said the man.

"Any *`choice'?*" asked the priest, quite agitated by the response.

"You didn't have *`any choice'?*" he repeated. "How could you not have *`any choice'* to kill *children?*"

The man was suddenly aroused. He turned on the priest with a fiery, vindictive sneer.

"Because they would have blown away my fucking *head!*" exploded the man. "You *got that, priest?* My fucking *head!*"

Father Mike fell away from the table at the man's sudden animation. He hadn't expected such a response, let alone the answer.

". . . my goddamn *head*, you see?" continued the man. "That's why I'm *here, goddamn it!* That's why I'm *here!*"

The man collapsed into his chair, stretched his arms across the table, dropping his head below his shoulders, and began to cry unrelentingly.

Father Mike starred wildly at the man, as Marcus Finley and the attorney stood vacantly with mouths agape. The man continued to cry. So, this was the answer. So, in this confession rested the rationale of the Immigration Court. This man was a confessed child killer.

Of course, the man couldn't go back. He knew too much—names, dates, circumstances, methods and procedures. Procedures! The priest had to continue.

"*How? How* did you kill these *children?*" asked Father Mike as he eased into a chair in front of the killer.

The man began wailing and writhing from side to side, his arms still stretched across the table.

"How did you have to *kill* them?" asked the priest, granting him the necessity of the man's own confession.

All of a sudden, the man stopped his moaning and became very still. Then he looked up at the priest and said in measured words, simply, "*Soup*," he said. "I *drowned* them in their *soup!*"

Chapter 23

By Their Works Ye Shall Know Them

Tanolito was hardly cold in the earth of a clandestine grave when they bore the bodies of Ana Fabiola, Meri Batos, and Isaiah Xolop to their funeral Mass. One by one the bell of the church tolled its grief as the citizens of San Felipe followed the small entourage up the steep tier of steps, across the wide portico, to the great doors, and down the long aisle to the altar.

Weeping silently in her scarf, María Xquic walked just behind Andres, her husband. Then followed in their turn Lucita María and little Manuel. Ahead of them, mounted high on the shoulders of the *auxiliaturas* of the *Cofradia of Santa Cruz*, moved the casket of little Ana Fabiola Xoy. When they reached the front of the sanctuary, the pall bearers stepped forward and placed the varnished wooden coffin beside the others on the altar now draped in black to receive its poor burdens.

María Xquic had attended the church on only the most solemn occasions. The last time—now more than three years before—had been the christening of tiny Matilde Barberena Somozo. Several of her young friends had been married there and not a few of San Felipe's citizens had preceded Ana Fabiola in their deaths, including little Matilde who had died from what everyone knew had been starvation.

Verse by verse, Sister Dona read the litany for the rite of the dead as the bell continued to toll. Outside, hundreds of Felipinos jammed the plaza, stopping to cross themselves in homage to the unfortunate young girl and her comrades. One old *campesino* climbed hesitantly up the steps, and reaching the porch at the top, slowly laid down his bags and knelt in prayer. When he had finished his salutation, he opened his *tzute* and took out a censor and a small handful of *copal*. Reaching inside his pants pocket, he retrieved a cigarette lighter and fired the charcoal through a small hole in the bottom of the tin can. In a few seconds, the incense was blazing, and he stood before the door of the church, joining perhaps a dozen others swinging the censor from a leather strap attached to the hanger wire that secured the can.

"*Ah, malaya! Señor!*" began the man. "*Jesucristo y Santa María!* Hear the prayer of your simple servant, Don Ronaldo Franco Roche. *Ah, malaya!* Blessed Mother of God. Hear the petition of a wretched *campesino* brought low in the dust of this poor earth. *Oh, Blessed Mother!* You know the pain of these, your people, the gentle ones of San Felipe del Lago. *Come* to us, Holy Mother. Come to us *now* and hear our grief. Come to us *now* and help heal our wounds of sorrow, and then lift our souls to your Blessed Heart, that we may find peace."

The *campesino* paused to shake his censor, and a stream of spent ashes drifted from the holes in the bottom of the can. Then he knelt again on one knee, swinging the censor slowly to the cadences of his sad prayer.

"*Ah, malaya!* The Blessed Mother of God is with me now, so come to me! Come to me, all you *alcaldes* of the world! Come here to me *now*, and receive this simple request. Before me, inside this Holy Church—*there!* Just there *inside!*—lies the poor clay of your tiny servant, Ana Fabiola Xoy, and two of her fallen friends. She was only a simple child of your devout servant Don Andres Menchu Xoy, but now, merciful lords of the night and of the day and of the wide heavens above all, this poor child of the corn lies now before us, oh, powerful lords, a slight and perishable thing who is restless for your peace. And so heavenly lords and *alcaldes* of the underworld, hear her story that you may understand and receive her in the bosom of your love."

Tears streamed down the old *campesino's* cheeks.

"What can I say, Great Fathers. Oh, *help* me, Blessed Mother!" continued Don Ronaldo. "In her love of another, this poor, little songbird gave up her own life that she and her violated, her murdered lover might find peace together. Hear now her story, mighty gracious lords, that she may find rest in the promise of your vengeance on those who continue to slaughter like lambs the gentle people of San Felipe."

Tears continued to flow down the chalky jowls of the *campesino* as he stirred the coals of his censor. Once more he steadied his balance, this time switching hands and knees at his place of prayer, and once more, the servant of the mighty powers of destiny continued his petition.

"So, hear me *now,* oh angry, lords. Hear the story of this tiny one whose only sin was to love too much. Ana Fabiola Xoy came from the earth only fourteen short rounds ago, not so long in the course of your timeless will, this I know. But this tiny servant might have known the face of many years, oh mighty powers, had not the *dogs of Satan* savaged her poor spirit."

The old man caught himself as he was about to lose himself to anger.

"I attended the birth of Ana Fabiola Xoy, so what I have to say, I know as her simple godfather," confessed Don Ronaldo, clarifying his own credentials before the assembled deities. "So, know that I speak the truth. This little girl was raised in the faith of *El Mundo* and his mighty servant, the *Maximón*, *Rila'j Mam,* the guardian of San Felipe del Lago, who blesses his people with health and his protection. Her soul was consecrated before the *Maximón* in the most solemn ceremony—did I not attend the offerings? —and from that day, Ana Fabiola Xoy never missed a day in sacred duties to the gods. And was it not the words of the ancestors themselves who taught the daughters of the corn to grind the *masa* and to shape the *tamales del lago*? To weave the threads of the village into fabric for the sacred *tzutes*?"

The old man shook his head wearily. "And what did she do to deserve this awful death, *oh merciful gods?*" pressed the *campesino* as he looked up to the heavens. "What did she do but to love another, the young man, Isaiah Xolop of San Felipe. *Ah, malaya!* No greater love is the devotion of a young woman for a man. Did not the ancestors themselves command the women to give up their lives to the men who would be their masters? Did not the ancestors themselves instruct the young men to honor their wives and to take them to their sides that they might seed the families of the earth?"

"*Ah, malaya!*" cried Don Ronaldo, his sorrow overwhelming him once again for the moment. "Hear me, Blessed Mother, and *oh, alcaldes of the heavens and the earth!* Was there ever a mother more *respectful* to the sacred duties on behalf of a daughter than María Xquic de Xoy? And did this small, crippled stalk of flesh ever fail in her responsibilities to raise up a Felipino child in the traditional ways and in accordance to the sayings of the ancestors? These things I know, *Oh, Holy Ones. Ah, malaya!*"

The old man ceased swinging the incense for a moment and bowed his head.

"So, what can I, only a poor *campesino*, know about such things?" apologized the godfather of Ana Fabiola. "How can a simple man such as I pretend to know why so great an evil has drifted from so far away to take root in such a humble place as San Felipe? And how is it that a poor man of the mountains can ever understand why hope has rotted in the fields, or that the womb of faith has borne only suffering for pious hearts?"

The distraught man picked up his censor once more, shook it twice to settle the coals, and began again its rhythmic swing.

"So, take her, dark lords of the earth and wide, blue heavens. Take her, lords of the high mountains and of the green fields of *maize*. Take this poor child, oh lords of the deep caves. Lift her high into the cliffs where the evil militaries cannot climb. Receive her fragile, little bones and lose them deeply under the hillocks of the tall corn where the truncheons of the *ejercito* will not pummel her little soul in its slumber. And *Blessed Mother of God!* Cradle the spirit of Ana Fabiola Xoy in the warm folds of your sacred bosom where the hounds of Satan will never drive her from your love!"

Tears poured from his eyes. The spirit of the old man was finally spent, and he could speak no more. He ceased swinging the censor and placed it carefully at his side. Taking a rag from his back pocket, he wiped the soot from around his eyes and face, and then bowed his head. The old man's anguish had finally become too heavy to bear, and, as his sorrow gave way to convulsions of unrelenting sobs, he collapsed face down on the steps.

The heavy air had broken into a steady drizzle, and the charcoals of *copal pom* began to crackle as light drops of rain sprinkled into the smoking censor.

The claps of the great bell began anew their awful, measured pace. Slowly, the procession bearing the caskets of the little Felipino girl and her comrades made their way from the altar out once again onto the portico of the church. When Don Andres spied the prostrate body of Don Ronaldo lying to the side of the steps, he stopped, and watching his footing so as not to slip on the wet stones, he carefully made his way to his side.

"She was your daughter, too, Don Ronaldo," Andres whispered. "Come, Don Ronaldo, join us now. *See!* Our little daughter waits for us, and we should not keep her anxious any longer."

Slowly, the old *campesino* turned and rose to his feet.

"*Come,* Don Ronaldo," urged the priest. "Take my shoulder."

The exhausted man reached down for his bag and censor. He placed his withered hand lightly on Andres's shoulder and followed him back into the procession behind María Xquic, Lucita María, and the sobbing little Manuel. In a solemn procession, the family and their friends made their way down the steps and entered the plaza where merchants were completing the disassembly of their stalls in the threat of an early evening rain. As the procession passed across the plaza, both the *campesinos* and the merchants removed their hats to honor the memory of the children, the story of whose deaths had already spread well beyond the *cantones* of Sololá. And the bell continued to toll.

Down through the community wound the funeral party. All along the streets, the Felipinos paused, the old men lowering their uncovered heads and crossing their breasts, the women lifting their fingers to the corners of their eyes. And the bell of the San Felipe church continued to toll. Little Ana Fabiola Xoy, Meri Batos, and Isaiah Xolop were passing on their way to paradise.

"*Ah, malaya! Mother of God!*" whispered old Tata Paco Albanes, as he stared ahead, twisting the rim of his sweat-stained straw hat.

"*What poor children*—poor little Ana Fabiola!" whimpered Sylvia Perez standing just out of sight, raising the corner of her apron over her mouth. "And María Xquic—what has *happened* to our poor families? *Oh, María Xquic de Xoy!* What have *you* done to deserve this?"

"Ah, what can we *do,*" cried Don Tupe Arredondo, "when the shadow of evil settles on a town?" He spit to the ground in defiance of the growing military presence in his *aldea.* And in the increasing rain and rolls of heavy fog, the bell of the church continued to toll.

At the edge of town, the small procession entered the gate of El Calvario and proceeded slowly up the hill to the tiny graves that had been opened among the respective families' tombs. Through the stinging drizzle and dense ground fog, the families divided and moved in close as the pall bearers lowered the caskets between them and nursed them into the shallow niches below. For a few moments, with their heads bowed stiffly, no one among the mourners seemed to move. Then, as if on cue, they turned away and drifted back down toward the cemetery gate. And the flat, doleful claps of the bell cracked the face of the night.

In one of those queer convolutions of Maya history, the evening of the funeral of Ana Fabiola marked the ancient anniversary of the conquest of the Tzutujiles. As the poor processions of families and friends returned through the streets of San Felipe, they were greeted by the aromatic waves of *copal pom* and the flickers of black candles which the Felipinos, in solemn commemoration, had placed at sundown in doorways throughout the *aldea* and in each of the villages all around the southern rim of Lake Atitlán.

Only a year before the arrival of Cristóbal Colón, the *auxiliatura máximo* of the *Rila'j Mam*, the revered *Maximón*, had cast the mixes before the gruesome god. Since that fateful day, *Atiteco* ancestors had told the story of how the horrible visage of the wooden idol had begun to twist and contort. Deeply within the soul of the earth—just beneath the compound of the *Maximón—El Mundo* convulsed, and a heavy quake sent tremors that erupted across the waters of the lake. The priest of *Maximón* emerged from the compound to announce the collapse of the Tzutujil nation by a foreign deity who would come among them followed by all the legions of hell. After the fateful prophesy, much to the horror of the Felipinos who had gathered about, the priest, as a token of his integrity, reached within his own breast, ripped out his heart, and pitched it into the coals of his censor before the mute and terrible *Rila'j Mam.* Within three decades, the guileful Pedro Alvarado lured the tall, proud Tzutujiles into the lake where an alliance of Cakchiquel and Quiché devils subdued them from the shores, sending a rain of arrows into the hearts of the proud warriors. Subjugation was nothing new to the Tzutujiles of San Felipe del Lago, and the peels of the all too familiar *sons* of sorrow drifted from the belfry of the church out across the trembling waters of Lake Atitlán.

In the grey morning, Lucita María donned the mourner's *sobre-huipil*, her ceremonial over blouse, and helped drape the same over the bodice of her mother.

"Come, Lucita María," called María Xquic. "Go to your father now before he returns to the compound for his prayers and consultations. You must tell him now."

"How can I tell him on such a morning?" pleaded the young girl. Lucita María's decision to enter the convent of the Sisters of St. Francis and to live in Antigua at the Convent of the Capuchinas would come as a heavy shock to a father who worshipped his daughters as much as his wife.

"Go *now!*" instructed her mother. "Your father *must* know. He should hear it from you and not from the American priest or one of the sisters. Go *now!*"

Don Andres, Lucita María's father, was deep in his morning prayers before *Santa Mesa* as his timid daughter approached. Already, the candles had burned down almost completely, and he was preparing the third grip of tapers for placement at the altar before casting the mixes. If she were to interrupt him at all, it would have to be before he began the final liturgy of the candles.

"*Papa!*" urged Lucita María. Lost in reflections and sad memories of his little daughter, and at the same time, absorbed in his prayers, Don Andres had not noticed Lucita María's approach, and her call startled him.

"Ana . . . *Ana?*" he mumbled without thinking.

"*Papa! Oh, papa!*" gasped Lucita María.

"*Oh, my daughter!*" whispered Don Andres, suddenly realizing his terrifying error, and in broken sobs, he dropped his chin to his quaking breast.

Lucita María moved softly to his side and pressed her cheek against his shoulder. For a few small moments, both wept openly together before the silent flickers of the candles. Then Lucita María reached before her father and picked up the third bundle of candles. Carefully, she untied the knotted wicks and began to spread the tapers in an even row before her father. The last one she placed into his listless fingers. Respectfully, she reached before him for the waning candle closest to her, nudged it from its stand, and held it to the exposed wick of her father's taper. At once, the string glowed, then flashed into a steady flame. Lucita María returned the fragment of candle once again to its place and then reached up and gripped her father's hand.

"For Ana Fabiola?" asked the girl. "Can we make a prayer for Ana Fabiola?"

"Of course, Lucita," returned her father. "But *of course*, my blessed child."

María Xquic watched the tender intimacies between her husband and surviving daughter for a few moments just out of earshot from their muted exchanges. A stream of tears traced the eroded paths of sorrow down her cheeks, and wiping her hands on her tattered apron, she rose from the last round of tortillas that she had just wrapped in the *servilleta*, then turned to Doña Mirna López de López y López, the wife of Don Francisco Ruano López y Lopez, *auxiliatura* of the *Cofradia of Santa Cruz*. She, along with Doña Marta Uco and Doña Pilar Humberto Mardriga, had stood in waiting for the wake of Ana Fabiola and would continue at the side of the grieving mother for the tenure of the mourning period—two weeks or longer, determined by the *alcalde principal* closest to the family—in this case, Don Pablo Manuel López y López. In her exalted position, the crippled, arthritic Doña Mirna would direct the support for their neighbor during the period of mourning.

"God bless, Doña María," said Doña Mirna, stretching out her stiff hands to the weeping mother. "What will you have of us?"

"Oh, my wonderful friends," said María Xquic. "You are *here*—each of you. That's enough. Thank you all. I asked my husband to say a special grace for you before *Santa Mesa*. There . . . there, you can see for yourself, *no?*"

"María," called Doña Mirna to her ward. "María Xquic, sit with us for a moment, and let us comfort you."

By custom, the *auxiliaturas* would minister to the mother of the mourners' house through a cycle of orchestrated grieving, counselling, and instruction. In addition, they prepared the meals for the family and facilitated the Masses at the church. The latter constituted a bit of uncomfortable syncretism in the case of a traditional, non-Catholic family. Such services were not always welcomed by the more conservative within the remote *aldeas*, but practices in San Felipe, a tourist stop, had become much looser over the past few years.

"Look at each of us, María Xquic," said Doña Mirna. "You are *trembling* so! Why don't you drop this mask? We understand your grief. Your sorrow is our *own.*"

María's heart raced. The blood swelled upward through her neck. Her glands throbbed, and a fever washed across her forehead. María Xquic flashed in a rage she had never known, and her anger spewed uncontrollably from her mouth.

"How *dare* you!" María cried. "How could you *possibly* . . .? How can you *possibly* know my, *my* . . .?"

"Your *hurt?* Your *pain?* But *María*!" protested Doña Mirna, "*Surely* you know, each of us has lost a friend, an acquaintance, *someone*—a *relative*, maybe. But we have borne our grief, as you must, in silence. Like us, you must learn to keep such great sorrow close to your heart and not give in to the anger that you feel, for that anger could bring ruin to all of us and destruction to San Felipe."

"*Ruin!*" cried María. "*Destruction to San Felipe!* How can you speak to me of *destruction?* Haven't I lost *two sons* and now my *youngest daughter?*"

"But *María!*" interrupted Doña Mirna. "Surely, you're confused—Ana Fabiola, *yes!* Our own precious child which is why we're here, but *for sure*, your *sons* are *alive and well* in their work on the *fincas!*"

María drew back in horror at the disclosure of a fear she had harbored secretly for so long. Her mind raced. The soldiers had come. Manuel had seen them talking with the soldiers just before they left for the capital—Tanolito and Miguel Mapa, and neither had ever returned. "Oh, yes! Of course, on the fincas of Retalhuleu. That's where they must be," she had told herself over and over, just as it had been for the past few years. They left. Months would go by. Then they would return. Why was this to be any different? But there was the day that Manuel saw them talking with the soldier. That was the only difference. Both had served in the civil defense patrol. Both had accepted their responsibilities to their community. Tanolito and Miguel Mapa, they wouldn't shirk such duty.

Hadn't she heard the stories. María had listened over and over again to the village talk of Miguel Mapa bringing in the two subversives, something which at the time had made her so proud. And she was, too. She was so proud of her sons for their example to the men of San Felipe. *And they would be home again. Or maybe not. She could hardly frame the thought, the idea that maybe—just maybe—they had died. Maybe they had talked with the soldier and left and died and gone, gone forever without a word to their mother.* And María Xquic was horrified at her own disclosure.

Don Andres and Lucita María sat stoned in shock to hear such fear expressed by a wife and mother, a confession that, up to then, she had been too frightened to share with any member of the family.

"Be *still,* María!" ordered Don Andres. "You are sad and angry. You aren't being *sensible* right now!"

María flashed at her husband—the first time in their married life together—her grief eclipsed by anger and rage. She quickly caught herself, however, and grabbing the front of her skirt, she withdrew inside and turned to the hearth.

"*María!*" started Doña Mirna, but then, in doubt, retreated among the other mourners behind the table.

Don Andres watched his wife turning the tortillas on the hearth. [Slap!] [Slap!] María's neck and head twitched in a kind of tick, the manifestation of a fury that would not be bridled.

"I cannot *accept* this, my husband," said María for only her husband to hear. "I will *not* accept these things that are happening to our *home* and to our *people.*" *And I won't be still! No, I won't be still any longer!*

[Slap!] [Slap!] María Xquic had found a new voice that surprised even her in its insistence and profound righteousness. *I will not accept this, my husband.* [Slap!] [Slap! . . . Slap!] *I will not accept this.* The thrice-turned tortillas were beginning to blacken on the hearth before her. *No! I will not accept this.* Dark smoke rose from under the tortillas as they began to crisp in the middle and curl up. *Miguelito went to the school the new red cap on his head for the teacher's dog he looked so funny with the ring on his neck when the teacher and the dog little Tano crawling on his knees*

"*No!*" María stammered audibly in the whirling of her reflections—

Never to accept this! How can I accept this? —in the corn beside the cat that the neighbor tried to steal for the mice and Miguel told him that the cat was his—

"*No! No!* I will *never* accept this!" she snapped out loud. [Slap!] [Slap!] The burning patties on the hearth blistered and cracked against the glowing sheet-metal surface. [Slap!] [Slap!] *Ana Fabiola's little white huipil, two days and already a black bean stain that wouldn't wash, so that Manuel's leg where the dog bit him, Oh, Maximón, Powerful Lord, heal this spot all red and swollen where two black holes and the fever for days, and the prayers of the Cofradia for my little son who liked to play with Ana . . . Ana Fabiola, little Ana Fabiola with the wide smile, her squeal when Manuel crawled under her little skirt to hide from the cat, the time that Ana Fabiola . . . No! No! Ana Fabiola! I will never accept this! I will never accept this! How can I ever accept this! her purple face above the deep red burn of the plastic rope, her lips slightly parted, eyes squinted tight under the rich black locks of hair her little hands pale almost translucent tied behind her back, tied behind, tied . . . tied . . . tied behind her back! How? How tied behind her back? Why? . . . Why tied? Why tied behind her back? . . . to accept this! Never! How? I never, never, never can . . .! I don't . . . I don't have to! I don't have to accept this! But how? . . . no matter! I just don't have to accept this!*

The old women were suddenly irrelevant, their counselling only so much blather, and her husband's order?—just another order. Nothing of the command that had now galvanized her unspeakable grief and horror into steel resolve. She knew clearly that she would *never* accept the death of Ana Fabiola, her purple face and hands tied behind her back, that she didn't have to accept what the *ejercito* had brought to her family and to her town, for that matter . . . and little Meri Batos and the Xolop boy! She had forgotten! Her embarrassment lingered but a moment as her anger seared white hot. She did not have to accept what was happening to San Felipe del Lago. She would *speak!* She would speak out . . . *here!* at *this moment!* She would speak *now* and in her *own home . . . starting right now! Here! To these people! To these people in her own home!*

"I will not *accept* this," whispered María, barely audible under her breath. And then again against the babbling of the loving, but trite village platitudes.

"I will not *accept* this," she repeated. And then again. And again. And then she exploded:

"I will *never* accept this!" she shouted, not so much at them as it was a declaration before her startled little congregation. And María Xquic de Xoy had crossed the line.

María's counsellors from the auxiliary of the *cofradia* left within the hour, and for more than three days a conspiracy of silence if not neglect—unnatural for a Felipino family in mourning—settled around the small compound of the Xoys. No one came up the path to seek out Don Andres who told María on the second day that, for the time being, he would take appointments only at the shrine of the *Maximón*. On the same day, Lucita María had left on the bus for the convent and girls' school in Antigua after a long conversation in private with her father, and little Manuel moved his toys next to his mother's *petate* from across the room so that he might be near her. It was on the afternoon of the fourth day that María received a visitor.

"I have come, María," said the striking young woman with the raven black hair, "because I know the others abandoned you, but don't hold that against them. They're only afraid."

The intruder stepped uninvited from the yard and into her house. Such forwardness was offensive, and María, saying nothing, continued to work grinding the *masa* for the evening tortillas.

"María . . ." said the stranger. "I know what has happened to Ana Fabiola and the other children." María continued kneading the *masa.*

"I only wanted to come to you to express my sorrow, *Señora*," she said, "and maybe to offer you . . . to invite you, to ask you to help us . . . to help the people of San Felipe to end this horrible violence in the town."

"Who are you?" María asked quietly, as she turned slowly to face the dark figure.

The stranger stood just inside the light of the doorway so that her face was silhouetted against the grey stubble of corn across the yard.

"My *name,*" started the stranger, "my name is . . . that is, in the mountains I go by `Linda.' But I am from Santa Lucía where I was named after the Blessed Mother, `María' like you. My name is María Paloma."

maríapalomaMaríaPaloma María "Paloma . . . María Paloma," she finally muttered. María Xquic began to tremble. Surely, this was not, but how could it be? Here, in her own home, the mysterious woman who had married "Lupe," the commander of the guerrilla squad that had chased the army throughout Sololá, the actual guerrilla who had set up "El Pesado." The same woman who was being sought by the *ejercito* in every *aldea* and *canton.*

María could only stare at the lithe figure of the *compa* still dark against her doorway. What could her presence mean? And who, if anyone, had seen her entering her own home? At once, María was terrified. A flood of questions raced through her mind. Did she know something of Miguelito and Tano? Had they become targets of the army or the insurgents? Or Andres? Had she come for her husband? What could it be? María was confused and frightened.

The Felipino's anxiety wasn't lost on the guerrilla, and she knew she had to press her issue carefully.

"I don't know how much more our people can stand!" said María Paloma. "Now they are taking the children!"

María Paloma turned her face from María Xquic in a heartfelt though somewhat orchestrated grimace of remorse, at the present more impatient with the Felipino's insecurity than empathetic with her personal anguish. There were always the larger issues before them.

María Xquic stood motionless, still paralyzed by the unexpected intrusion, her hands strapped within the folds of the ragged *servietta* which she used to wrap the tortillas.

"You don't have to *accept* this . . ." said María Paloma, turning her face squarely to meet the expression of the Felipino.

María Xquic blanched at the sound of her own words. Where could this guerrilla have heard her? She had said it only once, here, here in the intimate circle of her family and closest associates.

"*María!*" repeated the guerrilla. "*Listen* to me! I know your thoughts. I know that your anguish is deep, that the very soul of life has been ripped from your breast. Of course, I did not know your little girl, Ana . . .?"

"`Ana Fabiola,'" said María.

"`Ana Fabiola,'" acknowledged the guerrilla, "but *María!* Week after week, I have followed the daughters of Guatemala to their graves since I was forced into the mountains, and I know that even now, my *own* husband has found a rude grave somewhere at the hands of the army. Surely, you have heard the stories."

María Xquic continued to stare at the woman, unable to compass completely what was happening.

". . . I know your heart, María," said the woman, "and I have heard your cry. So María, that's why I am here. May I sit down?"

María Xquic looked around as if half expecting to find someone watching them. Then, wiping her hands inside the folds of the *servietta*, she nodded slightly and took an almost imperceptible step aside. The guerrilla moved into the hovel of a house and sat down on the earthen floor beside the hearth, the most intimate place *of an indigena's* home.

"María," said María Paloma. "We're all together in these things. All of us are targets of the rich and powerful, and the army is their right hand and the civil patrols their left. All across Guatemala, María, the army is attacking the villages of the *campesinos*. Three years ago, my own family was killed, and most of Santa Lucía burned to the ground. The army actually attacked our wedding and left us for dead in the tombs of the church. They attacked us only because we were teachers and spoke up for the rights of the people. So, we had to flee to the mountains and join with others to protect ourselves. And we have learned that the *militaries* appreciate only one thing: *power . . . this* `power'!"

The guerrilla pulled a small pistol from the folds of her wide belt. María Xquic stared at the pistol, incredulous and overcome by what was happening at her own hearth.

"María," confided María Paloma, "I am not asking you to join the *compas*. I am not asking you even to support us. We do what we have to do for Guatemala, for us all. But I can understand where you are, and I appreciate the danger for you right now in even talking with me, so I will not be long. But there is something very important for you, something that you must do for yourself and for San Felipe."

The guerrilla moved closer to the fearful woman, leaning over toward the bowl of *masa* in which María continued to work.

"Look, *María!*" said María Paloma. "When the time comes, María, you must find your voice. You *must* speak out. You must find the courage to speak your conviction, for just as certain, other daughters of San Felipe del Lago will follow Ana Fabiola to an early death, carrying within them the withered seeds of the town's future."

Tears were racing down María's face as the words of the guerrilla registered deeply. The notorious figure arose and moved close beside her, placing her hand on the diminutive Felipino's shoulder.

"You know I speak the truth—*your* truth, María," she said. "When the time comes—and that time is coming soon—you must speak that truth. What has happened to your little daughter—to you and to your family, María—you don't have to accept this, *okay?*"

The tall *ladino* guerrilla peered deeply into the eyes of María who jerked her head away, raising her two hands over her face. The Felipino mother nodded once, then twice, but was unable to look at her companion.

"Goodbye, María Xquic," said the *compa*, and then she paused. "But *listen* to me, okay? You are a strong woman. The future of Guatemala rests upon the shoulders of the mothers who will survive all of this. You have the courage to carry on, but if you need me, I . . . we're not far away from you. and we're here only to *serve* you."

María Xquic had never kept anything of gravity from her husband, but the interview with a *compa—and this one, among all of them, and in her own home!* —this was something impossible for her to relate to anyone, so terrified was she that word might escape and spread. If discovered, any contact with the guerrillas meant immediate kidnapping or disappearance, certain torture, and probably a lingering, horrible death at the hands of the army. No one could be trusted to know of this visit, not even her husband.

If she feared detection, she drew encouragement, nevertheless, from the words of María Paloma. Preparing the beans to boil for their supper, María remembered her declaration, "I don't have to accept this." As she walked carefully down the path, across the plaza, then over the paving stones to the lake for washing her laundry, María repeated to herself, "I don't have to accept this," and she knew that she would be ready.

"I don't have to *accept* this, Señora Salinas," she told her neighbor. "No, I don't have to *accept* this, and I *won't!*"

And to her neighbor's neighbor, Doña Lidia, "I don't have to *accept* this. It is *too much* for a mother. *No! No!* I can't *accept* this."

Within a week, María Xquic had found a new focus for her relationship with others in the town. Like others, now she, too, was a victim. Pirata Muñez, mother of the slain Remigo Peolido, confided with her at the market, "We don't have to *accept* this, María. My son did nothing wrong. Neither did Guadalupe, his wife, or their little baby, that they should die like pigs in a slaughter. No! María Xquic! We don't have to *accept* this from the *dogs of Satan!*"

And then, a week later, standing before the *alcaldes* in the town hall:

"We don't have to *accept* this at *all!*" said Señora Eva Alicia, whose son had been "disappeared" from his classroom at the university the year before.

"We Felipinos don't have to *accept* this!" said Don Turibio, whose son and his young friend had been shot and killed by the army in Suchitepequez.

"*No!* We don't have to *accept* this *any more!*" said Doña Consuela, *ladino* wife of the grounds keeper of the Director of Public Services in Sololá. A man of both conscience and courage, her husband had been killed after refusing to serve in the town's civil patrol.

"I think that we should tell the government that we don't want the army at our *fiestas* anymore," said Faustino Méndez Montenegro, a mechanic for the bus company whose brother had been found shot to death, at least as it was reported by the military commissioner.

"Or always traipsing through our stalls on market days, frightening our wives and sisters," said Anuncio Calél, the uncle of a young catechist for Father Jack who had been chopped in the head with a machete and left dead on a road outside Panajachel.

"I think that we should tell the government we don't want our fathers and brothers to participate in the civil patrols," said Francisco Pantzay, from his wheelchair, still convalescing after three years from the beating he had received from the Treasury Police for organizing the coffee pickers' union on Finca "Prospero."

"I think that we should tell the government that we don't want to be moved from our land where the parents of our parents rest beside their own," said Nito Bonaventura, survivor of an attack on his home by heavily armed men who stormed into the house one night in Santiago Poaquíl, murdering his mother and father, two sisters and baby nephew.

"Or seed the land with the blood of our families stolen away in the night and buried in clandestine graves beneath their own corn," said Victor Chomasay.

"I think that we should say to the government that we don't have to accept this anymore!" said María Xquic de Xoy, sitting among her colleagues at a meeting of the *Consejo de la Ciudad.* Don Fernando Fajardo, Mayor of San Felipe, nodded his head gravely.

"Surely, we can work together with the Army to find a path to peace," said the Mayor.

Behind a solemn frown, Don Lavendar Putmos, Vice Mayor, took his cue from the Mayor.

"Yes," said the Vice Mayor, "these are delicate matters that call for each of us to examine himself, to find a way."

"We all want peace in our time," said Jaime Chuchoy, member of the *Consejo*, pulling at the ends of his mustache, his glazed eyes lifted in pensive reflection.

"Who is your leader here?" asked Alberto Reyes Benitez, the interim military commissioner, still holding the position for almost two years following the murder of Madagascar Pecho, the much feared and detested "El Pesado."

Silence fell over the council hall as the military commissioner strained to penetrate the eyes of each of the speakers.

"Who is your leader—your representative here?" asked Alberto Reyes Benitez once again. Then, more conciliatory, "That is, which one of you should we consult with in these matters?"

Slowly, all eyes turned to tiny María Xquic in the second row of seats almost invisible behind the massive Victor Chomasay. María Xquic de Xoy was breathing rapidly, her heart pounding. In a moment, all the horrible details of the past month raced through her mind, and she remembered the words of the *compa*, the tall, thin guerrilla silhouetted against the grey fog drifting across the *milpa* behind her compound.

"You must speak the truth . . . your truth!" whispered the voice of María Paloma just over her shoulder. María Xquic de Xoy looked slowly from left to right, the collective power of their little federation lifting her courage. Never before had the crippled daughter of Don Vincente Marcos Xquic experienced such a nervous rush to service. The room fell silent, waiting. María Xquic de Xoy reached over to her husband's arm, and gripping it for support, she rose from her chair.

"What is *this,* María?" whispered a frantic Don Andres, stunned at his wife's surprising response. "María, what are you doing?

"I won't *accept* this," said María almost inaudibly, looking down toward her trembling hands. The *alcaldes* stared at the slight, crippled figure before them, vagrant strands of silver hair dishevelled within her head ribbon.

"What is *this?*" asked the military commissioner. "Speak *up*." María's voice tumbled over and over again in her throat.

"Say it *again* . . ." urged the military commissioner. "What did you *say?*" María's voice convulsed within her throat, catching in a knot behind her tongue.

"I . . . I don't have to *accept* this," stammered the Felipino woman.

"I . . . " she struggled, and then suddenly, she found her voice.

"I speak for the people," said María Xquic de Xoy, now with resolute power. "We—we don't have to *accept* this now. We won't *accept* this *ever again!*"

The *consejo* sat stoned in silence. The expression on the face of the military commissioner went blank. Nervously, Don Andres reached slowly up behind María Xquic and tugged lightly at the back of her *huipil*. María's lips continued to tremble with her message, and her eyes glinted in the strength of her rekindled anger.

". . . *Never!*. . . " she muttered. "*Never again!* . . . ."

Don Andres inched up from his chair amidst the small group of anxious protestors, looked hesitantly if not apologetically at the military commissioner Alberto Reyes Benitez, and then urged her down the aisle toward the door of the *palacio municipal*.

As if shocked from a trance, María looked lost, her wide eyes surveying the small congregation around her.

"Let's *go*, María!" mumbled Don Andres. "Come on. We have to *go* from here!"

"I couldn't help it," said María to her husband as she slipped a fresh faggot into the hearth. Don Andres stood in the shadows of the corner, his arms folded sternly across his breast.

"It was not your *place!*" he responded. "You are a *woman*, and *your* place is in this *house* and with our *children!*"

María blanched in a fury still new to her relationship with her husband.

"Your grief has made you *crazy!*" said Don Andres. "And what do you think will come from your . . . from *this* . . . this *`protest'* of yours tonight?"

María's back grew rigid as she slipped the last branch into the fire.

"You will have the army at our *own door!*" growled her husband. "For the last five years, we have enjoyed the support of the army. The soldiers have *protected* us from the guerrillas."

"The army has *killed* us!" cried María, unable any longer to resist.

"The army *protects* us!" shouted Don Andres.

"The *army* killed Remigo Peolido!" returned María, "and his wife . . . you *saw* what they did!"

"Remigo Peolido and his wife were `subversives'!" barked Don Andres. "They made danger for *everyone* in San Felipe!"

"Why do you say they were `subversives'?" cried María.

"How is it that *you* question *me?*" shouted Don Andres, now standing before his quaking wife.

"Because her arms . . . because they tied her arms behind her back and cut off her hands!" cried María. "The army . . . the army tied Ana Fabiola's arms behind her back, then cut off her hands!"

"*How? What?*" stammered Don Andres. "What are you *saying?*" The Tzutujil priest stepped back away from his wife, trying to make sense of what she was telling him. María was fighting a sudden nausea welling up in her chest.

"Before they . . . they killed her, they killed Ana Fabiola, . . . they tied her arms . . . her hands," she said. "They, they cut off her hands and then . . . then they killed her, little Ana Fabiola! They just killed her!"

The distraught mother collapsed at the feet of her husband who, at the moment, was simply unable to move to assist her, shocked speechless by her revelations.

"How?" he asked. Then, "why?" But then, how could she know such a thing that he would not have already known? She must be deceived. Surely, María was out of her mind with grief, perhaps a dream . . . that had to be it! Or a horrible rumor! But why would he have not heard such a thing himself.

Don Andres stared at his wife unable to believe such a thing. Had he not rushed to the sanctuary himself? Had he not seen with his own eyes the poor body of his little Ana Fabiola there behind the altar only moments after the priest had cut her down, the rope thankfully removed from around her neck—the pale, blue hands, her purple face distorted, that incongruous smirk frozen forever on her mouth. Had he not run his hands through her hair? But her hands! Then under the sheet, they must have . . . her hands!"

"I was *there*, María!" said Don Andres. "Did I not hold her to my heart? Would I not have seen such a thing for *myself?* Her arms were *not* tied! How could you *say* such a thing . . . her *hands!*"

María Xquic stared in horror at her husband. Of course, they were tied—it was all so very clear. She knew it was so! She had . . . had . . . had seen it herself. It had become so clear to her! and she had seen the hands herself, had seen them in the grave!

"Is this what has driven you so! To speak out against your community? To put our family at risk?" cried Don Andres. María glared at her husband in anger, registering only the stream of his passion. Then the words began to reconnoiter, and her mouth slowly opened, at first in disbelief.

But he was there! With his own eyes, he saw Ana Fabiola! How could it be something else? anything different from what he said? He was there! Of course, he was right! But her arms—they were tied behind . . . tied behind her back! It was so clear! Adrift among the ambiguities, María stared at her husband, her lips trembling as tears traced down her face.

The silver-white fog undulated across the road as María made her way through the gates of El Calvario cemetery. It had been five days since the confrontation before the Consejo, five days since Lucita María's departure to the convent of the Capuchinas in Antigua. Earlier in the morning before the dawn had broken over the eastern rim of the lake, her husband had returned to the compound of the *Maximón*. María had determined to visit the grave of her daughter. She had brought a small basket of sweet condiments, some of Ana Fabiola's favorites. Lost in thought, she reached the new grave's freshly mounded earth too quickly, and she shuddered at the unexpected vista. She stopped to catch her breath and to gather her bearings in the raw, cold morning. She set the basket down at the side of the grave, and wrapping her *peraje* tightly around her shoulders, she knelt at the cross bearing the painted name of her lost child.

María reached down and gathered a clod of dirt in her hand. Slowly, she began to turn it over and over. Flakes of the wet clay began to crumble as she continued to massage the dirt, and she determined to break up each of the larger chunks of soil at the head of the grave. With resolution she slipped both her slender hands into the rude, gummy earth, turning it over and over to lift out the larger clumps. Then, one at a time, she slowly and methodically kneaded the small mounds, driving her nails deeply into the clods until they crumbled into fine little tufts of moist earth that scattered over the face of the grave.

Having reduced the last of the clumps of clay in reach, María began driving the full length of her index finger straight down into the earth. A fourth, fifth, and sixth hole she drilled, then wiped her hands on the grass beside the grave and dried them on her skirt. Opening the folds of the *servietta* in her basket, she reached into the small collection of sweets and pieces of fruit and retrieved a handful of cellophane-covered hard candies. Carefully, she unwrapped six of the candies and deposited one in each of the shafts.

"You always liked the sweet candies, little one, so here!" said María, as she dropped the first into the small hole and gently coaxed the loose earth into it with the tip of her finger until the shaft was filled.

". . . the strawberry especially, so here's another," and she filled the second one in the same manner. In each hole she deposited an unwrapped candy offering to her little daughter.

"I don't like the lemon," Ana Fabiola had protested only a week before she died. "Why don't you trade it for licorice—a long, black stick of licorice!"

"The licorice costs 25 centavos," María had told her. "You know that's too much! We have to save our money. We can buy five hard candies for the same amount that we must pay for only one licorice."

"You bought licorice for Lucita María," observed a petulant Ana Fabiola.

"Of course!" retorted María, "but that is because Lucita María is going into the convent to study to become a teacher with the nuns."

"You like Lucita María more than me!"

"Of course not! Now, eat your candy! There! Right in there! That's where I put the strawberry. You like the strawberry."

"You always liked Lucita María more than me."

"She's only older than you. I had to teach her things."

"Why do you like Lucita María more than me?"

"Eat the strawberry. Have you eaten the strawberry yet? Let me see."

María dug out the strawberry candy and brushed off the dirt.

"You haven't touched the strawberry."

"I didn't have a chance. Put it back!"

"You don't like the strawberry."

"It's okay. Put it back."

María looked down at the gouge in the earth.

"You don't like the strawberry. But you always liked strawberries. Why are you doing this to your mother?"

"Put it back! I can't see it! Put it back where I can see it!"

María returned the strawberry candy to the hole and carefully covered it once again.

"Let me see your wrists."

"What?"

"Let me see your two wrists."

"Why, mother? Why do you want to see my wrists?"

"I want to see your wrists where they . . . where they hurt you. Just do what I tell you, please."

"Mother! I can't! I can't raise my arms! I have no room! See?"

"Oh, my precious little one! Can't I see your little arms, your hands and wrists?"

"Mother! I have to rest! I have to go! Now, please let me rest! I am so very, very tired!"

"So, rest, then, Ana. Rest there in the cold, hard ground. I will plant you flowers in the spring time and bring you candies and care for you, sweet one! Oh, my little Ana Fabiola! I hate to leave you so, there, all by yourself to sleep there in the hard, cold earth by yourself through the night."

María's delicate fingers pruned back the trace of fine roots protruding through the dirt. Carefully between her fingers, she ground away the grains of clay from the small filaments of root and sprinkled them back over the face of the grave. She looked slowly to the side and behind her over the mounds of turned earth. She would come another day, and with her little daughter's help, she would clean the rest of the clods.

The fog swirled around her legs as she rose to her feet. "Every morning!" María promised. She would come to visit her daughter. Here, beside her daughter's little plot she could find strength to continue through each day. With her daughter's help she would try to make sense of what was happening to her family and to the people of San Felipe del Lago. María took a last glance at the simple wooden cross with her daughter's name painted in the small, white letters.

"Goodbye, my precious one!" she whispered. "Goodbye, my darling, little girl."

The half wafer of the muted sun was burning softly through the blanket of clouds and fog that hovered about San Felipe and stretched across the lake. María climbed carefully down the path through the tombs of the cemetery toward the road that would take her back through her village. Two men in T-shirts, caps, and black leather jackets, and each smoking a cigarette stood leaning against the side of a Cherokee van. They talked casually as the diminutive Tzutujil woman approached.

"*Óla,* María! Where is your daughter, María?" hailed the smaller of the two who appeared to be in his late twenties or early thirties. He stepped in front of her, blocking her way down the sidewalk.

"*Mira!*" he said, "we have some important business with Lucita María. So . . . maybe you can tell us where we can find your daughter, *no?*"

Not understanding clearly all the Spanish, María nodded and moved to step around the man. Suddenly, she felt herself spun around, her upper arms locked in the tight grip of her assailant's steel-like hands. María's breath caught in her chest, and she felt, for the moment, unable to breathe.

"Su hija!" barked the man. *"Lucita María . . . donde está ella?"*

María's mouth dropped open as she gazed about herself. Suddenly, the man began shaking her violently, sending her head flopping back and forth from one side to the other.

"Lucita María?" he asked again. "*Donde está ella? Conteste me!*"

"*No cono'co!*" managed the hysterical woman. "*No cono'co!* I don't know! I don't know!"

"Look, you Indian *whore!* We know where your daughter is," interrupted the older man. "Your daughter's in Antigua with those fucking *nuns, right?*"

María was confused and terrified. Surely, the man was looking for someone else! There had to be a mistake! But her name—"Lucita María!" He knew her name! But why? Who was this? What could he possibly want with

Lucita María? And why this? Why this assault? Why was he doing this?

The younger man slapped her hard across the face.

"Now, listen to *me, bitch!*" he ordered. "We can take your daughter at any time. Maybe you've seen this little item before!" The man blew a stream of smoke in María's face. Then, he reached inside his jacket and retrieved a small, handwoven garment, the unmistakable *huipil* of Lucita María—wadded it into his fist, and shoved it into the María chest, sending her sprawling onto the pavement.

The next moment, the terrified mother was lying on the ground over her left arm. Suddenly, she was aware of a sharp, reverberating pain that pulsed up and down her arm from her shoulder to the wrist. Apparently, the blow had caused her to land on her arm, and María never heard the man's threat. Then her head exploded from a kick at the base of her skull. A splash of yellow and red light flooded the back of her eyes, and then the back of her head felt as though it had been struck with a brick or paving stone.

"Get *up!*" cried the younger man. María was groping, unbalanced; her eyes wide open, they flitted back and forth in a swirling blackness.

"*Listen, whore!* You better watch what you say from now on—who you *talk* to! *Understand?*" said the older man.

"*Dog shit!*" cried the younger man, as he gave her one last boot in backside. "Get this straight, you *cheap cunt*! We can take out your *daughter* any time we're ready! *See?*"

"Leave the shit *woman*," said the older man, "and let's get out of here."

María could hear their footsteps shuffling toward the jeep, the opening and closing car doors, and a final, indistinct epithet. She tried to make sense of what had happened, but her fear for Lucita María blocked all reason. Wasn't she *there?* Wasn't she just beyond this impenetrable *blackness?* Somewhere just to the left? Or to the right? If she could just feel her skirt, she would know Lucita María was safe there just next to her, and María Xquic reached tremulously about with her fingers, first her right hand, and then her left.

The vehicle raced away, throwing a rain of mud and exhaust over María's body. She lay dazed and disoriented, fading in and out of consciousness.

"*María!*" cried a voice. "*María Xquic!* What is the *matter?* Are you *okay? María!*"

María turned her head from left to right, trying to fix the voice.

"*María Xquic!*" said the voice. "What has happened? Are you *okay?*"

"*Lucita!*" mumbled María in her panic. "*Lucita María!*"

"*No,* María!" said the voice.

"*Lucita!*" then wailed María in a broken, agonizing cry. "My poor *Lucita!*

They have come for *Lucita María!*"

"Who, María?" queried the voice. "Who is `Lucita'? Who is `Lucita María'?"

The hands of the voice reached behind her head and then down behind her shoulders to give her support as María tried to find a point of balance. Two pigeons flew down from the nearby rooftop and began picking at the refuse, old peelings of bananas and oranges in the gutter at the feet of the Indian woman, remains from the market day activities the day before. Firm, angular palms steadied the Tzutujil woman's head and gentle fingers spread back her matted hair, twisted and confused in her unravelled head ribbon.

"*María Xquic!*" said the voice. "Are you okay? Who is `Lucita María'?"

"*Lucita María!*" repeated María. "They just came for my *Lucita María!* Oh, mother of *God! What can I do?"*

María Xquic turned her head away to hide the terror and her tears.

"Lucita María?" pursued the voice. "Lucita is your daughter?"

María Xquic nodded once as her tears flowed freely. The distraught mother began to tremble uncontrollably. She felt the taut, insistent hands pull her face upward and the arms cradle around her shoulders and back. She felt her musty face buried in the *huipil* of the voice and her quaking body rocked gently back and forth.

"We are here for you," said the voice. "You are a courageous woman, and we are here to support you. Let me help you up, and then you must come with me."

A wash of warm red light began to filter through María's eyelids, and María Xquic was suddenly aware of her blindness that was already receding.

"*Here!*" insisted the voice. "I have a vehicle for you. Try to stand, and I will help you to the car."

María Xquic accepted the support of the voice and made an effort to readjust her posture on the sidewalk in order to anticipate trying to sit up.

"That's good," said the voice. "Just take it easy. You've been attacked and hurt. Do you feel like anything is broken."

María Xquic began a slow, disoriented inventory of possible injuries. Her left arm and shoulder throbbed, and she winced in pain as an abrasion inside her elbow scraped across the fabric of her *huipil*, but nothing seemed broken.

"*Easy*, María!" said the voice. "Let me help you. Can you see?"

María blinked her eyes once, then again, as she found her footing under the support of her assistant. As she rose slowly, the first thing she could see was the blunted edge of the curb and fruit peels in the gutter below.

"Yes," she offered. "I think so. Yes, I can see."

A van pulled up beside them. A side door slid back and jolted open.

"*Hurry! Get in, María!*" cracked a voice from a spot in the back of the vehicle.

"Yeah! We're getting there!" said the woman's voice. "María's in rough shape. They just hit her."

"Just get her in!" came another voice from the driver's seat.

"*Okay! Okay!"* came the testy retort from the woman.

As María Xquic reached forward toward the floor of the van, two hands gripped her forearms and eased her inside. She heard the confident leap of her partner jumping in behind her and the race of the door to its jarring slam as the van lurched forward.

"Just stay down!" said the now familiar voice. María's face was lying on its side against a musty, muddy carpet.

"We'll just cruise around the plaza real slowly, maybe a round or two, and then we'll move out."

"What happened?" asked the driver.

"I'm not sure," said the woman's voice. "I was just coming to the corner to intercept her as she was coming back from the cemetery when I saw this Cherokee Jeep tear off to the right, and I found her in the gutter. I think they were trying to pick her up."

"*Bullshit!*" said the driver. "If they were trying to pick her up, she wouldn't have been there in the gutter."

"I guess you're right," said the woman. "She was saying something about a `Lucita María'—I think her daughter."

"Yeah, that'd be right!" said the driver. "It would make sense. They've got her number. They'll never let up. They'll take out her whole family—wouldn't surprise me."

María Xquic was starting to focus once again, and through a shimmering veil of pulsing reds and orange, she opened her eyes to see the dark *morga* skirt with the fine, silk *randa*—its alternating bands of pink, blue, green, red, and yellow, the patterns she had seen only once before in the *corte* of María Paloma, her guerrilla visitor of a week earlier.

María Xquic reached to the skirt and touched the thigh of María Paloma, her fingertips gently nudging the fabric. The *compa* took her hand and squeezed it reassuringly.

"María," she said. "María, you need protection, and we are here for you. Rest easy. We're going to take you to a place where you will be safe for the time being."

María felt the van pull slowly to a stop at one of the intersections and then start up again. She tried to rise but felt her shoulders urged back down.

"Don't try to get up just yet," said the guerrilla. "You need to rest. You've been through a very rough time. Just rest, okay?"

"Where . . .?" asked María? "Where are you taking me?"

"To a safe house," said María Paloma. "Only a block or two more, okay?"

The van continued slowly through the streets. She heard bottles rattling in cases beside her and smelled the sweet, tart aroma of papaya and oranges. Around and around the van seemed to go, cruising slowly through the streets of San Felipe. Then, after about twenty minutes, María Xquic felt the car turn and stop abruptly. The driver's door opened and closed. She could hear the movement of heavy, metal doors sliding away and the eager play of small children skipping around the vehicle. The driver's door opened and closed again. The van lurched forward and then stopped.

"Stay inside," ordered the guerrilla as she pulled back the sliding side door of the truck. María heard behind her the muted sound of heavy bars falling into slots inside the doors. Children clamored around the guerrilla woman as she moved away from the van.

A disgruntled dog set out an aggrieved howl that echoed from deeply down a hallway. Others responded up the street and in the surrounding homes. María could hear new voices, a woman and a boy talking with María Paloma, the driver, and the other man from the rear of the van. For several moments the muted conversation continued while the Felipino woman remained face down on the carpet.

"Okay, María," said the voice of María Paloma. "You can come out now. Here, let me help you. Watch your step."

Gently, the guerrilla reached under María's arm and eased her around to exit from the van.

"Come with me," said the guerrilla, "but watch your step. Don't trip over the fruits."

María Xquic took the hand of María Paloma as she stepped from the van and maneuvered past the boxes of fruit that had been stacked against the wall of the garage just inside the door. Several small avocados had spilled from a spilt crate and were strewn across the floor. Carefully, the two women made their way through the narrow corridor between the van and the boxes toward faint light filtering from around the corner. A few feet beyond the van, the two women turned into a small court lined with potted tropical plants—ferns and branching orchids, reedy, spined vermiliads, and spindly, arching cacti.

Just in front of the two women, a tawny young guerrilla stepped ahead, an automatic rifle slung casually over his shoulder. He escorted the two into the dimly lighted kitchen where a man, his back to the women, worked to finish counting a small stack of *quetzales* and change spread on the table before him.

"*Pase adelante!*" invited the escort as he turned aside to allow the women to pass before him. Startled by the interruption, the man spread his hands before him and rose slowly to greet the party.

"Ramón!" exclaimed the man as he recognized the party's guard. "Come in! And who do we have with us? María Paloma, of course! And María! María Xquic de Xoy! Come in, *companeros*. Ramón! Please! Bring in a couple of more chairs!"

"Don Fernando!" cried María Xquic. "Is it you?"

Surely, she was dreaming! María was astonished to find the mayor of the town in the company of María Paloma and her guerrillas. But for what reason? Why?

"María Xquic," said the man. "Come, sit down here. Something to drink? Some coffee, okay? Ramón . . . there on the stove. Make it two cups."

María was confused. Here were the guerrillas, and here was Don Fernando, the *alcalde municipal*. It was very confusing and disturbing. What could he want with the guerrillas?

"*Comandante!*" said Ramón as he presented the two cups of coffee to Don Fernando.

"That's fine," returned the *alcalde municipal*. "That's very fine! María?"

Don Fernando offered a cup of the steaming coffee to the perplexed Mayan woman. María Xquic accepted the cup timidly, still trying to interpret her situation.

"Will there be anything else, *comandante*?" asked Ramón.

"No, Ramón," returned Don Fernando. "That will be just fine. Thank you."

"Thank you, *comandante*," said Ramón, as he grabbed the strap of his rifle and readjusted it over his shoulder. Then he turned and assumed a position as guard just outside the door of the kitchen. Don Fernando turned to María Xquic.

"Drink some of this coffee, María. Perhaps it will make you feel a little better, *no?*"

María Xquic sat stupefied by the unfolding revelations.

"Go ahead, María," urged the *alcalde*. "You'll feel much better if you drink even a little. Sure, okay?"

Don Fernando turned to María Paloma. "What's the situation now?"

"Well, María was attacked, as we told you," said María, "and we've been in the van all day. María was in pretty bad shape, in and out of consciousness throughout the day. She really only came to in the last hour, so we decided to bring her on in where you could talk with her. She doesn't appear to have anything broken, but she's kind of out of it."

Words of the conversation lapped gently, dream-like on the periphery of María's consciousness.

"ComandanteDonFernandoalcaldeDonFernandocomandante—"

Nothing made sense any longer. *The alcalde municipal, Ramón, the guard, and the fruits boxes and crates of fruit, the money spread over the table and María Paloma who knew Ramón, the same one who called the alcalde municipal "comandante" not alcalde municipal by the guerrilla woman María Paloma, "I don't have to accept this" María Paloma said so herself I'm María, too, after the holy mother of god the guerrilla who went to El Pesado carrying the bottles of water who bled black blood and bile, his penis flipped in a corn row, just flipped off into a corn row, in the corn the black blood of El Pesado, Holy Mother of God, of the rich earth and the corn, just the tip, shriveled little finger of a penis—accept this, don't have to, to accept this, María Paloma with the gun in her hand from her belt, in her house, the gun, María Paloma the guerrilla, not alcalde, alcalde municipal, el comandante that, Ramón by the door,* "feeling better, María," *the rifle slung over his shoulder, who said "comandante!"*

" . . . better María? Are you all right now, María?" asked Don Fernando, reaching across the table to take her trembling hands into his own.

"Señor?" asked María. *I don't understand. I was with Ana Fabiola there, there at El Calvario, there with the strawberries, her little face . . . the strawberries in the dirt, and the man who hit me, knocked me down, so I got down in the van.*

"*María Xquic!*" barked Don Fernando. "*Look at me! Here!* Drink some of this hot coffee, *okay?*"

María opened her eyes and stared at the coffee, then reached for the mug of steaming coffee and slowly lifted it to her lips.

"*There!*" said Don Fernando. "That's *good!* Just take your time, okay? Try to relax. We are here for you tonight. You are safe. We're here tonight just for you, so don't worry any more, okay?"

María Xquic took another uneasy sip from the cup of coffee and wiped her lower lip on the back of her hand.

"Where am I?" she asked. "What do you want with me? Why am I here?"

"María," said María Paloma. "You were almost killed in the streets this morning. We found you and have saved you from certain death at the hands of the army. You are very weak and still disoriented, so we have brought you here. We have a bed for you in the next room, if you want to sleep for awhile."

"But my family . . . " said María Xquic.

"Manuel is with *Señora* María, your neighbor," explained María Paloma. "Your husband will be working late at the compound."

"But I must prepare his dinner," complained María Xquic. "I have to return!"

"No, María," returned Don Fernando. "The most important thing right now is for you to rest and regain your strength. And we are here with you to give you some time to rest, okay? Ramón!"

The guard turned toward the *comandante* without leaving his post just outside the door.

"Go to the roof . . . look around and make sure everything is secure," ordered Don Fernando. "Then come on back down here."

"*Si, comandante*! *Como no!*" saluted the young guard. Don Fernando turned once again to María.

"Come, María. Come to the back room where you can rest."

María Paloma moved to assist the Tzutujil woman who was struggling to move from the chair at the little table.

"Let me help you, María," said the guerrilla as she steadied the woman with her own arm.

"We'll talk when I get back," María Paloma offered the *comandante* as she stepped past him.

The guerrilla *compa* helped María Xquic through the back of the building, what she now recognized as the *tienda* next to the tailor shop just three blocks from the plaza of San Felipe. María Paloma ushered her into a tiny room that held a simple bunk and side table dimly illuminated by a single, exposed twenty-five- watt bulb dangling from an electrical cord above. María Xquic stood for a moment acclimating herself to the new room and took a hesitant step inside.

"Go ahead," urged María Paloma. "It's quite safe, and we won't leave you. You just lay down there and get some rest. You'll be okay."

María Xquic eased herself onto the bunk which held a musty, striped mattress and a feather pillow, both new to the Tzutujil mother who had rested on a woven, straw *petate* against the ground all her life. She sat down carefully on the edge of the mattress and caressed the fabric, tweaking the buttons sewn into the stuffing. She could never rest easily on such a soft padding. In the kitchen, down the hall, María was talking to Don Fernando. A dog barked forlornly at pedestrians' steps on the street outside. María looked over the mattress and scanned the soiled, damp walls of the small room. After a few moments, she slipped down onto the floor and curled up—her knees almost under her chin, her bruised, swollen elbow resting against her side. Her mind began to drift, and her reflections sifted into the voices of the night.

"accept this any more! any more! accept this! accept this! the strawberry candy in the face of Ana Fabiola who won't come home any more . . . any more . . . any moreAna Fabiolaanymore five cents the licorice candy who liked, she always liked the strawberry candy "in Antigua at the Convent of the Capucinas" *one-cent candy for the licorice, no! Ana Fabiola "if they already picked her up" Manuel's little cat, so cute! if she hadn't gone to the fiesta where the army in the plaza, their big guns, the way they always treated the naturales like animals, Isaiah—Isaiah Xolop—he knew the girls liked him more than the other boys, because Ana Fabiola liked him so much, didn't Colata Toj know a match when she saw one? so* "if they know she is in Antigua, at the convent, they'll have her on a stick before the end of the week when" *everyone knows a good match, Lucita María, too, the church, she never went to the church, she never went, so why the convent? know the nuns? She said prayers, the voices because her father could speak with the ancestors, Lucita María, he wanted her to, too, never could, I could never even when I tried, prayed, always, put the candles, the roses, bought the eggs and incense, never heard the voices, I never heard them, Andres could, I could never hear the voices, but Lucita María—when she was just a little girl, she was always so sensitive, she knew she had the gift, I didn't have the gift, I prayed, Lucita María, when Lucita María prayed I could tell, everyone could tell, Lucita María the nuns told her it was the saints, St James and the angel Moses, and the Jesucristo, Santa María, "the devil," that's what Andres said, "a trick," he said, he prayed before Santa Mesa, I prayed at his side for the truth in front of Santa Mesa, three turkey eggs,* "not a prayer of a chance if she's with the nuns in Antigua" *three turkey eggs we passed over the incense, lit the candles, four grips of candles, then three masses before the Maximón to seek the truth and protection for Lucita María from the devil,* "Crucified! God damn! At the Capuchinas! You've got to be lying! No, not crucified! My God! God damn!" *my little daughters, so precious! in the yard, playing with the hens and Manuel's little cat, rolling the tortillas, little Lucita María at her loom, the little muestra that she carried with her to the convent in Antigua,* "No! Andres! She will learn and she will return as a teacher to the children, she has to go, it is her only chance! You have to let her go! You have to let her go!" *he said she could go, there on the bus with her hands over her mouth and tears in the corners of her eyes, the bus so crowded, Lucita María's little face pressed against the glass as the bus just went away down the road,* "crucified in Antigua?" *So*

come with me, Lucita María. I have so little room, but you can lie down to rest, to rest beside me here in the dark, it is so quiet. Momi comes with sweets, she comes with sweets to put into our mouths. Momi has to place them in my mouth because my hands, you see, I can't find my little hands. Lucita María, oh, Lucita—why have you come so soon, so early in the morning, on a cold, wet morning? Momi won't understand. How can she understand? Why you have come, come on a cold and rainy morning the grey mist, the cold rain, grey and misty in the morning, that you come when they, through the rain, the cold wet clouds, to come by me, to lie with me here at my side, by my side, here in the silence, here in the dark until Momi comes to bring you little sweets, little sweets for Lucita María and poor little Ana, little Ana Fabiola, not Ana not Lucita, not Ana and Lucita anymore . . .

Chapter 24

I Am The Way

His heart was "filled with Jesus." Don J'cab turned haltingly through the "Gospel of John." His coarse fingers fanned over each page as if by nervous touch he might absorb the devotionals of the texts. Then he closed the book and held it out in front of him just so as to catch a ray of light drifting across the end of the table. Stroking the grain of the black cover, he felt a rush, a charge of excitement and fresh expectation, as if detached, his hands were animated anew. The Bible, of course, was as familiar as all the other religious paraphernalia—the icons, little altars, and all—that decorated *a campesino* community. But *this* book, this *particular* volume, with its Kingdom Throne Ministries golden logo embossed on the front cover, just this small volume *itself* was suddenly the missing piece. It was the touchstone that fulfilled a life which before now—before the Kingdom Throne crusade three weeks before, he knew looking back—had never been fully realized. The American evangelist and the Lord had changed everything.

Don J'cab closed the Bible and rose slowly from the small, hand-carved chair that had sat at the head of his table for more than twenty years. The whole setting—this tiny, dingy cubicle of a hut—seemed suddenly aglow, all its simple accoutrements rarefied blessings, each bathed in new meaning and value. Not that the table and its setting were all that *much*—just a hand-sawed board table, its legs nailed from the top. A flimsy, smaller chair squatted beside his own for his wife of twenty-three years. The table and chairs had stood in the middle of the packed, earthen floor just the way it was, only a step or two from the hearth, since, as boys, he and his older brother, Andres, and their father had erected the house more than thirty years before.

The utensils he had accumulated during two decades of often penurious drudgery hung on eight wooden pegs and less than a dozen nails: a couple of plastic buckets, a claw hammer, a worn file, a butcher knife, two ladles, one long-handled axe, two machetes, the rest—a few metal pots, a broken tortilla press. In the corner of the one-room house stood his grandfather's rusted, single-round shotgun, his sole inheritance following his father's death. All the rest had passed to his older brother, Andres, so renowned for his spiritual prowess. It was Andres, for instance, with whom his father had entrusted the *Santa Mesa*, blessing the transfer with the sacrifice of a turkey hen. It was Andres who had inherited the family Bible and their father's sacred bundle. It was Andres, of course, who accepted the *cargo* of the *auxiliatura maximo*, a decision undisputed by the *Cofradia of Santa Cruz.* Regardless that they claimed Andres himself had chosen the exalted *cargo*, J'cab knew better. Andres had been encouraged to do so by his father and the *alcaldes* themselves. In fact, Andres had enjoyed all the privileges of San Felipe, while J'cab, at forty-two, the younger by four years and obviously the lesser son, had been relegated to second station in just about everything.

No, J'cab had had enough of brother Andres long ago. Their mother had died young, but J'cab's resentment for the rest of the family ran deeply. For many years the two had not shared a word, J'cab choosing instead to banish the *name* of his brother from his speech, if not his thoughts. He had learned to keep the festering bitterness to himself. As long as he could feed his family and attend worship in his own way, he could survive outside the suffocating shadow of his brother's acclaim.

The division between the two brothers had roots buried in their childhood. Don J'cab couldn't remember exactly *when* he first noticed the discrimination. Maybe it was the time his father took young Andres off to the *milpa*, laughing together as they went and leaving the younger son behind. It might have been when the *alcaldes* of the *Santa Cruz Cofradia* had served only his father and Andres the *aguardiente* during the festival of Santiago. It didn't really matter which incident he selected. They all added up to favoritism which had hurt him deeply as a child. So when, outside village custom, he had taken Manuela Mendoza as his wife, he determined to make it on his own, without reference to Andres, his aging father, or, for that matter, the whole hierarchy of village authority. In short, like the family of his wife, he would become *ladino*.

Historically, the *naturales*, the "*real* people," despised *ladinos.* Originally, the *ladinos* were the Westerners—that is, the descendants of Europeans. *Ladinos*, too, were the mixed bloods. In the context of five hundred years of persecution and resistance, the indigenous people generally hated the *ladinos* for any number of reasons—for taking their land, for burdening them with intolerable taxes. They cursed them for sending their armies to intimidate and terrorize them, for seizing their sons for detestable military service. The *naturales* abhorred *ladinos* whose empiring and materialism represented a threat to everything they held dear. Through the strength of their communities and enhanced *constumbres*, the indigenous people struggled to resist *ladino* encroachment, and in sporadic reprisals over the decades, they had actually attacked and killed *ladinos*, even once many years earlier in San Felipe. Reviled the most, however, were those among the *naturales* who allowed themselves to be seduced by "Yankee" values, those who, in so doing, neglected, even rejected the old ways, those who spurned the community, those who turned on the *alcaldes* and *costumbre* itself in their selfish quest for personal wealth, position, and power.

From his point of view, it was not Don J'cab who had turned away from San Felipe customs. The old ways had abandoned him, not he the sacred traditions. If he had sought other opportunities outside the expected paths, it was not so much for himself as for his family, not so much to promote himself—to parade himself before his neighbors as something "better"—but rather to seek relief, he told himself, from the suffocating demands of a *cargo* system that only threatened to debilitate him without hope of compensation or restitution. If the truth be known, however, although he would not have articulated it so precisely, Don J'cab had become too proud to support his lower station in the community hierarchy any longer.

But the Kingdom Throne Crusade had changed all that. Now he could see through it all how the Holy Spirit had been directing him all his life, guiding him away from the loathsome bowels of paganism, coaxing him to that moment of deliverance by God, through the guidance of Brother Farrell and the Kingdom Throne Ministry. That night at the crusade, the Kingdom Throne "evangels" had explained it all—there on their knees beside him, holding his hands, anointing his head—they had shown him the way. He had felt the flush of God's irresistible grace fill his heart, and he would remember always the moment during Brother Farrell's call, his transformation by the Holy Spirit. And now, everything seemed so *clear!* so *simple! Truly,* Don J'cab had been "born again!"

The "love of Jesus" had made him a new person with solemn responsibility. Now, he was a minister for the "Truth," the charismatic "Truth of God" that was sweeping across the country, the same "Truth" that had finally reached his own heart and had "shown him the way." *Naturales* or *ladinos*—that incessant conflict was now curiously moot. He had been *saved,* and his strongest desire any longer was to share that salvation with everyone he met on the streets of San Felipe del Lago. Don J'cab was now a man with his own mission to the community.

Once the village's "prodigal" in his self-imposed exile from his family and, through their influence, much of the rest of the town, Don J'cab had returned as a new spiritual beacon, buoyed with the promises of the Kingdom Throne ministry—an enterprise of people and power, television and radio, a world-wide network of buildings and property—all that, and something else: *cash—lots* of it. Cash enough to erect a new evangelical house of worship. Cash enough to seed a new congregation. A commitment of cash enough to check the growing tide of the new Catholic *comunidades de base* that were beginning to socialize and politicize heretofore only nominally Catholic communities. And cash *enough*, at least, to challenge the supremacy of Don Andres Menchu Xoy, *auxiliatura* to the demon *Maximón*.

On the bus, returning home from that soul-saving crusade where, rising from the "waters of the Jordan," he had accepted "baptism of the Holy Spirit and Jesus Christ as his personal savior," Don J'cab had had time to reflect and dream. For the first time in his life, he had a place in a future that seemed clearly defined. Kingdom Throne Ministries would contact him within the month to announce plans for the new mission church. Their offices in the capital would complete all the arrangements for the purchase of the property and the processing of the deed. The Ministry office would also contract for the plumbing and electrical services and arrange for Kingdom Throne Disciple volunteers from Sololá who would construct the building. In addition to the building costs, two Kingdom Throne congregations in the United States had contributed the funds to sponsor the electronic cassette ministry and to purchase a piano for the sanctuary.

It didn't take long for word to spread about the proposed new evangelical church in San Felipe del Lago. For more than a week, Kingdom Throne offices in the capital announced plans for the church over its nightly radio broadcast, "Service of Praise." It was clear that, from their new mission outpost in Sololá, the Kingdom Throne Ministry was expecting wonderful things—*milagros estupendos!* And Don J'cab need not have worried about his introduction to the community, for the radio transmissions had broadcast his name nationwide for more than a week.

Don J'cab was only one of more than a dozen recently announced "pastors" for newly designated congregations throughout the highlands. From more than twenty years of experience in Third World nations, Kingdom Throne officials knew that "anointment" over the airwaves established immediate credibility in what otherwise could often be hostile settings. Certainly, for Don J'cab, his authority was clarified, and the news spread quickly. On the morning after only the first broadcast, word had filtered throughout San Felipe. While it was customary to regard public figures with deferential respect, it was clear to him, from the expression on people's faces, that he enjoyed unprecedented attention.

Heretofore only indifferent neighbors now expressed an eagerness to acknowledge him, and children of people whom he didn't even know smiled widely and giggled when they passed him, then went tearing off down the streets, little hands over their faces to muffle their embarrassment.

The first civil recognition came, most gratifyingly, from the mayor, Don Fernando Fajardo, himself.

"It's a wonderful *thing,* Don J'cab!" said the mayor. "It's truly a work of *God* to think that San Felipe has been chosen for this new mission church. You must feel very *proud!*"

The question of "pride" was a coded dart which Don J'cab would have preferred to dodge, but he extended the mayor the benefit of his confidence. Like Don J'cab Menchu Xoy, Don Fernando Fajardo was evangelical, at least in affiliation if not in practice. He had been carried into local office on the tail of the Christian Democrats with the popular elections in 1985. Wasting little time, Don Fernando had become something of a public voice in the town, bleating in fervent appeals for a return to morality and Christian principles. It was only incidental, of course, that he maintained close ties to the military and was, reputedly, one of the wealthiest *ladinos* in the area. Word had it that the good mayor had cut a deal with a general in the capital for the storage of cocaine on properties he held in El Quiché. Surely, though, they were only so many rumors, for the truth of Don Fernando wore a different face, indeed.

"*Sí*, Don Fernando," said the reticent pastor. "I am *very* proud, but . . . but proud *only* to do the work of the *Lord!*"

The energy he felt swelling behind his profession of faith—just the saying of the words which was so new to him—gave Don J'cab a little fever, made him want to add more. But the presence of the *ladino* mayor was more intimidating than he had anticipated, and in silence, he submitted to the civil protocol.

"Tell me, Don J'cab," said the mayor, "tell me about plans you have for this new church in our town. Where are we to *put* such a facility?"

"Don Fernando," said the pastor, "I have no answers to such questions just yet. The plans . . . Kingdom Throne Ministry is making the plans, doing the arrangements and all. They are supposed to bring the plans, maybe in a month or so."

"And how to *pay* for all of this . . .?" pursued the mayor. "San Felipe is not a wealthy community, as you know."

"Don Fernando," replied Don J'cab. "Don Fernando, the Lord has moved the people of the United States to pay for this, to pay for *everything*—the building, the construction, all the seats and tapes and *everything!*"

"Well," said Don Fernando, pleased and surprised by the disclosure of anticipated funding; he had some projects of his *own* that could use a little evangelical *boost!* "Perhaps this church, this mission will be very important to our town. You must work closely with this office, Don J'cab. Of course, there are rules—you understand, certain *regulations* that must be met when you anticipate building something like a mission church. The church will need to make certain *'deposits,'* you know. How shall we say? —*'good faith gestures,'* every now and then, to the community, *no?*"

The mayor rose and slapped the diminutive preacher on the back. "We all want to see this thing done *right!* Do we *understand* each other, Don J'cab?"

"But *of course!*" returned the pastor as he stepped ahead of the mayor in passing out of the office, full of the sense of his new commission, one ratified now by the mayor's own expression of good will.

Word of plans for building the new evangelical church were not so well received in the Catholic community. In fact, the idea came under attack after the very first broadcast. In Sololá Bishop Juan Pablo Ortíz was deeply disturbed and had summoned Father Jack to his offices the very next day.

"It's all so *clear!*" protested the Bishop. "Here we go *again!* It's the army's attempt to drive one more *wedge* into this community. It's no accident that this little fudge-faced *campesino* has been tapped as a `pastor.' He'll be in for a hell of a shock when the *real* administrator shows up from the States. I doubt the little snit can even read his own *name!* The only reason he's been selected as this preacher "front" is to counter the fanatical followers of his brother in the *Santa Cruz Cofradia. Jesus!* They've been doing this kind of thing all *over* the highlands, just to sow disaffection in the communities!"

"No question about it," returned Father Jack. "You could just see something like this coming. They say he was handpicked to attend the crusade in Guatemala because they knew of his abrasive relationship with his brother. They've been at each other for years, particularly Don J'cab. They say he's been on a slow burn most of his life. My housekeeper told me that he and the rest of the family have always been divided over Andres's so-called *`gifts,'* and that it's only the small handful of true believers who have kept the whole system propped up."

"Well, the whole damn *Maximón* thing is more complicated than that, but if there's anything under attack, here, though," said the Bishop, "it isn't Andres and the *Cofradia of Santa Cruz*. Oh, *no!* You can bet the real target is *you* and our operations over there in San Felipe—and all around the lake, for that matter. I don't have the slightest hesitation about that."

Father Jack looked down, trying to dodge the personal implications in the prelate's observation.

"*No*, Jack!" continued the Bishop, not willing to let the matter rest. "We've got to be exceptionally careful until we see how this whole thing is going to shake out. If it goes anything like that operation of North American missions up in Barillas, we're going to have serious trouble, and a lot of people are going to die. I just don't know what to do about it, and that's why I asked you to come over today. What do you think? How do *you* see all this coming down?"

Father Jack paused, wiping his forehead with his grimy handkerchief. The development of another evangelical church and clinic in Barillas had seeded only division and sorrow between the indigenous Christians of far northwestern Huehuetenango. After fifteen years of laboring, Catholics had established active social programs—a well-staffed health clinic and a literacy program in addition to its doctrinal instruction. The number of catechists who had matriculated from the Maya *cantones* had increased remarkably. And then, parading into the *aldeas*, came the Pentecostals, bristling with pious arrogance, moral indignation, and holy righteousness.

From the beginning, the Missionary Holiness Temple entered the ecclesiastical fray, declaring unrelenting war on "drunkenness, Satanism, and Catholic idolatry." Even before the doors of the new mission chapel opened for services, loud speakers mounted on the roof poured forth, in Kanjobal, nightly streams of condemnation and calls for "baptism in the Holy Spirit." A phalanx of ardent Temple "evangels" paced throughout the *cantones*, distributing to the illiterate Mayas religious tracts illustrating in simple line drawings scenes of heaven and hell. The tract with the more ominous implications featured the bleeding hands of Christ and the splintery cross anchored on the crest of a hill. Below the cross, a robed priest led a file of drunken Mayas into the unmistakable sanctuary of the parish church of Dos Puentes. The pamphlets made an impression. Night after night, dozens of Kanjobales drifted into the evening services until by the end of the first month, the new mission boasted a congregation of more than three hundred "conversions."

Social and political tremors racked the traditionally Catholic communities of Barillas. An attempt by the American priest of Dos Puentes to discuss the Holiness diatribes was rebuffed with the haughty sneer, "Our disciples will *pray* for you, Father!" The *alcaldes* of the various *cofradias* called a rare ecumenical summit to address the heavy charismatic thrust into their communities. The late arrival of the priest brought only distressing news: the local Holiness pastor in a neighboring *canton* had been holding secret meetings with the military commissioner. The information came like a shot through the room. Within two months, following the selection of mission leaders, their most disturbing fears were complemented when all the officers in the civil defense patrol of Dos Puentes were replaced by the entire deaconate of the Missionary Holiness Temple.

Harassment of the *cofradia* leadership picked up immediately with visits by small cadres of the civil patrol. They wanted to check papers, and the next night, to examine the same papers again. They questioned the wives and daughters almost daily about the routines of their husbands in the fields. They rifled throughout the meager holdings of storage bins in search, they said, of clandestine caches of arms and supplies for the guerrillas. Only two weeks after a reported second round of meetings between the Holiness pastors and the military commissioner, three recently confirmed catechists were "disappeared" and the families of four others threatened. Two days later, almost a hundred Catholic indigenous families crossed the border into Mexico, the first of more than twenty thousand who were to follow within the year.

Father Jack wiped his hands with the same handkerchief.

"To answer your question directly, I see a bloody, *bloody* cross, Father," said the American priest.

"Are you *afraid*, Jack?" asked the Bishop.

"Of *course!*" confessed Father Jack. "But not so much for me as for our people. *They* are the ones who will be the first targets. Then . . . then, maybe me. I don't know."

The Bishop rose and walked over to his book shelf, running his index finger indifferently along the spines of musty Bible commentaries. Then he turned.

"You know, Jack," he said soberly. "You know, you don't *have* to stay. You can leave. I can reassign you . . . right *now*, if you wish. All you have to do is say so."

His Bishop's offer startled him. Father Jack had never seriously considered leaving. He had made his commitment to the people of San Felipe a decade before, and while he remembered, from time to time, the admonitions of his family—his mother, particularly, he had never contemplated what life would be like in any other circumstances. Where would he *go?* What ministry could he serve more rewarding than where he *was?* No, he had made his place among the *campesinos*, and he suddenly felt the urge to rise at once to start the trek back around the lake.

"You're my Bishop, Father, and I'm not telling you anything you don't already know," said Father Jack. "But I'll say it anyway: a priest in Guatemala can't escape the shadow of evil, except standing in the light of his faith. I guess that sounds a little precious, but I'll tell you something: every morning, Father, I look out over the lake and watch the sun rise over the mountains, and you know, I really feel refreshed. It's only in the late afternoon, as the sun is setting and the cold fingers of fog steal down from the summit of Tolimán—I hear the wild dogs howling high up in the *milpas*, and I start to tremble. Sometimes, deep in the night, I turn over and think I hear the scuffle of boots up on the wall, and I think, *`My God!* Here they *come!* This is *it!'* And I'll tell you the truth: I'm just a man like any *other,* and I'm afraid, *really afraid!* But in the day . . . in the *day,* there's sunlight. The people flock around me, and they seem happy and confident. In the daylight, in the streets with the people, my life is full, and I don't think about the nights."

Don J'cab waited for more than three weeks for representatives of Kingdom Throne Ministries to contact him. In the interim he became much the center of conversation in San Felipe. Many wondered how God had come to choose such a man, one who had never showed an inclination to leadership before. But the Lord moves in mysterious ways, and following the radio broadcasts of Kingdom Throne crusade replays, all Felipinos were aware of the prestigious, new appointment.

The Kingdom Throne pastor warmed quickly to his sudden visibility. A growing cadre of Pentecostal disciples confided their own conversions to Don J'cab, and by the time the Kingdom Throne Ministries sent word to him by letter, about twenty followers had pledged their support in founding the new mission temple in San Felipe. They met together every day, just after the evening meal. Don J'cab would lead them in prayer, a litany in which each would offer up his or her ecstatic declaration of praise and call upon God to deliver their village from Satan and the evils of the Catholics and all other idol worshipers. Then, not yet having been counciled on the finer points of the evangelical world view, they called upon Mary and the saints to bless them and to remember them in their new venture.

When it finally arrived, Don J'cab immediately recognized the letter from Kingdom Throne Ministries which bore the organizational logo embossed in gold on the left side. He tore it open, then slowly removed the three-page message typed on the thin, onion skin paper. His eyes raced over and over the pages, franticly scanning the text for any familiar reference. His forefinger traced along each line. He strained to find a word in the Spanish letter that he could understand, but the third grade-educated pastor could only wince in chagrin.

Less than twenty percent of the Felipinos could read anything more than their signature. Don J'cab was not one of them. Rarely, however, had the anointed cleric been embarrassed by his illiteracy. Like his neighbors, he functioned on a limited cash/barter economic system that involved few contractual agreements that required printed or written negotiations. Literacy was never a factor in his military service, and the piety of his religious devotionals necessitated only work, not words.

"I have received this letter from Kingdom Throne Ministries," said Don J'cab Menchu. "I thought maybe you would like to see it."

The newly confirmed deacon took the letter from his pastor's hands and slipped the message from the envelope.

"Don J'cab," asked Deacon Julio Marcos Cabrerra, "this is the letter that you were telling us about—the one you have been waiting for?"

Don J'cab nodded his head, his weak smile somewhat belying his air of confidence, for he hadn't been able to decipher a single word of it.

The letter circulated around the table of the assembled deaconate. Each member received it cautiously, glanced quickly over it, and passed it to the next. After making its round about the table, Don J'cab accepted the epistle from Brother Julio Marcos and slipped it back into the envelope. Then piously, he crossed his hands over the Bible resting on the table in front of him and called the assembly to prayer.

"Dear blessed Jesus," intoned Don J'cab in his high-pitched, lyrical song. "We just ask that you be with us today and hear the prayers of your disciples gathered together . . ."

"*Amen! Amen!*" came the choral response from the deacons, their eyes tightly shut, one or both hands lifted heaven high above their bowed, swaying necks. Don J'cab, their pastor, had taught them all well—those, at least, who were new to the evangelical assembly.

"We just ask that you hear our prayers *now,* oh Lord," petitioned the pastor, "that you hear our prayers and that you wash away the mighty *weight of sin* that keeps us down, *oh Lord!"*

"*Amen! Amen!*" returned the chorus.

"*And Lord!* We just ask that you continue to rain your mercy *down!*" continued Don J'cab, beginning now to catch the rhythm he had found so appealing in the cassettes. "And *Almighty Lord!* We just ask that you use us today as `instruments of your peace'. . ."

Don J'cab liked the new words. He had practiced them over and over to himself, to make them familiar, and once comfortable, to use them in the embroidery of his pastoral insignia. Words of Kingdom Throne would become the symbol of his learning and their practiced style, his credentials. If he could not read the words, he could hear them, of course, and in the traditional way that all respected, learn to use them in formulas that everyone expected from an authentic leader of any new congregation.

"And now Lord," continued the pastor, "we would ask that you just hear the prayers of each of us, your disciples; that you just listen to our words of praise for you; and Lord, we just ask that your Holy Spirit join us now; that the mighty Holy Spirit might sweep within this room and find our hearts! And *oh! blessed Jesus!* We just pray here today, that you just send us *today!* that you just pour out upon these, your *disciples*! —that the gifts of the Holy Spirit just *wash over us* and just *lift us up* so that we may bring you *all the Glory!* We just ask that you *do it, Lord!* We just pray that right *now!* That right in *this* place and at *this* moment! That *here!* Among the assembled *brothers!* That you just *pour out your Spirit! Oh, do it! Blessed Jesus!"*

And he *did!* In the cold, damp hut of the pastor, the chorus was rolling from side to side and moaning, their individual prayers now commingling in a cacophony of ecstatic praise. Higher and higher swelled the powerful strains, louder and louder as each of the diminutive, black-haired deacons seemed heaven-bent in raising the ante on fervency. And then it broke.

"Diny-machu-tahni-loco!" shouted Hermano Jaime.

"Diny-loco-machu-tahni-taca-cami-poca-diny-machu!" Hermano Pablo, in a sympathetic rapture, responded.

"*Praise the Lord! Thank you, Jesus!*" cried the pastor, as around the table, the Kingdom Throne Disciples of the new gospel mission temple of San Felipe del Lago rose from their chairs, dancing and hopping about in a frenzied orgy of glossolalia. Around and around the table they moved, some clapping their hands to the beat of their own passion, others embracing in a flood of tears while Pastor Don J'cab stood back now as if frozen in place, his palms stiff and outstretched over his slightly cocked black head, his lips twitching contortedly, only the otherwise mute testimonials of a prayer rumbling deeply within his soul.

Hermano Jaime lay stiff on the floor of the hut, emitting deep gurgles as his bent arms twitched and jerked in spasms over his chest. The gift of the Holy Spirit had indeed flooded the room, and the disciples—with tears of great joy streaming down their cheeks—yielded up body and soul, a fitting climax to their investments of praise. Before it was over, each had collapsed on his knees or had fallen face forward, at least two chewing into the dirt in a personal gesture of their own wretchedness and unworthiness.

Moving slowly to one after another, Don J'cab bent over the feet of each and drew a dripping towel from a pot of hot water. One by one, he lifted the ankles and washed the feet of each disciple—just as *Jesucristo* had taught him to do.

"God bless you," offered Don J'cab as he finished with each of his parishioners.

The service of the foot washing was moving and did much to secure the sacramental image beginning to envelop the Indian "pastor." True it *was!* Don J'cab was not only a man of faith, but was to be a new seed of spiritual life in the community. Day by day, other Felipinos ventured by his home to greet him and to wish him well. Most expressed their interest in joining the new congregation. All were fascinated by widely rumored plans for the new building. In their enthusiasm to embrace the fashionable new church, they had many questions. The only thing that Don J'cab could do was to retrieve the letter from Kingdom Throne Ministries, showing them the prominent golden logo on the front of the envelope.

"All is well," reassured Don J'cab. "We will begin soon."

What else could he say? Don J'cab scanned the small gathering of well-wishers and smiled with confidence. They, in turn, nodded in respect and accepted the pastor's prayer for their health and good life.

"It is a good thing, the new church and all," said Mario Ortíz Bentrado to his brother, as the two coursed their way down the path from the pastor's small compound.

"Yes," agreed his brother, Luis Beltran Ortíz Bentrado. Excitement ran high among the evangelicals. They felt their own growing value and prestige in the community.

In one sense, the ambiguity of the undeciphered letter fed the enthusiasm of the growing congregation. Speculation about its content served only to strengthen the resolve of the deaconate to proselytize the community.

Don Fernando had it on good word that the letter placed the site of the new church at the crest of the hill overlooking the new tourist boat landing. The temple would greet each arriving group with its promise of salvation. During the evenings, the loud speakers would project the message of God's love and faith in the government across the waters to the neighboring communities. Of course, it was only one of several assurances that consigned the location of the new construction to the corner of the plaza where it would face off against the old Catholic sanctuary, or across the street from the *Cofradia of Santa Cruz*, or at the very gates of the military post where the soldiers could join the services of praise as they passed on patrol.

The period of construction, the clarification of donations, the proposed date for the dedication . . . the speculations swirled around the community, and not without consequences. Each new rumor registered in every corner of the town. The *cofradias* opposed the idea. The catechists opposed the idea. So, too, the *consejo* of the traditionals—the counsel of the *brujos*. All dissenters spurned the legion of evangelicals and their heavy-handed proselytizing. They had heard what had happened in El Verde Campo and San Antonio Nentén after the evangelicals opened their temples. The presence of the temples only exacerbated the divisions in the town and established alternative authorities and their bases. Within days, the mysterious letter and its consignee had assumed prodigious significance for all of San Felipe del Lago.

When Billy Ray Glover stepped off the bus, the great mystery was just about resolved. The Kingdom Throne administrator reached below his protruding belly and jerked up the front of his trousers to the proximity of a waistline and pulled down the back of his light-blue polyester Kingdom Throne jacket that had hiked up over his fleshy behind.

"*Two bags!*" he called up to the small *ladino* picking through the bulging luggage, baskets of fruits and vegetables, and nets of dried corn. "Two . . . Say, *boy!* D'ya *hear* me? *Two* bags!"

The *ladino* boy pitched down two of the large nets of corn and another of bilious cabbages, landing almost squarely on Billy Ray Glover whose urgency hadn't yet made an impression.

"*Say!* Looky *here!*" ordered the administrator, stepping back from the netted globes of cabbage. "*Two* bags! *Huh?*"

Perspiration drained from his hairline as Billy Ray Glover turned into the sun to catch a better angle on the operations above him.

"*Si, señor!*" returned the *ladino* boy. "*Two bags! Si, señor!*" The boy shuffled through the few bags atop the bus and found the two suitcases with the airline tags. He untied the loops of the hemp rope which, snaking through the various bundles and nets, secured the freight and baggage to the carrier of the bus.

"*Su equipaje, señor!* Two bags, sir!" he announced proudly as he presented the suitcases at the edge of the roof of the bus for the administrator's approval.

"*Yeah! Yeah!*" said the administrator, puffing under the strain of the humid morning.

The *ladino* boy maneuvered the bags next to the ladder attached to the rear door of the bus and motioned for the panting American to step below to receive them. A smirk of exasperation stretched across the puffy mouth of the sweaty administrator as he reconciled himself to the required effort and raised his arms above his head to receive the bags. Recognizing the ungainly predicament below him, the *ladino* boy stepped down the first two rungs of the ladder, pulling down the bag onto his back and then to his side before lowering it into the grip of the American. Then he scrambled back up the ladder, retrieved the second bag and passed it along in the same fashion before jumping past the last three rungs to the ground below.

"*Here y'go!*" Billy Ray Glover said as he passed along two *quetzales* in tip to the *mozo*. The boy took the two bills quickly, thanking his gratuitous benefactor, incredulous in the tourist's extravagance. Twenty-five *centavos* were usually more than what he expected from the common passengers of the "native" busses. The bus revved up and lurched forward. The *ladino* boy pocketed the money and dashed along side the bus toward the front entrance, jumping into the narrow opening just before the vehicle careened sharply to the left, leaving the administrator alone in a cloud of choking dust and heavy, black diesel grime.

"*J'EEZ-us!*" cursed the Kingdom Throne administrator as he turned his face from the fusillade of dirt and fumes.

Billy Ray Glover stood in the gritty street at the entrance to the town and took a quick look around as he struggled for his breath. In his rumpled, fleshy presence, he fulfilled the prophesied "second coming," following the crusade of the previous month, of Kingdom Throne Ministries to the highland *aldea* of San Felipe del Lago. For Billy Ray Glover personally, it was only his "first coming" to Central America after almost two years with the Ministry at the executive offices in Macon, Georgia. A "brilliant strategist" in an arena of flow charts and schemata, the Kingdom Throne administrator was experiencing all the on-site misgivings of a beached whale.

Billy Ray Glover looked around, mopping the sweat from his forehead and eyebrows against his shirt sleeve. Up the street he could see a circle of young merchants pulling together armfuls of ribbons and belts. A chorus of whistles erupted as the crew gathered its regalia and came racing toward the new arrival. Within moments, he was engulfed in a miasma of exotic cries, color, and competition.

"*No!* I don't think I want any today," said Billy Ray Glover. His insistence served only to redouble their efforts as they pressed the newcomer vigorously for a first sale.

"*No!*" protested the administrator. "I just *said* I didn't *want* anything! *Say!* what did I just *say, huh?*"

Around and around him went the Felipino girls, bumping him and grabbing at his jacket. This first trip into the highlands was proving very disarming for the North American disciple. He tried speaking a little louder.

"Y'all're lovely girls, lovely little girls," offered Billy Ray Glover, "but I just think I really don't want any right now, *comprende*?"

The tone of his voice registered only as a kindly reassurance of interest, and the sales girls continued to press the issue. Billy Ray Glover's *ad hoc* smile gave way to an anxious snarl, and he grabbed one of the girl's hands that was pulling on his left wrist and flung it away from him.

"I'm not going to buy anything, so you might as well leave me *alone!*" he barked. Like feisty mutts nipping at his heels, the Felipino girls danced around him. With the churchman's every remonstrance, their pleas became more insistent.

"You buy *ribbon!*" cried one.

"A beautiful *huipil* for you' lady!" begged another, holding up the first of three or four bright, new blouses draped across her left arm. "Which one? Which one you like?"

In exasperation, Billy Ray Glover turned to pick up his bags. In a chorus, the rebuked little sales team turned churlish, flinging epithets at his feet, defiling first his sister, wife, and mother, and then the administrator's entire extended family. Billy Ray Glover rebuffed them, one and all, with a fart from his backside, and with his two bags in tow, nudged his way through the girls and began the trudge up the street toward the central market.

"I be your guide, *okay?*" offered a voice just behind him as the church man reached level ground two blocks up from the bus stop below. Billy Ray Glover welcomed the interruption, for it gave him an excuse to drop the bags which had taken on enormous weight in his ascent.

"*Hey!*" returned the American, reaching into his pocket for the wad of *quetzales* he had purchased on his arrival at the airport the afternoon before.

"You wanna be my guide?" asked Billy Ray Glover now saturated with perspiration. "*Whooeee!* It sure is *hot* down here!"

"Where you need to go?" asked the small, stringy boy who appeared no more than eight or nine years old. He looked up at the American through listless eyes that seemed to glaze against the bright sunlight. Billy Ray Glover winced as he glanced at the boy's feet, scaled with dusty sores. Patches of light skin betrayed the extent of his malnutrition.

"Jacob . . . Jacob's place," said Billy Ray Glover. The boy looked puzzled.

"JAA-cob's place," repeated the American. The boy looked around, watching two cats pawing at a beetle struggling against the blazing white concrete paving stones.

"*No conozco,*" said the boy.

"No, I said *`Jacob,'*" repeated the administrator.

"I don't know no 'Jacob,'" explained the boy.

"This is San Felipy d' Lago, *no?*" asked Billy Ray Glover.

". . . del Lago," corrected the boy.

The phrase was lost to the American. "Say *what*?"

Staring now at each other, the two had reached a hesitant linguistic impasse. The boy turned his head back to the two cats. The enthusiastic felines had succeeded in dismembering the beetle. Billy Ray Glover handed the boy an additional *quetzal.*

"What do you *want*, boy? How much do I need to pay you? Is this what we're doing here? You need *another? Here!* Take *another!*"

The small boy drew back, perplexed by the American's sudden, inexplicable hostility.

"No," he said, and then he turned and ran off down the block, leaving the administrator flabbergasted and alone once more with his two overstuffed suitcases.

"Well, that *stupid, little runt!* That's the damnedest thing I've ever *seen!"* protested the American. He looked around for another prospective guide, but spotting no other Felipino child offering to assist him, he picked up his bags and began laboring up the street. He passed the Esso station where two mechanics tinkered under the transmission of a broken down 2 1/2-ton produce truck. The American sat down the bags and wiped his face again.

A battered, blue Chevy Nova pulled into the service station for gasoline, and one of the mechanics crawled out from under the truck to assist the driver. The administrator saw his chance and moved to ask for directions.

"*Hey!*" cried the American to the mechanic wiping his hands on his rag. The mechanic turned toward the voice.

"*Hey!* Looka *here!*" cried Billy Ray Glover. The mechanic raised his hand, saying something in Spanish which the administrator couldn't understand, and then he turned to the car. Once again, the American found himself stranded, and once more, he switched bags and ground back into the street, craning his neck around for any sign of help. Scratchy crackles from a loud speaker more than two blocks ahead gave him hope, and he changed directions at the corner in order to pursue the incessant din.

Irritated momentarily by a large horsefly that had targeted his sweaty forehead, Billy Ray Glover floundered up the sidewalk past a small open drink stand and *tienda* where three laborers set quietly at a table drinking cold beer. In the tailor shop next door, the owner of the shop sat behind his humming machine, slipping a bolt of dark-blue cotton underneath the needle. Near the front door, his small son smeared bootblack over the heels of a pair of worn boots at his own tiny shoeshine stall. Beyond the *tienda* and tailor shop, he struggled past three tiny yards where women sat under scrub trees weaving, squatting among small swarms of filthy, ragged children scurrying about, their dogs chasing at their heels. And then he stopped. Something in the voice blaring over the loud speaker on the corner caught his attention. While he couldn't understand the mixed message of broken Spanish and Tzutujil, the cadences of the message were unmistakably the rhythms of the Kingdom Throne cassette ministry. Billy Ray Glover gripped the suitcases more vigorously, and hurriedly, he stepped back out into the street.

He worked his way through the growing number of women at the corner who were converging from various side streets. As he reached the plaza, Billy Ray Glover discovered a small group of *campesinos* standing around a stall covered with a sheet of blue plastic. As he moved closer, he spied the "voice" of the message spitting into a microphone before a PA system rigged up on a rather flimsy folding card table. The Kingdom Throne disciple worked his way over to the young man where he could observe the operation more critically.

Moises Bámaca, one of the new deacons of the San Felipe congregation, was recruiting membership, reciting in a rather flimsy Spanish and a more robust Tzutujil, various "calls" for affirmations of faith and invitations to the community to seek peace through confessions of sin. Brother Moises yelled into the microphone, spewing short declamations in patterns of three—three phrases, three points. Although he couldn't understand even a single word, to Billy Ray Glover the rhythms and pacing of the delivery and the intonations, even the emphases of the inflections, echoed the unmistakable style of the Kingdom Throne cassette tapes. As he moved closer to the front of the table, he could see a crude rendering of the Kingdom Throne logo scratched out in pencil on a piece of repurposed cardboard.

Billy Ray Glover was exuberant. Even before the construction of the Kingdom Throne temple, the seed of salvation had already sprouted. He saw no reason to interrupt the young disciple. He needed only to find Don J'cab and to review with him the schedule for the purchase of property and the beginning of construction. The key to his instant support in the community was the gold Kingdom Throne Ministries logo on his own "gimme" cap which he pulled from one of the suitcases while listening to the young disciple. Immediately, the brilliant, embroidered logo flashed like a beacon to the few devotees standing around the table. One of the listeners could communicate in at least broken English.

"You King-doom Throne, *no?*" asked Eduardo Santa Cruz.

"*Yes!* Yes, I *am!*" exuded Billy Ray Glover, comfortable for the first time since his arrival in the previous hour.

"You just come on the boat, *no?*"

"Yeah! Just now," reconfirmed the American.

"You want to see Don J'Cab?" asked Eduardo Santa Cruz.

"*Yeah! Yeah!* That's the guy!" affirmed Billy Ray Glover. "Right away, *okay?*"

"Okay! Follow me," said Eduardo Santa Cruz.

"How much?" asked the American.

Eduardo Santa Cruz looked puzzled at the question. "What?" he asked.

"How *much?*" Billy Ray Glover repeated.

The Felipino only stared at the American.

"How *much?* How much do I have to pay you to take me to this `Don' fellow?"

The young Tzutujil appeared confused.

"Why, *nothing, señor!*" said Eduardo Santa Cruz, embarrassed by even the thought of payment. As a new disciple, the Felipino saw himself both apart from and above the simple street urchins who preyed upon the naive tourists. No more for him; Eduardo Santa Cruz envisioned himself as a servant leader to his community.

"Follow me," he said, and he reached for the bags of the surprised administrator.

The disciple took the lead and began maneuvering through the market crowd. Within moments they were clear and working their way up the hill from the plaza. The young man never slowed until he was forced to pause four blocks away from the path that led to the home of Don J'cab. Billy Ray Glover was far behind, having stopped several times to catch his breath in the higher altitude. After a laborious march, he had reached his guide, and together they turned up the trail before them.

Don J'cab was not at home when the two arrived, but he wasn't far behind. He was in town when Billy Ray Glover had been "discovered." He had raced to the broadcast stall to intercept the emissary, but he had missed him by about five minutes. The guide and his ward had arrived at his home just as Don J'cab and at least five of the deacons began the ascent of the path to his home.

It was a proud moment for the small, evangelical congregation gathered when Don J'cab took the hand of Billy Ray Glover. A fifth-year student of English at the IGA, the bi-national center in the capital before he had to drop out to return to aging parents, Eduardo Santa Cruz volunteered to interpret for both parties. Don J'cab invited all to enter his small house and ordered Manuela, his wife, to prepare a fresh pot of coffee and tortillas.

"*Bienvenida a San Felipe del Lago,*" offered Don J'cab. "*Sientase, por favor.*" Eduardo Santa Cruz slipped easily into his role as interpreter, following every sentence with his quick response.

"Please. Sit. Welcome to San Felipe del Lago, *señor*," repeated Eduardo Santa Cruz.

"Thank you very much," returned the American. "Nice place you have here." Eduardo Santa Cruz translated. The five deacons assumed a formal position in a line against the side of the room near Manuela's preparations of coffee and tortillas, each allowing the two leaders to become acquainted and each most eager to learn, first hand, any information about their new church and its construction.

"Well, I guess you know why I'm here," offered the American administrator. Eduardo Santa Cruz translated.

Each of the deacons assembled turned to Don J'cab with great anticipation. Don J'cab himself smiled in a knowing, self-assured kind of way, a complement to his exalted position in the proceedings.

"Of course," said the Tzutujil pastor. "We have been waiting for you ever since we received the letter."

Don J'cab pulled the letter from a small drawer secreted below the kitchen table and handed it to the American.

"Yeah, the letter," said Billy Ray Glover. "Let me look over the letter again."

The American slipped the letter from the envelope and held it under the light streaming in through the door. The sunlight illuminated the particles of unsettled dust that hovered about them, and the American swatted through the fine cloud with the stationery, irritated that he could not disburse it.

"Well, I think that pretty well explains things," said the American. "Any questions?"

Billy Ray Glover glanced around the room at the small assembly half expecting some kind of response, a question or two about the preparations of his own arrangements. The deacons deferred with a glance to their leader and pastor, Don J'cab.

Don J'cab looked puzzled for a moment, but refusing to be humiliated in the presence of his peers, he dismissed the assembly so that he might address the administrator, one-on-one.

"I hope you will excuse me, gentlemen," said Don J'cab. "There are some things we must discuss privately."

In deference to his position as their pastor, the deacons, with the exception of Eduardo Santa Cruz, filed quietly out of the house and descended the path. At the foot of the trail, they congregated casually, hoping and half expecting to be recalled to the discussions.

"Well, the first thing," said Billy Ray Glover, "I guess you're gonna need to show me where I'm going to be *staying.*" He looked at Eduardo Santa Cruz and nodded for him to translate.

"He wants to know where he is supposed to stay," said Eduardo Santa Cruz to his pastor. Don J'cab never changed his expression from the mien of a quiet self-confidence, while, inwardly, however, he was churning with agonizing insecurity. He had no place for the unexpected visitor and certainly no funds to support an extended stay in the two public hostels in the town. He needed more time.

"Thank you, Señor Glover," said Don J'cab. Eduardo Santa Cruz translated.

"We are very pleased to have you in our community," continued the Felipino. "Of course, we have expected you since we received the letter. We have very fine accommodations arranged for you, and we hope you will be comfortable. But you must allow me to send a runner to make sure all is in order and ready for you."

"Well, that's fine," offered the affable administrator. "That'll be just *fine, okay?*"

Don J'cab turned to Eduardo Santa Cruz and motioned with his hand his desire for a confidence.

"Eduardo," said the pastor. "Go outside and ask Don Ramiro to come back, okay?"

"*Como no!*" said Eduardo. Excited by the unfolding activity and eager to be a player in the proceedings, the young translator slipped out the door and scooted off down the path to the small group of deacons.

"*Fine* little place you have here!" exuded the American. Don J'cab struggled visibly to catch any semblance of meaning but masked his frustration with a languid smile.

"Yeah, really *fine* town!" said Billy Ray Glover, slapping his fat knees with his pulpy hands.

"*Si!*" offered Don J'cab in an attempt to complement the good-natured salutation.

"*Donde vive?*" asked the administrator. Don J'cab looked puzzled. Was this a test of some kind?

"*Bueno . . .*" said Don J'cab, offering the American an opportunity to clarify the incongruous question.

"*Uhhh, d-o-n-d-e-v-i-v-e . . .?*" Billy Ray asked a little louder a second time, confident in his command of the language. The two stared at each other, each hurtling toward another awkward impasse.

"*Uh . . . aquí!*" said the pastor. The American stared incredulously at the Maya sitting before him.

"Aquí . . .?" repeated the administrator. "`How are you?' and this guy says `here'!—now what kind of a dumb-shit answer is that?" he asked himself. "This guy's a chump for sure. The military sure knows how to pick'em!"

The two stared at each other across an unfathomable gulf. There would be no other question from Kingdom Throne Ministries at this time. The American savant had exhausted the full range of his linguistic acumen.

"Don J'cab?" came the solicitous voice of Deacon Ramirez. "*Con permiso,*" said Don J'cab to the perplexed administrator, and he rose to consult with the churchman.

" *`Con permiso'!* Sure!" said Billy Ray Glover. "Sure! *`Con permiso'!*"

Don J'cab motioned his Felipino friend to stand outside, and he escorted him over to the corner of the yard beyond hearing range of the American.

"Look," said Don J'cab. "We've got to find a place—a room—for Señor Glover. "Right now!"

Deacon Ramirez looked confused.

"Well," said the pastor, "I was supposed to find a place for him, but I never knew exactly just when he was coming, so see if you can get a room. Go to Señor Marco . . . Marco . . . "

"Marco Esparza, the furniture maker?" asked the Deacon. "He has a room?"

"Yes," confirmed Don J'cab. "Ever since his brother died last year. And Don Ramirez . . . *hurry, okay?*"

"*Como no!*" said the deacon. Brother Ramirez nodded respectfully, took three steps backwards, turned away, and went running down the path.

Billy Ray Glover stood up and surveyed the mean hovel of the newly anointed pastor. The smoothly pounded dirt floor was mottled with the droppings of small chicken pullets, cheep-cheeping behind two musty cardboard boxes filled with bulbs and seeds in the corner. More than twenty years of smoke from the humble hearth had blackened the mud-packed walls and rafters overhead. A rope strung from two of the beams stretched over the hearth on which two ragged *tzutes* and *servilletas* dried above the hot embers. Tall, arching sprays of dying gladioli were anchored in two cans of water on either side of a makeshift altar below the only window of the house. On the small stand stood a short, foot-high, elaborately carved crucifix over the arms of which hung a set of crystal rosary beads. The heavy aromas of freshly brewed coffee, hot tortillas, and two rancid cabbages choked the air, almost gagging the American emissary.

Manuela completed the coffee and was pouring it in two cups for her guest and husband.

"*Señor?*" offered Manuela de Xoy softly.

"*What?*" asked the startled administrator. "Oh . . . *no!* No thank you, honey!"

"No?" said Señora Xoy. *"No quiere algo tomar?"*

"*Sí, Señora!*" said Billy Ray Glover. "Nice *place! Nice* place!"

The American waved off the steaming, black coffee and glanced toward the two cabbages hanging in a net just inside the entrance. *"Goddamn! It stinks in here! How the hell can anybody with any self-respect live like this? J'eez-us!"*

He reached for his handkerchief in his back pocket and blew heavily from his nose.

"What in Chris'name am I doing here," thought Billy Ray Glover. "These people can't understand a word I'm saying. I'm just gonna have to take control. I can see that for sure!"

Billy Ray Glover turned his back to his host and walked out the entrance into the yard. "Goddamn! How does anybody live like this! J'eez-uschris'!"

"Hey!" Billy Ray called to the translator. Eduardo Santa Cruz turned from the side of the pastor and ran to face the American.

"*Sí, Señor!*" he said.

"Looka *here,*" said the American, delivering another blast from his nose into his handkerchief. "Tell `Don' fellow here that we can leave my bags. I've got the directions to the church site. We can go there any time he's ready—right now, if he wants to."

Eduardo Santa Cruz looked with amazement at the American as the meaning sank in. The message was almost too much to contain, and he virtually jumped into the face of Don J'cab. Billy Ray Glover watched with curious amusement at the almost boyish glee his presence was eliciting. Don J'cab's eyes brightened. As he received the announcement, the semblance of a smile spread momentarily over his face, but then dissipated just as quickly. The Tzutujil pastor slipped back behind the stoic facade, raised his fingers before his face in caution to the excited young translator, and then walked over to the American.

For a few moments the three huddled together in conversation. The American reached up with a sweeping gesture over his head and then followed the pastor's hand signals in the opposite direction. The conversation continued again, and then the three began their walk down the path toward the cluster of deacons squatting on their heels at the bottom of the hill.

The location selected for the new Kingdom Throne Temple was the site of the army's old boat storage shed. The facility, on an acre of prime land on the shore of the lake, had been abandoned for more than four years after the military had moved their operations five kilometers up the road from San Felipe. Construction was slated to begin as soon as all contracts had been awarded and the crews assembled.

Not surprisingly, all details and concerns were accommodated in a matter of four days. A spread of cash cleared all arrangements between Kingdom Throne Ministries and the city fathers through the good auspices of Alberto Reyes Benitez, the military commissioner, and a ground-breaking ceremony was scheduled, in accordance with the customary protocol, for the first weekend.

Word spread swiftly throughout San Felipe. Among the newly converted members of the evangelical community, enthusiasm was especially high. In the marketplace, the new "temple" was the only topic of conversation, and its presence assailed and praised by the partisans of each camp. By the end of the first week of discourse, the camps were clearly divided. Catholics sat mute, virtually atrophied in the unceasing cacophony of exuberant evangelical chatter that dominated completely every turn in the conversation. The few traditionals among the merchants huddled together at the back of their stalls, all but stupefied by the Pentecostal proselytizing at every entrance and turn of an aisle.

On the morning of the ceremony, volunteers unloaded folding chairs and sheets of heavy plyboard from the back of an army pickup truck and arranged them over a set of reinforced plastic coca cola cases. Within the same hour, a second supply truck arrived with a portable speaker's podium, a set of Guatemalan flags, and buckets of gladiolus sprays and bundles of birds of paradise blossoms. In short order, the platform was assembled and the chairs positioned for the invited guests and dignitaries.

A hundred or more Felipinos witnessed the affair. The principle figures sat on the small plywood platform. Billy Ray Glover, the representative for Kingdom Throne assumed the position of honor, ensconced between the *alcalde municipal* and Alberto Reyes Benitez. Don J'cab stood at the center of the deacons in a formal row on the ground just behind the officials.

To begin the activities, Don Ferenando, the *alcalde municipal*, welcomed the new addition to the life of faith in San Felipe. Alberto Reyes Benitez noted, not so obliquely, that the presence of the new congregation would constitute a new vanguard against the "heresies of certain political theologies."

Punctuating the military commissioner's observation with just the sheer weight of his presence but otherwise aloof from the rhetoric of the occasion, Captain Villalobos stood squarely behind the honorable Alberto Reyes Benitez, his arms folded and his face frozen behind his American military sun glasses in a posture that was unmistakable in its meaning to the Tzutujiles. On cue from Eduardo Santa Cruz, Billy Ray Glover stepped forward, removed his Kingdom Throne Ministries "gimme" cap, and addressed the crowd of both greater and lesser disciples.

"Today, *God* has arrived in San Felipy!" exclaimed the American administrator, and he nodded toward Eduardo Santa Cruz who moved closer to him in assuming once again his role as translator. At the American's opening exclamation, Don J'cab seemed to square his shoulders and raise his chin, affecting almost a military posture. On that cue, the Tzutujil crowd before them went rigid in a formality, a mien that Billy Ray observed with chagrin. He would have none of that, for sure! His intention was to establish a decidedly different tone for the occasion, and he turned to Eduardo Santa Cruz.

"I *said . . .!*" he gestured to Eduardo. "I *said . . .!*" he repeated. "I *said . . . GAW-uuDah! . . . GAW-uuDah* has come this day to San Felipy, d'Lago!" The administrator made a dramatic gesture to Eduardo Santa Cruz that he should try to emulate both tone and message. Eduardo Santa Cruz didn't miss the suggestion, and his rendition rocked the tiny platform. Suddenly, Tzutujil heads began bobbing from side to side. Don J'cab and the deaconate were visibly disturbed.

"Can you say *a-MEN!"* shouted the American as he turned and stared directly at the Maya pastor. Don J'cab winced visibly as a shock of embarrassment ripped down his spine.

"Get up *here*, boys!" cried the administrator. "Get up here and shout *'Hallelujah!'*" Eduardo Santa Cruz motioned to the deacons and the good pastor to step up onto the platform behind the community officials and the military commander.

"Are you too embarrassed to praise the *Lord?*" cried Billy Ray Glover. Eyes closed, and a murmur of prayer began to trickle through the diaconate.

"Can you say 'a-*MEN'?*" insisted the administrator.

"Amen!" said the men and a few of the other disciples standing in the crowd.

"Can you say 'a-*MEN'?*" repeated the American, and the crowd began to sense the rhythm.

"So! Say 'a-*MEN'!*" bellowed Billy Ray Glover, and the crowd began to sway back and forth as the "amens" began drifting through the assembly.

"So! Let's just say 'a-*MEN-ah!*" pleaded the American, and the disciples offered up a thunderous cadence of holiness. Billy Ray reached to the podium and retrieved his copy of the large, flimsy, leather-bound Bible, raising it high over his head.

"Pur-raise-ah-*Gaw-uudah!*" he ejaculated, shaking the Bible vigorously, thrusting it skyward again and again. "I say—say it with me, *now*!—I *say*-uh, Pur-raise-ah-*Gaw-uudah! A-MEN-ah!* Thank you, *J'EEZ-us-ah!* Oh, let me *hear* it, brothers! Thank you, *J'EEZ-us-ah!*"

"Thank you, Jesus!"

"I say-ah, Thank you, *J'EEZ-us-ah-ah!*"

"Thank you, Jesus" came the clamorous refrain.

"Oh, let me hear it from your hearts—I say, Thank-ah-you, *J'EEZ-us-ah-ah!*"

"Thank you, Jesus!"

"Oh, Thank you, blessed *J'EEZ-us-ah-ah!*"

"Thank you, Jesus!"

"Oh, praise-his-*name-ah!*" cried Billy Ray Glover, slip-sliding away from a little flash of ecstasy. "Don't you just love to pur-raise-ah *J'EEZ-us-ah!* Oh, thank you, Lord, for the gift of your son, *J'EEZ-us-ah!* Pur-raise his *name-ah! A-MEN-ah!*"

Eduardo Santa Cruz continued to work the now feverish crowd before the austere platform, the new Kingdom Throne diaconate, and the stolid, immovable Captain Villalobos.

"Ladies and gentlemen!" continued a flushed Billy Ray Glover, as he lowered and closed the Bible. "We are here today to dedicate a temple of praise and worship. We are here to dedicate a sacred temple of holiness in a place that God loves, in a place that is so *BLESS-id!*"

A smile suffused his face, and he beamed benevolently as he surveyed the crowd for the first time. He fixed on the quartet of little merchants that were hanging out on the edge of the adults.

"Have you ever seen such *cute* little *children!*" cooed the administrator. "Just *look* at them!"

Billy Ray Glover waved the limp Bible over the heads of the growing congregation flanked on each side by a pack of dirty, little Tzutujil urchins, their big eyes and easy smiles belying the destitution of their parents and general conditions all about them.

"Just look at them, sweet *J'EEZ-us-ah!*" cried Billy Ray Glover, raising his paunchy jowls beneath squinting eyes against the bright sunlight overhead. Then, all of a sudden, he remembered a favorite scripture. "Oh, God loves them so *much!* So much that he gave his only begotten *son!* That *whosoeverth* . . ."

Eduardo Santa Cruz stumbled over the King James effervescence, and repeated twice again the last familiar phrase he had understood so as not to lose the cadence. The American never caught the glitch.

"But my brothers in *J'EEZ-us-ah!*" roared Billy Ray Glover, as he suddenly rolled over the podium, thrusting his Bible out toward the crowd. "But do they know it? . . . Do these little children—" and he beamed benevolently again—"Do they know the love of *J'EEZ-us-ah!* . . . these precious little indians? . . . Do they know that *J'EEZ-us-ah*, that *J'EEZ-us-ah! died!* that he *dah-I-id!* for their *sins?*"

The crowd stood petrified before them as Eduardo Santa Cruz slurred through the awful challenge.

"Suffer not the little children to come unto me!" squealed the administrator. Eduardo Santa Cruz stumbled once again, and Billy Ray Glover was forced this time to rephrase a cardinal aphorism of Holy truth.

"Why don't these little children know the luh-uv ah-*Gaw-ud-dah?*" cried an angry Billy Ray Glover. "Why don't they now know the luh-uv-ah *J'EEZ-us-ah?*"

The crowd dropped its head as Eduardo Santa Cruz laid the heavy chains of responsibility upon them.

"Le' me tell you somethin', ladies'n gentlemen!" offered the administrator as he slipped his thumbs under his belt and hoisted his trousers back up over his ankles and stomach. "Let me tell you why these sweet children don't know the love of *J'EEZ-us-ah!*"

The crowd rolled their eyes upward once again expectantly, beseeching the truth from the divinely inspired Billy Ray Glover. The administrator sapped the moment dry, glowering now, fixing every eye. "It is *because!* . . . it is because of your *sin!*"

Billy Ray Glover slammed the floppy testament down against the podium. "It is because of an E-vil-ah that breeds like a lecherous filth across the face of this town! An E-vil-ah, I say, that knows not the face of *Gaw-ud-Dah!*—and the Holy Spirit of his blessed son, *J'EEZ-us-ah! A-MEN-uh!"*

Billy Ray Glover began a slow, deliberate thumping away against the face of the Bible.

"A *vile-ah wretchedness* has the soul of this town—this little town—set against one of God's special wonders—" roiled the administrator. "I say, a *sin* against the very *Holy Spirit of Gaw-ud-Dah!*—himself, weighs *heavily* on the life of San Felipy d'*Lah*-go!"

Billy Ray Glover paused magisterially to allow the damage of the awesome revelation to register. His head swayed heavily from side to side, his bulbous, swivelling, lizard-like eyes locking on each cowering parishioner before him.

Tears flowed down the cheeks of the diaconate. Don J'cab was shaken, and he raised his right palm high over his head while mumbling a prayer for forgiveness. Back and forth along the row of the disciples, solemn, agonizing prayers rippled over their lips. More hands sprouted aloft in praise, and one of the more enthused among the brethren dropped to his knees in sobs of mordant remorse.

And not without effect.

Before the platform, the reconstituted Tzutujil disciples of Kingdom Throne fell to their knees, pouring out wails of grief around them. Billy Ray Glover stalked the platform, waving the Testament over the *penitentes*, his own "Holy Spirit" in full throttle. As the wave of agony began to subside, he sauntered back self-assuredly over to the pulpit.

"But my friends," beckoned the administrator, "we have the key to hev-un right here in our hearts when we let *J'EEZ-us in-ah*. In *J'EEZ-us-ah* is our hope of salvation, and in *J'EEZ-us-ah* is the hope for San Felipy! If you just say *`yes-uh'* to *J'EEZ-us-ah*, you can save this town, this town on the lake, this town on one of the most beautiful little lakes I ever see!"

Throughout the distraught crowd, wet eyes peered up with restored hope into the confident, sparkling gaze of Billy Ray Glover, puckish dimples stretching away now from the corners of his mouth.

"Oh, *yes!* My *friends!*" cooed Billy Ray Glover as he extended the now open testament, its pages draped over his powerful left palm. "Oh, *yes!* My *friends!* We can say *`Yea-yus'! to J'EEZ-us-ah*, and we can save San Felipy!"

He preened again, stepping away once more from the pulpit, throwing his shoulders back, prancing like a feverish, randy cock before the fawning chicks in the hen house. The face of Billy Ray Glover was aglow with the love of God and the enlightenment of God's Holy Word.

"So, my friends," whispered the administrator. "I wanna ask you right now." Hungry hearts followed every word, every nuance, the *campesino* faces awash in tears. "Do you love *J'EEZ-uz-ah?*"

A chorus of anguished groans rose on outstretched palms from the pliant disciples below him. "Do you love *J'EEZ-uz-ah?*" he pleaded.

"O*h, yes! Oh, yes!*" came the reply.

"I just don't think I heard you now!" cried the administrator. "And if I can't hear you down here, how is the blessed *J'EEZ-us* gonna hear you way up *there!*" And up went the wings of the Bible.

"Oh, yes! We love Jesus!"

"I didn't quite hear you, friends!"

"Oh, yes! We love Jesus!"

"Oh, can you hear it, Lord *J'EEZ-us-ah*! . . . Oh, say it *again!*"

"*Oh, yes! We love Jesus!*" roared the disciples.

"Praise *Gaw-uhh-dah!*" exuded the preacher, as he paced back and forth across the flimsy platform. "Pur-raize *Gaw-ud-a-mighty!*"

"But *brothers!*" he cried, "Will you *serve* him?"

"Oh, *yes!"* came the cries.

"But *brothers!* Will you *work* for him?"

"Oh, *yes!*" came the response.

"But *brothers!* Will you *bring in* the *Kingdom of God* to this heathen town of San Felipy?"

"Oh, yes! Lord Jesus!"

"Oh, *brothers!* I just wanna *ask* you! Will you *drive out the devil* that has a hold-a-your-ah *hearts-ah?*"

"Oh, yes! Lord Jesus!"

"Will you fight the great beasts-ah darkness?"

"Oh, yes! Blessed Jesus!"

"Will you *drive out* the great *beasts-ah E-vile-ah* who hide behind the masks of *saints-ah?*"

"Oh, yes! Blessed Jesus!"

"Will you *save San Felipy* from the grips of the idol-worshipping *Catholics?*"

"*By our very souls!*" cried the pilgrims.

"And will you drive from your midst—today! I said today! Oh, my brothers and sisters! How can we tolerate even one more hour these demon-divining dogs of that Satan-sucking idol, `Mashy-Mon-ah'?"

"Before the dawn of another *day! Oh, come, Lord Jesus!"*

Chapter 25

Do Unto Others

Twelve troops sat upright, jammed together on the left bench of the truck, mirroring the same number of their nervous, weary counterparts to the right. Their newly issued M-16 A2's at the ready and alert for any interruption, the two soldiers on the end of the benches sat at the rear of the "deuce-and-a-half," the American-made 2 1/2-ton canvas-covered overland troop transport. On the floor board at their feet, the squad of soldiers guarded eight cases of the rifles, more than fifty of the units that would replace the older guns—some of them early 1960's models which had seen service more than twenty-five years earlier in the Mekong Delta of South Vietnam.

Less than twenty yards behind, four other vehicles, each ferrying duplicate cargoes, worked their way over the dusty ruts of the stretch of road that wound around the west end of Lake Atitlán toward the garrison of San Felipe. Their commanding officer, Captain Marco Menendez Villalobos, rode side by side his troops in the third truck. He always positioned himself inside an interior vehicle and next to the squad's radio operator. If their convoy were attacked, the first truck would probably receive the initial incoming fire, and the captain needed to be free to react, to direct the response of his squad, and to call up reinforcements.

The trucks ambled along, lurching and rocking back and forth, zigzagging across gouges in the road that would have grounded any passenger car. Dirt and grit billowed from under the wheels, blanketing the hot canvas tarpaulins in layer upon layer of fine, pale yellow dust. The drive from the *Bruceros'* Post #14 usually took about an hour and a half, but this time the convoy would require more than four. Ahead of them a squad of foot soldiers tramped along both sides of the road watchful for mines or crude booby traps while two helicopter gunships flew escort overhead, racing back and forth along the route to protect the rear from any surprise assault.

The troops were returning from three weeks of training on the same M16-A2's that they guarded at their feet, and they were exhausted. They had received instruction in assembling and disassembling their weapons and had spent more than three hours at a range learning how to fire from both prone and assault positions. Moreover, they had been subjected to full battle simulations in almost every terrain and condition found in the country. They rappelled off cliffs, shooting into jungle canopy at hidden "subversives" silhouetted on reinforced cardboard stakes. They fired on targets as they dropped from helicopters hovering over newly cleared jungle growth, landing swaths stripped away by gattling fire, another legacy from Vietnam. They trampled for hours behind armored escort vehicles and light tanks, and then laid down blankets of fire as they covered for their colleagues spreading left and right away from the vehicles, taking shelter in shallow ravines. They charged up the southern slope of Pacaya and then pushed across the valley to the north, chasing phantom subversives up and back down Volcán Agua less than ten kilometers from where they had engaged the *EGP*, the People's Army of the Poor, only months before. They had completed three days of training in the Petén, engaging in fierce hand-to-hand combat within their units in the steaming jungles once contested by warriors of the ancient Maya.

Now in the beasty heat, they were returning to San Felipe and the rugged little garrison still under construction. The five trucks continued up the road in the early afternoon, creeping along the south rim of the mountain past occasional traditional huts with their bamboo walls and dry thatch covers. Here and there, they passed concrete block houses with sheet metal roofs, one-room structures that had been erected from international aid following the devastating earthquakes of February, 1976. As the road turned again over the crest of the mountain and zigzagged down the north side and into the valley, the houses assumed the more traditional appearance. These had somehow survived the wracking tremors of the great *terremoto*. Up and down the slopes of the opposite side of the steep mountain, small clusters of Indian houses, straining under the massive weight of heavy, blackened roof tiles, hunkered down in the middle of cornfields in the rich volcanic soil.

The trucks continued their measured pace around the bends in the road. Ahead, the column of soldiers dropped into two single files as the road opened and stretched outward before them. As far as they could see to either side of the road, row after row of musty, dead corn stalks towered around them. As they passed, the soldiers could hear the withered leaves crackling in the faint breezes sweeping upward from the lake, while overhead, three buzzards circled lazily against the deep blue sky. The soldiers turned their heads carefully from left to right as they widened the space between themselves down the straightaway, a defensive tactic should guerrilla fire strike them from one side or the other.

As the last soldiers of the two columns came around the bend in the road behind them, the point man of the left column suddenly dropped to a crouching position, frantically waving his right arm up and down behind him, motioning his comrades to do the same. At once, the two columns knelt, their rifles aimed into the corn breaks on either side of the road. Ahead, a narrow foot path entered the road from the left. The point man had heard commotion in the fields just beyond the crossover. Not a soldier moved as each cocked his ears toward the sound.

Momentarily, the source of the noise was clarified as two emaciated cows lumbered out from the path and onto the open road. The two animals turned left onto the road away from the troops followed by a family of *campesinos*. A Maya father, in a homespun brown shirt, worn khaki pants, and rugged sandals, a high brimmed straw hat on his head, preceded his weathered wife. A short, rather squatty woman in a faded *huipil* and filthy *morga* skirt, obviously too preoccupied to even notice the soldiers behind her, she urged two playful, little girls on ahead of her to tend the cows.

It was the sound of the trucks and not the soldiers that seconds later attracted their attention. As the trucks approached the opening of the road behind the foot soldiers, the family of four stepped briskly aside to let the vehicles pass. The soldiers eyed the Indians carefully as they filed past. The Maya father removed his hat and, with a red and white bandanna, wiped the perspiration from his forehead.

As the trucks approached, the two cows continued to amble along in the middle of the road. The father shouted something, and one of his tiny daughters ran toward the nearest mound of corn by the side of the road. Throwing her spindly little arms around its dead stalk, she tugged and tugged until she had finally loosened it from its moorings in the soft earth and ripped it up. Then, brandishing the dead switch before her, the tiny Cakchiquel girl jumped back into the road and raced ahead toward the nearest cow. Not to be outdone in the potential fun of it all, her sister followed suit, pillaging another mound on the opposite side of the road. With their small fists clutching the long stalks high over their heads, they flailed away at the hind quarters of the two animals, grunting and shouting as they urged the cattle forward. At first the two cows seemed indifferent to the savage little commotion behind them. One even paused, raised its tail, and defecated at the bare feet of its pixy tormentor. After tolerating the growing nuisance long enough, however, the two animals begrudgingly drifted to the side of the road, and the five trucks passed on, leaving the family in a swirl of choking dust.

Despite the intense fighting the troops had engaged above Sololá the month before, the return of the convoy to San Felipe was uneventful. The trucks followed the two-foot columns all the way around the lake and entered the gates of the San Felipe garrison about four o'clock in the afternoon. Captain Villalobos ordered Jaime Cabrera-Toc and his unit to unload the crates of rifles from the truck and to move them into the arsenal located in a concrete-block structure in the middle of the compound. The corporal assigned drivers to the other four vehicles, and together they rolled up to the depot where the sergeant began logging each crate and its contents.

The San Felipe garrison was a relatively new establishment, opened only five years before, following the army's drives of 1982 and 1983 against the insurgency throughout the Lake District. The compound was about four city blocks in depth, stretching from the reedy lake front, back up almost to the road that led from the small, outlying *cantones* to the plaza of the town about five kilometers away. The primary purpose of the base was to act as a buffer between the communities to the south and east shores of the lake and those to the west and to the north. Its dormitories could accommodate four hundred active-duty men but could bivouac up to a thousand or more inside its perimeter in an emergency. The arsenal constituted the largest stockpile of arms and ammunition on the south rim of the lake. Two light-armored tanks were stationed within the compound along with more than a dozen troop transports. Surrounding the entire garrison, a heavy, wire fence stretched from a post anchored more than thirty yards out into the lake, and then back and upward toward the road. Six or seven yards from the road, the line of fence turned and came together at two concrete guard stations at the main gate of the entrance.

If the residents of San Felipe despised the military presence in their community, they came to resent it even more as the garrison expanded, taking on the appearance of a permanent installation. Such a suggestion was reinforced by the initiation of a wall just inside the gate beginning at the two guard stations. The stone and concrete structure had been only partially completed, extending about three to four feet high and away from the guard posts about forty yards on either side. Stones had already been collected for the side walls and had been piled up in twelve large heaps along both sides of the garrison compound. The various squads took turns working at the wall, building a little more each day.

It wasn't the concrete and mortar, the munitions depot, the fence, or even the growing wall, however, that so affected the Felipinos. What extended the garrison's heavy presence into every home and hearth was the military patrols.

In small squads of threes and fours, the soldiers were planted everywhere—on the steps of the church, in the stalls of the markets, at almost every street corner, and in front of their school. They seemed omnipresent.

Only a month after their arrival, the threats and intimidations began, followed by the first disappearances. The Felipinos became terrified. Tales circulated throughout the *pueblo* no more than a week after the fence went up—awful tales, stories about tortures in the interior of the main building where it was said that peasants had been thrown into circular pits more than ten feet deep, their floors littered with the decaying remains of severed limbs and the bodies of fellow *campesinos*. On excessively hot afternoons and evenings, the awful stench, some reported, drifted throughout the compound and far out into the lake. It was generally accepted that the heavy metal and *Latino* rock music that was broadcast occasionally on loud speakers over the compound in the early days of the garrison was meant not so much for the entertainment of the troops as it was to mask the screams of torture victims within the pits. Of those who had been incarcerated within its gates, rumors persisted—no one had ever come out of the compound alive. Others told how the sounds of trucks moving up the road after midnight were those carrying the bodies of the peasant victims to clandestine graves said to dot the slopes of the Volcan Tolimán.

In the beginning, that is to say, for about the first three months after the fence had been completed and the central buildings erected, no Felipino had been targeted for disappearance by the troops. But not long afterwards, the repression began to take its toll among the Felipinos themselves.

Perhaps it was because it was the first; perhaps it was the unique brutality, but the killings of Remigo Peolido and Lupe Sanchez Diaz sent a clear signal to other labor organizers and their fledgling union leadership: families would pay for the sins of their fathers and husbands. The civil defense patrols took courage from the army night raid, and the killings of the union organizer and his wife were followed by the two killings attributed to Miguel Mapa Xoy. The rationalization of his own brother's death was said to have had hardened "Pepe," the "killer beast," as he had come to be regarded by his tiny corp of operatives. Village reports of his involvement in the seizure of Don Pablo Poppe, the pepper merchant, had brought him his first record of accomplishment and acceptance within his unit. In fact, he had developed something a swagger in his gait which was irritating to superior officers.

Across the lake, however, María was experiencing a disturbing reaction from her neighbors. While many admired her privately for her courage in speaking up for the Felipinos against the military, they greatly feared the army's repercussions. Still others, however, had come to suspect her and her family of even more sinister relationships. Quite understandably, María might have denounced the military for their implicit involvement in the murders of Ana Fabiola and her little friends, but many Felipinos were frightened and angered by reports of Miguel Mapa in the service of a death squad. More than one Felipino claimed—anonymously, of course—that they had seen the same Miguel Mapa fleeing through the alleys the night that Don Poppe had disappeared. His mother's public denouncement, however, was something new for a woman in San Felipe, and because of her new-found activism, many of her closest friends and extended family had come to fear association with her. In one of those perverse turns within the life of a community, many other outspoken Felipinos had now shifted the blame for the entire military repression of the community to the diminutive, crippled María Xquic and her poor family. The unprecedented and growing declamations against the Xoy family, however, were symptomatic of the general diminishing stability within the Tzutujil community.

It was that very instability that Captain Villalobos was thinking about as he returned to his barracks after the long trip back. A green light from the colonel meant that within a matter of two or three weeks, the entire Lake District might be re-pacified. The thing was to find the one factor, the one lynch pin which, when extracted, would collapse the entire infrastructure of the town.

If he had learned anything from his training in the "School of the Americas," it was the value of what the Americans called "finesse." You had to be patient; you had to operate within a certain "window of opportunity," as the American commanding officer at the "School," Col. José Guttierez, had suggested. It was an international window with shutters that were sometimes open, at other times closed. When they were closed, an operator could do what he wanted without much fear of discovery and accountability. With them open, however, you operated under an international spotlight, and an agent had to watch it, to be careful, to move within an understood protocol. You could kill a few *campesinos* a day, maybe even a catechist or two, and shake off the repercussions. But with the international shutters open, you didn't take out a European or American priest or burn down another Spanish Embassy on a whim. At the moment, however, with the First World focused almost exclusively on events in Eastern Europe, the Guatemalan militaries could do what they felt like without too much fear of UN, OAS, or World Bank sanctions or reprisals, and according to the schedule of the captain, the next target was just another *campesino*: the *alcalde* of San Felipe.

Through the process of diminishing candidates, Don Alfonso Doq had finally outlived the other *alcaldes* of San Felipe. He now enjoyed the pre-eminence that came with such stature in a traditional community. As his health permitted, he would receive the citizens who daily filed past his home near the town plaza. From their meager returns, they would leave at his gate little tokens of respect and appreciation, an egg or piece of firewood, a spool of thread, or—although much more rarely—a live fowl or two.

In turn, Don Alfonso would offer his wisdom or advice, counsel that among the traditionals brought him the love and affection that someone like a foreign priest could only hope, in time, to garner within a community. Like the renowned Don Andres, Don Alfonso was a man of highly regarded spiritual gifts. While the former had been a seer, Don Alfonso's reputation was well established around the lake as a healer. People had come to San Felipe for more than five decades to receive his touch and prayers. It was said he could reverse the path of cold and warmth through the entire body. He could draw away excessive heat through a turkey egg placed at the top of the head, or he could warm another by rubbing an egg over patches of cold observable on the surface or even deeply within a person's body.

The Felipinos would never have anticipated an attack on Don Alfonso Doq any more than they could have foreseen the disruption that the seizure of such a leader could affect in a town. The disappearance of the *alcalde* would serve to throw the Indian hierarchy into complete disarray. Such a move on the part of the militaries, of course, had been clearly calculated. With the government among the traditionals interrupted, the evangelicals would be in a stronger position to increase their influence at a time when the Pentecostal fervor was still aflame. The *cofradia* infrastructure would be divided even wider, and the American priest himself would be increasingly isolated. It was the priest, of course, who was the real target, but taking him out independent of a clearly established context of counter-insurgency could provoke undesirable international attention at a critical time when the military seizure of the Lake District was essential to extending control throughout Sololá and north into El Quiché.

Captain Villalobos was confident, however, that the days of Father Jack and Catholic Action were numbered. Simply put, he would have already taken such independent action against the priest, but the cleric's days were registered according to some superior officer's calendar hanging probably in the National Palace.

But first things first: Captain Villalobos had his immediate orders to address. The arrest of Don Alfonso Doq was set for the next evening, and he was still awaiting the arrival of "Pepe," scheduled to arrive by helicopter from

Post #14 around noon. Captain Villalobos paced back and forth behind his desk as he listened to the whine of the helicopter engine and the "whump-whump-whump" of its rotors began to dissipate. He had yet to meet the already legendary "Pepe," the man who could rip out a human tongue with two fingers and flatten a subversive's head with a single blow.

"Come in," said Captain Villalobos at the first rapping against his door. He was surprised to find, instead of the towering "Pepe," his own attaché, Lieutenant Gomez, standing in the doorway wearing a look of urgency.

"Well, Lieutenant Gomez. Come in," repeated the captain.

"Thank you, Captain!" returned the Lieutenant. "I have a report that may be of importance to you just now—*now*, that is, before you speak with the guy from No. 14."

"Oh?" said Captain Villalobos. "Well, shut the door and come in."

The lieutenant closed the door behind him and took three steps toward his commanding officer.

"At ease, Lieutenant," offered the captain. "What do you have?"

"*Sir!*" said Lieutenant Gomez. "I got word from the new military commissioner of San Felipe—when you were gone yesterday—that María Xquic, the mother of "Pepe" and the wife of Andres Menchu Xoy, is making trouble in San Felipe. She gave a speech yesterday before members of her neighborhood denouncing the civil patrols and the arrest of her husband and the presence of all the troops in the community. But this is the first time she's ever done anything like this. The commissioner said she's had recent contact with the *EGP*. He said that the wife of "*Comandante* Lupe" talked with her and put her up to all this. That's all, Captain."

"Who else knows of this report, Lieutenant?" asked the captain.

"*Sir!*" said Lieutenant Gomez. "I think it's pretty well known to all the troops. I overheard the soldiers talking about it this morning."

"What do you think, Lieutenant?" asked the captain. "Are we looking at trouble in San Felipe?"

"I don't know, Captain," said the lieutenant.

"What is the disposition of the men?" asked the captain.

"They're nervous, Captain—the new recruits and all," said Lieutenant Gomez. "They know about the fight last month and about the killings of the guerrillas and all about what happened to the guerrilla leader. They know about his wife working in the area. They're pretty up for a round of their own. They don't understand why they weren't included in the action last month."

Captain Villalobos pulled the pencil from his shirt pocket and began striking it rhythmically across his left palm as he began to reflect on a new idea.

"Look, Lieutenant," said the captain. "I have this idea—look, I think I want you on this operation with Pepe tonight. I want you to watch him—see how he works, you know—and bring me a sense of the community. Hang around for a minute and join us in the briefing. Is Pepe out there? Is he ready?"

"I don't know, Captain," said Lieutenant Gomez.

"Well, why don't you sit down over there," said the captain, "and I'll get him in here."

The captain reached for the telephone receiver and called for a military policeman. Within moments, one was knocking at his door.

"Yes, Captain!" said the officer.

"Yes, Corporal," responded Captain Villalobos. "Bring in the guy in the black shirt outside."

"Yes, sir!" said the corporal as he exited, pulling the door behind him.

"Lieutenant Gomez," said the captain. "How will these recruits do in a fight? Do they have enough discipline?"

"I think so, Captain," offered the lieutenant. "They all say they want to fight. All of them have been in some action in the past eight months, but they don't like being holed up all the time in the garrison. They like the patrol duty in the village."

"Well, let me just ask it right out," said the captain. "Will any of them refuse to fire on civilians in San Felipe?"

"*No,* Captain!" returned the lieutenant. "Of *course* not! I can guarantee that. They're just *itching* for the moment, Captain."

"Well, we'll see. It'll probably come to that, the way things are going, I suspect," reflected Captain Villalobos. "I guess we'll see soon enough."

Both of the officers heard footsteps and voices approaching the office door, and they turned to receive the notorious "Pepe." Moments later, the giant of a killer was standing within their midst.

"So, this is the big man of *San Felipe!* Sit *down!"* said Captain Villalobos to both Pepe and Lieutenant Gomez. "Sit down, and let me go over tonight's operation with you."

The captain turned to the hit man and began relating his new idea.

"Pepe," said the captain, confident in the man's full attention. "I've asked the lieutenant to accompany you tonight. He needs the experience, and he understands how important it is to help us here. I have every confidence in him, and I know I can count on both of you. Now, get this: this whole thing is going to be strictly a civilian operation. The army has nothing to do with it.

That's got to be clear from the top, *okay?* So, here's how I think you ought to make this arrest."

The captain related the background of subversive activity over the past few weeks reported in and around San Felipe del Lago, but he decided not to relate the information about Pepe's mother's denouncement and her probable collaboration with the *EGP*. He didn't want anything to compromise his team's attention to the *alcalde* and the mission at hand. There would be time later for this other matter.

"Take one of the Cherokees into San Felipe tonight," explained the captain. "Park it about a block or so behind the tailor shop. That's about a block and a half from the old *alcalde's* house. He usually sits at his doorway to greet all the old drunks as they're wobbling home. Hang around the bar at the end of the block, or you can just sit in the van. Anyway, wait until you're satisfied he's about ready to turn in and its dark. We've already put out the street light this morning, so it ought to be real easy to drag the old man away unnoticed. You probably ought to secure him in the house, and then one of you go back up the alley for the van. You can be in and out in five minutes easy. Now, whatever you do, don't screw *around!* Get him back to the base right away."

Then Captain Villalobos added his own twist to the scenario.

"Now, listen carefully," he advised. "If you run into any trouble *at all,* if you think you're discovered . . . if something—*anything!*—goes wrong with the old man . . . if you get caught in a jam in the *streets!* I mean, if *anything at all* goes wrong, *don't come back to the garrison!* Take the truck back to the road and head all the way back to the Post. You got it?"

"*Yes,* Captain!" said Lieutenant Gomez. Pepe rose and shook the captain's hand, confident in the success of his previous assignment in dispatching the pepper merchant.

"I think we've got it, Captain," reiterated Pepe.

The Indian giant was something of a celebrity among the conscripts at the San Felipe garrison. Throughout the afternoon, the troops, many of them indigenous themselves, sought opportunities to steal a glimpse of the notorious hit man. Privately, however, the enlisted *Ladinos* resented the Felipino's popularity. Each felt his breeding, education, and training placed him far above and apart from this Indian's world, that the only element they all shared was a commitment to the same hierarchy of power. "Pepe" was nothing more to these enlisted men than a tool, like a hammer, a gun, a garotte, or like a well sharpened knife. Any bravado by a local paramilitary was out of line in a well-disciplined army unit. Any misdirected allegiance by the troops for anything other than the authority of rank was treasonous. The enlisted ranks had reason to fear this "Pepe," not so much for his legendary prowess as it was his potential threat to stability and discipline, any breech of which could compromise the very ends they were pledged to serve.

Pepe stayed within the compound out of sight for most of the day, following the usual operational procedures before a pick up. He spent the afternoon hours working out, exercising in the small barracks dormitory, doing push-ups, sit-ups, and running in place. He took pride in his physique and even more in his new-found brotherhood. For the first time, he was beginning to identify with "Pepe" and no longer with "Miguel Mapa," eldest son of a stupid *brujo*. He was developing his own *curriculum vita*, a resume which was beginning to give him once again that cocky, self-assurance he thought he'd lost forever, a sense of pride now tempered by the pervasive, institutional arrogance of the army affirmed in certain looks of respect or approval, not to mention a growing array of small perks. Each duty performed, each order served left him feeling more and more a sense of belonging to something larger than himself, but with increasing concern, he was beginning to sense his place in a social system over which he had no control. For the first time, his traditional roots had become embarrassing. Now, only "duty" and "service" had any meaning for him, and he was growing more and more confident in his commitment and resolve to both.

As dusk settled, thousands of little lights began to flicker on across the lake. The western sky over their shoulders, awash in crimson and gold, was hastened on by the wall of blackness that pushed across the lake from the east, as the rim of the sun dropped below the horizon. The air was still, now that the afternoon winds had calmed. In the garrison, two men stepped inside a dark-blue Cherokee land rover, fired the ignition, and moved cautiously toward the gate. Soldiers at the guard station unlocked the twelve-foot high fenced gates and swung them open to allow the vehicle to pass. The land rover exited the gate, paused for a moment at the intersection of the road, then turned left and began a slow crawl toward San Felipe, usually only about ten minutes away. Tonight, however, ground fog was beginning to set in, and the short journey would be more uncertain.

Half way between the garrison and the community of San Felipe, the Cherokee stopped at the old guard station, an abandoned outpost of the National Police that had been erected more than thirty years before during the Castillo Armas era as a check point against communist subversion around the lake. Lieutenant Gomez stopped the vehicle momentarily to communicate with the garrison about their progress toward the town. After a minute or two, the vehicle moved back out onto the road and continued on its way.

Clouds rolled down from the peaks of the volcanoes and were drifting in steely fingers through the pine breaks, obscuring the roadway stretching out before the Cherokee. Pepe and the Lieutenant strained to pick out the ruts crisscrossing in front of them. Unable to anticipate the slips and holes, they lurched and bounced along.

"God-*damn!*" said Pepe as his head struck hard against the ceiling of the vehicle. "That hurt like *shit!* Take it *easy*, man!"

The car engine died as the Cherokee bottomed out in a particularly deep rut. Lieutenant Gomez started the engine again and jammed the transmission into reverse, but the front wheel refused to crest the trench that had all but swallowed the front right tire.

"Wait a minute," said Pepe. "Let me get out and give it a nudge." He tried to open the door but found he could swing it only a few inches before it jammed against the roadbed.

"Move out, Lieutenant," ordered Pepe. "Move out, and I'll give it a little lift."

The officer opened his door and stepped out. Pepe maneuvered over the console and the gear shift and piled out behind the lieutenant.

"Okay," said Pepe. "Wait until I get in place, and then gun the *shit* out of it!"

The Felipino walked to the front of the car and assumed a squatting position over the bumper. He placed his massive hands under the bumper and set his shoulders.

"All right!" he said.

Lieutenant Gomez turned the ignition key, and the engine fired. As he felt the gear slip into reverse, Pepe strained upward, lifting the front end of the vehicle about five inches. Instantly, the tread of the wheel caught against the wall of the rut, and the Cherokee lurched backwards, shooting a stream of sand and gravel over Pepe's head.

The Indian turned away from the rain of dirt and grit, wiping his eyes against his shoulder.

"Sonofa*bitch!*" he shouted. "God-*damn!*"

Pepe stood up to brush away the remaining dirt clinging to his jacket and pants and shook his head, raking his hands through his thick black hair.

Even a few feet away, the Cherokee looked ghostly as it was engulfed in a pillow of undulating fog. Gingerly feeling his way along, Pepe returned to the vehicle, and once again they began the precarious trip along the next two kilometers into San Felipe.

As the car turned around the final bend in the road, the muted lights of the town danced and flickered in the fog which was now beginning slowly to dissipate. The two-man squad entered San Felipe from the southwest, avoiding the main street for the first alley. The rock-strewn passage was used typically by the truck traffic heading for the market, and the sound of the Cherokee would mean little to people accustomed to occasional rumblings of trucks throughout the late nights and early mornings.

Lieutenant Gomez dimmed the head lamps and drove hesitantly, pausing at every corner for any unexpected vehicles approaching the intersections left or right. One block up, a battered Toyota pickup truck choked and sputtered as it turned in front of them. A shirtless teenage boy sat in the rear helping to balance an unfinished chest of drawers. With a howl followed by an unrelenting stream of vicious, angry barks, a feisty, homeless terrier erupted from its sleep on the sidewalk and raced beside the rear tire of the Toyoto as it crept along over the bumpy cobblestone pavement. The Felipino boy yelled an expletive over the side of the truck as the rumpled dog finally gave up the chase in deference to some diversion in the gutter.

Lieutenant Gomez had pulled to the side of the street and turned off the parking lights while the truck continued on its way now several blocks beyond them. Two young lovers stood just inside a doorway, too absorbed in each other to notice much else in the night. The heavy fog had now completely dissipated, and a full moon rose over the plaza of San Felipe only two blocks further to their left.

"Let's make a pass around the corner and see if the old man's still out there," said Lieutenant Gomez.

"Right," said Pepe, and he reached into his jacket to reset his shoulder holster and the old United States Army issue .45 caliber automatic pistol. "If you go up two blocks, there's no doorway facing our direction for at least a half block, and we can park at the corner. There's just the tailor shop on the left. It'll be locked up. The only action will be the old farts at the *tienda* one block away around the corner to the left. There's nothing open to the right, so we can get to the old man quick and have him out before anyone knows anything."

"That sounds good," said Gomez, more reassured, and he maneuvered the car slowly up to the corner, turned right, and rolled to a halt only a half block from the house of Don Alfonso Doq. The lieutenant turned off the ignition and retrieved the keys, placing them deeply into the right pocket of his jacket. Like Pepe, he reached into his left side and readjusted his pistol, a 9mm Glock imported from Austria by way of Israel. He liked the Glock, preferred it over the Beretta, its Italian counterpart. With the Beretta, he felt he had better control over his pattern in practice rounds at the shooting range.

The two men looked forward and backwards, up and down the street. The immediate vicinity was quiet and tranquil. Carefully, but naturally, the lieutenant and his fellow agent opened their doors and stepped out of the Cherokee. Instinctively, they tugged downward on the front of their light jackets and crossed over to the opposite side of the street. The lieutenant reached into his shirt pocket for a cigarette, and Pepe lit it with his plastic butane lighter. The pause gave them both another few moments to reconnoiter from a more exposed position now that they were on the street.

"Let's go," said the lieutenant. At once they turned up the street and walked comfortably, adopting a smile now, affecting light but low conversation. Before they realized, they were only a few yards from the *alcalde's* home, and they could see the glow of a single, dim light bulb burning toward the rear of the compound.

"What do you think?" asked Pepe as the two paused no more than twenty feet from the old man's gate. "Should we walk on around like we said?"

"*No! Shit* no!" said Gomez. "Let's *take* the old bastard!"

"All *right!*" said Pepe.

At once, a rush of adrenalin shot through him, and he felt the now familiar swell of excitement. All his muscles began to tense. He felt the power pulse in the sinews of his arms. His hands tightened and began to perspire.

Lieutenant Gomez made one quick glance again left and right, and satisfied that they were still unobserved, growled sternly, "Let's *do* it!"

Pepe reached inside his coat pocket and retrieved his pistol, cocking it as he skipped over the old man's stone threshold. In four quick steps he was inside the three-room concrete block house, right on the heels of the lieutenant.

The light from the rear of the compound radiated across a tiny interior courtyard no more than sixty feet deep and forty feet across. Don Alfonso and his wife were at the rear wall feeding the hens and turkeys as the two men stepped before them.

"Don Alfonso!" cried the lieutenant in an almost muted order.

Surprised by the intrusion, the old man and his wife turned to face the two figures in their black jackets and khaki pants standing just inside the yard.

"Yes, what is it?" asked the old man, still unaware of the harrowing import of their mission. Just then, his wife, Doña Lucía Elena spied the gun in Pepe's hand.

"Oh, my God!" she cried. "Oh, my God! Are we dead?"

Pepe and the lieutenant were now at their sides. With one shove, the Indian sent the old woman sprawling on her face into the garbage heap, the hens and turkeys screeching and wings a flutter as they tried to dodge the falling woman. Immediately, two dogs, jolted from their early sleep in back of the adjoining pharmacy, sent up a livid howl.

"Hurry up," said the lieutenant. "Let's get this over with."

Stunned almost senseless, Doña Lucía Elena dug deeply into the refuse about her as if to secure some handle for leverage. With that one shove, Pepe had severed ties of family friends who had known him for a lifetime. The good neighbor woman had accompanied him on his first day to the public school in San Felipe, the largest boy of his age. She had sat with him when pounding fever and the red, itchy scabs had almost taken his life two years later, and his young friends wondered how the strongest among them could have been brought so low. And now the pathetic old woman grovelled in the trash and tailings of their small garden, frightened beyond all comprehension.

"What do you want from us?" shouted Don Alfonso in a breathless, shaking voice. "Who are you? What do you want with us? What's this all about?"

Dogs up and down the street began to take up the cry.

"Shut up, *loco perro*!" cried a young girl more than a block away.

"What's going *on?*" cried a Felipino voice on the other side of the street.

Don Alfonso turned and spied his wife of more than forty years still lying prone in the garbage.

"Miguel Mapa *Xoy!* Menchu *Xoy!* What have you done?" he stammered as he recognized Pepe for the first time. "What are you doing to your own *family* and *town?* How is it you have become *this,* this . . . `*dog of Satan!'*"

Don Alfonso had picked up a planting staff to strike a blow for his wife, but was blocked by the giant Felipino who had turned squarely to receive the puny gesture of the *old alcalde.* Pepe simply grabbed him at the throat, twisted him around, and, like some brittle stalk of corn, flung the old man to the ground.

"*Quick!*" cried the lieutenant. "Tie his hands."

Pepe holstered his pistol and pulled a stretch of heavy cord from his left pocket. After only two quick wraps, the old man's hands were trussed behind him. With one hand, Pepe reached under the diminutive man's arm and pulled him up once more onto his feet.

"*Hurry!* Let's *go!*" cried the lieutenant.

All but dragging the old man behind him, Pepe stepped briskly across the compound toward the house. The lieutenant spun around behind them to make sure the old woman represented no threat. In fact, Doña Lucía Elena remained prone, sobbing almost incoherently the name of her husband as she lay face down in the spread of refuse and manure.

Outside the front of the house, Simon Lucero, the neighbor across the street, had run to his door, followed by his thirty-year old daughter, to address all the commotion. He flew open the top of his door just as Pepe and the lieutenant appeared on the street. His daughter Martita was the first to respond.

"*No! No!*" she cried in her shrill, soprano voice. "*Help!* Someone *help!* They're taking *Don Alfonso!* Someone *help!*"

"What's going on?" yelled Don Mercio Steinholder, the old German pharmacist who had been visiting his ailing friend in the adjoining house.

"*Quickly! Quickly!*" cried Martita. "They're taking *Don Alfonso!* Oh, *help* him! *Help* him!"

Within a moment, the whole neighborhood had been aroused in complete alarm. Pepe reached inside his coat with his free, left hand for the pistol, but in the melee the handle had turned around, and Pepe couldn't find the grip.

"*Forget the gun!*" cried the lieutenant. "No *shooting!* I've got the *key!* Just get the bastard to the *car!*"

Suddenly, Don Alfonso fainted dead away. His body went completely limp, and as they were passing over the threshold, the cuff of his pants caught on the head of an exposed nailhead just at the base of his front door frame.

"God-*damnit!"* cried Pepe, as he repositioned the old man under his bulging biceps and jerked him loose, ripping the *alcalde's* trousers and tearing a gash mid calf all the way down the outside of his leg to his ankle.

Just then he looked up to hear the old Toyoto pickup truck lumbering up the cobblestones toward the scene. Noticing the skirmish at the gate of Don Alfonso, the driver flashed on his bright headlights. When he realized what was happening, "Porky" Baedra lay on his horn. At the other end of the street, a group of teenage boys had turned the corner, kicking a soccer ball before them. Immediately, they set out a yell.

"Let him *go!*" they cried. "Get the hell *out* of here! *Murderers! Butchers! Murderers!* They're kidnapping our *alcalde*!"

Buoyed by the many witnesses around them, the soccer team began a full run toward the assailants, shouting obscenities as they came.

"Let him *go!*" cried the lieutenant, now brandishing his pistol before him. "Let the sonofabitch *go*, and let's get the hell *out* of here!"

Pepe dropped Don Alfonso to the paving stones at his feet and ran into the street to meet the young teenagers confronting them. As the first approached, he grabbed the school boy by his shirt, lifted him off his feet with one hand, and flung him against the curb.

"Out of my *way!*" cried Pepe, now seething with a fury that was exploding from his hands.

The rest of the team broke to let the giant by, shouting at the now discovered figure as he passed.

"That's *Miguel Mapa!*" someone yelled across the street.

"That's *him!*" cried another. "That's the *killer of San Felipe!*"

"*Murderer!*" barked the tailor. "Miguel Mapa kills his *own family!*"

The whole neighborhood for blocks around had been aroused, and Felipinos were pouring into the streets. Lieutenant Gomez and Pepe reached the Cherokee within seconds, knocking aside every person who got in their way. As he reached the driver's side, the nervous lieutenant fumbled and dropped the key which fell to the street below the tire. With his head ducked beneath his arm, Pepe stood helpless to the passenger side, waiting for the officer to release the lock, but it was too late.

By the time the lieutenant had finally engineered the key into the slot and had opened the door, a jeering, angry crowd of neighbors was gathering about the van. Instantly, Pepe piled inside the vehicle as Gomez fired the ignition. Never bothering to find the lights, the officer gunned the car and headed straight down the middle of the street. Incredulous at the sudden attack in their restful evening and not yet fully awakened to the awful target of the assault, the Felipinos fled for the security of the sidewalk as the Cherokee sped to the corner, turned left toward the western exit of the town, and raced away in the direction of the garrison.

Lights continued to blink on throughout San Felipe. Up and down the streets, animals set out a chorus to match the Felipinos' clamor that drove the demon killers from their midst. All at once, the bell of the Catholic Church began to peel in shocking reverberations. In less than five minutes after the aborted attack, much of the town had entered the streets and began pouring, as if by instinct, toward the plaza and the church.

In swollen anguish before her tiny, makeshift altar of candles and rose petals, María Xquic turned suddenly at the commotion that echoed up the hill, and she gathered her shawl tightly at her throat.

"*Andres?*" she cried. "Could it be that my husband has come *home?*"

For the past five hours, she had sat at the hearth locked in panic. María had expected Andres the night before and all that day. She had sent little Manuel throughout the town three times to seek his father, but he had returned each time in tears.

"What else could it be?" the poor woman asked, locked within the narrow corridor of her mindless grief. She rose suddenly, almost losing her balance as her crippled ankle started to give way beneath her, but she was able to brace herself against the cool hearthstone. Her wretched foot was numb from the angle she had been sitting, and she lurched toward the door of her house.

"I have to *go!*" she cried. "I have to go down and meet my *husband!*"

Her grief had driven her almost mad, relieved only now with expectation. Slowly, the circulation had returned to her deformed ankle and foot, and María steadied her balance as she maneuvered precariously down the trail toward the growing crowd of Felipinos. She stepped carefully onto the sidewalk as her own path met the head end of the street. She grabbed at and held on to the top of a pickup truck parked at the curb, the first vehicle she came to.

"Did they not welcome Jesucristo with palms upon his return?" she thought. "And will they not bring me my husband with songs and the throats of paradise?"

María was beside herself with swelling joy as she stepped into the light of the street. She had released all lingering grief and fear in the anticipation of her poor husband's embrace, and she turned, peering left and right to catch the flow from where he would be coming.

"My husband, Don Andres?" she cried weakly. "Which way does he come?"

"Your husband, and maybe that *`dog of satan'* that nursed at your *tit!"* cried old Colata Toj, the weaver merchant. "Maybe they come from *hell together!*"

Chapter 26

Into the Night

María Xquic de Xoy was afraid of the priest and withdrew from the presence of the otherwise kindly American. She knew nothing of "America," and Father Jack—like "America"—was something mysterious and disturbing. María was equally leery, if not afraid, of the evangelicals who were posturing for recognition and influence among the indigenous of San Felipe. Her husband was greatly worried by the growing friction between the two religious bodies, and especially by suggestions that the San Felipe "traditionals" were "demon-bound" and "Satanic." Scurrilous rumors were drifting throughout the community—and with effect. Longtime family friends who had begun attending evangelical circles were dodging the Xoy family, and some of the children had started to laugh at little Manuel.

"Your daddy is just a crazy *brujo*! *Loco! Loco! Loco!*" And "Manuel Xoy is going to *hell!*" the older girls would say, teasing the little water bearer, sending the child in a tearful retreat from the school yard.

Almost daily, Manuel Xoy came home silently, slipping quickly out of his mother's sight to seek his cat among the rows of corn, or grabbing the plastic water pitcher to pursue his errands before she could see his swollen eyes. Manuel Xoy, however, wasn't the only member of the family suffering attack in the community.

Don Andres himself had noticed the changes sweeping through San Felipe. They were registered in little ways—the hollow glances, the feigned greetings from former patients, the deliberate crossings of acquaintances to the opposite side of the street to avoid the traditional homages paid to the wise ones. And then there were the open smirks by the proud converts among the evangelicals, some who would even point out the *jefe principal* as a heretic, or others who would laugh at the antiquated fool. The lines were drawn, and the situation tense. Any incident could spark conflict that might irrevocably divide and devastate the once peaceful community.

All of the leaders—the *ladinos* and the indigenous—of the community were nervous. Father Jack continued to orchestrate a frenetic schedule of activities designed to present a positive, activist image among the Felipinos, hoping to appeal to the younger adults who had been abandoning the Church for more than two generations. The priest started a drive to support young mothers with pre-natal care, developed a small distribution center for first aid care and milk, and organized additional literacy classes for women.

The evangelicals, divided between two Pentecostal churches and the old-line *ladino* Presbyterian congregation, had attracted more than 600 Felipinos, enthusiastic converts who preened themselves in the rarefied arena of a newly discovered international forum. Many had been bussed in to the capital to attend the Kingdom Throne Crusades and had been overwhelmed by the thousands of people who attended. They had stood side by side both fellow *campesinos* from throughout the country as well as apparently some of the wealthiest, most influential among the *ladinos* and their supporters within the military who sat in full, military dress in special sections set off for them near the platform. The traditionalists, led by Don Andres Menchu and the *Cofradia of Santa Cruz*, were clearly on the defensive, caught between the tightening vice of the Christian faithful on both sides—and all three groups under the watchful eye of the army.

The final "arbiter" between the two increasingly zealous sects and any other factions of San Felipe, of course, was the army. It was clear to both the Catholics and the Protestant factions that they were being played against each other by a military that appeared, more and more, to be siding with the most extreme among the evangelical sects. President Bustamante's own evangelical membership had fuelled anti-Catholic sentiment throughout the highlands, and even if the multimillion-dollar goal of North American donations had come up short, the visibility of the Kingdom Throne Crusades and publicity before a national United States audience had secured the confidence of the military power brokers behind the Presidential throne.

The rationale for evangelical support of the Guatemalan military was, ironically, theological. The enthusiastic, emotional clergy of charismatic evangelicalism preached fixation on one's after-life. Catholicism, on the other hand, had redefined its role in support of the world's poor and the disenfranchised and had placed itself in direct confrontation with traditional seats of power throughout Latin America. Catholicism had reversed an almost 500-year-old posture that in its politics had always stood guard ceremonially, if not functionally, behind the power structure. Traditionally in Latin America, behind every ascending general had stood a bishop ever so quick to anoint him, both in place and deed. In 1968, the meeting of the Latin American bishops in

Medellín, however, changed all that.

Vatican II, the first thorough-going review and reformation of Catholicism in a century, sowed the seeds of radical revolution within the church. Those seeds sprouted in Brazil, Peru, Colombia, and finally throughout all of Latin America. When Pope John XXIII charged the Church to address its role among the impoverished of the world, in Latin America, the distressed among the clergy—who long had identified with their parishioners—redefined the entire mission of the Church. From the Counter Reformation dating to the Council of Trent in the 1540's to the ingratiation of the ineffectual Pope Pius XII before the maddened Hitler and Nazi atrocities, the purpose of the Church was clearly an intellectual reclamation and restoration of the faith among the world's literati and their princes. With Medellín, the purpose of the Holy Church had changed fundamentally, and its rejuvenated clergy, walking side by side their impoverished parishioners, had become, in fact, a phalanx repositioned to do battle against those former alliances which they now recognized as responsible for the dehumanization of the masses. As well as for its eschatology, the new mission of the Church was to be understood in the light of Christian salvation and its implications for life in the here and now.

So, Father Jack continued to work with his people, celebrating daily with them in their common labor, witnessing from within his historical vision of the church among those who could only see his presence among them, doing what they were doing and walking along beside them. Father Jack loved the Felipinos, and he couldn't abide being away from them for any more than a week or so. Trips back to Oklahoma to be with his family were always warm and restful, but within three or four days, he found himself thinking in Tzutujil (which he had all but mastered during his tenure) and speaking the language aloud when he was certain others were outside of hearing.

The priest's most recent returns to San Filipe, however, had left him perplexed. Father Jack found himself increasingly nervous, even fearful for his people. He could never predict any more what he might find as he walked from the landing beside the lake up the long, steep path, through the busy market, and on to his church.

"*Father, Father!*" pleaded Sister Noelia upon his return after the New Year. "They came for Tata Alfonso after you left, and he has never *returned.* We fear that he is *dead!*"

Father Jack had called a meeting of the *alcaldes* of the *Cofradia of Santa Lucía* with whom the respected, old man had labored throughout his weary life. No one knew anything for certain, of course, but some had reported that a large man, wearing civilian clothes and working with one of the soldiers from

Sololá, had been seen earlier in the day milling about the town, and that a large truck was heard lumbering away on the road above the city just an hour after sundown. It was the work of the military dressed in civilian clothes, they said. It was the business of a military death squad that had taken him away to a certain death. Father Jack had never seen or heard from the seventy-nine-year old man again during the past two years.

Then it was Mildred Tierrez Albanes who disappeared with her sister and tiny niece. Then Amalcar Bañez, the teacher from the capital, who was dispatched by a burst of gunfire while working under the hood of the priest's jeep. Six months later, Father Niño de Rivera had had to leave under threat of death after a note and a black rubber glove filled with dung had been tacked to his altar only three months earlier. These were difficult times, and Father Jack sensed some kind of quickening in the expressions of his parishioners that seemed ominous to him.

And then it happened. On the day before Father Jack's most recent return, Don Andres Menchu Xoy, the old shaman of the *Maximón*, "was disappeared" into the night.

"They took him, Father," said Raul Pelax excitedly. He had run up to the priest just as Father Jack had approached the gate late in the evening of his return.

"They tore the place up," explained the young Felipino, his hat in hand as a gesture of respect as he spewed out the rough outline of the seizure to the priest. Two other young teenage boys, dressed in the traditional Felipino pants and dirty western cotton shirts, came running up to help their friend relate the story.

"His table, *Santa Mesa*, was broken up . . . scattered in pieces all around the room!" hastened Juanmanuel Tobias.

". . . the mixes, the holy things, his candles!" interrupted Claudio Sanchez, "They were all broken. There must have been a big *fight!*"

"And María?" asked Father Jack. "How is María? Was she there? Did she see anything?"

"No . . . well, I don't know, Father," said Claudio.

"No, she wasn't *there!*" said Juanmanuel. "She was away. She came home later and found the house all tore *up!* That's why I know she wasn't there. She came later and saw the house all tore up and all."

"Where was Lucita—what's her name? *Lucita—?*" asked the priest.

"`Lucita *María,*'" volunteered Raul, not to be lost in the conversation.

"`Lucita,' `Lucita María,'" echoed his two friends.

"Yes," said Father Jack, "and Lucita María wasn't there, either?"

"No, Father," said Juanmanuel. "They *killed* her along with Sister Juliana at the convent. They strangled Sister Juliana. Then they raped and *crucified* Lucita María in front of the *convent!"*

"Oh, my God!" cried the priest. *"That's insane! Just insane!"*

The boys stood motionless before the priest, having relinquished the most exciting news they could bring. They watched in surprise, however, as tears began streaming down the grown man's face, and their enthusiasm for their role as messengers suddenly dissipated.

"That's *incredible!*" said the priest. "Well, thank you, boys. Thank you very much. You've been a very big help. You all be careful going home, and *boys* . . ." he admonished them. "Go with *God!*"

"Thank you, Father," said Raul.

"Yes, thank you, Father Jack," said Juanmanuel, as the boys crossed themselves and tore away from the priest in the direction of the Xoy house far above the church against the hills pacing up the flank of Volcán Toliman.

How could it *be?* How could such a tragedy strike *again?* "And such blows to a single *family!*" thought the priest. "First the sons; then the daughter; and now, María's husband, the shaman himself."

He would have to go to her quickly. Although in all the years of his service to the Felipinos he hadn't held a single conversation with Maria Xquic de Xoy, it wouldn't be appropriate to miss her at a time like this, even on this first evening of his return.

Father Jack watched the three young boys race away across the open plaza and disappear beyond the perimeter of the single street light on the corner of the square and its intersection with the street, hardly more than an alley which wound across the town and down toward the military post a mile or so away. For a moment all was quiet, almost unnaturally still. The sound of the muffled crush of his shoes against the dusty, concrete pavement blocks beneath him were all that the priest could hear as he picked up his pack and old, weathered suitcase and trudged through the gate and across the church courtyard toward his quarters.

At the gate to his compound, Father Jack set down his luggage once more and reached for the key ring hanging from his belt. He never needed to look at the ring itself to find the key to the compound. Confidently, he fumbled through the keys, feeling for the shortest one with the rounded head, always on the end of the key ring next to the clasp of the flat, jadeite carving of the Maya head which always secured the key chain between his waistband and belt. His fingers and thumb easily isolated the small key and flipped it over to fit it into the lock of the heavy wooden door. Just as he turned the lock and released the bolt, Father Jack became aware of a presence that had moved up behind him.

Instinctively, the priest lurched to the left, falling away from the figure that had taken him so off guard, and tripping over his bags, he tumbled to the ground at the base of the gate. The figure gasped audibly behind him and jumped backwards to avoid the priest careening away from the surprising intrusion. Father Jack grabbed the handle of his suitcase and swung the bag in front of him, bracing himself to deflect any blow aimed either at his head or chest. As he was able to focus more clearly on the figure on the ground beside him, the priest caught his breath and released the suitcase, which slipped off his lap, and he moved to assist the slight, frightened figure lying in a small heap across from him.

Father Jack managed to stand up and took a step toward a diminutive woman, obviously embarrassed by the panic she had brought the priest. He reached down and offered his hand to the woman, careful not to assume to touch an Indian woman out of deference to her own customs. Somewhat hesitantly, she took his hand, and Father Jack helped her to her feet. As she found her balance, the Indian woman readjusted her *tzute* over her head, pulled it back around her hairline, and secured it below her chin with her tight little fist.

"*María!*" whispered the priest, obviously surprised in his recognition. This was the first time that the wife of Don Andres Menchu had ever approached him directly during all the years that he had served the people of San Felipe. Shaken by the confusion that she had caused, the Tzutujil woman looked down at the ground at the Father's astonished exclamation.

"I'm *sorry*, María!" said the priest. "I just didn't know who you were there behind me. I wasn't expecting you."

The priest spoke in disarmingly confident Tzutujil Mayan, relieving his ward of her initial anxiety.

María Xquic de Xoy tightened her grip on her *tzute*, continuing to stare into the pavement below. She would wait politely for the priest to invite her to speak before she dared to reveal her story.

"María," said Father Jack. "Come into the church where we can have some privacy." He withdrew the keys from the door and motioned toward the front of the church.

Father Jack knew it would be inappropriate for the woman to enter the private quarters of a priest, even though the front of the church was a long walk around. He turned to take the lead, well aware that it would be her place to follow behind. They moved into the shadow of the high wall surrounding the priest's compound and ambled to the corner, turned left into the plaza, and passed toward the front gate.

"I think I know why you are here, María," said the priest as he opened the door to the reception room just off the main sanctuary of the colonial church. María stepped in front of the priest for the first time as he motioned her to enter ahead of him. Beginning to tremble now, she turned toward her host and waited again to be asked to sit.

"Please sit down, sister, and tell me what has happened," said Father Jack. María stared into her *tzute* which covered her sweating, trembling hands.

"*María, look* at me!" commanded the priest, now beginning to take more control so that the distraught woman might be able to find her voice. "*Tell* me, María! I have heard about your husband . . . your husband, Don Andres! You are here to tell me about the disappearance of your husband, right?"

Never raising her eyes, the poor woman nodded only once.

"Today? Yesterday? When did it happen, María?" asked Father Jack.

María nodded once.

"Today?" asked the priest again, seeking clarification.

The woman shook her head.

"Yesterday?" . . . "It was yesterday!" said the priest, acknowledging the Indian's response.

"And you . . . sister, he just disappeared? Do you know anything at all about his disappearance?" asked Father Jack.

María sat inconsolable, obviously incapable of conversation. She shook her head again.

For a moment longer, Father Jack looked silently at María and then moved in front of her, pulling his chair up from behind. He reached over to her lap and gently took her hands into his own.

"María, I promise you that I will do everything that I can to help you find your husband. Do you understand me? . . . María, *look* at me!" commanded the priest. "I will do *everything* that I can to help you find your husband! You *must* believe me!"

The priest knew the import of such a meeting with a person so deeply involved among the traditionals, a community he had tried to influence for many years now. If he could help María in this awful time, he might win other supporters for the mission of the Church. María Xquic de Xoy looked deeply into the eyes of Father Jack, relinquishing all hope into his hands and then collapsing in long, anguished sobs against their entwined hands.

"How long, *Oh, Lord*! must these people have to suffer?" raised Father Jack in an almost forgotten English.

"See this woman, Lord," continued the priest—once more in Tzutujil—

"and comfort her in this desperate time. Seek out her husband, Lord, and hold him safely from all harm, and bring this man, your servant, Father, into the loving arms of his loved one before us here tonight."

María sighed deeply and seemed to take comfort in the familiar words. Father Jack stood up slowly, drawing María up with only the slightest touch to her shoulder.

"I am your *brother*, my sister," said the priest. "I am your *brother,* María." Father Jack looked into her eyes reassuringly, and then, reaching up with his thumb, the strange, mysterious American placed his nail just above the center of her forehead, drew a thin, faint line downward about an inch to a point between her eyes, and then crossed it with another light stroke from left to right, completing the sign of the cross and asking the blessing of the Virgin to preserve and protect the small, vulnerable woman.

For more than a week, Father Jack divided his time between his various administrative duties for the projects and a tireless search for any information about Don Andres. He followed every lead. Once, he even took the *ruletero* around the lake to visit a shaman who reported having envisioned Don Andres on a hillside overlooking a certain crossroad. Father Jack had paid the shaman with the prescribed contribution of candles and *aguardiente* for his service. He had long since learned to practice respect for the patterns if not the implications of traditional ritual among the indigenous. He had sat patiently through the complicated divination at the sacred table and had heard the name of Jesus conjured among the pantheon of Mayan deities and their various natural manifestations.

Father Jack had followed meticulously every direction of the traditional priest, his Cakchiquel peer. He had taken the launch to a point at the far southeastern end of the lake and had climbed up the steep paths that zigzag through the *milpas* up the eastern slopes of *Volcán* Tolimán. For more than three hours, the priest scanned the hills around him, the tree line far up the volcano above the corn fields, and peered back and forth over the trails that crisscrossed below him. Nothing of the Felipino materialized, and Father Jack left his post, frustrated at the futility of listening to "those damned shamans."

The most difficult thing for Father Jack was the hike up the trail from the plaza to the humble house of María where he had to confront the distraught woman with more bad news—his failure, time and time again, to turn up even a shred of hope for Don Andres's return. On each visit, María would sit quietly, without a stir, staring at the floor or into the burning embers of the fire in the hearth, or twirl the balls of rolled yarn at the frayed ends of her *tzute*, listening to the pained explanation of the priest who could keep only the spirit but nothing of the substance of his promise to her. After finishing his strained explanation, Father Jack would rise, wait for something of a response from the woman, and—receiving nothing—quietly but quickly take his leave. He didn't want his own presence to add more than what might be necessary to the poor woman's anxiety, for there was simply nothing more that he could do.

The good priest's anxieties were amplified by growing disquiet around the lake. The military presence was becoming insufferable. More than fifty soldiers bivouacked now every night at the small garrison that they had erected just three years before less than a mile away. Words were being exchanged throughout the market—*angry words*—and Father Jack feared the worst. If the worst came, it might be sparked by plans overheard to build a weapons depot at either San Felipe or San Pachula just five kilometers away. In either case, if that happened, the military presence in San Felipe would soar, since the village lay at the crossroads of commerce on the south side of Lake Atitlán.

What chilled the priest even more were the sacrificial claims of several young hotheads who had apparently circulated in some circles that they didn't care what the military might think or do. They were fed up, and if the people needed an occasion to trigger a rise against the army, they would be happy to comply. They weren't guerrilla factions, he didn't think, but when word leaked back across the lake to the military post, the whole town would suffer from whatever wretched squad down at the local garrison would receive the orders.

What the priest couldn't know was that San Felipe had been singled out as the location for such a flashpoint already. There would be no weapons depot at San Felipe, San Pachula, or at any other village around the lake. The guerrillas were committed to fight such a move and had decided to make a stand between Base 14, the home of the *Bruceros*, and Los Encuentros. They would attack any shipment that came into the Lake District, and they had already learned from informants in the capital that the first shipment of military hardware was slated to move from the Military Polytechnic to Base 14, a shipment of perhaps as many as 250 M16-A2 automatic rifles already received from the United States.

The plan had been drawn up hastily after confirmation of the shipment. Lupe's squad would be enhanced by at least one battalion that would arrive just two days before the scheduled shipment. The San Marcos battalion would remain in the hills overlooking the Sololá highway until given the word. Then they would sweep down the mountainsides and commandeer the highway, closing off all out-bound traffic from the lake. They would establish their site of attack at the narrowest point of the valley, relying on the steep, rocky crevices on the facing slopes for their cover from air strikes. When the trucks arrived, they would seal off the Pan American highway just south of Los Encuentros at the intersection of the Quetzaltenango/Sololá forks.

María Paloma was already preparing to join her husband's contingent and move into the hills when word came of the disappearance of the Sololá shaman.

When she learned of the news, María Paloma consulted with Lupe. What a perfect time for her to move into San Felipe across the lake. The attack would mask her movements like a diversion. They couldn't have anticipated the opportunity or planned one any better. It was agreed that she would move quickly down the highway to the lake. If she could make contact with the GAM in Sololá, she might even enlist the support of that more moderate faction that could be useful to them in the future. She might influence María Xquic to seek support through GAM. The victimized Tzutjujil had spoken out publicly before, and with these latest attacks, she might be ready to cross over. A strong spokesperson on the south rim of the lake would help seed the subversion they had already planned for San Felipe. She would attempt to persuade the wife of the shaman to become a voice for *"Madres de la Represión"* in San Felipe de Lago.

María Paloma gathered a small bundle of clothing including a San Felipe outfit. For the moment, however, she dressed in a traditional *traje* of Sololá and took a late afternoon bus from Los Encuentros to the lake. She would talk with the Father Juan Pablo Ortíz, Bishop of Sololá, her confidante for more than two years, and with "Piti" Ochoa Martinez, the local director of the *MR*, the "Mothers of the Repression," on the north side of the lake.

María Paloma had made plans to arrive on the evening before market day so that on the next morning she might mingle more easily with the large crowd and avoid standing out. She draped her *tzute* lightly over her head and took a seat near the rear of the bus. With its stops along the way, it would take the bus more than an hour to complete the route to Sololá. There was only one critical point on the route down to the lake. That was the *Bruceros* military district and post just two miles before the entrance to Sololá. Of course, María carried no *cedula*, and if the bus should be stopped—as it often was at the military check points—she could be detained for questioning, and she knew exactly what that would mean for any young woman, let alone a *ladino* in disguise. If any of the soldiers recognized her from San Felipe or even suspicioned her relationship with the attack on *"El Pesado,"* María Paloma knew that she would be brutally tortured and killed. This trip to San Felipe, then, was no small matter, but the chance to engage the wife of an *indigena* so well placed as Don Andres Menchu—at this most vulnerable moment in her life—was an opportunity that was worth some risk for the larger interests of the *EGP* and the popular revolution.

The bus stopped every mile or so to take on new passengers, most of them women and their small, ragged children on the way home, but others on the way to Sololá to make early preparations for market the next day. Throughout the cold night, they would sleep in small groups huddled together on the sidewalks near the plaza. Before dawn, they would be up, erecting the poles and tarpaulins over the rented space assigned to them for their respective stalls.

As the bus continued to stop for passengers, the aisle filled quickly with jostling children and their mothers trying to balance bundles of produce and personal belongings on their heads. The vehicle rambled along, missing none of the ruts and potholes that pocked the weathered, two-lane highway. Somewhere up the aisle and under one of the bench seats, a small child erupted in wails. Moments later, it gagged and vomited. In the tight quarters, the stench drifted quickly throughout the cabin of the bus.

Even without the putrefied smell, the rough highway and sharp cutbacks through the mountain passes made the trip tedious and uncomfortable. Nevertheless, there was only that one portion of the journey that María dreaded. That was the smooth glide down the highway that approached the Military Post #14. The passengers swung from side to side as the bus rounded the curves that entered the valley. After more than ten miles of winding pavement, the highway entered a straightaway for more than a mile before it turned sharply to the right in a course that would take it directly past the gate to the military compound. Along the stretch, tall cedars flanked both sides of the highway. The trunks of each cedar were painted white extending from the roots upward as high as six or seven feet off the ground. As the headlights of the bus flicked on to high beam, the trees took on a ghostly impression, appearing to hover a foot or more above the ground, intimidating the security of the vehicle as it passed through the small valley. For the first time, the air turned cool, and blasts of the fresh air rushed through the open windows, relieving some of the passengers' tension from being so cramped among the seats and aisle for so long.

The bus picked up speed as it raced along the road through the valley, but as it neared the end of the short run, the driver braked rapidly as he prepared to take the turn that would direct them to the check point at the military post. The bus slowed almost to a stop, turned abruptly to the right, and inched along to the first set of *tumulos*, the high, concrete traffic bumps that stretched across the road to assure compliance with the five-kilometer speed limit mandated by the military police.

As the bus chugged and lurched over the first set of *tumulos*, a small patrol of heavily armed *Bruceros* descended the hill from just under a concrete bunker and lookout constructed at the end of the wall of the compound. The soldiers carried Israeli automatic field rifles and long belts of ammunition over their shoulders. Their boots and pants seemed to be quite muddy and their gait disorganized and rushed as they stepped out of the shadows and resumed their hike along the roadside back to the post. Suddenly, as the driver down shifted and slowed the bus in its approach to the entrance of the compound, gasps went up from the passengers on the right side of the bus. Women and young girls—whose hands were free from the management and security of children or infants—covered their mouths and jerked their heads back in horror from the windows. Their terrified eyes quickly brightened and glistened with tears. Outside their windows they could see the still bodies of several men and boys, perhaps a dozen or more and all in the traditional *trajes* of Sololá, lying shoulder to shoulder against the gate of the post. Hoping to avoid distracting the soldiers from their notorious work, the women muffled their shock and pain as best they could, looking frantically at one another, almost suffocated with fright and anguish.

Apparently preoccupied with the removal of the bodies to some place inside the compound and obviously confounded and disturbed by the untimely arrival of the bus, the military police stepped aside and gestured wildly for the bus to move on. The bus lurched forward, bouncing heavily over the last set of *tumulos*. Cries erupted from the women as they moved into the deep shadows of the road well beyond the flood lights at the gates of the military compound. María was perhaps the only one on board relieved by the passage.

Past the post and its scene of massacre, the bus drove deeply into the night and resumed its winding course toward the lake. In a half hour that seemed to stretch to an eternity, the vehicle with its desperate passengers completed its route into Sololá, arriving at the central plaza in front of the great white colonial mission church, its facade shimmering in the cool moonlight. Immediately, the distraught women and their children poured from the bus, wailing as they scattered in every direction from the church and the parking lot. Lights popped on in the houses and shops near the plaza as the Indian women fled weeping and screaming up the blocks.

Within minutes, *Sololatecos* began amassing on the plaza. One hysterical woman shouted loudly, denouncing the military and crying out against the represssion of the town by the soldiers. Her cry was taken up by the waves of the protesters, brandishing their machetes and hoes, cursing the military, forced conscription into the civil defense patrols, and the unrelenting repression against their community.

María Paloma could not chance compromising her work and the objectives of the *EGP* by exposing herself to discovery in such a demonstration. As drawn as she was to the protest, she had to discipline herself, so, unlike many of the women who had returned to the plaza to join the protest, María had slipped away from the ensuing demonstration and sought the compound of the Bishop.

"What have you brought with you, María Paloma?" asked the Bishop as he carefully double-bolted the door behind her. The fifty-four-year old cleric never had to ask her if she had been careful making her way to his quarters or if she had been seen, any more than he ever mentioned the "movement" in which she was engaged. She had made late evening sojourns to his private quarters before—several times, to be sure. He had always found it in his best interest not to know too much about the *ORPA, EGP, FAR,* or the *URNG*; he would do what he could to support his parishioners, and that meant working with leaders of various "persuasions" committed to basic human rights for the *campesinos*.

"Father *Juan!*" exclaimed María. "The *ejército* has killed some of the men of *Sololá!* We passed them just now as we came in on the bus. The militaries had the bodies piled up just outside the gate of the post. The women are *hysterical*, Father! I am afraid what might *happen!*"

"Oh, *my!*" said the Bishop. "Perhaps I'd better go myself and see if I can calm some of them down. If they've been killing the men, it won't stop there if the rest of them get all riled up and march on the post or do something stupid like that. I'd better go see what I can do. You stay here, María. Don't open the door for *anyone! Okay?*"

Bishop Ortíz grabbed his coat, passed quickly from the room, crossed the patio, and ran toward the outer gate. He threw back the latches on the heavy, steel door of the gate and stepped out onto the sidewalk only to be almost knocked down by *Sololatecos* running in alarm toward the central plaza. He pulled his collar up around his neck to break the chill of the evening and moved into the flow of the crowd.

The Cakchiqueles of Sololá—the *ceballeros*, or the "onion growers, as they were called—were not new to the repression. Even before the guerrillas had begun operating around the perimeter of the lake six years earlier, the soldiers had established base camps near each of the twelve villages and towns. Fifteen community leaders had been "disappeared" from the municipalities of Sololá, and more than 100 had fled after receiving death threats. The arrival—if not emergence—of the guerrillas in the area in 1983 signalled the army to the seething resentment of the Indians for the military and their retrenchment into patterns of resistance which, in their creativity and intensity, hadn't been seen among the *indigenas* since the communist insurgency of the mid 1940's.

The military responded in wave after wave of assaults. From the Central Highlands, the repression swept north throughout the Petén and then stretched westward through Huehuetenango. During early 1982, few reports of the hundreds of massacres in the highlands ever reached the handful of journalists in Guatemala City who had pledged among themselves to monitor such activities. From a point of view in the capital, the Lake District had remained "tranquil." That is to say, the military had refrained from highly visible activities in the area because of the heavy tourist traffic and the growing, highly transient, international community on the north beaches in and around Panajachél. The new hotel consortium, controlled by the oligarchs in the capital, had brought considerable pressure against such overt tactics around the lake. So, large-scale military operations had remained in check—for the time being. But with the execution of "El Pesado," the first civilian military commissioner in the region to be assassinated, the situation changed abruptly.

The military's first heavy attack came to the Lake District in late October, 1983, when more than 500 ground troops with helicopter gunship support attacked the community of La Paz de Cristo, killing more than 100 *campesinos*, their wives, and children, burning the town and the surrounding crops. The men and older boys were caught in the open fields and cut down by bursts of machine gun fire from the helicopters. Two bombs destroyed the school and store on the plaza of the small hamlet. Ground troops arrived the next morning and finished their work on the remaining buildings, exploding them and burning them to the ground.

In diversionary raids, the guerrillas responded by expanding their assaults on bridges and power stations. They dynamited the bridge over the Motagua River just west of Dos Piñas. They raised two electrical towers at the power station at Santa Lucía Jutiapa and Santa María Necta. Then, after the soldiers had readjusted available manpower to guard the roads and public facilities, the *EGP* turned on their real targets—the wealthy land owners and their families whom they held responsible for the seizure of their ancestral lands. Don Enrique Esquivel, a retired colonel and Guatemalan ambassador to Italy in the 1970's, died in a hail of gun fire as he stepped from the Church of the Vírgin de San Juan in Milotenango. The body of Doña Celestina Walker, wife of the brewer and another retired colonel of the notorious *kaibiles*, the self-styled "messengers of death," was discovered shot to death in the back of her car outside a service station in Costa del Sol. Outside Cobán, the remains of Don

Marcos Reynosa-Estrada, shot once through the heart, turned up in a ravine three days after he and his body guard had disappeared on a trip to the capital.

The military response escalated until the bloodshed had taken the life of at least someone in every extended family in the department. No home was immune from the debilitating attacks. When the military assaults had ceased after more than nine months of unrelenting attacks, more than thirty percent of some of the *aldeas* had been killed. Then, the military shifted its tactics from the destruction of the towns to the occupation of the communities of Sololá. The soldiers—most of them young indigenous conscripts—patrolled each of the markets, intimidating the merchants and their customers. Convoys of trucks rolled up outside the churches during mass, and their soldiers paraded into the back pews of the sanctuaries, cocking their field rifles in ominous displays of power. They ransacked the libraries of several priests, looking for evidence of subversive connections with the *EGP*. When finding nothing of note, they destroyed the altars and stole the colonial icons and gilded religious relics as souvenirs of their campaign. On orders, they looted shops and demanded protection payments from cowering widows, and they entered the classrooms of local schools, tearing through books and papers, looking for lessons in subversion.

Bishop Juan Pablo Ortíz made his way through the crowd into the center of the plaza. He was a tall, attractive man, well-trimmed and energetic for middle age. To make himself appear more "available," he used to jog every morning through the neighborhoods. Frankly, he liked both the exercise as well as the attention it brought him. He was particularly flattered by notices of the women. In truth, he enjoyed the respect of many of the community leaders among the *Sololatecos*, since he was one of their own, having risen in the Church from among them.

In deference to Father Juan Pablo's high role in the Guatemalan church, the Indians dropped their voices as they spied their Bishop. By the time he reached the steps of the church, the distressed crowd had reduced its din to muffled sobs. The priest made his way up the steps and turned to address his parishioners.

"*Sololatecos!*" called the Bishop as he scanned the growing crowd.

"*Please! . . . Please!*" conjured the cleric. "We *must* have *calm!* We *must* have *calm!*"

Again, but only for the moment, the people were willing to let the priest have his say.

"Apparently, an awful thing has happened once again to our community," cried Father Juan.

A general cry of anguish rushed through the crowd.

"*But! . . . But!*" said the Bishop. "*Please! Please!* I *know* what you have been through. I *know* what we have been through *already* together over these past horrible *years*."

Suddenly, a wail screeched over the angry rumbling of the crowd.

"Migi! Mi Migi!" cried Doña María Mendoza. *"Mi Migi se ha ido! Mi Migi se ha ido! Mi Migi estaba trabajanda en la milpa larga! Ahóra, mi Migi se ha ido!"*

Miguel Mendoza was a worker in the farmers' collective that had been under increasing harassment by the military. He and the other leaders of the cooperative had left for the fields early in the morning with plans to attend a meeting of the leadership after their work. At once, the crowd realized that none of the cooperative leaders were present among them.

The rumble of anguish that had continued over and around the priest's petitions suddenly exploded into a heavy, universal outcry, and the Bishop, raising his hands on high trying to proselytize caution, realized that he had done all that he could, all that the crowd—now matastacising as a frenzied mob—would be willing to accept.

"Let's go to the *alcalde!* Make him *speak* for us against the *repression!"* cried Paco Mitla, a catechist in the Church of the *Vírgin* of San Juan who hoped in vain to support the Bishop's plea for more reserve and reflection.

"I've got *another* idea!" roared Alonzo Mario Xolop, a butcher in the Sololá market and not particularly a devotee of the Bishop. "Let's find that bastard *commissione*r and cut his *throat!* Let's *split him* like the *pig* he *is!*"

"*Yeah! Yeah!*" went up the cry from three or four of his inebriated comrades. "Let's *take* the bastard! Let's show him what we'll do to *los hijos de putas* who take our land and destroy our *families!* Search every *bar!* He'll be *drunk* tonight!"

"He'll be *dead* tonight!" responded others.

"*Yes! Yes! Death* to the fucking *militaries*!" cried the now encouraged butcher.

"*Yes! Yes! Yes! Death* to the fucking *soldiers*!" and the chant went up.

The crowd surged backward, away from the plaza and out into the streets in search of Albo Victore Moises, the detested *ladino* military *comisionado*, the lackey of the military commander of the Sololá post.

The Bishop was soon lost in the wave of angry protestors, and his pleas for a more sane resolution to the evening's tragic events dissipated in the evening breeze. He knew it could be easily misinterpreted if now he were to be seen among a mob of militant protestors, particularly if they were actually to riot against the military post itself. There would be more killings, to be sure, and the church would be identified clearly by his presence among them. He couldn't risk further those of his parish who were already under assault in the ensuing confrontation with the evangelicals and his catechists, particularly, who were immediate and constant targets of the military. At best, it was his part to return, and loosening his clerical collar, Father Juan took a side street back toward his quarters two blocks behind the church. He worked his way cautiously down the sidewalks, careful to watch on either side for any suspicious observers and alert to every footstep that might approach from behind. When he reached his gate, he was surprised to hear heated words from within his room.

María Paloma turned to the door at the sound of the Bishop's return and held up her hand to silence her insistent interrogator. The Bishop entered the dimly lit parlor, his robe and stole over his arm.

"I thought I heard a conversation," said the priest, "and María Paloma, who is our guest?" The Bishop turned to greet the large, Sololá woman sitting on the couch beside María.

"Father, I am sorry that we have taken liberties with your quarters," María Paloma apologized, "but given the circumstances outside, we thought it best to seek sanctuary here. Father, this is `Piti' Ochoa . . . `Piti' Ochoa Martinez with *Madres de la Represión*."

"Piti" Ochoa was an indigenous woman in her early forties. Both her husband and brother-in-law had been seized two years before and their disemboweled bodies dumped at the front door of the Hotel Cakchiquel where they were seen by many horrified guests. The killings and their rather histrionic display was an obvious effort to terrorize the local people and to intimidate the fledgling union movement in the hotels. Both had been employed as grounds keepers and were suspected of organizing the workers along the "gold coast" in Panajachél. Their murders had stunned the villagers and became a reference point for what they feared might follow. "Piti" was one of the courageous ones who, throwing caution aside, had committed herself to the movement and to activism aimed at discovering the details of the abduction and murders and bringing to justice the perpetrators. Her emerging connections with the national office of the *MR* gave her a reputation beyond the Lake District, but rather than drawing her own people closer to her, "Piti"'s new found recognition served only to distance herself from her friends and neighbors who became fearful of continuing their associations with her. Increasingly, she had turned to the *MR* for assistance, but the *EGP* was something quite different. She felt nervous and compromised both by the events of the evening swirling around them and this impromptu meeting in the quarters of the Bishop.

"Ah, yes, *Señora* Ochoa," said the priest. "I have heard much about the Mothers of the Repression, and I support their fine efforts for furthering human rights in our country. I understand that it is your purpose to start a group here in Sololá, is that correct?"

"Yes, Father, we have more than 150 widows, sisters, and loved ones who have lost their husbands and brothers in Sololá, and tonight apparently the number has risen even higher," explained the deeply disturbed Indian activist. "We want to bring the full pressure of the *MR* from the capital and all its resources to focus on what has happened here in Sololá."

"Yes, but we have other plans for the *MR*, don't you *see!"* petitioned María Paloma, opening their discussion once more, this time before the Bishop. "I don't know what has happened here tonight, but I know that we are ready to make a move here on the north side of the lake, and for the near future we need to develop our support in San Felipe! We've already made some decisions, and right here—*tonight!*—we're conducting an operation this very minute. I'm going to San Felipe where they've disappeared the *Maximón* priest. His wife could be a key to both of us. This is a particularly strategic moment, and we simply can't be distracted by anything . . . even *this*, these killings *tonight!* There is just too much at stake."

"I don't see how *MR* can relate in any positive way to a violent attack, if that's what you're getting at. The minute *MR* gets linked up with any guerrilla activity, all our work is compromised," protested "Piti" Ochoa. "We want the violence to *stop!* We want the government to represent us and to help us find our loved ones and to open investigations and trials, and bring these killers to justice through the *courts*—not through *more bloodshed!*"

"We are all the *same!*" pleaded María Paloma. "We are *all* fighting for *Guatemala!* There's no *difference!* Do you really think we will be successful if we work apart from each other. The *URNG* and *MR* . . . *MR* and the *URNG*—what's the *difference?* We are both seeking peace with dignity and justice. It's *you!* Right *here!* Right here in *this* place and at *this very moment* that you are dividing those who seek a *true* peace. You *must* help, `Piti'! I . . . *Guatemala* needs your help right *now!*"

"Piti" Ochoa was becoming increasingly angry over such incessant pressure as she realized more clearly the role that she and the *MR* were being asked to play in the operations of the guerrillas. She was aware of divisions within the guerrilla movement, and she was very leery about appearing to take sides. She wasn't the one to make such decisions. She simply needed to talk with her counterparts in the capital, and any commitment on her part now—and espe-cially under this kind of intimidation—could be very dangerous.

"María, you'll have to excuse me," said "Piti" Ochoa. "If I am even seen *talking* with you, the *ejercito* will come and kill even *more Sololatecos*!"

The *MR* leader turned to the Bishop.

"*Monsignor!*" she said, acknowledging the Bishop as she took her leave from the prelate's quarters.

"Piti" Ochoa rose abruptly, gathered her shawl over her arms, smiled tersely, and walked to the door. At the exit, she turned to an obviously perturbed María Paloma, and remarked, "I'm *sorry*, María. I really *want* to help! *Really!*"

"It's very simple to count," said María Paloma, something stern like a warning in her voice. "You count your friends one at a time; your enemies the same. There's nobody *else*, `Piti' Ochoa." To María Paloma, the *MR* leader obviously didn't understand the complexities of the Guatemalan reality.

"It is very hard," observed the Bishop. "This isn't good, María. There's too much division between our good efforts, and the people will suffer. I don't know what's going on tonight or what you have planned for San Felipe later, and I really don't want to know. But I think that if you're going to try to take advantage of the disappearance of the shaman, you may have been compromised by this thing here tonight. Word, I'm sure, is already around the lake, so you had better leave as soon as possible. I could offer you a cot again here in the compound tonight. Perhaps you should not leave, *okay?*—what with the trouble and all—*okay?*"

María Paloma smiled, scanning the face of the Bishop, and nodded her agreement. Father Juan reached for a small bell on his desk and rang for his servant. A small *Sololateca* came to the door from the kitchen annex, drying her hands on a towel.

"Yes, Father," said the servant.

"Lucía," said the Bishop. "Please show our sister here to the guest quarters. She'll be spending the evening with us."

"*Sí, Padre,*" said Lucía, as she stepped aside to allow María Paloma to pass into the hallway. The girl continued drying her hands on the towel as, unaware of the identity of their guest, she showed the guerrilla officer to the small dormitory room, a spartan closet with a narrow mattress on a small box frame and covered with a thin sheet and typical blanket from Momostenango.

The Bishop watched them pass down the hallway and into the room, and then turned to the window of the parlor to make sure that it was locked and the shutters closed. He walked hurriedly over to the door and placed the steel bar into the slots to secure the quarters for the rest of the evening. Then he retired to his private room for a final meditation. Through the walls and ceiling of his small chapel he could hear the commotion outside—the persistent but indistinct shouts far down the street and the occasional outcry of young teenagers running past the clerical apartments as they came to and from the plaza.

The Bishop looked at his watch and noted the late hour. He sat down in the rough-hewn, straight-back chair next to the small altar table that he had fashioned. In reality, it was one of the white pine, carved chests found throughout the highland markets. Over its top and running the length of the lid he had spread a Sololá *faja*, or Indian woman's belt. In the middle of the belt he had set up a handcarved crucifix. Two red glass votive candle holders contained the almost dissipated, perfumed tapers which he turned on end and carefully lighted. He sat back in his chair and leaned forward, resting his chin in his hands.

This is not the beginning of the trouble, he thought, for too many others had already died. But it was certainly not the end, either. Others would assuredly follow, and he knew that the church was caught in a desperate, three-way crossfire between the military, the guerrillas, and the evangelicals—indeed, a four-way shootout it you counted the Vatican itself. He couldn't keep walking the line much longer. He knew that with the next meeting of the Guatemalan Bishops, he would be forced to accept the growing sentiment among his peers for drafting a formal protest against the waves of violence which were sweeping the highlands, that the compromise worked out with the Bishops of Huehuetenango and the southern departments had been derailed by the massacres in Patozí and La Paz. Such a document would remove any doubt about the standing of the church, and he knew the army would react swiftly within the *aldeas* to check any enthusiasm for the position paper. If the military had had any doubt about himself at all, it would be resolved probably within the month.

The Bishop watched the candle flames quivering in the rose receptacles. Thin, wispy columns of smoke drifted around the base of the crucifix and seemed to gather around just under the outstretched arms of the crucified body of Christ, seeming from that angle to lift the figure before his own face. The priest stared intently at the image of the Saviour, trying to trace even the faintest trail of tears for the grieving wretched of the world. The essence of this Christ was sacrifice, and in Sololá that sacrifice was being hanged on a tortured, bleeding tree. That tree—his *own* cross, for *sure*—was looming larger and larger, and he was afraid. Simply that.

The Bishop shut his eyes as a tremble jolted his meditation. The events of the evening, more than at any other time, had brought to his own gate the inevitabilities of the repression—the panic cries for his support juxtaposed by the angry vigilance of the militant opposition. Certainly, the military had not been oblivious to the comings and goings and correspondences of the past three hours. There were informants everywhere who, to save themselves and their own families, were working clandestinely through the civil patrols against all alleged "subversives" in Sololá. His own days, the Bishop felt, were numbered. The only saving comfort was a curious fatalism, that he would follow the course laid out before him a step at a time and take satisfaction in each movement forward.

"Three of us working to help these people are still alive at this moment," thought the Bishop to himself, "so there is still hope for the *Sololatecos*." There could be no other consolation; how many other people had newly perished at this same hour? He could not know or even guess what might follow in the next few hours.

"Would you help me, Father?" said a voice behind him. The Bishop was startled from his reflections, and he turned to discover María Paloma standing behind him. In the dim candle light haunting the dark recesses of the simple chapel, María suddenly reached for the Bishop's right hand, drew it inside her thin, open blouse, and cupped it around the warm globe of her left breast.

"I thought that you might come back to me, my child," said the Bishop as he pulled her body closer to his own.

"Help me, Father," pleaded the guerrilla, standing next to him slightly higher than the seated celibate, her eyes flashing across his, searching for compliance. "*Help* me . . . help me find something to *confess!*"

Chapter 27

Rank and File

"He's big, *man!* I mean like, I mean, this guy's *big!*" exclaimed Jaime Cabrera-Toc. "I mean, like, I mean this guy's bigger than any man I ever seen, you *know!*"

"*Shit,* man," returned the first corporal. "I'm just glad he's one of *us, man!* I'm just glad he's one of *us! Shit!*"

"Hey, *Juan!*" said Jaime Cabrerra-Toc, the second corporal, to the first private. "Didn't you say that guy was from the capital?"

Juan José Soto-Soto, the first private, spit out the tail of a weed he had been chewing for the past few minutes. Like the rest of the new members of the squad, Juan Jose was a young, eighteen-year-old conscript. He and the others had arrived at the garrison outside San Felipe del Lago only two days earlier. They had missed the battle the week before, but the excitement had spilled over among all the new recruits. The focus of their conversation was the reputed giant who was alleged to have dispatched the head of the whole guerrilla contingent of Sololá.

"Yeah," said Juan José. "I heard he's been working for the Army ever since his brother disappeared two years ago. They said the army tried to make out like it was the guerrillas that choked his brother and beat him up and all. But some of them say *he* did it, killed him when he was down in one of those fuckin' pits, and he didn't know what he was doing. They say it was the army that made him do it and that they drugged him afterwards so he would do what they wanted, the army and all."

"Whatever," said the first corporal. "I'm just glad he's on *our* side."

"They said that was him," interrupted the second private excitedly. "They say that was him that tore the tongue out of that *guerrilla* guy—that "*comandante* Lupe"—the other day."

"*Yeah!*" said the first private. "They said he just grabbed the guy by the *jaws* and squeezed `til his mouth popped open, and he just reached back in his throat with his two fingers and out came this guy's *tongue!*"

"*Shit!*" said the first corporal.

"No *shit, man!*" echoed Jaime Cabrerra Toc. "I mean, I mean like . . . can you get *that, man?* I mean, the *whole tongue!* The *whole goddamn tongue!* You know what I *mean?* I mean like, I mean that guy's got *balls!* You know what I *mean?*"

"*Shit!*" said the first corporal.

"*Yeah!*" interrupted the second private. "And they said that guy—that *guerrilla* guy—just sat there in the chair and just looked at that big guy, like, I mean—`*what—the—shit—did—you—just—do—to—me?*'"

"*Goddamn, man!*" said the first private. "I mean, *shit!* Can't you just see that guy *sitting* there! Sitting there with his *thumbs* up his ass! `*Goddamn, guys!* You just ripped out my *fuckin' tongue!*'"

The squad erupted in guffaws and rolled backwards off the section of the garrison wall facing the lake front and still under construction.

"*No, man! No!*" offered Juan Jose Soto-Soto. "*Wait* a minute, guys! *Look!* Look *here!* Like *this!*" Juan Jose Soto-Soto mimed an attempt to cram both fists into his mouth simultaneously. His eyes rolled, and his head bobbed. He was very funny, and the squad rolled backwards again. Tears streamed down their cheeks, they were laughing so hard.

The young recruits laughed and threw good natured punches at each other. Moments later, however, they had regained their composure. If the captain of the small garrison had seen them acting like this on duty, they could have been shot. But Captain Villalobos was across the lake at Panajachél or Sololá—or somewhere—for the night and wasn't due back until noon the next day. The lieutenant was in San Felipe buying beer or liquor and probably embarrassing some Felipino girl or her mother.

"They say this guy doesn't care what the job is or *who's* the hit," continued Jaime Cabrerra-Toc, the second corporal. "They say he'd walk right up and rip the balls off the *Pope* if the captain ordered it. They say he doesn't care at all. Just give him an order, and that's all there is to it."

"I mean, who . . . who *is* this guy?" asked the second private.

"`Pepe,'" said Juan José Soto-Soto. "He just goes by `Pepe.'"

"I mean, where's he from," asked the second private.

"Somewhere around here," said Juan Jose.

"*No!*" interrupted the third private. "He's *Felipino!* He's from right *here!*"

"*No shit!*" said the first corporal.

"*Yeah, man!*" said the third private. "They say he's the son of the *brujo*, that guy, `*what'sis* name.'"

"The *Felipino?*" said the second private.

"Yeah, *that* guy—" said the third private, still searching for the name. "You know, the one who sees the lights, talks to the ancestors—the real *spooky* one."

"`Andres'?" offered the second private.

"*Yeah! That's* him!" said the third private, relieved with the revelation. "Yeah, *that* guy! *Yeah!* `Andres,' the *spook!* I heard they *`disappeared'* his ass!"

"*No!*" protested the first corporal. "Where'd you get *that?*"

"*Hey*, man! No *shit!* I heard one of his own *ancestors* got him!" claimed the second corporal, catching the vein of sympathy in his colleague. All the squad members laughed and laughed.

"Don't laugh, *dick heads!*" warned the first corporal. "That guy's the *brujo* of *Maximón*! No *shit*, man!"

The first corporal crossed himself over the forehead, his lips, and then his chest in obvious respect for even the mention of the idol. He looked around for any reaction, half expecting a challenge and ready to defend his own anxieties anchored in a common bank of community lore regarding the ancient deity.

The notoriety of the *Maximón* of San Felipe del Lago spanned the department of Sololá and beyond. Among its devotees could be numbered the governor of the department, every *cofrade, alcalde,* and *principál*, and—privately, of course—at least one Guatemalan bishop. Thousands of *campesinos* still feared the god and brought regular offerings from their meager returns. Many of the more urbane among the recruits, however, dared to mock their earlier faith and beliefs. Squad leaders encouraged a certain cockiness and irreverence toward local culture. It was part of the effort to break down resistance to military order and control. So, these young recruits had become smug in their small heresies. After all, they had been around; some had already had women. Each of them had killed at least once. It was enough that their captain had exploded in laughter while blasting to splinters Catholic statuary behind an altar with rounds from his M-16.

In the privacy of the squad, however, a soldier might still confess—certainly with caution—any lingering trepidation for the old ways, and for the first corporal, his respect for tradition was rooted in his implacable faith for the *Maximón*, albeit the *Maximón* of Chimaltenango more than three hours away. He still might want to go home some day, and it wouldn't do to break away completely. Any obvious practices of traditional faith on the part of a new recruit would bring a devotee endless rounds of insults and expressions of withering contempt, not to mention grunt assignments digging out latrines—or worse, like "pitching Indian *shit,*" the derisive expression for dumping the tortured and mutilated remains of guerrillas or other alleged subversives picked up by the army for interrogation.

"*Hey!*" cried Juan Jose Soto-Soto. "What if we could put up the *captain* against old *Maximón*!" He knew full well how the corporal would react whom he could see grimmace at the quip.

"Yeah, *well!*" retorted Jaime Cabrerra-Toc. "Captain Vargas is a *Brucero, no!* There ain't no god *safe* where the *captain* is!"

"Or a *virgin!*" returned the second private.

"Or her *grandmother*, for that matter!" smirked another.

All but the first corporal rolled again in laughter. Embarrassed by the earlier burlesque of the *Maximón* priest, the first corporal turned his head from the arrogance and irreverence of his comrades.

"What's the *matter*, `Meribela'?" cracked the second corporal, setting off a cacophony of howls and whistles.

"Meribela" was the nickname which had followed the first corporal, then only a private, from his training base in the capital to his first posts in the highlands, kidding elicited from his squeamishness about raping his first "subversive," one "Meribela Tupoy," a twenty-five-year old school teacher from Zacapa who had been accused of providing information about troop movements to "known guerrillas." The squad leader had ordered him to sodomize the terrified woman who had been stripped, then jostled back and forth between files of jeering soldiers. Troops in their squad had repeatedly grabbed and fondled her as they passed her from one to another. Before his peers, the first corporal had stood impotent and humiliated behind the woman tied face down over the edge of a table.

"What's the matter, Chico! Can't get it up?" barked the captain.

The first corporal's flaccid penis shrivelled even further in the wave of insults he had to weather from the captain. The officer motioned to one of the other recruits to step forward and complete the job.

"Maybe this soldier over here is a `real' man!" taunted the captain, as the second soldier stepped behind the woman. He fumbled with the fly of his uniform and after a moment or two presented his engorged penis and rammed it up the exposed woman. The slightly built teacher winced and clenched her teeth as the soldier pounded her furiously for almost a minute, and then, with a series of heavy thrusts, he ejaculated and withdrew.

"Well, `Meribella,'" continued the captain. "Have you learned anything useful from this little demonstration? . . . Well?"

"Yes, sir!" returned the first corporal.

"Well, `Meribella,' let's see what you have learned," said the captain.

Hysterical, the bound teacher was now hyperventilating and on the verge of passing out, her wild eyes staring blankly at the wall.

The first corporal approached the woman once again, but just as before, his penis, hanging limp from out the side of a pair of filthy briefs, failed to achieve an erection.

"Maybe the pretty `teacher' can help our `Meribella,'" said the captain as an afterthought. "Maybe our bonita maestra here can pump up a soldier's `ego.' Suck it, you fucking bitch!"

The captain grabbed the hair of the woman, writhing uncontrollably, and jerked back her head.

"Suck this dick `til it comes out your goddamn ears!" ordered the captain as he threw the side of her head down sharply against the edge of the table. The first corporal approached the woman whose face was starting to flush with a massive bruise emerging across her forehead and a swelling across her right eyebrow. The captain jerked her head back once more and motioned for the soldier to place his penis in her mouth. She was convulsing now, tremors of terror rippling through every muscle.

"Suck it, bitch!" said the captain to the trembling woman. The captain pulled her head over to the edge of the table where the first corporal's limp penis hung just beyond. The corporal laid the penis across his palm and slipped the head of it into her mouth. Instinctively, the woman gagged and at once drew back her head.

"Suck the goddamned dick, bitch!" returned the captain, and he slapped her hard against the back of her head. Her eyes now almost swollen shut, the woman gingerly inched her face along the surface of the table and, shaking violently, she accepted the head and then the shaft of the soldier's penis.

"Suck it! Suck it, you goddamn guerrilla bitch!" yelled the captain. "How many sons of bitches did you lay out there in the mountains, you fucking whore! How many dicks did you smack out there, huh?"

The woman clamped her lips loosely around the shaft of the flaccid member and began to stroke the tip of the head with her tongue, but once more she failed to control an overwhelming convulsion. Her chest heaved once, and then her mouth exploded with vomit.

The first corporal jumped back, his briefs saturated with the whole load of her evacuation. His "classmates" could refrain no longer, and they broke up in a round of laughter.

"Atención!" barked the captain. At once, the soldiers realigned their file to the side of the table as the first corporal tried to dump the woman's discharge in the direction of the drain under the table.

"I guess you're just about useless, bitch!" shouted the captain to the teacher now trembling in chills, the residue of vomit and stomach acid gurgling deep within her throat.

"I guess you're just about worthless as either a guerrilla or a fuck!" yelled the captain, striking her sharply again across the face with the back of his hand.

"Don't you pass out on me, you fucking guerrilla whore!" he continued. "Better yet, bitch, you might not want to watch what the corporal here's going to do to you."

The woman was convulsing rapidly, her chest jerking on the table as her arms and legs remained stretched and secured by straps to the front and rear legs of the table over which she was spread.

The captain withdrew his bayonet from its sheathe, grabbed the hair of the woman just above the forehead, jerked back her head, and drove the point of the blade almost two inches into her left eye. The woman sent out a shrill, curdling yell that reverberated throughout the complex. Blood spurted from the socket as the captain gouged out the eye with a single twist of his wrist, and the remains of the severed eyelid slipped down the woman's bloody cheek.

Then with the skill of a grizzled, journeyman oyster shucker, the captain scooped out the right eye with the same practiced finesse. With the exception of the profusely bleeding eye sockets, the woman's face blanched white, and her breath subsided into irregular, widely spaced gasps. She had lapsed into shock and unconsciousness.

"Well, `Meribella,'" coaxed the captain. "Come around to the front of the table."

The first corporal grabbed at his open fly to keep his uniform pants from falling off and moved around to the head of the table just beyond the crown of the woman's head, her sightless face now lying on its side in a massive pool of thick, dark blood.

"You're looking a little pale, yourself!" turned the captain to the nervous recruit. "Maybe a little thirsty, too, eh?"

"Here!" said the captain as he handed the sticky handle of his bayonet to the first corporal. "Zip up, lover, and cut the straps holding her wrists."

The soldier restored his zipper and then, slipping the blade of the bayonet under the cords that tied down the woman's arms to the table legs, he cut them both. At once, the woman's arms swung limp over the edge of the table, the fingers of her hands already blue.

"Now cut the ropes around her ankles and come back here," ordered the captain. The soldier walked briskly to the rear of the table, slit the cords, then

returned to the head of the table. He handed the bayonet back to his superior and took his position once more near the woman's face.

"Yes, sir! `lover!'" shouted the captain. "I think you look a little thirsty, no?"

"Soldier!" the captain barked to the recruit rigid in place at the end of the line.

"Hand me that jar on the shelf behind you," said the captain.

The young soldier turned smartly, reached for the glass quart jar on the shelf behind him, turned again, and stepped forward to the captain.

"Stand here," said the captain to the second soldier, as he motioned the first corporal to the side and assumed his station near the front of the table. Then the captain reached out toward the woman, grabbed her under the arms, and suddenly jerked her forward until her bloody head now hung all but lifeless over the edge of the table.

"Put the jar down here," ordered the captain to the second soldier, pointing with the bayonet to a spot on the floor below the woman's throat. The second soldier knelt down and placed the jar, as ordered, beneath the woman's head. The captain then grabbed the woman's hair and lifting it high, stretched the woman's neck forward from her shoulders.

"Slit her throat!" barked the captain to the first corporal, once again handing him the bloody bayonet. "Slit her throat, `Meribella,' and then maybe we can find another name more suitable for a soldier in my squad!"

But the name held, and the soldier's reputation seemed to precede him as he had moved to the next two posts with his small unit. It was the first time he had ever tasted human blood. Some of the older troops told crazy stories—how it made you see things, how it made you want to kill something. In fact, drinking the woman's blood had made him quite delirious for a while, and he had fought, unsuccessfully, from losing consciousness. He had passed out for more than an hour after he had topped off the quart and woke up on his cot in a pool of his own vomit. Nevertheless, the captain had been quite pleased, and the next day, he introduced the new corporal to the approval of the applauding members of the squad.

"Maybe this `Meribella's' getting thirsty *again!*" barked the first corporal to his comrades.

The other members broke into playful laughter and cut loose a siren of high-pitched, though good-natured whistles, and the sergeant slapped him respectfully across the back. If the young soldier still retained a thread of village superstition, there were few among them who would care to challenge him.

At Post #14 in Sololá, Captain Justo Vallez Otoñio awaited a briefing on the operation conducted throughout the Department of Sololá the week before. Captain Marcos Rufino Calles, the officer-in-charge of the "Mariposa" resettlement post in San Jorge Zuníl, sat beside him, completing the last drag on an American Marlboro.

"We beat the *shit* out of them, *no?*" observed Captain Vallez.

"We got lucky as *shit!*" responded Captain Rufino.

"Well, yeah! But I mean picking off `Lupe' like we did."

A chain smoker, Captain Rufino lit another cigarette and enhaled a deep draught, then released it slowly in the air above them. "Like I *said,*" remarked Rufino, "`we got lucky as *shit!*'"

"I'm surprised he got taken in the *open* like that," said Captain Vallez, interested in keeping the conversation focused. He was eager for more details from the reluctant Captain Rufino who had coordinated the assault with the rear flank along the southern rim of the valley. Privately, he was chagrined that he and his unit had not been included in the operation.

"We didn't take him in the open—that was all for the press," explained Rufino. "We caught him trying to make his getaway at Los Encuentros on one of the busses on the way to *Xela.* He was bleeding pretty badly, lying in the back seat. We found him when we got all the Indian shits off the bus. We dragged him off the bus and took him to the post. That big guy ripped out his tongue. The sonofabitch just sat there and bled to death. We never got even a grunt out of him. The mechanics had been servicing all the trucks that morning, so we stuffed him in one of those 55-gallon drums that was about half full of old motor oil anyway. We put it up in the back of one of the trucks and hauled it over to the garbage dump. We pitched a match in the drum and set it on fire. *Shit!* His ass just went up in greasy black *smoke.*"

Captain Rufino was tired. He hadn't slept in almost two days, and the idea of sitting through a briefing over his own operation in the assault only added to his misery. A chain of cigarettes kept him going.

The door of the office opened, and the two captains jumped up to attention.

"At ease," said Colonel Federico Altapaz. "Be seated. We'll be joined in just a moment by Captain Villalobos from San Felipe. Captain Rufino, you must be very tired. We'll make this brief, *no!*"

"As you will, Colonel," responded the officer.

"Captain Vallez, I've heard a couple of good reports on the civil patrol work across the lake," said the Colonel. "You need to keep the pressure up, you understand?"

"*Como no!* Colonel!" said Captain Vallez.

The door opened, and Captain Villalobos, with his cap under his arm, entered the room, clicked his heals, and saluted smartly.

"Páse, capitán," said the Colonel. *"Siéntase! Bueno! Todos estamos aquí!"*

"Gentlemen," said Colonel Altapaz. "It's not my intention to keep you very long, but we have several items of unfinished business to attend to that involve your squads."

Colonel Altapaz rose from his chair and stepped forward, sitting against the front edge of the desk.

"Gentlemen, you might be pleased to know that the shipment of M16's has been secured and will be delivered by truck tomorrow to your posts. They're the new A2's that will replace the units they're using now. As you might guess, then, the guerrillas, to say the least, were unsuccessful in their attack on our shipments. In fact, we made a major dent last week in the guerrilla cels around the lake," continued Colonel Altapaz. "We suffered only minor casualties, but we killed thirteen guerrillas including *Comandante* `Lupe,' apparently the coorinator of the whole operation. We have Captain Rufino here to thank for that. Good *work,* Captain!"

Captain Rufino jumped to his feet, saluted the Colonel, and sat down at the Colonel's nod.

"But we have to keep the *pressure* on," said Altapaz. "The MR must be shut down on both sides of the lake. I want all three of you to step up patrol activity, and I think we might just as well disinfect some of the leadership offices. If you don't follow me precisely, let me put it more directly. Hit the goddamned Catholics *hard!* You can start by taking out any of the catechists who are working with the priests. Are there any *questions?*"

"*Colonel!*" responded Captain Villalobos.

"Yes, Captain," said the Colonel.

"Does that include the *priest* in San Felipe?"

"*Especially* the priest!" said Colonel Altapaz, "and while you're at it, you can take out the mayor, too. In fact, start putting pressure on the priest, send him some notes—maybe he'll get the hell *out*—and I'll send `Pepe' to pick up the MR leaders here and then the mayor over there. Pepe's unit will set up at your base in San Felipe. He'll move in and out after dark. Fewer people are likely to recognize him then. They'll come in—probably in about two days."

The captains exchanged looks of satisfaction that the action would continue. All three were beginning to feel the heat from various "private sector" representatives who were agitating locals against cooperation with the army.

"In the meantime," said Altapaz, "I want the three of you to stay over tonight. In the morning we've arranged a training demonstration for you all on the A2. Captain Benton with the American Special Forces will be with us to provide the orientation and drill. Then you'll need to go back to your units and give them the same training you receive tomorrow."

The young captains were suddenly charged up. The idea that they might be the first at instruction on the M16-A2's was exciting to each of them.

"And one thing *more*," said Colonel Altapaz, standing before the desk now in preparation to dismiss his squad leaders. "Just one thing *more*. I got word this afternoon that the *wife* of `Lupe' was in Sololá the night after the attack and was planning to cross to San Felipe. Your boys might have some fun, whichever ones of them get to her first. She's useless otherwise, so you can dump her in the lake or whatever when you're through with her. Is there anything else?"

The three captains rose and saluted the Colonel, turned, and retired from the room. Colonel Altapaz walked across the room, opened the shutter on the single window, and peered out across Lake Atitlán. In the cool evening, all was silent. Lights twinkled over on the southern side—Santa Lucía, Santa Catarina, San Lucas Tolimán, Santiago, San Felipe. High above the villages, there on the balcony of Atitlán, Colonel Federico Altapaz felt secure in a week's work well done. It was refreshing to tie up loose ends, and at least one dating back to Suchitepequez; a thirty-seven year old high school grudge was finally settled. In the back of his mind, the colonel etched another knotch on his belt. No—the essential task in life was to keep score—take names, make lists.

The key to the good life, however, was to be in every affair—no matter how trivial—the designated score keeper. If life in the Guatemalan military had taught him anything, Colonel Altapaz learned early to win at *everything*—no matter the *costs,* a personal policy which could be translated quite literally most of the time as eliminating the opposition, either actual or potential. Nothing else mattered for a military man with a family to support and a career on the line. Officers who didn't advance always retired early and never enjoyed the perks of senior staff. You didn't make colonel at thirty-six—or general, perhaps, at forty-six—kissing babies' cheeks—or diddling their *mothers*, for that matter (a lesson apparently lost on Pablo Manuel Rigoleto). Drop those kinds of "condiments" before the recruits, and they'll never give you grief about anything of real consequence in the ranks.

Three taps on the door behind him stirred Altapaz from his musings. The colonel jerked around and instinctively slipped his right thumb in his belt just above the safety snap on his holstered Berreta automatic pistol.

"*Páse!*" said the colonel, straightening his shoulders to receive a possible superior. Not that he expected one in a post like this, but he had been startled once—quite severely as a matter of fact—when, as a young captain, the Minister of Defense himself had entered the commissary office of the Polytechnic Institute in the capital, and he had been caught with his back to the door. It was an embarrassment for the young perfectionist which resulted in the only reprimand on his record. Subsequently, he had been able to expunge the offense after some six weeks of extra duty for his commanding officer, but it had been a lesson he was never to forget.

"*Páse*!" repeated Altapaz, but the door was already swinging open.

"*Colonel Altapaz!* We meet *again!"* said the familiar American voice.

"Captain Benton!" returned the colonel. "It's good to see you. Come in and have a seat."

Captain Jeremy Benton, special assistant assigned to the United States Office of Military Affairs, stepped forward and took a chair in front of the colonel's desk. Altapaz himself released his thumb grip and reached over the desk to shake hands with the American special agent.

"That was a clean exercise last week in the capital," said Benton, relating to the assassination of the Director of Tourism at the Military Polytechnic. "I understand you and the subject were acquainted."

"Yes," concurred Colonel Altapaz rather perfunctorily. Quite frankly, he was uninterested in pursuing the subject at a personal level but felt constrained by the formal relationship between the two countries to acknowledge the interests of the American liaison and advisor.

"Yes," continued Altapaz. "We grew up in the same *aldea*—the same town, you know. Our fathers worked in the same company. But he was `soft,' if you know what I mean. It's a sad thing, of course, but he had lost complete control of security as an intelligence officer. He was fucking a couple of *guerrillas*, if you can imagine *that!* `Strange bedfellows,' I think you Americans say, *no?*"

"*May* I?" asked Captain Benton as he reached in his jacket for his cigarettes.

"*Por su puesto!*" said Altapaz. The American advisor lit a cigarette, took a deep drag, and offered the Marlboro package to the Colonel.

"*Grácias,*" returned Altapaz who favored American tobacco rather than Guatemalan *Rubios* or some of the other Mexican and Costa Rican brands preferred by some of the other Ministry officials. He popped up a cigarette and slipped it loosely between his lips, still anticipating a response from the American.

"Yeah," offered Captain Benton, "I guess so—`strange bedfellows.' But

I've heard of that before. We've had some interesting cases in Europe with Soviet agents. We had one operation that we were able to infiltrate with some of our own people. We had a couple of German girls who had reputations extending all the way back across the Atlantic to their work as call girls in the Bronx. These gals were pretty good—some of the best ass I've ever seen. They set up this East German and balled that guy for three years before he ever figured out what was happening. It's amazing how unsophisticated the East German operations could be! *Shit!* He just disappeared. One day he didn't show up at his office, and the girls were out of the country in two hours. He's probably pushing up *sod* in *Siberia* somewhere!"

Both officers chuckled at the suggestion.

"Look," said Altapaz. "Why don't we walk over to the lounge for a beer. We can continue our discussion over something cold. We've even got some `Heineken,' I think—or whatever you want."

"That sounds fine," said Captain Benton.

The American officer was an English teacher—a "professor of modern British literature and Romance languages." At least that's how he was carried on the roster in the American consulate. He had been registered as an "adjunct professor of language arts for teaching English as a second language." As part of his cover, he had actually been assigned an office at the I.G.A., although at this point he had yet to check in. Nor was it likely that he ever would. His real specialty was ordinance and counter-insurgency, and he had served for the past four years as an instructor of technical support at the "School of the Americas" in Fort Benning, Georgia. Captain Benton had accompanied the first shipment of M16-A2's to Guatemala about three months earlier and had been assigned as a training instructor on their use by the *kaibiles*. He was also monitoring their distribution to both the *kaibiles* and the regular forces for the C.I.A.

"Well, you got the shipment through, Colonel," said Jeremy Benton. "That was a pretty good operation, don't you think."

"Thank you, Captain," said Colonel Altapaz. "Our intelligence network has been improved sharply in the last five years, especially with the good help of the Israelis in our computer contract and continued United States technical support. We're in a war we can win, but it's going to take some time and continued training. The new rifles were really important."

"I was going to ask you about the report we received in Military Affairs last year," said Benton. "There's really no reason for that level of malfunction in these units."

"Captain," said Altapaz in a tone of confidence. "Captain Benton, I'm going to tell you the truth. I had one captain take his rifle and sling it across the fucking river into *Mexico!* He lost two men in a fire fight last year in El Petén because their rifles jammed on them at close range. Those sons of bitches are down *forty percent* of the *time!*"

"Colonel," returned the American advisor, "your men aren't *cleaning* their guns."

"Captain . . ." said Altapaz.

"*No!* I'm *telling* you, Colonel," interrupted the captain, "I'm telling you right *now* that your men aren't *cleaning* their rifles. Tomorrow, I'll examine the rifles of your captains there and two out of the three will have corrosion in the magazine chamber, they'll have . . . I'll tell you *what!* I'll examine their shells, and I'll show you *rusty* and *corroded casings*."

"Captain," interjected the Guatemalan officer. "These men are *kaibiles*! They're the best we've *got!"*

Captain Benton rolled the glass of beer between the tips of his fingers and turned his head to avoid the gaze of his complement across the table.

"Look, *Colonel* . . ." offered the captain. "No offence, *huh?* I know my business. I'm `School of the Americas,' *no?* And I'm telling you that tomorrow in two out of three units that I examine from these three officers I'm going to find chambers full of *shit!*—dirty carrier keys, and probably carbonized piston ends. I may even find a frozen assembly in one of them. So, don't *shit* me, Colonel!"

Altapaz was angry to the point of erupting, and the American captain could see he had made an effect.

"Look, Colonel," said the captain. "This is between two old veterans like ourselves, *huh?* We got the same thing in Nam. Those *jerkoffs* were cleaning their units with *shoelaces, sticks—Goddamn!*—just about anything they could ram down the *barrel!* Those sonofabitches were jamming up . . . *Shit!* They were blowing up in their goddamned *faces!* We were losing a lot of pretty good men, otherwise. So, Colonel . . . don't *shit* with *me, okay?* I've *been* there. Your recruits aren't any worse than *ours! Okay?*"

Acknowledging the "friendly fire" from his advisor, Colonel Altapaz lifted his mug, took a deep swallow of beer, and wiped his mouth on a paper napkin.

"Anyway," continued Belton. "You can put all that aside. We're looking at the A2's which'll relieve a lot of the anxiety we've all experienced up to now."

"Captain . . .?" asked Colonel Altapaz. "Captain, what are we *really* getting in these A2's? I mean, I know the generalities, and we've all passed the good lines around. But give me the specifics. I'm going to get cornered at some point, and I really need to know what I'm talking about."

"Well, it's all in the literature, Colonel," explained the American captain.

"*Yeah! Yeah!* I *know.* I can read the `literature,'" countered Altapaz, "but I'd like to hear it from *you, como igual a igual, me entiende*?"

"Si! Cláro, Colonel. Si, cláro!" said Captain Benton.

The American advisor reached to the side and pulled out a couple of paper napkins from the holder. With the first he sopped up the rings of water from the middle of the table and then laid the other in the clean spot. He took out his ball-point pen and drew two parallel lines down the napkin.

"Okay," said Benton. "Think of these two lines as the thickness of a man's body as you would see it from the side. Now think of this spot here" —and he drew a small round spot on the left line—"think of this spot as the entrance of a round. That's where the projectile penetrates the target—in this case a human body. Now what happens at *this* point?"

"Well," surmised Colonel Altapaz, "it just goes in or maybe through the body."

"`Or maybe *through* the body,'" echoed the captain. "And that's just the *point.* With a high-power projectile, you get a pretty clean wound, but one that is not particularly destructive. The ideal round is one that will penetrate the target, hang around inside, and tear the place up. Now that's what the A2 round does."

Colonel Altapaz continued to follow the discussion intently.

"In the older shells—the one that your troops have been using," explained the captain, "you often got `clean wounds.' That's because the Army changed the original design specifications. Those changes reduced the tumble, or the `twists' of the bullet. Now all that's been changed, and the original specifications have been restored or modified. We're using the SS-109 NATO bullet with the IMR powder rather than the Army's ball powder. This bullet has a 1-to-7 twist ratio that means when it penetrates the body, it's going to tear the *shit* out of the insides."

Captain Benton drew a small channel into the "body" on the napkin which flared almost immediately into a wide circle, still between the two lines. Then he began to blacken the interior of the circle.

"Now this is what's going to happen to your `subversive' before the shell exits—exits *`somewhere,'* I say, because that sonofabitch is tumbling *ever which* way, and there's no telling *where* that bastard is liable to exit. *Shit!* It may enter his *ass* and blow off the top of the bastard's *head*—fucking up everything in *between!*"

The two officers laughed heartily at the suggestions and then reached for their respective mugs. The captain picked up the illustrated "body," wadded it into a tight ball, and chunked it over his shoulder toward the overflowing waste basket in the nearest corner.

"Now, that's not all," returned Captain Benton. "The new A2's have a stronger buttstock. They have an improved front handguard. The barrel is heavier toward the muzzle end to accommodate the 1-in-7 twist I was describing. You've got an adjustable rear sight, and you can set the fire for single-round, three-shot, or fully automatic fire that'll release the whole magazine in less than *three seconds.*"

Colonel Altapaz sat across the table deeply absorbed in the details.

"Now," continued Captain Benton, "here's something else—with the new A2's, you're not going to get the jamming; the gas port pressures have been reduced, and that means that you're not going to encounter the parts breakage you've seen in the past."

Captain Benton was satisfied with his testimonial and broke for the final revelation. He turned the napkin around and drew a series of straight parallel lines.

"But the best part about the A2 is that you're looking at a whole *system*," explained the American officer. "You'll be able to up-grade and to modify each unit off the original rifle for more specialized work—for instance, in the tight vegetation in the Petén or scaling the cliffs out in Huehuetenango."

"A *system?*" asked Altapaz, still not understanding the concept.

"Yeah," said Benton. "A *`system'*—that means, you can by special parts—a shorter, collapsible stock, for example. You can get a shorter barrel, modified handgrips, special infrared night scopes. We've got a new grenade launcher. It's all in the literature, *amigo*!"

Never changing his expression of a stern dispassion, Altapaz sat across the table from his United States advisor determined to resist the clearly patronizing American captain, but he was impressed, to be sure.

"What do you think, Colonel?" asked Benton who had reached for a cigarette in his shirt pocket.

"What . . ." said Federico Altapaz as he took a drag on his freshly lighted cigarette. "What do I *think?*"

The colonel slowly exhaled a pair of smoothly oscillating smoke rings in the air above their heads.

"`What do *I* think?'" queried the Colonel. "I think we're going to—how do you Americans say?—I think we're going to `kick some Indian *ass,*' Captain!"

"I *like* that, Colonel!" exuded Captain Benton. "I *like* that! It'll be good for the Pentagon and State Department to realize something of value for its efforts, even though all this, of course, is a `private' venture, right?"

"Right," agreed the Colonel.

"Well, *amigo*!" said Captain Benton. "I think it's time for this old soldier to retire."

Captain Benton rose to shake the hands of Colonel Altapaz, all rank aside.

"Yes, Captain," said Altapaz. "I think you're right. Why don't we get some sleep. I'm anxious to get the shipment around the lake and into the hands of our young troops. The quicker we get them delivered, the quicker we'll be able to—how do you say it?—`waste some subversives,' *no!*"

"You *got* it, Colonel," conceded the Captain. "By *God!* I think you've *got* it!"

Chapter 28

Father, Forgive Them

August 1st, 1990
Dear Mildred,

While we met only this year, I feel somehow as though, in writing to you now, we've known each other for a lifetime. That's silly, of course, but then, everything seems so distorted, so unreal. My whole life is churning in a black whirlpool that just won't stop spinning. Every waking moment since that awful discovery, I've felt the horror of it gathering like a thunderstorm in the back of my head, its lightening flashing ominously there behind my eyes. If I thought it would change a thing, I'd open my mouth and scream at the top of my lungs. I'll be puttering around or doing something else, and all-of-a-sudden, I'll see his smiling, confident face. My breath rushes up but catches in my throat. Even now, my chest heaves in and out as I think about it. The "fact" of the matter is so simple: Father Jack is gone! My eyes have seen it. My mind can say it. I "know" the fact of it just the same as I can know anything. But Mildred, without Father Jack, everything has lost its moorings. Emotionally, I am adrift—just a meaningless piece of floating refuse, nothing but worthless debris, tossing back and forth between terrifying swells that have torn all the props right out from under me.

This isn't very lucid writing, I know. I just had to get it out—I won't even try to go back and edit it. I couldn't do that now for sure. Oh, Mildred! Where do I start? How can I begin? That night is still too fresh, the wound too deep yet to write about it directly. I have to find something else to write about, some other place safer to begin. The trouble is, there is no "safe place." Every subject of consequence about San Felipe seems to hinge on violence. Quite frankly, Mildred, I don't know how much more this town can take before we all go completely mad.

Of course, the whole world knows about the massacre earlier this year. I don't know what Father Jack may have told you. There were several different stories circulating. It really all started when a couple of guys in one of the army's paramilitary death squads tried to kidnap the retired mayor of the town, an old man and his wife whom everyone loves, but they couldn't do it. Some people saw them trying to drag him out of his house and started making a lot of noise and yelling. Pretty soon, just about everyone heard about it, and a big crowd started gathering at the plaza in front of the church. No one could stop them—Father Jack was across the lake—he wasn't there to try to reason with them. So about two thousand of them went up the road to protest, and the troops at the military post just started shooting. It was horrible! They killed thirteen, fourteen people and wounded a lot more! That was in December, December 2nd last year.

But the worst for me were the three children. This year we had had the fiesta of St. James—that was July 25th, the same week every year. There had been a huge dance in the plaza the night before. All the kids were excited about it because a rock band was coming in to play. They'll only make the long trip around the lake when they'll be guaranteed a good crowd. Of course, that's St. James Day in San Felipe. Well, as soon as the people started to arrive, here come the soldiers. I remembered them from the year before. It was just the same, although, when I first saw them, I had assumed that they were always there, just hanging around, you know. It took a year for me to learn differently. On my first day in San Felipe last year, I saw two of them in the church; they looked so young! They let me take their pictures. They didn't look like killers to me (but Father Jack clarified a few things for me a little later in the day!) Anyway, this year, after the dance the night before—well, the next morning, two of the kids—just teenagers!— were found dead beside the road leading out of town toward the military garrison—their heads cut off! Beheaded! Oh, Mildred! And that wasn't even the worst. I heard about that, but I didn't dare try to see them. I couldn't bear to witness something like that.

I didn't know what to do, so I went into the church to find Father Jack and to pray. I was so frightened. I didn't know what was going on; it was so horrible. I went into the church. There were two or three people leaving as I went in. I thought they must be hurrying down the steps to go see the bodies of the children. So, I went on into the church, thinking I might find Father Jack, but no one was there. Well, I was looking around for him, and then I thought, maybe he might be in the back of the altar area. Sometimes I had seen the cofradia working with the relics.

Mildred! When I went back to the chapel in the rear of the sanctuary, I stepped on something wet, some spots on the floor, and slipped down. I really hurt my shoulder and elbow when I landed. I fell down, and when I rolled over and looked up, I saw the body of one of the little Felipino girls hanging by the neck about twelve feet off the floor. Her forearms were bound behind her with rope just below the elbows, and Mildred! Her hands had been cut off! It was her blood on the floor! I can't stand it, Mildred! I just don't know what in the world is going on! I've never been so frightened in all my life! I ran screaming out the side door of the altar and ran right into Father Jack. I just collapsed. I was so hysterical I couldn't even speak. I just sat there at his feet sobbing and sobbing uncontrollably.

Father Jack left me on the ground outside the door, and he went inside. Then I heard him curse and swear. He was yelling at the top of his voice. It was the only time in the two years that I worked with him that I ever heard him take the Lord's name in vain. He just seemed to explode! It was horrible and frightening to hear him like that, because I knew that he was so shocked and hurt, and really, he was almost out of control.

Later, I learned that the little girl that I discovered was the daughter of the shaman of the Maximón, Andres Menchu Xoy. Among the "traditionals," he's probably the most respected man in the village. People really fear him. He is supposed to have incredible powers and spiritual gifts. There's a lot of speculation as to why the children were killed. Rumors are flying! Most think the little girl's murder is an attempt to target leaders in the community. Others think it is an attempt to divide San Felipe by pitting the major religious groups against each other. The oldest Xoy brothers have been active members of the civil patrol, and one of them personally killed two of the leaders of a neighboring aldea. Several people saw them talking with soldiers after the killings, and a lot of people think they're in pretty deep with the military and working against their father. Does any of this make sense?

It's so hard! It is so hard to live here and watch how these people suffer so! I know that I can leave at any time I wish, but the Tzutujiles have no other place to go. They go to their houses every night in terror that the killers will come and steal them away or worse yet, their children. And they wake up to a new day not knowing if the soldiers will surprise them in their homes to beat them, steal their meager possessions, or rape them in front of their own children. Why? How can they do these things? They weren't born like that! What happens to people that make them able to do these things to other people? And to children! I just don't understand! I'll never be able to understand!

Every morning, the tourists come here and see the soldiers walking around in the streets with their heavy field rifles, and they don't think anything about it. They've already seen them all over the capital, probably for the first day or so after they arrive or before they began their tour of the jade factory in

Antigua or the market at Chichi. So, by the time they cross the lake, they're more or less used to the idea of the troops. And it's the same thing they see from village to village. They'll stop them on the street corners and ask them to let them take their photographs—just like I did on my first day in San Felipe! Oh, I can't believe just how naive I was! I just thought they were so young and cute, just part of the exotic trappings along with the quaint Indians at their looms, the volcanoes, Tikal, and all. The tourists don't have any idea what the presence of these soldiers mean to the people. They are really afraid and have every right to be.

Oh! Here's one for you! I was talking with one of the catechists the other day. He was just about to go visit one of the widows who lost her husband in an accident two years ago, and she's been having a lot of difficulty raising her four kids. He was just taking off a basket of bread and beans to her house when an American woman came into the front of the church. We had heard the horn on the boat down at the launch about twenty minutes earlier, so we weren't surprised when she walked in with her video camera just a-rolling. Well, when she saw me, she came up to me and asked me where I was from, assuming from my long blonde hair that I must have been with one of the other tourist groups that had arrived that morning. Her name was Bertha something or other. She was from Dallas, and she dragged out of her purse this write up from the travel section of the *Dallas Morning News* extolling the virtues of the "land of eternal spring." She had some questions about directions to some of the places that she read about in the article. She wanted to find the Maximón compound and all that, you know.

Well, I was scanning the article, and when I turned to the second page, I found a little blocked off piece of text about the "political situation" in Guatemala. It advised travellers to Guatemala not to take too seriously somewhat "exaggerated claims of political turmoil in the country today"! I couldn't believe it! It went on to say something like that "while a small insurgency, in years past, had attempted to disrupt the country and to destabilize the government, with the help of military aid and training from the United States, the Guatemalan army had been able to eradicate political violence in the highlands caused by a few cadres of communist guerrillas." It added that "while charges of human rights groups in the past had decried the country's mounting toll of the `disappeared' and tortured, with the new president's assumption of office, the human rights record had actually improved dramatically and that travellers need take only the normal pre-cautions when traveling to the major tourist sites"!

I just wanted to throw up, if you'll excuse me! I mean, these people want to come down here, drag out the old credit card, sit out beside the pool at the Camino Real, and have some pretty little native girl bring them rounds of jizz-on-the-rocks all day until they're shit-faced by night, want to "oouuuuu and ahhhhhhh" at the ruins, and get pissed off if some one-eyed campesino with half a leg and a broken down crutch hits them up for a dime in the park. I'm sorry, Mildred! I really lost it! But I just can't help it. Father Jack—*Father Jack!*—there it is again!

You know, when I think about it, I think Father Jack really knew that he was a marked man. He was changed when he came back from Oklahoma last time. That's what they said. I had gone home for a little R & R, and when I came back, Santiago told me how it was before and then how everything started to change for Father Jack. Santiago told me that when Father Jack first arrived back in '68, there were a number of American priests and lay workers in San Felipe—Father Thomas and Father George, they were from Oklahoma, too. He said there were two Carmelite sisters, Jessica and María, and some Maryknoll Sister—I can't remember exactly who she was. That was back in the mid sixties. But by the late seventies, Father Jack was the only one left. I don't know why I'm going on about this—I'm sure you and the family know all about that. I was just trying to make the point that Santiago was so insistent on—that Father Jack was the one who stayed. He was the one who cared enough about the people not to abandon them. He was their shepherd who wouldn't run when the wolves were at the gate.

Father George never thought much about Father Jack when he first came—I know that. Santiago said Father George thought he wasn't very bright. He didn't think Father Jack would ever learn Spanish. But he did! He said he learned to speak pretty well in just the first year he was there—passable, you know, just to be able to get around, go to the market and all. What really made him special to the Felipinos, though, was that he learned to speak Tzutujil! I wonder, did he ever speak it around you and the rest of his family?

But come the '80s, he was the only one. He was the only one who stayed, and he learned to speak Spanish and Tzutujil, both. That's just incredible to me. I guess I'm rambling. Santiago told me how busy Father Jack always was. One time he gave communion to more than 3,000 people in just one day. He baptized more than 200 babies one Sunday. People were always around him. He was training people for the health clinic. He himself used to operate the bulldozer . . . he'd be working on it from sun up until five or six in the afternoon, conduct an evening mass and classes for Confirmation. Santiago said the man never stopped.

That's the same man I met when I arrived two years ago. What made the big difference just before I came, Santiago said, was the growing violence. I know that Father Jack wrote to you and your dad and mother back in Okarche, but I think that he must not have told them what was really happening here. I ran across a copy of a letter that he shared with the Archbishop last year on behalf of Father Arnulfo, the Tzutujil priest who was assigned to the parish at San Felipe three years ago. I know that Father Jack was very worried about him. In the letter to the Archbishop, he explained in great detail the difficulties that the Felipinos were facing at the time. I probably shouldn't have done it, but when I found a copy of the letter in his folder, I xeroxed it and am enclosing it with this note.

Oh, Mildred, I loved him so much! I have never met another person so completely dedicated to his work or to the people he served. I just can't believe what has happened! Why did a person as good as Father Jack have to be sacrificed to such an evil? And to what end? Don't they realize that they are only driving the people to the hills and into the arms of the guerrillas? Isn't that ironic? You know, Father Jack never supported the guerrillas. In fact, he warned the people about the dangers that that kind of activity could bring to San Felipe. Now, some of the people have fled to the hills. If the army will kill an American priest, the people feel they have no hope and are completely lost. Some of them, undoubtedly, will join the insurgents out of desperation, and I see no end to the violence.

Oh, it just hit me again! Mildred, being his sister and all, I'm sure you must be experiencing the same shocks that we are. They just come in little waves of reflections—I see something familar, something that I remember him working with—and I feel him standing there. In a moment, I relive that awful evening all over again. And it is these little things—just then, seeing the schedule of worship for the baptisms next week that we were working on for the last three weeks. *Oh, Mildred!* I just can't stand it. Who's going to tell the people? Who's going to be there for them when they show up with their little ones? Some of them will have walked for days to bring their infants to the church! What are they going to think? What are they going to do?—

Mildred, I'm sorry. It's been two days since I've been able to get back to this letter. I had to stop writing when I heard that the Sisters were returning and had to tell them what happened. They were just coming back from the capital and were really frightened. The military had stopped the bus at Sololá and ordered everyone off to check their cedulas. One of the little indigenous girls selling cashews at the roadside asked them if they had heard what had happened at San Felipe and then told them, I guess, the basic details. They were crying so! I had to spend the rest of the evening with them to help us all get through the night. Yesterday, all the people—I've never seen so many people in the plaza!—they all came together to protest the removal of Father Jack's body, and Don Fernando, the mayor, announced the results of his negotiations with the officials. They have allowed the medical authorities to remove his heart for burial in the church. *Oh, Mildred!* These people loved your brother so much!

I can't go on—really! I just have to stop and put this letter in the post, or I'll never get it finished. So, please know that I am with you. I really respect you and all the work that you are doing. I enjoyed meeting you last year and seeing you again this past April. Please know that I will be here for you and your family in any way that I can. I think that I can stay here and finish my work with the agricultural project either this month or the next, and then I'll have to reconsider my assignment. I had a meeting with a man from the American Embassy this morning. He was out here to pick up the rest of Father Jack's things. He asked me what I thought. I told him we had a letter of support from the military commander authorizing the fertilizer project, and he told me that he thought I wouldn't have any problem completing the work. So, I'll be here for a little while longer if you need my help in any way.

Yours in the faith,

Susan Simpson

P.S. I'm enclosing the copy of Father Jack's letter to the Archbishop in Oklahoma.

* * *

February 1, 1990

Dear Archbishop Merton,

Much has been written in the past few months about our situation here in Guatemala. Some of it is true, some exaggerated, and some apparently false. I am writing to you now to clarify that situation and, in its light, to ask you for your special help on behalf of an associate.

The political and military problems have been escalating over the past few months in a context of continued disenfranchisement and impoverishment of the Indian populations. All across the country, reports tell of army attacks on many of the aldeas. Some of the priests report whole villages wiped out and the deaths of thousands of campesinos. Many people have fled to the mountains and others, apparently, northward into Mexico.

Here in San Felipe we have suffered ten kidnappings and apparent murders in the last eighteen months. I say "apparent murders" because only two of their bodies have been recovered. I have no idea why they have been killed. The military came to San Felipe last year and said that guerrillas were living in and operating from San Felipe. I know that they came once—just a small group after the killing of the military commissioner. They staged a meeting—more of a demonstration—for about two hours in front of the church, explaining who they were and why they had killed the commissioner. Then they left. But the military says they came from San Felipe and that they were stepping up activities to destroy them. Certainly, none of the men seized so far, to my knowledge, had any connections with the insurgents. They were just peasant farmers who worked hard, were members of the church. They went early before sunrise into the fields on the slopes of the mountain and came home long after dark.

Now, 32 children have no fathers or bread earners for their families, and the six Carmelite sisters and I have been working with the widows to provide them enough food to stay alive, but it is really a sorry situation.

Just as ominous is the situation for Fr. Arnulfo Botel, my assistant. He has received two death threats, and we are all very worried for him. We think that he has been targeted because he is a native Guatemalan, the first to be ordained and assigned to this parish. Since the first death threat, Fr. Botel has been staying within the compound working with the Sisters to help with the literacy classes and preparing food for the destitute families I mentioned above. Now he has received a second threat, and we believe that, given the pattern of these things, this threat places him in imminent danger. It specifically tells him to leave the country or be killed.

Father Merton, I am asking that you send him a letter of invitation to come to Oklahoma for work in a diocese there until things settle down again here. I know that he could be of service in the clinics or at the hospital in Okla City. Your invitation would justify his request for a visa and work authorization and would give him an opportunity for an immediate departure. I think I can get him to the consulate in the capital without any complications if you can send the letter quickly, but if we wait very long, I don't know.

As for myself, I think that I am not a target, at least for the time being. Twelve priests have left the country under threat. Ten of them were foreigners, but none have been Americans. I won't hesitate to leave if I come under threat, because I don't want to endanger our workers and the catechists if I stay. Of course, I don't want to leave. I feel like my place is here, and the people have come to depend on me and the church during these difficult times. The shepherd cannot run at the first howl of the wolves.

I hope that you will keep much of this and especially the details private. I couldn't send it by regular mail for fear of censorship and possible reprisals. Please pass on my love and concern to Robert and Trish and to all my family in Okarche.

Love in Christ,

Jack

* * *

August 11, 1990

Dear Susan,

I appreciate very much the lovely letter of condolence that you shared with me. I found it when I returned from Okarche after the services there and in Oklahoma City. We had so much support from the people of Oklahoma. Archbishop Merton gave the eulogy and Bishop Paris conducted the Mass in the Cathedral.

What you said about Jack really moved me. I think many people shared close relationships with him, although every one was so special and unique as certainly yours seems to have been. I know that one family named their newborn son after Jack after he had saved the life of an older boy who almost drowned. Another time, he insisted on taking a young man to the hospital when he discovered a suspicious bleeding sore in his mouth. It turned out to be a malignant cancer. Jack paid for the surgery himself from a trust fund he used for emergencies. He was doing that kind of thing all the time, and the people really came to love him.

One thing I wish I could learn more about, however, is the report I have heard circulating stateside that Jack had had a confrontation with the army at some meeting in San Felipe. Have you heard anything about that? The reason I am so concerned about this is because I have heard that he had challenged the military commander directly and that that was what probably targeted him for assassination. I was thinking that it might have been the letter that guy sent to the Embassy, you know—the guy who stood up in the service last year who told Jack he thought he was a subversive and lying about the situation in Guatemala. I had no idea Jack had stood up to the military, if that's true. I would appreciate anything you could find out about that?

Susan, you have no idea how much your letter has meant to me. I can tell how much Jack certainly meant to you. We all share in the grief over his loss, but we must not lose heart and certainly not our faith. Jack was moving with the spiritual flow of things. I sense that, and I think you do, too. The blessing of God's love is more sacred than even the miracle of our lives; the embrace of the Holy Spirit warmer than the touch of death. And as you continue to step so tenuously there in San Felipe, go in peace with the knowledge that there is nothing that can separate us from the love of God.

Love to you and friends in San Felipe,
Mildred

* * *

August 25, 1990
Dear Mildred,

I was out of San Felipe for about four days after your letter arrived and didn't get it until I returned. Things are still very unsettled here. People are still very hurt, angry, and afraid. And I'm not so sure what to make of my own situation. I thought that it would be okay to continue on the fertilizer project, but I got word from one of the workers that most of them weren't coming back to the project. Two of them had received death threats. Word got out, and since I was a close friend of Father Jack, they assumed it was because of that. So, right now, I don't think we can return.

As soon as I read your letter, I realized that I hadn't mentioned the meeting of the military commander and the church leaders. I can't believe I didn't say anything about that. I must have just blanked out. I wasn't there, but Santiago was, and he was the one who told me about the confrontation.

Santiago said that about two months before the massacre in front of the military post last December, the military commander called a meeting of the religious leaders of the community. They all met in one of the evangelical churches. The commander got up in front of all these ministers and told them that the troops were in San Felipe because the guerrillas were still operating in the area. He said the guerrillas were responsible for all the disappearances and murders of the campesinos. He said that the army would stay in the area until the guerrillas and all their subversive supporters had been eradicated and the area made safe again. All the evangelicals nodded in agreement. One of them even stood up and told the commander how grateful the community was for the army's support.

At that point, Father Jack had heard enough. He stood up and asked permission to make a statement. He stood right up and faced the commander directly and told him that it wasn't the guerrillas who were killing the people, that it was the army. He said they had no disappearances and tortured bodies of the people until the army arrived. He said the first mutilated body appeared just two days after the troops arrived at the post. Father Jack said that if the commander was serious about bringing peace back to San Felipe, he and the troops couldn't leave soon enough! Can you believe that! He didn't give that commander any slack at all, but he spoke right up and challenged him face to face.

Santiago said that you should have seen the face of the commander. He took a step toward the priest and swung his machine gun right toward Father Jack. He was angry enough then to pull the trigger on him. Santiago said it was really tense. The commander couldn't say a word. When I asked him about it, Santiago said he really believes that this was the moment that probably sealed his fate in San Felipe. Santiago said that the commander just stared at him for better than a minute without saying a word. He just stood there staring at him getting madder and madder. Then, he turned around and motioned something to his attaché and the two of them left the church without saying anything else. Everyone was really frightened. But Father Jack was the only one who had the nerve to stand up and say directly what everyone of them knew.

That night, Santiago and the other catechists—three or four of them—and some of the other church leaders followed Father Jack back to the church rectory. No one said anything. Father Jack seemed sort of lost in thought. They all went into the library and sat down with him. Then Father Jack started talking very softly to them. He said he knew that they were all in great danger if they stayed any longer, that Santiago and the other catechists should leave as soon as possible. They all said they really didn't want to go as long as Father Jack was there, that they all felt their job was to be there to help him and members of the church, particularly the old people and the widows, who depended on them for so much. Father Jack told them that if they stayed, they all risked being killed along with other members of their families and friends. That made an impression on them, and they all gathered around Father Jack to tell him goodbye. I think they all knew what was happening and that this was probably the last time that they would be alone together with their pastor. It was very sad, and everyone was crying.

I heard one report that said that that was the same night that Father Jack was shot, but that's not true. It was like I said. It was sometime in October, about two months before the massacre. That's really all I know, just what Santiago told me. He was the only one who was there that's still in San Felipe. I hope this helps to clear up any questions.

Something else that's in the mix down here—we have a reporter from Texas—Marcus Finley, from McAllen in the Rio Grande Valley. He came down here at the suggestion of Father Mike, our priest at St. Michael's in

Brownsville. He arrived last week to do research on Father Jack and the mission here. He was doing environmental studies in Pasadena before moving to the *McAllen Star* several months ago. He said he got interested in Guatemala after talking with Guatemalan refugees there in Brownsville. I spent about three days with him, showing him the site where the people were killed in the massacre and the little study where Father Jack died. The Bishop has approved our making a chapel out of the room where he was killed. Father Jack was an unwilling martyr. He would have been embarrassed by all the attention he has received in death, but even after this short time, people have started to make pilgrimages to the church. They want to see where he died. Because they loved him so much, many of them are praying to him as if he were already a saint. It's truly moving, Mildred.

Marcus Finley, the reporter, is deeply upset with the violence. I think that Father Mike in Brownsville gave him a fair idea what was happening. He talked to me at length about the interview the two of them had with a couple of Guatemalan girls—well, I say the two of them, because apparently, Marcus had to wait outside while Father Mike counseled with them. But the sense of the reality of the violence, the human toll, the physical wounds, the emotional trauma of even a single act of violence against the people of San Felipe has been very difficult for him to process. It's almost as if he has suffered the wounds himself. He seems really battle scarred by this first visit. Anyway, he got a letter from a friend in New Orleans about two weeks ago, and he left a couple of days later. He's supposed to be back next week. He told me he was going to try to get some freelance assignments from a couple of papers in New Orleans for human rights stories. So, he's supposed to be back any day now. I told him he really had to be careful about how he approached people because he could get them and all of us killed if word gets back to the military about the kind of story he wants to do.

Mildred, I hope this letter finds you well in your work with the homeless there in KC. I know how much you care and are doing for them there. I have really enjoyed the growing correspondence with you. Your friendship is a living link with Father Jack and everything he meant to me. Write again soon when you have time.

Love,
Susan Simpson

* * *

October 14, 1990
Dear Mildred,

I am so scared! Marcus Finley is dead! I just received word this morning that Guatemalan police picked up his body beside the road on the other side of the lake just outside Post #14, the *Bruceros* garrison. He had been badly beaten and hacked several times with a machete. I guess I saw it coming, but I was just too paralyzed to try to do anything about it.

Early on, I tried to stop him. After he came to San Felipe several months ago—late July or early August, I can't remember exactly anymore—I could tell that he was greatly disturbed about what was going on in the country. In fact, after his first week or two, he was trying to figure out how to get in contact with the guerrillas. He was ready to go from house to house to find a contact. I finally convinced him that that would probably get a lot of people killed pretty quickly! What he really wanted to do was to find one of the guerrilla *comandantes* in the URNG high command and do an interview with him on the peace process in the context of the continued savagery of the war.

Then, just one morning, I saw him walking toward the boat landing. I hadn't talked with him for maybe two or three days. I asked him where he was going. He said that he was going back to the states, back to New Orleans. He was gone for maybe a month. No, I guess he was gone a good two months, now that I think about it. Anyway, he just showed up again at the project office without much to say at first.

I was surprised to see him. I asked him how the R&R had been in New Orleans. He said fine and didn't go into great detail. But then later that night, he told me an incredible story. A friend of his in New Orleans knew a Guatemalan refugee that he said he ought to meet. Marcus looked him up two or three days later, and the two agreed to meet later on that evening for a meal at a small cafe several blocks off Bourbon Street there in the French quarter. Marcus explained that he was a reporter and had been in Guatemala. The refugee told him a little about his own story, but not as much as he would reveal on their second meeting. Anyway, Marcus explained how it was his objective to get to the mountains to interview any one of the four commanders of the URNG, that he was freelancing now and thought it was good timing for a story on the peace process. The refugee had to go to work, but he told him to meet him at the cafe for lunch the next day, that he might be able to help him.

The next day the two met at the cafe. Marcus said that this guy must have been deeply involved in the guerrilla movement to have had the contact that he did. He said they talked for awhile. Marcus figures the guy was apparently trying to test him for his real interest in the project. They talked for a while longer, almost an hour, he said.

And then the guy said, "Let's take a walk."

"My name isn't `Juan,'" said the man. "But that's what everyone here calls me."

The two of them ambled over to the park just opposite the Cathedral in Jackson Square. Juan reached down and flicked off a mound of pigeon dropping caked on one of the benches and sat down, offering the cleaner spot to Marcus.

"Let me tell you a story, okay?" said Juan. "I grew up in Guatemala City, the capital, in zona 5, a pretty poor neighborhood. When the earthquake hit in February, 1976, I was a teacher in an elementary school. I was also a lay worker in an evangelical church and began working immediately to help organize relief work in the community. About five of us developed a plan for supporting the people around us for about twenty blocks, because the government wasn't sending anybody to help or even look at what had happened in our neighborhood."

"We worked very hard," said Juan, becoming more animated with the recitation. "We organized a clean up committee to check out the houses and pull down the structures that still might fall and hurt people. We created a small clinic with the help of one of the nurses from Roosevelt Hospital. She lived in the same area. She would finish her work at the hospital and then come back to the barrio and work an extra shift with the children and other injured people. She had contacts in the States at some church, and she was able to get bundles of medical supplies shipped in through the diplomatic pouch at the American embassy."

"I think that's what started bringing the attention of the government." Juan's voice began to drop a little.

"They started wondering where we were getting those supplies. People from other neighborhoods started coming into our clinic when the word got out. We started getting reports that we were being watched. I didn't care. We weren't doing anything illegal, and besides, we had the support of the whole American government! So, I didn't care. Let them watch."

Juan reached down for his cup of coffee and sipped a long draft, wiped his mouth on his napkin, and glanced around the cafe.

"Well," he continued. "One day I had gone to San Marcos with my parents for the weekend. That's where my grandparents lived, and my family always went to check on them and help them. Fortunately for them, the earthquake didn't destroy their house—it just knocked off the plaster on the walls and broke some dishes and things. They were very lucky, but we still went to see

them. It made them feel more secure, you know."

"So?" asked Marcus Finley.

"So," said Juan, "I had gone down the street—it must have been about 6 o'clock in the morning—to buy some rolls for breakfast. When I got back to the gate, I saw a motorcycle parked in front of the house next door. I didn't think anything about it particularly, just that I hadn't noticed it before."

"Well," said Juan as he took another sip of his coffee. "Well, I was about to open the gate when two guys walked up to me. One of them asked me if I owned the motorcycle. I said that I didn't. He asked me if I knew who owned it. I said I had no idea and started to open the gate."

"Well, just then," said Juan, his eyes beginning to squint. "Just then these two guys jumped me, and I knew right off that they were trying to kidnap me. I started struggling and screaming. Someone across the street must have been watching because they told my parents that these guys threw me in the back of a police van and drove off, but they never tried to stop them. I don't remember anything else about that because they must have knocked me out. When I woke up, they had me tied up in a room at the police station. I could tell it was a police station because I could hear conversations out in the hall. They were talking to people about police matters."

Juan finished his coffee and set the cup aside.

"I was tied to a chair for the rest of the afternoon," he continued. "Then after the sun went down, one of them—a big fat guy—came in and started smoking. He walked back and forth cursing me and asking questions about my guerrilla activities. He said he knew that I was a guerrilla. He said he had proof of it. He said it would go easier on me if I would just sign a confession that another guy was writing for me. I could hear someone pecking around on a typewriter in the other room. I could also hear some guys down the hall not too far away. One of them kept screaming every once in and a while. He'd let out a yell and a long groan. There was somebody in there beating on him. You could hear the whacks, you know."

Juan looked cautiously at the people strolling by, one couple pushing a stroller carrying a small infant. He waited until they had passed some distance before he resumed.

"Well," he continued, "I think he was just working up to beat me up, because the more questions he asked me, the more pissed off he got. He walked around behind me, and I felt his foot lift the chair rung and then push me over. When I fell, I hit the front of my head on the table leg. My head was just pounding after that."

"Then I felt being lifted up by the chair. They had tied some kind of rope

behind my back through the slats in the back of the chair and were hoisting me up."

Juan raised his hands slightly off the table to indicate the movement up, the only motion he had made throughout the recitation.

"They pulled me about four feet off the floor. I was just hanging there facing the floor with my back and arms tied to the back of the chair and my ankles tied to the legs. The other guy turned on a small radio that I hadn't noticed before. It was playing music from El Salvador. Both of them lit up cigarettes and started swinging me and turning me around and around."

"Who's your comandante?" one of them asked me.

"I don't have a comandante," I protested.

"Let me ask you again," said the policeman, and he started turning me slowly, around and around.

"I don't know any comandante," I said again. They started swinging me as I turned in circles.

"Let me ask you one more time," the policeman said. "Who's your comandante in the guerrillas?"

I didn't say anything because I thought it would only make it worse. I couldn't have been more wrong. All of a sudden, I crashed into the wall. It broke my jaw, and I could feel the blood streaming from my mouth where I bit almost completely through my lower lip. My whole head was throbbing. It hurt so bad I just wanted to pass out. They started swinging me back and forth. Every time, I bounced off the wall, crashing my shoulders and my head."

"I must have blacked out," explained Juan, "because I woke up after that on a mattress. When they saw me coming around, these two guys picked up a bucket of water and threw it on me. I was drenched. All of a sudden, something hit me; I don't know where. I started jumping all over from one side to another, over and over again. You're not going to believe this! The goddamn mattress was wired! I thought my head was going to explode. I remember screaming over and over for them to stop! They must have thought that was just about the funniest thing they'd seen all day! They never stopped laughing while I was flopping around. It was too much pain. I've never felt anything like that before, and I passed out again."

Juan reached in his shirt pocket, pulled out a cigarette, and offered another to Marcus Finley.

"No thanks," said the reporter. Juan lit his cigarette and took a slow drag, his attention momentarily fixed on a small group of tourists exiting the front of the cathedral. He flicked the long head of ashes from his cigarette and ground them into powder under his shoe.

"Just like that!" said Juan. "That's what the militaries and the richos want to do to the people, to anyone who steps up, to anyone who tries to make a difference, just a little improvement, you know. Just like that!" And he pretended to grind the ashes again under the sole off his shoe.

Juan inhaled a final drag on his cigarette and crushed the filter under the same foot, then continued his story.

"At one point," he said, "they dragged me out into the hall and propped me up in a chair. I was sitting next to two other guys, I think the ones that I had heard screaming down the hall throughout my interrogation. One of these guys had the end of his tongue cut off. Maybe he bit it off, I don't know. His face was all swollen. He was missing one eye. This other guy sitting next to me—his arms just hung limp to his sides. One of them was all twisted, so it must have been torn loose from the shoulder. He couldn't move either one. He looked at me and said, `You gotta hang in there, guy. We all heard you, and we're pulling for you. When they leave us alone, we both pray for you to make it and get out of here, okay?'"

"I couldn't believe what I was hearing," said Juan. "Here were these guys so badly beaten they were close to death, and they were worried about me! I never saw them again. They were probably taken out that same night and killed."

"How did you survive?" asked Marcus Finley.

"I had to sign a paper that said I was in a car accident, that the police had no responsibility for my injuries."

"You're kidding!" said the reporter.

"No!" said Juan. "I had to sign the paper or they would have killed me, no question about it."

"I don't know how you made it," said Marcus Finley.

"If it hadn't been for Dalila," explained Juan, "I wouldn't be here today."

"Dalila?" asked the reporter.

"Dalila," said Juan. "Yeah."

"Who is she?" asked Marcus Finley.

"Dalila?" repeated Juan. Marcus nodded.

Juan retrieved another cigarette and tapped the filter against the side of the pack.

"Dalila . . ." said Juan, looking away and pausing for a moment. "Dalila was a girl who attended our church. She was a student at the University of San Carlos. She had been active as a leader in the Student Association. She had been picked up by G-2 before and tortured, also. Well, she started coming by to see me. She could understand what I had experienced. To make it short,

after about a year we became lovers, and we moved in with each other. We had a kid, and after a while, I went back to teaching. Then, about four years ago, I got another death threat."

"Shit!" said Marcus Finley. "Why?"

"I don't know," said Juan.

"What did you do?"

"I got out," said Juan. "I left for the states."

"And Dalila?" asked the reporter.

Juan didn't answer straight away but took another long drag on his cigarette and stared off to the opposite side. Then he turned his head slightly toward Marcus Finley and said simply, "Dead!"

"Dead?" asked Marcus Finley, quite surprised. "But why?"

"Well," said Juan, "Dalila had been very outspoken as a student activist at the University. She had been picked up, like I said, before—in fact, twice before. Both times they had beaten her up pretty badly. Her uncle was a big-shit colonel, and he's the only reason that they let her go. The family kissed up to the President through this colonel, and he went to a G-2 contact he had in the National Palace and was able to get her released. But she knew a lot of stuff, you know, about the army—names, faces, techniques, places and all that, so they couldn't take the chance of her ever telling anyone."

"Did you know when it happened?" asked Marcus Finley.

"Yeah, I knew," explained Juan. "I got a call from her just before. She got picked up a third time, and when she was released, she was really scared. I could tell. She called me and asked me how to apply for an American visa. I told her, and she went to the consulate at the embassy. It took about two weeks for her to get the visa. On the night before she was supposed to leave, she made plans to go into the capital from Chiquimula. She was going to leave our son with a friend who lived in an apartment near the airport and then leave on the early morning flight for Houston. But she never made it to the apartment."

"What happened?" asked Marcus.

"Well, somewhere along the highway on the way into the capital, these two guys stopped her cab and pulled her out. They didn't bother the cab driver. He already knew the address where she was going, so he just went on to her friend's apartment and reported Dalila's kidnapping."

"And then?" returned Marcus.

"Well," said Juan as he fired up another cigarette. "Well, her body showed up three days later in a park in the capital. They had chopped her up with a machete. They had wacked her across the chest, cut off her hands, and tried to peel her face off."

Marcus Finley just stared at his informant. How could he even relate such a thing!

"Your kidding!" said the reporter.

Juan blew a stream of smoke over his shoulder and dropped his head for a moment. Then he reached into his back pocket and removed his wallet. Slowly, he fumbled through a bundle of loose receipts and folded bills and retrieved a worn clipping of a newspaper photograph.

"There!" offered Juan. "That's a morgue shot of what they did to Dalila. It appeared in the Guatemala press a couple of days later."

Marcus trembled as he took the fragile clipping. He stared at it for several moments and then returned it to Juan.

"That's incredible! Simply incredible!" he managed. "How is such a thing possible? How can one human being do something like that to another? That's just incredible! I don't know what to say! What can you say to something like that?"

Juan folded the clipping once again and slipped it back into his wallet. "Well, they do it! And somebody down there's probably getting it right now, I'll tell you that."

"Incredible!" offered Marcus.

"But that's not the end of it," said Juan.

"What do you mean?" asked Marcus.

"Well, about two months ago," said Juan, "I went over to the little restaurant where we were just now."

"Yeah!"

"I've got a friend who works on weekends—just to fill in—back in the kitchen," explained Juan. "He's Guatemalan. I go in there to drink a little coffee, get a bite to eat, and just pass some time, you know what I mean?"

Marcus nodded.

"Well, about two months ago," said Juan, "I was just getting ready to leave. I was walking from the bar through the front of the restaurant where we were sitting."

Marcus stared intensely at Juan as he related the story.

"Well, these two guys were sitting there. I hadn't seen them before because I had gone back into the kitchen to talk with my friend. So, when I came out, there they were."

"Yeah," said Marcus Finley, reinforcing his attention.

"Well, one says—as I'm just walking out—he says, 'Hey, paisano! Come on over and have a drink, okay?' So, I turned around and looked at them. They were just a couple of regular-looking guys, kind of young, you know."

Trying to anticipate the direction and resolution, Marcus was riveted to the unfolding story.

"So, I went over and sat down. We passed some small talk—how we liked New Orleans, and all. Then I asked them why they were here, when they had left Guatemala. One of them, the older one, said that they had been there for about a month or so, that they were taking a little needed R&R from the `fighting.'"

"From the `fighting'? I asked." Juan took another draw on his cigarette.

"Yeah," said the younger one. "The captain and me—we're getting tired of fucking around all those goddamn guerrillas, you know."

"You mean `fucking those goddamn guerrillas,' don't you?" joked the older one.

"Whatever!" responded the younger-looking one with a smirk and a jerk of laughter. "Whatever comes up, huh?"

And they both laughed.

"You guys aren't `military,' I said."

"The shit we're not!" the younger guy said.

"I said, `No, you guys are too young for military!' I couldn't believe they were military, they looked so young, you know. So this guy—the young one—whips out his wallet and flashes his military ID, and then he introduced himself as `Lieutenant Peréz,' and his buddy `Captain Salazar—he's a pretty big stick back in Guáte!' And the `captain' drew out his ID."

"I took the ID's," said Juan. "I just looked at them in amazement—they still looked so young. So, I handed them back, and I asked the younger one—he's the one who seemed to want to do all the talking so, I asked the younger one what he meant. He said—`now get this!' He said that `this "Captain Salazar" was the one who "fucked" that guerrilla bitch at the university!'"

"Man, I got chills all over. I said, `What guerrilla bitch?'—I just had this sense of where he was heading."

"He just looked me in the eye and said, `that guerrilla puta, Dalila!' Goddamn! I was frozen! I felt the hair stand up on the back of my neck. I couldn't even move. I just stared at him."

"And you want to know something else?" said the Captain, looking me cold in the eyes. "That bitch's `punch'—that bastard's living right here! Right here in New Orleans!"

Juan took a deeper drag on his cigarette which had just about burned to the filter and looked away. Then, he dropped it to his feet and slowly ground it with the toe of his shoe.

"Man!" he said, exhaling a fog of smoke from deep within his lungs. "I

mean, I really lost it. I told them that I needed to take a leak and got up to go back to the kitchen."

Marcus Finley sat stoned on the bench.

"I had never been so angry in all my life!" said Juan, just shaking his head. "I was going for the sonofabitches! I went racing back to the kitchen and grabbed a cleaver off the wall—I was going to split some army heads! My friend saw me. He knew that something had really got to me, and he wouldn't let me go back out to the tables. He just grabbed me until I got a hold of myself and asked me what was going on. I said, 'Look! Look at those two guys out there sitting at the table near the door!' My friend looked through the little window in the kitchen door out into the restaurant. He said, `Look at what?' `Those two guys!' I said. `What two guys?' he said."

"They were gone?" asked Marcus Finley.

"Yeah!" said Juan. "The bastards were gone!"

"It was a setup!" said the reporter.

"Yeah! No shit! A goddamn setup!" said Juan. "They were military, all right! Military intelligence! The bastards were G-2 all the way! Well, they got their message across. They know who I am, and it doesn't matter where I go or what I do, they can take me out! They know where to find me, and they can take me out any time they're ready!"

Marcus Finley rose and stepped away from Juan who was sitting on the bench, his face buried in his hands and his elbows planted deeply into both knees. The reporter drifted away down the sidewalk a few paces, his hands anchored in the bottom of back pockets. He paused in thought for a moment and then shook his head. He turned back to Juan who was already up and walking toward him.

"Look," said Juan. "You want to get to the mountains, right?

"Yeah!" he said. "You're damned straight! I damn sure want that story!"

Juan stared straight ahead for a second or two and then reached back for his wallet, looking left and right over both shoulders. Satisfied he wasn't being observed, he reached into the wallet and took out a small slip of paper.

"You got a pen?" he asked the reporter.

"Yeah!" said Marcus Finley opening up a small address book and clicking on his ballpoint pen. "Go ahead."

"Well, write this number down," said Juan. Marcus Finley copied the number from the slip of paper and handed it back to Juan.

"Wait until about 9 o'clock tonight, and then call this number. Ask for `María' and tell her that `Juan' told you to call her. Tell her what you want to do. I can't guarantee anything, and `Maria's just a go-between, but maybe she

can help you, okay?"

"Yeah! You bet!" said Marcus Finley. "Thanks a lot, okay?" Marcus Finley reached out and shook the hand of his informant.

"Look!" said Juan, appearing nervous and somewhat out of order. "I've got to go. If anybody ever asks, we never talked, okay? You've never met me. You've never even heard of me, all right? But call this telephone number. Good luck! Maybe I'll see you around."

And with that, Juan drifted into a group of elderly tourists who had just exited a bus for a tour of the square.

"Oh, you know what? I think I just broke a nail getting down from that bus!" a fussy woman in her mid-sixties said to her husband fidgeting with an umbrella handle in his Cartier carry-on. "Why I never!" she said.

For a moment, Marcus pondered the exchange, the gruesome story of Juan and Dalila, which horrified and, at the same time, fascinated him in every detail of the relation. But it was the photograph that had sealed his commitment. He had to get to the mountains. He had to write the story of the people's struggle. Through his newfound commitment, he had to make a contribution; somehow, he had to make a difference. Perhaps the key was in this telephone number to this "María."

Marcus Finley looked at the note in his hand with the quickly drafted number and rummaged through his pants pocket with his left hand for telephone change. Why wait another moment? He would take his chances with the rest of his day. He had nothing else pressing, now that Juan had departed. He looked past the little mob of tourists who were moving away from him and found a pay phone on the corner a block away.

Twisted roots flexed under his feet as he maneuvered up the steep trail, the turn ahead a ticklish step no more than the width of a tiny foothold skirting a thousand foot drop off. "María," a tiny little woman, sported a pack across her narrow shoulders that mirrored her own body weight in the transmitter of "La Voz Popular," the radio program of the guerrillas. Deftly, his guide tripped lightly over the rutted trail and disappeared around the corner of the bluff stretching away from him.

"Cuidado! Cuidado!" said María as she urged him cautiously.

The deep blue sky stretched up and away from him as he reached the edge of the path. One slip on the damp clay would send him flying over the edge, cheating the Kaibiles plodding up the trail behind them. As he placed his foot at the edge of the drop off, he felt coins slip down his pants leg from a hole in his left pocket.

"You dropin' you change, buddy, all ova' th' sidewalk, pal!" said the street

sweeper pushing a small pile of trash and dirt ahead of his broom.

"Oh!" said Marcus, jolted from his clandestine fantasy. "Why, yes! I'm sorry! I mean, thank you! Thank you very much!"

Embarrassed by his own clumsiness, Marcus Finley reached down to the curb and began collecting the trail of coins that were spinning off the side of his shoe. He wouldn't make it in the mountains if he couldn't keep it together on a flat sidewalk. He was suddenly startled that along with the coins, in his reverie, he might have dropped the note with the number, but he was relieved to find it still in his right hand.

"Get it together, fool!" he muttered to himself.

"`María' . . . " He noted his handwriting and the number below, reconfirming the reality of what he was plainly projecting as a touchstone in his career and life.

"`María' . . . not a name but a . . . a, a key to the path leading to the commandante in the mountains." Marcus Finley dropped the salvaged quarter into the telephone and slowly depressed the numbers on the face of phone.

"Let it be `María' . . . let her be home! Please!" And the phone continued to ring. `María' wasn't home.

"Perhaps I screwed up the number," he thought, and he dropped the quarter into the phone again for a second attempt. The connection engaged at the other end, and he waited for the first ring, then the second, the third, a fourth, one more—a fifth . . . `María' wasn't home.

"Shit!" he said. "Well, now what?"

Marcus Finley looked around and spotted the tourist group wobbling around the front of the church, craning their necks this way and that, taking in the sights. "She broke her fingernail! She broke her poor little fingernail! Imagine that! I've just seen a woman chopped to pieces with a machete, and she broke her fucking little fingernail! Isn't that the shits!"

Marcus Finley had time to kill—a whole day until nine o'clock that night. He hadn't anticipated a day off. There wasn't time for that. He could be back in the mountains. He could be interviewing the compas in their mountains and waiting for the arrival of their comandante. But no. Here he was four blocks off Bourbon Street in New Orleans with a whole wasted day before him.

"Well?" he asked himself. "What to do?"

He had options. Marcus Finley surveyed two or three alternatives. He could catch the trolley and slip over to Tulane University to view the Guatemalan collection and browse through the archives. Or he could hang out around the river and strike up some conversation among the locals and maybe get a lead on a follow-up to the last story he had written in Pasadena—the one on the irradiated pollutants he had heard about being dumped up river in the Mississippi. Or he could go over to the book shop on whatever the street was and pick up a Mesoamerican text—that was it! He could look for the Americas Watch publications that Susan Simpson had suggested. That was a plan that would take him to lunch anyway. It was well and good to have options!

"An educated man always has alternatives," he told himself. "Options set apart the professional from the mindless, floundering herds."

"God!" he said to himself as he looked up at the refurbished apartments. Marcus Finley never got enough of the French Quarter. The tall, lithe street lamps, the green frame shutters on the windows—intrigue behind every shade! It brought the writer out in him—`Maggie on a hot tin roof'! Somebody had to write that line— compose it at one time or another—just another writer, it could have been him.

"Maggie between the sheets! Soft, white, sensuous Maggie between fresh sheets just ripped off the clothesline behind the tenement house." Maybe he had something going there.

The quarter that he had been flipping as he made his way down the sidewalk toward the bookstore slipped off the back of his hand, tinkled as it hit the pavement, and rolled off the curb into the gutter.

"Buy that fo'bits off ya'," said a musty, little black boy.

"What?" asked Marcus Finley of the shoe shine boy who was slapping at flies with his shine rag as they landed in reach along the gutter.

"Buy that fo'bits, dude!" returned the boy.

What do you mean, `buy' this `fo'bits'?" said the reporter. "What'll you give for this quarter, huh?"

"I dunno!" said the shine boy. "Ain't got much, but I'll give you my lucky wood'n nickel!"

"A what?" asked the reporter.

"Lucky wood'n nickel!" offered the shine boy as he plunged his right hand deeply into his pocket.

"Here'y'go!" said the shine boy.

It was worth the dalliance. Marcus Finley hadn't seen a wooden nickel in years, ever since he was a kid and he had gone with his dad to Dallas to visit the State Fair, back in . . . in . . . in? He couldn't even remember, it had been so long.

Marcus Finley took the grimy wooden nickel from the small entrepreneur and turned it over to read the printed side.

"Plant the . . . ?" He couldn't quite make it out. "Plant the . . . the . . . the `what'? Plant the 'what'?"

" . . . the seed!" said the boy. "You gotta plant th' seed!"

"What `seed'?" asked the reporter.

" . . . seed!" reiterated the boy.

"Yeah, I know!" said Marcus Finley, "but what `seed'?"

"I dunno'," said the shine boy. "Jus' the seed, I guess. Jus' gotta keep on plant'n' the seed!"

"Well, I guess your right, Mr. Man!" said Marcus Finley. "I guess you're right, for sure! We just have to keep `plant'n' seeds' and see what sprouts! I guess you're right! Here you go. Here's your fo' bits, okay?"

"Clean them sneakers, mister?" asked the boy.

"What?" asked the reporter, preoccupied with the wooden nickle.

"Them sneakers!" repeated the boy. "White'm up real good fo' ya, huh?"

Marcus Finley glanced down at his shoes. "No! . . . No, thank you! Say! Listen, there! You've given me the best idea I've had in months. Here! Here you go! Take this and get you a good lunch, okay! And thanks a lot!"

Flushed with his new idea, Marcus Finley shoved a five-dollar bill into the fist of the small shoe shine boy. Wooden nickels! That was good! He'd stamp up some wooden nickels, a whole gross of them . . . what the hell! a thousand of them. They'd be light. If he left them blank, they'd get through customs without any problems, and he'd get a printer back at Panajachel, sure! There was the German hippie kid that did the silk screening. He had said he could put it on anything, right?

"Goddamn!" Marcus Finley would strike a blow for human rights in Guatemala: he'd plant wooden nickels outside every fucking military post across the country!

"Oh! I almost forgot!" he said, turning back once again to the surprised black boy, and Marcus Finley handed the boy the wayward quarter.

"Gotta plant them seeds, huh mister!" cried the boy after the reporter who went hustling off down the street.

"That whitey gonna harvest shit, fo' sho'!" said the shoe shine boy as he slipped the five dollars into a wad of twenties, fifties, and hundreds that he pulled up from inside his underwear. "Dum' sumofabitch, sho' nuf! That whitey! Shit, fo' sho!"

"Why don't you meet me in front of the library on campus?" asked María. I'm only about four blocks away, and I can drop off my work and meet you, say . . . in a half hour?"

It seemed more like an hour to Marcus who paced back and forth in front of the library, attracting the disturbing attention of one of the library assistants working at a receptionist's desk just inside the door.

"We don't allow subversives to hang around on campus," said the library assistant. "You'll have to move on, or I'll have to call campus security."

"I'm sorry!" said Marcus somewhat bewildered by her greeting. "I must have been day-dreaming."

"Juan gave you my name?" she asked as they shook hands rather formally on the sidewalk.

"Yes, that's right," said the reporter.

"Okay," she returned. "Look! It's warmer out here than I expected. Why don't we go over to the Union. We can find a booth and talk over there."

"Yeah," said Marcus Finley. "That's fine with me. I'll follow you."

María wasn't so far removed from his image of the compa in his fantasy that morning. A slight, small ladino woman, perhaps twenty-five, twenty-six years old. Wiry, acute, quick. Long, black hair that streamed freely down her back. Reserved. No room for maneuvering. Self-assured to a hair trigger. All business. Could blow it easily.

As they walked across the campus to the Union, Marcus Finley felt increasingly ill at ease. Back from only a brief trip to the highlands, he had no credentials for what he wanted to do. He didn't even know his way around well enough to take a local bus. How could he possibly convince her of his integrity in this matter?

María and the reporter continued their trek across the campus in the balmy evening air. Marcus Finley watched the precise, measured gait of the woman who, walking seemingly along side him, set both the direction and the pace. With each step, he became more and more nervous. There wasn't any way she was going to take him seriously. She walked straight and narrow. Looked at her watch twice. Kept stepping out front. No way—he might as well slip back, bow out with as much grace as possible.

For the first time in his life, Marcus Finley was embarrassed by his good looks that had always counted for so much whenever he wanted something from any woman. Now, confidence in his tawny, manicured body wilted in the presence of the fierce, determined lines and buckling brows of the tiny Guatemalan woman to his right, outstripping him in every way.

"Mr. Finley?" asked María. She stopped and turned around when she realized that the reporter was no longer beside her. "Is there something the matter?"

Almost immobilized by the wave of insecurity and self-doubt, Marcus Finley had sat down on a park bench, ostensibly to tie his shoe.

"No—ahh," he started. "No, that's all right—just . . . ahh, the shoe, just had to tie my shoe . . . there!"

Marcus Finley finished the bow in his shoe lace and began to rise slowly, uncertain how to proceed even after the borrowed time for recollection. He was even more uncertain of himself than ever.

"Look-ahh!" The reporter swept his lungs for a breath of courage to continue. "Look, María! Maybe this isn't such a good idea, after all."

"Mr. Finley," said María, stepping with obvious purpose before him. "I talked to Juan only briefly, but he said that you are very concerned about Guatemala, no?"

"Yes . . ." offered the reporter. "Yes, very . . . I'm very concerned about Guatemala. That's why I'm here, but . . . but I guess that it's just that I'm . . . I'm just so very new at all this kind of thing."

"Mr. Finley!" said María, as she looked firmly and directly into his eyes. "Mr. Finley, that's good! And that's the only reason I am here now!"

She continued to gaze into his eyes.

"Do you understand that?" asked María, never blinking or changing her expression. "There are so very few Americans who even know where Guatemala is or who could care less. You say you `care about Guatemala,' and okay! That's good! But . . . well, I don't know what you have in mind exactly, so I can't make any commitments until we have talked, and maybe not then, I don't know. But you seem very nervous and upset. Why don't we just sit down here and talk, okay?"

The two took a seat on a concrete bench under a large, moss-covered water oak tree.

"Am I that obvious?" asked the reporter, managing a nervous laugh.

María never smiled.

"I guess so," returned Marcus Finley, confessing only what was obvious to both of them.

"Mr. Finley," said María, pushing beyond the familiarities. "Why do you want to go to the mountains?"

Marcus Finley was startled by the abruptness of the question.

"What did Juan tell you?" he asked, dropping himself all pretense of social formalities.

"He told me that you want to go to the mountains," said María.

"And . . . ?" asked Marcus Finley.

"Why do you want to go to the mountains, Mr. Finley?" she asked again, reasserting her direction of the inquiry.

" . . . to . . . I want, I mean . . . ." Marcus Finley had never before suffered from such a breakdown of self-control. María looked away and tucked her palms between her clenched knees. Then she looked down, waiting for the

reporter to recompose himself and for his answer.

"Look," said Marcus Finley. "I'll tell you right out: I want to do a story on the guerrilla movement in Guatemala. I want to . . . "

Marcus Finley was beginning to reassert himself. " . . . I want to interview one of the—"

"Why?" interrupted María. "Why do you want to interview one of the . . . one of the commanders? I think that's what you were about to say, no?"

"Exactly!" said the reporter.

María rolled her shoulders back, looked to the side away from Marcus Finley, and let out a long sigh. Then, slowly she looked straight ahead and said, "Reporters don't just go to the mountains, Mr. Finley, and `interview a commander.' That doesn't happen."

"You're saying such a thing `hasn't happened yet'? or it `hasn't happened and it won't happen?'" Marcus Finley pursued more sharply than he actually had intended.

"Mr. Finley," said María as she rose and wiped crumpled dry leaves from the seat of her slacks. "You're probably a very fine reporter and a good person, but I think perhaps this conversation should end, okay? I'm sorry if you feel mislead, all right?"

"Wait a minute!" said Marcus insistently as he rose to meet María's rejection. "There are people dying in Guatemala, lady! And you can use all the help you can get!"

María turned squarely to face the frustrated reporter and looked straight into his eyes, flashing angrily.

"I know there are people dying in Guatemala, Mr. Finley!" sparked the woman. "Five of them were my own family! I don't think I need to hear a lesson in the Guatemalan repression from you! And I certainly don't think an interview between a commander and some self-serving gringo newspaper reporter is going to do much to change that, do you, Mr. Finley?"

Marcus Finley was shut down. He stood staring at the woman, unable to believe what he was hearing when he hadn't even framed his proposal. The woman was either blinded by prejudice, off balance, or both. Certainly, it wasn't anything he had said . . . "body language"? Maybe that was it—the way he carried himself or his looks. Maybe she just hated men! Hell! He shouldn't—didn't have to deal with that. The thing for him to do, quite clearly, was to check out of this situation with as much finesse as possible and to forget the whole thing.

"Look!" said Marcus Finley. "I've greatly offended you somehow, María—or whatever your name is—which is the last thing I ever had in mind, and I

certainly apologize for that. So, I tell you what—let me just say that I hope someday that peace can come to both you and your family and to all the people of Guatemala. And remember, please, that there are a few of us `gringos' who have come to know and love the people of Guatemala very much and are horrified by their tragedy and would do something, if only they knew how, okay?"

María stood with her arms folded across her breasts, a fixed stare riveted to her face that appeared to check any possibility of compromise.

"So . . ." said Marcus Finley. "So, María! Good luck, okay?"

Marcus turned away without offering even a handshake, shoved his fists into his jacket pockets, and walked away from the solitary figure, leaving her alone in the middle of the campus commons.

"What the hell did I do?" he couldn't help but ask himself. "Crazy! That's just crazy!" he said out loud.

The reporter walked slowly back through the campus to the taxi stand next to the convenience store on the corner and hailed the first cab that rounded the intersection. The drive back to his hotel was featureless as he became lost in the reflections of the day. Maybe he was in it for the sense of glory, the attention that would come if he was able to "score the big one." Perhaps he wasn't being "up front" in this thing. Maybe the Guatemalan people weren't the real priority for him.

"I mean," he pondered, "what if I got to the mountains? What would an interview with a commander really mean? What good would come out of it? Would it be worth the risk—to himself and everyone who would have to help him—what if it got someone killed?" Just maybe this whole thing was bigger than he had or could realize from such a limited perspective. Maybe it was he who was all off base. Maybe he was too naive to know what he was getting into. Perhaps he ought to go back to the bar at the hotel and drink a beer. That seemed something he could negotiate while he continued to sort out his feelings and plans at this point.

"Say! Say!" Marcus Finley cried to the cabby. "Say, forget the hotel, okay? Take me over to . . . take me over to the—the, let me see—okay, here it is!"

The reporter pulled a matchbook from his pocket. "Yeah, here it is—the `Fontainebleau Cafe.' That's about four blocks east of the hotel, okay?"

"Right!" returned the driver.

Something—maybe Juan's encounter with the Guatemalan intelligence officers—was pulling him back to the little cafe. There was something fetching about just being in the place where the international intrigue had been orchestrated. He imagined both the lieutenant and the captain hailing Juan as he walked by them toward the door. The streets were empty as the cab turned past the front of his hotel and proceeded the extra blocks to the cafe.

Marcus Finley paid the cabby and stepped out of the car into the heavy, humid night air, suffused with the muted strains of a wailing Dixieland clarinet.

Marcus stood back as the crusty cab pulled away from the curb, pulverizing the remains of a broken beer bottle under the rear tire. The reporter turned back to the door of the cafe, layers of dark green paint peeling away from the door frame behind the worn brass doorknob.

Inside, the Fontainebleau Cafe smelled like scorched grease, its dominant hue, a shadowy yellow brown. Two local shrimpers, in sweat-stained T-shirts and soiled jeans, rolled the swells of their bulging stomachs over the edge of the pool table in the rear of the saloon. Their Cajun swearing had distracted two rather dowdy, working women who swooned in laughter at the pool players' robust allusions to New Orleans whores, the punch line of an earlier joke.

Engulfed in a cloud of cigarette smoke at the end of the bar, both women appeared to be in their late forties or early fifties. The louder of the two had long since succumbed to a massive weight problem. Rolls of limpsy fat undulated inside her purple sweater and hot pink, polyester stretch pants as she swayed from side to side in a spasm of raspy laughs and coughs. Her flat-chested, anorexic partner stared into the mirror behind the bar where the two of them could watch the patrons come and go. Her sunken cheeks inflamed in rouge, she darted glances at the handsome reporter, sizing up opportunity from under false eyelashes flitting over her liquid gaze like a pair of venus fly traps.

At one of the four tables in the front of the restaurant, two middle-aged men, probably in their fifties, one in a muddy T-shirt, the other in a plaid flannel, long-sleeved shirt, swigged two beers on tap. Across from each other at the farthest table next to the planter, two Hispanic laborers whispered under the closing refrain of the clarinet solo. Overhead, secured on a wall mount, a color television set broadcast a round of CNN news, the cadences of the pert, blonde news anchor tripping off sound bites over the wail of Pete Fountain. Marcus looked over at the bar on his left and decided to take a stool on the end next to the door.

"What'll it be, jack?" asked the bartender, wiping a spill from the countertop.

"Whatever you've got on tap, okay?"

"You got it!" said the bartender. The two women glanced over at the

reporter and exchanged winks and a smile. The shrimpers broke another wrack of pool balls, the clatter bouncing off the high ceiling.

"That'll be three-fifty," said the shiny, black bartender in his black bow tie and heavily starched white vest. "Here . . . have some chips, jack," and he slid a basket of potato chips toward Marcus Finley from the corner of the bar.

"Goddamn! Mardi Gras robbery!" thought the reporter, as he retrieved his wallet from his jacket.

A map of Mexico and Central America blew up over the shoulder of the CNN announcer.

"Today, there comes a story of tragedy in Central America," said the hair-sprayed, bottle blonde. "Outside Antigua Guatemala, a bus carrying forty-five members of a folkloric ballet from the Mexican state of Chihuahua plummeted over a sixty-foot embankment, killing twenty-five people including the bus driver, sponsors, and seventeen young people, sixteen to twenty-five years old. Reporters on the scene . . . "

"Where'd that happen?" asked the platinum anorexic.

"Where'd what happen?" asked the other, coughing on the exhaled smoke of her cigarette.

"That accident—where all those people in the bus . . . " said the first.

"What are you talking about?" asked the other.

"That accident, there on the news . . . " replied the first. "Antigua or something."

"Shit!" said the second. "How would I know. I don't even know the name of the bar down the street—hey, Slappy! Turn that goddamn channel to something interesting, huh?"

The bartender finished drying a wine glass and winked at the patron. "Whad'a'ya want? The `one-900' numbers?"

"Yeah! That's all right!" said the anorexic.

"Put it on that talk show," offered the second. "You know, where they badger those drag queens, those fags and all."

The bartender pointed the remote-control channel changer toward the monitor and flipped through the stations to "Wheel of Fortune."

"How 'bout `Wheel of Fortune'?" he asked.

"Yeah," said the first. "That's better than that `spike a dike' show, no shit! Bring me another beer, will you, sweetheart?"

"You know," confided the blimp. "I get so tired of all that news crap anyway, you know what I mean? It must be a dull-ass day in the studio if they gotta drag off to bum-fucking Egypt for a story! Jee-zus Christ! Hey, Slappy! Make that two, okay?"

His initial reaction was to make a move on the conversation, but Marcus Finley only sat still and stroked the condensation from the side of the mug of beer.

"That's the American bitch goddess!" mused the reporter. "That's the mother of just about the whole American public!" he thought to himself. They'll never care about what's going on in the world, because they're too busy splayed over bar stools while sitting on their thumbs `fist-fucking' themselves, smugly satisfied in the general consensus of just how great they are. No, if anything is going to be done, it's going to be done in spite of the American people, not because of them or even in reference to them. And that will be the really `revolutionary' element, not that they would ever recognize it or be touched by it until Japan or the rest of the Pacific Rim corners the market again on cellular phones and the price of fresh strawberries in December jumps to $20 a basket. No, they just think they understand revolution and revolutionaries. `Revolution' is a fine and righteous thing when it means rolling back school taxes and throwing out the bastards. Anything else is "just plain 'commie-nist,' by God!"

"Kiss my ass!" cried the pool player in the T-shirt. "Wrack'em again, you sorry somovabitch!"

"There you go!" thought the reporter. "`True' Americans," Marcus Finley pontificated, "`True Americans' are about fifty-five years old, two hundred and sixty pounds, bald and color-blind to anything but red, white, and blue. Outside of what touches their pay check every two weeks, they care practically about nothing. Forty hours with benefits, cheap day care, big tits and country music, `Playmate' cheer-leaders and Monday night football, Jesus and the preacher, the local chiropractor, a wide-ass waitress and chicken fried steak—that's about all that matters. Back in Texas, Pasadena couldn't have cared less if Sims Bayou had glazed over thick enough to skate on. They don't have the foggiest idea about what their government is really doing out there in the world. And in the cause of social justice—here or anywhere else, for that matter—the American people are simply irrelevant."

Marcus Finley could just see the Bishop of Brownsville commiserating with the "Queen of Sheba" at the other end of the bar. You might as well throw into the mix the "soup guy" back in Harlingen, an old geezer of an oligarch with a sticky eye on an adjacent "unpopulated" 300,000 acres, a State Department bureaucrat at the Latin American desk with only two years left to learn Spanish before retirement, every junior high school PTA vice president in America, any "Republican" president, a bored, overstuffed Guatemalan general, a lean, ambitious colonel, a couple of grunt soldiers from Patozí,

Cardinal "what's'isname," the Pope, and a hell-raising Pentecostal Sunday School teacher, a U.S. immigration judge with an honorary degree from the local junior college, and—what the hell!—probably a pre-menstrual guerrilla combatant (if they're all as confused and crazy as this one tonight, you'd only need one!) Stir 'em all up, and there you have it!—all the makings of a fine little holocaust!

"Why?" Marcus Finley asked himself. Why is it so hard to awaken the American people? Why is it impossible to persuade our own government that a policy that will tolerate the wholesale slaughter of men, women, and children in the name of some smoothly worded, cotton-mouthed rhetoric is simply wrong? Why?

The reporter began doodling on his napkin—little "x"s and circles, then circles around "x"s, then other lines and circles and more "x"s. Then it hit him—American foreign policy is written in Washington, not in a place like San Felipe del Lago. If all the bureaucrats in the State Department had grown up on a finca in Guatemala and then gone on to graduate school, they wouldn't be writing the kinds of policies they're writing. And another problem—they were all "Sunday-schooled" before they were "educated"! They all went off to their fine eastern colleges and universities with certain gilded truths already jingling deeply in their pockets. They all grew up trusting authority and authorities, already pledged to studying and mastering the same systems and processes to the same self-end of someday controlling their own little fiefdoms. Each one of them had matriculated up the ladder, confident in the common knowledge that America had cornered the market on absolute truth, never once questioning that the whole world wasn't naturally metamorphosing into the image of a red, white, and blue-collar America.

The surface of Marcus Finley's napkin exploded in clusters of little "x"s and circles.

"There you go!" he smiled. Then you let all these little Sunday-schoolers move into state offices, and what do you expect? You're going to get policies articulated to defend every little doctrine that got gold-starred on Sunday mornings.

Suddenly, it had all come together, and the reporter slammed the point of the ballpoint through the napkin, breaking it off into the top of the counter.

"There you have it: perfect little scholastics, every one of them!" Marcus Finley delighted in the wash of his fresh insight. Quintessential little deductivists—the whole damn crew of them—all of them completely comfortable in their tidy, little syllogistic view of the rest of the world! They sit around the offices all day with their feet propped up, so what do you want?

What else could you possibly expect? Just let some unfortunate bit of inductive data cloud up their pristine little definitions, and they'll just close their eyes, reach deeply into their pockets, and throw up fists full of taxpayers' dollars—their answer to anything even a little disconcerting. Well, fuck 'em! Screw 'em, every one!

Marcus Finley crumpled the napkin in his fist and pitched it over his shoulder.

"We don't have a lot of extra help to clean up after inconsiderate patrons, mister!" said the bartender.

"What . . . ? asked the reporter, incredulous at the banality of the previous remark.

"Oh, I heard you!" said Marcus Finley. "Here . . . here, chump! Have another one!"

Marcus Finley wadded up a second napkin and flipped it toward the bartender.

"Hey! Look here, bub!" said the bartender, a deep scowl dropping from his forehead. "Why don't you just find somewhere else to . . . "

"Yeah! Yeah!" said the reporter. "Okay, okay! "I'm outta here!"

Marcus Finley rose, pushed the stool up under the bar, and turned to leave.

"Look!" he said. "Look! I'm sorry! I guess I just let something get to me. I'm sorry. That's not like me usually. I'm really sorry, okay?"

Marcus Finley waved off the bartender and moved toward the door. Then he remembered the tip. As he reached into his pocket, his fingers found the wooden nickel. He pulled it out and turned it over to look at the words one more time.

"Plant-the-seed," he repeated just under his breath. And then to the bartender, "Here you go!"

Marcus Finley smiled and pitched the disk to the bartender, then walked out the door.

"What th' hell!" said Slappy, holding the wooden slug in the open palm of his hand.

"Plant the seed . . ." he mused as he held it under the light next to the cash register. "Plant the seed? What the hell?"

The evening air was thickening, a slight drizzle misting the sidewalk and windshields as he began the stroll back to his hotel.

"What a screwed-up evening!" he thought. A couple of teenagers embraced in a doorway as he passed. A taxi honked at a dog that had drifted into the street. Marcus Finley stopped at the first intersection, trying to decide

whether he was hungry enough for a club sandwich or a "subway" before he turned in.

"Oh, hell!" thought the reporter. He had left the rest of his money in his wallet in the other jacket back in his room. He'd have to go back there before he would have enough to buy a meal, and it wasn't worth all the effort. He would just go on back to the hotel and rethink what he should do. Burks, his contact at the Journal, wouldn't be back in town before midnight or one o'clock, so he would have to wait until he returned to his office the next morning. He wasn't looking forward to reporting the dissipation of his plans and the possible loss of his contracts.

"That's a bummer! said the editor. "What're you going to do? What do you have in mind."

"Well," said Marcus Finley. "I'd like to come by and talk with you. I've got a couple of ideas I've been thinking about and . . . "

"Yeah, well," said Burks, "I just got back in late last night, and I gotta lot of stuff on the desk I've got to do this morning."

"What about lunch?" asked Marcus Finley.

"Yeah, that might work," said Burks. " . . . no, shit! I gotta staff meeting. Hey! I tell you what? Why don't I get back with you tomorrow or the next day. We can get together, maybe and . . . "

"No, that won't work," said the reporter. "I've got to get back down to San Felipe. My plane leaves tomorrow night. I can't afford to change my flight schedule. I'll lose about a hundred dollars if I change it now . . . "

"Well, look!" said the editor. "You go on back down there, and if something hits, send it up. I'll see what I can do, okay?"

"Well . . . " said Marcus Finley somewhat reluctant and disappointed. "I'm really short on cash. You don't think you could advance me a little stake in a couple of stories, do you?"

"Well, Marcus," said the editor. "I really wish I could, but things have changed a lot around here. I can't do that anymore. We've got to send all these story ideas up the line. Four or five supervisors have to check off on these things. That's just about ended most of our freelancing. You do what you can, and I'll see what I can get for you. But an advance is sort of out of the question. Gee, I'm sorry, Marcus, but check back in as soon as you can, okay?"

"Yeah," said Marcus Finley. "Yeah, I'll do that!"

"Son of a bitch!" thought the reporter. "Goddamn! Son of a bitch!"

Marcus Finley was disappointed and angry at the unexpected turn in his plans. No one had ever thought to go to the mountains with the guerrillas. It was a story he knew would bring international attention to the repression and one that would secure his own credentials as an international investigative reporter. This wasn't to be the end of it. Surely, he would find another connection. New Orleans couldn't be the end of the line. If he had another day he would lay over in Houston, but that wouldn't work either. He had just about burned his bridges there.

"There's got to be a connection in Guatemala!" he thought to himself. He began to survey his options in the lake area. The EGP had been operating around Atitlán for the past decade. Of late, the attack on the military commissioner, the attempted seizure of the weapons within the last two months—someone had to know something. Someone was a conduit in San Felipe, and he would be able to find out when he returned. In fact, that was it! The little wooden nickel project! He would seed a few of them discreetly in the streets of San Felipe and watch the fuss. For sure, the army would come in looking for subversives and blame the guerrillas. People would start talking. They would never suspect a gringo reporter working with the church; he'd be too obvious. The Felipinos would remain hush-hushed until after the army quit prowling around. Then, as soon as they were gone, people would start chattering away. He would make contact easily.

Marcus Finley pulled the New Orleans yellow pages from the desk drawer and began thumbing through the index. Where would he look? He hadn't even thought about how to purchase something like wooden nickels until that moment.

"Novelties!" That had to be it. Quickly, he began flipping through the pages of the phone book. "`Novelties . . . novelties'! Let's see . . . ." Marcus Finley scanned the pages of the novelties section but to no avail. He found not even a single clue to "wooden nickels." Then he thought about ad agencies.

"Yeah!" he said aloud. "Ad agencies. At least they'll be able to steer me in the right direction!"

Before the afternoon was out, Marcus Finley was returning to his hotel with a large box of wooden nickels. He had paid just under $200 for 10,000 smoothly machined wooden disks. The problem was his suitcase. He would have to all but empty the luggage just to accommodate the "nickels." He was allowed only two check-on bags and two carry-ons. If he worked at it, he could figure out a way to get the disks into his larger suitcase.

"These appear to be highly irregular, Mr. Finley," said the customs official at La Aurora International Airport in Guatemala City. "Perhaps you should come with me."

"But I have to return to the lake," said Marcus Finley. "I am going to print

them tonight and scatter them at the military posts. Each soldier will read one of them and shoot their captains, don't you see?"

"You are a subversive, Mr. Finley!" said the customs official.

"Not at all!" protested the reporter. "It's just that I've come to save the indigenous people from genocide, so I have prepared these wooden nickels, you see."

"No," insisted the customs officer. "Mr. Finley, you are a subversive. It's subversive to try to save the indigenous people. They are all subversives, too. They have no rights. They are all squatters on the land of Guatemala. They have to leave. They have to leave or be killed—men, women, and children! All of them!"

"But why the children?" protested the reporter.

"Because," offered the official. "Because, if these little rats are allowed to grow up, they all will become activists! They'll want to be educated! Then, they'll all start whining about better wages, and that will ruin the economy! You see, communists want to destroy the economy. They just want to destroy Guatemala! So, they have to be eliminated."

"Now, about these wooden disks . . . " said the officer. "These are very suspicious, so you must be a subversive, too. I think that the captain in G-2 will have to have you executed before you leave the premises. We can take care of your car. Don't worry about the fine. We can arrange to have the fines reduced or even eliminated, so the captain can execute you without compromising the state on the extended parking fee. We'll go back and make everything right in the books, so are you ready, Mr. Finley? Are you ready to be executed, Mr. Finley? It won't take very long. Are you ready, Mr. Finley? – Mr. Finley? . . . Mr. Finley?"

Marcus Finley lurched forward, horrified by the incredible vision. "Sons of bitches!" he muttered to himself.

He might not be able to change the system, but perhaps he could be at least a small factor, even if it meant spinning only a single thread of doubt in the minds of the poor, unfortunate little campesino kids who happened to get drafted because they were in the wrong spot at the right time for the Goddamned army!

"I may not be able to change the mind of a general," said Marcus Finley, "but every time one of these foot soldiers is ordered to kill a kid, he's going to have to make a decision! Maybe I can prod the process just a little."

Outside the post, Marcus Finley could see troops gathered about the gate and a small unit—probably a patrol—milling around the others preparing back packs. One was obviously a radio operator with what looked like a transmitter strapped over his shoulders. Three of them carried large field rifles, the others, small machine guns. From his vantage point at the mirador overlooking the south rim of the lake, he had trouble making out any other activity in the small post.

Marcus Finley walked back to the car which he had borrowed from Johann Studeker, the German who operated the silkscreen shop at Panajachel. The young printer had refused to take any money for the job which took the two of them almost an entire evening to complete. They had built a template from a piece of three-quarter inch plyboard by drilling rows of evenly distributed holes across the surface. When it was finished, the template held one hundred disks. The screen was framed to fit against two corner braces tacked to the top and side of the template so that they could control the placement of the screen over the template of disks. They had to print all the disks on the first side, drying each rack of printed disks with a hand-held electric hair dryer. The two had worked throughout the evening, each getting more and more excited about the prospects of the protest. It wasn't the first clandestine print job that the young German had completed since his arrival in Panajachel several years before.

Studeker had printed some placards for students at the University of San Carlos for distribution at the May 18th parade in the capital. He had been well-paid by the San Carlos students, but this job was different. This was a direct challenge to military authority, and he had rejected any compensation. Anyway, the novelty of the whole concept of "wooden nickels" had intrigued him.

Marcus Finley was trembling with anticipation as he walked back to the rear of his car. This was to be the last "seeding." He had placed about five dozen of the disks—the last of the "nickels"—in a small belted bag that was originally intended as a tourist's camera case. Carefully, he looked around as he opened the trunk. He reached into the floorboard and retrieved the belted bag and tied it around his waist. Then readjusting it so that the zippered bag hung just in front, he unzipped the top of the bag and reached for one of the "coins."

"Niños, No!" The sharp, clean letters in bold, jet black were striking in their simplicity. He flipped it gingerly over to the reverse and read, "Capitanes, Sí!" The concept was so simple. If a captain orders you to kill a child, you've got two choices: you can shoot the child, or you can shoot the captain!

Well, after Marcus told me what happened in New Orleans, he just sort of disappeared, taking his box of disks with him. Then one day, oh—maybe about three or four days after I had last seen him, some soldiers came to our project. One of them, the captain of the unit, was really angry. He made us all come out and stand in front of the little house. They asked each of us for our identifications—the *cedulas* for each of the Guatemalans and my passport. Then he slung four or five of these wooden nickels on the ground and started asking questions.

That was the first time I had actually seen any of the coins. Everyone looked shocked. I think I was the only one who really knew anything about them—at least of their connection to Marcus. Anyway, the soldiers made us all stand by the wall on the outside of the house while they went inside. They tore the whole place apart, I guess looking for more of the disks or anything else that might look suspicious. After about an hour, they all left. I think that the only reason that they didn't rough any of us around is because I was with the Peace Corps and had my American passport.

The last time I saw Marcus alive, he was really frightened. It was just before midnight when he came into my room which was next to the sisters' quarters in the rectory. I had never seen him so disturbed, completely overcome by fear. It was in his eyes, and the way he moved his head as if he were dodging something coming too close too quickly. He could hardly speak without shaking.

"Marcus! What's the problem?" I asked. I was still dressed but lying in bed reading with just the sheet pulled over me. I ripped back the sheet and reached out for him. He just collapsed beside my bed. It was so . . . so unlike him. I never thought of Marcus as a weak person. But this time he looked really weak and completely vulnerable, like a small child, and he started shaking.

"They're coming for me!" he managed.

"*Who,* Marcus?" I asked in fright. "Who's coming for you? What are you talking about?" His terror was really infectious, and I started trembling right along with him.

"Marcus?" I pleaded. "Marcus? *Tell* me! Who's coming for you? What are you saying?"

"The army!" he cried. "The soldiers from the garrison! They've sent patrols out to find me! They're working their way around the lake from both the west and the east. They've commandeered the boats at Panajachel, and they're stopping all the traffic from this side! They've stopped every bus tonight, checking *cedulas* and asking for me!"

"*Oh, Marcus!* Are you sure?" I cried. "Are you sure it's you they're after? Oh, surely not! Not you!" I didn't realize until later how superficial that must have sounded to him. It wasn't at all comforting. What he wanted was a place to hide.

"Look!" he cried as he bolted away from me. "I've got to go! I've got to find some place where I can get away, at least for tonight!"

"Marcus!" I cried. "*Wait!* Where are you going? There's no place to go tonight? Where do you think you can hide from them? Shut the door! Come back over here!"

"No!" he cried. Tears were racing down his cheeks. "I can't be found here—you! You and the sisters! You would all be killed! I love you all too much, and you've been a big help to me, but I have to go! I just have to go!"

Then he was gone. Oh, Mildred! That's the very last time I ever saw him. A week later, I heard they found his body over on the other side outside the garrison, found his body all . . . I just don't think I can stand it much more! I'm going to have to leave because I heard that the army has said that we are all supporting the guerrillas, that we are all subversives. We're all targets, even the Peace Corps volunteers. And that's the first time for us! Two of the other workers from Xela are leaving tomorrow. I'm going to try to meet them at Los Encuentros around four tomorrow afternoon. We'll go to the embassy in the capital. They'll be able to get us on a flight, and we'll be secure until we have to leave.

Just to be safe, I'm going to leave this letter with the sisters to mail after I'm gone. There're some things I've written here I guess that might be dangerous if they found me carrying it. So, I may be back stateside before you get this letter through the mail from here. I'll call you as soon as I get back to Texas. Please say a prayer for all of us and especially the people of San Felipe.
Love,
Susan

Chapter 29

Among the *Compas*

With only a jacket tied around his waist, Marcus Finley fled the rectory even as the grinding engines of military trucks rumbled through the western entrance to San Felipe. He raced down the side streets, pausing in the shadows, secured from the barking animals whose alarm all but published his retreat. In panic he collapsed on his haunches beside a trash barrel, panting for breath, and trying to assuage the terror that rippled through every muscle.

Where could he go? How could he escape now? There was no time to plan, to chart a course; he had only to *run* and to run *fast!* But that was no answer. Run where? Where could he flee that he might escape the troops whose trucks had already found the plaza and disgorged their terrible messengers of death? Not here. This place—here in the shadows—was only a respite. His car keys? How could he have had forgotten them at such a time as . . . *Car keys!* Was he already *mad?* He had to get control. He couldn't afford to lose it now, not now with the bastards already chasing him up the streets. *Move!* He had to move *on!*—the dogs barking now only two blocks over from where he had just *passed!*

His *breath*—he had to catch h*is breath!* Save hi*s energy!* Take th*e easy step!* He had to find footholds against the smooth cobble stones that could send him sprawling. Away he sprinted up the alley once again, dodging the glow from windows as he ran. Off he sped up the footpaths that turned and twisted upward from the last earthen hovels at the base of the mountain that rose sharply behind the town. Crashing through the rows of crackling corn stalks stumbled the reporter, the treads of his Reeboks sending clouds of fine powder up from the base of each hillock. Up, up into the evening fog he fled, his hot breath puffing before his mouth and into his eyes. High above, he could trace the lower rim of an outcropping. If he could make it, he might stop long enough to catch his breath and scan the town below. Lying flat on his stomach, he might be able to spy the movement of the troops and better assess the success of his escape.

Before he could drop, however, the earth gave way below his feet, and down he slipped, toppling the crisp, brown stalks of maize beneath him. Over and over he rolled, his pin-striped Van Heusen shirt shredded from his ribs and shoulders. Sharp, throbbing pains lanced his scalp just above his left ear and eye. A wash of warm blood momentarily blinded him. He ripped off a shred of the shirt, wiped his eye, and then packed it tightly over the tear in his forehead. Aware of his possible exposure, lying, as he was, between the rows, he rolled over on his stomach in the debris of crushed corn stalks and their mangled husks, then looked from left to right, trying to reconstruct his bearings.

Through the swirling filaments of ground fog, the reporter could see the faint patterns of street lights in the town below. The clipped staccato of captains' orders filtered through the slight rustle of the seared, dry corn husks. The howl of an anxious dog just off the central plaza was answered sympathetically in frustrated barks of other animals aroused farther up the street, their useless protests falling away toward the lake front. Apparently, the soldiers were moving away from him, and Marcus Finley dropped his face in the dirt, relieved for the first moment since his flight began. A fine mist peppered the broken leaves, split and cracked on their stalks. Over the rustle of the burned-out husks, the promontory of rock still stretched up and away above him.

Suddenly, he choked, erupting in a coughing spasm, a stream of flem and bile spewing from his mouth. Again and again, the reporter convulsed, his enraged throat rasped and burning. He rolled over, burying his mouth in his hands to muffle the convulsions, but as they subsided, he was relieved to hear the rumble of trucks proceeding out of the town. He strained to follow their every nuance until they had rounded the bend at the edge of the lake. If they were retreating to Sololá, it would be more than a half hour before he would hear them again chugging up the incline toward the crest of the mountain on the other side of the inlet. He felt secure enough for the first time to sit up and take stock of his wounds. He rolled off a particularly sharp stalk of corn, and as his face turned up to scan the ridge line above, a handful of pebbles sprinkled down onto his head.

Marcus Finley froze. His eyes raced across the horizon, coursing up and down the ridge row. A small breeze unsettled the cloud of mist enveloping the stalks above him, and he strained to catch any hint of movement on the ledge, but only the ripples of the waving corn husks disturbed the damp night air. Somewhere far in the hills beyond, a wild dog barked twice, then sent a howl that drifted in shallow waves over the placid surface of the lake. Then, he heard it—the unmistakable, frantic scuffle of feet only twenty feet above him followed once more by a rain of dirt and gravel. Instantly, he pushed away the loose earth around him and rolled over next to the hillocks of stalks to his right. His heart raced, and his temples throbbed. Any moment now he would be discovered.

"Up! Up! You gringo son of a bitch!" barked the soldier. Marcus Finley felt the sharp thrust of the man's boot crack the side of his left rib cage.

"Up! Get up! You bastard!" repeated the soldier.

The reporter dredged the very pit of his stomach for the energy to turn, but all he could feel was the imprint of the boot still throbbing in his side. He reached up with one hand in a limp gesture to ward off a second blow only to feel the razored edge of the soldier's bayonet plunge into the side of his throat, the fiery burn of the raw cut and the hot, pulsing flow of the blood pumping from his artery. The rubble of the dead corn began to bend down and then whirl in a blur around him. He struggled after the fading light drifting about and gradually dimming from his eyes.

"Get up!" cried the soldier. "Get up! Get up! Get up, you son of a bitch! Get up! "Get up! Get up! Get up, you son of a bitch! Get up!"

And then the chorus: "Get up! Get up! Get up, you son of a bitch! Hah! Hah! Hah! Hah! Hah! Hah! Hah!

Marcus Finley grabbed at his throat, the tender skin wet with perspiration. The jolting vision of his own death had stunned him, but the pungent, fetid odor of musty earth under his chin and nose shocked him back to his senses. The pelting of stones only moments before, however, had not been a dream, and he lay still and prone, listening for something more, anything that might clarify his situation. For a moment, only the dry crackling of leaves answered his fear. Then he heard, *"Ssst!"*

It was a voice somewhere close by. But surely not! Certainly, it was only a conspiracy of his over-ripened senses.

"*Ssst!*" again came the hesitant call. Again, Marcus Finley refused to believe what he thought he had heard.

"*Ssst!*" came the call once more, this time more insistent. Slowly, the reporter turned his head, but could see nothing.

"Ssst! Ssst!" came the call for the fourth time, now clearly from the ledge above him.

"Up here, *señor!"* It was the high-pitched voice of a small child, perhaps a boy—he wasn't sure. Cautiously, the reporter peered above, craning his neck to find the source of the calls.

"*Ohhhh!*" cried the voice, as down the ledge bounded the blurred image of some animal that came crashing through the brittle corn stalks. Marcus pitched over to avoid the flying figure.

"*Jesus!*" protested the startled reporter, as he bumped the bloody wound over his eye on the fragment of a corn cane.

"Señor!" cried the fragile, little voice again in its broken mixture of Spanish and English. "Come *up!* Come up *here!*"

As his eyes readjusted to the breaking fog, Marcus Finley could make out the faint outline of a small black head peering from over the ledge ahead of him. His left knee throbbed as he took his first tremulous steps up the steep incline toward the ledge.

"*Aquí! Aquí!*" said the voice as the reporter reached the top.

"*Okay!*" said Marcus Finley, anxious to discover the source and nature of all the commotion.

"Sígueme! Follow me!" insisted the small child, a boy who emerged from around a shaft of dry corn behind the rock escarpment. Taking charge, the young man motioned the reporter to follow him into the corn rows. Up the narrow path he scampered, the grey wisp of the animal—a small cat—racing before him. Marcus Finley untied his jacket from around his waist and slipped his bruised arms into the sleeves.

Up and up they climbed, the young boy and his pet fading in and out the heavy patches of fog enveloping the *milpa.* Marcus Finley reached the end of the row, almost knocking down the Tzutujil boy who had turned to await his charge, an outsider obviously unfamiliar with the terrain of the field.

"*Oh!*" cried the reporter. "*Disculpe!*"

"*No me preocupa!* Don't worry!" said the boy. *"Sígueme! Arriba allá!* Climb up here!"

"*Whew!*" said the reporter, struggling to catch his breath in the increasingly demanding climb. "*Wait* a minute! *Wait* a minute! Let me catch my *breath!*"

The boy stopped and turned, correctly interpreting the situation if not the words.

"Where are we going . . . where . . . ?" asked the reporter, panting and searching his embarrassingly limited Spanish. *"Adónde . . . ?"*

"*There!"* cried the boy, pointing to a dark slit barely visible in the side of the hill, still a good twenty yards above them.

"*Venga conmigo!* Come with me, *señor!"*

More determinedly, then, Marcus Finley looked up at the spot to satisfy his curiosity, almost forgetting momentarily the fear which had sent him flying through the streets less than a half hour earlier. The Mayan waif reached the crest of a small rise just at what seemed to be the narrow mouth of a cave and disappeared. Marcus Finley slowed as he approached the same, knelt down cautiously at the black opening, and peered within.

"Pasen! Pasen!" came a second voice, this time the dark, insistent appeal of a woman from some muted corner deeper within the hole. Marcus bent down and rolled over onto his stomach so that he might slip backwards into the cave feet first. Slowly, he worked his way down into the passage. Unlike the cool, moist soil of the *milpa,* the earth beneath him appeared to be a finely ground pumice. Increasingly, he sensed the aroma of the familiar, sweet *copal pom*, the incense used in ceremonies performed by the indigenous priests. Just as he was beginning to get his bearings, he was startled by the striking of a match behind him. In a second, a soft glow radiated against the blackened wall of the cave behind him.

"Welcome, *señor!"* said the low voice of the woman. Marcus Finley turned his head. There behind him, silhouetted against the dim, red glow of a candle were the faint outlines of two women and the young boy. The reporter was startled at the response in sharp, secure English.

"Marcus? . . . *Marcus Finley?*"

"Why, *yes!*" said the reporter.

"Come, Mr. Finley," said the woman. "Come further back so that we can see you better and talk. You are safe here with us, okay?"

The reporter was completely disoriented by the greeting and what had transpired in the last few moments. Who were these people who knew his name and could speak English? Susan Simpson was the only person he had found in San Felipe with whom he could communicate comfortably. He had no idea that there might be another in the whole town.

"*Quickly,* Mr. Finley!" insisted the woman. "Come back and find a spot with us so that we can put out the candle."

"*Yes!*" said the reporter. "Yes, *of course!*"

Immediately, Marcus Finley shifted around, rose into a low crouch, and waddled back to the rear of what now he discovered to be a substantial, vaulted room completely blackened with soot and ash. He slipped next to the woman who extended her hand to help him settle comfortably.

"Are you *okay*, *señor?"* asked the woman.

"Yes," said Marcus Finley to the figure veiled in shadows squatting next to him. "Yes, yes I am. Thank you."

"*Good!*" said the woman. "Then we can put out the light."

The woman reached around and pinched out the candle burning softly behind her.

"Perhaps I misjudged you, Mr. Finley," said the woman.

Trying to explore the cave from the disadvantage of the darkness, Marcus Finley was too preoccupied to catch the woman's last remark.

"I'm sorry?" he said.

"In New Orleans—" said the woman. "I think I perhaps misjudged your intentions when we met in New Orleans . . ."

Marcus Finley was stunned.

"María?" he asked.

"Yes," said the woman, still hunched down, her arms wrapped around her knees.

"What . . . ?" stammered the reporter. "I don't understand. Just six weeks ago you were in New Orleans, and now . . . ."

". . . and now the mountains, *no?"* said the woman.

"*Yes!*" said Marcus Finley, surprised and animated by the whole curious and bizarre circumstances.

"Yes, `the mountains,'" echoed the reporter. "But this is all so strange! What in the world are you doing here—what were you doing in . . .?" Marcus Finley thought best to check himself.

". . . `in New Orleans' I think you were about to say, Mr. Finley," said the woman.

"Well, yes, I guess I was," said the reporter.

"Mr. Finley," confided Maria, "from Geneva to this hole in the side of Atitlán—it's all a seamless tapestry. From the fine speeches of the High Commissioner on Human Rights in Switzerland to the last bullet of *the compas* on the other side of this volcano, we are speaking with a common voice. All of us are working for peace and justice in Guatemala."

Marcus sat speechless in his new-found security and the restored confidence of one who had seemed his nemesis only a few weeks before.

"I must apologize for the way I reacted to you, Mr. Finley," said the guerrilla. "But you must understand how *careful* we must be in everything we do and with everyone we meet."

"But what were you doing in New Orleans?" asked Marcus.

"`Acquisitions' and other things," said María.

"I don't understand," said the reporter. "*Guns?* You were purchasing *guns?*"

"*Please!*" María interrupted. "That's all I can *say!*"

"Yes . . . of course—`careful'—you have to be careful what you say," said Marcus Finley. "But now, *here?* How did you happen to be *here* . . . and *tonight?*"

"Well," said María. "We are here for the people. The army is continuing its campaign against the people of Atitlán, the same campaign that took my husband just a few months ago and more than two hundred *compañeros* around the lake in just the past year."

"I'm sorry," said Marcus Finley. "I didn't know."

"It's hard, Mr. Finley," said the guerrilla woman. "It's all so very *hard!* But I am only one of more than 45,000 widows in Guatemala who must struggle without their husbands. It's so very *hard!* But we have to continue the struggle for all of the people. Our common grief makes us strong, and the people *will* prevail! *Someday,* Mr. Finley! *Someday,* the people will overcome the racism and evil that has intimidated them for 500 years. The people are awakening. The people now understand that in their struggle for basic human rights, they are struggling for their very *lives!* Mr. Finley, no one on this mountain was *born* with a gun in his hands! Our spilled blood has given us the right to defend ourselves and to struggle for a peace with *justice!*"

"María," said the reporter. "You have to know—*really know!*—that you are not alone, no more alone in this struggle than the very fact that we are here together. Right *here!* Right *now!*"

"I know," said María. She reached out toward him and took his hand, slipping one of the reporter's wooden nickels into his palm. "I know that *now*, Mr. Finley."

For a moment, the reporter was unable to respond. He accepted the disk and squeezed it tightly in the palm of his hand, as a tremble rippled down his back.

"It was *crazy,*" said Marcus Finley. "It was such a *silly* thing to do!"

"Yes . . ." said the guerrilla. "A *very* `silly thing'! The kind of `silly thing,' that will probably get us all *killed,* but maybe save the life of a *child!* Who's to say—perhaps the lives of a hundred, a *thousand* children! *Yes*, Mr. Finley! A *very* `silly thing'!"

"Where did you find this . . . this one," asked Marcus Finley.

"In the jacket of a soldier we captured last week," explained the *compa.* "He had slipped it into his front jacket pocket. I could see its shape right there in front of his uniform. It's a wonder his captain hadn't discovered it *before!*"

"What did he say?" asked the reporter.

"About . . .?"

"About `this'?" he clarified.

"Nothing," said María.

"Nothing?" asked Marcus Finley, somewhat surprised.

"*Nothing,*" she reiterated. "He couldn't *read!*"

"*Oh!*" stammered the reporter, set aback by the unexpected revelation of illiteracy among the troops.

"Hardly any of the soldiers—the conscripts—can read their own name," said María.

"That's *incredible!*" said the reporter. "There's a school in every *village!"*

"Where did you hear *that?*" she asked.

"Well, I've seen them *myself*—in every village," he said.

"No," she said. "You've apparently seen only the municipalities. Back in the *aldeas,* in the *cantones*—there are few schools. Anyway, even those who go seldom complete more than three years. Mr. Finley, less than one percent of the people ever attend a university."

Marcus Finley was not so interested in the country's educational profile as he was intrigued by the uncanny nature of the whole set of circumstances and the mysteries, up to this point, of this inscrutable woman.

"Where did you learn to speak such good English?" asked the reporter.

"At the IGA—the binational center in the capital," explained María. "I studied for five years. After I married, my husband and I practiced English for our work among the *compas.* We had to. Then, I have been in and out of the states off and on in the past three or four years."

"And you?" asked the reporter. "You attended the university?"

"I have a degree . . . a degree in the humanities," she said. "I studied dance—dance education."

Marcus Finley paused. He couldn't say it out loud, but he had to ask himself—privately anyway—why *dance*? In a country like this, with so much poverty, with less than one percent ever attending a college of any kind, "Why *dance*?"

"Because life is *art*, Mr. Finley!" she said, "Here in the highlands, the first art is music, and dance is the expression of the music of the heart. Look at the people around us—so *poor*, so hungry and wasted, the little ones with the big bellies—they are starving. Over half of them will die before they are five years old. The people suffer so much. But when they come together, they bring the marimba and the *chirimia*, the *tun*, and the harp. They play the flute and the marimba. The old *alcalde* places the reed in the head of the *chirimia,* and with his assistant following him, beating out the rhythm of the drum, they lead the procession of the musicians and the people to the town plaza, and when the music comes together, they dance."

Increasingly infatuated, Marcus Finley sat still, listening to the *compa's* moving explanation.

"Everyone dances, the young people and the old," said María. "They dance and dance, the slow, sad, gentle *`sons.'* I grew up with dance—with the music of the marimba and the flute. I learned to dance, Mr. Finley, holding onto the skirt of my mother as she swept the earthen floor with her soft, graceful steps. I learned to walk by dancing, Mr. Finley. My soul comes alive in the dance."

The other woman sat still and silent beside María. The little boy was gathered up next to his mother, cradling the fuzzy cat in his lap. Neither seemed to have moved during María's explanation. When María had finished her remarks to the reporter, the woman whispered softly in the guerrilla's ear.

Marcus Finley could see faintly María's insistent nod and the finger raised to her mouth. Then María slipped forward onto her knees and moved up toward the mouth of the cave. Marcus panicked momentarily, thinking that she might be leaving them alone deep against the back wall, but he could barely make out her silhouette at the mouth of the cave, enough to realize that she had stopped well inside the entrance. After a few moments, María returned and slipped beside the reporter.

"We have only a few more minutes," she said, "and then we must leave?"

"*Leave?*" asked Marcus Finley. "Leave *tonight?*"

"*Yes!*" she said.

"What about the soldiers?" he asked. "Have they *gone?*"

"No, not all of them," she said. Marcus Finley panicked again, and he could feel his legs quivering uncontrollably.

"I thought they had left—I heard the *trucks!*" he protested.

"Of course!" she said. "They have gone for the others. They will be back. So, we must leave soon."

"But they might be on *patrol!*" said the reporter.

"No, probably not *these!*" she said, "but we don't take unnecessary chances."

"What do you mean?" he asked.

"These are recruits from the post," said María, "but they aren't men, not *kaibiles*. These boys usually won't patrol up *here!*"

"Why? asked Marcus Finley. "Why not? How can you be sure?"

"Because *we're* up here!" she said. Marcus Finley failed to register the implication.

"How can *we* stop them?" he asked.

"*We* can't," she explained, "but the other *'we's'* can and *will* if they try to follow us up the mountain."

"What do you mean?" asked Marcus Finley.

"What I *mean* is . . . ," said María. "What I *mean* is that we're not alone on the mountain. These troops that just arrived are not *kaibiles*. They won't come up on this mountain tonight. They know that they would be cut down before they got as high as we are now."

"That's *incredible!*" said the reporter. "Coming up here, *I* didn't see anyone!"

"Of *course* not!" she said. "That's why you're still alive right now—not that they would have harmed you, but if you could have seen them, the soldiers down in the valley would already have spotted us, too. We would be in a firefight right *now!"*

"So why do we have to leave *tonight?*" asked Marcus Finley.

"Because by morning," he explained, "these troops in the town will have reinforcements, and the helicopter pilots will be able to spot our retreat."

"So we're leaving *now?*" he asked.

"Shortly," said María. "We'll leave in just a few minutes."

"Where are we going?" asked Marcus Finley.

"Over the top," said the guerrilla.

"Over the *top*? . . . the top of the *volcano?*" he asked.

"Straight over the top."

"Why not around?" he asked.

"It's quicker over the top, and it's more secure," she explained. "The other routes around the perimeter are watched. We'll climb straight up until we reach the trees, and then we'll stay just inside the tree line and make our way around the summit."

"How long will that take us?" asked the reporter.

"Normally, about five hours," said María. "But it will probably take us longer with her and the boy."

"Who is she?" asked Marcus Finley.

"María Xquic, the wife of the priest," said María Paloma.

"Oh, I heard about her," he said. "She's the one who stood up in the council and denounced the repression."

"Yes," said María, "and then her husband disappeared, right before the priest."

"And her *children . . .?*" queried the reporter.

"Gone," said the guerrilla. "All gone except this little boy, the little boy and his cat."

"That's *incredible!*" he protested.

"Yes, *incredible*!" she said. "*Wait* a minute!"

María Paloma turned her head toward the front of the cave. As Marcus followed her attention, he saw the shadow of a man sitting at the entrance.

Without a word, María reached behind her and grabbed a shoulder bag, strapped it on, and snapped her fingers toward María Xquic and the boy.

The boy reached up toward his mother's ear, and then she motioned him to the back of the cave.

"*Quickly!*" she said. The little boy retreated to the corner of the cave where Marcus could hear him urinating in the corner. The cat brushed slowly against the reporter's foot and then bounded off toward the boy as he finished.

"Let's *go!*" said María Paloma.

The first steps out of the mouth of the cave were frightening. The little boy gathered his cat, slipped it inside his shoulder bag, and then maneuvered between his mother and María Paloma to avoid exposure to the corn rows on either side. The small party moved quickly into the well-worn path that wound up the side of the foothill overlooking the village. Up ahead, the guard paced some twenty yards in front, pausing every now and then to count heads of those behind him. Then all at once, the small group stopped. The guard waited patiently as the two women seemed to be discussing something, but when it became clear that they were not to resume their climb, he ran back to the group.

"What's the problem?" he asked.

"María has to go *back,*" explained María Paloma. "She has to return to her house."

"That's *impossible!*" said the guard.

"*No!*" said María. "She *has* to go . . . she has left something very important."

"What?" asked the guard.

"It doesn't *matter,*" explained María Paloma. "She has to return."

Manuel, María's small boy, began to cry softly and tremble, too afraid to speak up but too moved to contain his fear. He clutched the cat close to his chest.

"They'll be looking for her," said the guard.

"Probably," said María Paloma. "Perhaps *I* should go. That's *it!* *I'll* go back down. I can be back in thirty minutes."

"You're *crazy!*" said the guard. "Let's *go!*"

"*No!*" said his insistent colleague. "You work your way back down to the cave, and give me thirty—make it forty minutes at the *most.* Then, if I'm not back, I'll catch up. I've got to do this for María. She has paid too heavy a price for the people. I'll be back."

Then the *compa* turned her back, slipped behind a corn row, and disappeared without a sound.

"Let's *go!*" said the guard. "Let's get back to the cave. Quickly and *quietly!*"

Marcus Finley followed the frightened and distraught Tzutujil woman and her son back to the cave. They slipped easily into the mouth, but this time remained close to the opening, more confident that if anything went wrong below, all attention would be fixed there instead of scanning the corn fields above.

From the mouth of the cave, it was impossible to see much of the village proper because of the height of the dead corn stalks of the field in front of them. Marcus Finley peered out beyond the tops of the dry husks, trying to imagine María Paloma's descent back into the town which unrolled before them in a mosaic of faintly outlined rooftops below. The tedious minutes staggered by, each passage marked by a chorus of impatient sighs and worried glances. María Xquic drew the little boy under her arm and wrapped her *peraje* over his shoulder. Manuel reached into his bag to retrieve the cat only to suffer the sharp rebuff from his mother.

"*No!*" she said. "We have to be ready to go in only a moment!

Manuel frowned, but then nestled more securely against her side. The fog was thickening again in the last few lingering moments of the old day. Within a few minutes, visibility from the mouth of the cave extended no further than the third row of corn stalks in front of the cave.

"*Good!*" said the guard as he discovered the ghostly image of María Paloma step from the corn rows into the trail just below the cave. "Let's *go!*"

María Xquic emitted a tiny gasp of relief to see her helpmate making her way on hands and knees up over the ledge and returning to the entrance of the cave.

María Paloma greeted the mother and small child with a strong hug and handed the anxious Tzutujil woman the small bundle which she slipped into the folds of her *huipil* and skirt. Tears of relief and joy streaked down her cheeks as she reached up, took the head of the *compa* between her palms, and kissed her repeatedly on the forehead.

"Gracias, María Paloma!" whispered the grateful woman. "God bless you forever and *ever! Gracias, María Paloma!*"

"Let's *go!"* ordered the guard. Quickly, the group gathered itself, and Marcus Finley held back to allow the women and boy to exit before him. Out on the ledge, however, María Paloma insisted in bringing up the rear. Down the crumbling edge of the escarpment they slid, brushing off their pants and skirts once they reached the open trail.

"*Here!*" said María Paloma as they stopped for a short break more than a half hour later.

"Eat some of these," she ordered as she took from her shoulder bag a *servietta* stuffed with chilled, moist tortillas. Manuel brightened and shoved the thick pastry into his mouth in a single bite. To Marcus Finley, the patty tasted bland and chalky, but he was grateful, nevertheless, for anything, even this. Each ate two or three of the tortillas. María Paloma waited until the others had finished and then ate the last two herself.

"Okay," she said. "That will have to do until we reach camp."

On up the slopes they climbed. Try as he could, however, Marcus Finley felt himself falling further and further behind, his chest heaving for breath and his lungs burning in the higher and higher altitude. Both ahead and behind them, the trail was completely obscured. Three paces either left or right, and the reporter would have been lost. María Paloma's easy pace and steady breath behind him, however, was reassuring.

"It's okay," she volunteered. "We can stop as often as you need to. I know the way."

Marcus Finley was too vulnerable in his exhaustion to find excuses, and without a word, he all but collapsed at her suggestion. María stopped at the edge of the trail to listen for anything moving up from behind. Satisfied that they were secure, she moved closer to the reporter and knelt beside him.

"You . . . you don't *think* much of me, do . . . do you?" Marcus Finley asked, panting. "A man . . . a man who can't *climb* . . . climb a *trail.*"

"*Look,* Mr. Finley," said María Paloma. "Up here in the mountains, the values we live by are very different. Up here, we learn to be very patient. We all look out for each other. We have to, or we die. It's real simple: if a *compa* gets wounded or injured, another doubles his load and picks him up. But everyone understands and accepts that if a *compañero* gets wounded so badly that he endangers everyone else, he'll put the gun in his mouth, and that's it."

Marcus Finley was still wheezing, still fighting to regain his breath. Misinterpreting her meaning, he looked over at the guerrilla and shook his head.

"*Look!*" he said. "*Forget* it! Forget *me!* Let me go. You go on and look after the others."

"You're not injured or wounded, Mr. Finley," said María Paloma. "So I can stay with you. You can be helpful to us. Get your breath and let's *go.*"

Marcus Finley placed the palm of his hand on the loose ground beside the trail and steadied his balance.

Once again, they resumed their trek up the trail through the heavy ground fog. For more than two hours they climbed steadily, pausing from time to time to rest. With the last conversation, they had come to an understanding that needed no further elaboration. During their breaks from the steep climb, then, they spoke little. In another three hours, the dawn was breaking as the fog began to dissipate. They had finally reached the tree line where the last of the *milpas* gave way to flinty crags. Always wary, María Paloma was satisfied that, for the past hour, they had not been pursued.

Marcus Finley, however, was enthralled by the vista stretching before him as he scanned the summit rising less than a half hour of hiking above him. Far below, the lake looped around the base of the mountain through the early morning mist. The reporter wrapped the collar of his jacket tightly against his neck as the cold wind whipped about them on the exposed slopes.

"Where are the others?" he asked, as María reached him from behind.

"Up there and down the other side," the *compa* replied.

Marcus Finley finished snapping his collar and stepped aside as María Paloma motioned with her hand to let her pass. She moved quickly now in the daylight and seemed to be setting the pace for them both. As they moved to the very top, they stepped through rough volcanic rock. To his right Marcus caught glimpses of the deep, grey bowl of the volcano plunging away into a basin of heavy clouds. Carefully, they maneuvered around the sharp boulders that had cracked and fallen away from the rim. Then, as María Paloma dropped from sight, Marcus Finley panicked.

The wind had picked up. A steady gust whipped at his cheeks and whistled in his ears. He blew hastily into his cupped palms and scanned the unmarked path that she had taken only ten or fifteen yards ahead of him.

"*Down!*" came a voice, broken and distorted by the wind.

"*Down! Down!*" came the voice more urgently.

Marcus Finley knelt and then dropped flat as he finally spotted the arm of the guerrilla motioning to him decisively from behind a large, flat slab of rock ahead of him. María Paloma was peering out and down the slope on the other side of the rim lying just beyond his sight. The reporter felt his heart pounding in his throat as he tried to imagine what it was that had so startled his guide. In front of him, he could see only the feet and cuffs of the pants of María Paloma and her hair blowing wildly above her shoulders. It seemed that they lay prone for more than fifteen minutes before María Paloma pushed herself up with the palms of her hands and crawled backwards on her knees toward the reporter.

"The *PAC!*" she said. "The civil defense patrol of San Jorge—they're on the path down below the tree line. They're moving away from us, though, so in about an hour or so we can move on. But we have to wait. They sometimes leave a rear guard to watch and wait for the *compañeros.* We'll just have to wait."

In a low crouch, María Paloma waddled away from the reporter back up near the rim where she could continue to watch the trail below. Marcus Finley pulled the cord to the hood of his jacket tightly below his chin and tied it off in a bow. All that he could hear with any confidence was the rustling of his jacket billowing around his shoulders and over his back in the cold, fierce winds that were now whipping the summit.

For more than a half hour, the two clandestines lay still against the sharp volcanic lava. The reporter felt his nose and forehead beginning to burn in the bright sunlight. His mind raced back to his conversations with Father Michael Justice. Never in all his wildest projections could he have foreseen himself like this "in the mountains." A shadow flitted quickly over him, and he turned his head in time to catch a glimpse of a buzzard drifting on an air current just over the rim and then disappear. He shuddered in its ominous suggestion.

"*Okay!*" called María Paloma just beginning to rise to her feet ahead of him. "We can *go!*"

There was no discussion or explanation. The guerrilla escort rose and signalled to the reporter behind her, and they continued their slow, precarious movement around the rim of the volcano. For more than an hour they climbed on a slightly elevated grade around the huge crater always to their right until they had skirted the eastern flank and were then facing south and southwest. Before them now, the flatlands of Retalhuleu stretched down toward the Pacific, the wide expanse of the ocean lying beneath a dense grey haze on the horizon. To the northwest, rising above the mist, towered the rugged peaks of San Marcos. The reporter's nose and forehead were now tingling in blistering pain, and the backs of his hands were turning from a light pink on his fingertips to deep red at his wrists. As he worked his way behind his guide, he tried to pull his hands up into the cuffs of his jacket.

Finally, they began their descent. The south rim lay under the great slip in the rim of the crater through which the lava had flowed periodically for probably thousands of years. The footing was treacherous. Great sheets of frozen lava cascaded downward. Each measured step held a peril that threatened to send them sliding to a horrifying death, stripping away every exposed inch of skin against the abrasive sheathes of lava and pumice.

The two moved steadily if not rapidly, crossing the lava flows without mishap. Like a pair of ants against a grand curtain, they traced their way to the bottom of the lava cap and disappeared into the tree line. Under the first shade, Marcus Finley collapsed and released the cord of his hood. The incessant winds of the summit had now dissipated into a cool, though gusty breeze. María Paloma had sought the privacy of another tree and returned shortly to her companion.

"Very well, Mr. Finley," said the *compa.* "We made it. Maybe you could use *this, no?*"

María handed the reporter a small square of plastic sheeting. At first, Marcus Finley appeared puzzled.

"How shall I *say?—*" suggested María Paloma, "A `sanitary *napkin'?*"

"*Oh!*" said Marcus Finley, and accepting the swath, he walked away toward a clump of weeds at the base of two of the larger pines.

"Where are the others?" he asked upon his return.

"Just beyond us—over *there,*" she gestured.

Marcus Finley looked in the direction of her signal but saw signs of no one.

"How can you *tell?*" he asked.

"Behind those other pines . . . " she said, smiling.

"*Oh!*" he laughed. "We're leaving a trail like *they* have!"

"We'd better *go!*" said María Paloma with a snicker.

Marcus Finley followed closely at the heels of the guerrilla as they proceeded through the sparse tree cover down the slope of the summit.

"*There!*" exclaimed the reporter as he spied a trail breaking through the undergrowth.

"*No!*" cautioned María. "We never take the trails. Over *there!*"

María Paloma pointed to a dense clump of trees and growth extending down into a ravine below a sharp ridge. "*That* way," she said. "Down there we'll find the others."

Carefully, the two of them made their way into the trees. Almost immediately, she bent down and picked up a tuft of fur from a thorny scrub.

"The *cat!*" she said. "*See!*"

María Paloma knelt down and pointed to faint scratches on the trunk of a small sapling.

"Here's where the boy's cat stretched and clawed the *tree,*" explained the *compa*. "It caught its fur in the thorns as it backed *up!*"

Marcus Finley merely shook his head in amazement.

"Out here," said María Paloma, "you learn to notice things, or you *die!*" Then she brushed the clump of hairs from her fingers.

"We're almost there," she said.

"Have you ever been here before?" asked Marcus.

"You mean `right *here,*' at this very *spot*?" she asked.

"*Yeah!*" said the reporter. "Right *here*."

"Never," she said.

"Then how do you know that they will be around here?" he asked.

"Mr. Finley," confided the *compa*, "we've been on this mountain for *seventeen years!*"

The two continued through the tree line just above and inside the point where it plunged downward toward a stream that raced through the ravine. Gusts of wind whipped through the trees. An occasional bird cried out in alarm as they approached.

"We'll find the sentry shortly," said María Paloma.

Within moments, María Paloma heard the familiar "*Chau! Chau!*"

"*Chau!*" she responded as a small, puckish Mayan boy, his M-16 at the ready, stepped cautiously from behind the lightening-blanched trunk of a stumpy, dead pine tree.

"*Hóla! compañero!*" said María Paloma as she greeted the young man.

"*Recto!*" said the sentry. "Straight ahead, *por favor!*"

In deference to her sex, age, rank, or possibly all three, the sentry stepped aside as María Paloma reached him. María Paloma led the reporter past the guard and down the narrow path through the windswept trees.

"*Hóla! Qué tal, compa?*" came another greeting for the guerrilla woman as she stepped into a small clearing in the underbrush. It was a man in worn jeans and an olive drab military-styled shirt, a belt of grenades slung across his waist. He rose at the entry of María Paloma and the reporter.

"*Los otros e'tan allá,*" he said, gesturing back over his shoulder.

A squad of perhaps thirty or more guerrillas were sitting or squatting in small groups beneath trees under which scrub and bushes were thinnest. Some were talking quietly, smoking on the stubs of cigarettes, or drinking only lukewarm coffee. A small bed of coals still glowed under an outcropping of rock. The weak trail of smoke that rose from the fire dissipated quickly in the gusts of wind that sliced through the trees. Standing together, isolated from the others, María Xquic and her little boy seemed nervous and disconcerted. For the first time, Manual appeared lost and frightened even as he stood within the shadow of his mother.

"Why don't you go to the fire," said María Paloma to the reporter. "Take a cup of coffee, or we may have some sweet *atole* left. You can just ask that guy there to use his cup, *okay?*"

María motioned to the man in the loose, camouflaged jacket bending down at the fire, stirring the coals with a small twig.

"What is his name?" asked Marcus Finley.

"`Donaldo,'" she said. "Here in the mountains he goes by `Donaldo.'" Marcus Finley turned and made his way across the camp toward the fire.

"Donaldo" was a wiry, middle-aged Tzutujil Maya whose rich, black hair glistened in the mottled streams of sunlight that poured through the leaves. He was dark and sinewy, his sculpted hands suggesting something other than the much heavier field work of other *campesinos*. He squatted low to the ground, his knees spread wide apart as he filled two abused tin cups with steaming but very weak coffee.

"*Hóla! amigo!*" greeted Marcus Finley. The man turned his head slightly in only the most brusk response. Donaldo rose slowly, careful to avoid spilling even a drop of the refreshing drink.

"*Permiso,*" said Donaldo as he turned and moved from the fire in the direction of María Xquic and the boy.

"Here," said Donaldo to María Xquic and her frightened son, as he handed them the two cups of coffee. "Maybe this will warm you up, *okay?*"

María Xquic was surprised and grateful for the unexpected gesture. She smiled courteously to her host and took the two cups for herself and Manuel.

"You are very courageous, María Xquic," said Donaldo deferentially to the surprised and nervous Felipino. "There is much talk of you and what you have dared to risk on behalf of your family and the people of San Felipe. So, if I can be of any help to you, Señora. The others, you know . . . most of them don't speak *Tzutujil*, coming from another area and all. So, you come to me, okay?"

"Thank you," said María Xquic most gratefully. "Thank you very much—for *both* of us."

Donaldo bowed slightly before his neighbor and started to turn away when María Xquic exchanged a glance that must have revealed a hint of the terror and uncertainty she was feeling.

"Doña María?" questioned Donaldo.

María Xquic raised her hand slightly toward the gracious man and asked, "Maybe Don Donaldo . . . perhaps you could stay with us, my son and me, for just a moment. We have lost everything, *señor.* And now they have come . . . the army, down *there!* Maybe . . ."

In unmistakable fright, her eyes now beseeched the man to stay, and he moved toward her, inviting the Felipinos with his hands to sit down as he squatted on a rock beside them.

"You shouldn't fear," he said. "We're *safe* now. The army doesn't come up this high. It's down there—where the coffee grows high up against the *milpa. That's* where we have to be careful."

"But the *civil patrol* . . . ?" asked María Xquic hesitantly.

"No," said Donaldo shaking his head. "They'll be gone until tomorrow night. They'll change shifts today and start out again in the afternoon. They won't be back today."

María sighed and pulled her son, preoccupied with his cat, closer to her in the chilly, early morning air.

"Don Donaldo," asked the woman. "Where is your home, and how long have you been with the *compas*?"

Donaldo shifted his weight off a sharp rock gouging into his buttock. Then he turned to answer María's question.

"My home was San Martín Comitán," began Donaldo. "My family lived there for more than one hundred years, maybe more. Maybe we lived there for *one thousand* years? How to *know* such a thing!"

The light glinted through the strands of his raven black hair as he twisted the point of a twig back and forth, digging a small hole in the ground between his knees.

"There were twelve of us," he continued. "My father's father when I was young. But he died. My father's brother, my uncle. But he died crossing the lake during the *xocomil*."

Donaldo continued to twist the small twig, penetrating deeper and deeper into the earth. María Xquic readjusted her shawl over her shoulders to block out the cool air from her neck.

"My father and his father were woodcarvers," he explained, "so I am a woodcarver, also. I had a small shop. I made furniture. When the army came, we had a very rough time in San Martín. They came in and accused all of us of being subversives, of helping the guerrillas. The guerrillas had been working in the area, just like in San Felipe. But we only wanted peace. We didn't support the guerrillas or the army. We tried to explain that we were neutral. But the army didn't accept that. We had to be for the army, or we were all subversives and would be killed."

Accidentally, Donaldo broke the stick in the dirt and began sifting through the leaves for another. He found an even longer twig and stripped away the leaves, then continued his penetration of the hole.

"I was elected *alcalde municipal*, just about one month after the army arrived," said Donaldo. "No one else wanted the job. I had been elected once before, maybe ten, maybe fifteen years before all the trouble started. I knew how to get along with the *ladinos* from the capital. So, they came—a group of them—they said, 'Don Lazaro' . . . "

Donaldo stopped twisting the stick. He had just broken one of the rules on the mountain—never, *never* to mention a person's real name.

"That's my name in Comitán," explained Donaldo. "In the mountains we all have *another* name. In the mountains, my name is Donaldo . . . but they came to me. They said that I should run for *alcalde municipal*, that because I could talk with the *ladinos*, maybe then I could talk with the *ejercito*, too. I knew Spanish from working in the shop for so many years, *ladinos* coming in and out. I knew some German and a little English. So, I said, I *guess* so. Maybe I could try. I just wanted to help."

Donaldo plunged the stick in and out of the hole, smoothing out the edges. He couldn't look María in the eye.

"I went to the priest," said Donaldo. "I asked him to pray for me; I didn't know what to do and all. So, we prayed about it. I felt a lot better after we prayed. I had been working with our father for several months in the `*alfabetación*.' I had taught all the new catechists some Spanish. They did pretty good. They all got to where they could read a little bit, you know. Then one day I got this message. This guy came into my shop. I had never seen him before. He told me I had to go to the military post to meet the colonel. I was really *scared*."

Donaldo seemed to stumble for words. He looked at the point where the twig had slipped fast into the small puncture in the earth. He paused for a moment longer and then continued.

"I had to walk for almost thirty kilometers," said Donaldo. "I was so tired when I arrived, but more than tired, I was very worried. I thought maybe the colonel was going to take me, maybe `*disappear'* me. Better *me* than to lose my whole *family*. My family was all I could think about over and over as I made the trip out of the valley and up the highway to the military post. But nothing could have prepared me for what was to come—the most *horrifying day* of my life."

"Is *this . . .?*" started María. "Is this the story of the *five boys?*"

Tears began to flood from María's eyes, and she grabbed the corner of her shawl and raised it over her mouth and nose to hide her uncontrollable sobs. Donaldo himself dropped his head between his arms, his shoulders convulsing in revisited terror and grief.

On the other side of the camp, the *compas* began to stir and rise. Three turned toward the opposite end of the ravine where the stream took a sharp turn downward and to the left down the slope. Then the rest of the camp took interest and began moving toward whatever it was that had first attracted the others.

"*Donaldo!*" said a heavily armed guerrilla who had stepped beside the distraught former *alcalde*. "*Donaldo! Quick!* They're *coming!*"

Donaldo lifted his head, turned, and jumped up, grabbing María Xquic by the arm and motioning her and the boy to move out in front of him toward the others. The mother and her boy returned a terrified look to their confidante.

"What *is* it?" she asked. "What's *happening?*"

"We're moving out," explained Donaldo. The sentries are returning, so we'll be moving down to base camp. No problem, *okay?* We're *alright!*"

María was relieved. She looked down at little Manuel and patted him on the shoulder. "It's *okay!* It's *alright*."

Reassured, the boy returned his attention to the cat that was pulling upward onto his shoulder, and he winced as the cat's claw caught the skin under his shirt.

María Paloma stepped ahead of the others to greet the first of more than a dozen men and teenage boys who were flowing back into the camp.

"What's the situation?" asked María Paloma.

"We'll be breaking base camp right after the broadcast this afternoon," said the sentry. "After the killings at the post and all the protest, the army is building up for maneuvers, it looks like, on the other side. The Postman says we should move the transmitters to the *finca* just to be safe."

"And *this* unit?" asked María Paloma.

"`Rear guard,'" returned the guard. "They'll move out ahead of us, so we just go on down. The Postman said that the troops have moved into San Felipe and will probably be attempting to follow us. We'll know if they bring in the helicopters."

"*Okay! compa!*" said María Paloma, saluting the soldier who snapped to attention before her. "*Rafael!*"

María Paloma turned to the young man beside her who was carrying the radio receiver on his back.

"Radio ahead and tell them we're moving," she said.

"*Sí, comandante!*" said the boy, and he knelt down and began preparing the radio for the transmission.

"*Felix*!" Another teenage boy ran toward her, saluting as he stopped.

"Get them *together!*" she said. "We're moving out and down to base camp. Tell them `rear guard,' and tell Donaldo I need to see him."

"*Sí! comandante!*" returned the youth as he adjusted his M-16 over his left shoulder.

Donaldo, who had been watching the proceedings, didn't have to wait for his instructions which he already anticipated, and he stepped past the messenger, waving him on in a friendly gesture.

"Sí! comandante!" said Donaldo, standing at attention before his commanding officer.

"Take María and the boy since you speak her language the best," said

María Paloma. "I'll stay with the reporter. If we get into a scrape, try to get her and the boy behind the line. We're `rear guard' this time. You know what that means, so if any of you get hit, you know what to do. You know what they'll do to the woman and boy."

"*Sí! comandante!*" returned the old mayor. The soldier winced as memories too fresh flashed across his imagination. "*Sí, comandante!* I understand. You can count on *me!*"

María Paloma moved through the *compas* busy gathering up their few items—cups, ammunition clips and belts, and ponchos that had been stretched out for drying over low hanging branches. As she stepped toward a small group of seven or eight soldiers on the opposite side of the clearing, Marcus Finley was just rising as one of the guerrillas pulled the commander aside.

"So what do we do with *them—those* two?" asked the soldier, his older model M-16 cradled across his arms.

María Paloma turned sharply to the young guerrilla fighter. "What do you mean *`do with them'?*" she barked. "You know *exactly* what to *`do with them'!* We've *settled* all that, and *you* have your *orders!*"

The young man hung his head as he heard the commander's response. He stuck the toe of his boot into the thin dirt and rocks at his feet. "*Sí, comandante.*"

"*Now!*" she said.

"*Sí, comandante . . .*" said the young man dejectedly.

"You don't *get* it, *do* you!" snapped María Paloma. The guerrilla *comandante* reached inside her pants and withdrew her automatic pistol. "Bring these two over *here!*"

Two middle-aged indigenous men, sitting cross legged on the ground against the base of a large boulder, exchanged looks of terror at each other as they registered the commander's orders to their guard. They began to rise as María Paloma approached with her gun in hand, but then they fell backward over themselves as she motioned to the guard to secure them.

"What is this *about, comandante?*" said one of the two *campesinos*. "What is this all *about?*"

"You *know* what this is `all about'!" said the commander. "You two tried to flee the area; you tried to leave. *No one* leaves the *compas*. You're *orejas, both* of you! So, you're going to *die!* Right *here!* Right *now!*"

Donaldo was helping María Xquic to her feet when the two shots blasted through the trees. Everyone was startled.

"*Madre de Dios!*" cried María Xquic. Donaldo turned toward the direction of the shots, his mouth gaping in surprise.

"Let's *go!*" cried the voice of María Paloma from within the small group of *compas* that had gathered across the clearing. "*Quickly! Quickly!*"

Immediately the five or six disbanded and began moving with their commander away from the two bodies that lay slumped up against the wall of rock. Donaldo stood for a moment transfixed, his mouth still locked open. Then he found his voice.

"*Why!*" he muttered vehemently but just under his breath. "*Why!*"

Donaldo turned to María Xquic and motioned for them to follow the others. Manuel fled in front of his mother, the shock of the repercussions still ringing in his head. He ran to the opposite side of the clearing and then turned back to steal a glance at the two bodies behind them.

"What *happened?*" he cried as he looked up to Donaldo who had once again come up to them.

"I don't know," said the old fighter. "I think they were very bad men."

María Xquic glanced sharply at Donaldo. They were Tzutujiles from one of the other villages, perhaps San Martín. Something wasn't right. Donaldo knew more than he was saying.

"Very bad men, *no?*" said the ex-mayor. He reached down and muffed the hair of the young *campesino*. "Perhaps they were very bad men. Who's to say?"

"What did they do *bad?*" asked Manuel. The *compa* kept up an even pace, watching the trail before him, glancing every now and then behind them to make sure the last few units of the squad were still trailing at regular intervals from back down the path they were making through the sparse trees.

"What did they do *bad?*" repeated Donaldo. He turned his head to catch the boy's small eyes. "I think . . . I think maybe they *lived* too long."

"*Come!*" snapped María Xquic, as she gathered her son to the other side, stepping between the boy and the angry *compañero*. "Sometimes you ask too many *questions*, Manuel! Step *ahead.* Watch the *cat, okay?*"

Manuel looked away from his mother, tears swelling in the pockets of his eyes. Two men who had been sitting there just talking . . . then two shots. Now they were dead. Just like that, lying back there against the rocks, their arms stretched out limp from their sides. And the woman who had helped him and his mother, the woman who was a friend of the American, she had shot them both. How could she be a friend to his own mother and then shoot the two men who were lying back there behind them, their legs and arms stretched out, who fell backwards when the two shots rang out? Was she going to shoot anyone else? Who would be next? She wouldn't shoot the American, would she? Who was next? Not Donaldo who spoke so clearly. He could understand

Donaldo. If she shot Donaldo, who would he talk to?

Tears ran down the face of Manuel Xoy. If Miguel Mapa would come back, he could make the woman stop shooting the two men. She wouldn't shoot Donaldo, the one who could speak so clearly the Tzutujil.

"Look," said Donaldo, pulling the boy aside. "You don't have a thing to fear, *okay?*"

The *compa* nudged the boy to a position directly in front of him. He reached up with his thumbs and wiped away the boy's tears.

"These two *guys* back there . . ." Donaldo paused to weigh the options. "These two men . . . they worked for the army, *okay?* They were telling the army about us, maybe things about you and your mother there, *okay?* They were working for the army . . . *orejas*, telling the army things so that the army would come and *hurt* us, maybe even *kill* us—you and your *mother!* They were *bad* guys, so they had to die. But they won't ever hurt anyone else. So you don't have to worry, *okay? . . . Okay?* Now everything's going to be *alright.* You don't have anything to worry about. You just watch out for your mother and the little cat there. Everything's going to be *fine!* So be a *man* now, and dry those eyes. We've gotta lot of looking and seeing ahead of us today, and you need to have *good* eyes for *seeing!*"

Manuel bowed his head and wiped his cheeks on each shoulder, leaving a heavy dark smudge of grime on the cloth. Donaldo rose and muffed the boy's hair again, turned him around toward his mother, now further up the trail, and gave him a pat on the behind. Manuel offered up something of a conciliatory smile and bolted toward his mother. Donaldo stood up slowly and watched the boy streak away. He wiped his own brow across his sleeve and took a long breath.

"Shit!" he muttered to himself. Donaldo turned away from the *compas* passing him slowly as they continued maneuvering up the trail. In a fit too powerful to resist, he kicked at the base of a tall *chocón* stalk, its heavy leaves shaking a cloud of dust across his chest. High above, the sun had climbed atop the summit and had begun its slow descent in the early afternoon. They had seen no sign of either the civil defense patrol or the army regulars. The air was clear. No trace of an airplane had broken the rush of the breeze.

Throughout the late morning and deeply into the afternoon, the unit of the "Guerrilla Army of the Poor" trudged slowly around the slope of the volcano. At irregular intervals they would stop, and a scouting party would back track in order to secure their position from behind. The larger unit, a team of more than 200 troops, would continue to move on toward base camp, a location about half way down the southern side of the mountain. This rear-guard patrol would bivouac overnight a good two hours climb from the main unit. In the event that the larger team engaged the army, the rear-guard patrol would remain in place to secure a retreat.

The sun had settled like a large wafer against the horizon, slowly evaporating in a grey mist as it slipped closer and closer to the rim of the Pacific Ocean. Tired from the long trudge around the perimeter of the volcano, most of the *compas* took a few moments to witness the spectacular scene. Several stepped from behind the tree line to take a clearer view from a promontory of rock jutting more than fifty feet out from the side of the mountain. They took bets on how long it would take the sun to set completely over the horizon. Intent in their wagers, they reacted only reluctantly when they first heard the drone of the helicopter.

"Son of a *bitch!*" cursed one of the *compas*, still counting the seconds as he slowly rose from the promontory, leaving the shimmering globe only halfway dissolved in the ruby-grey ocean.

"*Move!*" cried another. "It's the *military!*"

Shocked from their gaming, at once the small group sprang backward from the promontory, scrambling for their guns. As the helicopter swooped low overhead directly above them, the *compañeros* threw themselves into the nearest shrubbery, hoping that their negligence hadn't compromised the unit's location.

With the others, María Paloma had ducked back into the trees. After the helicopter had passed, she called for her radioman who was already adjusting his earphones.

"*Rafael!*" cried María Paloma. "Call the base camp. *Postman!* Get the *Postman!*"

Rafael adjusted the frequency knob and antenna, and then began carefully pronouncing the codes. All others were taking cover, preparing for a second pass of the military helicopter. Rafael completed the connection and handed the earphones and microphone to his commander, María Paloma.

The guerrilla commander took the receiver from her radio operator and began trying to confirm any hostile activity at the base camp more than five kilometers further down the slope. María Paloma listened intently and then returned the receiver to Rafael.

"I think we're okay," she said. "There's no activity at base camp."

María Paloma walked to the middle of the reassembled patrol to explain what had happened.

"The helicopter was military from the Brucero post," she said. "Apparently, it was on reconnaissance, so we have to assume we've been spotted. Base camp is breaking up and moving back up to reinforce us. We're going to set charges back up the trail and then move a little higher up the slope just below the caves."

María Paloma stepped further into the middle of the units and gave her final instructions.

"*Everybody!*" she directed. "Everybody check your *supplies* and *weapons*. We don't want to leave *anything* behind. We'll leave in *five minutes. Rafael!*"

The commander turned again to her radio operator who began to prepare for their last transmission before the evacuation.

"Tell the Postman that we're moving now on up the slope to the caves—use the *code!*"

"Sí, comandante! Como no!"

Rafael found the frequency and passed on the message to the operator at base camp.

"*Está bién!*" he said when the message was through.

"Good," said María Paloma. "Now *listen, all* of you. Be on the lookout for the helicopter again. The army will assume we know we've been spotted and that we'll move out from the promontory. Esteban! You take your units up to the cave. You all will be point this time. The rest of us will fall behind to cover you. Rafael will stay with me, so we can be in contact with the CB. We're going to try to take the copter out if it returns. *Donaldo!* You take the woman and her son with Esteban and get them into the caves. Mr. Finley, you can do as you like—go ahead or stay behind with the rest of the unit."

Marcus Finley was savoring the moment of his first maneuvers with the *compas* against the army. He elected to remain behind, anticipating the ambush on the helicopter. Within moments the two groups had secured their supplies and weapons and began moving up the slope just inside the tree line.

In the twilight, Esteban's squad trudged up the side of the volcano, moving higher and higher toward the caves. In reality, the "caves" were nothing more than a row of acute overhangs formed when earthquakes had broken away large slabs of the volcanic lava, sending the broken debris rolling away down the slopes. What remained were long, broken outcroppings under which as many as two or three dozen people could take shelter from the weather or hide from anyone above or at the same level. The cave in which the reporter had discovered the two Marías had been formed in a similar fashion apparently as two different layers of volcanic slag had separated and fallen apart, leaving a gaping, angular rift or hole in the side of the mountain.

María Paloma led the major body of the squad to a spot just inside the tree line approximately two hundred meters from the caves. From there they could step out away from the trees to attack a helicopter from behind following a low pass and still remain secure from sight on any approach. Esteban's units would be the visible decoys, but they would be in easy reach of the caves just above the clearing.

Marcus Finley followed closely upon the heels of María Paloma. He watched the sure and steady movement of her small feet and thin ankles. He imagined the shape of the calves of her legs and the sinewy muscles of her long, lithe thighs. He wondered what making love to her might have been like with her husband, with someone she really cared for, but he let it pass. He couldn't even frame the fantasy as a lover. Her image as a *comandante*, the shooting of the two *campesinos* were too powerful, too intimidating. On the contrary, he felt most secure around her, completely trusting of her experience and the apparent respect for her of everyone in the unit.

The squad moved into position at the tree line within sight of the sharply defined ridge row of the "caves" away and above them. Rafael confirmed by CB the arrival of the point team. Everyone was in place for an army fight if it was still to come. For more than three hours, the two units held their positions. As the sun began to set, once more María Paloma called Esteban above and instructed him to prepare to receive the rear guard. Then María Paloma began organizing her team to move on up.

"You never saw *anything?*" asked Esteban as María Paloma met him under the ledge.

"No, *nothing,*" she said. "We might as well settle in under the caves tonight and prepare to meet the rest in the morning."

In the rapidly fading light, the units began to select spots up under or close to the ledges. There would be no fires tonight. Several broke into their sacks for strips of dried venison, a staple on the long treks up the slopes. Donaldo had prepared tortillas two days earlier and had saved back several for the hike to base camp.

"Here, María," he offered as he handed the patties to María Xquic and her hungry, young son. The boy waited until his mother indicated her pleasure with a nod, and he took one of the tortillas from the *compa.*

"I'll rest beside you tonight," said Donaldo, knowing that the offer would give his wards a sense of security. Both were completely exhausted from the day's march, and Donaldo himself would find the rest most comforting. He urged the two Tzutujiles to take the highest positions up under the ledge so that he could respond during the night if the patrol was disturbed in any way or outright attacked. The latter seemed most unlikely, because there would be no fires to give them away. Manuel Xoy pulled the cat from his bag and fed it some small pieces of his last tortilla, then released it into the night to scavenge.

Satisfied that María and her son were secure under the ledge, Donaldo took a position only a foot or so from the edge of the overhang. He slapped at something crawling down his neck, a spider whose web he had disturbed as he had inched back down the slope. He placed his assault rifle on the ground beside him, its barrel pointing downward and away from mother and child now settled in behind and over him. As he lay still, all he could think about was the shooting earlier in the day.

"Why?" he asked himself. Josue Reynalde Osco and Pascual Tierrez Sic, two workers from San Martín, Don Luis Armando Osco, his father—a good man who raised the melons, the best melons in the *canton*, a good man who kept the old ways, had moved with great respect through his cargos, never a better man—Don Luis, and his son, a lazy boy, not bad, just lazy—the vultures drifted in wide circles over the clearing—they could not, they wouldn't compete with the rats and wild dogs already at work, tearing back the shredded shirts to gnaw at the open wounds, stripping away the hot, moist flesh.

"Why?" asked Donaldo. So they left the area, maybe to get a little drunk, maybe to find some work down on the *fincas*, maybe they saw the army, talked with some soldiers, maybe someone saw them talking with the army, or maybe they just said they did, someone in the civil defense patrol who needed a hit, had to show loyalty, needed a target, they were easy, they had left the area. So nobody—neither side—could trust them, they had to die.

"Shit!" cursed Donaldo. For what *good?* The army was running the *compas* all over the mountain. Last month they had lost two commanders and more than twenty comrades. The month before, more than fifty. This month two had died when they stepped on land mines that had exploded under them just off the trail as they returned from reconnaissance. It was hard to find new recruits. Everybody was afraid of a rumored new army offensive. All the *campesinos* in the aldeas were terrified. A person didn't even have to be suspicious, didn't have to do anything but to be hanging around when the soldiers came, and then to die! But not just die, but to be slaughtered like barnyard fowls—slit and gutted before their own families, or dragged and beaten so ferociously until they bled from every pore. So, what to do? You run away to the mountains to find the *compas*, hoping that they'll have a gun for you—not to save Guatemala, whatever that means, but to give yourself an equal chance in a tight.

"Shit!" cursed Donaldo. One by one, the vultures drifted slowly downward. Just above the tree tops, they began flapping their wings in a languid descent, committed to the brutal fray below them. Sleep came only in

bumptious fits and starts for *Compañero Donaldo*.

Overhead, the stars spread across the deep night sky in a spray of shimmering lace. The moon's sharp sickle hung low in the southeast. Down the slope away from the caves, two sentries sat fifty meters apart, staring at each other's silhouettes, slapping at gnats and flies that had somehow found their faces, having finessed the breezes that stirred the trees around them.

Sometime in the late hours, the air grew still. A mantle of clouds rolled in from the Pacific enveloping the summit and slopes of the mountain in a heavy dew. As the grey dawn broke, Donaldo suddenly lurched up as two replacement sentries slipped by. A few seconds later, he heard his name.

"Don Donaldo," whispered María Xquic. "*Don Donaldo, Señor!*" Donaldo turned on his elbows to face the Tzutujil woman craning her neck from under the ledge above him.

"My *son,*" she said, "he has to pass."

"*Oh,* okay!" said the *compa*, and then to Manuel Xoy: "Follow the sentries there. They can watch for you. Run, boy, and go with them."

Manuel scurried after the two guerrillas as they were preparing to move down the slope. The two paused to allow him to catch up, and the three of them disappeared down the side of the mountain toward the sentry posts, a grey fluff of cat racing after them. Donaldo turned back to Maria Xquic who was inching precariously from under the ledge.

"*Señora,*" said Donaldo. "We will have a beautiful *dawn, no?* The clouds will lift soon."

"A beautiful dawn," responded María Xquic, "but the *day?* What about the *day?*"

María looked searchingly at the featureless expression on the face of Donaldo and then turned her attention to the drop off over which Manuel had just disappeared. The air thickened, and the dewy mist gave way to a steady drizzle. María slipped back up into the obscurity of the ledge. Donaldo reached into his back pocket for a strip of rag to give María to wipe her face. He himself was climbing up under the ledge when it started.

Without a warning, the morning erupted in explosions. One after another, a stream of mortars screeched down and exploded into and around the small clearing. Machine gun fire raked the wall of the embankment. All the guerrillas began to cry out and race about for their guns. Bullets whipped through the air like needles, ripping through the leaves, stripping the bark, and sending up puffs of dirt as they blasted into the rocks and ground. Screams and moans of *compas* wounded in the fusillade surrounded María and Donaldo as they huddled together under the rocks.

It took several moments for María to realize that they were under attack by the army, and then she remembered Manuel.

"*Mi hijo!*" she cried. "Where is *Manuel,* my little *son?* Where *is* he? What are they *doing?* What have they done to my *son?*"

María began to push at Donaldo who had wedged into the crevice tightly against her to keep her from being hit. Now she was mustering every bit of her strength to extricate herself.

"*No, señora!*" urged Donaldo. "*Please!* You can't go *out* there! You will be killed for *sure! Please,* don't *move*!"

"But my *son!*" she protested. "My little *boy!* I have to *find* him. I have to make him *safe!*"

"*No,* María, *no!*" cried Donaldo over the din of the battle. "We will *both* be killed! You have to *stay!* What can you do for him if you are wounded or dead *yourself?*"

María Xquic gave in, collapsing against the body of Donaldo in convulsions of grief and anguish. The ground fire had lasted no longer than five minutes, when two helicopters swooped into the area and began strafing the compound and the ridges above. At times, they seemed to hover close enough to touch the rungs of their landing gear, but there was no room to set down. After a minute or two of ferocious firing, each plane backed away and dropped out of sight further down the slope of the mountain where fierce fighting apparently continued from base camp. Then, about as quickly as it had started, the shooting stopped.

Neither Donaldo nor María dared move or speak a word for what seemed an hour, fearful that an army patrol might be waiting in an ambush, but the fighting had clearly passed on down the slope to base camp. The cries of the wounded and dying were terrifying. In vain, they were forced to endure the slow, agonizing deaths of their comrades who lay across the compound, from the little they could see below, strewn like limp rags over the ground. Then, from somewhere away to the left, amid a stream of wrenching groans, a shot rang out, followed by a staggering silence. One of the desperately wounded *compas* had managed to end all the suffering. Moments later, on the opposite side, a second shot blasted the morning. María's eyes flashed in terror, and Donaldo clamped the palm of his hand over her mouth, fearful that she might cry out. That these shots were not answered by the reaction an army reconnaissance team would have meant, Donaldo suspected that they were alone, but still he couldn't be sure.

Miraculously, neither of them had been hit during the entire fire fight. After the first hour had passed, neither still appeared ready to withdraw from their sanctuary. By midday, the heavy smell of powder had dissipated, and the clouds had burned off. For the last two hours, they had heard nothing from either their friends or from possible military activity. Donaldo made the first attempt to move, still careful, however, for fear that he might set off a small avalanche of rock and pebbles that could give them away in the event that the area was still being monitored. Slowly, he extended one leg and then the other and finally slipped from the side of a trembling María Xquic.

As he moved from under the ledge, Donaldo could see nothing but human debris scattered about the narrow clearing. Bodies lay twisted and grotesque, their backs and limbs, broken and distorted, great pools of blood already blackened where they had seeped into the porous ground beneath. The smooth, easy glide of vultures' shadows slipped across the compound, circling again and again, waiting the opportunity to descend upon the carnage.

Donaldo stood slowly, his own muscles cramped and stiff. He looked slowly from left to right and back again to reassure himself of their security.

"María," said Donaldo. "You can come out now, but be careful. It's very *ugly!*"

María Xquic slipped quickly but cautiously down the incline from under the ledge and took Donaldo's hand to steady her rise. Her eyes filled with tears as she looked about her, and she turned quickly, about to vomit from the pent up fear and anger that had gripped her unabatedly throughout the morning. She dropped to her knees as the convulsion finally seized her.

"That's *okay, mujer!*" said Donaldo, choking on his own sobs. "I feel like doing the *same!*"

Cautiously, the old *alcalde* began moving from body to body looking for any signs of life. All were dead. As he moved closer to the edge of the compound where it slipped off down toward the tree line, he could see a circle of five or six bodies, those of comrades who had been caught by a mortar round.

The body of their commander, María Paloma, had been flung against the trunk of a tree, her face and long hair matted into the bark. Donaldo stood over the diminutive body, immobilized in the presence of the woman whose grit and steel courage had so inspired him upon his arrival in the unit so many months before. It was impossible that it was over. He looked down at her legs pro-trudeing from the pants that had been all but torn away in the explosion. Her exposed flesh seemed so pallid, almost white, it was so pale. Donaldo could see old scar tissue from various wounds tracing up and down the inside of her right leg and just below the knee and down the calf of her left. Suddenly, he felt very embarrassed to be witnessing such exposure of one whom he had grown to love and respect, and he had the urge to cover her. Tears streamed freely down his face, and he dropped to his knees in silent, unrelenting grief.

"*Manuel!*" cried María from across the clearing. "*Manuel! Oh, Manuel!*"

Donaldo was shocked and somewhat angered by María's outcry, first for the intrusion upon on his own horror and sadness and then for the renewed fear of their discovery. He jumped up and turned to see María peering out over the incline down toward the tree line. He had no idea what she had found, but he expected the worst. He raced to her side, pleading with her as he approached to be quiet. "*Señora! Please!*" he begged. "The soldiers, they may be around us—here, over there, *anywhere!*"

Covering her mouth, María raised her other hand, pointing to a small mound of a body down the slope seemingly thrown up under a boulder.

"It's my little *son!*" she cried, tears washing down her cheeks. "My poor little *son!* It's my little *boy!* My *Manuelito!*"

"You *wait, please!*" said Donaldo. "You wait, and *I'll go* down. *Please!* You wait *here!*"

Donaldo slipped over the side of the embankment and slid down to the outcroppings of rock where several of the bodies were resting. Gingerly, he turned them up searching for any signs of life and to identify their faces. Satisfied that all was lost, he then worked his way down to the last body lying against the larger boulder.

Up above, María held her breath as she watched the guerrilla standing over her son. Surely, he was still alive! Surely, there was space for hope! Holy Mary Mother of God, *alcaldes* of the father son and mother moon, and of the four sacred points, hear this poor woman, your servant. *Ah! Malaya!* Gracious God! . . . María tripped through a spasm of prayer, crossing her forehead, chin, and breast as she craned from side to side, watching Donaldo struggling below at the base of the incline, trying to turn the body of her little Manuel.

Donaldo bent over and fumbled through the clothing of the corpse for several seconds and then rolled it back over face down. Then he turned back to face María and, looking up, only shook his head. María gasped and struggled to keep from pitching over and rolling down the slope. Her head was spinning and her heartbeat erratic.

"*Oh, my god! Oh, my god!*" she cried, and she slipped off her feet down to the ground. Slowly, Donaldo made his way through the fallen *compañeros* back up the slope to María.

"*Oh, my god!*" sobbed María Xquic. "*Oh, my god!* My little *son!* My poor, precious little *boy!* Who *am* I? And without *Manuelito,* what is to become of this poor mother?"

Donaldo raised his hands and shook his head as he worked his way back up the slope toward the distraught woman.

"*No!*" he said as he reached on the edge of the clearing. "*No!* It's not *him!* It's not Manuel . . . *Manuel Xoy!*"

"*What?*" exclaimed María. "It's not *him?* But, I can *see* down there . . . there against the rock at the *bottom!*"

"*No!*" repeated Donaldo. "It's not him. It's very bad, only *part* of . . ."

"It's not *him!*" exclaimed María as tears flooded her eyes. "It's not *him! Really?*"

"*No!*" said Donaldo. "It's not your son, not Manuel, *Manuelito Xoy!*"

"*Ohhhhh!*" cried María. "Then *where?* Where *is* my *son?*"

María turned left and right, stretching her neck, straining to peer through the high shrubs and trees that ringed the compound. "We have to look *again!*" she cried. "We have to keep *looking!* We have to find my *son!*"

Donaldo reached the top of the embankment and sat down to catch his breath. "*Yes!* We have to keep *looking.* We will look *everywhere.* We have to *find* him!"

"What . . .?" María Xquic ventured to explore. "What . . . if, what if he's *dead!*"

"Look, *María!*" said Donaldo, turning to the panicked mother. "He may *be* dead. You stay here, and I'll look. I'll look *everywhere*. You just go back up under the cave out of the sun. I'll look, *okay?*"

"*No!*" protested María Xquic. "I have to go *with* you. I have to see for *myself.* I am his *mother.* Alive or dead, he *needs* me. I am his *mother!*"

Donaldo couldn't debate such an argument, and he rose, brushing off his pants. Standing beside María, he joined her in scanning the clearing more carefully.

"Let's start over there," he said, pointing toward the most congested clump of undergrowth at the far end of the clearing. María preceded him down the slope to the tree line. As they moved carefully on through the brush, they began to realize the intensity of the attack. Trees with trunks and branches as thick as a forearm were splintered and broken. Already withering leaves carpeted the ground like an impromptu autumn shedding. At first, María was reticent to touch the bodies. Everyone had suffered terrible, bloody disfigurements from the heavy machine guns and mortar explosions.

After they had turned four or five of the bodies, still clinging to hope that one might have survived, María began eagerly to turn their faces, placing her own cheek to their mouths, trying to catch even the faintest trace of a breath. Nowhere, however, could they find any sign of Manuel Xoy. Twice, and then a third time, the two swept the area. Each time they failed to discover the boy, María's hopes grew stronger that he might have run away, that somewhere down below in the thick undergrowth he might be nestled against a tree with his cat.

"The *cat!*" cried María. "Maybe we will find him with the *cat.* The cat may return for scraps of food. We could set some out and *watch tonight*!"

"We can do that," said Donaldo. "We can set out some scraps of tortillas and dried meat, but we'll have to go back down and search the bodies for any food."

By mid-afternoon, the sweet, rancid smell of death permeated the air. María covered her mouth and nose as she moved once more among the violated *compas*. When she stumbled upon the body of María Paloma, María Xquic gasped and fell back. It was the first moment, in the panic over her son, that she had even thought about the brave *comandante* and her only confidante on the mountain. María Xquic knelt down at the feet of the dead commander and wept. At once, she felt so lost, so very lost and isolated. Completely alone. Stripped finally and completely of everything of her life. Completely desolate.

After a few moments in her solitude, María rose and turned to find Donaldo standing only a few paces behind her. The look on his face shocked her.

"*María!"* he said.

"Don Donaldo?" she asked.

"You have to *come!*"

"Come?"

"Yes, come. But it is very *bad*."

"*Manuel! . . .* You've found *Manuel?*"

"No . . . not *Manuel.* Not really *Manuel.*"

"Then? . . . Then, then *what?* What *is* it?"

Donaldo reached out and took her hand to help her move carefully from around the bodies. "Over *there!"*

Donaldo pointed to a weather-spent tree stretching out and over a clump of undergrowth. There was the cat, Manuel Xoy's little strip of grey fur hanging dead from a low branch, a *compa's* shoelace knotted tightly around its neck.

"Madre de Dios!" cried María. "Oh, mother of god!"

Donaldo placed his arms around the woman's shoulders to lend her support, and María Xquic suddenly knew. In a rush, it came to her that the *ejercito*, these crazy, bloody jackals had taken her son.

"*Oh, my god!*" cried María, as the shadow of a vulture swept silently over their path.

"We have to go," said Donaldo. "*Tonight, tonight* we have to leave."

So, everything was settled. In silence, they picked their way back up to the clearing, collecting what scraps of food they could gather from their comrades. The breeze had shifted mercifully, so that as they sat once more in the late afternoon, the wind carried the charnel odors away from them. It seemed somehow appropriate that they slipped into the same position under the eaves of the rock ledge, laid down their bodies, and drifted into sleep.

Sitting in the sweat bath she was still chilled, her back in an ache that wrapped around her lower back and rolled into a tight knot below her stomach. Her legs and knees trembled, her hands limp masa, almost ready to fall away from the stubs of her wrists. Even at that, the birth of this fifth child had come quickly and easily, slipping from her loins like a tamale from its wrapper. The aches would last for two, maybe three days, and the sweat house helped. In two days they would take the afterbirth and bury it at the corner posts. Doña Marina would come by, and they would determine the Tzutujil name. Her husband had already conducted a blessing ceremony before the Maximón and received the prayers of the cofradia. They still had to register the name with the alcalde. From its lines, the baby looked strong; from the length of its feet, it would be able to climb the steep trails to the milpa high above the town. From the width of its brow, the little boy would be sensitive to others and grow in wisdom, earning the respect of the alcaldes. Perhaps he would come himself to serve the cofradia before the Maximón. Tano and Miguel Mapa, no. Maybe this little boy, though. That would be a blessing and an honor to its father. If not, then maybe another . . . another child. Making the baby had become so rough. Andres with the liquor, Andres who demanded so much, with the liquor, when he came from the milpa—he had prayed to the alcaldes, he said, he had spoken with the family, he said, and the liquor—he poured in solemn prayers before the sacred table, the Holy Mesa, lit the candles, poured the liquor, so rough when he took her to make the baby, whispering in a rush as he made the baby, spraying the seeds to make the baby, so rough, spraying the seeds that had made the baby. The baby's water spewing from her loins, the cat, so she spread her legs, rolling on the petate, her back writhing in pain, her bloated stomach churning, the muscles of her stomach convulsing in spasms, the little claws of the hind legs first, the wet tail wrapped around, around its claws drawn up under its stomach, "Once more!—there! now almost the head! Ah! Malaya! Madre de Dios! the head with the bloody shoelace around its throat, the dead cat slipping from her loins, dead the cat, slipping from between her legs like a Christmas tamale from its wrapper, María Xquic, the wrapper of the cat, dead the cat, María Xquic to go, the time, the cat the tamale cat, "to go," *María, María Xquic to* "go, María Xquic! *Señora!*"

María Xquic rolled her head to the sound of the insistent voice as Donaldo gently nudged her shoulder.

"*María!*" he said again, confident now in her attention. "Let's *go.* The clouds are heavy. We can make it by morning to the coffee."

"Yes," said María, still adjusting from her deep sleep.

Quickly, she slipped from under the ledge of the rock and began to gather her small personal bundle and the package of tortillas and dried meet.

"We have to take a cup and small dish, the lighters and some dry charcoal," explained Donaldo. "But no guns. We have to go as partners, as a family, the two of us. If we have guns, they will *kill* us, *sure!"*

Then, Donaldo was struck by an insight. "The *cedulas!* The *sub-comandante* kept his wife's *cedula.* We have to return to his body to find the *cedulas.* If I can find them, then we are safe. We will go as 'Rosalina' and 'José Martín Guerra'!"

Donaldo slipped from her side and disappeared like a spirit into the thick, black fog. María Xquic drew her knees up under her chin, suddenly feeling the urge to pass. She gathered her small, personal bundle and slipped from under the ledge. As she felt her way along the edge of the rock overhang to the end of the escarpment, she could not hear a sound—the whir or chirp of a bird, the movement of the trees, the rustle of leaves, anything. She had remembered a spot inside the underbrush away from the bodies where she might relieve herself.

Donaldo worked back up the slope with two small pieces of paper in hand, two tokens of a new identity. María Xquic had already returned as he stepped out of the black fog.

"For now," said Donaldo, "for now and the next few days we are `Rosalinda' and `Martín.' So, we can go."

Without a word, the two, then, began their exodus from the compound. María Xquic followed her new guide away from the terrifying clearing, placing her own feet in his tracks, no more than a yard behind. For more than two hours they worked their way along the edge of the tree line to avoid losing their direction through heavier underbrush further down the slope.

Somewhere on the southwest side of the volcano, Donaldo stopped and motioned for them to rest, taking a seat on a downed tree. Still, the night slumbered about them in an eerie, almost resonant silence.

"We must work down to the road to San Martín Comitán," explained

Donaldo in a whisper that violated all caution they had faithfully observed over the past two hours. "When we reach Comitán, we can take the vegetable truck of Juan Gonzalez that leaves every week for Huehuetenango. I have some *quetzales* from Rafael, the radio operator. He carried the money for the unit. So, from Huehuetenango, we can take the bus to Barillas. If we get off at Santo Domingo, the *compas* will give us an escort to the border.

It was almost a day later before they were able to reach San Martín Comitán. It was market day, and the streets were filled with women and little children racing through the stalls. Already the market was teeming with activity when Donaldo found his old friend preparing to load his truck with freshly netted cabbages. Over two bags of soda, the former mayor explained only the most general outline of the necessity for sequestered travel to Huehuetenango.

"*Sí, Don Lazaro! Como no!*" said Juan Gonzalez, the vegetable dealer. "Back behind the cab, around the cabbages, *okay?*"

"*Ah, amigo! Una benedición! Muy amable!*" said Donaldo as he embraced his long-time friend.

"It has been very hard for us since you *left,* Don Lazaro!" explained Juan Gonzalez. "We all understand why you had to go, but every day, more *disappearances!* Our priest finally left three months ago. Look *about!* Looks *normal, no?* But where are the *men, huh?* I'll tell you something: not up *there!* Not in the *hills! Me entiende*? So many women are *alone* now, no husbands or brothers, little work. No *hope!* No *future!* Just waiting for *death! . . . Well?* What *else?* And for *me?* Well, I keep hauling the vegetables for the little bit of money, you know, running them down the highway. But who knows how *long, no?* Then someday, maybe tomorrow, maybe today, *eh? Boom!* The *ejercito* might stop me, take the truck. And Juan Gonzalez? Dead on the side of the road, waiting for the *buzzards!* Who can *say?* So . . . we *go!* Get up in the back, *amigo*, you and the lady. If I don't ask any questions, then I won't have anything to *explain, no?*"

Donaldo and María worked down between two nets of cabbages at the front of the bed up against the cab of the truck. When he was satisfied that Maria was settled, Donaldo pulled the tarp back up almost over their heads. There was still space enough to squeeze into below them on the very bottom of the bed if it looked like they were going to be stopped. Juan Gonzalez had arranged a signal of three taps on the cab if he saw an imminent stop ahead at a military or police check point along the highway. There was always a check at Dos Pilas, but he was on his regular schedule for a market day, and the militaries knew him and usually just waved him on. Still, he had to be careful.

This morning, as it turned out, was no different. The soldiers, preoccupied with a group of school girls who had stepped off the bus to stretch, never even looked up as the cabbage vendor chugged up to the *tumelo*, bumped over, and sputtered on its way up the highway.

In season, Juan Gonzalez made an extended drive up to Huehuetenango every two weeks, a trip of more than six hours from San Martín Comitán. He would take the load of cabbages to a wholesaler in Huehuetenango right next to the large bus depot. There he would pick up *campesinos* from the north and transport them back down to Sololá en route to the *fincas* for harvesting the coffee. He could make enough on one trip back to pay for the upkeep on the truck and fuel for the month. Once he made it into the city, his two passengers might get up into the cab. Anywhere along the highway, however, they could be stopped, and it would be risky if any of the national police along the road who knew him saw him transporting a couple of riders.

In the bed of the truck María Xquic strained with every lurch up the road from San Martín. For more than an hour, the truck rattled along, bouncing and bumping through the ruts and holes. After about two hours, the truck turned westward onto the Pan American highway. Donaldo and María hadn't said a word to each other during the rough passage, but as they entered the smooth highway, Donaldo called out for his sequestered partner.

"Are you okay, *Señora*?"

"Thank you, Don Donaldo," said María. "Very sore, but okay, thank you."

"We can rest easier now," he said.

"Yes, I hope so. How far is Huehuetenango?"

"Many hours . . . maybe four, maybe five or so. Can you make it?"

"Yes."

The air grew cooler as the truck continued on up the highway, climbing higher and higher into the mountains. On some of the steeper grades, the truck all but broke down, leaving Juan Gonzalez racing through the gears, struggling frantically to finesse the last gasp of energy from the old engine. Horns blaring, arrogant bus drivers whipped their overladen vehicles around the truck, leaving the cabbage driver and his clandestine guests suffocating in thick, black clouds of diesel fumes.

Somewhere up the road, Donaldo was awakened from a spotty, troubled sleep by the shift of the engine into low gear and the sense of braking for an impending stop. It was late in the afternoon, almost twilight when Donaldo heard the three taps from inside the cab.

"*Señora!*" said Donaldo. "*Doña María!*"

"*Sí, Señor!*" said María. "I hear."

"We're going to stop. Can you move further down to the bottom of the bed?"

"Yes."

"Okay, then. You move on down. I'll come behind you and secure the tarpaulin over the cabbages."

As quickly as they could maneuver in the tight quarters, they inched and squirmed to the floor of the truck bed. Donaldo pulled the net of cabbages over him and secured the cord of the tarp around the cinch hook welded to the highest brace on the back of the cab and pulled it taut. Donaldo had no sooner settled in place than the truck swerved to a stop on the side of the road. A moment or two later he could hear some conversation ahead of the truck. The driver's side door creaked open, and Juan Gonzalez slammed the door behind him, saying something to another man further away from them. The din of passing trucks and busses obscured the conversation for a few moments. It was only as Juan Gonzalez and the other man returned to the truck that Donaldo could understand them.

"Sí. Como no!" said the driver. *"Cuarenta y cinco, y cincuenta quetzales."*

"Cuarenta y cinco, cincuenta . . . cincuenta quetzales, okay," said the other. "Pasen, pasen a la izquirda. Cuidado! Cuidado!"

"*Gracias! Muy amable,* officer!" said Juan Gonzalez as he stepped back into the cab. Donaldo and María held their breath as Juan Gonzalez struggled to turn the engine. Finally, it started, and the truck jumped forward as the gears ground into first. Slowly, the vehicle climbed back onto the highway. After they were well past the check point, both heard the tapping which meant they were all clear.

"Sons of *bitches!*" cursed the driver out the window.

It was well after nightfall when the truck with its load of produce and clandestines pulled into the outskirts of Huehuetenango, the capital of the department. Juan Gonzalez pulled the truck into the first service station to add two quarts of oil.

The station was all but closed, only an old attendant sleeping heavily on a broken chair just inside the door. Donaldo pulled the truck up to the far edge of the drive so as to avoid disturbing the attendant.

"*Okay!*" he called through the cab to Donaldo and María. "I'll help you *out* now!"

María's legs were completely numb from the cramped position she had had to endure during the past few hours; Donaldo, hardly better. They could hear Juan Gonzalez untying the tarpaulin over them and ripping it off the load of produce.

"Okay, my *friends!*" he said triumphantly. "We are in *Huehue!* We have made it at last. You can come *out* now!"

Slowly, the nets of cabbages rolled off of them, and María and Donaldo looked up at clear air for the first time in several painful hours.

"*Easy*, my friends!" said the driver. "Let me help you to your feet. *Slowly* now!"

Carefully, he urged them up to a sitting position onto one of the nets of cabbages. "Why don't you just sit here and rest for a moment while I add the oil. Then we will be on our way to the bus station. We're only about three kilometers away from the city, maybe fifteen, twenty minutes from the bus line."

Juan Gonzalez reached into his shirt pocket, retrieved a packet of cigarettes and offered one to Donaldo. The former *alcalde* looked nervous and distracted, his hand shaking as he tried to fire the lighter.

"What are you going to *do, amigo*?" asked the driver of his lifelong friend.

At first, Donaldo only stared at a hole in the sky somewhere far over the horizon. Then he took his first long drag, looked up vacantly at his friend, and shook his head.

The truck driver glanced over at María Xquic and then beyond her, suddenly distracted by a pair of dogs in heat courting coitus a few meters away beneath a stand of dead brush and weeds just behind the service station. Juan Gonzalez watched without humor the futile attempts of the smaller male mongrel attempting to mount the exasperated bitch, her back arched and rigid in anticipation.

"You can't come back to San Martín," said the driver. "There's nothing there that's the same, except the buildings. Most of them are empty. Everything's changed. The army might as well come into Comitán and burn it down, so much for the life of the people there, *verdad*?"

The bitch snarled and turned on her hapless suitor, slashing at his left hip as he reeled backward in retreat.

"*Shit!*" said Donaldo. "There's nothing back there for me in Comitán. And the mountain? Everything's rotting up there on the mountain. No one's left. They're all dead. There's nothing up the road—just more of the same *shit, no*?"

María Xquic had climbed down from the truck and was walking slowly back to the shadows beyond the light of the one bulb which illuminated the drive of the service station. As she approached the side of the building, the bitch dog caught up to her and followed along beside her into the privacy of the weeds.

"What was it *like* on the mountain?" asked Juan Gonzalez.

"On the *mountain?*" said Donaldo. He looked down and wiped the palms of his hands down his filthy pants.

". . . on the *mountain!* Well, I'll *tell* you! I'll tell you straight up what it's like on the mountain. I just don't care any more."

The driver handed Donaldo another cigarette.

"I went to the mountain almost two years ago," began Donaldo. "I went to the mountain first out of anger after the five boys were killed. I went to the mountain to get revenge on the army for what they did to the five boys and their families. If I had failed those boys and their families, it wasn't my fault, but somebody had to *pay, verdad*? So, I went up to the mountain really *mad.* I really wanted to *kill* some *militaries*."

Juan Gonzalez stepped a pace or two away to give his friend space enough to think, to measure his words carefully. He wanted to know as much as a friend would share with him, but a man has to have some space to tell such a story.

"*Entonces . . .*" said Donaldo, his acknowledgment of the courtesy and his signal that he wished to continue. Juan Gonzalez turned back to face his friend.

"*Entonces . . .*" repeated Donaldo, "I had trouble at first. I wasn't used to the long hours on patrol and the constant climbing. The ground was never *flat,* never *level, verdad*? Always climbing up or down, slipping this way or that—I had *trouble, no*?"

Donaldo inhaled another draft from the cigarette.

"You just don't go up on the mountain and start popping *kaibiles*," confessed the *alcalde*. "You . . . I wasn't used to all the waiting, and the climbing, and the constant hunger. That's all I could think about—*eating, verdad*?"

"Almost everyone had worms," said Donaldo with disgust. "All you wanted to do was eat—you were always so *hungry!* So, you'd try to eat something—*anything!* That would *do* it! All you could do for two or three days afterwards was just grab your stomach, roll on the ground, and *puke*. And *shit!—man!* You'd shit for *hours,* nothing but *sopa verde*. Remigo died from the worms. We'd fix tea for him, *te yerbamora, te manzanilla—shit! Nothing* worked. He just died in a puddle of *green soup, verdad*? One time, the whole unit was down—everybody rolled up behind some bush, shitting green soup, spitting up blood."

Donaldo turned his head to spit out fragments of tobacco from the cigarette.

"You want to know what it was like on the *mountain?*" he laughed sardonically. "*I'll* tell you what it was like—you'd get *sores* all over your arms and legs, great white, pussy *sores.* If you scratched them, they would spread all over your body. Everybody scratched them, you couldn't help it. We made this salve from aloe leaves. That was good for the sores—took the sting and pain away for a little while, but you were almost always covered with these sores. Once they were open, they healed pretty quickly. But it would take the whelps for days to ripen—maybe five six days before they would fester and you could open them. *Shit!* You want to know what it was like on the *mountain? Shit!*"

Donaldo looked back behind the station, half expecting to see María return. He took another pull on the cigarette and spit.

"You have to be pretty *tough*—tough and *lucky* to live very long on the mountain," Donaldo continued. I always hated to leave the camp. Some of us would have to go into the *cantones* for supplies. You always had one or two people you could count on for a little something—an egg, maybe—some *masa.* You know—just a little something to take back. But you never knew who might be watching, never knew who was the *oreja* for the *militarie*s or the civil patrol. So we had to be careful. One time Remigo—you know, the guy with the worms—he went down to San Mateo Concepción. What did he get? Two *eggs!* Two fucking *eggs!* Next day, you know what happened. The *militaries* came into San Mateo—wiped out six families! Just dragged them out of their houses, women, kids, the goddamn *dogs!—everybody!* Just blew them all *away!* For two *eggs! Two fucking eggs! . . . Shit, man!"*

Juan Gonzalez dug his heel into a break in the driveway slab, his hands buried deeply into his front pockets.

"We'd get these new recruits from the *city!"* laughed Donaldo. "The *guys* especially! They thought they were better than anyone *else!* They'd be dragging their butts before they ever got to camp—like that American *reporter* guy last we*ek! Shit!* The older guys— they'd always say, `Send them up to the front. They're all dead, *anyway!' Shit!* No one wanted to go out with them. They were *`monkeys'*: that's what everyone called them—*`monkeys,'* you know. We'd all laugh at these young *`monkeys'!* They thought they were so *hot*—for the *first* few days. Always flirting with the *compañ*eras. It didn't matter, you know, their *compañeros.* These guys were from the city, so they thought they'd just move in, the *compañeras* would just roll over and spread their *legs! Shit!* Well, I mean *everybody* flirted. What else was there to *do?* But *shit!* You just didn't move in on someone's *compañera.* And the *compañeros* wouldn't have to say a thing. The girls would take care of these city guys. They'd drive them up as point on patrols and laugh at them from behind about how slow they were, what cowards they were. No one wanted to run off a new recruit, because then you'd probably have to slit his *throat.* If he'd been to base camp, he already knew too much. But still, they had to learn. And they *learned!* Or they *died! Shit!* Up on the *mountain* . . ."

Donaldo looked up to see María returning from behind the station. The stories of the mountain had been interrupted. Juan Gonzalez took leave to change the oil so that they could move on to the bus station. María Xquic walked softly back over beside Donaldo. She had been standing behind the station waiting for the men to complete their conversation, but returned as she sensed the importance of their time. She knew they had to reach the bus station if they were to make connections that night for Barillas.

Juan Gonzalez completed adding the oil to the engine, closed the hood, and was wiping his hands on a rag as he stepped back around to the couple.

"You have really *changed,* my friend," he said to Donaldo. "We've *all* changed—the killing, all our families destroyed. We've all changed, but *you,* Donaldo, my *friend!* You have lost something, that *something* that always set you apart, that something that all the rest of us looked to for support, for leadership. What *is* it, Lazaro, my friend? What *is* it?"

"`Hope' . . ." stammered Donaldo. "`Hope' that this will ever change for the people. I've *been* on the mountain. I've *been* there! I took my *`hope'* to the mountain, but I *lost* it. I'll tell you something, Juan Gonzalez. I'll tell you something for *sure, verdad*? *You!* . . . *Me!* . . . the *lady* here! *She* can tell you—*I* can tell you! Anyone who's been on the *mountain* can tell you. We *indigenas*, we've only got two choices—*where* and *how* do we want to *die!* You can stay down here and get your throat slit, or you can go up on the mountain and die in a puddle of *green soup!* And if you think you've got any other options running *cabbages* back and forth to Huehuetenango . . . well, my wonderful friend, Juan Gonzalez . . . you're just *fooling* yourself, *verdad*?"

"If that's the case," offered the driver, "then why don't we all just go up to the military post and turn ourselves over, just give it all *up?"*

"That's what they're doing right *now!*" said Donaldo. "At Nebáj, Cotzál—some of them are so fed up with the starving and diseases that they don't *care* anymore. So, they're coming down out of the hills, down from the CPRs and throwing themselves at the mercy of the jackals."

"Why?" protested Juan Gonzalez. "Going back with their kids and all from the CPRs. The military says they're all *URNG.* That's a *death* sentence. Why would they do *that?* Why in the world go *back?*"

"Because there's only so much a human being can take before he breaks," said Donaldo, "and then it's over."

María Xquic crossed her arms, cradling her elbows in her hands. How easy it was for some to talk. How can you speak of hope—how can a mother speak of hope when all she has ever known and loved has been torn from her heart? How can anyone talk of hope when fear crowds out every other human feeling? But how could anyone think of going back, back to face the bayonets of the army, back to face being burned, and cut, and tortured? How can two feet do anything but run when the wild dogs are at their heels? After the death of little Ana Fabiola, it was all well and good to have spoken up to the military commissioner at the *palacio municipal*. That was the right thing to do! But it was not all right, then, to lose Lucita María! It was not all right to lose her sons! And it was not all right to lose her husband! There was no life left for her in Guatemala, nothing but death—a horrible death. What else was there for her to do but to run, to try to reach safety in Mexico. In Mexico she could rest, regain her strength, and think—think about what she had to do, gather her thoughts, look for a way. Others were there already, other *Guatemaltecos* living in the camps. She had heard. She had heard about the camps. The people were alive. They had food, a place to live, a roof over their heads. She would be safe in the camps. Donaldo was going to take her as far as the camps of Margaritas. He had a brother, maybe it was a cousin—at least he knew someone at the camps of Margaritas. They would be safe there, there among the *Guatemaltecos* in resistance.

Chapter 30

Career Service

Julius Parker had worked for State for almost fifteen years. The Guatemala Desk was a step up . . . or sideways, or maybe it was just a change. He had held a number of posts in the region: political advisor in El Salvador, assistant cultural attaché and later public affairs officer in Honduras. From 1975 through 1982 he had directed the bi-national center for "Service" and in the Consular division at the Embassy in Guatemala. From 1982 to 1987 he had worked around the Caribbean basin, a "donkey" as he preferred to call himself (if not a "mule" for C.I.A., as he sometimes suspected). He could manage "Desk." After all, he needed a little stateside R&R. Most of the corps dreaded reassignment stateside, but he needed to be back. He needed to "ease the tension in his backside *state-side*," as he had quipped in his transfer interview.

Julius Parker wasn't just "Service," but rather, "*Career* Service," although his early enthusiasm had long since lost its edge. He had seen just about all of it: the rise and fall of every little "ism" in the Caribbean. He had played a role in Grenada, "ferrying pouches" for the military attaché in Trinidad and Tobago that he felt sure fixed the targets for the invasion. And he knew his way around. He could pick up the phone to Paris and reach "Papa Doc," and he despised Daniel Ortega from earlier contact, viz-a-viz. "This guy was all bluff outside his own taco stand," he was fond of sharing. Why, "that little *fart* couldn't find his *asshole* with a heat-seeking *missile!*"—another cliché he enjoyed passing around State. But he was getting tired, and Julius Parker really didn't care where he played the last hand or two, and the Guatemala Desk "would work just fine." It would put him in line for a few serendipitous perks, he felt certain. He surely wouldn't be the first in line for a little "double dipping" with some "after-glow" contracts. The only real ambition he harbored was to lose about twenty-five pounds off the old paunch; at least he would feel more comfortable a little lighter around the "Californians" in State's secretarial pool.

He had been in D. C. for more than a month, looking for temporary lodging around Alexandria; he didn't mind the commute. He had done it all before. His ex-wife, ex-daughter, ex-mistress—they had all checked in, off and on, during the month. He had found a little two-bedroom job that wouldn't cost him more than a left "tes-*TI*-cle," but it would let him provide a little classy hospitality when the "Californians" began to line up—in his *dreams! Right?*

The light changed, and "Gua-*TEE*" Parker turned on the street leading to the alley that entered the rear to his condominium. The movers would be arriving in the afternoon, and he envisioned his walls redecorated in "highland *tzute.*" If there was anything particular about Guatemala that retained any fascination for him, it was the cottage textile industry, the determination of these Indian women to keep turning out these weav . . . . No, it wasn't all *that.* It was the weavings *themselves*, but not just any weavings, but the ones *he* owned. That was *it.* What he had really taken from his experiences in Guatemala were a few prized weavings and the stories of each. For of course, each had its own story.

He had framed one from San Juan Comalapa. He had purchased it on site at the weaving co-op. The drive there from Guatemala had been atrocious. The road out to the village off the Pan American highway was unpaved and deeply rutted. Even the Embassy's Land Rover's four-wheel drive was challenged. His back ached for two days after his trip. He remembered how thirsty he was for anything to drink, but after the `76 earthquake had levelled much of the town, and even seven years later, the drinking water still wasn't safe. He looked for a bottled soft drink, but it was more than an hour before one of the little urchins showed up, accepting a *quetzal* for his effort, plus two more *quetzales* for the drink. It was the kid's sister, close behind, who had reached into the folds of her *huipil* and produced the panel of cloth that he later had framed for hanging behind the head of his dining room table.

And then there was the *morga* of Sacatepequez—a surprise gift from his lover, the sister of his secretary at the bi-national center. After a wild evening's tryst, he found the heavy Indian skirt with its embroidered seam, folded meticulously at the foot of his bed, crossed by the limp, long-stemmed red rose that he had given her early in the evening before as they had entered his hotel room.

Of course, every weaving had its private story. No one would ever know the hours he had spent just touching them, looking at them. That's all. Simply looking at them. He would spread them out on the floor, angle them all around his lounge chair, and then just stare at them and know that they were *his.* Then he would pick up each one, fold it carefully, return it to its plastic bag, and tuck them all away in his chest of drawers. Everything else about Guatemala was messy and of little interest outside the variety of his daily activities for State. But the *weavings!—these* were the constant.

Julius Parker turned into his parking space under the carport behind his back door. He turned off his ignition, engaged the auto alarm system, grabbed his briefcase, and locked the car as he exited. He slipped his fingers along the key chain until he found the coated key—the key to his back door—unlocked the door, and entered the back-entry hall leading to the kitchen. Quickly, he reached for the alarm panel and cleared the switch, set his briefcase on the kitchen counter, and grabbed a cold beer from the refrigerator. The first sip of the cold malt caressed his lips, his tongue, and the walls of his cheeks. The refreshing lager fizzed on the back of his tongue against the roof of his mouth as he swallowed deeply from the can.

Julius Parker looked around the room and then removed the morning newspaper from over the telephone answering machine to check for messages. The red message light was flashing.

"Julius . . . sorry to disturb your evening. Give me a call as soon as you get in. We've got trouble brewing in Guatee." It was the voice of the Assistant Secretary for Latin American Affairs, his boss, Bill Boyer.

"Trouble, my *ass!*" Julius protested. "It can damn sure *wait* until I finish this *beer.*" He pushed the "erase" button and dissolved the remaining message and then sat down in one of the kitchen chairs around the dinette. After glancing over the frontpage headlines for a few moments, he turned the can on end and swallowed the last drop of the lager. He tossed the empty can into the plastic trash basket in the corner of the sink and then reached back for the telephone at the end of the counter.

"Put me through to Boyer," he instructed the front desk.

"Hey, *Bill,*" Julius said.

"It'll hold `til in the morning, but I just thought you ought to know we've got some heavy press coming out of the highlands," said Boyer. "Things are starting to get a little warm again. Seems like the Indians organized a demonstration at Sololá and the army opened up on them. Looks like we might have taken a couple of American casualties. First reports seem a little exaggerated; you know how that goes, so you'll be getting some inquiries. We want to deflect as much *enthusiasm* as we can—if it *develops,* you know. Anyway, I just thought it best to alert you tonight so you'll be prepared when you get in in the morning. In fact, why don't you stop by my office about six o'clock, and I'll brief you on what we have, *okay?*"

"Yeah, yeah, *sure!*" said Julius. "Yeah, I'll see you at six."

He heard the phone release on the other end. He stared at the receiver for a moment and then slammed it into the base.

"What the *shit!*" he said to himself. "The first god-damned call is going to be *Amnesty*, for *sure!*"

Julius Parker didn't much care for *Amnesty International, Americas Watch*, the *Washington Post*—it didn't matter. "They're all the same; they have such a way of *personalizing*—I mean, *trivializing* these things," he thought to himself. "You don't move a Third World nation into a free-market economy and democratic society overnight. What's even a 1,000 to1 kill ratio compared to the *GNP*? These lily-lipped *liberals* never understand the *larger* picture. In a country like Guatemala, it was a matter of selective education, a slow accretion of skills and investment among a tight, targeted elite that gradually builds a base of competency in these nations, and that just doesn't *happen* like *that!* What the hell are these *Indians* going to do to improve *anything?* They're prejudiced against *real* statehood, *anyway*. But you let a handful of disgruntled hot-heads among them start agitating and stirring things around, and the power base in Guatemala isn't going to stand for it. You're going to get these incidents *every time!* And then you get *Amnesty* and every other `yippie-hippie' on his *`high moral ground'* making lists and taking names. I mean, *JEEZ-US Shit!*"

Julius Parker glanced up and grimaced at the clock. "So that means I've got to drag ass in before six in the *Indian-fucking morning*," he said to himself. "Those poor bastards," he said out loud. "When in *jesusname* are they ever gonna *learn* something about *political expediency?* Well, anyway, here comes the *beer*. I guess I'd better take a leak."

By day break, Julius Parker was already entering his office. He passed through the third-floor corridor, past the security desk, waving at the guard over his shoulder as he reached for his badge. He couldn't work it out of his pocket, so that he was forced to stop, set down his briefcase, and work the plastic sleeve loose from his overstuffed pocket. His shirts were too small and pinching him under the arm. Little inconveniences like this exposed his pudgy weight to fools around him, and he was irritated with the whole security system that refused to acknowledge career people like himself whom they and everyone recognized anyway.

The security guard acknowledged his photo I.D. with a smug disregard for rank and privilege and noted the passage on his clipboard. The buzzer sounded, and Julius Parker entered the reception area for Latin American affairs. He walked over to the "Californian" waiting for him or anything else to sign the register, positioned himself in just the right spot to observe her split skirt revealing a pair of sun-drenched thighs, and winked at the "little party favor" still absorbed in her fingernails.

"Has Secretary Boyer arrived yet?" he asked.

"Mr. Boyer?" responded the blonde "Californian."

"Secretary Boyer, yes," confirmed Julius.

"Yes, I think so," reflected the "Californian." "You can check the roster there, if you like. Just turn the page back."

Julius flipped back the top page and turned to the bottom of the previous registrations. Quickly, he scanned for "B"s, but he was unrewarded.

"*Julius!*" barked a voice behind him. It was Assistant Secretary Boyer. Surprised by the unexpected exclamation, Julius jumped, and then laid the book down on the counter. The "Californian" kept grooming her nails.

"Hey, *Bill!*" said Julius. "I was just about to look you up on the *registration.* Don't you *work* here anymore? Or is it you just don't have to *sign* in since your *promotion?*"

"Good to see you," said Boyer. "Sorry to have to drag you in here so early, but you can probably imagine what the day is going to be like. You remember that incident up at San Saba, don't you?"

Boyer didn't have to ask him about anything in Huehuetenango. Julius Parker had interviewed a dozen or more who had made it into the Center nine months earlier. They had come into the Center with the Bradley kid from Casa "Guate Libre." Julius didn't have to guess twice about the probable "American casualty." "Buster" Bradley was a Mennonite from Ohio who had come to Guatemala to "minister to the poor." From the "hairlip" hospital in Antigua, he had bounced out west to the orphanage outside of Colotenango where he had gotten caught up in the Catholic Action thing. They didn't have much use for him there, either, after the Puente Alto affair in July, `82. He had made it a point to protest the massacre to the *comandante* of the post himself, and the Bishop began receiving interesting correspondence about a week later. So, the Bishop asked him to leave for his own and the security of the whole community. He showed up the following month in Guatemala as a sort of self-appointed "representative" to the displaced. He would bring in these Kanjobal Maya kids into the Center for English classes. He said he had support from Mennonite groups stateside, and he had determined that what they needed was English classes as part of their ticket out of the country. Julius Parker began to get a clearer picture a little later when four or five of the Bradley "students" began showing up "wet back" in Harlingen, Texas.

"It's pretty rough," said Bill Boyer. "Now it's a couple of Michael Justice's crew from South Texas. We've got a Marcus Finley, a reporter, and a Susan

Simpson down there in the morgue. The National Police picked them up outside of Sololá at the military post early yesterday. It was pretty much the same sort of thing. They'd been roughed up pretty badly. It looks like the girl had been "poled" and the reporter burned with electric shocks and cigarettes before they cut him all up. The Ambassador is on his way back now . . . Well, he should be leaving in about two hours. He's supposed to be escorting the remains. The *President's* pretty pissed. This Susan Simpson was a Peace Corps worker and had a distinguished teaching record at UCLA."

"*Christ!*" remarked Julius Parker. "We're going to have American `martyrs' on every goddamned *plaza!* What's next?"

"Well," mused Boyer, "the Secretary and the Ambassador will sit down this afternoon to review some options, and we ought to know in another day or two. The Ambassador has already lodged a response to the Bustamante government, so we're already `on record.'"

Julius Parker walked over to the side window of the office and reached for a cigarette, pulled one from the pack, and slipped it between his teeth, musing nervously over the images of torture that he couldn't quite escape. The massacre of San Saba brought about three hundred calls, telegrams, and letters to the Embassy. He had been working in the Consular Division for about three months at the time, and more than 3,000 Guatemalans converged on the Embassy for visas in about a four-week period. Old toothless, bristle-chinned *campesinos* stood in lines wrapped around the embassy and stretching for three blocks, political beggars—each and every one—with their wrinkled, thirty-year-old crones for wives and their barefooted menagerie of runt children in their miniature jeans and dirty, wide-striped T-shirts. Consul approved two asylum cases: a teacher who had lost an ear—said he had been hit upside the head with a machete—and a catechist whose family had died in the melee and had presented a death threat notice splotched with blood alleged to be his daughter's. The rest had been turned away. Of course, these things are almost always messy and bad for image.

"Nobody wins in these massacres," muttered Julius Parker. He couldn't shake the image of some "long-haired, hippy-looking" girl hanging from the rafters by her wrists with a bloody broom handle shoved up through her cunt just about all the way up to her throat. It was a rough way to die. He hadn't ever seen it himself, but a Military Attaché had described it to him years before.

"They tie the woman's wrists together and throw the end of the rope over the rafter and tie it off," he could still hear the agent explain. "Then they make her stand on a chair and bend over. They grease the end of a broom stick and force it up into her, threatening her with burning cigarettes if she kicks or protests. Next, they tape her feet together with the broomstick between her ankles. As soon as she straightens up, they pull the chair out from under her, stick the end of the broomstick in a hole in the floor just below her and leave her hanging there, twitching. Of course, her instinct is to pull herself up with her wrists. The whole system works like a Roman crucifixion: every time she twitches, the pole works up a little further until her arms give out completely. When she finally collapses, the pole glides up into her body cavity until it breaks through vital organs, and she slowly dies, depending on the path of the pole up through her."

". . . before they arrive. *Okay, Julius?*" Julius had heard only the last phrase.

"*Okay, Julius?*" returned Boyer.

"Yeah. I mean, *what?* I was drifting, I guess. Tell me again, Bill," Julius Parker responded.

"I said," said Boyer with some irritation, "that I need you to run point on this for State, Julius, and break the news to the families, cover all the arrangements."

"Yeah. Okay, Bill. Yeah, I'll get on it today . . ." said Parker.

"This *morning!*" insisted Boyer. "Right *now!*"

"Oh, *yeah!"* echoed Julius Parker. "That's what I mean. I'll go on down to the office right now."

Julius Parker turned a sluggishly animated left and ambled over to the "Californian."

"Hi, honey. Look," said Parker, "call down to my wing and see if Cindy's here yet . . . Oh, *hell!* She won't be here for another hour. Never mind, honey."

The Californian continued to scan the health and fitness section of the morning's paper. Parker turned to his boss who was about to say something else.

"And Julius," returned Boyer. "We've got some staffers coming up here from the hill . . . from Congressman Sheranski's office to pump us about that last military shipment. The Senate Foreign Relations Committee is warming up for a full-scale review of Senator Freeman's activities in all that, and we may have to do some clean up. Make your calls and then go over to the files and see what you can pull up. I've already called in clearance."

"*Right!*" said Parker as he walked past the Californian through the security doors into his corridor.

Julius Parker didn't want to call either the Finley family or the Simpsons.

"Notices" were always unpleasant, and he didn't enjoy being "point" for State. He opened the door to his office, ready to tell Cindy to get him the numbers when he realized that he was alone.

"*Jeez-us Christ!*" he said aloud. He despised everybody else's "nine-to-five," but he grew exceptionally impatient with the inference that he himself might be shirking duty when he split at 2:30 or 3 o'clock. Sometimes you just had to do what you had to do. "*Jeez-us Christ!*" said Parker.

Julius Parker stopped at his secretary's desk, set his briefcase down, and thumbed through the few envelopes and interoffice files. Nothing of pressing importance surfaced, and he picked up his briefcase again and entered his own office to face the inevitable. "*Jeez-us shit!* What a fucked-up *world*, and I've got to debrief the whole goddamn *show! Shit!*"

His thoughts drifted back down the corridor to the pretty little "Californian" sitting at her desk. Parker pictured her tan thighs stretching up under the finely finished hem of her fashionable, high-cut skirt.

"*My, oh my!*" he thought to himself. "Just one night in *paradise! . . . Shit!* They *gotta* know what they're doing—sitting there with the goddamn hemline high enough to check out their *slit.* I mean, *goddamn!*"

Julius Parker picked up the telephone and dialed the switch-board.

"Get me 'Brownsville, Texas—I mean, 'information' in Brownsville, Texas—`information'," he said. "*No, honey! Texas! Not Arkansas!*" pleaded Parker to the switchboard operator who had obviously miscued.

"Yeah . . . '*Brownsville,'*" said Parker to the South Texas operator. He just couldn't stand the country drawl of Texas operators.

"No fucking *class!*" he thought to himself.

"*Yeah*, honey! I need the number for a 'Ronald W. Simpson' listing."

"Is that a business or residential listing, sir?" asked the operator.

"Is that a *what? . . . No! No!,*" protested an exasperated Parker. "Residential, sweetheart! *Residential!*"

The dial tone suddenly hummed in his ear.

"Well, the *goddamned little bitch!*" said Parker as he slammed down the receiver. "That *goddamned little bitch* hung *up* on me! Why, that *goddamned little bitch!*"

Julius Parker was furious. He kicked his briefcase that had been sitting at his feet, knocking over the trash can beside his desk. "What a *goddamned, chickenshit little bitch! Goddamn!*"

Parker threw himself back in his chair and slipped his finger in his collar to loosen his tie. His face was flushed, and he felt his blood pressure rising. He was panting, trying to catch his breath.

"God-*damn!*" he said. Then he reached for the telephone again.

"Yeah, I'm sorry, sugar. I must have been disconnected. Get me 'Brownsville' again, would you, honey?" Julius Parker pleaded with the switchboard operator once more. He heard the connections crackling down line and the operator at the other end.

"This is 'Brownsville,'" said the voice of a male assistant. Parker was momentarily stunned, half expecting to hear the same woman who had just dispatched him.

"*Oh! Yeah!*" said Parker. "Yeah, *Brownsville!* Get me . . . I need the number for `Ronald W. Simpson' . . . that's a residential listing."

"Yes, sir," said the operator. "Please hold for your number."

"The number you requested . . ." said the mechanized voice. Julius Parker reached over his desk for a pen, a pencil, *anything!*

"*Goddamn!*" he said. "Not a fucking *pen* or *pencil anywhere!*" His pudgy hands slipped in and out the pile of loose papers, notes, and folders that cluttered the top of his desk.

". . . may be dialled automatically for an additional charge of fifty cents by pressing `0' now," finished the phone message.

"Well, *Goddamn!"* said Parker to himself. "Sometimes you fucking *win!*" And smiling to himself, he pressed "0," and settled back deeply into his reclining swivel chair.

Julius Parker listened to the distant rings at the other end of the line . . . a third ring, then a fourth. And finally, he heard the receiver lifted and dropped with a clatter. He had obviously awakened the party.

"Hello," came the muted and congested voice of a woman.

"Yes, *uhhh* . . ." stammered Julius Parker. "*Yeah,* I'd like to speak to Ronald W. Simpson, please. This is the United States Department of State, Julius Parker at the Guatemala desk."

"What? *Who?*" said a woman's voice.

"Yes," said Parker, finally beginning to find himself once again. "Yes ma'am. I'm sorry to disturb you so early. This is Julius Parker, Guatemala Desk Officer at the United States Department of State. I'd like to speak with Mr. Ronald Simpson. Have I reached the correct party?"

"Yes. This is the Simpson residence, but my husband isn't here right now. This is Bonnie Simpson, his wife. Can I help you?" asked the woman, now quite alarmed.

"Yes. Well, Mrs. Simpson," said Julius Parker. "I'm afraid I am calling to share with you some very bad *news* regarding your daughter, Susan, in Guatemala."

"*Susan?* What about *Susan?*" cried the panicked mother. "What *about* her? Is this some kind of *joke?* Who *are* you?"

"Mrs. Simpson," confided the officer. "We've just received a report, and while we don't have all the details, the basic facts have been confirmed."

"What are you *talking* about?" stammered Mrs. Simpson.

"Well, I'm afraid," said Parker, "that I have to be the one to tell you that your daughter Susan has been killed. We've received a classified telex just . . . just this *morning,*" he lied, "and it seems that Susan was killed in an attack on her village by guerrillas. We don't have the whole story, so I'm afraid that there isn't much I can tell you now, but let me give you a telephone number where you can reach me during the next few hours as we try to get more information."

Margaret Simpson was sobbing openly on the other end of the line, and Julius Parker could hear a male voice in the background, also alarmed, pressing her for information.

"Yes," said Parker. "Here is my inside number at State so that you won't have to go through the switchboard."

Julius Parker called out the number slowly and then repeated it to the hysterical woman. The male voice took the telephone before he could finish repeating the number.

"This is Ronald Simpson, *Junior,*" said the stern voice of a young man. "What's going *on!* What's this all *about!*"

Parker expected as much.

"Yeah, this is Julius Parker at the Guatemala Desk at the State Department in Washington," explained Parker. "Yeah, Mr. *Simpson!* I'm calling with some very disturbing news about Susan Simpson. Are you her *brother?*"

"Yes, that's right," said an obviously frightened young man.

"Yeah. Well, as I was saying to your *mother,* Mr. Simpson," said Parker. "Are you with your mother now?"

"Yes. Yes, I *am,"* said the teenage boy, increasingly nervous himself.

"Well, we have just received and confirmed a telex regarding your sister, Susan. It seems Susan has been killed in some kind of guerrilla raid up in the highlands—probably sometime last evening," explained Parker, now in more control. There was only silence on the other end, interrupted by muffled sobbing.

"Mr. Simpson . . . *Mr. Simpson!*" called Parker. "Are you still *with* me?"

"*Yes, sir!*" cried the boy.

"Look, son," said the desk officer, trying to sound as empathetic now as possible. "Make *sure* that your mother has my number . . . and I'll tell you what," said Parker in a moment of weakness. "Let me give you my *private* number . . . well, I guess my inward number at State will be best because I'll be beeped automatically if I'm not there."

Parker had caught himself almost giving out his unlisted personal number, and that wasn't the thing to do. "*Goddamn!*" he said to himself. "That was a *close* one!"

Julius Parker repeated the number again to the son. "Now, you or your mother—your *dad,* there—you call me at any *time.* I know this is a terrible thing, and you need to know that we're here to help you in every way possible. . . . That's *right.* . . . That's *right! Any* time! . . . *Okay?* . . . *Okay!"*

Parker hung up the receiver and settled back in his chair, loosening his collar a little further. He grabbed a cigarette, fired up, and made one slow spin in his chair.

"*Slit-high!* . . . *Goddamn!*" he mused. "Those *Californians!* They just *gotta* know!"

Chapter 31

The Visitation of the Virgin

Not a breath of air stirred the jungle. Donaldo sat at the banks of the Usumacinta River, a wide expanse of churlish, grey water cutting through steep jungle embankments. The river marked the boundary between Mexico and Guatemala, and it was as far as he would go. María Xquic stood at his side, a pace or two away, looking hesitantly through the branches at the deep flowing current, the whir of cicadas buzzing in the steamy jungle behind her. Tomás, the "mule" for the URNG, was behind them both, steadying the waterproof pack containing María's shoulder bag, her American dress, a few of his own items, and a three-day supply of food, enough to get them to a camp in the *selva* of Margaritas, to one of the *CPR's,* the so-called *communities of population in resistance*, located throughout Chiapas in the broad stretch of jungle ranging along the western and northern borders of Guatemala and Mexico.

This was perhaps the most perilous juncture of their flight. The passage through the jungle had been exhausting for sure. For eight days they had suffered angry insect bites and had fought dehydration. María had finally overcome a bout with diarrhea after the first night in Huehuetenango and a flea infestation in the *pensión*. The proprietor had awakened them in the middle of the night when he dumped a plastic milk jug of urine down the middle of the hall which emptied into a drain just outside their door. Even the meager fifty *centavos* he had charged the two of them for the two-bunk room had been a rip off and the source of anything but a good night's rest.

Tomás was a stoic Mam Maya from the department of San Marcos. For eight years he had fought with *ORPA*, the Revolutionary Organization of the People in Arms, one of the four guerrilla groups. For the past few months he had been "working the river," assisting in the smuggling of weapons and supplies across the river from Chiapas. As time and opportunity permitted, his unit worked as "mules," ferrying refugees into the camps that dotted the jungles of Margaritas.

For United Nations monitoring and funding purposes, the Mexican government recognized only 45,000 Guatemalan refugees. That was far less than half the projected 200,000 that human rights agencies estimated living in countless squalid camps flung across the southern and eastern stretches of Chiapas. As a consequence, most of the Guatemalans lived precariously on only the fringe of any aid and obscure from, at best, only fleeting international attention. Constantly in competition, hence at odds with their reluctant Mexican hosts in the dense jungles, the Guatemalans felt very much isolated and alone. The only reliable contact they had at all with their countrymen was through the guerrillas who had become their eyes, ears, and security from attacks at the hands of the "locals" and occasional sorties by the *kaibiles* themselves.

Tomás was a well-trained, no nonsense combatant for *ORPA* who knew the precautions that meant so much to the success of their operations along the Usumacinta. He had trained initially in Cuba back in the early `80's, so he understood something of the international dynamics of their cause. He had spent five years in the mountains of San Marcos and the past two years in Chiapas among the refugees. He worked with a unit of five others who patrolled about a ten-kilometer stretch of the river. They coordinated ferries back and forth across the river, maintaining radio communication both with each other and with their base camp. They suspected, however, that the army had monitored their broadcasts in the past, so they preferred to work with visual signals whenever possible, particularly for daylight crossings. Such move-ments, however, were exceedingly dangerous, subject to sightings by both the Mexican *federales* patrolling the increasing narcotrafficking up and down the river and by the Guatemalan army's daily helicopter sorties over the river and the adjoining interior.

Tomás stepped forward just behind María and carefully pushed back a branch obstructing his view across the river. Without moving a muscle, he steadied the limb as he scanned the opposite bank. María started to sneeze, and immediately, Tomás reached around her from behind and covered her mouth tightly, holding the limb in place with the other. Satisfied María's spasm had subsided, Tomás released his grip and glanced at his watch. They were right on time.

Across the river a flash of light blipped once and then twice more. Tomás grabbed María's arm and forced her down. Donaldo dropped behind the bush. Tomás reached into his pocket and pulled out a small piece of chrome-plated metal, moved it into the light in front of the bush, and flicked it back and forth in the direction of the reflections from the other side. In a moment, a burst of flashes erupted from across the river.

"We'll be going in about a half hour," said Tomás. The boat will pick us up in just a few minutes. We can rest here while we wait."

Donaldo reached into his pocket for his pack of cigarettes and lit up a smoke. He had almost completed his contract with María and, for that matter, with the whole revolution.

"It's not a question of right or wrong anymore," Donaldo had said a week earlier as they waited for their meal before leaving Huehuetenango. "It's not a question of change. It's not a question of the past, the present, or the future. It doesn't have anything to do with you or me or them or us. It's not even a question of *sense* or *nonsense.* In fact, I don't even think it's a question at *all.* It's that it just doesn't *matter* anymore, whether I go or stay, whether I go back, or *whatever* I do. Nothing's going to change. It just doesn't *matter*. There's no connection for me anymore."

"So, what will you *do?*" asked María. She had no idea what all the rest of it meant.

"I said I'd take you to the river," said Donaldo.

"And you won't come to the camp?" she asked.

"It doesn't *matter,*" he said, as he looked away, signalling an end to the conversation.

After about fifteen minutes, Tomás pointed to a small, hand-rowed skiff slipping out into the middle of the river at the head of the northern bend. A single *compa* rowed steadily, maneuvering the boat into the main current that shifted toward their side of the bank about two hundred yards ahead of them. The landing was no more than five or six meters of open bank straight down and away from where they were waiting in the bushes above. They continued to watch as the boat slipped silently below them and beached on the bank. The *compa* jumped from the rear of the boat onto the land and raced quickly up the incline to meet them.

"*Hola! Carlos!*" said Tomás. "How was the crossing?"

"*Easy!*" returned the *compañero*. "No *problems!* But we better get going. The *federales* came by here an hour ago. They'll probably be making another sweep back up the river in another hour or two. We usually see them twice if they come by at all."

"Well, you're right," said Tomás.

"How many do we have?" asked Carlos. "Just these *two?*"

Donaldo pitched his cigarette to the earth and crushed it slowly with the toe of his boot. María looked over at him from the corner of her eye.

"How *many?*" repeated Carlos.

"Both . . ." said Tomás, but María Xquic knew better. She turned her head now to catch Donaldo's response. The *alcalde* raised his head and looked upstream away from the group, his lips pursed tightly into something of a grimace.

"Just *one* . . ." he said. "Just the lady."

And that was all. His relationship with the rest of it? Well, it just didn't *matter* anymore. When María stepped in the boat, it would all be over. Donaldo sat down slowly on the ground beneath the bush and lit another cigarette, waiting for the rest to pass him by—this transfer, the revolution, the history of it all, and everything yet to come.

"*Señora?*" called Carlos. "*Lista?*"

"*Sí!,*" she said. "*Sí, señor.*"

María looked down at Donaldo who sat solemnly, staring at the burning end of his cigarette cupped inside the palm of his hand. She paused another awkward moment to give him a final opportunity to say anything, then picked up her bag, stepped in front of him, and followed Carlos through the brush to the boat.

While Carlos adjusted a strap that had slipped on his pack, María stepped out into the water knee deep to push the bow of the boat further up on the narrow beachhead.

"*No!* Not *that* way!" said Carlos, motioning for her to stand back until he had entered. "Let me step in *first* so I can help you."

He climbed into the narrow boat and turned around to take her hand. Holding her sandals, María first stretched out her crippled foot over the side of the boat. Then taking Carlos's hands, she eased herself behind the bow and started to sit down.

"No, *here,*" said Carlos, indicating the middle of the skiff. "Sit *here* so that we can get more lift from the bow. It'll be easier to land on the other side." María understood where to sit, although the rest of the explanation was lost to her.

With that, Tomás, standing at the edge of the bank, pushed off the boat, and out into the heavy current they drifted. Quickly, the water swept them into the channel of the river. With a smooth stroke or two of his oar, Carlos sent the skiff to the middle of the current and then across to the other side. María glanced back, shocked when she realized that she had no idea from where they had departed. All of a sudden, she seemed frightened and exposed. For the first time, she felt as though she was totally alone and on her own. Everything that she had ever loved and lived for, she now was leaving behind forever. Tears filled her eyes as images of her family, her husband and children, drifted through her imagination.

Little Ana Fabiola crying in her arms after her first day at the ladino school, Tanolito on the horse that the captain had sold to the alcalde that didn't want to go—the horse, Miguel Mapa, the girls who used to giggle when he walked by, so big with his muscles, the gold chain around his neck that he had bought in the market from the merchant of Sololá, on her knees beside her husband Andres before Santa Mesa, praying for illumination, beseeching the alcaldes for their blessing and for the gift of speaking, communing with the ancestors, Andres scattering the sacred mixes, casting for the illumination, the divination, shaking as he slowly scanned the mixes below his open palm, feeling the heat of her body, stroking her arms with the silver and coral chachales with its talismans, praying that the alcaldes might intercede with the spirits of the ancestors, that she might feel their love, that she might receive their warmth, that they might speak of the past and its lessons, that she might receive their instructions, the blessed alcaldes who consult the ageless wisdom of the ancestors as Andres slowly stirred the mixes, sensing their message, taking to his heart all that he could learn from their love, that she might come to know, that somehow she might come to hear the voices, to bathe in the radiance of their cool presence, their luminous spirits gliding over her shoulders, down the smooth lines of her arms, their shimmering blue halos dancing off the tips of her fingers, Andres, her intercessory, Andres, who trembled in the pale blue lights drifting over his shoulders and across the back of his neck, praying that through the warmth of his prayer and the touch of his hands María Xquic de Xoy might come to know the blessings of the alcaldes of the heavens, that she might come to hear the voices, when Lucita María would slip to her side and ask, "Mother, why does father tremble at the Santa Mesa, so stiff and tremble, Mother, why?" Why, Mother? Why the smooth water with the deep brown and silver-lined . . . the frothy bubbles that churn beside the boat, the steamy warmth in the heavy air that came down to the water and back up through the trees where the compas watched from the shore that Donaldo, the old alcalde, wouldn't go . . .

The crack of the gun ripped through the trees, its echo ricocheting off the cliffs, bouncing back and forth before and behind them. María shot up straight, her heart throbbing, fearing first that they were under attack in the middle of the current.

"Everything is *okay!*" cried Carlos. "We just keep going." María turned her head back to Carlos for reassurance.

"But the *shot*?—that was a *shot!*"

Carlos correctly interpreted the expression if not the words.

"Not for us," he said, waving off her obvious concern. While he wasn't fluent in Tzutujil, Carlos could communicate in simple phrases and understand enough himself to sense her anxiety.

"But the *shot . . .!*" stammered María, still failing to comprehend.

At first, Carlos resisted explaining, not wishing to panic his passenger, exposed as they were until they could reach the security of the shoreline still a hundred meters or so downstream. But then, with second thoughts, he relinquished the truth.

"Donaldo," he said without elaboration.

"Donaldo?" thought María. Then, "*Donaldo!*"

She suddenly understood. But *why? Why Donaldo, the shot, Donaldo, who said it just didn't matter! Donaldo who gave up hope in the mountains, then why all this way? Why come all this way just to . . . just to . . .?*

Stunned, María sat shaking in the middle of the boat, confused now even more by the shot and her own precarious circumstances.

"How far?" she asked herself. "How far must I go to find rest?" Now, more than ever, she longed for the camp. She stepped out onto the water ahead of the boat, jerking the rope, sending the boat racing along behind her.

With measured strokes, Carlos guided the boat downstream, carefully angling the craft between large branches and limbs, snagged and hung up here and there in the shallows below. María sat tense now in the floor of the skiff, her hands gripping the railing on each side. She looked straight ahead, her long, tangled hair flowing gently back over her shoulders. Contemplations of the future were as dark as were her poignant memories of the past. She had to put them in order, and she would begin with the most immediate, the most personal necessities. It was disturbing, for instance, that she hadn't wrapped her hair since she had fled to the mountain more than two weeks before. That was it—the first thing that she would do when she arrived in the camp would be to put her hair up in a ribbon. Then she would feel more comfortable approaching others, people she would have to confront and address.

In Margaritas, soft rays of sunlight drifted down through the cool trees. Beneath mottled reflections dancing over their heads and shoulders, young children, playing a rhyming game, held hands and tripped around a circle. Women walked casually through the streets, laughing gently to themselves as they bore large bundles of laundry on their heads. At the pilas, as they doused their garments into the frothy suds, the women gossiped about market the day before and speculated about markets yet to come. They growled over the apparent aimlessness of the older children, or whined resentfully about their restlessness that might someday take them away from the camp. They whispered playfully about the love match of the week and the glee with which they had preserved their little secret from the respective fathers far away in the selva. Tilling the fields all day, the men had little time for domestic chatter when they came home so exhausted each evening. Every day they came back to their wives and children, their bags bulging with frijoles. Racks of corn rose tall in the sheds. Every kettle was boiling with fresh water. The children's cheeks were fat and healthy, their eyes sparkling with good-humored mischief. Awash in the ceaseless stream of the people's thanksgiving, the jealous, peevish gods of Margaritas slumbered heavily in pillows of satisfaction.

As the boat shifted across the channel of the river, the sunlight flashed in María's eyes, shocking her from her reverie. Ahead of them stretched the seemingly impenetrable jungles of Mexico. The current shifted to the opposite side of the river and carried them quickly into the shadows of the trees. Carlos sounded the bottom with his oar to avoid any reef extending from the shore. They glided silently into the overhang of branches reaching out from the thick tangle of trees anchored in the river's edge.

"Here," he said. "Grab that branch and steady the boat while I tie up."

María snagged the tree limb overhead and held on as Carlos maneuvered the stern of the skiff up against the bank, the whole craft well concealed under the overarching branches. Carefully, Carlos held the boat steadily against the tree limbs while María stepped out onto the muddy bank, her heels sinking into the spongy soil. Then he made his way to the front of the boat and climbed out himself. He tied the anchor rope to a trunk of one of the saplings and took María's bag over his shoulder. María slipped out of her sandals and rinsed them in the water, then put them back on her feet. Carlos jumped ahead to hold back the limbs of the tree before them and gave María a hand up the loose, slippery bank.

Once she found a point of balance at the top of the bluff above the boat, María looked around at the thick brush, vines, and thorny undergrowth.

"How far are we off from the trail?" she asked.

Carlos only smiled. "*I* am your `trail,' *señora!*"

"*But . . .?*" María protested. "How do we get *through* this?"

"We will work our way slowly," he explained. "Higher up, when we get over the next few hills, it opens up more. Or at least the foliage is different—not so many vines. But we can't afford to leave so easy a trail behind us. If I used the machete, the whole Guatemalan army could find us and follow us right into camp." For the most part, he had been talking to himself.

Carlos took the lead through the dense jungle. Clouds of insects—a myriad of gnats and large, black and iridescent green flies—bit at their exposed arms and faces. At one point, Carlos stopped María and pointed to the tree limbs directly overhead. A swarm of hornets hummed about the thick drum of their nest, a paper swirl as wide as the barrel of a man's chest, that completely encircled the crook of a tree. Hundreds of testy, little yellow hornets plunged in and out the curved cornucopia from an opening at the base of the hive. María turned icy with chills that crawled over her skin, tingling the back of her neck and scalp.

"Cuidad!" said Carlos. *"Cuidad, Señora!"*

María understood. Carefully, Carlos released the branch that threatened to disturb the nest, and they moved on into the undergrowth. Everything they touched or that brushed against them seemed to prick or leave behind a sticky residue. Within an hour, María's left eye was swollen almost shut. A deep, reddish blue scratch raced up her right forearm from just above her wrist to beneath her armpit where a sharp thorn had threatened to rip open her arm. Stinging whelps dotted her feet and ankles where ants had attacked her legs. Both their clothes were completely saturated in oily perspiration. María became embarrassed by her own acrid body odor which the sweltering heat only aggravated. At one point, Carlos stopped María, reached down, and lifted up her skirt almost to the knee. A two-inch long, black leech had attached itself to her leg just above the ankle beneath the calf of her left leg. Carlos drew his knife and carefully peeled it away.

"*Awwow,*" cried María, and Carlos slit the writhing slug curling on the ground before her. She reached down to rub her leg only to wipe away a sticky patch of her own blood already coagulating over the wound.

"Here," said Carlos, as he reached down and scooped up a pinch of the rich, deep humus and packed it over the abrasion.

It was more than three hours before they reached the clearing, just on the edge of darkness. The sun had already drooped behind the highest canopy of leaves in the tall, jungle trees, some towering more than sixty feet into the azure sky above. They had found their way to a small campsite less than a kilometer from Tecún Umán. Carlos motioned for María to stop at the foot of a narrow path. Then, shouldering his rifle, he ran briskly over the smooth ruts up the trail.

A wasted, little hamlet of palm and bamboo shanties, Tecún Umán was named for its more opulent counterpart on the other side of the frontier. It was only one of perhaps more than a hundred—maybe closer to two hundred campsites and tiny, makeshift settlements that lay sprinkled throughout and around the periphery of the dense, sultry jungles no more than an hour beyond the Guatemala-Mexico border. Virtually all were without public services. None of these small camps could claim electricity or even a tap for water. In fact, for most, water had to be transported by hand in large canisters from many kilometers away due to the threat of surprise by clandestine Guatemalan commandos. From time to time, the *kaibiles* would sneak across the border to terrorize the camps that had been erected too close to the ponds. At other times, Mexican *vigilantes*, rogue gangs intent on keeping the intruders nervous and off balance, would sweep into the villages or sit in ambush along the trails, hoping to intercept the meager trickles of United Nations aid donated by the international community.

Carlos stepped quickly back down the trail and motioned for María to join him in the hut. The old peasant woman stood at the edge of her lean-to watching the new arrival making her way up the path.

"Well, *señora*," said Doña Martita, "you have had a long journey. You must come in and have some coffee and fresh bread."

María could make out the friendliness and the Spanish references to bread and coffee, but she had entered the world of *ladino* Spanish where she felt estranged from everything of her Tzutujil culture. She could live on *"maize," "frijoles,"* and *"pan"* if she had to. Those words she could understand, but the necessity of accommodating herself completely to the various social arenas of Spanish in a *ladino* world was most unsettling.

"*Que habla?*" asked Doña Martita. "What language, *Señora*?" María Xquic dropped her head in embarrassment, unable to understand or to respond appropriately. She felt very foolish and ignorant.

"`Tzutujil,'" said Carlos. María Xquic quickened to the name of her own people, looked up at Doña Martita, and smiled demurely.

"`Tzutujil,' *sí*," echoed María as she glanced at Carlos for reassurance.

"`Tzutujil,' *pues!*" reiterated Doña Martita. "`Tzutujil,' *claro!*"

Doña Martita turned to her oven, retrieved the loaves of bread, and placed them on a metal sheet that she used as a cooling pan. María watched the stooped, old lady pinch the steaming rolls, tweaking each one to see that it was done.

"*Ladino* bread," thought María.

María had little use for ladino bread. Like the idea of ladinos themselves, it always cloyed her stomach. Ladinos were very different from indigenas. They lived, how to put it? . . . They lived `back away from' the earth. They were too removed from the land. They were too arrogant and disrespectful. They had rejected the old ways. She had never seen a ladino taking food to the graves. She never heard a ladino woman talk of her cargo with the pride and care of an indigena. The ladinos rejected the Tzutujil cofradia. They made fun of the indigenas who worshipped piously in the old ways. They never honored *the earth with their sacrifices. They never burned the candles for El Mundo. They never blessed their houses or gave back to the earth a portion of their fields. When they died, ladinos preferred the tomb instead of a grave in the earth so that this poor little bit of flesh might go back to renourish the mother of all life. No, if she had to eat ladino bread, she would accept the roll out of courtesy to her guest in light of the circumstances, but she wouldn't have to like it.*

"I bake the rolls for the *ronda* every afternoon and evening," explained Doña Martita. "The boys get so *hungry*."

"La ronda"—that was another term that meant something to María, and it wasn't anything particularly positive. The "ronda" of San Carlos Mixco, a village not far from San Felipe del Lago, was a civilian patrol organized by the city itself, a self-styled alternative to the military civil defense patrol. Men and boys volunteered themselves to make the nightly patrols of their community, insisting over and over again that they didn't need a military commissioner or instructions from the army commander to police their own village. The ejercito had disagreed, and several of the members had been threatened with death if they continued to serve in the voluntary brigade. Miguel Mapa used to laugh at the idea of the Mixco ronda. He called them "las guias," swishing his hips like the ladino girls.

A wave of anxiety rushed through the Tzutujil woman. A *ronda* meant no security at all, as far as María was concerned, and she looked around her at the deep shadows of the forest wondering from behind which trees the *kaibiles* in their gruesome camouflage and greased faces might approach them unawares to slaughter them like animals in the night. Had they not butchered more than one hundred people at San Andres Jocopilas? Already, María was beginning to have grave doubts about her situation in the camps.

"*Bueno,* Doña!" said Carlos as he finished stuffing a couple of the fresh rolls inside his shirt. He reached over and took the old woman's hand and gave it a strong shake. "I have to go. Maybe you can get the lady to the camp tomorrow. Thank you if you can help with her tonight."

"*Bueno* . . . " said the woman, as she shrugged her tired shoulders. "Be careful, son. Be careful, and come back for some more of Martita's rolls, *no?*"

"Okay, *vieja!*" Carlos picked up his rifle and lifted it jauntily over his shoulder. He waved to the "old woman," his friend of many past sorties, as he sauntered back down the trail toward the jungle. Doña Martita smiled at María Xquic and motioned for her to come further into the lean-to.

Before Carlos could have reached the bottom of the trail, the leaves of the jungle canopy started to crackle as rain drops began to fall. The shower was a surprise, coming so late in the season as it was. Doña Martita looked anxiously toward the loaves and then out into the darkness at the rain beginning to filter through the leaves.

"Sit down," she said as she motioned toward a grass mat next to the hearth. María took the offer and sat down, pulling her skirt over her swollen feet. The ant bites were still quite painful. Overhead, the rain began to break through the high awning of the tall trees and their blanket of leaves and vines. The usually sharp, bitter cry of a macaw was strangely muted against the steady shower of rain.

Doña Martita fussed over the kindling beside her oven. The work of the *ronda* was always frustrating in inclimate weather like this. With the mud and rain, the work of the patrol would be hard. They would want as many rolls as the indefatigable woman could bake. With only the light of the hearth, the old lady reached into her sack of flour and began preparations for baking off another pan of the little breads.

Fatigued from worry and uncertainty, María watched her host with little more than casual interest. Besides, she had never worked with flour before, always able in the past to buy *ladino* bread in the market for the few times a year her husband called for it. Charitably, Doña Martita offered the Tzutujil woman one of the rolls, fresh and hot from the hearth.

"*Gracias,*" said María, accepting the bread which she placed carefully on the mat beside her. She was surprised at the soft texture and the vapors of heat still rising from the loaf. Strange to the idea of eating freshly baked bread, she would wait until it had cooled and hardened. Doña Martita only smiled at the simplicity of her guest. The rain began pouring harder. All the busy jungle sounds that had accompanied them in the afternoon were lost in the incessant drenching. All at once, exhaustion overcame her, and María rolled over on the *petate* to stare off down the trail and out across the small compound into the black depths of the surrounding jungle.

Miguel Mapa stepped into the lean-to and took off his hands, placing them on the hearth to dry beside Doña Martita. His massive hands were blistered from lifting and transporting the heavy sacks of sand. He sat down near the fire where Doña Martita was rolling the dough into the loaves and, when she turned away, stuck the stumps of his arms into the fire. The exposed flesh began to crack and sizzle, and Miguel Mapa howled with pain as he yanked them free.

María Xquic stepped over to her son.

"Why do you burn your arms like that?" asked María.

"Because the captain told me to," he said.

"Don't go near the soldiers," admonished his mother. "The soldiers come and take the boys from their homes and make them do terrible things to their mothers."

"I will have to kill you someday, mother," said Miguel Mapa to María.

"That is a horrible thing to say to the mother who loves you and feeds you."

"In the future I will have to come for you. The soldiers said that I would have to kill you because father is crazy in the head with the religion. You and father. I was the one who came for the Holy Table, but you weren't at home. I was going to kill you then, but my arms hurt so badly where I burned them. See?"

Her son held out the singed stumps of his two forearms for her to examine. Bits of charred flesh fell onto her skirt as he lifted them into the light for closer examination.

"Are your hands ready, Miguel?" asked Doña Martita.

"No?" he said.

"Why are you warming them so?"

"Because they were so cold."

"They have the smell of Tanolito. I can smell your brother even here!" said María Xquic.

Miguel Mapa only looked away.

"Why do they smell like your brother, Tanolito?" she pursued.

"Because I killed him in the pit. I can't get the smell of his blood off my hands."

"Why did you kill your brother, Señor?" asked Doña Martita.

"Because he was in the pit, his tongue ripped out, so that he couldn't say, `I am your brother.'"

"So you killed your brother, Tanolito?"

"Yes."

"With your hands?"

"Yes, with those very hands."

"Those hands? Those at the hearth? But why?"

"Because the soldiers . . . "

"Don't go near the soldiers, Miguelito," warned Doña Martita. "The soldiers come for the young boys and take them from their mothers. Then they send them back to do terrible things to their families. Don't go near the soldiers, Miguel Mapa."

Miguelito flew over toward the old woman rolling the loaves of bread and landed on her shoulder. Doña Martita pinched off some of the raw dough and gave it to the large black bird.

"Here," said Doña Martita. "I have a favor to ask."

Doña Martita reached into the folds of her skirt and retrieved the severed hands of Ana Fabiola. María Xquic gasped at the disclosure.

"Take these," she said, "and place them in the little one's grave. I can't believe it has been so long that she's been without them. How is she to eat her mother's candy?"

Miguel Mapa pecked at the shriveled hands, black from their exposure to the damp air, and folded each of them under his wings.

"Take them," she said, "and place them over her small breasts where her mother may find them, so that she can feed her precious little one. It's a good thing for a mother to feed her children sweet candies."

Miguel Mapa ruffled his feathers under which he had secreted the hands and pecked lightly at the ear of Doña Martita. "I will tell the colonel," he said. "I will tell him just how helpful you have been against the guerrilleros!"

Doña Martita turned and smiled, knowingly.

"We have to be careful in the camps," she said. "If they ever suspect that we are working for the army, things would not go well for us, verdad? I will feed the boys poisoned bread so that their guts will tie up in knots and they will fall to the ground, retching in agony. I will bake more bread for the subversives yet to come. I have elotes, Miguel, saved from the corn shed. You may rape the young compas with the fresh elotes. They will lie writhing in the dust with fat elotes swelling in their bowels—five, six or more, and in the spring we will harvest their little crops, no?"

Outside the lean-to María could hear the clandestine whispers growing closer. In the thatched palm overhead. There behind the hearth. Coming up the trail—the whispers and the heavy boots, mounting the wall around the lean-to, jumping down inside the compound, their heavy boots, the jingling of their metal grenades, the clapping of the plastic butts of their rifles against the metal belts and canteens. Miguel Mapa smiling. The soldiers whispering. Miguel Mapa laughing. The Guatemalan captain whispering a name in the ears of the federales, in the fat, wide ears of the Mexican troops, rolling a fresh elote between his palms.

"For María Xquic de Xoy when you find her," said the captain as, with a wink, he slipped the shank of the pendulous corn cob into the hand of the toughened Mexican soldier.

María Xquic shrank in terror around the edge of the lean-to just as two Guatemalan compañeros ran into the shelter from up the trail. Miguel Mapa squawked in irritation at the interruption.

"We've had a report from the river," said one of the young men.

"Oh?" said Doña Martita. "What report?"

"The kaibiles came into the town just after sunrise, more than fifty of them in their awful uniforms with the huge guns, axes, and machetes. Right away, they set up a camp at the end of the town, just next to the bridge that crosses the gorge. There must have been an oreja in the community who had been helping them because they brought the alcalde from his house and then his whole family. They brought them down to the bridge. They took his wife first, they dragged her by the hair to a concrete block that they placed in the middle of the stone bridge that crossed the deep gorge below. They forced her head down onto the block. She was screaming the whole time, and her children, and her husband watching—what could they do, no?—the alcalde begging the soldiers not to hurt her, and with one blow of the machete, they cut off her head, her blood spurting in great streams over the concrete block and down all over the bridge. Then they just rolled her body off the bridge down into the raging waters and picked up her head and threw it over after the body, down, down into the water below. Only the blood remained. Her husband couldn't believe it, he just cried so. Next, they dragged his daughter over to the block. You wouldn't believe the horror in her expression as they forced her face down into the sticky blood of her mother, and as she screamed in terror, they just cut off her head, and threw the body and the head after her own mother, down, down, down into the swirling waters, the deep swirling waters below. The poor alcalde fell over stiff onto the ground, his mouth locked open and his eyes staring straight ahead. The soldiers started kicking him, trying to make him come around. They got really angry at first, so they began beating him. When they couldn't get him to speak, they just dragged him over to the block, and in one, two strokes, they cut off his head and sat it on the block, facing toward the foot of the bridge from where they would bring the others. When the others saw the head of their alcalde staring at them with those two fixed, blank eyes rolled back, his bloody severed head just sitting there on the block, they went crazy with fear and started hitting at the soldiers with their fists, trying to get away. But the soldiers just kicked them and kicked them over and over again until they couldn't resist and they pulled them by the hair or by their clothes over to the block and just chopped off their heads. After about the first ten or fifteen people—there were some small kids and the first women—the others tried to flee. They ran up the trails and into the fields, but the soldiers had completely surrounded the town. There was no escape. One after another, the soldiers forced the people to the bridge where they cut them apart. After a while, some of the soldiers just went crazy, but really crazy! Others joined,

swinging the long machetes, cutting off arms and legs, the old women's breasts, throwing them into the water below. I swear to God! We both saw it all, José Mancheco and me, Julio Bera. We saw it all from under the rocks on the other side of the bridge, way up high where we could see it all, no?"

"We knew them all, no?" cried José Mancheco. "We knew them all! We saw all our friends die by the soldiers, there on the bridge where the soldiers cut them up and threw them into the river!"

"The soldiers never stopped all morning," said Julio. "They kept up the killing until the afternoon. We wanted to move, to take a leak—both of us, we had to go so bad that we just pissed all over ourselves, because we didn't dare move!"

"No! Not move!" repeated José.

"We stayed there until after all the soldiers were gone," said Julio. "All that night we stayed there under the rock, looking for camp fires that would tell if the soldiers were still there."

"But we didn't see any fires all night," said José. "So, we supposed they were all gone."

"So, in the morning," said Julio, eager to break in, "we made our way down the path from up on the other side of the mountain."

"That's where we were hiding!" interjected José.

" . . . down the trail to the bridge," continued Julio.

"It was awful!" interrupted José once more."

"Really awful!" reiterated Julio. "The smell was so thick in the air, even before you reached the bridge."

"The whole bridge was just covered with blood!" cried José. "It was so deep, it covered your whole foot, right up to the ankle bone!"

José made a slashing motion above his ankle to emphasize the point.

"We tried to cross the bridge," said Julio over José's gesture, "and José just went down, right down on his back in the sweet, sticky blood. I helped him up, and we had to slip and slide along, holding onto the rail of the bridge, the black blood oozing between our toes and under our heels, until we finally made it to the other side."

"Julio was the first to . . . first to get sick!" said José.

"We got so . . . we got so sick!" explained Julio. "We couldn't stop—you know—for maybe an hour? An hour or so? We were just so sick at the sight of that sticky blood all over us. There was no place to wash it. The soldiers had thrown bodies into the pila, bodies just floating there face down in the washing tank. So we couldn't wash . . . the awful, oily water."

"But those were the only people we saw!" said José.

"Yes," said Julio. "We couldn't see any of the other bodies. We went to the edge of the gorge and looked down into the water below. But we couldn't see anything—none of the people. We made our way down the path to the bottom of the gorge—it took us more than an hour, we were so weak. But even down there we saw nothing of any of the bodies. Then José, he said, `Look!' `Look!' he said. `Down there!' We looked down toward the bend in the river, down there where the whirlpool goes around and around. We climbed over the boulders and sharp rocks, cutting our feet on the sharp edges, climbing up and over the large rocks until we made it to the whirlpool that spins around and around."

"And there we found them!" cried José.

"Yeah," said Julio. "There they were—just, just . . . the bodies—swirling slowly in the current, around and around, bobbing up and down. Slowly, they circled around and around. We moved closer to the edge of the water. We took a limb with a crook in it. We used it to coax the heads and arms closer to us, and we just started stacking up all the pieces in a great pile on the shore just behind the trees so that no one could see them from the other side of the river or from back along the edge of the water on our side. We cried and cried as we found what was left of our friends and families, but we couldn't stop. We couldn't stop once we had started, because we were determined to lift out every last one of our friends, the pieces that the soldiers had just chopped away and thrown into the river."

"So that's what happened," said José Mancheco.

"So that's what happened at the aldea," said Julio Bera.

"So that's what happened at San Andres Jocopilas," said Marco Soccoro who had heard it first-hand from Julio Bera.

"What can I say?" apologized Silvia Guerrero. "So that's what happened high in the mountains at the aldea that morning."

"And would Silvia, my own sister-in-law—how could she make up such a horrible thing?" protested Doña Marta María Taxco de Ramirez. "I say she tells the truth, and if the truth, then what a horrible thing! I couldn't even talk about such a thing like that!"

And so the story made its way, flashing like splintered lightening throughout the highlands, and to effect—rumors raced back and forth: an hour ahead, an hour behind, the terrible kaibilies had been spotted here, there, just on the other side of the ridge, or over there, just beyond the edge of the jungle. In San Vincente, they said, the soldiers had destroyed the town hall and all the records and then shot every fourth man or boy as they stood in line for inspection. In Chalotenango they had raped all the women and slashed the infants with their bayonets. At the crossroads south of Sierra Palma, the militaries stopped all the outgoing busses, robbed each of the indigenous passengers, confiscated their cedulas, accused them all of supporting the guerrillas, and threatened all of them and their families with torture and death. North of Barillas, just beyond the pass that dropped down to the Mexican border, the helicopters had strafed the remnants of the people of Dos Pueblos who were preparing to flee across the frontier, killing more than thirty men, women, and children along with their livestock. At Cuarto Pueblo . . .

The beasts of her nightmare crashed back and forth through the jungles as María tossed and rolled against the blackness outside Tecún Umán. In semiconsciousness, María held them at bay just out of reach, just behind the tree line, just beyond the low stone walls of her dreams.

"Twice," said Doña Martita, as she stirred the bright young embers of her new hearth just at the first musty light of dawn. "Twice the soldiers have come through the settlement in only the last six months. *Me entiendes?*—Do you *understand* me?"

All along the path through the village, María made her way, warily but hurriedly, past the teetering shanties of the settlement, past the fearful glances of the precautious residents. The air was stifling, choked in the fetid smells of rotting vegetables and stale urine. Toddlers in filthy t-shirts, naked from the waist down, raced around her while their mothers called to them in panic, suspicious of a stranger in their street. Snarling, emaciated dogs nipped at her skirt. She had to make it to the highway where some ten miles away she might take a bus to Comitán, anything to flee the terror and the rancid stench of Tecun Umán.

María felt the roll of bread in the small bag within which she kept her precious cargo and the *quetzales* which Doñaldo had lifted from the dead *compas*. She could buy a ticket on the bus, said Doña Martita, as it stopped along the highway. The bus would take her to Comitán where she would be safe, far away from the *federales* that attack the camps in the night, far away from craven, old *orejas* that conspire against the *Guatemaltecos*.

"*El camino*? You want the highway, *Señora*?" said the corn vendor. He shoved awkwardly out from under his pickup truck, his hands laced with grease. "Maybe fifteen, sixteen kilometers. Where are you going?"

María Xquic smiled graciously at him unable to comprehend the question. The corpulent Mexican struggled to his feet and wiped his hands on the rag hanging from a belt hidden somewhere beneath the globe of his huge, protruding stomach. He looked over the Guatemalan peasant with some interest. "I said, `where'? Where . . . `*donde*'?"

María stared at the man, trying to fathom his question.

"El autobus . . ." she offered. *"La ciudad."*

"For Comitán?"

"*Sí, Comitán!*" she repeated eagerly, recognizing the name of her destination. "*Gracias.*"

María looked back behind her in the direction of the wretched settlement and the jungle she had just fled and then up the rutted dirt road twisting away beyond the truck driver.

"*Gracias,*" she said again as she secured her shoulder bag and began walking past the truck.

"*Hey!*" cried the man somewhat gruffly.

María turned around to face the man struggling to communicate with both a stranger and a woman. He dropped the abruptness, feigning a cheery confidence. María felt very awkward and wanted to keep walking, for something about the apparent insistence of the man was unsettling.

"*Bueno . . .*" said the flatulent driver wobbling toward her on short, pudgy legs. "*Mira, mujer!*"

The driver continued to wipe his hands in the same greasy rag, at best only transferring the grime from one hand to the other.

"Look here, *woman!*" he blundered again, his eyes beginning to glisten with expectation. "You have money, *verdad?*"

María looked hesitantly at him with uncertainty.

"Money! You know—*dinero! No?*"

Still unsure of the man's real meaning, she had no intention of revealing the little money she had managed to secret away deep within her *bolsa.*

"To buy a ticket, *no?*" he continued, still making his way over to her. "*Bueno*, you give me *money*, I take you to *Comitán, okay?*"

María frowned, still wary of his question.

"*You!* . . . in my *truck! Vale?*" he barked loudly. "*Vamos a Comitán? Okay?*"

María was starting to get the drift of his proposition, and she began to drop her stony reserve. She pointed to herself and then the truck.

"*Sí!*" responded the man with instant satisfaction. "*Sí! Sí! Sí!* In my *truck! Okay? Sí! Sí! Sí!*" And then not to lose the moment, he insisted, "*Para $20,000 pesos solo! $20,000 pesos, no?*"

María looked lost again, and she drifted once more behind her mask.

"*No, no, no?*" said the man, recognizing the difficulties in his tenuous proposal. *"Vamos ahora! Vamos ahorita!"*

He would collect later.

The driver turned his back toward the truck, his sweaty t-shirt hiked up over his pants that hung down low, revealing the dark cleavage of his buttocks. He reached down and pulled up his trousers which immediately slipped back to their accustomed position beneath the mounds of flesh draped over his narrow hips.

"*Vamos!*" said the man as he finished beating loose the thick layer of yellow sand and dirt from the back of the seat and wiping the cushion of the passenger side of the pickup truck. The door squeaked on rusty hinges as the driver forced it open the rest of the way for his passenger. María was worried about having to reveal the small roll of money in her bag, and she hung back hesitantly. The man smiled at María standing several paces yet in front of the vehicle and motioned insistently for her to climb in.

"*Pasen, por favor!*" gushed the driver. María was afraid not to respond. She managed a quick smile but turned her head demurely to avoid any eye contact as she gathered herself and small bag of belongings, walked over, and climbed into the truck. The driver grabbed her elbow and helped steady her as she lifted herself into the passenger seat. He eased shut the creaky door and then slammed it hard to secure the latch.

"*Bueno?*" puffed the man with satisfaction as he lumbered around the front of the truck. "*Comitán, sí! Vamos!*"

He turned the key, and after a few hesitant rolls, the truck started. The driver eased the vehicle out onto the rutted, one-lane stretch of road. Almost as an afterthought, he reached over and switched on the radio which erupted in a spasm of Mexican band and balladry.

"*Ahee! Yoop! Yoop!*" he cried as he turned to María and winked. "Old Vincente, *el taxista! No?* Old Vincente, the taxi driver! Going down the road with . . . going down the road with? *Como te llamas?*"

María looked straight ahead, already growing suspicious of the man. She wished she were out of the truck. Back in the jungle. Back in the rain on the *petate* under the lean-to of Doña Martita, the *oreja*. Back with Donaldo when he said it didn't matter anymore, before they crossed the river when the shot echoed back and forth against the steep walls of the river. Back to the graveyard when she stuffed the candy into the mouth of Ana Fabiola, her long fingers guiding the candy rocks through the earth into her little daughter's petulant mouth. Back to her father's revelation about his little weaver bird.

The driver slapped her knee and squeezed her thigh, a wink and a twinkle in his eye. "Old Vincente, *el taxista con . . .?*"

"*María!*" she suddenly blurted, thinking perhaps that cooperation in this small matter would buy her more time and security.

"Old Vincente, *el taxista con `María'!*" he laughed. "*Con María*, the blessed mother of God! What an opportunity for this old *taxista, no? Bueno? María!* So off we go to Comitán, old Vincente and the mother of God! *Es un milagro increible! Madre de Dios!* It gives this old taxi driver a hard just to think about it, no?"

María was trembling as she stared straight ahead. The driver glanced over at his passenger, little black turds for pupils peeping expectantly over the mounds of his high, fleshy cheeks. He turned his attention back to the road as they dodged a particularly deep rut only to fall axle-deep into the adjoining one.

"*Ha! Ha! Ha!*" roared the driver as the engine raced and screamed, the front wheels straining to rip out of the hole. After another futile attempt, he grabbed the gear shift stick, jammed it into reverse, and slipped the clutch. As the truck lurched backwards, the front wheels jumped out of the hole, bumping the heads of both driver and rider sharply against the roof of the cab.

"*Mother of God!*" cried the driver, rolling in a barrel of laughter. "*Ahheeee! Es un milagro, por supuesto! Ahheeeee!* What do you think, *María! Es un milagro de María, madre de Dios!*" María's shoulder was throbbing where she had struck the door of the truck coming down from the jolt.

"*Es un milagro!* Don't you *think, María!*" said the driver, the expression of his voice now turning dark and ominous. María failed to respond.

"It's a fucking *miracle*, you goddamn Guatemala *fuck!*" he cried. The driver reached over to his passenger and backhanded her across the mouth and face. Then he jerked her over beside him, ripping her dress down the seam from under her arm all the way to her waist. "Get your fucking *ass* over here by *el taxista*, you goddamn Guatemala *whore!* You can help old Vincente drive this stick till we get to Comitán, and then this old pecker's got *another* stick you can drive, no *shit!*"

María's face was quivering in fear and pain, ashamed that her only dress was now ripped and her modesty compromised by such a man.

For the next half hour, María sat beside the driver, thankful at least that the condition of the road demanded his hands on the steering wheel and gearshift for the duration. It was more than an hour after their departure before they reached the paved highway which turned west toward Comitán thirty-five or forty kilometers away. The truck pulled to a stop behind a bus, a large Mexican scenic cruiser that had paused to pick up more than a dozen passengers for the otherwise already overloaded cargo. The *mozo*, or assistant to the bus driver, raced about like a little fyce at their heels, scurrying to grab their bags and stuff them into the undercarriage of the bus.

María longed to run into the crowd, to disappear into the pool of passengers already aboard, but she was afraid that she should not be able to open the door of the truck and escape before the driver could grab and probably hurt her. María watched in panic as the *mozo* secured the last bundle in the luggage bay and locked the door. In a blast that was obviously his signature, he whistled to the bus driver in a long, trailing wail and scampered aboard just as the cumbersome, green and chrome-trimmed liner swayed back onto the highway. As he pulled the truck onto the road just behind the bus, the driver turned to María and smirked, "*Ahhee! Increible, no? Old Vincente con la madre de Dios!*"

Still trembling, María reached for her shoulder bag and clutched it to her bosom up under her folded arms. The driver began chuckling deeply, slowly at first, and then in an uncontrollable spasm of abusive, arrogant laughter. "*Dios mio! La madre de Dios y old Vincente, el taxista!*"

María Paloma stormed across the clearing, pulling the heavy automatic pistol from under her shirt. Two guards held the driver tightly under his arms up against the pine—the driver, laughing above the din of the helicopters hovering overhead, pouring a rain of withering fire into the remaining compas hiding behind the cover of trees and the caves above. "We won't tolerate an arrogant, fat taxi driver," said María Paloma, as she blasted two rounds into the protruding stomach of the surprised Mexican driver. There were answers for men who blaspheme the mother of God! There were answers for those who belittle the true faith! But the driver just laughed and laughed.

The corn merchant turned up the radio as loudly as it would play, the music spilling from the rickety truck. The minutes stretched to more than an hour before billboards outside the city limits of Comitán began to pop up, accumulating left and right along the highway. The closer they came to the city, the more hostile the driver. His movements at the wheel, his feet on the clutch and brake became heavy and jerky. Grimly, he scanned the streets and seemed to stare out the window as if looking for something in particular.

"Well, *María!*" said the driver as they passed into the broad boulevard that stretched through the center of town. "*Bienvenido a Comitán!*" Sweating profusely, he still refused to look directly at his passenger. He pulled the truck to a stop at the red light just before the Mexican office of *inmigración* in the next block.

Her face and jaw still tingling in pain, María watched a stream of people standing around the front of the building, a line of cars and trucks in the long, muddy parking area. The Mexican immigration officials ambled slowly and deliberately from vehicle to vehicle, looking suspiciously at each occupant.

"We're going to make a stop a little further up," said the driver.

María never moved. The light changed, and María watched the stalled lineup of cars and trucks drift by as the driver turned at the stoplight and lumbered on past the immigration office. They passed house after house, only smudged adobes squatting behind their grassless yards filled with litter and abandoned junk, parts of old, rusty vehicles, washing machines and refrigerators, kids in rags chasing mongrel dogs through the hot, dusty air, the truck's radio still blaring in rhythms that seemed to match the pounding of its overheated pistons.

"Just a little *further, María!*" laughed the driver. "Just a little further to *paradise, no?*"

The houses began to thin and the road turned sharply into row upon row of maguey fields, the few houses now set off from the road. They were passing once again into the steamy, sweltering Mexican countryside. Little streams of perspiration trickled down her face, and María was panicked, her heart racing now, her elbows trembling against her sides. Her stomach was churning, and she felt her bowels convulsing.

The truck was speeding now, dust belching from underneath, leaving a dense cloud of grime trailing away from them, obscuring all hope she felt that lay behind them in the city.

"Here we *are!*" said the driver as he slowed to a crossroad and turned.

The dusty road gave way to nothing more than a gravel path that approached a small complex of dilapidated houses and a barn. Grabbing lethargically at flies, two old *campesino* men never even bothered to look up from their perches on makeshift chairs shoved up under the eaves of the first house. The driver pulled the truck into the compound. They passed the side of the two houses, finally lurching to a stop next to the back of the barn amid the rusty debris of abandoned farm implements. Slowly, the driver opened his door, laughing again as he violated the mother of God.

"*Bueno, mi bonita madre! Bienvenido a paradiso!*" he smirked as he ripped open the side door. A mange-infected dog lifted a hind leg against the back tire of the truck. "Get out, you fucking *bitch!* You owe old Vincente a little something for the ride, *no?* And this old pecker's about to *collect!*"

Hail Mary, full of Grace. Blessed art thou among women, and blessed is the fruit of thy womb, Jesus. Holy Mary, Mother of God, pray for us sinners, now, and at the hour of our death. Dios te salve, María. Llena eres de gracia. Benedita tu eres entre todos las mujeres y benedito es el fruto de tu vientre, Jesus. Santa María, madre de Dios, ruega por nosotros pecadores, ahora y en la hora de nuestra muerte. Amen. Hail Mary, full of Grace. Blessed art thou among women, and blessed is the fruit of thy womb, Jesus. Holy Mary, Mother of God, pray for us sinners, now, and at the hour of our death. Dios te salve, María. Llena eres de gracia. Benedita tu eres entre todos las mujeres y benedito es el fruto de tu vientre, Jesus. Santa María, madre de Dios, ruega por nosotros pecadores, ahora y en la hora de nuestra muerte. Amen. Hail Mary, full of Grace. Blessed art thou among women, and blessed is the fruit of thy womb, Jesus. Holy Mary, Mother of God, pray for us sinners, now, and at the hour of our death. Dios te salve, María. Llena eres de gracia. Benedita tu eres entre todos las mujeres y benedito es el fruto de tu vientre, Jesus. Santa María, madre de Dios, ruega por nosotros pecadores, ahora y en la hora de nuestra muerte. Amen. Hail Mary, full of Grace. Blessed art thou among women, and blessed is the fruit of thy womb, Jesus. Holy Mary, Mother of God, pray for us sinners, now, and at the hour of our death. Dios te salve, María. Llena eres de gracia. Benedita tu eres entre todos las mujeres y benedito es el fruto de tu vientre, Jesus. Santa María, madre de Dios, ruega por nosotros pecadores, ahora y en la hora de nuestra muerte. Amen.

A hundred prayers, a hundred "Hail Mary's" wafted to paradise on the lacy fumes of a hundred votive candles. Three chimes of the bells, the Holy Eucharist offered up on high, raised to the communion of the mysterious angels and the benevolent saints, the Holy Faith celebrated in the Mass, then distributed among disciples and servants of the Lord, remembering in their prayers the old and feeble, the weak of mind and body, the children of the Passover, those who called upon the name of the Lord in their great pain and suffering, those among the idle rich who still remembered their alms, those who labored in the fields, those who had died in childbirth, and those whom the Lord had raised up as leaders, those who had fled the persecution, those among the damned for whom God's wrath is everlasting, those who have hungered and thirsted after righteousness, and those who had been cast among them, desperate.

"My peace I leave with you. My peace I give unto you. Peace be with you."

"And with you, Holy Father."

"Amen."

"And Amen."

"And Amen."

"And so we prayed for you, sister," said María Marta. "We have prayed for you now for these twenty days and more, and *see?* The Lord has heard our prayers, beautiful lady."

From the scratchy tacking of the cornhusk mattress, María Xquic stared up into the face of the Mexican woman. Slowly, in smooth, even strokes, the woman washed her forehead with the damp rag. Suddenly, a tremble rippled through the Tzutujil refugee. Nothing in the small room around her seemed familiar—the white plaster walls, the single crucifix above the foot of her bed, the sprays of red and yellow gladiolus in the bucket beside her next to the little table, the bowl of water, and the humble Mexican woman ministering to her in a voice just above a whisper.

María glanced from side to side, her mind frantic to connect somehow with the strange circumstances about her. She tried to lift her arm but felt a sharp pain lance her elbow. The tremor shot up and down her right arm from the elbow to her wrist. When she attempted to raise her left arm, she became aware of a throbbing ache across her rib cage and over her shoulder.

"You have to rest," said the kindly woman. "You've been hurt very badly. You have to rest now, *okay?*"

Understanding very little, María nevertheless registered the abiding concern in the woman's insistent eyes.

"*Really!*" she urged. "You have to rest. It is very *dangerous* for you! You've been hurt pretty badly, so you have to rest, maybe for a day or two more."

The room, though spartan, was clean for a poor *campesino* clinic. The nurse reached below a sheet that was covering María from the waist down and lifted her feet. Her right knee was swollen and badly bruised, apparently from when she had fallen.

"It may take another day or two before she is ready to try to walk again," she said to the doctor standing beside her. "I'd like to see her removed to one of the sister's quarters a little later today. She'll be able to rest more comfortably, and we can use the space for sure. I'm surprised she's even alive, she's taken such an awful beating."

"She has several massive bruises that she'll start feeling once the sedative begins to wear off," said the doctor, "but that's the best we can do. No, I think you're right; she'll be much more comfortable around someone speaking her own language."

Ricardo and Sylvia Pertierra were Guatemalan refugees themselves, Tztutujiles from San Francisco Xojalá, a small *aldea* nestled against the south-eastern slopes of the Tolimán volcano. They had lived in Mexico and Comitán for almost ten years since they had fled, accused of being guerrillas by the army and the military commissioner of their village. After receiving numerous death threats—the last one passed along by their own neighbor of more than twenty years, they realized that they had to flee. Ricardo and Sylvia worked in the clinic as volunteers through their church, *La Iglesia Merced de Guadalupe*. In turn, the priest found them odd jobs in the community. Along with the other refugees—about twenty or twenty-five of them, they ate one meal a day at noon, a modest plate of rice, beans, and tortillas. Mostly, around the clinic, they were valued for their translation skills. In addition to Spanish, Ricardo spoke both a smattering of Mam and Quiché, as well as Tzutujil, his native tongue; Sylvia spoke both fluent Spanish and Tzutujil, and a passable Cakchiquel that she had picked up over the years in the markets of Sololá.

Sylvia was bathing María's forehead when she awoke again the next morning. She continued to sponge her patient's face lightly with the damp rag. María looked up at the rich olive complexion of her nurse, her smooth, greying hair wrapped in the swirls of the familiar red and green headband of a Guatemalan town.

"Oh, it's *good* to see your bright eyes, *Doña*," said Sylvia as she smiled reassuringly.

María Xquic was startled when she realized that Sylvia had addressed her in her own idiom.

"Where . . . where *am* I?" she asked as she became aware once more of the throbbing aches throughout her body.

"In *la clinica Merced de Guadalupe*," replied Sylvia. "My name is Sylvia. My husband, Ricardo, and I—we're Tzutujil from San Francisco—San Francisco Xojolá. You must be from San Felipe, *no?*"

María was surprised.

". . . yes," she offered somewhat tentatively in more of a question than a confession.

"Your bag, the *huipil*," said Sylvia. "It is very beautiful."

"My bag, my *huipil*!" exclaimed María. "You've seen my bag, my *huipil*?"

"They're both right here . . . right *beside* you," said Sylvia, picking them up from the foot of the cot and holding them up for María to see.

María's eyes teared, and she gasped, reaching up and covering her mouth to mask the sobs rising in her chest.

"They're *fine!*" said Sylvia. "They'll be right *here*."

Comforted in a renewed sense of security for the first time in days and relieved in the rediscovery of her personal belongings, María rolled over on her side, her swollen eyes away from the nurse, and lapsed once more into sleep.

As she drifted off, a kaleidoscope of comforting images swirled in her head. *Lucita María was still working at her loom, the little muestra at her side. Oh, how she glowed when her daughter poured over the intricate patterns, studying every nuance of relationship, working awkwardly with the pick at first, but learning quickly until, in time, a style of her own had emerged, her deft fingers coaxing the fiesta of fibers in and out the warp, the bouquet of floral designs billowing around the neck, the animals parading in uniform rows across the shoulder panels and down the front and back. Lucita María, holding her mother's textile in her lap, turning it at angles back and forth to check the accuracy of her own work. Lucita María who smiled when the German lady gave her the first payment, the enormous pride she took in her mother's and grandmother's approval, and Ana Fabiola! turning up her nose, piping up so frivolously, "Anybody can weave!" and running off with her friends down the path to the market. Because Lucita María knew that when the German lady, who gave her the money that Ana Fabiola would never, ever weave the way and her grandmother frowning and turning her back, that look that Andres thought so haughty of her, coming back, coming back, coming back up the trail, the water pitcher brimming, couldn't have been Ana Fabiola! the scream, the seething anger, because he hurt her so, the little huipil, not the huipil! Oh, please, the huipil of my poor daughter who was not her daughter anymore, anymore her daughter, not her daughter anymore . . .*

For more than two days María Xquic slept fitfully, all the while with Sylvia at her side, dabbing a wet rag on her lips to cool a fever that during both days would seem to rise and subside, rise and then subside again. Periodically over the next two days, María would groan and roll over, grabbing at her stomach and pulling at her mutilated dress. Sylvia had placed a cheaply framed reproduction of the *Virgen* of Guadalupe beside her cot. On each evening, she lit a candle before the icon and recited her rosary and prayers on behalf of her troubled and injured ward.

". . . ly Mary, Mother of God, pray for us sinners, now and at the hour of our death." Sylvia completed her round of prayers just as María Xquic began to stir late in the evening. The candle burned to nothing much more than a filament of wick in a pool of swimming wax in the center of the little, cracked ceramic dish. The nurse's aid reached over and pulled back the hair from María's face. María opened her eyes to see the tiny flame flickering within an arm's reach of her face.

"Oh, *Holy Blessed Mother of God!*" cried Sylvia, so thankful to see her Tzutujil patient beginning to come around. "*Ricardo! Ricardo! Come see!*"

Sylvia fled from the side of the bed out the room to find her husband who had returned only minutes before from chores outside the clinic.

"Praise *God!*" cried Sylvia as she reached the side of her husband. "She has *returned! María!* She is going to be all *right!* Come and *see!*"

Sylvia tugged at her husband's sleeve and then fled back into the adjoining room. She knelt down beside María and stroked her forehead to check for the fever. She was cool.

"*María!*" she called in a low voice. María Xquic turned to the familiar face and smiled.

"You're *okay!*" said Sylvia. "You're *okay*, María!"

María Xquic smiled again, then slowly turned on her side and began to sit up. The nightmare was over. She was rested, but very hungry and thirsty. Sylvia helped to steady her as she slowly lowered her feet to the floor beneath the cot. As María began to take her bearings once more in the room around her, Sylvia reached to the foot of the bed and retrieved María's shoulder bag and laid it beside her. Grateful for the thoughtful gesture, María looked down and stroked the *bolsa* lovingly.

"I have fresh tortillas, some rice, and *frijoles*," Sylvia said with satisfaction, and she rose to return to the kitchen. In a few moments, she reappeared with a small plate of food.

The two women sat beside each other, María still in place on the cot with Sylvia at her feet. The steaming coffee that her husband brought them finally quenched María's deep thirst. Silvia brought another candle from her blouse and lit it from the last flickers of the retiring wick. Well into the early morning hours of the night, they continued their soft conversation until María could fight back a yawn no longer. Sylvia smiled, excused herself, and slipped quietly back toward the door.

"Sleep, María, in the love of Our Lady of Guadalupe," prayed Sylvia, mumbling to herself as she turned one last time to make sure that María was comfortable before leaving her for the side of her husband.

Over the next two days, Sylvia helped María to walk and to regain her strength through light, brief exercises. On the third day, María was able to join Sylvia at work for an hour or so in the kitchen. The following day, she spent most of the morning and afternoon with Sylvia. They continued small domestic chores throughout the rest of the week, and María was beginning to find a peace she had not known for many, many months. Then, just as quickly as she had found security, everything changed.

The sun was not yet up one morning a week later as the two women met each other at the hearth. Sylvia stripped the husks from the last corncob and handed it to María who was carving the dried kernels into a bowl.

"We are leaving tomorrow," said Sylvia.

"*Leaving?*" asked María, startled at the announcement.

"Yes, we are leaving for our pilgrimage to the basilica of the *Virgen*, and you can go with us, María, if you like."

"I don't understand," said María.

"To the capital to honor Our Lady of Guadalupe, the Blessed *Virgen*," explained Sylvia. "Every December, we make the trip to Mexico to honor the Holy Mother and to pray for her intercession. Really, María, you must *go* with us."

Sylvia smiled encouragingly, hoping to interest María in joining them. Then earnestly, she confided, "Look, María, I know something. I have to tell you something. I know that the *Virgen* awaits you."

María Xquic shuddered visibly. Deeply disturbed, she continued to stir the bowl mechanically, not daring to look up from her labor. Her hand plunged back and forth into the corn, sifting them over and over in a blind search for bad kernels. This was something startling and unnerving. María knew of the preparations and had watched the members of the church mounting the elaborate decorations on the truck which would carry them so far. It never dawned on her that she might be extended such an opportunity. She had decided herself that she had to move on somehow. For days, however, she had sought work in the *cocina*, begging off every invitation to leave the building. Each new male voice sent shivers of fear through her, and she was comfortable in the presence of even Ricardo only in the company of his wife. The only thing that she had thought about for the past several days was moving on, "going north," as Carlos had tried to explain, north through Mexico, north to the United States where she might find freedom and sanctuary. But Sylvia's invitation brought complications for her as she reflected on the prospects of confronting more strangers and especially unfamiliar men.

Suddenly, her trembling hands slipped from the bowl, knocking it over into her lap. It was too late to catch them as the bowl pitched over, and the freshly shaved kernels of corn scattered over the floor.

Sylvia watched the bowl roll over on María's skirt, and she sprang forward in a futile attempt to catch the corn spilling onto the floor.

"*María!"* she cried. "Are you all *right?*"

María seemed momentarily stunned, unable to respond, but merely stared ahead in a kind of stupor. Then, seconds later, she came around, and her mouth dropped open as she surveyed the ruin of the morning chore.

"I'm . . . I'm sorry," she whispered, embarrassed by the accident. "I'm *very* sorry."

"We have more corn," she offered, brushing aside the accident. "I'll get some more, but María, you don't need to *worry, okay?* I think that you will be safe in Mexico and also on the highway with us. We don't take strangers into our vehicle. Ricardo and his two brothers from the church will drive the truck. The only others will be the two sisters from the convent. We will stop as we have to just for water and a little rest. It will take us five nights on the highway. We'll always sleep in the bed of the truck under the canopy. When we get to Coahuilas just outside the city, we'll stop at Concepción to buy the wreaths that we'll carry before the *Virgin*. Oh! It will be a *wonderful* pilgrimage, *María!* Every year since the earthquake destroyed the chapel twenty-five years ago, our members have made the pilgrimage from the altar of the new chapel to the basilica to give thanks to Our Lady of Guadalupe."

Silvia, the faithful, moved closer to María and took the bowl, setting it aside so that she might share a confidence.

"I will tell you something, María," she urged. "I will tell you why we go and why you will be blessed. The *Virgen* herself has visited our small *iglesia*!"

Sylvia paused to check María's reaction, but María looked away, avoiding her eyes.

"After the awful earthquake destroyed the church and much of our town," continued Sylvia, pressing her appeal, "the *Virgen* came to us in a visitation to Sister Juana. She was dying. Her family and the two sisters from the convent were all about her, waiting for her passing. In the middle of the night, Sister Juana began to stir. Her breathing, it had been very . . . very, how do you say, very erratic, very uneven. She was choking, gasping. It had been like that and getting worse for four or five days. She was very hot with the fever. Someone stayed by her side just wiping her face and arms. Then, Sister Juliana, she was sitting beside Sister Juana. She said that Sister Juana opened her eyes and turned her head toward the door. A radiant smile came over her face, the face of Sister Juana. All of a sudden, her raspy breathing was smooth. She just turned her head over onto her pillow. Her fever was gone. The next morning, Sister Juliana had gone to her room. When she returned, Sister Juana was on her knees before the altar in the little closet. It was the first time that she had been to her prayers in more than three weeks. She was crying. She told Sister Juliana that it was the *Virgen* who had come into their room the night before. She told Sister Juana not to worry, that her faith had healed her and that she was to be a blessing to all who knew her and through her would come to serve the Lord. That very day, we received a gift of more than one million *pesos* to rebuild our church."

María turned to face Sylvia, tears streaming down both their cheeks.

As the small party entered the outlying *barrios* of the capital, the last few miles of the pilgrimage were some of the happiest moments of María's life. Silvia and Ricardo had become far more than her nurses. They were her friends and Sylvia, the only spiritual link with her beloved highlands. Throughout the thankfully uneventful excursion from Chiapas, the two women had laughed and cried together, day after day, until they were both emotionally drained and physically exhausted. They had relived their Maya youths and had celebrated the most memorable moments of their village life. In understood confidences, they reconstructed the finest nuances of their great loves and various disappointments. They recounted the horrors of giving birth and the great pains of loss. They reconstructed the awful events of the more recent years and months that had forced them to flee everything familiar to seek sanctuary abroad with no prospects for a future. In short, they had become confidantes in the most vital elements of their lives. Each night of the long trip, they had fallen asleep at each other's ear, whispering into the night their gratitude and prayers, so that as they approached the great Mexican megatropolis, they arrived with hope and mounting expectations.

Sisters Veronica Ortíz and Rubia Ordoñez, members of the convent of Our Lady of the Immaculate Conception, had decided at the last minute to join them, and their late preparations had made their departure from Comitán a little tardy. Throughout the journey, the two sisters attended their prayers—for more than twelve hours at a sitting—and when not in prayer, they sang softly the radiant *canciones* of their praise, rocking back and forth, their eyes shut tightly as their fingers caressed their crystal rosaries.

Don Pedro Parriera's brother Don Rodrigo had been saved by the *Virgen* following an accident in the mountains as a youth, an injury that left him with one leg slightly shorter than the other and a foot, like María's, that turned slightly inward and under. Rodrigo had fallen off a precipice and landed on a mound of sharp, flinty rock, a spire of which had penetrated his left lung. He was all but dead when he and his brother Pedro had finally arrived at the hospital. The American doctor had given Rodrigo little or no hope for recovery. During a mass before the *Virgen*, however, he had regained consciousness and in two days was taking food. It had been a miracle—nothing short of it. The priest himself wouldn't deny it.

During a fervent prayer for his brother's life before the statue of the Holy Mother, Don Pedro had seen the faint impression of the *Virgen* in the dim evening light in the chapel and had felt her warm, kindly grace—had heard her own voice tell him, "Rodrigo is my own. Worry for him no longer." Don Pedro and his brother had missed the pilgrimage only twice in the past thirty-two years and only once since they had taken work together in Comitán some fifteen years before.

The truck never "arrived" in Mexico City. It seemed, rather, to merge with the sprawling slums that stretched for miles in all directions like a seething, undulating flotsam across the valley. It was more of a passage than an entry, more a factor of time, of becoming than distance to or from. It was different in the *campo*.

Out in the countryside, you'd be driving along and come to a *tumulo* across the middle of the road. You'd slow down to an almost imperceptible crawl and then cross over the hump with a lurch. Before the bump, you could say you were "outside San Cristobal," or you were "outside San Miguel," or you were "outside Concepción." On the other side, clearly you were "in San Cristobal," "in San Miguel," or "in Concepción," and you would leave on the other side of the village, crossing another set of traffic bumps, just as distinctly and decisively, just the same as you had entered. But you "processed" into the capital. Suddenly, one discovers that he is "de Mexico" rather than just "en Mexico." He is breathing differently, feeling differently. For the first time he anticipates rather than merely perceives; he relates to things left and right rather than to those just straight ahead. What he hears has more than melody; it has cadence, a distinctive rhythm. Except for true believers. For them the flow from the *aldea* to the capital is a smooth undulation of spirit from the meanest shrine back in the village to the grand altar of the Holy Mother, only the humblest path of faith, patience, and endurance. And that's why the *Virgen's penitentes*, streaming incessantly into the capital, stand apart so severely during their nine-day period of adoration.

From her view under the canopy in the back of the truck, María was overwhelmed by the ever-unfolding confusion of traffic and pedestrians, the rows and rows of countless little *tiendas*—the whole stuffy, irritating cacophony of image, noise, and odor so intrusive and obnoxious in their persistent pounding and grinding on her senses. Gone was the familiar flight of the truck through the countryside, its smooth gliding up and around and down the mountains. Gone was the rush of cool air that streamed through the slits in the tarpaulin. Gone also was her sense of progress, of destination. Now they only lurched, jerking along in rude fits and starts, breaking every few feet at unpredictable stops. For hours during their passage through the city, her head had been throbbing in pain. Her lungs were congested from the clouds of diesel fumes that fogged the narrow lanes at every intersection as they inched along behind the Mexican city busses.

As the afternoon drew on and dusk approached, the truck passed slowly through the *barrios* of Mexico City. From their view in the rear of the truck, María and the women could see more and more devotees filling the lanes behind them.

The days of the adoration of the *Virgen* was a festive time. Cars and trucks were decorated with brightly colored streamers, flags, and banners. Many of the larger trucks had strings of twinkling Christmas lights stretched up and down the wall of the canopied beds and looped gracefully over the hoods and windshields. Others sported great wreaths of flowers featuring images of the *Virgen* at their centers.

As they approached the Boulevard of Guadalupe, the streets became more and more congested. The great Boulevard itself would be closed off from all vehicular traffic. Some people parked many miles away in church lots. Ricardo preferred to park the truck as close as possible to the boulevard and then to walk the more than a mile or two up the street to the great plaza and basilica of the *Virgen.*

As the afternoon drifted into twilight, all the earlier, irritating commotion became focused. The air was scintillating with anticipation and expectation. Through the blaring din of the streets, María could hear the sounds of small brass bands and the steady, pounding beats of drums echoing off the tall buildings. Ricardo blew his horn at a flatbed truck carrying an effigy of the *Virgen* with banners of Chiapas. It was a truck that they had passed several times in the last few days on their long drive up from the south. Inside the cab of the truck, the family turned in the cab and waved back, delighted in the recognition.

The two sisters were as excited as a couple of young school girls on a vacation outing. They had been to the basilica many times before, and on each occasion, they always found renewal and confirmation of their past year of service. Every time they had made the pilgrimage, from the moment they stepped through the fenced gates of the grand plaza, they were on their knees—both physically and spiritually—in a flush of praise and adoration, an orchestration of thanksgiving for a year of petition, cajoling, and negotiation with the Holy Mother for the sacred incidentals of daily devotional life.

The Boulevard of Guadalupe stretched straightaway from the grand plaza of the basilica toward the crowded mercantile district of the city. For the visit of the Pontiff five years earlier in 1985, the street had been divided by a wide, enclosed esplanade through which the "Popemobile" had maneuvered past the more than 400,000 devotees who had crowded on either side to witness the leader of their faith. On this afternoon anticipating the midnight High Mass, the boulevard swelled to overflowing with jubilant crowds.

Up the esplanade came indigenous groups, church ensembles, singing groups, and bands, horns blaring and drums rattling. Dancers in elaborate costumes—men, women, and children—outfitted as animals, clowns, pre-conquest warriors and Spanish soldiers, feathered Nahuatls—descendants of the ancient Aztecs. Slowly prancing up the boulevard, they twisted and twirled around, stretching and flinging about their decorated arms and hands overhead, driving themselves into frenzied entries toward the basilica.

By the time the Chiapas devotees arrived at the narrow entrances into the plaza, some 10,000 people had already assembled inside the gates of the great shrine. Behind them, another 30,000 would clamor up the boulevard and join them before the joyous midnight Mass. The dusk had slipped into darkness, and the glaring lights from the altar deep within the modern edifice streamed through wide portals, washing the celebrants in a rich, amber glow. The soft, steady pounding of drums reverberated across the plaza, beating out a ceaseless rumble.

María Xquic and the two sisters followed Ricardo, Sylvia, and the two brothers, winding stiffly, shoulder to shoulder through the *penitentes* just inside the gates. They carried with them rolls of blankets which they planned to use as bedding inside the alcoves of the basilica. María was terrified by the thought of being separated from her friends, but Sylvia thoughtfully left the side of her husband and stepped back to hold María's elbow as they continued to pass toward the center of the plaza where the crowd was thinner. All at once, Sylvia collapsed, tripping over the prone body of an old *aficionado* who had fallen in the press of the people. Sylvia tried to right herself and avoid being trampled at the same time by those behind them unaware of the difficulty. María Xquic turned around, raising her hand to guard herself and her friend. Those behind stopped patiently until Sylvia had worked her way back up on her feet. Then the two of them reached down to assist the fallen man.

The old *abuelito* appeared inebriated and dazed. He seemed distracted by the fall and embarrassed by all the attention. Carefully, Sylvia helped steady the old one. Without looking at his helper, he fumbled to brush off his straw hat as he slipped back into the stream of people.

"We must stay close, María," said Sylvia.

Once again, they began to inch their way through the crowd, blocked here and there by small groups gathered around isolated troops of festive dancers pitching about wildly in rhythm to the syncopated drums. Two by two and never really more than a few yards apart, the group maneuvered through the people. Sylvia and María finally managed to reach the center of the plaza where the crowd had thinned, and within moments the *Chapines* had once again reunited. Ricardo pulled Sylvia aside as the two sisters brushed themselves off and readjusted their habits.

"I think that we better go on into the basilica before the crowds move in if we're going to get any place at all to sleep," suggested Ricardo, always the practical one anticipating their next move. "Are we all together now?"

"Yes," said Sylvia, looking about to make sure that María, the two sisters, and the brothers were along side.

The shift to the center of the plaza had given the group time to orient themselves before pressing into the great throng of devotees already making their way inside the basilica. María was awestruck by the spectacle unfolding even outside the massive edifice. She craned her neck to get a better sense of the place. To her right was Tepeyac, the hill, the sacred mount where the *Virgen* was believed to have appeared to Juan Diego, the hill below which the original church had been constructed. Now in a state of partial ruin, this mid sixteenth-century structure had been abandoned and sealed off. Behind her, on the opposite side of the plaza, was a second chapel, also dedicated to the Blessed *Virgen*. High above her, mounted at the very top of the hill was the latest chapel, outside the basilica itself, of course.

"I guess we better go in," said Ricardo to the small entourage.

Upon the cue, the two sisters dropped to their knees. Their fingers caressed the crystal rosaries as they fell into the litany of their most solemn prayers in preparation to witness once again the ancient *tilma* of Juan Diego. Both Sylvia and Ricardo, in complement to their fellow pilgrims, knelt down themselves and offered up a heartfelt rain of "Hail, Mary's." María joined the two brothers, kneeling beside them at the opening of their own prayers, and in kind, she crossed herself reverently over the forehead and breasts.

As she knelt, María began to sense the deep spirituality around her in the devotion of the thousands of pilgrims pressing forward to enter the sanctuary. In the heavy crush, she felt very small and insignificant. Who was she that she should somehow be included among these disciples?

"Ah, malaya!" cried Andres Menchu Xoy. "Blessed fathers of the earth and sky, come to this, your humble servant, and hear his fervent . . ."

"Enough!" cried María. For the first time, she felt embarrassed by her husband's faith and the quaint rituals of the Sacred Table. What was that splintery toy compared to this? Everything about her was new and awesome, and in the immensity of the spectacle of it all, both terrifying and overwhelming.

Sylvia was radiant. The glow of the basilica's light enveloped every strand of her hair and illuminated the edge of her collar and sweater. María was completely disoriented, much the way—she now recalled—she felt only once before, at the revelation of her father so many years earlier when he had informed her that she had been chosen as a bride for the most revered and respected young man in all of San Felipe. That same frightening sensation now gripped her again. She felt that she had been caught up in something larger than life itself. She was being transported beyond the capacity of her senses to register. If Sylvia and Ricardo, if the small group were somehow to abandon her, she would surely be lost and swallowed up. She couldn't let herself think of such a thing.

"Mother! The candles! See the candles!" cried Lucita María.

"No! No!" protested María Xquic. Her imagination was racing wildly. She had to take control, but mounting fears and insecurity were swamping her sanity. She thought again of the Mexican nuns at the church in San Felipe, curious that she hadn't remembered them for so long. She thought of Father Jack, seeing him playing with the young children outside the gate on the street. She remembered that awful moment in the night by that same gate, the night when her husband . . . No! she simply couldn't tolerate the thought. Then suddenly, the veil of fear and apprehension that she had harbored so many years for the North American priest had been lifted, and she felt a quite peace wash over her. María shuddered at the revelation.

As they inched their way in the dense crowd closer and closer to the wide front of the basilica, a swell of organ chords engulfed the parishioners. Tears filled the eyes of some; others dropped their heads in simple reverence. María began to feel light headed, as if somehow her feet had left the pavement below her and she had been suddenly wafted off her feet, drifting now through the entrance. The heavy air about them seemed tense and rarefied. As she looked ahead, María could see nothing but the shoulders and taller heads bobbing slowly before her. She glanced up as they worked their way finally under the great eave of the building and past the support pillars. Then, as the ethereal chords began to spiral toward their sustained climax, the floor suddenly pitched downward, and the undulating wave of people fell away in front of her to reveal the great hall of the basilica itself.

Deep into the cavernous building and against the far wall stretched the massive altar, a platform raised above the congregations wide enough to hold comfortably a dozen or more of the small bamboo shacks of San Felipe. A cherry-white communion table, about as long as the village boat dock, was draped in pearly cloth in the very center of the high altar. Three tall pulpits, one just off center and the other two on either end were festooned in long banners featuring sharply stylized symbols of faith. Draped behind the altar across the slatted louvered walls, a massive Mexican flag provided an expansive cyclorama of red, green, and white, diminishing the almost doll-like figures—

the few acolytes and altar boys—who were beginning to crisscross the stage, initiating what would be more than two hours of preparations for the High Mass at midnight.

"Over *there!"* called Ricardo. "I think we can find some space over there behind that altar. María turned to look in the direction that he was pointing. Against the back wall was a small encased figure of some Catholic saint. Behind it she could see people standing about and others dropping down, adjusting blankets and bedding. Sylvia and the two sisters turned and followed him toward the back of the building. As they approached the wall, they could see a few people already stretched out and asleep, wrapped up in ragged covers.

"There . . .!" said Ricardo. "Back *there!* We can lay out there." The group followed him back to the corner next to the doors to the restrooms where a steady flow of people was streaming in and out.

"We're lucky to find a *spot!"* said Sylvia. "In another few minutes all the spots would have been gone." Already, the remaining places along the wall that arched across the back of both sides of the building were quickly filling. The two brothers dropped their bundles and sat down against the rough brick wall. The two sisters knelt down and began arranging their covers.

"Here," Sylvia said to María. "Why don't you take this place."

Sylvia pointed to the last place next to the nuns, indicating that she and Ricardo would take their places on the other side of the restroom entrances. María nodded her assent and sat down, grateful to be off her feet for the first time in a couple of hours. Don Pedro called Sylvia over to his place. After a moment, she stepped back to María.

"Don Pedro has offered to stay with our blankets if we want to go on up to the altar," said Sylvia. María smiled.

"Thank you," said María. She was extremely tired, but exhilarated at the same time and didn't want to miss anything. Already the heavy organ tones had subsided, giving way to chants and drum beats pounding from the wide center aisle of the building.

"Look," said Sylvia. "Look up at the altar ahead of us. Let me show you where we are going."

María turned and scanned the crowd now standing shoulder to shoulder across the expanse of the floor. To the left, groups were maneuvering toward the front, some carrying tall banners with images of the *Virgen* bouncing slowly up and down. To her right, a central aisle had been roped off to allow other groups and ensembles to salute the altar and its sacred shrine. As she looked over the thousands of heads between them in the back of the building and the expanse of the central aisle, she could see only the bobbing of the massive headdresses and the tall, flower-enveloped *altares*, shrines fashioned from an assembly of decorated poles crisscrossed in large frames and lashed together, and carried high over the heads of the devotees as they approached the grand altar. One by one, the groups approached the altar and its shrine to the *Virgen* of Guadalupe, receiving the blessings of the priests standing at the foot of the altar, dispensing sprinkles of holy water with feather dusters over the parishioners.

María was drawn to the dancers and the companies of worshippers. From the simple preparations of the nuns, the brothers and her friends, Sylvia and Ricardo, she hadn't anticipated the color and immensity of the spectacle about her. She inched along toward the central aisle, moving at one point even ahead of Sylvia.

"*María!*" cried Sylvia over the surging organ music. Five or six women turned around.

"I'm *sorry!*" said Sylvia, somewhat embarrassed to have disturbed them. She stepped deftly through the line of people moving like María toward the central aisle, reached ahead of two of them and grabbed the sleeve of María's dress.

"*Ssst!*" she called. "*This* way! Back *here!* I want to show you!"

María stopped and worked her way back against the crowd to follow Sylvia.

"Before the lines become too congested," explained Sylvia, "I want you to see the shrine of the Blessed Mother."

"The *shrine?*" asked María.

"*Yes!*" exclaimed Sylvia, shocked by the realization that she had told her *companera* nothing of the tradition of the *tilma*, the focus of the complex pageantry unfolding around them.

"*Yes! The shrine!* That's why the people are *here*! That's why *we* are here!"

María stood beside Sylvia, eager for the explanation. "Tell me," she said.

"*Look!*" said Sylvia, pointing to the wall behind the altar. "See the flag?"

"Yes," said María.

"Now look above it, above the flag."

"Yes," said María.

"What do you see?"

"I see the picture," said María. "I see the picture of the *Virgen*, just like we see there, and over there, all pictures of the *Virgen* with the halo around her." María seemed confused by the rather obvious question.

"But *María!"* confided Sylvia. "That picture over the altar. That is the sacred shrine, the holy *image*, the very *miracle* of Juan Diego!"

María seemed puzzled.

Sylvia's eyes brightened with the opportunity for telling the ancient tale again.

"That's the *tilma*—the *robe*—of Juan Diego, the *campesino* to whom the *Virgen* appeared in 1531. She told him to tell the Bishop to construct a temple in her honor up there on the hill, atop the mount of Tepeyac, just outside. The Bishop didn't believe him. He went back twice after the *Virgen* kept reappearing to him up there on the hill. The last time she told Juan to gather roses in his *tilma* and take them as a sign to the Bishop of her seriousness. When Juan opened his robe, the roses fell out at the feet of the Bishop, and in the cloth was the Blessed Mother's own image. And there it is, María—the Holy Mother's gift to us today. Through her image she continues to reach out to us, to bless us and heal us, and to bring us peace. Oh, María, the Holy Mother *waits* for us. *Oh, María!* The Blessed Mother of God is waiting for *you!*"

María stared at the gilded framed image now for the first time in its full meaning, and she wondered why its significance had not dawned on her earlier, what with the people about her, the great piety and solemnity of all who approached the high altar before them.

As they moved down the side aisle, the crowd of people grew denser until, very respectfully, they stood shoulder to shoulder. A weathered matron of more than ninety years stood beside María Xquic clutching a worn frame, probably lifted from her bedside. Another woman pushed along a small child, a little girl in a ragged red sweater. The tiny devotee carried a small, felt banner on a pencil staff bearing the image of the *Virgen*.

The organ music wafted about them, the rows of pipes ranging along the wall on either side of the great hall. Young couples stared ahead in awe of the spectacle. Tears streamed down the face of another worshipper, a mother who held to her sagging breast the wrinkled photograph of a child for whose health she pleaded before the miraculous image. An old man inched along in the press of the crowd, gesturing with a crutch as he muttered to himself beneath leathery eyes.

Steadily, the line of the true believers slipped down behind and around the rear of the massive altar. The peals of the organ seemed to roar above them in heavy rolls, but below, a blanket of reverent silence enveloped the long line angling toward the conveyor path that took them in two files for some sixty feet across the very feet of the sacred image. As each person stepped onto the conveyor beltway, he or she, with lips trembling, turned eyes upward toward the image of the Holy Mother.

María Xquic dared not lift her eyes from the back of the parishioner inching along before her, fearful that she might slip and fall as she stepped onto the wide belt. Then, she watched her feet step gingerly, first one and then the other, onto the moving mat, and she felt herself jerked slightly to the right. Instinctively, she grabbed the sleeve of Sylvia who had moved in behind her and saved herself from falling. Catching her breath, María turned and looked up over the hat of the *Mexicano* in front of her, and she caught the sweet sublime expression of the blessed *Virgen* herself.

And then it happened. *Ah, malaya!* The *alcaldes* of the west, the *alcaldes* of the east and south, the venerable *alcaldes* of the north bowed once and stepped aside. María's eyes started to mist, and her heart began to rush. As she blinked to clear her eyes, she perceived a faint, tremulous blue aura tripping just on the crests of her cheeks. Wasn't this it! The gift of her beloved husband! Her breath swelled in the back of her throat. Fear and joy at the same time gripped her heart, and she dared not take her eyes from the face of the Holy Mother. Then, though she could not so much as see it, a mantle of blue light drifted down and began undulating over her shoulders, wafting its way up and down the form of her arms and tingling at the tips of her very fingers. Soft, unearthly whispers tripped in her ears and behind her head. Breathy voices beckoned, pleading and gently chiding. And the Blessed *Virgen* turned and smiled upon the daughter of Guatemala.

Chapter 32

Elotes

"Did you drop this?" he said to Sylvia, as she and María Xquic returned to their blankets at the rear of the basilica. Sylvia looked around at the inquirer, surprised by his question. A sophisticated young Mexican in his early thirties was holding out María's *huipil.* Instinctively, María Xquic gasped and grabbed at her bag, dropping her hand deeply into its folds. "My *huipil*! That's my *huipil*!"

Sylvia brightened at the kindness and took the weaving from the young man. "Where did you find it?" she asked.

"When you slipped down in the plaza, maybe it fell from your bag, *no?*" offered the good-looking young man, the sharp, angular features of his face accented by his neatly swept-back long black hair. He turned to María. "Guatemala, *no?*"

"*Sí*, Guatemala," said María.

"Atitlán, no?"

"*Sí, señor. Lago Atitlán.*" María appeared puzzled by the rather abrupt, personal inquiries.

"Refugiada?"

María Xquic looked querulously at Sylvia.

"Can I help you?" asked Sylvia. "She knows only a little bit of Spanish."

"I thought so," he said aside, returning his attention to María's companion and the weaving. "I thought it must have come from somewhere around that area. I've been all around the lake. I recognized the designs. I guess things are getting pretty rough down there, *no?*"

"Yes," said Sylvia. "Things are pretty hard for the people. Why are you so interested in María?"

"`María'?" he asked. "`María' is her name, huh?"

"`María,' yes," acknowledged Sylvia.

"It's incredible, *no?*" asked the man.

"Incredible?" said Sylvia.

"The crowd—all this, the Mass and all," he explained.

"Oh, *yes!*" said Sylvia. "It's really incredible, for *sure.*"

"Look . . .," said the man as he glanced away from Silvia, ". . . about María. Is she in trouble? I mean, does she need help? I was thinking maybe that she is going north, *no?*"

Sylvia knelt down and began to fuss with her blanket, looking for a graceful way out of what was becoming a rather awkward conversation. The last thing she wanted to do was to compromise her friend, María, who had had enough difficulty already as it was. She kept working to spread the covers.

"Look," said the man, "my name is Luis—Luis Pérez. Luis Pérez of Nuevo León. I was in the capital on business, and my wife wanted to attend the Mass. I don't mean to be nosy. I'm getting ready to go back to Nuevo Leon in the morning. My wife and I could use a passenger."

Sylvia looked up at the man from her blankets and then said, "You say `you and your wife' . . .?"

"Yes, my wife," he said, pointing toward the nearest exit to a chic young woman with short, black hair wearing a fashionable leather jacket, loops of gold chain around her neck, tight, form-fitting jeans, and slim black boots. "We have a pharmacy in Nuevo Laredo at the border. We're taking back medicines and supplies for the pharmacy. We'll be back there in two days. If she needs to go any farther, we have some contacts who can help her, *verdad?*"

"How much?" asked Sylvia.

"`How much'?" repeated the man.

"How much do you want for your . . . for your `services,' *señor*?"

"*Oh!*" he said. "Why, nothing . . . nothing at *all!* Perhaps you're misunderstanding my intentions! In fact, she will be a big help to us. Sometimes both of us have to leave the car for a little while, and she could stay with the car and guard the supplies. I was going to have to hire someone anyway. You can't trust the street kids, so she'll be a help to us and save us some money, too. When we get to the frontier, well, maybe we could help her."

Sylvia looked over at María who was standing silently and seemingly aloof from the conversation.

"*Look!* I can't answer for her," said Sylvia a little testily. "I'll have to *talk* with her. She is very frightened and has been through so much already. I just don't know."

"That's fine," said the man, attempting to wave off her misgivings. "Why don't you talk with her tonight. My wife and I will be back in the morning. We can meet you at the front gate . . . say, seven-thirty?"

"We have to talk, *okay?*" said Sylvia. "We just have to *talk.*"

"Well, my wife and I will be out there at the gate just down the ramp in the morning," he said. "We'll wait for a while, and if you come down, okay. If not, we'll just go on. God bless you, *Señora.*"

María Xquic looked away, her hand to her mouth. She sensed something of the subject of the discussion, and she was uneasy about Sylvia's report.

"What did he want?" she asked Sylvia, as the man stepped away beyond hearing. Sylvia finished smoothing out her blanket and motioned to María to join her on the bedding.

"He and his wife were just returning your . . ." Sylvia began, but then paused, recognizing in María's expression that she must have caught the drift of the exchange. "They're from Nuevo Laredo on the border—up on the border. They're returning north tomorrow. They asked if you might want to go. They said they can help you get to the United States."

María began to twist the blanket into little cones between her fingers but said nothing. Sylvia watched for a glimmer of response on the inscrutable face of her friend, but could read nothing. María only sat with her head down and cocked to one side, appearing to concentrate on nothing but the little twists in the blanket.

"What are you thinking, María?" Sylvia asked. María continued to twist the fibers of the wool blanket.

"María," offered Sylvia, feigning truth with her counterpart for the first time, "you don't have to go *anywhere*. You can stay with us as long as you like. You can work for us in the clinic. We'll find a way somehow, María. You don't have to go anywhere, okay?"

María turned her face away from Sylvia. She rose slowly and seemd to study the people milling about the entrance to the restroom. After a moment, she knelt down on her own bedding. Slowly and methodically, she smoothed out the kinks in the blanket and lay down on her side as the organ began to swell and the entourage of priests began to fill the altar.

"María," said Sylvia, as she pulled out an undergarment from her own bag. ". . . before you go to sleep, I'm afraid you're going to lose your bag. You'll need to wear this."

Sylvia rose and extended a hand to help up María and then escorted her *compañera* into the women's restroom. It was some time later in her sleep that Sylvia seemed troubled.

"María?" Sylvia called out. It was still sometime before daybreak, and someone stumbled at the foot of her blanket, awakening her. Sylvia sat up, thinking to find María. An old man wobbled past and into the darkened restroom. Sylvia looked over to the other side to check on María, but she was gone—María, her blanket and bedding, everything gone.

Sylvia threw off her covers and nudged Ricardo still deep in sleep. "*Ricardo! Ricardo!*"

Sylvia's husband grabbed at his blanket and lifted it over his head.

"*Ricardo!*" she cried again and reached over to tap him on the shoulder.

"*Ricardo! Wake up!*" Sylvia urged. "It's María! She's *gone!*"

"What?" he cried, finally coming around. "What's the matter?"

"It's *María!*" Sylvia explained again. "She's *gone!*"

Ricardo sat up and looked toward the empty spot on the floor where he had last seen María fast asleep on her grass mat, the *petate*, and blankets after they had returned from the Mass at about 1:30 a.m. María had slept through it all. Ricardo and Sylvia had held a whispered conversation throughout the service trying to determine how best to advise María about going north. Both had agreed that their guest had long since passed her stay. Food and provisions were running low, and the doctor had been urging them to make the break.

"What do you mean she's *gone?*" he asked.

"She's *gone!*" exclaimed his frightened wife. "She's just *gone!* I looked over there and she's *gone*—her bedding, *everything!"*

"Maybe she got up and couldn't find her way back," offered Ricardo. "That's probably it."

"But her blankets?" insisted Sylvia.

The two nuns were now awake and curious about the stir. "What is it? What's going on?"

"It's María Xquic!" said Sylvia in an aggrieved undertone. "She's *gone!*"

"But *where?"* whispered Sister Rubia Ordoñez.

"Yes, but *where?"* echoed Sister Veronica Ortíz.

"I don't *know?*" said Sylvia. "Perhaps Ricardo is right. Maybe she just got lost last night among the people. Why don't we divide and each take a corridor."

"I'll go out front onto the plaza," said Ricardo. "I'll meet you back here."

The four of them separated, and Ricardo began making the long circuit around the hall to the entrance of the basilica. As he neared the front of the building, he could see the first faint trace of grey light anticipating the dawn. The facades of the churches and the hill to his left were pasted darkly behind a murky fog that suffused the area. To his right and on the opposite side of the plaza a single light bulb radiated a faint orange aura marking the gate and the way to the streets beyond. As he scanned the plaza from left to right, he caught a glimpse of an old groundskeeper, stick in hand and bag over his shoulder, already making his way through the debris-strewn plaza. It seemed his only chance, so Ricardo decided to risk the effort.

"Señor!" said Ricardo as he approached. *"Perdoneme!"*

The old apparition turned non-committally toward the voice approaching from behind. He reached down and pulled off a wad of tamale wrappers and discarded service bulletins from the nail at the end of his staff and dropped them into his shoulder bag.

"*Señor,*" said Ricardo once more. "I am so sorry to bother you like this, but I need some help. I'm missing some friends, and you might have seen them. It would have been some time early in the morning, still in the night."

"Lots of people, *no?*" said the man as he turned his attention once more to the trash at his feet.

"*Sí*, lots of people, *yeah!*" said Ricardo handing the man a few *pesos* for his trouble. The man glanced down and took the worn bills and slipped them into his pocket.

"Then, maybe," said the man as he stabbed another tamale wrapper and slipped it into his trash sack trailing behind. "There were three people earlier—maybe an hour or two ago. A couple and a woman—she had a kind of limp."

"*Yes!*" exclaimed Ricardo. "That's *them!* Where did you *see* them."

"Over there," he explained. "Over there leaving through the gate."

"That's *them!*" said Ricardo. "Where did they *go?*"

"What did I say, *amigo*?" explained the custodian, "—out the *gate!*"

"*Thanks, fellow!*" said Ricardo as he slipped the old man another fistful of *pesos*. "Thanks *very* much. You've been a real help."

The groundskeeper never looked up but continued his slow deliberate course toward the next mound of debris. Ricardo turned and trotted back toward the entrance.

"We couldn't *find* her!" said Sylvia as she and the sisters approached Ricardo.

"*No!*" said Sister Veronica. "We couldn't find any *trace* of her."

"She's not here," said Ricardo.

"I know," said Sylvia.

"*No!*" said Ricardo. "She left."

"She *left?*"

"Yes," he said. "She left with the other two more than an hour ago."

"*How?*" said Sylvia. "How could that *be?* She wouldn't just *leave* without telling *us!"*

"All I can say is what the groundskeeper just told me," explained Ricardo.

"He saw them himself as they left through the gate—María, and that Mexican couple."

"I don't *understand!"* said Sylvia. "She wouldn't just *leave* without telling *me*, without saying *something!*"

Tears filled her eyes as she tried to understand, but Sylvia was lost for an explanation. "It doesn't make any *sense!* She wouldn't just *leave!* It just doesn't make any *sense!*"

"It does if she *had* to," offered Ricardo.

"What do you *mean?*" pleaded Sylvia.

"If they *forced* her to go with them," said Ricardo. "If they *kidnapped* her!"

"*Why . . .?*" asked Sylvia, startled by even the suggestion.

"Why would anyone kidnap *María?*"

María Xquic sat in the back seat of the Mercedes as it sped away northward through the outskirts of the capital. Her head was spinning, her heart racing toward convulsion. She had been surprised from at best only troubled sleep by a hand over her mouth and the cold steel muzzle of a pistol behind her left ear. A firm hand under her arm lifted her up while the figure of a woman had scooped up the bedding behind her. They had proceeded out of the basilica, walking casually across the plaza so as not to raise suspicion, and exited the gate without a word of explanation.

Neither of the two had said a word during the hour and more that they had been speeding along the expressway through the capital and out of the city. As the pale rose and aqua washes of the eastern dawn began to paint the horizon, the man muttered something to his wife and pulled off the highway into a gasoline station for fueling. The man stepped out of the car and spoke to the attendant who reached for the gas nozzle and began filling the tank of the car. Casually, the woman opened the door to the other side of the car and, pulling the front seat forward, motioned for María to get out and to follow her.

María walked slightly ahead of her abductress who directed her toward the rear of the service station. Preoccupied with their work under the hood of a wrecked produce truck, two mechanics never noticed the horror on María's face. The woman nudged her elbow to move her on. When they reached the rear of the station, the woman slipped a cloth belt out of her purse along with four long, knotted plastic bags, each containing a fistful or a little more of a white powdery substance. Holding the bags and belts in one hand, she stepped in front of María, reached down to the bottom of her skirt and raised it all the way up to her waist. Instinctively, María grabbed at her skirt, but the woman pushed her strongly back against the wall and pulled the small pistol out of her purse. María blanched at the sight of the gun. The woman handed her the belt and indicated for María to tie it around her waist under her skirt.

María took the belt in her uncertain hands and tied it loosely around her waist. Obviously dissatisfied, the woman holstered the gun in her purse and set it down with the plastic bags beside her on the ground, then reached up and jerked away the belt. She tied it around María's waist again, wrapping it twice about her before tying it in a double knot in front. Confident that the belt was secure, the woman retrieved each bag and tied them in tight knots around the belt so that they hung down between María's legs and out of sight beneath her skirt.

"*Vamos!*" said the woman as she gave María's shoulder a smart push.

Deliberately but slower now, the two emerged from behind the station and walked past the two mechanics, guffawing in reaction to a joke about "the *stupid indio* and the *ladino* landowner." María looked toward them, hoping to catch the eye of at least one of them, but the woman intercepted her glance and maneuvered quickly between them and rushed María along past their sight. María's last hope had dissipated.

In a moment, the trio was back out onto the highway and cruising northward. *Drugs! So, they're running drugs, these two.* María had heard about drugs, had heard about the women in other *aldeas* who were selling the little bags of drugs at their fruit stands or in the markets along the sidewalks. The European tourists were particularly savvy about drugs, and some of the American young people, too, were aggravating the problem. The civil patrols had been instructed to react aggressively against any drug trafficking, but she had heard also that their policing was particularly selective, that at Chimaltenango and other communities along the highway, the military controlled the sales of the little bags and kept up a regular supply to shop owners who catered to the tourists.

In the languid afternoon, María stared out of the window as the car ripped along through the steaming Mexican countryside. Tiny twisters raced across the fields, whipping up little clouds where their tails touched down. They passed from hamlet to hamlet, linked valley by valley between endless stretches of cactus and fields of the prickly maguey. Gradually, the road began to roll and turn as it rose from the *Valle de la Revolución* and up into the foothills of the Sierras just south of Monterey. How would she sleep without her blanket and bedding? And why had the woman discarded her bag? A sudden rush of appreciation for Sylvia swelled in her heart—she still had the *huipil*. After all she had been through, at least she had that yet. María trembled, fearing what lay ahead but too horrified by the past to even think.

She had to keep watching the countryside blitzing by her.

At one point, the car passed over a low water bridge and glided up the escarpment on the other side. Looking back over her shoulder, María followed the streamer of deep, rich green trailing away from them farther and farther below. As the car climbed higher, the lush, verdant ribbon looped in great arches as far as she could see until it disappeared in the musty blue haze against the horizon.

María's thighs itched where the plastic bags rubbed together under her skirt, and she crossed her legs to allow the bags to slip under her to hang near the floor of the car. Her forehead almost touching the glass, María could make out the faint outline of her own face, the liquid fear in her eyes staring back at her from across the hot Mexican wasteland. Suddenly, she felt adrift in time and space, slipping further and further away from these people, this car, this whole terrifying experience. María imagined herself floating freely, somehow in concert, out there just a little way from the movement of the car itself. In the reflection, all that she had lost or left behind came flooding over her. Curiously, after all that she had risked to secure it, the roll of the tiny *huipil* felt out of place, a pathetic stranger cradled in her bosom. She followed the lines across her brow and out the corners of her eyes which seemed to burn and ache with every beat of her pulse. A shadow flitted across the window, startling her from her preoccupation and the irritating bags of white powder under her skirt. María glanced up to catch a buzzard wheeling in a wide arch toward them in a path that would intersect the highway ahead of them. She tried to project their speed and the point before them where the vulture and the car would meet. She crossed herself to avoid a wreck of the speeding car at such an ominous intersection.

The driver reached over to the tape deck beneath the radio and inserted a cassette. Instantly, a *mariachi* trumpet chord blasted María from the speakers mounted in the back-windshield dashboard behind her. María lurched forward in surprise. As she did, the cargo of bags slipped down further from her lap. Instinctively, she slapped at her dress to keep from losing the them.

"What are you do*ing?"* barked the woman, as she grabbed at María's arm and threw her back against the seat and the door.

María flashed in horror unable to understand. The woman reached down and ripped up her skirt to check the bags.

"What are you *doing?*" the woman screamed. "What are you *doing?*"

María huddled against the door in terror, her lips trembling visibly. The woman starred fixedly at María, never taking her eyes from the disheveled Mayan. She meant to keep her off guard for the duration of the trip, given what lay ahead of them at the river. She didn't want María to be getting ideas of her own.

Ana Fabiola twisted and attempted to roll over in the dark. She would be hungry, of course! How long had it been? Three weeks? Three months? She had lost all time since the firefight on the mountain where Donaldo and she had looked for little Manuel, the dead cat that he loved so, little Manuel who must be looking for his mother still there, high up on the slope of the volcano. The sweets for little Ana Fabiola, but she had nothing but these two bags and Lucita María's huipil rolled inside the cups of the bra Sylvia had showed her how to wear. Lucita María would never forgive her if she let anything separate her from the precious little cloth again. Once was enough, and so close! The throbbing pain in her crotch where he had hurt her repeatedly. The little boy who had kicked the dirt in her face, the redness, the blood from her mouth and nose, her side that was still so raw with pain when she turned in just a certain way.

And so the afternoon passed into nightfall. Still the car continued on with stops only for gas and a toilet every now and then. The man and woman alternated driving. Throughout the trip, the man had ignored María, and she had discovered sleep, pretended or otherwise, could be an effective dodge to further assaults by the woman.

It was the slamming of the driver's door that awakened her in the night.

"Wake *up!*" said the woman as she nudged María's shoulder. "*Wake up and get out! Quickly!*"

María shook her shoulders to break off the drowsiness. At the second nudge, she raised her knee to ward off what she feared would be a blow. She opened her eyes enough to see the woman motion toward the door. María found the handle of the door, eased it open, and stepped outside. Immediately, a draft of cold, northerly wind enveloped her, chilling her to the bone.

"*Hurry!*" urged the woman. "*This* way!"

María struggled to assess her bearings, but nothing suggested anything familiar. Except for the silent, twin taillights of a car drifting away from them, the night was completely black with a canopy of stars that stretched across the sky. María heard the voice of the man and then that of a stranger talking softly only a few feet away from her behind the car, but she could understand nothing more than gestures the stranger was making with his arms toward some place beyond the car. The man then turned toward the woman and motioned for them all to move forward.

"*Go!*" said the woman as she nudged María's arm, indicating for her to move just ahead.

María stepped up behind the two men working their way up an ascending slope angling sharply away to the right. She felt awkward enough with the difficulty of her foot, but the deep blackness on every side of the incline almost paralyzed her with fear.

"*Here!*" said the man, as he turned back to give her a hand. "*Cuidad! Careful!*"

María reached up and felt the man's hand squeeze tightly around her right wrist. She took one hesitant step and then seemed to mount the crest of the ridge with ease.

"There it *is!*" said the stranger. "The *river!*"

María steadied herself on what now appeared to be a narrow embankment that fell sharply away below her where her eye caught the shimmering reflection of a sliver of the moon suspended above them. As she looked left, she followed the water gliding away until it curved off into the shadow of the land.

"Fifteen," said the stranger wearing boots, dark trousers, and a black leather jacket, the very mirror of her assailant. "Fifteen at the most. They come just about every forty-five minutes to an hour, so you've got to move now. It's too late if they spot the car. Mario's your contact. He's just a mile straight away on the other side. He'll be driving a light blue Ford Ranger."

"*Check* her," said the man, motioning to the woman.

"*Ugh!*" grunted María, as suddenly she felt herself jerked down from behind. She landed abruptly with a jolt to her left hip.

The woman muttered something gruffly and obscene as she threw back María's skirt to examine the bags. She tugged at each to check their security and then pulled María's skirt back down.

"Get *up!*" she snapped just above a breath, and she gave María another shove. María dug her heals into the loose dirt, pushing herself back from the woman, rolled over onto her knees, and managed to gain her footing once again.

"*Here!*" said the man as he reached out to her and looped a hemp rope around her waist. He grabbed both her hands and clasped them around the rope in front of her. The other end, more than fifteen feet or so, stretched back and was tied around the waist of the woman who would be bringing up the rear. "Let's *go! Cuidad!* Be *careful!*"

Slowly, the team began a single file descent of the embankment toward the glistening sheet of river. The stranger never paused as he reached the edge of the water, but stepped smoothly into the current. María felt the rope draw taut and the sharp, insistent pull on her waist. At the water's edge, the earth gave way to a slippery mud, and María felt her feet almost fly out from under her, but with a tug at the rope in front of her she was able to maintain her balance.

Into the swirling, silver water, María glided ankle, knee, and then waist deep. She felt her skirt swell out from around her thighs and the plastic bags of drugs rise up uncomfortably under her crotch and behind her. She kept her attention fixed on the man maneuvering slowly through the water before her, his right hand extending out behind him along the rope as he guided María along.

Suddenly, María felt her ankle snap. The gravelly bottom of the river gave way, and in a swift surge of the current, she was quickly pulled under. Water filled her eyelids and nose, and still under water, she coughed up what seemed to be a lung full of river silt. The rope around her waist popped sharply, and for a moment she thought she would pass out. As her face finally surfaced, a stream of acrid, muddy river water exploded from her mouth, and she erupted in an uncontrollable spasm of vomiting.

"Get her *up! Quickly!*" shouted the stranger. "We don't have any time to *lose!* The *helicopter!"*

Off to the right, the team could make out the barely audible but rattling drone of a helicopter.

"*Goddamn!"* shouted the man. "*Quick!* Get her up on the *shore* and grab the *bags!*"

The woman helped secure the line and to steady María who kept stumbling back into the strong river current.

"*Awwooo!*" cried María as she reached for the shoulder of the woman who had worked her way up behind the distraught Mayan. María couldn't put any weight on her left foot without a jabbing pain shooting up her leg and spine. The woman called her husband for assistance.

"*Goddamn!*" he swore. "We've got to get the hell *out* of here! What's the *problem?*"

"She's *hurt*," said the woman. "Turned her ankle or something. I don't know—just help me get her to the bank."

The two worked their way slowly with María Xquic cradled between them. As they reached the bank, they carefully laid her back onto the mud.

"Get the bags, *quick!*" said the man. The bags of dope were all twisted under María. Unceremoniously, the woman reached down and rolled María over on her stomach and pulled up her skirt to get at the packages. In the dark, the woman was having difficulty finding the fourth bag which was still caught under María's thigh.

"*Shit!*" cried the man. "*Here!* Use the *knife!* Just cut them *off* and let's get the hell *out* of here! *Jeezus!*"

The woman took the knife and slipped the blade up under the neck of the plastic bags and sawed back and forth until the bags slipped free.

"*There!*" she said. "Let's *go!*"

In a moment the three had disappeared only moments before the helicopter reached the river upstream and began to turn its spotlight up and down the banks. Within seconds the border patrol helicopter was hovering over the still, prone body of María Xquic de Xoy.

"She was running drugs," said the lieutenant to his captain. It was almost 3:00 a.m. before they had finally made it back to the office and the small two-cell lock up in Mission. "No question about it. She wasn't alone. There were tracks all over the area. Must have been three or four others. She had this belt around her waist under her skirt."

Out of an evidence sack, the officer dumped the cloth belt with the knots from the severed plastic bags still attached.

"One of the others apparently cut the dope loose and left her behind," he explained. "She can't walk . . . must have twisted her ankle in the river. I tried to talk with her about an hour ago, but she doesn't speak any Spanish or she's a good faker."

"Find any actual dope on her?" asked the captain.

"No," said the lieutenant. "We'll have to wait for a lab report on her dress. We found this . . . this `blouse,' I guess you would call it, stuffed in her bra. Must be a keepsake or something. She really fought Shirley when she stripped searched her and found it."

"Well," said the captain, "log it for the record. We'll hold her for the marshal. Go ahead and pull a car up, and we'll take her on over to Chamayo."

Fifteen racks of stacked cots, two high, and forty units deep filled the dormitory on the third floor of Compound 7 at El Chamayo, the INS detention center thirty-five miles north of King City. Cot 14B, the top one, was assigned to detainee No. 1548922. A tissue-thin, bleached bottom sheet was issued once every two weeks. The one stained, lumpy pillow with feathers escaping the rip above the seam had disappeared two days after her arrival and hadn't been seen for more than two weeks now. The US ARMY-issue woolen blanket was a patchwork piece, a reconstruction from two wars and a fifteen-year protracted police action in a tiny corner of the world a generation, three U.S. presidents, and two recessions back. With its patched, restitched rips, the mattress beneath the covers bore the pulsating, rhythmic graffiti of four federal prisons and a small, stained hole burned in its belly.

The air in the light-grey dormitory was institutional air conditioning regulated by a thermostat set at a constant 75 degrees which vacillated back and forth between 85 and 95 in the summer, depending upon the number of inhabitants in a given hour. Light streamed into the room from sealed windows installed just below the ceiling and stretching the length of the east wall. Like the air, the view was institutional as well: the roof line of the adjacent woman's dormitory, visible only by inmates assigned B cots, the top bunks.

Evacuated during the recreation hour, the dormitory room was disturbed only by three cleaning ladies, their mop buckets, and custodial carts. In their institutional "whites," they moved down the rows of cots making wide swipes under the bunks and down the rows behind them, picking up trash and depositing it in plastic-lined garbage pails installed in the backs of their carts. Each seemingly absorbed in music streaming from earphones, the large, black women strained for breath as they swung their mops.

"*Praise!* . . . . *Praise!* . . . . *Praise*-an'-th'-*Glawwwry*," sang one of the custodians in rhythm to the gospel tape in her cassette player. Raising the outstretched palm of one hand, she pressed down the handle on the mop bucket ringer with the other. Across the room, her colleague raised her own hand above her head in sympathetic unison.

"*Praise!* . . . . *Praise!* . . . . *Praise*-an'-th'-*Glawwwry*," belted the first in an exuberant refrain as she lifted the mop from the ringer and slapped it to the floor. She hummed as she finished the aisle and, dragging the mop behind her, pushed the bucket to the end of a bench sitting against the wall. Slowly and deliberately she turned around and, with her left palm pressed against the wall, eased herself onto the bench.

"*Lawd!* . . . *Be!* . . . *Praised!*" she exclaimed as she struggled to catch her breath. "*Whew!* I think I just about push' the paint off the *flo',* honey!" she laughed to her partner as the other finished her own aisle.

"I kno' *das*'right!" said the other.

New to El Chamayo, thirty-year-old Tamika Rawlins had been transferred, upon her own request, from the minimum-security prison in Parkerville about seventy miles further west. Work at the federal detention camp gave her two extra hours a day otherwise lost in driving time which she could now devote each evening to her dying mother resting in a nursing home in Brownsville.

"They got some *crazy* women in this place, don't you *know* it!" said Mattie, Tamika's co-worker, who had maneuvered her bucket and cart to the other end of the bench.

"Come on down here, *woman!*" bellowed Tamika in her deep, hoarse throat, pitching her invitation to Sister Jessie still ringing the muddy suds from the tangled, string mop. "I need one a yo' *cigarettes, ger'l!*" she laughed.

Tamika Rawlins was a two-pack-a-day asthmatic suffering from the early stages of emphysema. "Looka-*herrah*, honey. What you mean `crazy'?"

"Don't get close t' thissher *bucket,* now!" interrupted Sister Jessie. "*Lawd,* I believe they all on the same *rag!* These Mes'kins mus'sa past it *aroun'!* I neva seed th' *like! Lawd*-amighty!"

"You gonna get the *AIDS* from some Mes'can *'ho', woman!"* laughed Tamika. "*Eewwwwheee!* Don' roll that bucket *ovaherrah! Sho'*nuf!"

"I tell you su'thin' *`crazy,' ger'l*!" protested Mattie, in a loud voice above Tamika's jest. I tell you *su'thin'! Lis'n . . . Lis'un* to *me, herrah, woman!* . . . I *tell* you! *Say! Looka-herrah!* They's com'n' up herrah *wet back* to git yo' *job,* honey! Now, ther's su'thin *crazy*, if you as' *me!* They's com'n' in herrah *wet back* to get yo' *job!* Y'*hearrah?* I mean what I *say, now* . . ."

"Gimme one u'them *cigarrettes, honey!*" said Tamika. "You got a light, Sister Jessie?"

". . . Ther's su'thin *crazy,* if you as' *me!* They ain't gonna get *my* job! Tha's fo' *sho'!* They c'n *all* git th' AIDS, fo' all *I* carrah!" protested Sister Jessie as she reached under her bra strap for a book of matches.

Sister Jessie was a forty-nine-year old mother of four girls and two boys, a grandmother of seven, and a great grandmother of a two-year old with another one on the way. She supported eight people in her house and was proud of the fact that she had never been on welfare. In fact, she was most proud of the plaque awarded her by the First Baptist Church as "Mother of the Year" in 1979 for her success in putting both of her sons and two of the daughters through college on the salary of a custodian.

. . . "Fo' *SHO!* They ain't gonna git *my* job, *NO* way!" insisted Sister Jessie.

"Now, *looka-herrah,* Sister Jessie," said Mattie. "Herrah's wha' *I* wanna know. Why they's all up herrah in the *fus'* place? Now, who' gonna ansame *that!"*

"*G'erl*! Wha'd I jus' *say?* You lisn'n to me, or *what?*" retorted Sister Jessie. "They's com'n up herrah *wet back* for work `cause they ain't no *work* down *therrah!*"

"Well, they's truck'n'm outta herrah putty fast," said Mattie. "I seen a bus load of 'm on the way out'n herrah jes this *morn'n'.* Som'f'em ain't got no *teeth,* you know what I *mean?* They ain't got no *teeth, sho'nuf!* They's *Injins* or som'fn lik' *at.* An' com'n' in herrah *smell'n'* lik—*lawd*-amighty, I nevah see'd *nuff'n* like it *befo'!*"

"Finish that *cigarette, ger'l.* We gotta 'nother *flo'* to *go* 'fo' we *outta* herrah," said Sister Jessie.

The three women began to pull themselves up from the bench and maneuvered their carts toward the dormitory exit. Just as they reached the door, the buzzer sounded above them, the signal for the returning detainees. Within five minutes, the dormitory would be filled with Central American refugees.

Down the hall at the stair well, steel doors creaked open, and a stream of orange-red suits filed through into the wide corridor leading to the dormitory door. Each suit was distinguishable from any other only by the number inked on the front jacket above the pocket and, much larger, across the shoulders in the back. One size fit all except the extra large. On the third floor of Compound 7 there were no "extra large" occupants.

Slowly and aimlessly, the women returned to their bunks, each carrying a plastic bag containing their personal hygenic items, meager cosmetics, and a fresh bath towel. Fresh towels were issued every other day after exercise in the "courtyard." Detainee No. 1548922 walked cautiously back to her bunk, still nervous about the theft of her pillow, an item she had never used before but one for which she felt responsible. She was also frightened about the prospect of trying to climb unassisted to cot B, her assigned mattress on top. The strain in her ankle was still not healed, and she was quite frightened by the necessity of asking for help. She was still too disturbed and uncertain to speak with anyone and fearful that her limited Spanish might sound strange. If anyone should laugh at her, she would be humiliated, but worse yet, she would be singled out, and people would start to notice her. Perhaps someone would try to harm her.

No. 1548922 tried to hide her pained ankle by adopting a slow glide, masked, she hoped, by the large, baggy cuffs of the uniform, but she winced, and her eyes began to tear as sharp jabs of pain ripped through her foot. Still, however, she made her way among the others toward her bunk, her anxiety increasing as she turned down her aisle and hobbled toward her station.

"You gonna need some *he'p*, lady," said the guard.

No. 1548922 was suddenly paralyzed with fear. Over her shoulder stood a tall, elegant African-American woman in a starched, ironed uniform wearing the wide, shiny INS badge over her left pocket.

"Let me *he'p* you up onto your cot, ma'am," the guard offered.

No. 1548922's head began to spin. She was nervous beyond control and was now completely exposed. She felt a great urge to urinate and had to fight back tears which suddenly erupted in uncontrollable sobs, and then she collapsed.

They wheeled her down a long corridor. It seemed like forever, the gurney gliding silently from one annex to another, faster and faster. The sheet kept slipping off, and her sore ankle was perspiring and itching. She tried to reach it to scratch behind her heel, but she couldn't touch her foot. The sheet kept slipping off and someone put it back on, and the gurney slipped silently into another corridor. At the end of the hallway a bright light radiated through a window in the door. A figure stood to one side to open it to allow the gurney to pass through. It was Ana Fabiola with her full, little breasts arching under her fresh huipil! "Mommy, Mommy, I have been waiting for you!" the girl pleaded, and she pushed the metal door open to the emergency room with the bloody stump of her thin, little arm. The gurney slipped past her anxious daughter. "You must make the tortillas for me tonight, Ana Fabiola! I might be late tonight. Don't come looking for me tonight, my precious one. Don't talk to the soldiers who laugh when the Padre offers the Mass!" Ana Fabiola must make the tortillas tonight. She must pile them high above the fire and keep them warm. Miguelito can eat a stack of tortillas. He is big and strong, and he can eat the stack of the milpa when the corn rack under the cat if Manuel Xoy with the water. "Don't talk with soldiers, Manuel Xoy, like Tano and Miguelito. Sprinkle rose petals over the stack of tortillas for El Mundo, and ask your father to read the maguey seeds. He can heal your throat where they cut you, if you go to your father. Did he not heal General Francisco Palma?" No. 1548922 was running across the creek bed. Her foot slipped in between the slimy, moss-covered rocks under the cold water, and she felt the knifing pain as her tiny foot turned, and she began drifting down the stream with her face down in the cold, clear water. Then she rose from the stream and began to float swiftly above the water below and felt the warm rush of the wind as she was swept up into the sunlight over the trees and then drifted down and down, down into the little Mexican hamlet of Taxco, outside Comitán where the two old men on the porch, next to the pigs and the flies swarming around the garbage, the refuse pile of corncobs and the plastic bolsas with the filthy, sticky straws that the dusty little boys sucked whose little penises projected under their distended bellies, laughing at her lying in the shadow of the adobe wall in the garbage, the pig rutting under her arm and face, the lice-infested little boys whose little penises projected under their distended bellies, laughing at her and sucking on the grimy, plastic straws of the bolsas. The gurney stopped outside under the tree. "Let me buy your tortillas for la cena," said the corpulent, perspiring, Mexican vegetable merchant—the truck driver, twisting the end of his white mustache as he winked at her under the sheet, the gleaming golden pendant of the Virgin dangling on a gold chain over his sweaty, hairless Mexican belly. "Venga! Venga, aquí!" he urged. "Let me help you inside where we will eat some hot elotes!" And he laughed as he passed his wide pudgy hand under the sheet, over her knees, and up between her thighs. "I have hot elotes and cool, smooth chocolate," he whispered into her ear, and he laughed as his pudgy fingers entered her. She rolled onto her side as the elote pulsated and twisted deeply within her. And Miguel Mapa stroked her hand and wiped her tears and threw fists full of dirt over the sheet. "But Chico has some hot elotes for you, mi madre, and for Lucita. See, her belly is filled with elotes! See for yourself, mother!" offered Miguel Mapa. Lucita moved to the side of the gurney as No. 1548922 struggled to repulse the elote twisting and throbbing within her. Lucita unwrapped her morga and lifted the skirt of her huipil to reveal the massive belly with the shapes of the pointed elotes projecting in all directions from within. No. 1548922 reached out to caress the engorged belly of her oldest daughter, Lucita María, and she felt the hot elotes swelling within herself, twisting and turning as she pleaded with Miguel Mapa who stroked her hand and laughed. And she cried as she began to urinate on the gurney, staining the sheet. And the photographer laughed. And the priest reached into his tunic and placed the Eucharist on her tongue and then stood back with crossed hands, and he laughed and laughed, and threw dirt over the outstretched stumps of Ana Fabiola. Don Andres, her husband, genuflected before the priest and took a spent bullet from his mouth and placed it in the offering plate. Lucita ran her hands over the projecting elotes stuffed within her belly and laughed a rolling laugh, and the photographer reached into his bag and retrieved a gleaming, silver butcher knife and slit the priest's throat and then placed, the sticky, dripping blade under the sheet of the gurney and laughed and laughed and laughed while the pig rutted between her thighs as she continued to urinate in thick, yellow streams, and Manuel Xoy sucked on dirty straws with his little penis arched from under his little round, distended belly. And No. 1548922 cried and cried until she found the still tacky, bloody blade, holding it tightly between her breasts and squeezing it until it began to slice into her palms. Then slowly, she began to roll over and over as her body, with its engorged belly, filled with hot elotes and the smooth, chilly, chocolate, rose up over the gurney, and, still clutching the knife between her breasts, No. 1548922 drifted far, far away, high above San Filipe del Lago into the cool, tall pines toward the light.

The light intensified as the doctor at Brownsville Municipal Hospital adjusted the spotlight over the examination table. No. 1548922 lay immobile in a prenatal position, her knees drawn up tightly under her breasts and her two hands locked in a fist on either side of her face, in what appeared to be a catatonic state. The nurse wiped her forehead with a folded damp towel.

"How were her vital signs when you examined her this morning, nurse?" asked Dr. Lawrence.

"It's on the chart here, Doctor," said Nurse Adamson, as she handed him the clipboard. "They appeared normal with only a slightly higher than normal white blood count. She has been fighting an infection in her ankle from a sprain."

"For how long?" asked Dr. Lawrence. He was a person of few words.

"Maybe two, maybe three weeks," said Nurse Adamson. "The nurse at the Chamayo clinic wasn't sure. These women are so frightened that they would rather go quietly, even in extreme pain sometimes, rather than do anything that would draw attention to themselves. They are so intimidated by what is happening to them."

"Remove the sheet and let me examine her ankle," instructed the doctor.

The nurse pulled the sheet back up to reveal an extremely swollen left ankle and a striated red and purple bruise that extended from the bottom of her foot high into her calf.

The doctor felt the patient's toes, squeezing them sharply to check the circulation.

"She's getting circulation, but we need to send her over to X-ray anyway. When she returns, elevate the heel and place it in a bandage and check her circulation and vital signs every four hours, nurse," said Dr. Lawrence. "If it's broken, we may still have to operate."

The doctor made a few final notes on the charts for No. 1548922, turned off the spotlight over the examining table, placed the clipboard over the hook at the foot of the patient's bed, and left the room.

The nurse called for the interns to help her move No. 1548922 to the bed, and the orderlies returned the patient to the hallway outside the Emergency Room for transfer to X-ray.

María's ankle had been broken, and the doctor had operated. As the days in recovery slipped by, María's greatest fear had materialized: all the commotion over her broken ankle had guaranteed the attention of the officials. People were trying to talk with her. She had been brought to the office of some man in the detention center whom she couldn't understand, who had tried repeatedly to talk with her. The second time, three others were in the room with her. One of them was an American priest, a young guy, about five feet, six inches tall with a short black beard, who had lost the crown of his hair. He had escorted her back down the hall to the women's compound, trying to talk with her in Spanish; she really couldn't make anything out.

María's ankle and left leg were in a cast. Every day, a woman in a white dress took her out for a walk down the hall. She talked all the time to the tall black woman whom she couldn't understand either. The woman in the white dress took her to a room where there was a set of steps. María had to try to climb up and down the steps while the woman held her elbow. It wasn't too bad because she smiled all the time and always patted her on the back. Then the black woman would kind of coo in her ear and pat her on the back also. After a couple of weeks of walking up and down the halls and going to the little room that had the steps, the woman in the white dress started taking her outside into the women's compound again.

María liked it there when it wasn't cold and raining. Usually, it was warm. She liked sitting with the other women even if she couldn't understand them. They were all in the same situation, and words didn't matter much between them anyway. Together they would often laugh at their attempts to communicate. They had a kind of sign language that enabled them to get around. María liked just about all the detainees except the big one who always hogged the food in the cafeteria line.

One day the woman in the white dress left her sitting on a chair alone in the room with the steps. When she came back into the room, María saw the American priest following her along with a nun wearing a white habit. She was a Mexican woman, very short and smiling. The priest said something to María and motioned to the nun. The nun approached María and sat down on the chair next to her.

"My name is Lucía," said the nun. María sat stunned to hear her own language, even in the strained nuances of a Mexican dialect. Tears filled her eyes, and she dropped her head in the embarrassment of overwhelming joy.

"My name is Lucía," repeated the nun. "What is your name?"

"María" was all she could manage.

"*`María,'*" repeated the nun. "Well, *María!* Father Michael Justice has asked me to come here to meet you today and to offer any help to you."

María Xquic raised her eyes for the first time to look at the sister.

"*Thank* you, sister," she said. "*Thank* you."

"Where are you from, María?" asked the nun.

"San Felipe," offered María. "San Felipe del Lago."

"Oh, *yes*," said the sister. "I know San Felipe. I visited there before. I lived in Santiago Atitlán for more than three years, and then I was in San Martín Comitán for five years before that. That's where I learned to speak Tzutujil, *no*? I left San Martín just a year or so before the big violence came to the lake."

The words of the nun were the warmest expressions that she had heard in weeks. Immediately, María felt giving herself in confidence to the sister without saying a word. There was just that immediate connection.

"María," said the nun, drawing the Tzutujil's attention to her face. "*Listen* to me—*please,* María. Do you know why you are here?"

"No," said María, shaking her head.

"You have no papers?" asked the nun.

"Papers?"

"A passport? Birth certificate? Visa?—*Any* official travel papers."

"No, nothing."

"Then you came into the country without papers, to the United States without official recognition, *no?*"

"I don't know," said María, failing to comprehend all this talk of papers. "I was forced to come across the river in the night."

"You were *forced?*" asked the sister.

"Yes," explained María. "By three people, to carry their drugs. Then, after we crossed the river, they left me."

"That is *bad*," said the nun. "That is very *bad* for you, María . . . Look, María, would you—I mean, can you tell me—why did you leave Guatemala, María?"

"The violence, the repression," said María. "I lost *everything*—my daughters, my sons, my husband—*everything!*"

Lucía paled at the explanation. "I'm so sorry, María. I don't know what to say."

"What do they want from me? Why am I here?" asked María.

"This is a detention center where they put people who come across illegally . . . without the right papers, without permission to come to the United States. They put the people here and other places like this," said Lucía.

"How long will I have to stay here?" asked María Xquic. "When can I get *out?*"

"You have to talk to the judge," said Lucía. "You have to tell him your story and ask him if you can stay in the country. You have to ask for asylum."

"I don't understand," said María.

"*`Asylum,'*" repeated Sister Lucía. "It's the only way you can stay in this country. You have to go to the judge and tell him your story and tell him that you can't go back to Guatemala, that you are afraid to go back. That's the only way."

María Xquic looked away from the nun. She was afraid of the prospect of going before a court in the United States. This was her fear, had been her fear if she had to go to the hospital, and now *this!* This was *it!* Noticeably, María began to tremble across her shoulders and down her arms. The sister reached over and took María's hand.

"I know that this is very difficult," she said. "It always is. But María, you are not *alone.* These people here, they can *help* you. There are people here who will go to the court with you and speak for you before the judge. All *you* have to do is to tell your story."

"But who will understand me?" María asked.

Sister Lucía looked surprised.

"But *I*, of course," she said. "*I* understand you. *I'll* be in the court to help translate for you. I speak Spanish, English, and this little bit of Tzutujil!" Sister Lucía's pride in her language facility was clear.

"What will you *say . . .?*" pressed María. "What will you say to the court?"

"What will I *say?*" repeated Lucía. "But only what you *tell* me to say! I will tell your story to the judge."

"*My* story?" María thought. She looked away once again as tears erupted from her eyes and spread down her cheeks. Sister Lucía squeezed her hand once more to reassure her.

"That's *okay,* María," said the nun. "I am here to help you. God above, He is here to help you. You can put your faith in God, that He is *here* for you."

Sister Lucía reached over and sponged up the tears from María's cheeks with a tissue that she had pulled from her sleeve.

"What's the matter?" asked Father Mike. "Is she *okay?*"

"Oh, yes," insisted Lucía. "She's only frightened and nervous, but she's okay. She has witnessed much tragedy, and this is very difficult for her."

Father Mike looked at the nurse in the white uniform.

"We can come back at another time," he offered, "but I think that the court is in a disposition to move quickly on her case. They believe they have a federal indictment here on drug charges. I would really like to get some kind of statement from her if we can."

"She says that she was forced to bring drugs across the river by three other people," said Lucía. "They grabbed the drugs and ran off apparently and left her behind."

"Oh *boy!*" said the priest. "All the more reason we need to talk with her now, if she can."

Father Mike moved closer to María and laid his hand on her shoulder as Lucía passed the tissue to the distraught Tzutujil woman.

"Ask her . . ." said Father Mike. "Ask her if she will give us a little bit of her story now. Maybe that will get her to open up a bit. Tell her we can step out of the room if she prefers and leave you and the nurse to help her."

"That might be better," agreed Lucía. "I'll ask her."

The nun accepted a chair that Father Mike was bringing her from across the room and sat down directly in front of María. Then she reached over again and took María's hand.

"María," she said. "María, *listen* to me! Try to tell me a little of your story. That is very important. Can you try to do that? Just a little?"

María looked up at Sister Lucía and then burst into inconsolable sobs. The nurse winced and looked up at the priest, pleadingly.

"This isn't going to work, I think," she said. Perhaps it is better if you come back. Maybe give her the weekend to think about it and then come back on Monday or Tuesday."

Father Mike was a little irritated at the suggestion, interested as he was in helping the Maya woman if he could but concerned about an already tight schedule the following week.

"Well, if we have to . . ." he said.

"Yes, I think that is best," said the nurse. "She is still recovering from the surgery and is very nervous around others. I think that will give her some important time for reflection."

"Perhaps you're right," said the priest reluctantly. "Okay, Lucía?"

"Yes," said the nun. "I think that is a better idea. You just call me when you are ready. I can come back."

"*María!*" returned Lucía to María. "*Look, María!* You rest now and think about what we have told you. We are here only to help you. Why don't you think about what you want to say over the next two or three days. We'll come back on Monday or Tuesday, and then we can talk. And then we can talk, *okay?*"

María never looked up but nodded slowly as she pressed the tissue to her eyes. *What will you tell them, María Xquic de Xoy? What will you tell them that justícia norteamericana will hear and understand? What will you tell them, María Xquic? Will you tell them that your son ripped the heads off two subversives with his bare hands? That Ana Fabiola lies restless in her grave, hungry yet for the little nuggets of hard candy? That your husband was disappeared, the laughing stock of the evangelicals? What justice, María Xquic? Who will believe a poor indigena? What will you tell them, María Xquic—that it is because of your clumsy foot? That the compas who went upon the mountain were violated and slaughtered like silly swine, that little Manuel who was chasing his cat when Donaldo who wouldn't cross the river so he shot himself when you were in the river with Carlos, the compa? What justice, María Xquic de Xoy? Qué justícia norteamericana, that a poor indigena?*

Because what will you show the judge, María Xquic?—where he hurt you? the elotes chicos swelling in your belly? When they came for Lucita, Lucita María that the tiny little huipil that Lucita where she was taken from the sisters of Antigua and . . . but what justice, María Xquic de Xoy? that Lucita, who would rise to make the tortillas when she said, "I—not I, because we don't have to take this any more" that the military commissioner, sweet little Lucita in Antigua, Antigua de los Caballeros de Santiago where Lucita María, where Lucita . . . what possible justice? . . .

For more than three days and into the fourth, María's mind was flooded with such uncertainties and confusion, the same confusion with which she anticipated the meeting with Father Mike, the Mexican sister, and the attorney. If she had to tell her story to the judge, then why first the nun and the attorney. It didn't make sense, and María Xquic felt compromised and angry.

"Is this where I meet the *judge?"* she asked Sister Lucita as they walked down the corridor to the attorney's office.

"No," explained the nun. "We are meeting with the attorney today. This is where I will translate your story."

"I thought I was supposed to tell my story to the judge—the North American judge," said María.

"You will," said María, "but you will have to tell your story first to the attorney."

María Xquic's lips pursed tightly, and she turned away her face, an expression of frustration that Sister Lucía recognized from her own experiences among Tzutujil women recounting their little domestic horrors while washing their clothes at the *pilas*. Lucía had assisted one other asylum hearing, but it had been unsuccessful. She sensed it best to let María feel her way along the process, to make her *own* assessment of the players—herself, the attorney, Father Mike, and all—that if she felt too intimidated, the attorney wouldn't be able to get the information he needed to represent her adequately.

"Sister, come in," said the attorney, in a friendly but subdued tone as the two women entered his office. Father Mike, who had arrived only moments before, stood up and approached the nun and María, escorting them to two rather questionable folding chairs in front of the attorney's desk.

"Sister Lucía and María," said the priest. "Let me introduce you to Mr. Carlos Figuera. Mr. Figuera is an attorney here in Harlingen who has agreed to represent you, María, in your hearing."

Slowly, the nun translated for María who listened intently and then nodded solemnly at the attorney.

Carlos Figuera was no stranger to Guatemalan asylum cases. He had represented perhaps ten or twelve Guatemalans in "hearings on the merits" over the past five or six years. While he was well aware of their plight, he had made only the tourist circuit throughout Guatemala. In fact, what had attracted him initially was the possibility of quick turn around on some investments. His introduction to asylum work was a Guatemalan case involving a Guatemalan business acquaintance. The refugee project in the Valley had coerced him into taking the other cases over the years. As a rather hard-nosed attorney, however, he was frustrated that he had not been more successful in his represent-tations, only one of his clients in the past having been awarded asylum.

"María," said Figuera, "the purpose of our meeting this morning is for me to hear your story about coming to the United States and what happened to you in Guatemala that made you have to leave."

María turned to Lucía awaiting her translation.

"Mr. Figuera wants to know why you came to the United States," said the nun.

"I *had* to come," said María.

"You `had to come'?" said the attorney. Lucía continued to translate between them.

"Yes," said María.

"Why?"

"They *made* me come. They had a *gun,* and they forced me to come with them. I didn't want to come, but they *made* me."

"*Who . . . who* made you? *Who* made you come?"

"*They* did . . . the man and the woman."

"`The man and the woman' . . . *what* `man' and *what* `woman'?"

"The two Mexicans, the two Mexicans who made me go with them."

"Why did they make you go with them?"

"I don't know?"

"You don't *know?* You don't *know* why they made you go with them?"

"No."

"María," said the attorney cautiously, *"Look!* I have a copy of a report from the people who arrested you. They say in this r*eport* . . . ." Figuera methodically opened a fresh manila folder and flipped through the corners of the police report. "They say *here* . . . they say, María, that you are part of some Mexican *drug* ring . . . some people who have been bringing illegal drugs into the United States. What can you tell me about *this?* Is this *true?"*

María was deeply embarrassed by the suggestion that she had anything to do with drugs. That was something the *ladinos* do and the bad *indigenas* at that—the shopkeepers along the highway who sell to the tourists, the prostitutes, and the others. The more she thought about it, the angrier she became. She turned her head away from the attorney and Lucía. For a moment the room was silent.

"*María!*" called Lucía. "María, you can tell Señor Figuera the truth. He wants only to *help* you, but you have to tell him the *truth.*"

María continued to look away. She was most uncomfortable with the whole proceeding. She wished she could talk with Sylvia. She wished she were back at the clinic in Comitán. She could only imagine their fear and frustration in not knowing what had happened to her. She was never comfortable confiding in a *ladino*—Guatemalan or otherwise, and there was something about this American lawyer she didn't like—the messy office, his condescend-ing air of friendship, whatever. Lucía reached over and touched María's arm. She had correctly interpreted the Tzutujil woman's reserve.

"It's *okay,* María," said the nun. "You can *talk* to this man."

María paused for another moment, framing her response carefully so as to avoid any misunderstanding. "I never helped *anybody* with drugs."

"What about the *belt* that was tied around your waist," pressed the attorney. He had to clear up the obvious obstacles to any hope of an asylum case. He had to get past this drug thing. María was silent.

"María . . ." said Figuera. "The report describes a belt with knots of plastic sacks still tied to them. Apparently, the rest of these, these *bags* had been cut away. What was in the *bags*, María?"

"I don't know," she explained.

"You don't *know* . . ." repeated the lawyer. "Well, can you describe what was in them."

" . . . Yes."

"Well—"

"It was some kind of powder, maybe white powder."

"Heroin . . . cocaine?" said the lawyer. "Did you ever hear anyone around you say what was *in* the bags?"

" . . . No."

Figuera paused for a moment, glancing casually at the priest and the nun. He would give his client some relief from the drug issue.

"Well, María," he said, twisting a freshly sharpened yellow pencil between his fingers. "Why don't we start at the beginning. Where is your home in Guatemala?"

"San Felipe," said María in a subdued tone that failed to communicate to the lawyer.

"I beg your pardon," he said.

"San Felipe," repeated María, "San Felipe del Lago."

"*S-a-n-F-e-l-i-p-eeee,*" the attorney scrawled across the top of his legal pad. "Has that always been your home, `San Felipe'?"

"Yes."

"And you are married."

"Yes," said María as tears began to fill the corners of her eyes.

"And what is your husband's name?"

"Andres . . . Andres Menchu Xoy."

"And what does *he* do, Andres . . . *campesino*? Farmer?"

"No."

"Farmer?"

"No, priest."

"Priest?"

"Yes, priest."

"What *kind* of `priest,' Catholic or Protestant . . . *evangelical*, that is?"

María looked toward Lucía.

"What was the question?" Lucía asked the lawyer.

"Catholic or *evangelical*, I think they call it down there.

What kind of *`preacher'—`priest,'* whatever?"

Lucía turned to María and whispered an explanation under her

breath. María looked surprised and then shook her head.

"Neither," said Lucía. "He's *brujo*."

"`*Brujo*'? A *brujo!*" said Figuera. "Ooooh-*kay!*"

María caught something of a smirk in the corner of his mouth that made her angry. There wasn't much more she felt willing to share with this man.

"S*ooooo—, María*," said the lawyer, "you're married to a *brujo* in San Felipe."

María looked down at the floor, unwilling to accept any besmirching or brutality to her husband's memory.

"Well now, María," continued the attorney. "Do you have a family, any *children?*"

"Yes."

"And how many?"

"Five. Five children," said María as a tear slipped down her cheek.

"Five, you said?" asked the attorney, barely able to understand and looking toward Lucía for clarification.

"Five, yes," said the nun.

"F-*i-v-e-c-h-i-l-d-r-e-nnnn,*" wrote the attorney. "Very good. Now, María, please give me their names and ages."

Lucía translated.

"Miguel Mapa—twenty . . . *no!* twenty-two."

"Twenty or twenty-two?" asked Figuera, pausing for her reflection.

"Twenty-two," confirmed María.

"*T-w-e-n-t-y-t-w-ooooo*," drawled the attorney. "It is so important to be *accurate* in all these little details . . . go ahead."

"Tanolito, twenty," continued María, "then, Lucita María, seventeen—*no, eighteen.* Ana Fabiola, fourteen. And Manuel Xoy Menchu, eight."

The attorney took the translation from Lucía and wrote it carefully onto his tablet. "Okay, I think I've got it."

"How is she doing?" asked the attorney of Lucía.

"Okay, I guess," said the nun.

"So we can go on? We can continue, *no*?"

"Yes, I think so," said Lucía.

"Okay," said the attorney, "because I have to get into some pretty rough questions here, *okay?"*

"Well," said the nun as she looked toward the subdued client.

The attorney rolled around in his chair and turned directly toward María, motioning Lucía to move her chair in closer between the client and his desk. "I don't want to misinterpret any of her answers at this point."

Lucía angled her chair so that her knees all but touched the front of the desk.

"Where is your family now?" asked Figuera.

"They're in Guatemala," interjected Lucía. The attorney frowned.

"That's what she *told* me," said the nun.

"Well, that's fine, but I need to hear it from María herself," insisted Figuera. "Please translate the question."

Lucía turned her face to María and posed the question.

"Where is your family?" asked Lucía.

"What?" asked María.

"Your family, María?" explained Lucía. "Where is your family *now?"*

"My family, my husband, my children—each of my daughters and sons . . . but Miguel—*dead."* And then she paused, "No . . . They're . . . they're *all, all dead.*"

"All your family—your husband, *he's d*ead?"

"Yes."

"Your *daughters*—they're deceased as well?" Lucía translated.

"Yes," muttered María.

Figuera paused for a moment to allow María to catch her composure. "And your sons, María . . . what about *them?* What about your *sons?"*

María could only nod as the tears flowed freely down her face. Even hope for Manuel had shaken free in the trembling of her spirit.

"What *happened?"* asked the attorney. "Can you *tell* me?"

"It was the war," offered Lucía. "They were all killed in the fighting."

"Well, I understand," said Figuera, "but she can't win asylum on that. I've got to have something more. I know it's hard, but I have to hear from her something that I can reconstruct for the court, or she's probably facing some hard time in a federal penitentiary."

The nun bit her lower lip and stared at the attorney. Certainly, he couldn't be serious, but then . . .

"María," Lucía said to the Mayan. "You'll have to tell him more. He has to know more about what happened or you *might* . . . well, he just has to hear more of your story."

María closed her eyes and took a long breath. "I left Guatemala because of the repression. The military came to our village, and many people began disappearing."

"Why did the military come to your village?" asked Figuera, picking up on her opening to probe further into her past.

"They said that we were working with the guerrillas, that some of us in the town were subversives."

"`Subversives'?"

"Yes."

"Were there guerrillas operating around San Felipe?"

"Yes . . ."

"What were they doing?"

"Organizing the people . . ."

"What do you mean, `organizing the people'?"

"Trying to recruit the people, trying to turn us against the government."

"Why was *your* family attacked—were they working with the guerrillas?"

"No! Of course not!"

"Who attacked your family, María?" continued Figuera. "Was it the military or the guerrillas?"

"The army," said María.

"How do you know? How do you know it was the army?"

"Because I saw Miguel Mapa and Tano talking with the soldiers."

"Talking?"

"Yes, they were talking with the soldiers, and then they just disappeared."

"Had your sons—these are both your *older* sons?—Had they done anything against the army? Anything to make the army target them?"

"No, *of course not!* They worked *for* the army."

"`For the army'? How? How do you mean, `worked *for* the army'?"

"They were in the civil patrol."

"I don't understand—what's the *`civil patrol'?*" asked Figuera, feigning ignorance.

"The `civil *defense* patrol,'" explained María. "Every man had to work in the civil patrol."

"What *kind* of work?" asked Figuera.

"Well," said María, "they had to patrol the town to keep out the guerrillas."

"So they *patrolled?*"

"Yes."

"Well, did they ever do anything to make the army mad at them?"

"No," said María. "In fact, Miguel Mapa was a leader."

"How did he become a leader in the civil patrol?"

"Well," explained María, "he went out on patrol and captured . . . he brought in two guerrillas."

"You hesitated for a moment, María," said the attorney. "What were you about to say?"

"*Nothing*," snipped María quietly almost under her breath.

"*Look, María!*" said Figuera, "You really have to tell me what you know so that I can help you in the court."

Lucía tried to soften the tone of the attorney's admonition, but María could understand very well his inflections.

"They *killed* them," said María, just above a whisper.

"They *`what'?* They `*killed* them'?" pressed Figuera.

"Yes."

"Your two *sons?*"

". . . No."

"*Who*, then . . . who *killed* them, these `*guerrillas.*'"

"Miguel . . . Miguel Mapa."

"Miguel Mapa killed these two guerrillas, *no?*"

". . . Yes."

"Did Miguel Mapa . . . did he know them?"

María dropped her eyes.

"María, I'm just trying to find some reason why the army would want to attack your family," explained Figuera. "Now, it might be important to know if he knew these, these two `guerrillas,' because if he knew them, maybe there are some other people who might have had *reasons* to attack him and the rest of your family."

"I think so," said María.

"You `*think*' so," pressed the attorney. "You `*think' so*, or you `*know' so?*"

"Miguel, he knew them," said María softly. "They were two boys from San Jorge."

"San Jorge?" asked Figuera. "That's a town close to San Felipe?"

María nodded.

"Were they guerrillas, these two boys from San Jorge?"

"I guess so," said María softly.

"You `guess so'?"

"Yes . . ."

"María," said Figuera, "you say that it was the military that attacked you, but the way I see it, it was the *guerrillas* who did it."

"No," said María, shaking her head. "It *couldn't* have been the guerrillas."

"*No!*" interrupted the attorney. "Now *listen* to me! Of *course,* it was the guerrillas—*couldn't* have been the military! No *way!*"

María looked aside, away from the faces of the people around her. She was deeply insulted by the contradictions to her story.

"*Look,*" said Figuera. "I hear what you're *saying,* and I know that's what you *believe.* But María, let me show you something. Come over here for a minute."

Lucía signalled María to follow Figuera into the next room. Father Mike and the nun slipped in behind the Mayan woman to give her the reassurance of their presence in what was obviously becoming a very confrontive encounter with the attorney.

"*Look . . .!*" said Figuera, motioning to a table piled high with black, three-inch binders of photocopy. "See *that?* That's the Guatemala `theme packet.' That's the *whole history* of *violence* in your country from 1981 to the present. *Lookahere,* let me show you how it works. See *this?*"

Figuera lifted the top binder and thumbed through the pages. "See *that?* . . . `forced recruitment by the guerrillas' . . . `persecution of the church' . . . `guerrilla attacks on non-combatants' . . . the *whole story!* Now what we do, what we'll do with your story—and you've given me enough, *okay! Trust* me!—What we'll do with *your* story is pull up articles from these newspaper articles, book chapters—from all this *stuff*—we'll pull up stories similar to yours that will show the judge that what you've told him is supported by years of research. Then, I've got a guy—I have this professor over in Edinburg—he knows all *about* this stuff. He'll come into the court with us, and he'll corroborate everything you say, *no kidding!* We've got a strong case, but you've *got* to say that it was the *guerrillas.* If you say that, then we've got a case for `imputed political opinion'—that you're anti-communist, that your sons were in the civil patrol fighting the communists and that you supported the government, and that's why the guerrillas attacked you and wiped out your family. You don't have a thing to *worry* about, María, but you've got to keep your story *straight!* You just talk with Sister Lucía here, she'll help you to understand and get it right. You got any *scars?*"

María had drifted off. She hadn't heard the question or anything else Figuera had said and was startled when the attorney took her hands by the wrists and began to turn her arms over to examine them. She flashed a look of horror at Lucía.

"*`Scars,'*" he explained, "you know, places where they cut you or *hurt* you?"

María still didn't understand.

"It's better if you can show the judge where they hurt you," said Figuera, a little louder. "No, *I'll* tell you all something, for *sure!"*

The attorney looked around him to secure the attention of the priest and the nun. "I had one of these hearings—" he said, releasing María's wrists, "Oh, I don't know—maybe six or seven months ago now. He was Cuban. *Hell,* he had a little *cut*—a little scar tissue on the back of his hand, *right?* Well, *hell!* We played that little scar for all it was worth, how he'd been cut by a bayonet trying to escape one of Castro's *firing squads!* I mean, we had that judge in the palm of our hands. He had asylum in fifteen minutes. But I'll tell you something *else.* I know another attorney who was working a Salvadoran case `pro bono'—just last *year,* just about a *year* ago—I mean, this guy was a *sight.* He'd been tortured and all and all broken up! *Hell,* he'd been *all* cut up! We even had him take his shirt off right there in the court. Think it meant a *thing? Shit!* The judge found him `uncredible' and had him shipped out in two weeks. He almost threw him back in the *hole,* know what *I me*an! I've been thinking about writing one of those `My Turn' columns, you know, that they publish in *Newsweek* or *Time* or whatever. Call it the `*Tissue* Test for Asylum.' If you're Cuban or Nicaraguan, all you need is a fresh hanky in the hearing and you're *in, right?* But if you're Salvadoran or Guatemalan, it better be *scar* tissue and it better be *fresh!* Know what I mean? *Shit!"*

Figuera erupted in a high-pitched, staccato laughter, turning toward Lucia and Father Mike for their approval. The priest, who had been silent throughout the proceedings, motioned for the attorney to step outside the office.

"What do you think you're *doing!*" flashed the priest in anger.

"What do you *mean?*" reacted Figuera.

"*I'll* tell you what *I* mean!" snapped Father Mike, rising to meet the attorney face to face. "You've got a *woman* in there who's completely lost and *panicked!*"

"*No!*" retorted the lawyer, stabbing his finger into the shoulder of the priest. "*I'll* tell *you* what I *got* in there—I got a *woman* who's been caught *red-handed trafficking in drugs* and who's looking at *thirty years in the federal penitentiary!* Now, I don't really give a shit *what* her story is! Oh, we're gonna go through the *motions* and all, but I'll tell you *this:* the best thing we can hope for is to get her shipped out of here because Judge Harwell's gonna find her uncredible no matter *what* she has to say. She could come into his court with th' goddamned assassin at her *heals,* and with the evidence *he's* got, Harwell would just laugh in her face as the marshals were dragging her *away!*"

María had not slept well at all the night after the interview with the attorney. She had overheard the argument in the next room between Figuera and the priest. Her memory of it was so unsettling; there was too much *fury* and *uncertainty*. The air about her seemed heavy, and María felt her lungs grow cloudy. Her lethargic breathing became a strain. When she reached the door at the foot of the stairwell that would take her outside into the exercise yard for the women, she felt edgy and nervous. In her mind, she kept reviewing the argument between the lawyer and the priest—not the words, which she hadn't comprehended, anyway—but the *anger* and the *hostility,* that was *clear.* Then she understood: the lawyer didn't trust *her* anymore than she trusted *him.*

The detainee ahead of her pushed open the door for María who had decided to use her crutches for the walk up and down the stairs. Out in the yard she would leave them beside a chair and extend her walk to three laps around the yard before sitting down to rest her ankle. Her group of sixty or more would have thirty minutes in the yard to work out. Most preferred to spend their time at the fence talking to the men. Husbands and wives had been separated, and it was rare when they had the same exercise period. Most couples had to communicate through intermediaries who would pass messages back and forth. Younger women would gather in groups of twos and threes to joke or flirt collectively with counterparts in the male compound.

María found a chair close by the door which was usually occupied by the time she made her way through the group. The vacancy was a surprise, and she pushed along hurriedly not to lose the opportunity. She sat down for a moment, securing the tops of the crutches across the back of the chair. Slowly, the women milled around the yard, and María felt relaxed. It always made her nervous to walk with the crutches up and down the stairs. It was good to sit down and collect herself. The grey drizzle had subsided in the past few minutes, and even the saturated clouds seemed to be breaking up a little. The women had fanned out into their little groups, and the men on the other side of the fence had gravitated toward the women. María scanned the fence line, and then focused further into the compound on a column of new arrivals meandering out the door from the men's dormitory. Even in something of a slump, one man stood out from the orange-clad group a head taller than the others. When he turned around, María recognized the unmistakable high cheekbones and wide forehead of Miguel Mapa.

Chapter 33

The Magic Kingdom

The ears were too big—even the smallest set of the "Mouse-ka-ears" still slipped down over her forehead and threatened to roll off every time little Olivia María turned her head.

"You're so *silly, chica!*" chided her mother, Patricia Dona.

"You're so *silly, Olimía!*" playfully echoed her older sister, Carmela Teresa Altapaz. The two girls nudged each other in a mock rumble and quickly turned their big grins and wide eyes back out the window of the monorail car cruising slowly across the lagoon toward the Magic Kingdom.

It was the girls' first vacation in Disney World. Six months of fancy and endless nights of tremulous dreams were rewarded now beyond their wildest expectations. All the commotion of the preparations, the scramble at the airport to find her mother's lost diamond and gold bracelet in the bottom of the military car, their father's unexpected delay from the National Palace that had grounded the whole jet airliner for more than forty-five minutes—all the frustrations were behind them. The children were sailing along high above the zebras and antelopes cavorting below them. As the sleek, futuristic monorail turned into the glinting sunlight, ahead of them towered the blue and white spires of Cinderella's Castle.

Patricia Dona was almost relaxed, the bearer—as usual—of all the paraphernalia that came with orchestrating a family outing with two children and one of the up-and-coming military personalities for a husband.

"Don't put your face up against the glass, *chica, mi amor!*" admonished Patricia Dona. "You don't know who might have wiped their *noses* on the same *glass!* Sit *back* some!"

The five-year-old pouted as tears swelled up in her eyes, and then suddenly, she exploded into convulsions of screams. Sister Tita laughed at her young sister's expense, covering her mouth in mischievous mirth.

"*Look, Olimía!*" called her mother, trying to distract the aggravated child whose histrionic little outbursts were beginning to irritate others. "*Look,* sweetheart! There it *is!* Cinderella's Magic *Castle!*"

The announcement brought on an elfen outcry. Other children rushed to Olimía's side of the car, each eager to catch a first glimpse of the enchanted shrine. The little boys and girls cheered and rushed into the aisles against the advice of the audio recording urging caution as the monorail eased into its berth.

Slowly, the cars pulled into the station and came to a stop. Mothers grabbed at big bags and bundles and little hands and arms as the children scampered out the doors, racing to be first in line at the many rides and attractions.

"*Carmelita! Olimía!*" called Patricia Dona. "Be *careful, niñas*! Wait for your father and *me!*"

The two little girls, giddy with delight, turned in deference to their mother's call.

"Hurry! Hurry, Mómi!" they cried.

"Okay, *chicas!*" replied the mother, almost dropping one of her bags. "Please, Federico! *Please!*" Patricia Dona turned to her husband who had slipped into the aisle behind her and handed him her bulky carry sack with the children's hats and towels for use on the beach at the lagoon later in the afternoon.

"*Cómo no!*" replied her husband accommodatingly, as he accepted the bag of little domestics. He had been distracted by the contours of a deeply tanned, young blonde wearing sheared off blue jean shorts and tank top who was just stepping out of the car ahead of them. It was the second time that morning he had spied her. That was the kind of "fairy godmother" he had had in mind as he envisioned the attributes of the Magic Kingdom. He was rewarded further when he caught the profile of her ample breasts. "*Bonus!*" he said to himself, just out of his wife's earshot.

"Let's *go!*" cried Patricia Dona. "*Federico!* The *girls!*"

"*Right!*" he answered. "*Right,* the *girls!* Let's *go!*" Federico followed the North American with his eyes until she disappeared in the crowd. "It's a good thing—*vacation!*" he thought to himself.

The family made its way down the flight of steps to the lower platform of the station and out onto the walkway that opened onto "Main Street, U.S.A." On both sides of the street, brightly painted store fronts, bristling with all the busy knickknacks, fringe, and gewgaws of the Victorian nineteenth century, lured the passersby with sweets, souvenirs, and entertainment. Vendor's popcorn on the corners competed with the strawberry, chocolate, and vanilla ice cream cones dipped straight from the organ grinder's freezer. The bells of a

San Francisco trolley alerted wayward pedestrians as it slowly glided along its tracks in the center of the thoroughfare. As they slurped their ice cream cones, the little sisters were startled by the eruption of a Dixieland band just behind the trolley. Its red and white-striped members were riding in the jump seat of a model-A Ford. The driver squeezed off honks on his horn in time to the festive rhythm, and Carmelita and Omilía soon caught the spirit, their little "Mouse-ka-ears" bobbing up and down to the cadences.

"Oh, *Federico! Look* at them!" exclaimed Patricia Dona. "They're so *precious!*"

"Yes," acknowledged Federico Altapaz. ". . . so precious, *sure!*"

The smartly groomed colonel, in his tight-fitting leather jacket, green alligator pullover, and starched khaki pants, was already getting bored, and he looked beyond the fond expressions of Patricia Dona, his twenty-nine-year old third wife and her two children, hoping to catch another glance at the well-endowed North American mother who had slipped out of sight minutes before at the terminal. Without such distractions, it would be a long day before his appointment.

It was just another bright, clear morning in Orlando, but it had been raining for more than three days in the Rio Grande Valley. On the morning of the fourth, thunderstorms that earlier had drifted across the Valley erupted in a deluge in Harlingen, Texas. That was the same morning Carlos Figuera and Sister Lucía escorted María Xquic de Xoy into the Office of the Department of Justice for her merit hearing. María was soaked by the heavy rain before she had been able to make her way across the compound from the women's dormitory to the attorney's car. She entered the courtroom shivering, wearing Figuera's coat across her shoulders.

"She's very upset," whispered Lucía to Figuera, momentarily forgetting the language barrier separating them from their client. "She's really worried about something. She told me she was afraid to go in."

"Well," allowed Figuera, "that's not particularly surprising, given what she's facing. She might find herself on the way to the county jail before the day's over if the judge decides to hold her over for any more DEA examination. Her troubles might be just *beginning!* Did you have a chance to go over her story with her one more time?"

"Well, sort of, but that's just it," said Lucía. "I hope we don't have a problem there. It was confusing to her, and she wouldn't stop shaking the whole time I was with her. I thought she was going to be sick, so I had to stop."

The hearing room was cramped. Three solid, oak straight-backed benches—more like primitive church pews, were positioned at the rear of the room and so closely together as to jam the average person's knees. In front of the benches stretched a varnished plywood partition, separating the spectators from the clients and their attorneys. Up-scale a cut or two from the benches behind them, two six-foot long, dark oak tables served as desks for the two attorneys. Mounted on the respondent attorney's desk were three mikes, one for the lawyer, another for his client, and a third for use by any additional witnesses. In front of the two desks loomed the raised platform and judge's bench, the same dark oak veneer as the two attorneys' tables. To the right was a computer console, a microphone, and a padded swivel desk chair for the interpreter. On the wall behind the judge's bench hung, quite noticeably off center to the right, an extruded plastic, four-foot wide circular seal of the U.S. Department of Justice. There were no windows to relieve the harsh glare from florescent lighting fixtures lined up across the ceiling, illuminating every smudge on the industrial grey carpet across the floor. The drab, institutional chamber was empty as Maria's party entered the door.

"Well," said Figuera, "I guess it's always good to be a little early. With traffic like it is on the highway coming in sometimes, you never know. I guess we can go ahead and sit down at the desk."

María and Lucía followed behind the attorney who laid his briefcase across the desk and motioned for the two to join him on the right side. María was trying to shake her hair dry from the drenching earlier in the morning, still worried about what her disheveled appearance might mean to the judge. Figuera looked up at the clock to the left and checked the time on his own watch. As he was starting to sit down, the door to the judge's chambers opened, and a middle-aged woman came in and looked around.

"Are you Carlos Figuera," she asked, "the attorney for the respondent?"

"Yes," said the attorney, "Carlos Figuera, *Señora.*"

Figuera stepped around the table and approached her to shake her hand.

"Thank you, Mr. Figuera," she said. "My name is Alicia Hernandez, Judge Harwell's secretary. Have you seen the others?"

"The trial attorney?"

"*Sí,*" she affirmed.

"Well, no," said Figuera. "We just arrived ourselves, and no one else was here as we came in just now. If I remember correctly, Mr. Martin is the Service attorney for this hearing."

"Oh! Well, he was," said Mrs. Hernandez. "However, he's in San Francisco on assignment. I believe Ms. Leasure has been assigned to the case—Ms. Barbara Leasure from Brownsville."

"*Ms. Leasure?* Well, *this* should be interesting," said Figuera to himself. He had worked opposite her once before on a Central American case. "Pure *bitch!* Pure, twenty-four karat, gold-plated *bitch!"*

"And our hearing?" asked Figuera, "We're on time today?"

"As far as I know," said Mrs. Hernandez. "Judge Harwell will be in shortly. He's reviewing some of the documents for the case."

"Very well," said the attorney.

"Please have a seat," said the clerk. "He'll be with you very soon."

Mrs. Hernandez smiled graciously and stepped back out of the courtroom.

"Well," said the attorney. "I guess we wait."

María was chilled from the rain, but her trembling stemmed from her growing nervousness about the hearing and the shock of discovering Miguel Mapa in the compound. *What could it mean—Miguel Mapa in the detention center? Why would he possibly come to be in the camp if he weren't following her? Surely, he had been sent to Texas because she was here. He must have been following her all the way from Mexico? But where? Had she seen him before?*

María Xquic's mind raced back over the past days of her flight to Texas, back even further to their encounters along the way to the basilica. *Surely, it wasn't Ricardo and Sylvia? Did she have an enemy among those who had seemed her friends? That must be it—someone was an oreja, a spy reporting on her! She was right, after all. She just knew she was! Someone was working for the militaries. Someone knew her every movement! Someone had been spying on her and knew where to find her, even in the refugee camp, even in—that's it! It was the old woman in Tecún Umán! Of course, who else would have had any reason to turn her in? Had she not been warned in her dreams?*

"*Ohhh!*" cried María, loudly enough to alarm Lucía sitting across from the attorney.

"*María?*" she asked. Lucía looked across at María who was embarrassed that she had revealed her anxiety.

"María? Are you *okay?*" asked Lucía.

María Xquic nodded her head slightly and looked away. The nun rose and moved her chair to the other side so that she might sit next to the Mayan obviously disturbed by the whole situation of the morning, the place, the insecurity of the hearing, and her mounting terror of deportation. Lucía crossed herself as she prayed silently that María might not be turned over to the Federal authorities. She hadn't mentioned anything of that possibility, fearful that María might panic and become confused about her story.

"You're okay, *really?*" insisted Lucía.

"Yes," she nodded. "I'm okay. I'm okay." *But if he is here, then why? Why would Miguel Mapa come all the way to the United States? If the militaries wanted her, why send Miguelito? Why, if not to attack her, if not to keep her silent before the American authorities? But how could he possibly know about her hearing? About her request for asylum? And where is he now? Could he be here in the court this morning? Could he be here to speak against his own mother? Was he . . . was he here in this building, this very chamber? Was he possibly here, there—just in the next room?*

As she stared at the door to the judge's office, María began trembling with the thought of the presence of Miguel Mapa, and Lucía reached around her and squeezed her shoulders.

"It's okay," reassured the nun. "We'll be starting *soon*. Don't *worry!* You just have to remember your *story*, María."

Her story! Her story! *What* story? What story could she tell but her own? What story could she possibly relate but the murder of her precious children, the disappearance of her husband, Andres, and the awful flight over the mountain! What story? What other story was there but her *own* story! She would tell her story, all right! The only story!—the story of the destruction of her family and of their village, how the militaries had torn her family apart and had driven her fleeing for her life. And if Miguel Mapa, if he said one word—even one word against her and their family, then she would rise to tell him to his face and before this American judge that he was a conspirator against them all, that all that they had suffered was because of Miguel Mapa Xoy, a traitor to all the Tzutujiles and their families. *What* story, *indeed!*

"*Whew-eee!*" exclaimed Lieutenant Montez.

"*Ahhh! Chingada!*" echoed Lieutenant Gonzalo. "*Qué lástima!* What a *place!*"

The two Guatemalan officers stepped out of the Disney shuttle at the entrance to the Reception Office at Disney World.

"Is this *incredible, huh?*" said Montez.

"This is *worth* it, *no?*" responded Gonzalo.

"There's gotta be some women in here looking for a *good time, no?*"

"Check out the one ahead—the one up there behind the desk."

"*Jesus!* No *wonder* they put *her* at the front desk!"

"Well, as soon as we check in, I'm going to find me a bar and get drunk, *okay?* There's gotta be more women like *her* who aren't working so *late!*"

"Sounds like a plan, *amigo!*"

The two had arrived on the afternoon Greyhound bus from Columbus, Georgia. The trip to the resort climaxed their training for the past eighteen months at Fort Benning's "School of the Americas." They were two of seventeen Guatemalan unit leaders who had completed intermediate training in counter-insurgency and security operations, complements of the United States Army and the American tax payers. All graduates enjoyed a four-day R&R at Disney World, also at U.S. tax payers' expense. It was just one more part of the Army's "Operation Friendly Neighbors" designed to ingratiate client forces to the south who were already favorable or who might otherwise be susceptible—at a *future* date—to U.S. "influence in the region."

Neither Montez or Gonzalo had been in Florida before, and they were looking forward to taking the bus to Miami after their fling at the Disney resort. On the ride over, they had sifted through the Disney tourist packet, all the brochures and schedules for various activities in the theme parks.

"Check out *this* mama!" said Montez as the two spotted a young bride who had left her husband with their van while she stepped inside to register.

"*Hey!*" said Gonzalo as he nudged his partner. "Take a look at that *van!* What does it say, "J-u-s-t m-a-r-r-i-e-d . . . Just *married!*"

"*Shit!* She hasn't even been *gored* good!"

"Oh, *yeah?* Give the stud out there in the car about another half *hour!* He's steaming up the windows *already!*"

"Maybe we'll get a room next to *theirs, no?*"

"*Shit!* We wouldn't get a minute's sleep!"

"Well, then, maybe you could take his place when he gets *tired!*"

"*Hey! That's* a possibility! Why don't you go ask *him*, and I'll check with *her!*"

"*Shit,* man! Let's flip a *coin!*"

"*Next!*" said the attentive, bubbly receptionist. "Welcome to Disney World! How can I help you!"

"*Tell* her, *man!*" whispered Gonzalo under his breath as he jabbed his unit buddy in the back ribs.

María Xquic was worried. They had been waiting for almost an hour when Mrs. Hernandez returned into the courtroom.

"I'm sorry, Mr. Figuera," she said. "Judge Harwell just heard from Ms. Leasure. She is running very late. Apparently, she was in a meeting in Brownsville and had completely forgotten about the hearing this morning. She asked the judge not to postpone the hearing, though, if that's agreeable to you."

"Forgot the *hearing!*" said Figuera. "Forgot the *hearing!* That's *incredible!* And now she's going to be another forty—forty-five minutes getting here, and she wants us to agree to continuing the *hearing?*"

"No, she said she's already on the way."

"That's still the most *arrogant* thing I've ever heard in my *life!*"

"I beg your pardon, Mr. Figuera, but I have to let the judge know something now."

"Well, what about his docket this *afternoon*—can he suspend his afternoon hearing?"

"I don't know, sir."

"Well, I have Professor Johnson coming all the way from Edinburg in about fifteen minutes for expert witness testimony. We've gone to a lot of trouble for this hearing. I really think we have a strong case here, and it's just *incredible* that we would have to cut the hearing short just because Service can't get its act together."

"Mr. Figuera," said the sympathetic secretary, "I'm sorry for the delay, and I can understand your difficulty. All I can do is relay your concern to the judge. I'm sure he will work out something."

At that moment the door to the chamber opened and in walked a tall, bearded cerebral type in a dark grey suit carrying a large catalog satchel bulging with printed materials. Figuera rose immediately to greet Dr. K. Walker Johnson from Pan American University at Edinburg.

"*Dr. Johnson!*" said the attorney. "Good to see you this morning. I'm glad you could make it."

"No problem," said the professor, stroking his well groomed, short black beard. "I was worried that I might be late."

"No, no problem here," said Figuera. "In fact, the attorney for the Immigration Service *forgot about the hearing*—can you believe *that?* Actually *forgot about the goddamned hearing!* That's just about the most *arrogant* thing I've ever *heard! Forgot about* the *goddamned hearing!*"

Dr. Johnson only frowned and stroked the narrow point of his long, angular chin. "What does this mean? We're not going to have the hearing today?"

"Well, I don't know," said the attorney. "I don't know how we'll be able to get in María's testimony and yours, too, even if we started now. I know Harwell has another hearing scheduled for one-thirty."

Dr. Johnson stroked his chin again and looked down at the satchel of materials. It was the first time that he had been asked to give testimony in an asylum hearing. It was an opportunity that he had prepared heavily for, and it was clear that he was irritated that his testimony might be jeopardized.

"We'll just have to see what the judge says about his afternoon docket," said Figuera.

Dr. Walker retreated to one of the chairs beside the attorneys' desks and began sifting through his bag of readings. Figuera continued with small talk between himself and Lucía about María and the case. After about ten more minutes, the outside door opened and in walked the attorney for the Immigration Service, a thin, blonde woman wearing a somewhat rumpled three-piece yellow suit, who flung herself through the gate and dropped her briefcase, keys, and purse on the table.

"Look, I'm sorry to have kept you waiting," she offered in a brusk apology, more irritated than embarrassed by the attention given to her late arrival. Without another word or an offer to shake Figuera's hand, Ms. Leasure opened her briefcase, sat down, and pulled out the file and dossier for the hearing and began flipping mechanically through the pages.

"Look, Dr. Johnson," said Figuera, "why don't you sit back there behind the gate until Ms. Leasure and I have cleared this whole thing up with the judge."

Dr. Johnson nodded, picked up his satchel, and was stepping through the gate to the spectator benches when the judge entered the chamber. A slightly built man in his early forties, Judge Arlen Harwell, in a long, flowing black robe, entered the room followed by Mrs. Hernandez, who stopped inside the door a few feet while the judge ascended the steps to his bench in front of the chamber.

"All rise, please, for Judge Arlen Harwell," announced the secretary.

María and Lucía rose, following the cue from Figuera. Ms. Leasure sprouted from her chair, pulling down the back of her jacket which had slipped up over her flat, narrow buttocks. As Judge Harwell nodded, she pulled a comb through her shoulder-length, thin blonde hair and slipped it back into her purse as she took her seat.

"Ms. Leasure—good *morning!*" said the judge with a hint of irritation.

"Your *Honor,"* said Ms. Leasure, without acknowledging her counterparts in the hearing room. "I sincerely *apologize* for being late. I completely forgot about the hearing. I got my mornings confused, I guess."

Judge Harwell looked over the rims of his half glasses, stared blankly at the Service attorney for a moment, then broke into a simpy little smirk.

"*Well, Ms. Leasure*," said Judge Harwell, knowing that he had her cornered, "I'm sure we're all *pleased* to see you *at all* this morning, and we thank you for all your trouble."

"I'm *truly* sorry to have inconvenienced the court, your Honor," said the contrite attorney.

"Well," said Harwell, as he turned to the business at hand. "Mr. Figuera, what do you think? Can't we get through this hearing pretty quickly?"

"Your Honor," said Figuera. "With all due respect, I would like to request a continuance on this hearing. We have lost almost an hour and a half this morning only because Service here was late and . . . "

"*Mr. Figuera!*" said Harwell, "there's not going to be any *continuance* on this hearing. *That's* just not going to happen. You're aware—as we're *all* aware—this client has a strong breech of credibility, even at the outset here, and I just don't have a lot of sympathy in prolonging this case *at all.*"

"*Your Honor,*" said Figuera, "I think that we will be able to show very clearly that our client was *framed*—if I'm reading your implication correctly, and I . . ."

"*Mr. Figuera,*" said Harwell, "I'm sorry to interrupt again, but let's get on with it. Either we hear the case this morning, or I'm going to order this client held over for further investigation relative to a range of possible federal drug charges."

"Well, your Honor," said Figuera, quite frustrated, "I guess that settles it. There's no question, then, that we're prepared to go on this morning."

"Is the client to be your only witness?" asked the judge.

"The client," said the attorney, "and I have enjoined the service of an expert witness."

"An *expert witness?*" asked the judge.

"Yes, your Honor," said Figuera.

"Is your *expert witness* present in this court right now?" asked Harwell.

"Yes, your Honor," said Figuera, pointing behind him toward Dr. Johnson.

"The gentleman behind you?" asked Harwell.

"Yes, your Honor."

"And his name?"

"Dr. Johnson," said the attorney.

"Doctor—?"

"Dr. K. Walker Johnson, your Honor," elaborated Figuera. He caught Ms. Leasure rolling back her eyes and heard her sigh in what had to be some feigned expression of exasperation.

"Okay—any *others?*" asked the judge.

"No, your Honor—well, just Sister Lucía here, but not for testimony. I have asked her to come as a translator for my client who speaks little Spanish and no English. Sister Lucía here will translate from Tzutujil into English, your Honor."

"All right," said Harwell, "and do you have any other documentation to submit."

"Well, yes, your Honor," said Figuera. "Dr. Johnson, here, has prepared a set of documents supporting his testimony."

"What sort of documents?"

"Well, he's brought copies of various things—books, articles, that kind of thing, information relevant to his testimony."

Harwell looked over at the attorney and frowned. "Well, that's a little *irregular*, Mr. Figuera. It's standard procedure in hearings like this to submit copies of such documents in advance. I suppose he has extra copies of each for the court and Service here."

Figuera was beginning to get frustrated with Judge Harwell's abrasive manner. "I'm sure we can arrange to have photo copies of whatever we need, your Honor."

"Your Honor," interrupted Ms. Leasure. "With all due respect, your Honor, this all seems a little premature since this man hasn't even been certified yet as an expert in this hearing."

"That's fine, Ms. Leasure," said Judge Harwell. "We're getting there. The court is just trying to identify the substance of the respondent's testimony to determine whether or not there will be a hearing at *all.* If respondent's attorney is prepared to *obsfucate* this hearing with a lot of superfluous testimony, then the Court might just go ahead and remand the respondent here over to the DEA this *morning!*"

Dr. K. Walker Johnson took the intentional slight without visible reaction, but Figuera clearly bristled as Ms. Leasure smiled demurely, darting a look of haughty triumph at her counterpart.

"I think, your Honor," said Figuera rising from behind the table, "the Court will find Dr. Johnson's testimony most germane to this hearing. With the time remaining, we are prepared to use every moment to the client's direct support."

"Thank you, Mr. Figuera," said Harwell. "Well, Ms. Leasure, if Service is ready, then I think that we will proceed first of all to the certification of Dr. Johnson here."

"I have no objection, your Honor," conceded Ms. Leasure.

"Mr. Figuera," said Judge Harwell, "please have Dr. Johnson approach the bench for swearing in."

"Thank you, your Honor," said Figuera, motioning Dr. Johnson to step before the judge. "Would you raise your right hand, please," said Harwell. "Will you swear that the testimony you are about to provide this court is the truth and nothing but the truth, so help you God?"

"I do," said Dr. Johnson.

"Very well," said Harwell, "please take a seat at the end of the table and move that microphone on the end there closer to you. Speak plainly and respond only to the questions that the court, Service, and respondent's attorney here may direct to you."

"Yes, sir," said Dr. Johnson.

"You may begin, Mr. Figuera," said Harwell.

"Very good, your Honor," said Figuera. "Now Dr. Johnson, you have provided the court with a copy of your résumé, and I would call attention to the court and Service copies which I have provided with the respondent's dossier."

Ms. Leasure appeared to be caught off guard with Figuera's reference to a résumé. She frowned and began flipping clumsily through the pages of the rumpled manila file.

"I'm *sorry,* your Honor!" protested Ms. Leasure. "Respondent's representative apparently has *overlooked* the Service's copy. I haven't seen any such document. In fact, I had no notice *at all* from the respondent's attorney that he was anticipating expert testimony. I have to protest that this is all *highly irregular* at this late date, particularly since Service hasn't had prior opportunity to review this person's vita. Service is prepared to ask the respondent's attorney to withdraw this request for certification proceedings."

"Judge Harwell, *please!*" interrupted Figuera. "I can't answer for Service's *negligence.* The court's secretary, Mrs. Hernandez, confirmed that Dr. Johnson's résumé had been received in a timely manner and that all copies were in order for this hearing this morning. Service's objection to certification of Dr. Johnson is *way out of line*—not warranted, your Honor!"

Figuera was reaching a boiling point. Despite Ms. Leasure's reputation and his past experience with her, he hadn't anticipated the acrimonious barbs so early in the hearing.

Judge Harwell looked over his glasses at Ms. Leasure. "Well, Ms. Leasure, why don't you look one more time near the top of the dossier there. If Mrs. Hernandez said that she had received the résumé, I'm sure you'll find everything in good order."

It was becoming clearer to Figuera that Ms. Leasure had made no preparations for the hearing at all, had probably not even opened the dossier before this morning in the hearing room, and was clearly flustered by the prospect of an expert witness. Harwell, on the other hand, was apparently amused at the situation and was angling her along, something that was making the Service attorney even testier. Nevertheless, Figuera knew that Harwell was clearly prejudiced against his client and would be prepared to favor Service on every major point.

Ms. Leasure found the résumé behind the cover sheet in the proper order. "Thank you, your Honor."

"Please procede, Mr. Figuera."

"*Thank you,* your Honor," said Figuera, satisfied that he had survived the first joust. "Now, Dr. Johnson, please begin by stating your full name."

"Colonel Federico Altapaz, lieutenants," said Altapaz to officers Montez and Gonzalo, as they stood on the bridge of Cinderella's Castle. The two lieutenants, dressed only in civilian clothes, had been caught completely off guard by the colonel who had been following them after taking leave of his wife and two children earlier in the morning. He had been waiting for the two young Guatemalan officers at the monorail station at the very same spot he and his family had exited some three hours before. He had learned that the two had passes that day for the Magic Kingdom through a unique channel. Sergeant Montoya Díaz, a social service coordinator in the Office of Hispanic Relations at Disney World for the past three years, was, in fact, a G-2 plant and the intelligence liaison officer with responsibility for oversight of all Guatemalan graduates of the "School of the Americas" during their R&R in the Florida resort. This wasn't the first time the international playground had been used for clandestine operations. That morning, Diaz had posted a groundskeeper with a two-way radio outside the officers' suite. It was easy for Diaz to estimate their probable destination for the morning and was ready when Altapaz had telephoned his office.

"Your papers, *señores*," said Altapaz as he slipped his military ID back into his wallet.

"*Sí*, colonel," said Montez and Gonzalo as they reached for their own.

"And your passports and visas, *por favor*," ordered the colonel.

The two lieutenants looked at each other momentarily as they reached into their jacket pockets for their remaining documentation.

"Thank you," said Altapaz.

A cheer went up from the crowd that had gathered about them on the bridge and around the moat of the castle. Eager little children strained their eyes toward the highest spire of the castle where the figure of a girl in green tights and the pixie costume of "Tinkerbell" appeared in the lookout portal of the spire. The popular little "fairy" was preparing for her noon flight down the three hundred- foot high wire that stretched from the castle across the concourse to the adjacent amusement building. All at once, music from "Peter Pan," the movie, began wafting across the grounds, and "Tinkerbell" waved toward the crowd below. With the onset of the familiar music, more and more families had now maneuvered around the front of the castle for a view of the anticipated flight. It would still be another five minutes before the fairy would streak down the wire over her applauding audience, enough time for Altapaz to complete his assignment.

"*Mira!*" said Altapaz. He reached into his shirt pocket and took out a photo. He handed it to Lieutenant Gonzalo and said, "Look at this picture carefully. Memorize every feature."

Gonzalo stared at the photo for several seconds and handed it to his colleague. "What's this all about, Colonel?"

"Do you know this man?" asked Altapaz.

"No," said Gonzalo.

"No . . . well, maybe," said Montez. "Isn't he that *indio* from San Felipe, that "Pepe" guy?"

"Yes," said Altapaz. "He's the one who left the unit with the *Bruceros* three months back. We've traced him to Brownsville where he got picked up about two weeks ago. North American INS has him in El Chamayo right now. He was arrested after he tried to pass false papers at the bridge in Brownsville. The Americans probably don't know who they have yet, and he's not likely to tell them anything that's going to get him deported as an `undesirable.'"

Gonzalo stole a glance at Montez. He was beginning to get the drift of the colonel's suggestion.

"In a few moments," said Altapaz, "you are going to leave Florida for El Chamaya. As soon as you get there, you're to take out `Pepe.' Do you understand, officers? This is an official commission."

"*Sí,* Colonel," said Montez. Lieutenant Gonzalo nodded in agreement.

"*Mira!* Those two men over there—" Colonel Altapaz pointed to two uniformed men standing under the shade of a tree across the walk from the bridge where they were talking. Both were watching the proceedings between the three Guatemalans with some interest. "INS," said Altapaz. "When we finish here, they are going to come up here and take you away."

"But we have *papers*," Gonzalo protested.

"You have *what?*" returned Altapaz with a smile as he tucked their visas, IDs, and passports inside his jacket. Lieutenant Gonzalo looked startled.

"Don't worry," reassured the colonel. "You men were handpicked for this commission. You do your work in El Chamayo, and you'll return to Guatemala in three weeks as `captains,' *no?*"

Gonzalo finally got the picture and gave his colleague a quick glance of satisfaction. "*Sí, Colonel, cómo no! A sus ordenas!*"

Altapaz reached out and shook hands with both men and then turned away. Immediately, the two INS officers were at their sides.

"*Papeles, señores?*" asked one of the officers. "Your *papers?*"

"No," said Lieutenant Montez.

"And you?" asked the other of Gonzalo. The lieutenant only shook his head.

"Gentlemen," said the first officer. "You are under arrest. Let's go."

"That's all *I* have, your Honor," said Figuera, as he completed his questions of Dr. Johnson.

"Thank you, Mr. Figuera," said the judge. "Ms. Leasure?"

"Thank you, your Honor," said Ms. Leasure. "Yes, Mr. Johnson, I have some questions and, quite frankly, great reservations about your qualifications to testify in this hearing. Now, Mr. Johnson, you have testified that you have worked in Guatemala for some twenty years or more, is that correct?" She would continue to ignore the doctorate for the remainder of the hearing.

"Yes," said Dr. Johnson.

"And this work was with the . . . what did you say? The Ministry of *Education?*"

"Yes."

"I see," said the attorney, "and you said that you were in Guatemala sometimes three or four times a year . . . that was each year over the past twenty years?"

"That's correct."

"And what was the *longest* period you ever spent in Guatemala at any one time?"

Dr. Johnson paused before answering. Figuera raised his eyes and pursed his lips. "I hardly see where this line of questioning is leading, your Honor."

"Mr. Figuera, you've *had* your time!" snapped the judge. "Let the man *answer!"*

Figuera looked away, obviously agitated over the severity of Judge Harwell's rebuke.

"Go ahead, Mr. Johnson," said Ms. Leasure.

"Ten days, maybe two weeks."

"*T-e-n-d-a-y-s,* maybe *t-w-o weeks*," she said as she made a flourish of writing the same across the top of her legal pad, another ploy of intimidation she liked to introduce early in a hearing.

"Now, Mr. Johnson," said Ms. Leasure, twisting the blunt, yellow pencil in her hand. "Now, Mr. Johnson, it appears at the most—at the *very* most—you have never spent more than a month or two in Guatemala in any one year, is that right?"

"Yes, that's right."

"Okay," said Ms. Leasure, scoring another point for herself, obvious in the tone of her voice.

"Now, Mr. Johnson," said Ms. Leasure, "your bachelor's degree—what was your major for your *bachelor's* degree?"

"English. My B.A. is in English."

"*E-n-g-l-i-s-h*—" repeated Ms. Leasure, as she wrote the word in a strained scrawl across the pad. "And your Masters degree? What was your major for the Masters degree?"

"English, also."

"*E-n-g-l-i-s-h a-l-s-o*," emphasized the Service attorney, checking the previous entry on her pad and then tapping her yellow pencil on the desk. "Literature? Drama? Poetry? Criticism, I suppose?"

"Yes, that's right."

"And your *doctorate?*" continued Ms. Leasure. "What about your doctorate? What was your specialization for the doctorate?"

"American literature."

"American *literature?*—okay," said Ms. Leasure, making a dramatic gesture in placing a third check on the pad. "Now in a doctoral program, Mr. Johnson, I suppose you wrote a dissertation of some kind?"

"Yes."

"And what was the subject of that dissertation?"

"Mark Twain."

"*Mark Twain?*" she asked with affected disdain.

"Yes, Ms. Leasure, I wrote a dissertation on Mark Twain."

"The *literature* of Mark Twain?"

"The title of my dissertation, Ms. Leasure, was `*The Rise and Fall of Mark Twain*!"

"Thank you, *Mister* Johnson!" said Ms. Leasure in obvious disinterest for the additional data.

"Now, *Mister* Johnson," pursued Ms. Leasure, "certainly a scholar of your caliber would know if Mark Twain ever traveled in Guatemala. Did *Mark Twain* ever travel in Guatemala, Mr. Johnson?"

"I don't think so, Ms. Leasure."

"You don't *think* so, or you don't *know* so?"

"Yes, I *know* so, Ms. Leasure! Mark Twain never *set foot* in Guatemala. As a matter of fact, since you seem so interested, the closest he ever came was aboard ship off the coast of *Nicaragua!*"

"That's . . . that's just *fine, Mister* Johnson!" retorted Ms. Leasure. "Thank you very *much!* I think you've established clearly enough your authority in the field of American letters, but what you're also telling the court at the same time is that you're a specialist in a field that has nothing at all to do with Latin

America, is that right, *Mister* Johnson?"

"Not exactly . . ."

"But as a matter of fact—as you like to put it, *Mister* Johnson, have you ever completed a *single course* in Latin American literature for either your bachelors degree, masters degree, or your doctors degree?"

"No," said Dr. Johnson, "but with all due respect, Ms. Leasure, my specialization rests in something *other* than my academic work, and you *know* it. I have already testified to my human rights work for both Guatemala both in Mexico and in the United States. Graduate schools don't award many doctorates in `*Guatemalan death squads,'* Ms. Leasure!"

"Well, then, Mr. Johnson, let me ask you this," pressed Ms. Leasure. "In all those publications and materials you have brought with you today—does any of it contain published documents reflecting your *own* research on Guatemala?"

"No, no it *doesn't,*" said Dr. Johnson.

"Just . . . just one *more* question, then, Mr. Johnson. Have you *ever* . . . have you *ever* published a single word in any scholarly journal on any subject even *remotely* related to *Guatemala?*"

"Well, no . . . " confessed the professor.

"*Your Honor!*" interrupted the Immigration Service attorney, as she slammed her pencil to the desk, "I wish to reiterate my original complaint against this . . . this rather *self-styled `expert'!* Nothing in this man's credentials even *remotely* reflects expertise related in any way—at least according to any *traditional* standard defining `expertise'—to the business of this hearing *today*, and once again, I request that the court reject respondent's attorney's request to seat Mister Johnson for expert testimony!"

Judge Harwell leaned back slowly into his chair and pondered Service's petition for rejection, glancing once again over Dr. Johnson's résumé attached to the dossier. Then, slowly and methodically rubbing his eyes against the palms of his hands, he leaned forward, crossed his arms over his desk, and addressed Carlos Figuera.

"Mr. Figuera, I'm afraid I have to concur with Service's petition to reject Mr. . . . that is, *Doctor* Johnson's testimony here. While I appreciate Dr. Johnson's travels and the record of his frequent lectures and presentations, the list of video titles, etc.—all of which register his obvious *concern* for the plight of the Guatemalan people, I also question his academic credentialling for testimony in this particular hearing. Lots of people know about the civil war in Guatemala, and lots of people have expressed their revulsion of the many atrocities so many have experienced—on *both* sides, I might add—but they aren't lined up outside Immigration hearings across the country projecting themselves as `experts'! So, while I appreciate your efforts in coming to Harlingen this morning, Dr. Johnson, this court must adhere *very strictly* to only the *highest* standards of comportment, and I will ask you, in all due respect, to excuse yourself from any formal participation in this hearing today. Of course, you're welcome to stay, if you like, as an observer. That's up to you. Thank you, Dr. Johnson."

Dr. K. Walker Johnson looked stoically at the judge, rose, nodded at Carlos Figuera, and with his satchel in hand, walked through the gate and out the door. Following an afterthought, Carlos Figuera stood up and asked the judge for a five- minute recess in order to chase down Dr. Walker. Judge Harwell acceded, and Figuera rushed from the room only to catch Dr. Johnson driving off from the front of the building.

"Shit!" shouted Figuera. *"Goddamn it! Shit!"*

Figuera turned around and, spying the men's room down the corridor, decided to relieve himself before returning to the hearing. He entered the restroom and locked himself into the last of the four stalls. Finding the sports section of the daily paper abandoned against the paper dispenser, Figuera opened it up and began to scan the headlines. Moments later he was startled to hear the voices of Judge Harwell and the administrative assistant of Judge Tarper, the other resident immigration magistrate in the Valley, as they entered the john. Assuming positions over respective urinals, the two were commenting on the morning's dockets.

"*Yeah!"* said Judge Harwell, "we had a little *surprise* this morning when the *pro bono* attorney tried to seat an *`expert witness'!* It caught her way off guard, but I sure wish you could have heard Barbara! I mean, when she gets *cornered,* that gal's a *ball* buster—I mean a four-wheel drive, corrugated *bitch!* She has absolutely no respect anyway for these `Ph.D' types. Somebody told me one time she just about flunked out of law school when she and one of her professors got `crossways.' Everybody figures she had been screwing him or something, and he was trying to break it off. From what I heard, she just about broke *his* off! Anyway, this morning, she really had this Pan American University guy on the run. She's a real piece of work, I'll tell you! You should have seen Carlos Figuera, the respondent's attorney, suckin' his gums. It was during cross examination, so he couldn't say a word. Unless I'm really surprised, I don't think he has any kind of case with this Guatemalan woman. The border patrol caught her just about red-handed transporting cocaine—or *whatever*—back in December. She was wearing this belt under her dress. She was *obviously* trafficking, but the bags of drugs had been ripped or cut off. She was a `mule,' *for sure!* The only trouble is that the DEA lab report came back negative. They couldn't find any trace of drugs on her dress, so the feds didn't have much of case for an indictment. Unless she indicts herself during testimony in a few minutes, we'll save the state some money if I just hold her over for deportation."

As they were zipping up, Judge Harwell and his colleague were surprised by the flush of the commode in the last stall.

"Well, guess I better get back to the bench," said Harwell. "See you at the tournament this weekend?"

"*Yeah!* Bright and early! *Adios, stick!"*

Figuera had been humiliated by the exchange, but he was pleased to have overheard the outcome of the lab test. If he could keep his cool for the next hour and a half, his client might sidestep incarceration in the county jail, and she could return to El Chamayo where at least she knew some people—*if* he didn't lose it with this Service attorney. He was deeply embarrassed, however, for his expert witness. He felt he had lost Johnson's trust and support, and he wasn't willing to jeopardize a professional, even a *social* relationship over a bitch like *Leasure!* In his gut, he wanted to go back into that court room, take her by her stringy blonde hair, and just slap the *shit* out of her! He was professional enough to realize that she had a job to do, and challenging expert witness credibility was just part of the territory. But for some reason, challenging credentials was never enough for Leasure. He didn't know what it was with her, but the law school thing with the professor perhaps explained part of it. She was probably *lesbian*—that's what it *was!* or maybe one of those "women *libbers*" who hated *all* men, *categorically!* What she really needed was a goddamned *dick* shoved up her ass! A good *horse fucking* about once a week might *cure* her of some of that bubba-bashing *bullshit!*

"That's *good!* I *like* that!—`four-wheel drive, corrugated *bitch'!*" he said outloud as he adjusted his tie, preparing to reenter the hearing room.

"Is that *right*, *Mr. Attorney!*" said Barbara Leasure who had been walking down the hall just a few feet behind him. Figuera was so stunned to hear her voice that he fell back from the door speechless, letting the Service attorney enter in another little triumph ahead of him.

Still stunned and uncharacteristically embarrassed, Figuera followed Ms. Leasure through the gate and took his seat at the adjacent table without even a glance at Service.

"*Jesus!*" thought Figuera. He had to get himself *together!* He couldn't let this *rattle* him this way!

"Explain to María," Figuera asked Lucía, "that her story is next. Tell her not to be nervous. Tell her to answer my questions directly. Tell her to act very certain about her responses, and we'll get through this thing. And tell her not to worry about Dr. Johnson. Just tell her he gave his testimony and that everything's okay."

"Well," said Lucía as she turned to María sitting stiffly beside her. Lucía reached over and took María's hand. Figuera could see María's arms start to tremble as Lucía passed on his instructions.

"It's *okay*," said Figuera in English, trying to reassure María, and he reached over and patted the clenched hands of the two women. "It's going to be *okay!*"

Seconds later, Mrs. Hernandez reappeared, followed by Judge Harwell.

"Give me a moment, ladies and gentlemen," said the judge, "while I adjust this tape recorder." The judge slipped a cassette audio tape into the recorder, ran it forward past the leader footage, and pressed the "Record" button.

"Transcriber, this is tape 1-side 1 of hearing on the merit in the case of María—María—`Keesh'?" Harwell stopped the tape and asked, "I'm sorry, Mr. Figuera, but tell me again how to pronounce respondent's last name."

"Sh-e-e-*KEEK,*" said Figuera. "María She-*KEEK* de *KOY*. That's close."

Harwell punched the "Record" button again. "This is a record of a deportation proceeding, the respondent, María Shee-KEEK—transcriber, that's spelled `x-q-u-i-c' de Koy—spelled `x-o-y.' The hearing is being conducted by Immigration Judge Arlen Harwell on Thursday, March 21, 1992, in the Harlingen Office of the Executive Office for Immigration Review. Language will be in Spanish and `Zoo-too-*HEEL*'—that's spelled `t-z-u-t-u-j-i-l.' The court recognizes Sister Lucía Perez as the official interpreter for this hearing. Trial attorney is Ms. Barbara Leasure, general attorney of the Brownsville District INS. The respondent is present in person with Mr. Carlos Figuera, an attorney who has filed an I-589 on behalf of the respondent, María Xquic de Xoy. Ms. . . . I'm sorry, *Sister* Lucía, will you please translate exactly each of the questions for me and for the attorneys, and please translate exactly what Mrs. Xquic de Xoy says in response."

"Yes, your Honor," said Lucía.

"Now, ma'am, what is your full, true and correct name, please?" Lucía translated the question.

"María Xquic de Xoy."

"Ms. Xquic, I'm Judge Harwell. I'm an immigration judge and we're here today to have a hearing to determine whether or not you could be deported from the United States. Do you understand?"

María Xquic nodded her head.

"You must answer directly—with *words*, please."

Lucía translated, and María responded, "Yes."

"Also during the hearing you'll have a chance to apply for any relief from or alternative to deportation you may be eligible for. Do you understand that?"

María looked bewildered, and Carlos Figuera asked Lucía to have María simply answer yes.

"Yes," said María.

"Also, during this hearing, you have the right to be represented by Counsel. That might be an attorney of your choice and at your own expense or it might be a representative of one of the agencies in this area that sometimes provide free legal services for aliens. Did you receive a list of agencies and a notice of your right to appeal from the Immigration Service?"

Figuera coached Lucía to have María answer in the affirmative.

"Yes," said María.

"Do you wish to be represented?"

Carlos Figuera nodded, signifying that she should say yes to Lucía's translation.

"Yes," she said.

"Who is your attorney, ma'am?"

María pointed to Figuera.

"Let the record show that respondent has pointed to Carlos Figuera, attorney-at-law, who is also present in the court room."

Judge Harwell paused the tape for a moment to rearrange the papers of his dossier before him, released the pause, and then proceeded.

"Mr. Figuera, are you prepared to proceed today on behalf of your client?"

"Yes, Judge," said Figuera.

"Very well. Now, Mr. Figuera, did you or respondent receive a copy of the Order to Show Cause dated January 14, 1992?"

"Yes, Judge."

"All right. That will be Exhibit 1 as entered into the record at this time. Now, Mr. Figuera, have you advised the client of her rights and the procedures in these hearings?"

"Yes, your Honor."

"Do you wish to have me read and explain the allegations and the charge to her and receive a pleading directly from her or would you waive that and enter a pleading on her behalf?"

"We'll waive the reading, Judge, and enter a pleading."

"How would she plead to the two listed allegations of fact?"

"She accepts these two allegations, Judge. She would admit to entry without inspection and would concede deportability."

"Okay, Mr. Figuera. Now, should her deportation ever be required, what country would she designate?"

"We would decline to designate at this time, your Honor."

"Then, Mr. Figuera, I would designate by regulation, Guatemala, the country of her nativity and citizenship."

The judge returned to the dossier once more and reviewed the first page of the I-589. Then he continued. "Mr. Figuera, what relief are you seeking?"

"Mrs. Xquic is seeking asylum, your Honor."

"All right. Mrs. Xquic, have you applied for asylum before in the United States?" Lucía translated.

"No," said María.

"Very well. Mr. Figuera, I show an item, an application showed received on January 28, 1992, in Brownsville, Texas, apparently signed by the respondent. Is that so, Mr. Figuera?"

"Yes, your Honor."

"Any objection to its admission?"

"No, Judge."

"I show another item, an advisory opinion from the United States Department of State, an `an intention to deny,' prepared in response to the narrative attached to Exhibit 1, is that correct, Mr. Figuera?"

"Yes, Judge."

"Any objection to its admission in this hearing, Mr. Figuera?"

"No, your Honor."

"Ms. Leasure? Any objections?"

"None, your Honor," said the Service attorney without looking up from an apparently aimless flipping back and forth through the I-589.

"Very well. Let the record show a three-page response from the United States Department of State, dated—let me see . . . February 12, 1992—a response from the Department of State as Exhibit 3."

"Now, Mr. Figuera," continued the Judge. "Are there any other documents which you wish to submit for admission in this hearing this morning—off the record, you had mentioned something at the beginning this morning."

"No . . . no, your Honor," said Figuera, still frustrated with the failure to seat his expert witness earlier in the hour.

"Then, are you prepared, Mr. Figuera, to proceed with this hearing on the merits on behalf of the respondent."

"Yes, your Honor."

"Any objections, Ms. Leasure?"

"No, Judge," said Ms. Leasure. "Service is fully prepared to proceed."

"Very well, then," said Judge Harwell. "Mr. Figuera, you may call Mrs. Xquic to the stand."

Lucía indicated to María that she should rise.

"Now, Mrs. Xquic, do you swear that any testimony you give today will be the truth, the whole truth, and nothing but the truth?"

Lucía translated, but María was trembling and seemed strangely distracted.

"*María?*" questioned Figuera. Lucía looked worriedly at the attorney.

Harwell repeated his question. "Mrs. Xquic, do you swear that *Miguel Mapa who is in the next room that he could say if he was in the next room, could be, and little Ana Fabiola whose precious tiny hands across her breast when Andres didn't even return, she was so panicked! even the priest who looked for days and couldn't find her husband, the crazy, crazy, with the fear that she couldn't even move or talk about her story, if she could just remember her story that the attorney who was trying to trick her if Miguel Mapa was in the next room, but how could Lucía? Lucía just wouldn't do such a thing because the church! the sweet little candies that Ana Fabiola liked so much!* "the truth and nothing" *when she would lean over beside her grave* "but the truth, Mrs. Xquic de Xoy?" *Ana, little Ana Fabiola without any hands any more that María? the ejército!*

". . . Okay, Mrs. . . .?"

María's lips trembled, but she could form no words.

"That's all right, Mrs. Xquic," said the judge. "Just take your time. We're not going to be here very long, and there's no one here who wants to hurt you. We're here today only to determine whether or not you qualify for remaining in the United States. You've already said you understand that, so just try to relax. I'm going to ask you some questions. Your attorney, Mr. Figuera, here, will have some questions, and then Ms. Leasure will have a few questions probably to ask you. So take a deep breath, relax for a moment, and then we'll continue."

María stared blankly at Lucía as she translated. Suddenly, she bowed her head, and a shudder rushed across her shoulders.

"Do you think your client can continue this?" the judge asked Figuera.

"I . . . I think, I . . . I don't know, your Honor," said Figuera. "I hope so. Give her just a minute to get herself together. She knows what she has to . . . what she *wants* to say, that is, about her story."

From her little smile, it was clear Ms. Leasure hadn't missed the slip.

Figuera looked quizzically at Lucía. "Do you think she can continue?"

Lucía turned to María and whispered into her ear. María listened and slowly nodded her head. The nun stroked her wrist and squeezed her hand reassuringly.

"She's okay," she said softly to Figuera. "She said she can continue. She's just a little frightened and got mixed up, but she says she's okay."

"Fine!" said Figuera. "She's going to be okay, Judge. We can continue."

"Very good, Mr. Figuera," said Harwell. "Now, Mrs. Xquic—please translate, Sister."

"Yes, your Honor," said Lucía. "Now, Mrs. Xquic . . . "

María looked up at her companion, this time more attentively.

"Mrs. Xquic," continued Judge Harwell, "I just need for you to say if you will speak the truth today."

Lucía translated, and María nodded.

"Let the record show that the respondent nodded in the affirmative that she will speak the truth today. Very well. Now, Mrs. Xquic, you have sworn to tell the truth. Now, Mr. Figuera, your attorney, will begin with some questions to you, and Sister Lucía will continue to translate, *okay?*"

María listened to the translation and nodded again.

"Very well, Mr. Figuera," said Judge Harwell. "You may begin."

"Thank you, Judge," said Figuera. "Now, María, what country are you from?"

"Guatemala," said María.

"From Guatemala," repeated Figuera. "And have you always lived in Guatemala?"

"Yes," she said. *When he brought the water, she had seen the tears in his eyes anyway, the tears in the eyes of little Manuel, but she never let on. Manuel, he was always so proud of helping his mother, if only the cat! If only the cat . . .*

"Now, María," said Figuera in a confidential tone. "I'm going to have to ask you some questions that are going to be very painful for you to talk about, but just take your time and do the best you can, *okay?*"

María nodded. *Manuel would be about this tall against the corn. He would never catch up with Tano or Miguel—Miguel, with the strong hands and broad shoulders. He used to strain so under the heavy bags of sand—whatever it took for one or two more quetzales.*

"Now, María," said Figuera, "let's talk about your family. I know that's painful to you, but we'll get through this quickly."

María nodded, looking down in her lap. *Andres, Miguelito,Tano LucitaMaría,Ana FabiolaAndresMiguTanoLucitolaMiguelAnaMaría . . .* She couldn't make the count, and María was beginning to panic.

"Mr. Figuera," said Judge Harwell. "Move the microphone closer to your client—all the way to the edge of the table, if you have enough cord there."

Figuera slipped the cord of the microphone from around his briefcase and eased the small table mic stand up to the very edge of the table.

"That's better," said Harwell. "Go head, please."

"Thank you, Judge," said Figuera. "María, please speak directly into the microphone, *okay?*"

María nodded.

"Now, María, once again," said Figuera, "would you tell me about your family. Where is your home in Guatemala?"

"San Felipe," said María. *San Felipe of the powerful Maximón where Don Andres healed Generalisimo Francisco Palma, San Felipe of Colata Tój with her weaving bundle, the old pepper merchant—he always scared the children so with his coarse, gruff laugh.*

"San *Felipe?* San Felipe . . . is that the full name of your town?"

"San Felipe del Lago," said María.

"Where is that? In Guatemala?"

"En el centro," she said. *In the center where the army came from two sides so that they had to flee over the mountain or chance a boat crossing on the lake, in the center of the cave—they could leave in a hurry or retreat even deeper, in the center of the clearing where the bullets poured, cutting down the compañeros, their cries and wailings in the center of the horrible rain of bullets.*

"In the center," interpreted Lucía.

"In the center of Guatemala," added Figuera. "Now, María, please identify the members of your family."

María bowed her head, and Lucía saw tears beginning to form in her eyes again. She reached into her purse and pulled out a small packet of tissues and handed one to María. María glanced at Lucía gratefully and wiped her eyes.

"Your *family,* María?" pressed Figuera.

"Andres . . . " began María, his hands passing cautiously over the maguey beans, clients outside the concrete block house awaiting their reading before the silent, dour, the inscrutable Maximón.

"Andres . . . Andres is your husband?" asked the attorney.

"Yes," acknowledged María.

"I tell you what, María," said Figuera, "let me ask you about your family and you just nod yes or no. Maybe that will be easier since we've already talked about this, *okay?* Now, you told me that you're married, is that right?"

María looked up gratefully.

"And that your husband's name is Andres, right?"

"Yes."

"You told me that you have five children, is that correct?"

"Yes . . . *iolaManuelMiguelitoitoTananafabiolandres*" said María as tears spilled from her eyes anew.

"Miguel Mapa—you said he's twenty-two, and he's your oldest child, right?" *Twenty-two, of course. What could this man possibly know about her family! Twenty-one—twenty-two, then! Had he been talking with Miguel Mapa in the men's compound? This man who could come and go who must have talked with Miguel Mapa! What did he say, Miguel Mapa? Did he tell this man about how he talked with the soldiers—don't go near the soldiers, I said, I said to Miguel Mapa, and don't go near the soldiers to Tano—what they do to the mothers of the sons of the mountains, don't go near the soldiers! Could—did Miguel, this man? near the soldiers? Could Miguel—Alfonso Doq, Tata Alfonso, so hurt—Miguel? unthinkable! have to think of something else! unacceptable! so Manuel! So she had to flee over the mountain, over the—*

"Twenty . . . twenty-two, yes," said María. *Miguelito Miguel Mapa with the broad shoulders who turned the heads of all the girls, that the soldiers came to Miguel Mapa who—but how? That she had to flee, and here! but here? How here? Now?*

"And then Tano, your second son. He's twenty, I believe."

María nodded again, wiping her eyes.

"Now, you and Andres have three other children—two daughters—Lucita María, seventeen, and Ana Fabiola, fourteen, right?"

María nodded again. *They were not here. Miguel Mapa was not here. Lucita María,Ana Fabiola,Manuel—that was better, more control, she had to get the count, to get the count right, to somehow find the count, to make the count—not here.*

"And then . . . then, let me see here—Manuel, eight years old, is that right?"

" . . . yes," she said softly, *who loved Miguel Mapa and chased after him when the soldiers left. "Where are you going, Miguel Mapa? Why were you talking with the soldiers? Momi said don't go near the soldiers, don't go near the, Momi said don't . . . "*

"And these—*María!*" interrupted Judge Harwell. "These are all your children by your husband, Andres?"

Lucía translated.

"Yes," said María, *by Andres Menchu who brought me bougainvillaea in bundles over his outstretched arms, who warmed me in the chill of the night, long after the embers had lost their glow in the hearth.*

"Thank you," said the judge. "Please continue, Mr. Figuera."

"Thank you, your Honor," said the attorney. "Now, María, how big is your town. How many people live in San Felipe del Lago?"

María looked somewhat confused.

"How many people live in San Felipe del Lago?"

María thought for a moment. "Maybe . . . maybe two, maybe three thousand people. San Felipe is not too big" *and less the old pepper vendor, minus the American priest, less than Lucita María and Ana Fabiola, much less than Andres, father of Tano who never came back . . .*

María looked at Lucía for confirmation. Lucía shrugged her shoulders, "Maybe. Maybe more."

"Three or four thousand," corrected María.

"Thank you, María," said Figuera. "Now, María, how old are you?"

"Forty—forty-one," said María. She never knew. She had been forty-forty-one for a long time now.

"And have you lived all your life in San Felipe?"

"Yes."

"Did you go to school?"

"Yes." *The holes in her skirt where the girls laughed and teased her because she couldn't make the count—`add'? Who was the ladino teacher who sometimes didn't come on school days after the children had walked so far.*

"How many years of school have you completed?"

"Two. I went to school for two years when I was very young," said María. *She wouldn't sit next to Carla López Mejia, the ladino girl who came to school in store dresses and could make the—could `add.' She never understood how Carla López Mejia could add!*

"Did you ever travel very much from your town?"

María looked confused, and Lucía rephrased the question.

"Sometimes."

"When did you first leave your town?"

"When I was a girl."

"Where did you go?"

"Across the lake." *Her father had been so worried about them making the passage across the great lake, she and her mother, across the deep, blue water, the xocomíl—the great wind—that blew their boat to the north side, away from San Jorge and Panajachel.*

". . . lake?"

"Lago Atitlán," said María.

"Is your town on the lake?"

"Yes." *The crystal blue waters of the Tzutujiles.*

"Why did you go across the lake?"

"To sell my weavings?" *The third but only the first complete huipil that she had dared to let for sale and two head ribbons that the German woman bought for the old lady.*

"You were a weaver?"

"Yes."

"So, you went across the lake to sell your weavings. How many times do you think you left your village to sell your weavings?"

"I don't know exactly . . . but maybe, maybe three . . . three or four times."

"Three or four times . . . " said Figuera. "And these are the only times that you ever left San Felipe del Lago."

"Yes, I think so."

"No other times, then?"

"No."

"Not until when?"

"En . . . octubre." In the black of the night when the soldiers came from both ways, the large trucks with the soldiers.

"October? October when?"

"Octubre pasado."

"This past October, is that right?"

"Yes." *She could feel the thunder of the terror that awful October night still pounding in her heart.*

"María, why did you leave San Felipe this past October?"

"Because of the violence," she whispered, almost inaudibly.

"I'm sorry . . . ?" said Figuera.

"The violence . . ." said María. "I left because of the violence."

"You say there was violence in San Felipe?"

"Yes."

"Was this violence . . . ? How would you describe this violence?"

"Fighting." *The crash of the guns at the entrance to the town and the dogs barking, going crazy, their yelps rising higher and higher in the milpa above San Felipe where the guerrillas ran.*

"*Fighting?*" asked Figuera. "Who was *fighting?*"

"The army," said María. "The army and the guerrillas."

"So, there was a lot of fighting around your town. Just *your* town?"

"No! There was fighting all around. In many towns." *All the women cried when the men came home lying in the backs of the military trucks.*

"Around the lake?"

"Yes."

"Was there fighting in every town?"

"Yes." *In the night the fires were burning the fields way, far away, on the opposite side of the lake, the bombs exploding, their muted concussions floating on the wind.*

"Why was there fighting in San Felipe?"

"Because the army came and the people began to disappear and then the guerrillas came and said it was because of the army . . . that the army did all these things, but the army said it was the guerrillas."

Lucía translated, but was interrupted by the judge once again who had to turn over the tape.

"I'm sorry, Sister, but I'm going to have to ask you to repeat your translation. Please start from the beginning."

Lucía started the translation once again.

"Thank you, Lucía," said Figuera. "Now, María, were any of your family involved in the fighting?"

"No." *Don't go near the soldiers, Miguelito! Don't go near the soldiers!*

"No?" asked Figuera, looking confused. "But María, didn't Miguel Mapa, your oldest son, serve in the military?"

"No."

Figuera cleared his throat and leaned over the table to look María squarely in the face.

"You *told* me, didn't you, María, that Miguel Mapa and Tano served in the civil defense *patrol*, didn't you?"

"Yes."

"*Okay!*" said Figuera, somewhat relieved. He had to establish the military connection, but for a moment, he had seen his whole case beginning to unravel before he even began.

"Now, María," continued the attorney, "please describe the civil defense patrol. What was the civil defense patrol?"

"Well," said María, "the men had to go out at night on the patrol." *The rain poured and poured, drenching the national flag which clung in saturated pleats to the staff of the patrol leader the night they attacked the guerrillas in San Jorge.*

"*All* the men?"

"Yes."

"Why? Why did they have to go out on patrol?"

"To keep the guerrillas from coming into the town."

"The *guerrillas?* But who wanted the guerrillas out of the town?"

"The army."

"The *army?* The *army* didn't want the guerrillas in the town?"

"Yes."

"So . . . so, the *army . . .?*" Figuera was struggling to find the right spin on the question without appearing to lead his witness. "María, who made the men of San Felipe serve in the civil patrol?

"Señor Pecho."

"*Señor Pecho?* Who is that?" asked Figuera. It was new information to him.

"The military commissioner."

"The *military commissioner?*" continued Figuera. "Señor Pecho was the military *commissioner*. Then, did he work for the army."

"I guess so."

"What?"

"Yes, he worked for the militaries." *Strange men in dark sun glasses—people who were not Felipinos—often accompanied the fat man into town, men who only stared at people and never said anything.*

"So Señor Pecho worked for the army, and he organized the civil defense patrol for the *army?*"

"Yes."

Figuera smiled. He had made the critical link. "So, if Miguel and Tano served in the civil defense patrol of San Felipe del Lago, they were working *for the army, no?*"

María herself caught the connection. "Yes."

"Yes, *what?*" pressed Figuera for clarification.

"Yes, Miguel and Tano were working for the Guatemalan army."

Barbara Leasure had sat silently long enough, and this was to her a most leading question. She rose from her seat with a rush, gesturing widely with her hands. "*Your Honor! This!* . . . This is *beyond* leading the witness! Respondent's attorney might as well just read the script *himself!*"

"Objection overruled," said the judge. "Let her answer the question, Mr. Figuera."

"Thank you, your Honor," smiled Figuera. "So, if Miguel and Tano—your oldest sons—were working in the civil defense patrol of San Felipe, then they were working for the Guatemalan army, isn't that right?"

"Yes," said María. *The captain used to whisper to Señor Pecho who whispered, in turn, to Miguel Mapa who gave the orders to the civil patrol.*

"*Thank you*, María!" said Figuera with obvious relief. He had cinched the foundation of his case.

"Now María," said Figuera from a stronger sense of his own direction. "Now, María, you told me that . . . or—*well,* did Miguel and Tano participate in any violent act while serving in the civil defense patrol?"

"Yes," said María hesitantly.

"You say they did?" insisted Figuera.

"Yes."

"Would you describe the kind of act? What did they do?"

"They killed two guerrillas."

"They killed two *guerrillas?"*

"Yes." *She had heard that all the mothers in the towns shut and barred their doors on the stormy night the patrol returned with the bodies of the two guerrillas.*

"You are certain that they were *guerrillas?*"

María sat silently pressing the small tissue into a tight wad in her fist.

Figuera repeated his question. "Miguel and Tano—they were sure the two people were guerrillas?"

"Yes . . . maybe . . ." said María.

"But you're not sure?"

"No."

"Well, María," asked Figuera, "did your sons know these two people, these `guerrillas' they killed?"

". . . yes, maybe," said María.

"Well, they *did* or they *didn't,*" said Figuera. "Do you *know* if they knew these two guerrillas?"

"Yes."

"Yes, *what?*"

"Yes, they knew the two boys, the two people they killed," said María, now beginning to express herself more freely. "They were from San Jorge."

"*San Jorge?*" asked Figuera. "That is the name of the town of these two people, these two *guerrillas?*"

"Yes. San Jorge."

"So Miguel and Tano *killed* these two men from San Jorge as part of their work for the civil defense patrol in San Felipe del Lago—is that *correct?*" asked Figuera.

"Yes."

"Okay, María," said the attorney. "What happened after they—your two *sons*—killed the two guerrillas?"

"What do you mean?" asked María.

"Well," said Figuera, "did that stop the violence in San Felipe?"

"No."

"What happened? Did the violence continue?"

"Yes."

"Please explain, María. What happened?"

"Well," said María, "they killed Señor Pecho."

"`They' killed Señor Pecho—the military commissioner of San Felipe?"

"Yes."

"Who is *`they'?* Who killed Señor Pecho?"

"The guerrillas."

"The *guerrillas?*" asked Figuera. "How do you know it was the *guerrillas?*"

"Because they came into town—after they killed the commissioner, the guerrillas, and they made everyone come into the town square in front of the Catholic church. They made a speech. They said that the army was bad. They said it was the army that was making the civil patrollers kill their own people. They said that *El Pesado* was evil . . ."

"*El Pesado?*" asked Figuera.

"Señor Pecho—the people called him *`El Pesado'*—the `heavy one.' He weighed as much as a truck, they said."

Everyone snickered but Ms. Leasure who appeared only bored and increasingly restless.

"Okay," said Figuera, "go ahead.

". . . that Señor Pecho, he was carrying out orders for the army and that he was attacking the girls in San Felipe," said María. "Everyone knew he was a bad man."

"What did the people of San Felipe think of the guerrillas, about what the *guerrillas* said?" asked Figuera. "Did they support what the guerrillas *said."*

María hesitated. "It was very hard for the people."

"What do you mean?"

"Well, some of the people, they thought about what the guerrillas said."

"And . . . ?"

"Well, some of the people, they believed the guerrillas."

"Some of the people of San Felipe who heard the guerrillas, they believed them, is that *right?*"

"Yes."

"Were they guerrillas, too?"

"No. I don't think so," said María.

"Why was the army against the guerrillas, María," asked Figuera, maneuvering for the first time toward political alliances.

"Because the guerrillas were fighting the army," said María.

"Well, yes, I know they were fighting each other," said Figuera, "but why didn't the army like the guerrillas?"

"I don't understand," said María.

"We'll, María," said Figuera, trying another approach. "Did the *army* ever call the people of San Felipe together to hear speeches?"

"Yes."

"Yes?"

"Yes, many times," explained María.

"Did they talk about the guerrillas, the *militaries?*"

"Yes."

"What did they say?" asked Figuera. "What did they say about the guerrillas?"

"They said they were bad, that they were subversives."

"*`Subversives'?* Is that what the army called the *guerrillas?"* asked Figuera. He was looking for another word. "Is that the *only* thing the army called the guerrillas?"

"What do you mean?" asked María.

"Any other words they used to describe the guerrillas?"

"They said they were `subversives.'"

"Yes, *`subversives,'* but anything else?"

"Yes, *`communists.'* They said the guerrillas were all `communists' and `subversives.'"

"What does that mean, María?" asked her attorney. "What did the soldiers mean by *`communists'?"*

"They said that communists were bad, that they wanted to take all the land and make the people attack the government."

"They said that the guerrillas wanted to *overthrow* the Guatemalan government?"

"Sí!"

"Did you ever hear the guerrillas *say* that?"

"Qué?"

"That the guerrillas wanted to *overthrow* the government?"

"Well, they said that it was the army and the government that made the people poor. They said that it was always the army that was killing the people in the *aldeas*—in the towns and the cities."

"What did *you* think, María?" asked Figuera, addressing the most important question of the hearing.

"I don't know," she said.

But that wasn't the answer he needed. He pressed more specifically, delicately skirting, he hoped, the charge of leading his witness again. "Did you believe the *guerrillas . . . no! María! Look! María,* did *you* want to overthrow the government?"

"No, *of course* not." María looked terribly shocked and surprised.

"So, you supported the government?" he asked.

"I *object!* Your Honor, respondent's attorney continues to *lead the witness*, and I have to *object* to this whole *line* of questions!" exploded Ms. Leasure.

"Mr. Figuera, I'm going to sustain Ms. Leasure's objection this time. Even I can see where you're trying to direct the respondent. Please rephrase your question or pursue a different matter."

"Very well, your Honor," said Figuera. "My apologies to the court."

Figuera paused for a moment while he reconsidered his approach.

"Excuse me, María," he said. "A different question. María, did the guerrillas ever try to recruit people to help them or to join them."

"Yes," she said. "Every time they came into San Felipe, they tried to get people to support them."

"Did they ever try to recruit *you?*"

"No."

"Did they ever try to recruit Miguel Mapa or Tano or your husband?"

"No."

"Why, María?" asked the attorney. "Why do you think they never tried to recruit you or other members of your family?"

"I guess because Miguel Mapa and Tano were members of the civil patrol."

"Did they ever attack members of the *civil patrol?*"

"Yes."

"So the guerrillas wouldn't be interested in trying to *recruit* members of your family, but they might *attack* your family because they were members of the civil patrol in San Felipe, is that right?"

"Well, maybe."

"Well, María," said Figuera, "you have said already that Miguel Mapa and Tano killed two guerrillas from San Jorge, isn't that *right?*"

"Yes."

"Wouldn't that make the guerrillas angry?"

"Yes. I suppose so."

"Were you ever worried that the guerrillas would attack your sons?"

"Yes . . . *always.*"

"Because they were members of the *civil patrol?*"

"Yes."

"Because they had *killed* two guerrillas in San Jorge?"

"Yes."

"Were you ever afraid that the *soldiers* would attack your *sons?*"

"Why . . . why would they attack Miguel and Tano?"

"That's the *point*, María," said Figuera, satisfied that he had finally connected.

"The point *is,* wouldn't you agree . . .?"

Ms. Leasure readied to rise again in objection.

"Let me rephrase that, María," said Figuera, catching the chuckle of the immigration judge. "You tell *me* why the army would not want to attack your sons."

"Because they were good workers for the civil patrols. They were leaders. Everybody looked up to them."

"Even El Pesado?"

"Yes, he liked Miguel Mapa especially. He called Miguel Mapa `*el jefe*.'"

"`El jefe'—the leader!"

"Si!"

"So, Miguel Mapa was a leader in the civil patrol?" asked Figuera.

"Yes, I guess so."

"Well, then, as a *leader*, did he—Miguel—ever have contact with the army directly?"

"Yes."

"What kind of contact? Did he talk to the soldiers? Did the soldiers ever come to your home?"

"Yes."

"They came to your home?"

"Si!"

"Did you hear what they talked about?"

"Yes."

"Well . . ."

"Well, they told Miguel Mapa and Tanolito to come to the capital, to the National Palace."

"To the National Palace? What *for?*"

"They said a colonel in the National Palace wanted to talk to them."

"About *what?*"

"I don't know, but they were very excited about going. They thought the colonel was going to give them a special assignment."

"And did they *go?*"

". . . Yes," said María, dropping her eyes and tightening her grip on the tissue.

"So they went to the National Palace in Guatemala City?"

"And what happened?"

"They . . ." María couldn't finish her sentence before erupting in silent convulsions. Lucía leaned over and clutched her shoulders. Figuera had struck a line of the narrative he wasn't sure he should pursue, but curiosity drove him on.

"So, what happened, María?"

María Xquic whispered something to Lucía.

"They never came back," translated Lucía.

"I don't think we got Mrs. Xquic's comment, Mr. Figuera," interrupted the judge. "Can you rephrase your question?"

"Yes, your Honor," said Figuera. "María, after Miguel and Tano went to the capital, did you ever see them again?"

Lucía translated Figuera's question slowly. Suddenly, María turned pale in horror and stared at her translator. Trembling and on the point of hysteria, she rose and fled the hearing room, sobbing, "*No! No! No! Never, never again!*"

Lucía took a cue from Figuera and followed her out of the chamber into the hallway.

"Your Honor," said Figuera, rising from his chair behind the desk. "I'd like to request a recess for just a few moments so that Mrs. Xquic can compose herself and return to the hearing."

"That's fine," said Judge Harwell. "We'll take a ten-minute recess."

Ms. Leasure rose and, without acknowledging anyone, stepped briskly from the room. In the hall, Figuera found María sobbing openly, her head buried in her hands as she leaned over in Lucía's lap.

"It's *hard,*" said Lucía. "It's very *hard* for her."

"I know," said Figuera. "She has a very horrifying story."

Then he had an idea. This emotional collapse would work very well into the emerging scenario.

"María," said Figuera, as he knelt down in front of his client. "I know that this is very difficult for you. Look, María, I'm not going to ask you to tell everything about what happened to your family. Is that okay?"

María nodded slightly through her sobs.

"I'm only going to ask you just one or two more questions about your family, *okay?*" asked Figuera. María nodded again.

"I'm going to ask you, María—`Were the other members of your family disappeared or killed also?'" said Figuera, "and all you have to do is nod your head, *okay?* Is that *okay,* María? All you have to do is say yes and nod your head, *alright?*"

María nodded slowly in agreement.

"*Good!*" said Figuera. This was working out well because now he could avoid the untidy complications that María's fuller story would necessarily reveal, and he could move on to reconstruct her flight to the United States. Lucía helped María up, and the three of them stepped back into the hearing room. The judge and the trial attorney were already in place.

"You may continue, Mr. Figuera," said Judge Harwell as he pressed the "Record" button on the audio cassette player.

"Thanks, Judge," said Figuera. "María, I have just one more question to ask you about the other members of your family—your two daughters, your youngest son, and your husband. Isn't it true that they, too, were either disappeared or killed?"

María wiped the corners of her eyes with the tissue and nodded slowly.

"Let the record show that the respondent nodded in the affirmative to the last question of her attorney, Mr. Figuera," said Judge Harwell.

"Thank you, your Honor," said Figuera, appreciative of the sympathy of his response.

"Please continue, Mr. Figuera," said the judge.

"Very well, your Honor," said the attorney. "Now María, according to the narrative of your application for asylum, after—after the loss of your family, you left Guatemala. Is that true?"

"Yes."

"When you left Guatemala, where did you go . . . what country did you go to, María?"

"Mexico . . . I went to Mexico," said María.

"Why did you go to Mexico?"

"I was afraid."

"Why were you afraid, María?"

"That I would be killed, too."

"*Killed* if you stayed in Guatemala?"

"Yes."

"So you went to Mexico, is that right?"

"Yes."

"Now, María, can you remember exactly when you went to Mexico from Guatemala?"

"In November."

"In November? Last year? November, 1991?"

"Yes."

"On what day, do you remember?"

"No."

"Okay," said Figuera. "Where did you go in Mexico after you left Guatemala?"

"Comitán."

"Comitán, Chiapas?"

"Yes."

"Where did you stay in Comitán?"

"In the medical clinic."

"In `the medical clinic'? Why were you in a clinic?"

Once again, María dropped her eyes, and Lucía moved her ear to María's mouth to catch her whisper.

"She was attacked," said the nun.

"María," said Figuera, catching the judge's cue. "You were in a medical clinic because you were attacked, is that right?"

"Yes," said María.

"María, who attacked *you?"*

"A man. The one who gave me a ride to Comitán."

Figuera paused for a moment to allow María to compose herself once more. He had no plans to pursue the details.

"Thank you, María," said Figuera. "Now, how long were you in the clinic?

"Four or five weeks."

"Four or five weeks," repeated Figuera. "And where did you go when you left the clinic?"

"Mexico City, to the basilica."

"To the basilica—the basilica of the *Virgen* of Guadalupe?" "Yes."

"When was this?"

"In December."

"How did you get there?"

"With Ricardo and Sylvia . . . from the clinic. They were going, and so they asked me to go with them."

"To celebrate the *Virgen* of Guadalupe."

"Yes."

"Where did you stay in Mexico City?"

"In the basilica."

"You stayed in the basilica? They have rooms in the basilica?"

"No," explained María. "We slept in our bedding along the wall."

"Oh, I understand," said Figuera. "So, you were there only a short while, is that right?"

"Yes."

"How many nights did you stay in the basilica?"

"Just one."

"Just *one?*" asked Figuera, somewhat surprised. "Why only *one?"*

"Because they came in the night and forced me to leave."

"Who forced you to leave?"

"I don't know their names."

"Well, can you describe them? How many of them? Why did they make you leave with them?"

"A man and a woman."

"A man and a woman? How did they make you leave with them?"

"Well, it was in the middle of the night. They came to me and they had a gun. The woman put her hand over my mouth and put the gun at my head, so I wouldn't make any sound."

"So they forced you to go with them?"

"Yes."

"Why, María? Why did they take you?"

"I don't know?" María was on the verge of breaking down once again. "They . . . they thought I was going north."

"Why? What would give them that idea?" asked Figuera. He was fishing for any kind of credible response. This was sounding pretty farfetched up to this point, and he was clearly uncomfortable.

"They found my *huipil*," said María.

"Your *huipil*?" asked Figuera. "What is that—your *`huipil'?"*

"My blouse from Guatemala," said María, "the one I made for Lucita . . . for Lucita María."

"How did they find your *huipil?"*

"I guess it fell out of my bag, and the man, he brought it to Sylvia and asked if it was mine. Then he asked if I was Guatemalan. He knew from the designs on my blouse that I was from a village around the lake. He knew a lot about Guatemala. He asked Sylvia if I wanted to go north with them. Sylvia said they sold medicines and they needed someone to go with them to watch their car. She said they could take me to the border if I wanted to go across to the United States."

"What did you say?"

"Nothing. I didn't say anything."

"Why?"

"Because . . . I was afraid of them, and Sylvia said I could go back to the clinic."

"So, Sylvia wanted you to go back to Comitán?"

"She said I could go."

"Is that what you wanted to do? Did you want to go back to Comitán?"

"No."

"Why?"

"I was afraid."

"Afraid of *what?* What were you *afraid* of, María?"

"*Orejas*. Informers."

"Informers? Informers for whom? For Guatemala?"

"Yes."

"Guatemalan informers about what? I don't understand."

"For the army, the *kaibilies*."

"What are the *kaibilies?*"

"The soldiers, the Guatemalan militaries."

"Why would the Guatemalan army be interested in you?"

"They think that the refugees are guerrillas, so they chase them across the border into Mexico."

"Oh, I see. You were afraid because you had fled that the Army—the *Guatemalan* army—would be looking for you?"

"Yes."

"And not the *guerrillas?*"

María was silent, and Figuera restated his question.

"And not the guerrillas? Why wouldn't the *guerrillas* be looking for you, too?"

María paused for several seconds before responding. "I don't know. I don't know," she said.

"But you were afraid to go back to Comitán, is that right?"

"Yes."

"María, what would happen if the Guatemalan *army* found you?"

"I don't know?"

"If you don't know, then why would you be afraid of *orejas* for the army in Comitán?"

María looked down again, unable to respond.

"So, María, this is *important*—what would *happen* to you—*no!* What are you *afraid* would happen if the Guatemalan army *found* you?"

"They would *kill me!*" said María finally, just above a whisper.

Figuera glanced up at the judge to make sure that he was satisfied that her response had been recorded. Harwell nodded and indicated for him to continue.

"They would *kill* you because they might think you were a *guerrilla,* is that right?"

"Yes."

"Even though Miguel and Tano had been working for the army in San Felipe?"

"Yes."

"And if they thought you were a guerrilla, then they would also think that you were a subversive, a *communist,* is that correct."

"*Objection, your Honor!*" spouted Ms. Leasure.

"Objection overruled this time, Ms. Leasure," said the judge. "Respondent has already confirmed the link between the terms `guerrilla,' `subversive,' and `communist' sufficiently, I think. Please continue, Mr. Figuera."

"Thank you, Judge," said Figuera, mentally chalking up a mark for himself. Ms. Leasure pursed her lips and began drafting a flurry of notes across her tablet.

"Now, María," said Figuera. "About this man and woman who made you go with them—did they *harm* you in any way?"

"No."

"Did they *threaten* you anymore with the gun?"

"Yes."

"When?"

"When she made me put on the belt."

"*Belt?* What *belt?* The belt you mention in your application?"

"Yes."

"María, describe this belt, please."

"It was just a cloth belt, and it had some plastic bags tied to it?"

"*Plastic bags?* Could you . . . did you know the contents of these bags?" asked the attorney.

"No."

"Well, you described the contents as a `white powder,' is that right, María?"

"Yes."

"Well, what did you think this `white powder' might be?"

"Drugs," María said just under her breath.

"*What?*" pressed Figuera. "Did you say *`drugs'?"*

"Yes," María said softly as she nodded affirmatively.

"María," said Figuera, slowly and pointedly. "Did you offer . . . did you *willingly* put this belt on for the lady?"

"Well, I *had* to."

"Why did you *have* to? Why did you *have* to put on the belt?"

"Because she put the gun to my head and told me to put it on."

"Because she *threatened* you with the gun if you did not put on the belt—the belt with the bags of white powder, is that *right?"*

"Yes," said María, obviously frightened by her disclosures.

"Now, María, just a few more questions," said Figuera, beginning now to complete his presentation. "How did you travel with these two people?"

"In their car."

"By car. Okay. How many days were you with them?"

"Three days."

"Three days—so they came straight to the border, is that right?"

"I guess so."

"How do you mean?"

"Well, I slept some of the time."

"In the car?"

"Yes."

"So they never stopped?"

"Well, for gasoline, for food, and to go to the bathroom."

"And that's all. They never stopped at a hotel or other house for rest?"

"No."

"Now, María, you said earlier that you thought they were carrying medicine, that they wanted you with them to help watch their car because they were carrying medicine, is that right?"

"Yes, that's what Sylvia said."

"Well, María, did you ever see any medicine in the car?"

"No."

"Well, did you see anything else? Baggage? *Equipaje?"*

"No."

"So they were driving straight from Mexico City to the border of the United States, does that seem right?"

"Yes."

"When did you get to the border of the United States?"

"It was night."

"So this would be the *what?*—the *third night?"*

"Yes," said María.

"Can you tell the court what happened?"

"Well, the car stopped. The man said something to the woman and then he got out of the car. The woman pulled out her gun and made me get out. There was another guy there, there by the car. They were talking, that guy and the man, and then we had to climb up on a ridge. That's when I could see the river. It was shining in the moonlight. I could see the moon in the river and the man tied a rope around me and then we all started walking down to the river. The other man said something and then we just started wading out into the river. I was very frightened. The woman with the gun, she was behind me."

"She still had the gun?"

"Yes."

"Did you think about trying to escape? It was night!"

"No."

"Why?"

"Because the woman was very angry with me and pushed me, and she had the gun."

"And the woman threatened you with the gun?"

"Yes."

"So, there was no chance for you to escape, right?"

María nodded tearfully. "I *couldn't!*"

"María, during the three days that these people forced you to go with them—wasn't there ever a time that you could have escaped, that you could have gone for help?"

"Well, at the service station."

"At the *service station?*" asked Figuera.

"Yes. At the service station, there were these two guys working on a truck."

"Okay . . ."

"Well, I tried to get their attention . . ."

"And . . .?"

"Well, the woman, she saw me looking at them, and she got between me and them and made me walk fast past them so they couldn't see me."

"So, you wanted to escape, is that right?"

"Yes, of course!"

"But that was the only chance you had, is that right?"

"Yes," said María, beginning once again to cry openly.

"And you never volunteered to go with them?"

"No!"

"But they forced you the whole time to go with them and to wear the bags on the cloth belt, the bags that you suspected had drugs in them, is that right?"

"Yes."

"Okay, María," said Figuera, maneuvering now for his last questions. "What happened as you crossed the river?"

"I slipped and hurt my ankle."

"Actually, you *broke* your ankle, is that right?"

"Yes, I guess so."

"And how did you get out of the river?"

"They dragged me out."

"They dragged you out . . . out *where?* On which *side* of the river? Did you go across or did you return to where the car was?"

"Across . . . they took me to the other side."

"Okay," said Figuera. "Now, María, when the car stopped at the river, what country were you in?"

"In *Los Estados Unidos*—the United States."

"*No!* When the car *stopped!*"

"*Oh* . . . in Mexico."

"You were in Mexico when you got to the river, is that right?"

"Yes. In Mexico."

"Okay, María," said Figuera. "When they dragged you out on the other side of the river, what country were you in?"

"In Los Estados Unidos—the United States."

"In the United States, right?"

"Yes."

"What happened *next?*"

"Well, I was very *hurt.* I don't remember clearly. But some men came down in the helicopter and took me. That's all I remember."

"And the *others*—where were *they?*"

"I don't know—gone."

"And the *bags?* Where were the bags with the white powder?"

"Gone."

"Gone? Gone where?"

"I don't know?

"You don't know what happened to the bags with the white powder in them?"

"No."

"You never saw them *again?*"

"No."

"You never saw the man and woman and the other man *again?*"

"No, *never!*"

"María," said the attorney. "My last question—did either the man or the woman or the other man at the river offer or actually give you any money?"

"No!"

"You were not helping them *willingly* to bring drugs into the United States?"

"*No!*" said María with a horrified expression.

"Now, María," said Figuera. "What would happen to you if the court today rejects your application for asylum and you have to go back to Guatemala?"

María bowed her head once again and said, "They would *kill* me."

"`They would '*kill you*,' is that what you said, María?" reiterated Figuera.

"Yes."

"And *who* would kill you?"

"The army."

"And why would the *army* want to kill you?"

"Because they would think I was a *subversive*, a *communist.*"

"No further questions, your Honor, although I would request a few moments at the end for a final summary and wrap up after rebuttal," said Figuera with satisfaction, confident in his closing line of questions and grateful for a well rehearsed, articulate respondent.

"Very well, Mr. Figuera," said Judge Harwell. "And what is your pleasure? Do we need a break before cross examination of the respondent, *huh*, Ms. Leasure?"

"No, your Honor," said the INS attorney. "Service is ready to proceed. Service certainly wouldn't want to deny the respondent another moment of her *due process!*"

"Mr. Figuera?" said the judge. "Is the respondent ready to proceed?"

"Do you need a break, María?" asked Figuera. "*Lucía*?"

Both women shook their heads no.

"Yes, your Honor," said Figuera. "I think we're fine. Let's continue."

"All right, Ms. Leasure," said Harwell. "You may begin."

"Thank you, Judge," said Ms. Leasure. "Mrs. Xquic, I have only a few questions for you, if you don't mind."

Barbara Leasure flipped slowly through the eight legal pages of notes that she had scrawled throughout the hearing, tapping the yellow pencil on the desk beside the pad.

"Now, Mrs. Xquic, I would like to begin with some questions about your statement and then proceed to some remarks you have made in your testimony this morning."

María appeared very tentative as she watched the Service attorney and the pages of notes she continued to scan.

"Mrs. Xquic, you have said in the narrative of your application that all the members of your family were killed in the violence between the army and the guerrillas, is that right?"

María nodded again. "Yes," she said.

"Why do you think you were spared? Why weren't *you* killed?"

"I don't know?" said María.

"Doesn't it seem strange to you that everyone *else* in your family—even your two *daughters* would be killed? How old were they, did you say—*seventeen? fourteen?* and your little *son?* How old was he—*eight?* Why would the guerrillas want to kill *them?* Did they serve in the civil defense patrol, *too?"*

"No," said María.

"Well, it just seems a bit strange to me that the guerrillas would attack your small *children."*

María darted a look of horror at Lucía and dropped her eyes to her lap.

"I know this is difficult for you, Mrs. Xquic," said Ms. Leasure, "but there is just a lot I don't think we have heard yet that is important to the interests of the court this morning, and we're just not going to be able to avoid some of these hard questions, *understand?*"

Lucía translated slowly and then reached over and stroked María's hands, setting off the trial attorney once again. Ms. Leasure had been irritated all morning with the little personal exchanges between the translator and the respondent, but she had waited until the first such incident in her cross examination to respond.

"Your *Honor,*" said Ms. Leasure, rising from her desk. "I simply have to register Service's concern over what appears to be a less than *objective* relationship between the translator here and respondent, and if Service can't be reassured of the total impartiality of the translator in the proceedings, then Service must demand that this translator be *dismissed!*"

"Objection sustained, Ms. Leasure," said the judge, turning to Carlos Figuera. "Mr. Figuera, I must ask you to instruct your translator to act with more discretion in her expressions of support for the client. The court has a right to demand complete impartiality in these proceedings if we are to determine an unprejudiced ruling this morning."

"I understand, Judge," said Figuera. He turned and whispered an apology under his breath and a brief explanation to Lucía who clearly flushed in embarrassment.

"Please continue, Ms. Leasure," said Judge Harwell.

"Thank you, your Honor," said the Service attorney. "Now, Mrs. Xquic—

about the *guerrillas* in and around San Felipe. Did they ever kill members of *other* families—their children, *particularly*."

"No . . ." said María quite hesitantly.

"*No!*" said Ms. Leasure in mock surprise. "Then why would they single out only *your* children? In other words, Mrs. Xquic, could it not have been some agency *other than the guerrillas* that killed your family—your *children?*"

María nodded slowly as she buried her face in her hands.

"Is that a *`yes,'* Mrs. Xquic?"

"Yes," said María. It was Figuera's turn to roll his eyes as he could see the first thread of his own case beginning to unravel.

"Mrs. Xquic, who were the first members of your family to die?"

"Ana Fabiola," whispered María.

"Ana—?"

"Ana Fabiola," María repeated.

"Ana Fabiola—your *youngest daughter*, I believe?"

"Yes," said María.

"What *happened* to Ana Fabiola?"

"She went to the dance one night and she didn't come home."

"What *happened* to her?"

"They found her in the church."

"Dead?"

"Yes."

"How did she die, Mrs. Xquic?"

María was sobbing openly and struggling for breath.

"Your *Honor!*" protested Figuera, "I *hardly* think this line of questioning can lead to anything productive. All Service is doing is merely trying to *intimidate* the witness in the most *insensitive* manner *imaginable*, and I . . . "

"Your *Honor!*" retorted Ms. Leasure, "that's the *farthest* thing from my mind, and Mr. Figuera knows it full well. Service has a *right* to cross examine both respondent's narrative and testimony on any point and to try to determine the *verity* of . . ."

"The *court* doesn't need a lecture on procedure from *Service*, Ms. Leasure—objection *overruled,* Mr. Figuera," said the judge, "but the court will remind Service to probe judiciously. I think it's clear that the respondent is close to collapse here, and I hope that we can move with both care and caution to preserve the integrity of the witness's testimony."

"Thank you, Judge," said Ms. Leasure, and she returned to her question regarding the death of María's daughter.

"Mrs. Xquic, it may help the court to better appreciate your testimony this morning if you can share some of the . . . some of the more difficult details of your family's death and disappearance. Please understand, it is certainly not my intention to bring more *hurt* to you—only to get at the *truth* to help the court make a judgment here this morning. All *right?* Can you continue?"

María blew her nose in a fresh tissue and wiped her eyes, finally nodding in agreement.

"Very well," said Ms. Leasure. "I have to come back to Ana Fabiola and how she died. *Okay?*"

"Yes," said María.

"Mrs. Xquic, how did she die?"

"With a rope . . . *they*—"

"With a *rope?* She was *hanged?*"

"Yes."

"In the *church?*"

"Yes."

"Is that *all?*"

"What?"

"She was *hanged*—is that *all?*"

"No," said María, shaking her head sharply from side to side.

"What *else*, Mrs. Xquic—what *else* happened to her?"

"Her *hands!*" said María. "They cut off her *hands!*"

Ms. Leasure grimaced herself at the disclosure and retreated to the security of her legal pad.

"In San Felipe, Mrs. Xquic?" continued the Service attorney. "In San Felipe del Lago—is that the way the *guerrillas* attack people?"

"No."

"How did the *guerrillas* attack people in the conflict around San Felipe?"

"They *shot* them."

"So hanging *children* and *mutilating* them—that wasn't like the *guerrillas*, then?"

"No."

"Thank you, Mrs. Xquic," said Ms. Leasure. "Now, I need to ask you some questions about Lucita María, your other daughter."

María nodded.

"Lucita María—she was your oldest daughter, is that right?"

"Yes."

"What happened to Lucita María, Mrs. Xquic?"

"She was in Antigua," said María.

"She was in—in '*Antigua'?*" asked Ms. Leasure.

"Yes."

"Where is Antigua—in Guatemala?"

"Yes, of course."

"Thank you," said the attorney. "Now, what was Lucita María *doing* in Antigua?"

"She was living with the nuns in the convent, studying."

"She was a *student?*"

"Yes."

"What was she *studying?*"

"She wanted to be a teacher."

"What happened to her in Antigua?"

"They *killed* her!"

"*Who* killed her, Mrs. Xquic?"

"I don't know?"

"How did she *die?*"

". . . on a *cross,*" said María. "They put her on a *cross* in front of the convent."

"They . . . they *crucified* her?"

María leaned over and collapsed in convulsions of grief on the shoulder of Lucía. Neither the Service attorney or the judge felt inclined to protest, given the circumstances of her testimony.

"I'd like to declare a five-minute recess, Ms. Leasure," said the judge, "and would you please approach the bench—you too, Mr. Figuera."

Carlos Figuera left his client in the arms of Sister Lucía and joined Ms. Leasure before the bench.

"Y*our Honor! Clearly, . . .*" said Figuera.

"I *know!* I *know!*" said Judge Harwell. "Ms. Leasure, I'm inclined to accept the testimony of the respondent on these points, and I guess I just need a clearer sense of where all this is leading."

"Your Honor," said Ms. Leasure. "I *know* this is all very painful, but what I'm trying to establish is what the respondent *really* thinks about who killed her family. I don't believe for a minute from her testimony this morning that she really thinks it was the *guerrillas* who killed her family."

"*Your Honor!"* interrupted Figuera.

"*Come on, counselor!*" said Ms. Leasure. "I know *exactly* where you're going in this case, and that old `imputed *political* opinion' dodge isn't going to wash in her case, and you *know* it!"

Figuera shrugged and looked down at his shoes, slowly shaking his head.

"Okay," said Judge Harwell, "where are we? How much more time are you going to need, Ms. Leasure? We can extend this into the lunch hour, if we need to."

"Just a few more questions, your Honor," said the Service attorney. "Maybe fifteen minutes?"

"Okay," said the judge, "and Mr. Figuera, I'll give you both five-minute wrap ups, okay?"

Both attorneys nodded and returned to their desks. Figuera leaned over to speak with Lucía, and she indicated María's readiness to continue.

"Mrs. Xquic," began Ms. Leasure, "if the *guerrillas* didn't do these kinds of things to the people of San Felipe and around that area, then who *did?*"

María strained at Lucía's translation. Lucía repeated the question more deliberately, and once again María dropped her eyes.

"El ejército . . . "

"*What?*" pressed Ms. Leasure. "*What* did she say?"

"The `army,'" said Lucía.

"The *`army'?*—is *that* what you said, Mrs. Xquic?"

"Yes, the army."

"How do you *know* it was the army that killed your daughter, Ana Fabiola?"

"Because Celina Marquez said Ana Fabiola was dancing with a soldier at the dance and afterwards, the soldiers, they followed Isaiah and Meri Batos and took them away," said María in a wash of detail new to both the narrative and her previous testimony.

"*Wait* a minute! *Wai*t a minute!" said Ms. Leasure. "You're losing me, *okay?*"

"Well, Ana Fabiola wanted to dance with Isaiah, her boy friend, but he liked Meri Batos. Celina, she said that Ana Fabiola got mad at Isaiah and Meri because they were dancing together, so when the soldier asked Ana Fabiola to dance, she told him that they were helping the guerrillas. That's when the soldiers followed them after the dance."

"What happened to *them*—to Isaiah and Meri?"

"They found them . . . they found them the next morning. They didn't have any *heads*."

Ms. Leasure paled at the disclosure and turned a page or two in her tablet. Figuera stared at the microphone in front of him.

"And that's when you found Ana Fabiola—the next *morning?*"

"They found her in the church, the American."

"The *'American'*?"

"The American who was working for the *padre*."

"And so you believe that it was the *army* that killed Isaiah and Meri Batos and Ana Fabiola?"

"Yes."

"And *not* the guerrillas?"

"No."

"Now, Mrs. Xquic—about Lucita María? Why do you think the *army* killed her?"

"Because they said they knew where she was and that they could hurt her whenever they *wanted* to!"

"Who is *`they'?*"

"Two men—two guys who attacked me in the street. They said I was working for the guerrillas and they beat me up. They told me not to speak against the government again."

"When did you speak against the *government?*"

"I *never* spoke against the government."

"Well then, why would they *say* something like that?"

"Because I told the mayor and the military commissioner—I told them that we didn't have to *accept* the violence anymore."

"When was *this?*"

"The night before at the town meeting—after they killed Ana Fabiola."

"And so the next morning, you were attacked in the street?"

"Yes."

"Can you describe the men who attacked you?"

"They were *ladinos*. They had guns, and they wore *boots* like the militaries wear."

"Were they wearing uniforms—*army* uniforms?"

"No, just the *boots* like the militaries wear."

"So, you believe that they—well, who do you think they *were?*"

"I don't know."

"How did they know about Lucita María?"

"I don't know."

"When did you learn that Lucita María was *dead?*"

"That same day."

"How did you find out?"

"I heard them. They said she was dead, that she had been put up on the cross."

"*Who*, Mrs. Xquic? Who *told* you that?"

"Some people—the people who found me."

"*Who?* Who *found* you?"

"María . . . María Paloma."

"*María Paloma?* Who is *that?* A *neighbor*?"

"Yes . . . no. Not *really?*"

"Who was María Paloma, and how would she know about Lucita María?"

"She didn't. It was the others."

"*What* others? Mrs. Xquic, I need more *details.* I don't think you're telling me everything you *know!*"

"They were the people who were working with María Paloma."

"*What* people? Who *were* they?"

"The *guerrillas!*" exploded María, rising from her chair. "María Paloma was the leader of the *guerrillas* and she was my *friend* and she tried to save *my life and Manuel* and she took us up on the *mountain* to get away from the *soldiers* after *Lucita* was killed because she said that they were going to kill *me* and little *Manuel.* So in the night we went up on the *mountai*n and the army *attacked* us and María Paloma was *killed! Everyone* was killed but *Donaldo* and me, and Manuel *disappeared!* That's what happened to Lucita and Manuel and to María Paloma and the *others* and that's why I had to *leave Guatemala!*"

María Xquic collapsed into her chair in inconsolable grief, and Figuera rose and helped escort her from the courtroom.

"Well, Ms. Leasure," said Judge Harwell. "An interesting turn, wouldn't you say?"

"I think I've heard enough, your Honor," said Service.

"*No, no!*" said the judge. "I wasn't rushing you—you take as much time as you need."

"No, I think you're right. I think I'm ready for wrap-up, Judge."

"Well, you do what you need to do, *okay?*"

"Yes, your Honor."

"I think I have some questions, and we'll get Mr. Figuera's closing argument, and then I think we'll be done and still have time for lunch."

The judge looked toward his door and called for Mrs. Hernandez.

"Yes, Judge?" said his secretary as she opened the door.

"Mrs. Hernandez," said Harwell, "why don't you step out in the hall and check on Mr. Figuera and Mrs. Xquic. I'd like to get through with this, if we can."

"Of course, Judge," said Mrs. Hernandez, and she stepped through the hearing room and out the entrance. Judge Harwell returned to his own set of notes and the narrative attachment to the asylum application. Moments later, Figuera and María returned to the room followed by Mrs. Hernandez. "I think they're ready, Judge," she said as she passed the bench to return to her office.

"Very well," said Judge Harwell.

Ms. Leasure was making additional annotations on a sheet of tablet paper that she would use for her wrap up. The judge allowed María to reseat herself and confer for a moment with Lucía who had remained at the desk during María's last rupture in the hearing.

"Mr. Figuera," said Judge Harwell after another minute or two. "Service has indicated readiness for wrap up. I have just one or two questions or so, if you're ready to proceed."

"Yes, thank you, your Honor," said Figuera, squaring himself in his chair and glancing over at Lucía who seemed prepared to continue with her translation.

Judge Harwell leaned forward on his bench and deliberately addressed María.

"Mrs. Xquic," began the judge. "I want to commend you on your candor, and I sympathize with the pain you must feel right now."

Judge Harwell leaned back and allowed Lucía a long space to translate his concern. Then, he leaned forward again. "Let me remind you that we are here this morning to determine if you should be allowed to remain in the United States. The court has to decide this question based upon two things: first, a *credible* story, and second, a *clear* expression of *fear of persecution* if you were to be returned to your country—in this case, *Guatemala*—based upon a *reasonable fear* of persecution upon return because of your nationality, race, membership in a social group, your religion, or your political opinion."

Judge Harwell leaned back again while Lucía struggled to complete the translation of the complicated explanation.

"Now, Mrs. Xquic," said the judge as he leaned forward again, "I have to confess some very deep reservations on *both* points. I have seen many `tears' in this court room, and I have heard the testimony of many `fearful' people in the past. But I cannot be swayed by tears. I have to look for the truth and base my opinion—that I'll have to render here this morning—on a credible story rather than emotion. Now here's the problem, Mrs. Xquic—"

Once again, he interrupted his statement for translation.

"Now here's the *problem . . ."* he repeated. "A *'credible'* story is a *consistent* story—at *least that!"*

Lucía translated.

"And your story—at *this* point—is *not* consistent. So let me try to clear up this first problem with a question or two, and you must answer me directly and truthfully, *okay?*"

"Yes," said María.

"In your written statement, you say that it is the *guerrillas* who have been persecuting you, that it is the *guerrillas* who attacked and killed members of your family, is that *right?*"

María hung her head and thought for a moment before responding.

"No," she said softly.

"No, it was *not* the guerrillas who attacked and killed your family—is *that* what you are saying, Mrs. Xquic?"

"Yes," said María just as softly.

"Mrs. Xquic, look up at me—*look* at me!" demanded the judge.

"Mrs. Xquic, if it *wasn't the guerrillas* who attacked and killed members of your family, then who do you *know*, or who do you *believe* attacked and killed your husband, your sons, and your daughters?"

"The army."

"The *Guatemalan* army?"

"Yes," said María.

"And you are telling me the *truth* now," pressed the judge, "as you *know* it or *believe* it to be so, is that *right?*"

"Yes," said María.

"*Okay!*" said Judge Harwell. "If you are telling me the truth *now*—and I accept what you are telling me *now* is the *truth, okay?*—then, *why*, Mrs. Xquic, did you say in your narrative—not *once!* not *twice!* but *three times!*—that it was the *guerrillas* who killed your family? Can you answer me *that?*"

A look of terror washed over María's face as Lucía completed her translation of Judge Harwell's question. Her word had never been so compromised before, and she felt cornered and trapped for the first time.

"Can you *answer* me that, Mrs. Xquic?"

" . . . no," said María. *Miguel Mapa smiled at her from behind the face of the judge, laughing and laughing. "I am waiting for you, madre, with the soldiers. I have come for you, silly mother, and you thought you might escape the soldiers! Don't go near the soldiers, mother! Don't go near the soldiers!" And he laughed and laughed and laughed.*

"All right," said Judge Harwell, "now to the *second* problem."

The judge sat up straight, squared the loose pages of the dossier, fastened a paper clip to the top corner, and returned the secured papers inside the legal file.

"Mrs. Xquic," said the judge, "were you ever active in *politics* in San Felipe?"

María was trembling and looked confused.

"Did you ever work in a political *campaign*, or were you ever a member of a political *party* in your town or anywhere *else* in Guatemala?"

"No."

"All right," said Harwell, "before you left Guatemala, were you a member of any *organization*—a *labor union, women's organization, human rights group,* or anything like *that?*"

"No," said María.

"Okay," continued the judge, "were you active in a *church* or *religious organization?*"

"No."

"You weren't a member of the *Catholic church* or *protestant church* in San Felipe?"

"No." *The face of the Maximón broke into a smile.*

Figuera just shook his head. What kind of point could he make with the court about her *brujo* husband? He just chuckled to himself, checked his watch against the clock on the wall, and leaned back in his swivel chair.

"Were people ever persecuted in San Felipe just because they were *women* or maybe because they were *Tzutujiles?*"

María was growing more and more confused, and Lucía sensed that she was beginning to drift away. The whole process at this point was merely mechanical.

"No," said María blankly . . . *to make the count again—Andres, Migtno,MaríaFabiolaMan Manmanhe cat thathechasedintbiola . . .*

"So Mrs. Xquic," said the judge slowly, "you have no reason that this court can accept for fearing persecution if you return, is that *right?*"

María hadn't heard a word of Lucía's translation.

"No," she said.

Figuera bolted up from his chair, sending it sliding away behind him across the floor, and he paced up and down behind his desk with his hands planted deeply in his pants pockets.

"*Mr. Figuera!*" said Judge Harwell sternly. "Please take your *chair!*"

"Yes, of course, your Honor!" said Figuera, collecting himself again. Ms. Leasure smiled.

"Ms. Leasure," said Judge Harwell, "does Service wish to make a final statement?"

"Yes, your Honor," said Ms. Leasure. "Service finds the testimony of the respondent *completely inconsistent* with the narrative of her application, a contradiction *clearly* the product of poor coaching, probably by *counsel here*, your Honor. Because of the obvious inconsistencies, Service finds the respondent uncredible and recommends that the court reject respondent's application for asylum and further that the court dismiss respondent's appeal to voluntary departure because the witness's own incriminating testimony, and that further, the respondent's deportation be expedited in the most timely fashion to avoid continuation, if not expansion of her own *admitted criminal activities!* I believe that's *all*, your Honor."

"Thank you, Ms. Leasure," said Judge Harwell. "Mr. Figuera, you have five minutes for a response."

Carlos Figuera sat at the desk, staring blankly at the microphone before him.

"*Mr. Figuera . . .?"* said the judge.

"Uh . . . yes, your Honor . . ." said the attorney. "Well, *no, Judge* . . . the respondent rests her case."

Chapter 34

Greater Love Hath No Man

The morning of the funeral was dismal and wintry. A steady drizzle pelted the otherwise lush Texas valley. The Simpson family had remained isolated as much as possible from the media and the on-lookers, the thousands of the curious who had followed the horrifying story for days in the newspapers and who had shared in the grief when Susan's body had finally come home. Julius Parker had made himself available to the family who had received him indifferently at best. Susan's father had expressed what many members of the family had kept to themselves throughout the ordeal: "We've had *enough* of government in *this* family."

The Byner Funeral Home of Brownsville had opened three parlors to accommodate the guests on the night before the Simpson service. A constant stream of visitors filed into the low-ceiling room past the phalanx of flower arrangements to view the girl's body wrapped around the shoulders in its long, blue, tie-dyed Mayan shawl and San Felipe *huipil*. The fine lines of her powdered face seemed fixed in an imposed peace masking some fierce, though inexplicable resolve. Her pale, almost translucent hands clutched the silver-beaded chain of a rosary that had been blessed by the Pope on his visit to the shrine of Hermano Pedro at the Church of San Francisco in Antigua. The rosary was an heirloom given to her by one of the long-time patrons of the Church who believed fervently in the powers of the legendary Franciscan.

The most revered religious personage in Guatemala, Hermano Pedro was an early eighteenth-century Franciscan Brother, a large, overbearing presence in the Spanish colonial capital, celebrated and beloved, even in his own life, for his absolute devotion to others. Dedicated especially to the sick and the poor, Brother Peter developed a hospital in Antigua and worked on their behalf until he died at the age of forty-three. Throughout the decades, the Indians prayed to Hermano Pedro, beseeching their servant to intercede on their behalf. More than a hundred times in the three centuries after his death, devotees reported sightings—miraculous visions—of the good Friar in and around the old church and in the vicinity of the ancient hospital. A favorite haunt was his chapel, a three-hundred-year old ruin that had weathered more than a dozen major earthquakes throughout its history. Hundreds of crutches, photographs, and letters lined the walls of the alcove which bore the sarcophagus of the beatified remains. Each relic—a piece of clothing, a worn photograph and faded letter, or little mirable—silver-plated images of an arm or leg—each item testified to a parishioner's deep devotion to the ministries of the fabled Friar and hope for an orphaned child, an old woman, someone's grandfather, or tiny baby.

Miracle upon miracle were attributed to the Franciscan's intercession. Day by day, both the old and the young stood side by side in line for their moment to kneel before the entombed casket of the Brother, reaching across the guard rail and through the locked wrought-iron bars to rap on the old smooth, wooden panels that separated the poor, tired bones from their petitioners. The San Franciscans of Antigua, both the ladinos and the Indians, provided solemn maintenance of the shrine, sweeping up the fallen flower petals and scraping the remains of votive candles from the altars at mid day and each evening after vespers.

"Hermano Pedro has the ear of Our Father. He will protect those who call upon him. You take this rosary, Susanna," said Doña Petrona. "This rosary has rested for twenty-four hours among his bones and has been blessed by the Holy Father himself. Your faith is strong, and Hermano Pedro will watch over you, reina."

Susan Simpson's faith, indeed, had been strong, and she had deeply cherished the rosary that Doña Petrona had passed to her almost a year before. Although she had been only nominally Catholic before her arrival in Antigua, her work in villages had quickened her devotion, and she had begun regularly to accompany her new Quiché Maya friends to mass. She always wore the rosary to the services, but at night or during field work in the mornings, Susan would leave it in the little drawer with her Quiché testament. It was there in her drawer when she had been abducted at the pila, and it was there when the American consul had come for her effects. It was the Quiché priest who, through his interpreter, had explained the significance of the rosary to the consul.

"She was such a *sweet* child!" sobbed Miss Jenny, Susan's third grade teacher, as she reached into the casket and placed her hand over the cold, pallid fingers of the young woman. "A sweet, *sweet* child!"

Patricia Meyers, Susan's first cousin and constant companion through high school, peered down at her friend, stunned for the first time by the sense of the awesome reality of death. She had never understood her cousin's sense of calling to Guatemala, of all places. Before Susan's excited telephone call explaining her Peace Corps assignment in the highlands, Patty had been aware of nothing more about the country than the tiny image of the quetzal bird printed on a postage stamp in her grandfather's album. Now, looking closely at the tightly drawn eyes of her relative, Patricia felt hurt and angry. She realized, for the first time, just how far away from all their childhood, hometown fun and silliness her friend had drifted. A part of her felt cheap and trivial in the face of Susan's enormous sacrifice, and in a rush—in just a fleeting, intuitive flash—Patty caught the sense of a quiet nobility in Susan's martyrdom. At the same time, Patricia was terrified, and she began to tremble as she clutched the side of the casket. As the tears began to stream down her face, Patty Meyers felt very small and insignificant—helpless, in fact—in the face of an overwhelming, suffocating phenomenon over which she had no control. And in its wake, Susan, her friend, was gone forever.

The Simpson family sat together in the funeral parlor alcove off to the right of the casket's flower-covered bier. Father Mike sat with Susan's mother and father, holding the mother's left hand between his own while she wiped her tears with the other. At the prearranged time, the funeral director rose from his seat on the front row of the chairs and turned to the growing congregation.

"If you will all be seated, we will ask Father Mike to conduct the Rosary service," said the director.

One by one, those in line turned, looked across the extended parlor, and moved to take their seats among the mourners. Father Mike relinquished Mrs. Simpson's hand, rose, and took from under his robe the Guatemalan hand-woven stole, bowed his head, and draped it evenly over his shoulders. He clasped the hands of each of the family members on the front row and walked slowly to the pulpit just a few feet away from the family.

"We are here today to praise God and to honor the life of our sister, Susan Simpson," said Father Mike. Throughout the room, sniffles and muffled sobs began to erupt.

"Let us join together in a worship of the Lord, Our God, the giver of life and all good things," invited the priest.

"In the name of the Father, and of the Son, and of the Holy Spirit. Amen," echoed voices throughout the room.

"You call this a *good thing*, *PRIEST!*" came a blast from the back of the room, interrupting the opening of the Rosary.

"You call this—this *murder!* You call this some kind of *`good thing'?*" mocked the voice.

The almost muted plea in the voice of a woman urged silence and respect.

"No, I *won't* sit down! And I'm gonna have my *say!*" said the voice bellowing from the back of the room.

Father Mike stared blankly in disbelief toward the fountain of frustration and anger.

An enormous, sweaty man, in a light blue leisure suit, rose from a chair at the rear of the parlor. He was an ungainly figure of what must have been close to 350 to 400 pounds, the bulk of his weight splitting the seams of his shirt and protruding in rolls of fat over his belt. His face was bright red below a sunburnt forehead. The hams of his biceps extended out to his sides, tapering only slightly to pudgy, weathered hands that seemed out of place and useless in such a public forum.

"Junior" Waller was the captain of a shrimper that docked at the Brownsville port. Three years her senior, "Junior" had been Susan Simpson's silent admirer since their early days together in the Brownsville public schools, although his only attempt to date her had been kindly rebuffed more than eight years before. At twenty-eight, he had followed at a distance her work in college and later had clipped the two or three newspaper articles that announced her graduation from UCLA and, sometime later, her acceptance in the Peace Corps.

"Junior" Waller rose from his seat and began crowding his way down the row of chairs, stepped into the aisle, and walked up to the front of the parlor and turned at the head of the casket to face the shocked congregation.

"I ain't gonna be at the service tomorrow, so you folks don't have nuthin' to worry about, but tonight I'm gonna have my *say* before . . . before this *`priest'* over here gets into all this religious . . . *stuff!* I just got one thing to say: I *loved* this girl ever since I set eyes on her mor'n ten years ago. She never knowed it, I guess, `cause she was always a step out a head of me, even me bein' older and all," said the giant of a man.

"But I'm gonna tell all `a ya' somethin'," exclaimed the distraught tonnage. "This angel up here was *murdered* for *nuthin'!* . . . I mean *nuthin'* that's anything to *Amer'cans*! And as long as we keep listen'n to these *goddam' sap priests!*—"Junior" Waller shot a look of contempt and anguish at the clergyman.

Gasps erupted from the congregation, and two of the funeral home assistants rose, unbuttoned their coats, and stepped toward the shrimper.

"Looka *here!"* said the speaker, addressing the approaching attendants. "I ain't here to make no trouble. I'm just here to tell you that you don't have to look outside this *room* to see who stole this *angel* from us!"

"Why don't you just come back and sit down," pleaded one of the assistants in a low but firm voice, and he placed his hand on the shrimper's sleeve.

"Why don't I jis' belt the *shit* out'a you!" exploded the fiery fisherman, as he jerked his arm away and made ready to swing his pudgy fists.

And then as if awaking from a dream, the giant of a lover stopped and took two steps backwards toward the open end of the casket. Obviously disarmed by his own eruption, he glanced wildly around the room at the stunned mourners, turned his head slowly toward the ashened, painted face of the corpse, and collapsed on his knees in a heap at the head of the casket.

For a moment, the two attendants stood in their tracks, and then after glancing at each other, moved slowly but deliberately toward the shrimper, placed their hands under the man's arms and urged him to his feet. "Junior" Waller looked up helplessly and then maneuvered to a crouching position, accepting the support of the attendants. Audible sighs of relief amid an outpouring of anguished sobs rolled around the room as the two funeral home employees escorted the man to the side door opposite the beleaguered family.

Father Mike left the pulpit as the strains of organ music began to assuage the grief-strickened supporters and friends. The priest walked back into the midst of the family that had now arisen and taken positions of support around Mrs. Simpson who had collapsed across the lap of her husband.

"I'm so *sorry,* Father!" exclaimed Susan's sister, Marilee. She turned to the priest, and in a flood of tears, she fell against his breast and shoulder.

"That's okay," urged Father Mike. "The poor man couldn't help it. He must have loved her very much."

The evening's service passed. The mourners left the parlor after Father Mike had finished the Rosary. "Junior" Waller was too embarrassed to face anyone and had ripped away from the funeral home in his pickup truck, leaving a trail of rubber snaking off the parking lot and well out into the intersection. Members of Susan's family gathered around the open casket, speechless and unreconciled to their inexplicable loss. Father Mike remained beside Mrs. Simpson, her husband, Marilee, their daughter, and Ronny, Jr.

"Can you help me to understand, Father Mike?" asked Mrs. Simpson as her eyes remained fixed on the powdered corpse of her oldest daughter. She clutched the soaked handkerchief that had collected her tears throughout the service.

"Why would anyone *do* such a thing as this to Susan?" she asked. "She wasn't a *soldier!* She wasn't a *threat* to anyone! All she *ever* wanted to do was to *help* people! From the time she joined Indian Princesses, Susan wanted to help *people!* She said one time . . . one time she said to me, `You know, mother, I just can't *stand* it when the other kids say those mean things about the teacher. I wish I could make them see the teacher the way I do.' That's what she said. She only wanted to *help* other people. And they would do a thing like this to my *daughter!* Help me to try to *understand,* Father! What kind of *barbarians* are they in Guatemala? Why does God allow such a thing like this to happen to people so *innocent* and so *good?*"

Father Mike offered the parents a seat in the Chaplain's office just away from the chapel. He removed his stole and hung it over the coat tree behind the desk.

"Bonnie," offered the priest. "How can I say this?—the evil in Guatemala is a phenomenon. It's greater, somehow, than the sum of its parts. It's larger than the collective victims that it leaves in its wake. It's greater than all of those wretched individuals who commit these heinous atrocities. And it's endemic, like a fungus that has found its way into the tiniest filaments of the society's root structure, sapping the very lifeblood of the culture. It demands the absolute allegiance of everyone who cannot escape and crushes, in the most violent, malevolent ways, those who step forward to challenge it. Susan was destroyed physically by a phenomenon so vast and pervasive as to defy conception."

"But, Father, if you *knew* all of this, why did you *help* her? Why did you encourage her to go *down* there?" cried the mother. "She wouldn't have even *known* about Guatemala if you hadn't *told* her all about it."

Father Mike leaned forward, his elbows propped up on his knees and his forehead resting in the palms of his hands. For a moment he was silent, staring down at the insteps of his soles beneath his open robe. He was finally being forced to respond to questions he had been asking himself throughout the week, and he had no ready answer. As he struggled for the first words, he knew he wanted to avoid sounding irresponsible or disingenuous, but at the same time, he knew that the world view from which he had encouraged his young ward was one that they would probably not understand, least of all accept. It was a world peopled with thousands of martyrs for a cause—many martyrs and many causes. It was a world divided between an absolute good and an absolute evil, populated with agents on both sides who, both wittingly and unwittingly, contributed to the machinations of two opposing and irreconcilable scripts.

The priest wanted to say something like "Susan was a free spirit who wanted to make a difference," or "Susan was a big girl who made her own choice," or "Susan understood the meaning of sacrifice," or "Susan *this* or

Susan *that,*" but right now, the necessities of the priest's broader vision of the dilemma of evil were irrelevant to a mother looking not so much for an explanation as she was for something—something or even someone to blame. Nothing that he would say was likely to mean much unless he was willing to bear Susan's cross, quite literally at that moment, on his own shoulders, and Father Michael Justice was not ready to accept that burden just quite yet.

"I'm *sorry,* Bonnie, so *very* sorry," confessed the priest.

It was a lie, of course. He was far from sorry that the young woman had died; not, to suggest, however, that he had ever willed her death. Sorry more, he was, that the influence of her testimony would be limited to the grave and not to her continued good work among the people. The power of symbol could atrophy, he well knew, without constant attention and focus. But that was not likely to be the case, either, for there would be many more who would die. Nevertheless, on the night before her funeral, you just don't tell a parent that his or her oldest child has been a necessary or inevitable pawn of prophecy.

It was the nature of the war that those in solidarity had been waging, a war against an intransigence that would not be ameliorated by words or will but rather by the sheer, crushing weight of sacrifice, a sacrifice so raw, so ugly, so horrifying and repugnant that it might not any longer be ignored in the most lethargic corners of the First World, a sacrifice of such magnitude as to influence the collapse of the entire infrastructure of an evil society.

But how could he communicate this revolutionary faith to the shrimp boat captains, to the INS officers, to farm workers and school teachers, to even his own faithful—to his secretaries and church assistants, let alone to the Rafael Nuñezes—the small but disturbingly problematic little power brokers of the world. Sometimes his heart was bursting with the collective grief of those Mayans who, for want of respect and a little spot of land, had sacrificed so much to preserve the pleasure and power of the few. He often struggled for the words that he would say, and tomorrow he would have a platform and a forum for the small congregation who might hear.

"The Lord be with you," said Father Mike, standing before the celebrants of the funeral mass at St. Cecilia's Catholic Church in Brownsville.

"And also with you," they responded as they waited at the entrance to the church's sanctuary behind the pall and the white-draped casket.

Two golden ribbons about ten-inches wide crisscrossed at the center of the casket. Father Mike dipped his fingers into a goblet and sprinkled holy water over the head of the white draped coffin. Behind him, resonating from the range of pipes of the organ towering over the altar, a full chord anticipated the entrance song.

"When morning fills the skies,
My heart awakening cries,
May Jesus Christ be praised . . ."

The organ and chorus swelled as the mourning worshippers filed down the aisle and passed off, left and right, into the pews. Outside the church, and in a band of dismal weather that stretched from two miles up and down the Gulf Coast, the Rio Grande Valley was blanketed in a cold, penetrating drizzle. A lone crow shivered at the top of the mesquite tree outside the service.

"*Caw!*" protested the bird as it dropped into a lazy, uninspired drift from the tree and disappeared over the roof of the church.

The music of the chorus was muted by the trucks and cars, passing slowly toward the red light at the corner. The neon sign illuminated the first three letters of the name of the hamburger stand across the street. Just inside the restaurant's drive, a Brownsville police car, its lights flashing, sat behind a teenager's classic `66 metallic blue and flat white pickup truck as the officer checked out the vehicle's license. An empty melon truck spewed a cloud of exhaust as it revved up and lurched forward into the intersection at the change of lights. The driver of another car, loaded with teenagers, honked their horn and shot the derisive finger at their peer awaiting processing by the officer still absorbed in the cab of his car as they raced past the melon truck and on up the street.

". . . eez-sus, Christ *beee*-puraaaaiiiised!" finished the chorus. Most of the friends and acquaintances had found places among the pews, perhaps as many as two hundred, maybe three. Many others were still filing in from the side entrance closest to the adjoining parking lot next to the supermarket.

Father Mike stood up from his chair and approached the center of the altar, motioning for all to rise. Ronny Simpson, Jr. approached the priest and handed him a small Bible. It was Susan's own testament which had been retrieved from her room in Guatemala and returned with her effects.

Father Mike accepted the worn, pocket-sized scriptures and stepped down to the side of the casket and placed the book at the juxtaposition of the golden bands of ribbon.

"Give our sister, Susan, eternal rest, O Lord, and may perpetual light shine on her forever," recited Father Mike from the scriptures. Sobs erupted from the members of the family sitting in the reserved pew next to the young priest.

Following the "Mass for the Dead," the pall bearers removed the casket to the hearse waiting under the awning just outside the family alcove. The family took its place in the limousine behind the hearse, and the cortege began to move out of the parking lot and into the cemetery grounds. More than fifty cars pulled slowly into the procession while a hundred or more on-lookers afoot walked across the quarter of a mile across the cemetery lawns to the back of the grounds to the Simpson family plots.

Father Mike stepped out of the second limousine and walked toward the family's vehicle and opened their doors. One by one, members of Susan's family emerged and stood outside the car while the pall bearers removed the casket from the rear of the hearse. Susan's mother gripped the arm of her husband as the funeral party marched slowly up the incline to the grave site just atop the slight rise above them.

The thick fog began to change to drizzle as the family entered the small tent at the mouth of the grave. The others moved in closely under the mesquite trees that ringed the tent. Julius Parker and Bill Boyer took positions discretely behind the last row of mourners. The pall bearers slipped the casket onto the bier, removed the carnation boutonnieres from their lapels, and then took their positions behind the casket and the mound of covered earth. Father Mike stepped forward in his white robe with his Guatemalan liturgical sash around his neck, folded his hands over a *New Testament*, and scanned the line of the family members before him.

"The Lord be with you," said the priest.

"And with you," returned the Catholic faithful.

"We are here to say farewell to our beloved daughter and sister, Susan Marie Simpson, beloved of God and lifted by her martyrdom to the very presence of Our Lady of Guadalupe and Our Lord Jesus Christ for whom our sister lived and died in faith, Our Father who taught us to pray, saying:

"`Our Father, Who art in heaven; hallowed be Thy name; Thy kingdom come; Thy will be done on earth as it is in heaven. Give us this day our daily bread; and forgive us our trespasses as we forgive those who trespass against us, and lead us not into temptation, but deliver us from evil. Amen.'"

Father Mike reached down to receive a bell from one of the two young acolytes who assisted him on his right. He took the bell and rang it three times before returning it to the robed assistant.

"Hail Mary, full of grace, the Lord is with thee; blessed art thou among women, and blessed is the fruit of thy womb, Jesus. Holy Mary, Mother of God, pray for us sinners, now and at the Hour of our death. Amen."

"Glory be to the Father, and to the Son, and to the Holy Spirit. As it was in the beginning, is now, and ever shall be, world without end. Amen."

"Dear friends," said Father Mike as he raised his outstretched hands first to the family and to the others huddled under the eaves of the tent and the trees beyond.

"We weep today for the inconceivable loss of our friend and servant of God. Susan Marie Simpson died in her faith and in service to her adopted people, the poor and the afflicted Maya who have suffered so much in their simple quest for dignity and respect. She became caught up in their plight, and in her solidarity with them, paid the supreme sacrifice that others might be free," said Father Mike.

And then it happened—just as he fixed on the folded hands of Susan's mother, just as he as he turned and touched the head of the now sealed casket. For a moment, his voice stopped as he sensed a fullness begin to swell from somewhere deep within his soul. And then the fullness surged forward, and Father Mike's lips began to move as if controlled somehow from without.

"There is a spirit loose across the face of the planet," said the priest, "a spirit sowing its seeds in the hearts of the race. `It is time to come together,' it beckons. `It is time to celebrate a higher happiness.' It dances lightly over the tombs of the great missiles, rusting in their darkened silos. It kisses promiscuously all that is with the lips of its blessing and plays coyly with our finest sensibilities. It sutures and sifts and swells and soars. We must move in time to its rhythm; we must follow its way through the night. In humility, we must receive its all-encompassing embrace and be swallowed up in its perfect vision. For in the end, it will not be denied. `It is time to come together,' whispers the Holy Spirit of God."

"Amen," said the priest.

"Amen," returned the small congregation.

A pair of mockingbirds chirped brightly overhead and then wheeled skyward in great arches before alighting in trees several yards away.

Father Mike stepped forward to extend his support for the last time. On the fringe of the group, Julius Parker and Bill Boyer watched patiently as the priest passed from one member of the Simpson family to another, receiving their embraces and thanking the young priest for his message. Then they rose, approached the casket for the last time, standing for a moment in silence to witness their private meditations and prayers. Then, the priest stepped back, and together, the family moved out into the misty rain and walked slowly back to the waiting limousine.

"Those were beautiful words, Father," offered Boyer rather gratuitously as he and Julius Parker accompanied the priest back down the slope of the hillside and approached their cars. Then, almost spontaneously, the Desk officer stopped and placed his hand on the priest's shoulder.

"*Wait* just a moment, Mike," said Parker. "*Wait* just a minute. I mean, the way I see it, I mean we've got little pockets of *corruption* here and there throughout our government, but *shit!* Father, the American government isn't *evil*! . . . You know, Father, we aren't *evil*, eh?"

Father Mike smiled rather incredulously at the overstuffed Foreign Service officer, not quite believing the candor he was hearing from the dilapidated agent. Then he said:

"You haven't got it *yet,* have you, Parker?" The priest just stared at him. "You still haven't *quite* gotten it."

Chapter 35

Benediction

María Xquic de Xoy rocked back and forth. On the morning of her scheduled deportation, María was confused and frightened. Her hands rested on her thighs just above her knees. Mechanically, her fingers drifted back and forth, down and up and down again, over and over the thin cotton fabric of her dress, smoothing the wrinkles away from her and over the ends of her knees. Almost imperceptibly, María rocked back and forth in rhythm to the cadence of her hands. How could she return to a place that had taken her husband and destroyed her children? How could she return to a place where her oldest son had turned on his own people, to do such terrible things? How could she return to Guatemala?

Back and forth, back and forth, María rocked. María rocked back and forth, back and forth and back and forth. How could she face her own people in San Felipe? How could she bare the stares as she passed them through the streets? María's shoulders rocked back and forth. How could she survive her neighbors' silence, their spitting across her path? She knew their anger, and in that fierce hatred, she knew they would not accept her grief as sufficient penance. Even though she shared their affliction, María knew that she would not be welcome, even to visit the graves of her precious little ones. Where would she live? What would her first hours be like in a place where she was despised?

Rocking back and forth, María Xquic de Xoy suffered as she waited out the final hour. Tears streamed down her cheeks. Her throat was tight and tense, her stomach churned, and she couldn't stop the trembling. Would she be able to move? Could she make the walk across the yard and step up into the bus? It wasn't a matter of her ankle; it was fear, simply enough, a pulsating anxiety that stretched across her violated breasts and wrapped around her shoulders. Her temples throbbed. Her feet and thighs were chilled. And María Xquic de Xoy could not stop the trembling.

For most of the morning she had tried to concentrate on mechanical things, the correct placement of the few objects she carried about her. María Xquic sat on the edge of her cot, her cane resting across the end of the mattress. Her small bag of personal effects—the health kit with its almost full supply of tooth paste, the unopened plastic vial of hair shampoo, and an unused bottle of roll-on deodorant—all of it rested just under her right elbow, a mute remnant of her stay in detention.

Disposing of the foodstore plastic bag never crossed her mind. María Xquic of the Maya simply had no conception of choice in the matter, and she adjusted completely to accommodate the impertinence of accoutrements for which she had no use. The presence of the health kit, however, was not even an inconvenience to her. As something imposed, she assumed, from the authorities, María would simply do what she had to do to tend it. Like her cedula, she had long since accepted the bag as something necessary, so she determined to carry it with her as part of the *cargo* of her assimilation into the camp community.

Deportees from three stations were moving that morning—Salvadorans mostly, a few *Guatemaltecos*, some Haitians—perhaps more than a hundred, maybe two hundred both men and women. María couldn't know. She had watched the sad parade drift silently each morning just beyond her cot, or walking past her as she returned from the showers—particularly, the poor people who had exhausted all hope—the sick and infirm ones, the very saddest of them all.

As "D Day's"—*deportation days*—approached for the detainees, they became more and more withdrawn and subdued. The women would smile at each other, darting furtive glances from side to side, as if to protect what little arena of personal space they had left. They would sit on their cots looking about themselves, silently measuring the moments passing slowly but inexorably to the morning of their return. The detention busses always rolled into the camp an hour before dawn and parked in rows, usually five to seven vehicles long. The drivers and guards would stand at the gate, exchanging cigarettes and shop talk about night raids, river blockades, and INS assaults on sanctuary houses.

"I'll tell you *what*," said "Bubba" Sanchez, a veteran guard from Brownsville with more than thirty years in the Service. "I'll tell you something. We got us one of them little *`hippy'* types here back a year or so ago."

Sanchez turned his head and spit a wad of chewing tobacco across the curb and into a shrub.

The driver took a final drag on his cigarette and, with measured deliberation meant mostly for effect, flicked the butt to the pavement at his feet and ground it into pulp with the heel of his boot.

"I mean we *nailed* her," Sanchez exclaimed, his eyes twinkling. He reached into his hip pocket and retrieved a canister of tobacco, secured a pinch between his thumb and first finger, and slipped the wad between his cheek and gum.

"We nailed her little ass *cold* for running these Central American wetbacks up to `Sanan-tone,'" said Sanchez. "We watched her for more than a month. She'd pick 'um up outside of `Casa,' you know—right outside the *gate!* [Spit] *Hell,* she didn't care *who* saw her! We had thish'eere stand about 100 yards back of the compound, and we could see her—*hell,* we could see ever' move she made. She never made any attempt to hide what she was doing. [Spit] *Shit!* She'd put two, three—maybe four or five wetbacks in the back of her van—and her kid strapped-in, right there in the front seat. *Shit! She* didn't care!"

The driver stuffed his hands under his belt and deep into the crotch of his jeans and rolled back under his "gimme" cap. "Wonder if she *balled 'em* all before they got to `Sanan-tone'!" he offered as he broke into a guffaw.

"We watched her for a month or so, like I said," continued Sanchez. "We had her nailed on a good thirty, thirty-five counts. [Spit] We could've locked her ass away for sixty-five years, you know! *Shit!* And that *judge? Shit!* [Spit] That jackass give her just *six months!* I can't *believe* that! Can you *believe* that? Only *six months!* But it sure put a kink in their little `railroad,' I can tell you *that!*" [Spit]

Cynthia Cramer had been out of state on the day the judge found her guilty of transporting an illegal alien in Texas, the first prosecution and actual sentence of a refugee operative in the Southwest. "Sanctuary congregations in solidarity with Cynthia" throughout the nation paid for her legal expenses and child's day care while her husband continued his job during her incarceration in a minimum-security unit outside El Paso. The court intentionally sent her six hundred miles away as an intimidation ploy, making it twice as difficult for her husband and young son to visit her. The "congregations in solidarity" responded with a shower of cash and a network of prayer partners. Every evening at ten o'clock (Mountain Time), Cynthia would join a national prayer chain celebrating their commitment to the Central Americans and their challenge of what they perceived as an immoral foreign policy and a whimsical, if not out-and-out corrupt Immigration Service.

Cynthia Cramer served her time with dignity and a busy schedule. Every morning she facilitated a reading clinic for fellow inmates and conducted a non-denominational devotional just before lunch. In the recreation yard, she developed two competing track teams and taught them all the finer points of volleyball. Each afternoon, she spent two to three hours answering the stack of mail she received from well-wishers and sent personal epistles to more than two hundred churches, encouraging them to keep the faith and buoying their support through her acknowledgments.

By the end of her sentence, Cynthia Cramer had become a symbol, if not something of an icon. "Remember Cynthia" T-shirts and "Free Cynthia" bumper stickers circulated throughout the hemisphere. Thousands of letters pillaged the INS, and political advisors urged the Republican President to ease the pressure on the Sanctuary Movement, all the while the INS itself kept stepping up its prosecution of the "illegals."

Although she had no reason to suspect it or could have appreciated the larger political framework in which she found herself, as 1548922, María Xquic de Xoy was only an alien number in a calculated entrenchment of INS policy and a tiny factoid in a bellicose reaction to an increasing social consciousness and its small but emerging national outcry.

Clutching the rosary around her neck, a gift from Lucía, María sat on the edge of her cot, rocking and rocking back and forth, smoothing out the wrinkles in her skirt. Her bunk mates didn't need to ask her; they could tell; they knew that today was María's "D-Day," and they gave her space. At 7:00 a.m. the buzzer sounded at the end of the dormitory, and on cue, the detainees slipped from their bunks and filed to the door and the stairwell that took them to the dining hall for breakfast.

Slower than the rest to rise, María stopped the almost ritual rocking and reached beside her for the cane she had checked out from the infirmary. She no longer needed it, but the cane gave her security. She rose from the mattress, straightened her shoulders, and turned to look at the health kit spread over the rumpled sheets. She looked at the cane and then back again at the plastic bag, and then she placed the cane on the bed beside the health kit. She would walk to the dining hall unassisted for the first time in weeks.

"You're doing just fine, Miss María," said Amanda, as she placed her hand on María's shoulder. María froze at the touch that set her trembling once again. She stared straight ahead, fearful in just the first instant, that the time had already arrived unexpectedly, that she might be escorted to the bus on the spot, desperate that she might miss the breakfast pastry that she ate each morning. With her nervous stomach, María was in no shape to eat it or anything else at the moment, but she was counting on the breakfast roll to steady her when she would no longer be able to suffer the pangs of hunger sometime tomorrow or the next day, given whatever fate might bring her.

Sergeant Becker sensed María's fright and moved gently from behind her to face her horrified ward.

"Don't you be frightened of *me,* sweetheart," said Sergeant Becker. "I'm here just to be *with* you, honey."

Sergeant Becker took María's two hands and clasped them between her own, drawing down the fragile Mayan woman beside her on the mattress. María was too embarrassed to look up at her patron who had become attached to her through her medical ordeal and subsequent INS hearing. Both eased slowly to the mattress, and Sergeant Becker looked at the olive complexion of her distraught friend.

"I wish you could *understand* me, María. I wish I could get through to you just *once*, just *somehow*," said Sergeant Becker, as she looked over María, into her hairline and around the frame of her rough, deeply lined face.

Without ever looking at her supporter, María withdrew her hand from the imploring embrace of the Sergeant's clasp and spread her fingers down her thighs and over her knees, and then she turned her head slowly toward the door at the end of the corridor. She sensed the Sergeant's genuine interest, but she was embarrassed by her inability to communicate and too intimidated by the barricade of the Sergeant's officialdom. By the end of the day she probably would be far away, and the earnest Sergeant would be beyond her reach and any help. Any expression of sympathy now was a wasted gesture.

Speechless, Sergeant Becker was astonished by the rebuff and sat mute on the edge of the cot beside her ward. After a moment, she rose beside María and looked down at the Indian woman. And then it came to her: this Indian woman—she was beyond either her personal or official support. In the depth of some personal grief for which the Sergeant had no access, this diminutive woman was not meant to assimilate. There had been no recourse from deportation, even from the beginning, and because of that cold, precise reality, there could be no relationship beyond the perfunctory, beside the official one of a guard for a prisoner. For the first time in more than five years of service, Sergeant Becker felt empty and alone behind her badge. Perhaps it was always this way, although the Sergeant had tried, in each case, to extend her evangelical Christian friendship to the detainees in her charge. Sergeant Becker took four steps back, turned, and walked away. María sat on the edge of the cot, waiting, and trembling.

Light poured through the opaque, industrial window panes along the top of the walls just below the ceiling. Shadows of the detainees drifted down the aisles, sweeping the legs of the cots and ends of the mattresses. Quietly, in single file with hardly a word, the indigenous women filed passively toward the stairwell at the south end of the floor, and, with their exit, the sun brightened across the room, illuminating the silent, lone figure of María Xquic, bowed and convulsing in inaudible sobs.

"Okay, we'll be moving out, then, around 0:900. We'll have to bring them across the compound," said Captain Peterson, the director of operations at El Chamayo.

The compound was an open commons just inside the gates of the detention camp where husbands and wives were allowed to mingle under the watchful supervision of the camp guards each morning, usually in groups of thirty to forty for periods of half-hour intervals. The compound grounds stretched between the circular drive, where the busses always parked, and the fenced exercise yards adjacent to the men's and women's dormitories.

On "D-Days" the deportees would always cross the commons on the way to their busses. They would file out of the dormitories and go to the Central Processing Station in the main building where they would be identified, their passage recorded, and retrieve any personal effects from storage. After processing, the women would walk single file down the steps which exited the Central Office, take the right fork of the sidewalk which split immediately to the left and right into the respective exercise yards, pass through the commons, out the gate, and into their assigned busses.

The walk across the wide courtyard had been dubbed years before as *"El Paseo de los Muertos,"* the macabre "Passage of the Dead." Characteristically, there was seldom a word spoken until the deportees reached the commons where frequently they would receive the well-wishes of friends and a last embrace from spouses who, for whatever reasons, were being retained. For almost all who had fled their countries originally seeking asylum, the *"Paseo"* was a frightening, desperate experience—a passage that lead only to horrifying prospects which, of course, the deportees had sufficient time to amplify in their imaginations.

María glanced around her bed—the sheet and U.S. Army blanket and the bunk number "14B"—now she would leave it all. But would she have a blanket tonight? Would she be cast out among the homeless on the streets of the capital? Where could she get the fare to take the *ruletero* to the Lake? What would she eat tonight? Must she become a wretched beggar, her hands out among her own people?—*the disgrace!*

"Madre de Díos!" she exclaimed. She would lose the breakfast roll if she wasn't in line. She had to make her way to the cafeteria this last time. Almost mechanically, María rose from the side of the lower bunk and took the first few

steps hesitantly and then moved steadily toward the dormitory door far at the end of the aisle.

Cautiously, María pushed the crash bar opening the steel dormitory door and stepped into the stairwell. As she began her descent, she could hear the muted din from the cafeteria two floors below. Without her cane now, María relied on the hand rail for support, and she passed down the stairs with measured reserve. When she reached the end of the stairs, she was comforted to notice that she wasn't too far from the end of the line. Apparently, the serving line had been delayed in opening, for the otherwise stoicism of the indigenous women had tightened into deep-seated consternation evidenced in pursed lips and in the tight, wrinkled lines about their eyes.

But the line was moving now, if only slowly. The Indian women pried loose the chipped and cracked cafeteria trays from the two stacks at the head of the line. Curiously selective, they took set-ups of silverware wrapped in cheap, thin napkins, and then two-stepped down the serving line, inches at a time, from right to left. The black and Hispanic servers behind the food lines scarcely looked up at the morning's deportees as they turned the heavy steel spoons over the steaming row of scratched and cracked plastic plates. In a numbing rhythm, the slotted serving spoons slipped in and out the orange powdered eggs, the soybean "sausages," and the mound of grits bubbling in the heated pans. [Slap!] [Slap!] [Slap!] the mush fell onto the plates which the plastic-gloved hands of the kitchen help spun along the stainless-steel food rack.

One by one, the Indian women took their plates and a glass of water or cup of lukewarm coffee to their trays. At the end of the serving line, they could choose from a pan of large, puffy cheese biscuits or heavy, dry rolls plucked from under a red and white checkered towel covering the bread tray.

María stood at the end of a line of more than forty women in front of her. She took a warm tray from the top of the stack but declined the napkin and silverware; her stomach was far too unsettled to tolerate even the bland eggs and grits. She was anticipating the breads far down the line to her left. With every other step or so, María managed a glance at the diminishing mound of rolls and biscuits.

"*Algo comer*—sunthin' t'-*eat?*" asked the short, squatty Mexican-American server behind the counter. As the Indian woman seemed pre-occupied, she wouldn't ask twice, and the server scraped the eggs off the platter under the food rack into her garbage pail. María moved along, indifferent to the server's impatience, but as she turned in sight of the open bread tray and biscuit pan, she was surprised to see only two rolls left. In a wasted gasp, María flashed in shock to see the last two rolls withdrawn in the mealy grip of "Tia Taco" who stuffed them quickly into the folds of her shawl. María froze in place, her last hope dissipated before her very eyes.

As María slipped past them at the tail of the file of detainees, the help quickly shut down the warmers and began lifting the trays of unserved eggs and sausages out of the food line. Mechanically, María turned and followed "Tia Taco" past the end of the counter, bearing her empty tray in front of her, walked softly to an unoccupied table to the side of the room, and sat down. For a moment, as she stared at the tray, her heartbeat rushed, and her breath quickened into a frantic panting. After a few moments, a violent convulsion swept through her, and unable to restrain herself any longer, María placed her hands to her face and sobbed.

"Take the women first," said Captain Peterson. "Let's try to get them through processing this morning before the men. You manage `storage,' Amanda. Here, take the clip board."

A row of duty officers sat before the Captain ready to receive the schedule and appointments for the day. Peterson always operated from the policy of juggling assignments through his guard units so that each person would become familiar with the various steps in processing. It gave each of them a stronger sense of ownership in the total operation. But there were always hitches; he had turnovers every month or so, and education was a continuous function.

Sergeant Amanda Becker reached across the corner of the Captain's desk and took the warped clip board from her supervisor. She would be responsible this morning for coordinating the return of deportee properties from the storage cages. Rows of the meager artifacts were stuffed away in cramped, wire-mesh baskets jammed into the industrial metal shelves. Each basket was identified by the deportee's registration number scribbled on a cheap, perforated label that had been slapped over a layer of former, now otherwise "processed" cases.

The Sergeant's job was a simple one, but still no small task. Not all the baskets were in order. Amanda Becker had to coordinate the checking of the order against the manifest on her clip board, and she had only an hour before the deportees were to begin processing. She still had to find two of the guards from "B" complex to assist her, and she knew that both of them had to be watched at every turn to keep them from really screwing things up. She had worked with them both before, and the problem, the Sergeant surmised, was perceptual. She couldn't just hand over the clipboard to the two, because in thirty minutes they would have all the racks in complete disarray. To begin with, only one was even marginally literate, and she had no sense of sequencing at all. The older of the female guards, she always confused the long registration numbers and had never caught on to the concept of reading the last three digits in the registration numbers first. To avoid confusion at the processing gate, Sergeant Becker would probably have to stand over her assistants and point out just about each basket.

Sergeant Becker left the meeting and headed straight to the intercom where she called for the two guards from Complex B. Then she left the office for the property room down the hall. Inside the property room, the thick, musty smell was stifling. The stench of refugee garments was compounded by the chilly dampness in the usually locked quarters. Rats were a constant problem, and the sweet odor of decomposing rodents, poisoned from the baggies of dry pesticide thrown into the corners, enriched the aromatic bouquet. Sergeant Becker gagged and coughed as she entered the property room. Light streaming into the small room revealed the stiff remains of a dead rodent on the grey military desk just below the receiver of the telephone—this from just over a weekend!

Sergeant Becker brushed the dead rat into the trash can and turned on the light. She peered at the ceiling-high racks of wire baskets that extended ten rows to the rear of the storage room. The belongings of today's deportees were scattered throughout the racks. She looked at the manifest for the initial entry and made a mental note of the row and file where it should be. She walked back to the third row and slipped down the narrow aisle to the assigned slot for the basket. To her surprise, it was exactly where it was supposed to be. So was the second, the third, and the fourth.

"Sergeant Becker?" said a voice from the doorway. It came from one of the two duty officers reporting from Complex B.

"I'm back here—row three!" called the Sergeant. She turned back down the aisle and approached the two recruits to this morning's processing.

"We have only about twenty minutes, ladies. Come on back with me. The list is really complicated. We have a whole mix today of Salvadorans and Guatemalans, and about half of these have been processed on the West Coast, so their numbers, you know, are going to be the short ones, categorized by the ordinal `A' numbers, you remember, don't you—just the last three numbers of the `A' numbers."

Sergeant Becker knew better than to try to make any sense of what was going to be a confusing morning.

"Come on back here, both of you, and let me show you again—just to remind you," she instructed the two duty officers.

The first officer, a guard for more than fifteen years at El Chamayo, had invested her entire career in a cushioned, straight-backed military office chair behind a desk with its sixty-watt light stand, just outside the door to the second floor of the women's dormitory in Complex B where she had read more than two hundred and a dozen or so second-hand romance novels. Her partner, the illiterate one, slipped behind the first and drifted into the stacks of baskets.

"Start with the first file," said Sergeant Becker, "right there, just above your left shoulder."

The first officer looked up and scanned the numbers on the crinkled and smudged labels.

"What's the number?" she asked.

"The number?" repeated Sergeant Becker. "The number—the number . . ." she said, as she flipped back a page on the clip board.

"1548922—9-2-2, *-9-2-2.* You go by the *last* three numbers," instructed the Sergeant, somewhat exasperated.

The older officer stared up and down the rows of wire baskets. She finally spotted what she interpreted to be the correct basket and pulled it off the rack from a slot just above her head.

"*No!*" said the Sergeant. "That's the right *`last three numbers,'* but not the rest of them. Look down the row to the *right.*"

The officer turned to the right and began pulling at the fronts of the wire baskets, sliding them out into the light. She finally spied the correct one and started to pull it from the shelf when suddenly she jumped back, letting the basket fall to the floor in front of her.

"Gawd-*amighty!*" said the older officer as she clutched her throat. "Most scared the lights right *out'a* me!"

"What's the *problem?* What *happened?"* asked the Sergeant, as she hurried down the aisle to assist the officer who was leaning heavily against the opposite rack of shelves.

"Look!" she said, as she pointed toward the wire basket with its wad of material spilled from beneath the rim.

"What is it?" asked Sergeant Becker.

"*Rats!* Somofabitch is fulla god'am *rats!*" returned the duty officer. "Little baby *rats*—a whole *nest* of'um!" she exclaimed.

Sergeant Becker kicked the collapsed basket slightly with her feet, hoping to send any reluctant rodents scurrying away from them. Then she heard the cries of the newborn rats squealing inside. Cautiously, she lifted the end of a Guatemalan *huipil* which fell apart as it dangled in the air. Five small, grey rats fell out of the debris back into the basket and scurried for cover in the folds of a ragged skirt. Wheeling backwards, the Sergeant dropped the rag remaining between her fingers, catching herself against the steel shelving to keep from falling.

"Dam' *rats! Oh,* I *hate* them!" cried the first officer as she fetched the basket a sturdy kick and sent it skidding down the aisle.

Back at her cot, María Xquic de Xoy waited out the final moments of her detention. In only a few minutes she would be escorted through central processing, cross the yard to the gate, and step onto a bus that would take her to a big city far away, a place one of the guards called "Houston." There she would be put on a plane that would fly her through the skies. María tried to think about that for a moment. *It was a new idea; she hadn't allowed herself to focus on the meaning of a plane flight. Now that her departure was imminent, however, she began to tolerate the idea, but she simply had no conception. Perhaps it might be like a seed in the craw of a water bird wheeling in sweeping arches over Lake Atitlán, or a sip of aguardiente in the throat of the Maximón as he passed secretly over the streets, up the paths, and over the crest of San Pedro towering behind San Felipe del Lago.*

"Let's *go,* ladies!" barked the duty officer at the door of the dormitory. At once, a general stir and commotion rumpled through the bunks as the deportees for the day turned toward the dreaded sound. It had finally come, the incisive interruption that would divide them forever from the wide, open plains of North American freedom and its promise of hope.

Doña Petra rose from her bunk and smoothed the cover up to her pillow. Standing slowly, Tita Sevedra pulled the shawl over her shoulders and wrapped her arms within its folds. Leaning forward, "Chacha" Segunda turned to the nearest guard, shot her the finger, and spat into the aisle to demonstrate her disgust for the humiliating body search the guard had forced upon her at her arrival. One by one, the day's deportees filed into the central aisle of the dormitory and worked their way to the door.

Clutching her cane, María Xquic of the Maya stepped behind Doña Matilde de la Piedra, the "stone one," her stiff, deformed shoulders hiked above her neckline and the bulge of her hump rising beneath the blanket which she had received from the evangelicals. The "stone one's" limp set the pace for the emerging line behind her, and the women assumed a similar slip along the sweating, concrete floor. Each reluctant step brought them closer to the gate and departure on the industrial blue prison busses and the long flights back to their several respec-tive countries.

At the base of the stairwell, the long, mute line filed to the Central Office for processing. Each shuffled past a table and took a set of sweat pants and shirt, changed in one of the five or six cramped cubicles, and turned in the detested uniform. As each returned in her orange uniform, Sergeant Becker checked her number embossed on the wrist band against the roster and called back into the racks for the deportee's personal belongings. The "stone one" craned over the counter, attempting to peer between the rows of baskets to follow the guard groping through the labels to find her things. After more than a minute, the guard came forward with the basket bearing the sad woman's purse which contained the photograph of her husband, a *campesino* from Morazón Province in El Salvador, and an address book with contacts in Mexico and the United States, names of whom she had been unable to locate through her *pro bono* attorney prior to her merit hearing and subsequent deportation order. When Sergeant Becker slid the basket across the counter to the "stone one," the decrepit lady stretched a tremulous hand slowly inside, feeling for her bag. Slowly, prayerfully, she lifted the musty purse from the basket, held it to her breast, and then parted the seams to reveal the open, broken zipper. With her hand inside the mouth of her purse, the "stone one" turned away to indulge just a moment of privacy.

In the adjacent storage room, the wall phone rang—probably a call from the Captain. Sergeant Becker motioned to the older guard to take her place at the counter while she took the call.

Following Doña Matilde, María moved to the front of the line and stood before the duty guard with the clipboard.

"W'as yo' *numba*, hun'y?" asked the guard.

María smiled slightly, acknowledging the question without understanding.

"I *said,* `W'as yo' *numba,' huh?*'" the guard repeated.

María smiled.

"Gimme yo' *numba!*" the guard demanded irritatedly.

María smiled.

The guard reached across the counter and grabbed María's right arm. The fragile, nervous Indian woman winced as the heavy guard jerked it toward her so that she could position María's band under better light.

"1-5-4-8-9-2-2," barked the guard. "*-9-2-2!*" she returned, remembering the coded last three digits from the West Coast "A" numbers.

The younger guard could be heard rummaging through the baskets, pulling them out, then sliding the wire containers back in their slot. For several moments the commotion continued.

"Wha's dat number ag'in?" shouted the guard from deep in the racks.

"*-9-2-2!*" barked the older guard. "*-9-9-2!*"

More commotion, baskets banged around.

"Ain't *chere-rah!*" came the report from the racks.

"-9-9 . . ."

"Ain't *chere*-rah!" came the return.

Overhearing the racket, Sergeant Becker came forward from the stock room in the rear.

"*9-2-2?*" she asked.

"Yeah, Sergeant," said the perplexed guard still poking around the baskets.

"That's the one, the one with the *rats*—over there in the corner," explained Sergeant Becker. "*I'll* take care of this one."

Sergeant Becker worked her way past her perplexed help and retrieved the deserted, rodent-infested basket against the wall. Picking up the basket, she approached the Mayan woman waiting silently and placed the basket before her on the counter.

María trembled as she anticipated the return of her clothing—*the huipil she had worn as she fled San Felipe, the blouse that she had woven as a muestra, a model for Lucita María more than ten years earlier when her oldest daughter was learning the craft of backstrap weaving and the traditional patterns of the village. María had worked for more than four months at the loom to prepare the two panels of material for the huipil. Every row of tightly aligned little animal figures—the tiny chickens, the parade of venados—the noble deer, the files of spreading peacocks—each had been crafted with the care of a master weaver. María had used her grandmother's own pick and batten, the most prized elements of the weaver's art, heirlooms that Doña Audelia had passed on to María on her deathbed thirty-two years earlier only one week after María had finished her panel of material for her own first huipil. Lucita María had followed her mother's designs, tediously copying the knotted figures, spreading the warp threads with her pick and pulling the colored yarns into position to build each delicate image.*

María had had to carry her *huipil* in a small bundle in the bottom of her bag in order to mask her identity as a refugee during her passage to Mexico City. Sylvia had found a dress for her at an evangelical center in Comitán. When her bundle was stolen during her first assault, she despaired throughout the day, not about the savage rape and beating she had suffered at the hand of the truck driver, but rather for the loss of her most cherished possession, the only physical link with her homeland. It had been a small boy who had found the discarded garment behind the town latrine and returned it to the desperate refugee. He had found the Mayan woman bruised, frightened, and trembling at the creek bed at the end of the maguey rows behind the chicken farm. Expecting a reward, the young boy kicked dirt in her face as she tried to explain that everything had been stolen from her.

Now María was awaiting her only keepsake, the little *huipil* that she would carry with her on her return to Guatemala. As she looked through the wire mesh, however, something was strangely distorted; something wasn't right. She stared at the garment within as Sergeant Becker slid the basket toward her.

"*Rats!*" apologized the Sergeant.

María stared wildly at the shredded fabric, at first failing to understand, and then horrified at the realization of the destruction. At once, her hand flew to her mouth, and María turned her back to this unimaginable affront to both her dignity and identity. Without turning back, María reached out her right hand to the counter for support, caught her breath, and then slowly followed the line of deportees ahead of her toward the door.

What would Lucita María think to know that the muestra was lost forever? How would she be able to learn and to follow? What would the other young girls of San Felipe think when Lucita María, her oldest daughter, could not complete her own huipil? What would her neighbor, Doña Petrona, think when María could not attend the services for want of a dress? What was her own mother to think that she, María, had been so careless as to risk the heirloom of her own daughters?

María stepped into the bright morning light as she exited the Central Office building. Absorbed in the loss of her *huipil*, María had not noticed at first the movement of the line across the women's exercise yard and the commons just around the corner to the right.

"So, *this* is how it will be," thought María. *"So, this is how it is!" insisted another voice, suddenly communicating from somewhere deeply in her consciousness. Her heart was beating rapidly and her breath hard to catch. Startled by the intensity of the moment, María sensed, for only the briefest moment, that she had stepped outside herself and was now watching herself go through the efforts of walking. Somehow, she seemed to be just floating slowly along beside herself, observing intently from right angles each step of her uncertain walk away from freedom.*

And then, in an instant, the two voices within her disintegrated as she turned the corner in the women's compound to enter the great commons. There were the men, perhaps 150 to 200 of them, milling around in small groups, a pair here and there, clusters in pockets along the fence and others positioned near the gate to watch the women go by.

Suddenly, María froze, unable to take another step. Her eyes had traced along the group of men near the gate when she spied him—her evilness, the image of absolute blackness in her soul, Miguel Mapa, her son! *Strang*ely, she had not thought of him once on this horrible morning. But *now!* There he stood by the *gate!* Had it come to *this?* Had Satan at last shackled her *here—here* in these *last few paces,* to suffer even one final *assault?*

And as if her own thoughts had directed her fate, Miguel Mapa turned and stared at his mother, isolated and distanced from the moving line ahead of her. He stared at her, fixed and stern.

All her fears now rushed through her. Her son—was he not the assassin sent from her own womb to destroy her world, and, in a last, desperate act, now cut off the very root of his own life?

Never had María known such absolute terror, an immobilizing physical fear that locked her spine from the nape of her neck to her heels. Instinctively, María closed her eyes and prayed.

"Sacrada Madre, Madre de Diós! Holy Mother, Mother of God! And all the alcaldes of the earth, the sacred sky, our Father God! El Mundo! Spirit of the Universe! Hear now this poor piece of cake, this sorry meal that stands begging before you. Jesucristo and the Santos Sacrados, in the name of a poor brujo who served your people faithfully in your tiny aldea, San Felipe, come to me now, come and hear your servant, this paltry, this . . . this rotten elote in this strange corner of your great and vast harvest. Attend me now and protect me from an evil that has stolen my heart away. Have I not burned my candles and paid my fee for such a moment as this? Come to me here and be my shield."

María's prayer was uttered not so much as a litany as rather a grievous wailing from the pit of her soul, a passionate desperation flung at the powers of destiny in full expectation of a reprieve. Her concentration fixed in the sharply defined silhouette of her son, a figure stretching a foot higher than almost every other detainee around them.

Miguel Mapa had not yet seen his mother, had not even known she was there. Now, he was electrified by the sight of her standing in the women's line, filing toward the gate. The recognition of her among the morning's deportees sent him reeling backwards against the gate post for support. Three and a half years of misery, grief, and self-hatred rushed like a flood through his heart, and he stood terrified and condemned before the only person that could any longer give his cursed life any meaning.

For more than half an hour, Miguel Mapa had been fleeing the death squad that had arrived in the detention center only the night before. It had been Geraldo Mendezalba, the Honduran in the bunk above him, who had first heard the rumor about the arrival of the two-man Guatemalan hit team. Like a ricochet, the news had reverberated through the men's compound.

"In the morning in the showers," someone said, "Watch *out* for the new arrivals."

"In the compound mess, in the shadows of the workout room, behind the commissary, watch *out, Miguel Mapa!* They have *come* for you!" whispered another.

"Nothing but to *run!*" he thought, "only to flee with the morning's deportations. To flee out the gate and into the safety of numbers, he would lose himself among the deportees and then jump the bus somewhere, somehow—only now to outpace his assassins who were crossing into the compound at the very moment.

"*Ssst!*" said a confederate. "There they *are!*"

"Over *there,* Miguel, watching for the *break. Look!* See them pacing slowly, like two *cats* that have cornered their *prey!"*

Just outside the rear door to the men's dormitory, the two assassins stood on the small rise of dirt that had accumulated against the fence. From that vantage point, they had a clear view above the heads of the other detainees. To any Guatemalan in the camp, it was the short-cropped hair that suggested military association. They were *ladinos*, these two, and clearly, they were ostracized by the others. They couldn't have been more obvious if their orange uniforms had been painted green.

"With the *line!*" he had thought. "With this line of *women,* and then the *men!*" He would slip casually into the line up with the men, his blanket wrapped over his shoulders and down his back to mask the orange uniform.

"*Miguel!*" said the old man next to him who had agreed to assist him in his flight. "Look, *Miguel!* They *come!* They're coming for you, *Miguel!*"

Terrified, Miguel glanced toward the fence at the rear of the compound and saw the two assassins slip slowly from their perches and begin to move through the loose body of the men. Intently, he followed their movement through the men until light reflected from the window of the dormitory above flashed in his eyes, momentarily blinding him. As he threw back his head to dodge the reflection, he saw María standing in line among the women.

"Mother? My *mother!*" he exclaimed under his breath. "*Oh, my God! My precious mother!*" He flung himself forward from the gate and lunged through the line of women inching their way along toward the busses.

"*Oh, my blessed mother! Oh, mother of God!"* he cried over and over as he stumbled through the surprised women who fell back clumsily to let him pass.

María stood transfixed at the sight of her son pushing and shoving his way toward her.

"*María, Holy Mother of God!*" she exclaimed within her heart. "*Oh, blessed Mother of God! Is this it? Is this how it is to be? That a mother's oldest son, that a mother's first-born child should now turn on her? To knock her down? To trample her poor soul and spirit into the earth? Oh, Holy Mother of God! Give me strength to even bare the shame!"*

"*Miguel Mapa!*" cried María, holding up the cane before her. "*Miguel!*"

Miguelito stood frozen before his mother, his face an expression of terror and confusion.

"*I am María, your mother!*" she suddenly cried out, finding her voice at last. "I am your *mother!* And as I *die!* As I *die*, you shall hear from me in my dying breath what you have *done to our family!*"

Miguel Mapa stared at his crippled mother and the cane extended feebly as if to brace a blow. And then at once, his mother's words came rolling down like a thunder. Without taking his eyes from hers, his legs suddenly gave way from under him, and he collapsed at her feet in an eruption of pain and grief.

"*Oh, my mother!*" he cried. "*Oh, my poor, blessed mother! I am lost!* So very *lost!* I *fled,* oh, mother! I fled them *all!* I fled after Manuel . . . what they *did* to him! I saw him—what they *did* to him, his little *face* . . . the *bowl* . . . the *soup! Oh, God forgive me! Oh, mother! Forgive me!* I killed my *captain!* I *killed* him, mother, for what they *did* to Manuel. I *killed* him for what they *did* to him when they brought him down from the mountain. So, I ran from them. Across the mountains and through the jungles. Across the plains of Mexico, I ran and ran. I never stopped running for weeks, sleeping in the ditches by day and running, never stopping in the nights, never stopping until at the bridge, there at the river, when they asked me for the papers that the man had made for me in the night . . ."

Miguel lay prostrate before María Xquic, his mother, his large firm hands now pulpy and limp, wet from the flush of his tears. Whether it was the shimmering lace of the blue lights or the soft, muted voices whispering just behind her—which came first? María hadn't even considered the question. It didn't startle her this time as it had before. The pale blue light, an evanescent aura rose from just beneath her eyes across her cheeks, down her shoulders and arms, a faint but radiant blue glow enveloped her hands.

And the voices said, just beside her and behind her eyes—

"But look, my precious wife—look at our son before you!"

"Yes, look! Mómi! Look down at him!"

And yet another, so tiny and frightened.

"See . . . See, it's Miguel!"

And then the gentle chorus.

"But mother, look down! Look down at him. This is Miguel," they said.

"This is Miguel Mapa, and he's our brother!"

María looked down at the sobbing, prostrate giant at her feet and tapped his shoulder lightly with her cane. Then, she bent over and stroked his matted, knotted hair. Slowly, her desperate son rose and found his feet, squared his shoulders and looked away, still unable to face his mother. María reached up and turned his head deliberately in front of her own. She peered silently, deeply into his soul, studying the strong profile of his nose, his wide, high Mayan cheeks, and his blanched, terrified eyes. Then, without a word, María reached up slowly and traced the sign of the cross upon his forehead, turned, and stepped aside. María Xquic of the Tzutujil Maya walked slowly through the gates and boarded the bus for deportation.

CPSIA information can be obtained
at www.ICGtesting.com
Printed in the USA
LVHW010206031219
639238LV00004B/16/P

9 781733 472203